# VLADIMIR GONIK

# ORCHESTRA

AD VERBUM


Published with the support of
the Institute for Literary Translation, Russia

# ORCHESTRA

by Vladimir Gonik

Translated from the Russian by Christopher Culver

Published with the support of the Institute
for Literary Translation, Russia

Editing by Richard Coombes

Proofreading by Michael Wharton and Jonathan Campion

Publishers Maxim Hodak & Max Mendor

© 2021, Vladimir Gonik

© 2021, Glagoslav Publications

www.glagoslav.com

ISBN: 978-1-912894-39-0

First published in English by Glagoslav Publications in January 2021

# VLADIMIR GONIK

# ORCHESTRA

Translated from the Russian by Christopher Culver

Published with the support of
the Institute for Literary Translation, Russia


GLAGOSLAV PUBLICATIONS

# CONTENTS

Day turns into night
As we journey through space.
Chance, groping its way along,
Risks flashing into reality.




The power of coincidence pervades all
and subjects everything to it.

*a personal observation*

═══ 1 ═══

The ways of chance amaze me. How can one comprehend its power, its vagaries, its greatness and caprice, its waywardness and willfulness, its sheer implausibility? Like a mischievous youngster, chance acknowledges no laws, cares little what people want, and only rarely bows before the inevitable course of events.

Division X received a visit from one Captain Shilin, a military pilot and an undisputed and unrivaled ace, one capable – unlike most of the population – of flying a military aircraft at high speed at a significant altitude. It was early March, when winter was still in full swing and was not yet thinking of letting up, had not yet given a nod in the direction of spring. Someone who had completely lost track of time would have been quite unable to tell what month it was from the weather outside: frost, snowdrifts; proper winter.

A keen eye would nevertheless be able to make out where the snow had settled and darkened, where moist depressions had formed in the snowdrifts around the trees. When a thaw was just starting, the cold air took on an elusive smell of watermelon and apples. Few city people know the airy smell of meltwater, renowned for its healing properties. Country people know how it boosts one's health and brings relief to a weary body. It is no wonder that birds and other animals rush to drink from a fresh patch of melted snow, and if you water wilted indoor flowers with snowmelt, they will spring up and grow.

This is not what Shilin was thinking about, however. If the smell of spring suddenly catches a man unawares in the wintertime, do his thoughts turn to the possible advantages and benefits of it? Does he find himself harassed by corrosive self-centeredness? The faint, barely perceptible smell unsettles the blood, weighing on the heart and mind. Hope awakens in the breast, growing stronger with each minute: we have survived the winter, and now we can live, and live well, until fall!

 

The pilot stepped off the bus, and waited for the shaky old vehicle to rumble off, taking with it its smell of rusting iron and the acrid fumes of gasoline. The bus gave out a moaning, screeching sound, as if it suffered from chronic shortness of breath and was aching in its worn-out bolts. The fumes and soot hung over the road, but as the decrepit old bus slowly vanished, the air cleared, and a boundless stillness stretched off in all direction.

Rare indeed was the silence that settled in. The highway curved through the fields and was lost among the snowy hills. The pilot stood, absent-mindedly looking out over the landscape, listening, and breathing in the clean, cold air. Tall trees grew along the bends of the river and on the slopes – black trunks amid the immaculate whiteness. The crest of the road revealed birch groves, and meadows beside the river. Further off, the river valley was walled by forest; the nearby hollows were lined with thick undergrowth, and one could readily see how nature would flourish here when the warm days came.

Where the pilot had come from, the landscape was depressingly featureless: bare fells, stunted and windblown forests, gnarled trees, impassable swamps, lifeless rocks, and tundra, tundra, a mossy wasteland without end or edge.

His garrison was located in the Arctic circle. The settlement there boasted few inhabitants or visitors: dull buildings perched on the slopes, featureless streets, pipes running from small boiler rooms, trash dumps, scrub land, and finally the airfield off in the distance, its runway blasted and hacked into the rocks. It was a stone's throw from the sea, where no two years were the same: one year the bays would be frozen solid and passage could only be secured by an icebreaker; the next, the life-giving Gulf Stream would tame the bitter cold, warming the sea and cloaking both the dry land and the sea alike in an impenetrable fog.

## 2

Chance had brought both me and the American colonel to New York. We were both staying in the guest rooms of the Yale Club, a thirty-story building at the intersection of Vanderbilt Avenue and 44th Street, right next to Grand Central Station. These lodgings were meant for graduates of Yale University, though I, unlike the colonel, had gone to medical school in Riga. I was on a business trip, and the Yale Club had agreed to give me a place to stay while I was in New York.

It was chance that brought the colonel and me together. One morning I was taking the elevator to the twenty-sixth floor to have breakfast in the restaurant there, when halfway up the elevator became stuck and I found myself trapped with a tall, lean American, no longer young, but athletic and youthful. He resembled an aged Hollywood actor who had spent his entire life playing cowboys and sheriffs: gaunt face, gray hair cut short and parted to one side.

While work went on to extract us from the elevator, we exchanged a few words on our predicament. I liked the fact that he did not make a great drama out of our enforced confinement. On the contrary, he grinned, and used the intercom to ask how long our sentence might last, and could we possibly be served breakfast there in the elevator. By the time we finally reached the restaurant, we were like old acquaintances. The maître d' assumed we were dining together and guided us to the same table. Neither of us objected.

As I recall, we were seated in a corner, and on two sides the table was bordered by glass walls, revealing a view of early-morning Manhattan. The streets were like gorges, slashed between the roofs and teeming skyscrapers, down below were crowds of people and an endless flow of cars, and everything was enveloped in exhaust fumes. At the height of the twenty-sixth floor, small clouds hung, light and white, the remaining shreds of night-time fog, while far below us the city sizzled with life.

For those first few minutes, I felt uncomfortable, even afraid. All that separated us from a bottomless abyss on two sides was the glass. Our table, with its checkered cloth, brightly-painted chairs, and the two of us seated opposite each other, seemed to be floating bizarrely in the sky above the city. Merely looking down made one's heart stop from the height and the endless expanse. The emptiness was frightening, and my head spun; I was not used to this.

"I think we've flown too high," I said, glancing down fearfully once more. "It's time to land."

"Maybe we should keep flying a while," the American countered. "I'm used to this, though I rarely get the opportunity these days."

"Are you a pilot?"

"I was."

"Civil aviation?"

"Military. B-17s. I'm Colonel Steven Creighton."

My new acquaintance had been retired for some years now, and as we ate breakfast I learned that he had fought in World War II, in which he had flown a "Flying Fortress", bombed Germany, and managed to get through a year and a half of the war unscathed. In the end, however, he had been shot down, and after a time as a POW he had served in the occupying forces, then later in Korea, after which he had gone on to command a strategic B-52 wing over Vietnam. After he had had enough of bombing, he retired. Naturally enough, once the war against Germany was over, the American had done what he could to counter the Communist menace, whether in Europe, the Far East, or Southeast Asia – in whatever place the Reds might choose to descend like locusts.

A Hispanic waiter brought me fresh melon, strawberries, and juices. Colonel Creighton, like all Americans, started his day with a cup of coffee and a roll with jam.

"So," I asked, "they sent you from Germany to Korea?"

"I volunteered to go," the colonel answered gruffly, as if my question had annoyed him.

After the war, Germany was like heaven for the occupying forces. Canned meat, a pack of cigarettes, or a bottle of whiskey could be traded for all kinds of wonders. Some of the men made good money, or even a sizable fortune. The post-war devastation created conditions which certain enterprising people found good for doing business.

The colonel did not argue with me when I brought this up. His reply was restrained. "In Germany we didn't live badly," he said. "The thing was, though, in those years we were constantly expecting war with Russia. Day in, day out. They had Stalin and we had Truman. A fight could break out at any moment."

"Who would have won?"

"Frankly, the Soviets could have grabbed all of Europe. Their tanks could have reached the Atlantic in a matter of days. We thought a new world war would start just like that. Our air force in Germany was directed toward the east."

Waiters moved hurriedly around the floor. Now and again the elevator discharged hotel guests coming from various floors. Some of these found themselves turned away by the maître d'; no admittance without jacket and tie. Well, when in Rome… A jacket and tie it was, then, and only on Saturdays was one allowed to have breakfast in shabbier attire.

Soon the restaurant grew crowded, and a light hubbub floated above the tables. The two glass walls came together at the corner behind me, and the colonel and I leisurely ate our breakfast at a dizzying height in the sky above New York. In front of me and just to my right rose the sharp tip of the Chrysler building, while further afield I caught a glimpse of the famous skyscrapers of the Mobil corporation, the *Daily News*, and the Ford Foundation. Among the buildings, like a flying saucer, loomed the round dome of Grand Central Station at the corner of neighboring 42nd Street.

"You know, when North Korea attacked the South, we were shocked. While we were still figuring out what to do, Kim Il-sung reached Seoul. Just a little longer, and it would have been too late. I decided my skills were needed."

Steven Creighton had piloted a bomber over the 38th parallel and had been lucky: his plane was never shot down. American B-29s hammered North Korea, and the front was gradually pushed back. Then the Chinese became involved, saving Kim Il-sung from total defeat. There were so many Chinese that the allies pressed up against them as if they were a living wall. The UN forces barely managed to restore the border between North and South. Yes indeed: a million Chinese soldiers proved to be a serious obstacle; even the American army and air force could not manage to demolish this wall, built as it was out of Chinese cannon fodder.

"In November '50 we first met the Russians in the skies," the colonel said. "They were protecting Kim Il-sung from the air. I remember those days well. We'd been flying almost without cover, and suddenly the Koreans started shooting us down. We figured out right away that it was Russians flying with Korean markings."

"Did they shoot down a lot of planes?" I asked, trying to sound completely clueless in order to conceal my interest. "Were there major losses?"

"Yes, major losses," the colonel bowed his head and fell silent, as if now fully absorbed in his memories; then he began to speak again. "They had MiG-15 fighters. We were covered by F-80 Shooting Stars and F-84 Thunderjets, but their MiGs shot them down. We were completely gobsmacked. Our boys were taking off and flying straight to the slaughter. American taxpayers and the government had to shell out for new F-86 Sabrejets."

"Did it get easier then?"

"It did, but things were never as calm as they had been before. We knew all the Russian aces by name. Ten or fifteen guys. We'd get warning over the radio when any of them took off. Everyone was on the alert for them."

I knew that the Soviet 64th Fighter Aviation Corps had shot down a large number of American planes in Korea. Well, war is war. Many of my patients from Division X had passed through the Korean school. In little more than three years, nine air divisions had fought in Korea, though our involvement had been kept carefully hidden. Now I had an opportunity to talk to an American pilot who had fought in Korea. Without any hurry or anger, we calmly, discussed these events from long-ago.

It was hard to say that any one plane was superior to the others. The MiG-15 could take off faster, it had a shorter run-up and gained altitude swiftly, and it would have the advantage from above. The F-86 Sabre, on the other hand, maneuvered better and could fly longer distances.

"What do you remember best from the war?" I asked, when we had compared planes.

Colonel Creighton thought deeply for a moment, then took his knife and fork and simulated a dogfight.

"You might know how counter-attacks work. The Russian could come swooping down from high altitude – up there, the MiG was the master. But at low altitude, Sabrejets had the edge. When we were on a collision course, closing speed could be 1,200 miles per hour. We were coming at each other so fast, the pilots had no time to react."

"Now they fly even faster," I remarked.

"They do. Every generation of pilots does better than its training. Back then we thought a dogfight was the limit of what we could achieve. I've got to hand it to the Russians, though – they fought pretty well. They had this pilot, Captain Nikolai Sutyagin. He shot down twenty-two of our planes. All our aces went after him, especially our top boys, Joseph McConnell and James Jabara. But even they couldn't get Sutyagin. Our commander, a chap named Colonel Harrison Thyng, set every squadron onto it in a different way, but no one could shoot Sutyagin down. I hear he's already a general. Honestly, the MiG-15 was better equipped than the Sabrejet."

I felt a certain pride at hearing that: the colonel had recognized the skill of our weapons designers. He was right, of course. The MiG-15 had been armed with two 23 mm and one 37 mm cannon. These were distinguished by their high rate of fire and precise aim, and they could penetrate any armor plating. The six Colt-Browning machine guns with which the Sabre was equipped were inferior by every measure.

In Korea, Colonel Creighton had flown a B-29, the famous long-haul bomber, which was equipped for night flights. Pilots would sleep during the day, go up at night to drop their bombs under cover of darkness, and return to base by dawn. The Soviet 64th Fighter Aviation Corps gradually became masters of night-time dogfights, which led to a marked increase in American losses of B-29 bombers. A certain Major Karelin had managed to shoot down six Flying Fortresses on night fights. Recalling his name, the colonel grew visibly upset; clearly he had taken part in those battles and lost some of his comrades. He looked around distractedly, his pale eyes wandering around the New York skies, ringed by skyscrapers on this morning in late summer. I can still picture that scene in my mind now. A time that the Russians called "old lady's summer" and the Americans "Indian summer".

The colonel suddenly broke off our conversation and inexplicably disappeared, though physically he did not budge from his place, remaining seated at the table exactly as before. He was far away though, off in some unknown place beyond the horizon, his mind roaming in time and space. Steven Creighton was lost in thought, in his reminiscences, but I listened to the silence, tuning in to another frequency. This ability is something that the Chinese Taoists have, adept as they are in the wordless intercommunication of souls. In Division X we had intently studied the secret abilities of the followers of the Tao, which means the Way, and their teacher Lao Tzu, called by his contemporaries, all those thousands of years ago, the "Ancient Child".

We were seated together in New York at a single table, but Steven Creighton was flying at a dizzying height in the night-time skies. The crew of his B-29 were working a little sleepily but still competently in the darkness dimly lit by the glow of their instruments. None of the crew members knew what might be waiting for them. Abruptly, the skies lit up with gunfire. Anti-aircraft rounds could not reach the plane at that altitude, but it was obvious that the alarm would have already been sounded at the airfields, and the Russian pilots who had been on duty and waiting would already be taxiing to the runway.

The crews of the bombers flew calmly on, untroubled, but inside, everyone was expecting the Soviets' snub-nosed MiG-15s to appear out of nowhere and pounce. The B-29 echelon kept a formation that ensured each gunner could cover his neighbors with crossfire, and while everyone held the formation it would be hard for anyone to sneak up on them. With time, though, the Russian pilots developed a dogfighting tactic that brought them success. First a wave of interceptors would rush in. The American Sabres and the Russian MiGs would clash, pairs of opposing jets flying all over the place with incredible aerobatics. Then a second wave of interceptors would fly in from different directions and try to disrupt the bombers' formation.

It was never the case that everyone made it home from a night flight. The Russian fighters merely had to disrupt the squadron, and then each bomber would have to fight its own battle, and fending off the enemy alone was not easy. Once they lost their formation, the slow and unwieldy bombers became easy pickings for the fighters.

In Vietnam, Colonel Creighton commanded a strategic wing and flew the new B-52. In the air they were covered by supersonic F-4 Phantoms, a plane which had just been introduced into active service. The subsonic MiG-17s and MiG-19s flown by the Vietnamese and Chinese were slower than the Phantoms, and the story was the same as it had been in Korea: at first the Americans felt safe and at ease in the skies above Vietnam, and at the high altitudes unattainable by the enemy's fighters they would arrogantly comport themselves, completely carefree, as if they were the lords of the skies, conquerors of the heights.

No one would dispute that the strategic long-distance B-52 bombers were a technical marvel of that era. They could fly in any weather, they could easily cross an ocean and back, and their distance, speed, weight capability, and ceiling were impressive. The B-52 had no equal in the precision of its bombing, and furthermore, it was the first time a bomber had been equipped with rockets guided by on-board radar.

By every measure, the B-52 was a perfect plane, and when it was accompanied by F-4 Phantoms, it was well-nigh invincible. Not even the Soviet forces, let alone the Vietnamese or Chinese, were capable of opposing it. Later, when Vietnam had received the new MiG-21 supersonic fighters, and when the local pilots, slowly and with difficulty, had mastered the art of flying them, flying a B-52, too, became a dangerous job; the risks increased considerably. Later still, the Soviet Union equipped Vietnam's anti-aircraft defenses with surface-to-air missiles. The need for fighter planes was reduced, and they gradually disappeared entirely.

We continued to sit in the restaurant of New York's Yale Club on the twenty-sixth floor, but the colonel was somewhere else. He had forgotten all about me; he was absorbed in his thoughts and said nothing. Steven Creighton was still far away in the night skies above Korea, above Vietnam, seeing his comrades perish, and he was gripped by the same fear that he had felt then, his world growing dark and his thoughts gloomy.

"Maybe it's time for me to go." I spoke up in order to bring him back to himself. The colonel glanced at me in confusion, as if only half-awake. He looked around the room, apparently baffled, wondering where he was and what had happened to him. Then he pulled himself together, regained his composure, and nodded, as if he had made the entire journey back from there to here in an instant.

"Sorry, I got lost in thought," he excused himself, and shook his head in shame. "Bad form to do that in company."

"It's no problem," I reassured him. "I still don't know whether the Russians actually fought in Vietnam or not. What do you think?"

"We all felt certain the Russians were fighting there, though we didn't have any real proof. But the planes the Vietnamese had were Russian, and the way they flew left no doubt. They fought in the air like Russians – obviously the Russians had taught them how to fly and how to fight. We lost thousands of planes. And the pilots – what about them? If you weren't killed, you still ended up a prisoner."

"It wasn't the Russians who started it," I said, despite myself. I did not want to get into an argument. Petty arguments often lead to pointless hostility.

"North Vietnam started it, just like North Korea," Colonel Creighton explained, convinced of the rightness of his position. "We couldn't accept that, we had to get involved. Then the Russians came in as well."

"Of course they did. Could they really have stayed on the sidelines?"

"No, they couldn't, but that doesn't make things any easier. We had to sort out the whole mess."

I thought how ultimately the entire world had turned into an arena in which our two countries vied with each other. Sad as it was, our entire existence was stained by a merciless rivalry. Both they and we were subjected to a brutal struggle, and everyone suffered. How many lives were cut short on both sides; how cruel fate had been.

Nothing could be done now, however. We sat there quietly, neither of us saying anything. The atmosphere around our table grew strange at the Yale Club restaurant, where the Manhattan skyline was right there outside the glass and the crowds of people on the street far below were like ants. The gloom that hung over our table was understandable. I even felt remorse; it was my fault that this had happened. Yes, it sometimes happens that undesirable events result, uncontrolled and unexpected, from a chance conversation between two strangers stuck in an elevator, who otherwise would never have met.

A punctilious waiter in a red waistcoat brought the bill, and we settled it – naturally, each paying for himself, as is the done thing among civilized people. Especially considering that I was spending money meant for official business. Unlike me, Creighton left the waiter a generous tip, but I was a simple Soviet man… No, not a prisoner, as the famous song goes, but I had been sent on a mission, and I could not allow myself to squander money, to carouse and live high on the hog. Now all that remained for us was to stand up, walk out, and say goodbye to each other forever. Nothing tied me to him; it had been a chance meeting at a place where our paths had crossed.

I said goodbye, left the hotel, and flagged a taxi. From the restaurant on the twenty-sixth floor, New York had seemed majestic and solemn, like a great big organ in a church, but down below, gloomy Vanderbilt Avenue resembled a dim subterranean passageway. At street level, the city looked anxious and agitated, passersby rushing along with exaggeratedly serious faces, as if everyone was worried about the exact same thing at the same time. Crowds of people swarmed around the entrance to Grand Central Station, where cabs in their black, yellow, and gray colors would fly in from everywhere and then speed off.

Among the passersby, from whom one got a clear whiff of the dull weekday grind, only a couple of young blacks brought life to the joyless scene. They flashed dazzlingly white teeth as they laughed heartily, making their leisurely way in brightly colored shirts and pants. With merry and exaggerated gestures they swept past us and then vanished, like clowns who had just been gaily performing at a carnival and then suddenly found themselves in Manhattan, among ordinary city folk at a random hour between breakfast and lunch.

I, too, had to quicken my steps, for before I flew out of New York the next day, there remained things to be done. On trips abroad, one day is never enough.

After I had eaten breakfast at the Yale Club restaurant, I spent the entire day in various visits and meetings, and I returned to the hotel only in the evening. In the spacious lobby, with its striped sofas and soft armchairs, a porter and some messengers were standing behind a wide wooden counter to the left of the entrance, dressed in colorful uniforms and round hats. Here I met Colonel Creighton again. The bellhop had just taken his luggage out of the elevator, and I took it upon myself to walk the colonel to his car. We stepped outside together and stood at the entrance under the wide awning that covered the sidewalk. The colonel was waiting for his daughter Cindy, who lived in New York, to come and drive him to the John F. Kennedy International Airport, where he would board a late-night flight to Seoul.

Creighton himself, incidentally, lived in San Francisco, and usually saw his daughter each year in September, when he would visit her in New York or, more often, she would come to California.

The colonel's son Michael was also a military pilot, serving in a fighter wing at the Misawa Air Base in Japan. Each year in late August or early September, Colonel Creighton would go from San Francisco to New York to visit his daughter, and then he would fly on to South Korea. As a veteran of the Korean War, Colonel Creighton was entitled to visit Seoul once a year, and he would spend a week there as an honored guest, with all expenses paid by the South Korean government. Usually his son Michael would try to arrange his leave at the same time and fly from the island of Hokkaido to see his father. They would ordinarily meet in Seoul before the rainy season, though this year was an exception to the rule. This time Major Creighton had flown to San Francisco, the city where he had spent his childhood, and he had spent two weeks with his father and his childhood buddies. Father and son had then left for New York for three days, and that night they were to fly together to Seoul. From Korea, the major could easily return to his base on Hokkaido.

"I'm sorry, I never asked you where you're from," the colonel suddenly said.

I did not hide the truth. "The Soviet Union," I answered.

"You've immigrated here?"

"No, I live there."

"Oh, Lord!" Steven Creighton said, and slapped his forehead. "And there I was, running my mouth off! I can imagine what you thought of me."

"No, no, it's fine. After all, we were allies once."

   

"Of course, of course!" the colonel nodded. Chagrin remained clearly visible in his face, but behind that chagrin one could guess at other thoughts that had just arisen and would not let him go.

Neither of us noticed a silver Ford turn the corner of 44th Street, jauntily pull up to the sidewalk, and stop sharply at the entrance to the hotel.

"Hi, Daddy!" A redheaded beauty jumped out of the car and, without slowing her pace, came up and kissed her father, deftly spun round on her high heels, and then opened the door for him.

The colonel meanwhile was frozen in a strange stupor. Only slowly did he come round, as if he had been pondering an urgent problem, seeking a solution for some pressing business.

"Daddy!" the young lady called to the colonel. She urged him on and danced impatiently on her long, slender legs. It was obvious at once that she regularly visited a gym to work out, went running and swimming, and in general paid a great deal of attention to her physique. I must admit, I very much admire sporting types, especially women, who take care of themselves and do not let themselves go.

The colonel, though, seemed to be somewhere else. He was far away from the Yale Club hotel, from Vanderbilt Avenue, from the city of New York, and from reality in general.

His behavior was indeed very odd. His daughter's eyes opened wider than the door of the car, and she seemed quite unable to make any sense of her father's strange demeanor. He himself did not notice her astonishment, and was in no hurry to say goodbye to me and get into the car. He gazed absently about him.

Moving slowly, as if with difficulty, the colonel turned to me. "When are you heading back?" He asked the question stiffly and timidly, as if something important to him hinged on my answer.

"Tomorrow. I'm taking a roundabout route, though. I'll only get back to Moscow ten days from now."

"Are you going to Italy?" the young lady suddenly asked. My, she was uncommonly attractive. Her pure skin shone like fine porcelain and her eyes were dazzlingly bright.

"How did you guess?" I asked, in great astonishment. She had knocked me off balance; it was as if she already knew something about my movements around the world.

"It's the Venice film festival," she said, speaking as if nothing out of the ordinary had happened. "I'd been planning to go myself, for my job."

"Are you not going, then?" I asked, with a mixture of hope and a sinking feeling.

"It didn't work out this year. Maybe next year if things go well."

Honestly, Cindy had stunned me with what was either female intuition or a lucky guess, or a keen sense. In any case, her intuition had not misled her. Her unexpected question had been right on target. Perhaps, for some inexplicable reason, Cindy had tuned into my own thoughts and could tell which way they were going.

Scientists in Division X examined the noetic symptoms that relate to intuitive understanding. We studied the nature of random guesses, coincidences, prophetic dreams and the gift of foresight. We arranged experiments, gathered statistics, and searched for natural laws. And now this young American lady had shown an interest as if she was experiencing a premonition of things to come.

Yes, I admit that I had business in Europe, but it was not about that. When my superiors at Division X had sent me abroad, they decided to kill several birds with one stone. On the way back from America, I was to remain in Italy for a time on an intelligence-gathering mission. Cindy naturally could not have known anything of my plans to gather intelligence, nor of the reasons why I was taking this particular route.

Firstly, passengers coming from the USA did not attract special interest. Secondly, at the film festival it would be easier to disappear among the crowds, or at least to attract less attention. Thirdly, I would not need to fill out yet more forms, obtain visas, and generally be conspicuous at the border. Fourthly, there were material benefits: government accountants labor tirelessly to reduce costs, and if two trips can be combined into one, money is obviously saved. Not to mention that I had some selfish interests of my own, for if a person got a once-in-a-lifetime opportunity to visit the Venice Film Festival, with the state paying for it, O lucky man, it would be foolish to refuse: Venice, the island of Lido, a hotel room booked, all-inclusive. Any way you looked at it, it was a dream come true. However, the Americans did not need to know any of these details. I had no intention of involving the Creighton family in my plans.

Meanwhile the colonel was sadly shaking his head and continuing to mutter, "It's a pity I didn't meet you before. A real pity!" His sadness seemed boundless, sincere, overwhelming, and inextinguishable. He stood still among the rushing passersby, like a player unsure who to pass the ball to. Then he went on, timidly, as if afraid of being met with a refusal, "Forgive me, sir… But if you could… I know how ridiculous it sounds, but… there's no other possibility. There won't ever be one. I know it's an awful lot to ask. I don't want to trouble you, but please listen for a moment, I won't keep you long. This is something that's really important to me. Afterward Cindy can drive you wherever you want to go. Please!"

His daughter said nothing; she was staring at her father silently, as if seeing him for the first time. She could not understand what was going on with him, and was completely baffled by his behavior. The colonel, too, stood there motionlessly, as if his fate was in the balance, as if his life depended on my answer. What can I say; we had been brought together by a mysterious whim of chance, but now it was I who had the power to move forward toward the mystery, or take my leave of him and walk away.

I glanced down Vanderbilt Avenue and found no answer there as it stretched away, narrow, gloomy, and sullen. To be honest, I failed to find any answer, no matter how hard I tried to look for it.

"I need to make a phone call," I said in a rather guarded tone, without particular enthusiasm. I was now being forced to change my plans on the hoof.

"Thank you, sir." The colonel sighed with relief and bowed ceremoniously. "You can call from the car, we've got a radio telephone."

I called the place where I was being expected and put my meeting back to a later time. Meanwhile Colonel Creighton had shoved his bag into the trunk. We sat together in the back seat, and he placed a narrow case on his knees.

"What's that?" I asked out of nothing beyond mere curiosity.

"A flute," Colonel Creighton answered. "I play it sometimes."

The car set off, the streets and avenues of Manhattan shining through the window. I felt a light dizziness, as if the reality around me held a promise of bold new experiences: my nose for these things rarely let me down. I frankly had no idea what was to come, what risk I might be taking, but better that way than the horrible monotony of everyday routine.

3

Nikolai Shilin had come to the Arctic from Germany. In those days, a top student could choose his own place of assignment after flight school, and the newly-minted lieutenant chose Germany, the Western Group of Forces. From the airfield in Potsdam, fighters would occasionally take off to make interceptions, to fly along the border, or to patrol the air corridor leading to West Berlin. Naturally the entire territory was kept under vigilant guard. Radar operators had their sights on Europe, but they kept especially close watch on airfields nearby that were directed toward the east. A plane needed only to take off in an easterly direction and immediately Soviet interceptors would take to the air. Based on the guidance of the radar station – course, altitude, bearing – the interceptors would stick close to the target plane until it landed, or they would move to patrol a section along the border.

Of all the occupying forces, the Americans were the most brazen in the sky. The French and English behaved themselves, but the Americans would often soar recklessly, openly bullying the Soviets; they might feign an attack, or violate East German airspace in order to locate the radar stations there and determine their communication frequencies and codes, or simply to play on the nerves of their former allies and make them lose their cool.

One could hardly catch any sleep as a fighter pilot. The situation on the border of the occupied territory grew increasingly tense by the day, and the level of determination rose with each new order. Day and night, the squadrons kept a sleepless vigil, their ears sharp at all times. They kept watch over the sky like a diligent landowner over his garden. It often seemed as if a fight was just about to break out, a battle in the skies, but at the last minute the American Spitfire would pull away, as it knew precisely the boundary that could not be crossed without bloodshed ensuing.

At the airfield, the pilots stood watch, ready to scramble at any moment. They sat in the cockpit with their flight suits on, their fuel tanks full, their weapons armed, and the aircraft connected to the power supply. As soon as the order "Airborne!" was given, they could take off immediately – the entire process took only three minutes.

The skies above Germany seemed awfully cramped to these pilots. A plane had only to take off, maneuver, gain altitude and set a course, and Western Europe seemed already to be rushing straight at it. At those speeds, the entire continent was a stone's throw away, and you could violate another country's airspace before you even knew it.

This represented a real headache for many Soviet pilots, accustomed as they were to their spacious homeland. Back in the USSR, there was plenty of room to move around, and one could fly on and on in any direction, but in East Germany the border was always right there, and the pilots felt as if they were cooped up and on an invisible leash. If you so much as blinked, you were already over foreign territory, and if you were not intercepted, then be happy, your luck was in.

Shilin knew many of the American pilots and ground operators by name. In turn, they knew everyone in his squadron and his regiment. The Americans would often broadcast on the Soviet regiment's frequency, and sometimes they would be the first to congratulate officers on a promotion, one day, two days, or even a week before the message came down from headquarters. This was the Americans' distinctive swagger, a demonstration of their capabilities, of their ability to gather intelligence: fly on, little one, you just fly, we know everything about you. They knew the Soviet pilots' entire service records, and sometimes even details of their families. In the Cold War, playing on the opponent's nerves was fair game.

Germany was dramatically different from Russia. Ah! The old cities of Saxony and Harz: Quedlinburg, Wernigerode, Königstein, and the rest. They were like enchanting dreams, pages from children's picture books: knights' castles on hilltops, walls and towers, mossy bulwarks, moats, drawbridges, narrow, medieval lanes, cobblestones, houses that looked like gingerbread, tiled roofs, everything impeccably clean… From the walls of the fortresses, one looked down onto a dense expanse of sharp roofs, steeples, weather vanes, and chimneys.

Unforgettable were the cozy little beer halls, the merry, good-natured burghers and the way they sat on the heavy wooden benches as they drank and sang in a chorus, the oak barrels, their wood darkened by time, the firm smell of good beer and fried sausages that the walls had absorbed over the centuries.

Sometimes the pilot sat there – "*ein Bier, bitte*" – among the upright and smiling Krauts, craftsmen and artisans, adherents of the Lutheran Bible, frugal-minded folk with their quiet and measured speech. There was none of the swearing, shouting, scuffles, or brawls, none of the dirt-spattered floors, sticky tables, or foul-smelling and suffocating air of provincial institutions back in Russia, where morose drunkards whiled away their lives.

Indeed, as long as Shilin sat there silently, no one would have taken him for a Russian. There was something European in him, though you could not tell right away what it was. His features suggested membership of a northern race. In other words, Nikolai Shilin looked more Scandinavian or Anglo-Saxon – a rare trait for someone who hailed from Siberia. His face held not the slightest hint of the prominent cheekbones of the steppe peoples, those bow-legged, swarthy, slant-eyed, stocky, horse-riding nomads. A facial feature that had been gifted to the Slavs by the Turks, and the Scythians, Khazars, Kipchaks, Cumans, and Mongols…

When the pilot was in Europe, he did not feel as if he was in a foreign land, though he had been born and raised in Siberia. He felt as if unknown lands had been revealed to him in childhood, or even earlier, before he was born, in the mists of the past, but what lands, where? His intuition, his gut feeling, suggested somewhere to the west. There, faintly and dimly, in the murk beyond an unseen boundary, as if in forgotten dreams, he felt a foreign presence, and he sensed strangers to whom he strangely felt attached. Part of Shilin's own nature seemed to lie there among them.

If you asked Shilin what these unlikely suspicions meant, he would not know the answer. But sometimes – not too often, but sometimes – he would find sneaking up on him the absurd notion that only part of him was in Russia, and somewhere beyond the horizon, in some other reality, was to be found the rest of him.

Thus it was that military aviator Nikolai Shilin came to Division X at the beginning of March. On the snowy hill behind the trees, he caught a glimpse of an Orthodox monastery which, as was the custom in the Middle Ages in Russia, had guarded the approach to the capital: high towers, walls, embrasures for firing arrows, golden domes. This was so unexpected a sight that doubt and bewilderment arose within him, like a sleepy bird: had he come to the right place?

Before leaving his place of assignment, Shilin had received orders setting out the route he was to follow, and as a military man he had executed them to the letter. He had even taken a local bus from the station to the indicated stop and then walked, following his instructions. According to the paper, the captain had arrived at his destination, but now here was a monastery staring right at him. Atop the hill, an impregnable fortress rose above the forest. The mighty walls and towers inspired awe, as does any building that has stood for centuries. This stone fortification resembled an ancient city in the sky, something fantastical, something out of childhood fantasies. Before he approached the massive gates, the pilot looked around hesitantly, not quite believing, as if searching for a government office where he should go to report his arrival, present his documents, and hand over a sealed package. He apparently did not know that after the Revolution, the Bolsheviks had housed many secret institutions in monasteries. He did not know, or had forgotten.

The pilot had come into the world in a camp for enemies of the people, shortly before the end of the war. His mother had given birth to him in the small prison hospital, which lacked any special maternity ward. It is true that prisoners were categorically forbidden to have children; the Great Leader had prudently banned the ideologically harmful from reproducing. However, the pilot had been conceived while his mother had still been a free woman, so it was too late. The only thing that remained was for him to come into the world – a bold step under these conditions and maybe even a turn for the worse.

Soon after Shilin had been conceived, his mother had been arrested and immediately sentenced – the tribunal at the front did not bother to go through the ritual of a prosecution opposed by a defense. His mother gave birth to him when she had already spent a summer, fall, winter and part of spring in the camp.

Did the infant, as he was being born, know that he was an enemy of the people? No one had ever pressed any charges against him personally. He had wound up in his prison camp without any trial, and just by coming into the world he had sentenced himself to ten years without any right of appeal. He served his sentence in full, without parole, and his birthday fell on the day of his release. As one can imagine, little Nikolai firmly believed that the world was one big prison, for the camp was all he knew. The untrodden taiga stretched all around him, and a bumpy unpaved road led from the nearest pier to the camp – a day's journey on a creaking truck.

For reasons that were not explained, in the camp the boy was given the nickname of "the American". This nickname originated in the camp offices, where the case files were held. No one gave him any details, no one explained the reason. The women prisoners mocked him, the camp personnel smirked at him. The child lived in complete ignorance, but he grew used to being referred to as the "American". After all, why fight it, when there were worse nicknames around: one of the camp guards was known as the Ghoul. And the Great Leader and shining light of Communism was known in the camp, for some odd reason, as Minai, though when he was a child and still living in his native mountainous region, he had also been given the nickname Chopur after suffering from smallpox; "Minai" means "pockmarked" in Georgian. Shilin's nickname of "the American" seemed to mean something beyond the child's ken – some kind of contempt, spite, or reproach. It hinted at a mysterious guilt.

After the death of the official in charge of the entire prison region, the camp administrators reviewed the cases and many were released. Nikolai's mother served her whole sentence, however. She served every day to which the tribunal had sentenced her, for the Great Leader may have already been laid to rest but the Soviet regime had not gone anywhere and could not forgive a Soviet officer, let alone a political operative, for a monstrous crime such as hers. In the end, the military interpreter served ten years, plus an extra month due to the perennial inaccessibility of the place: only rarely could a ship make its way up the shallow river, and they were lucky to catch one.

To reach the pier, they spent an entire day in the back of a truck, and then for a week they floated downstream on a barge hauled by a little tugboat, until finally they reached the Yenisei. Then for two weeks they suffocated in the stinking hold of an old steamboat whose shuddering wheels would slam into the water in a difficult battle with the impetuous current of the mighty river.

The Shilins settled in Krasnoyarsk. Nikolai's mother did not have the strength to make it all the way back to Moscow, where she had been born and from where she had been sent to the front. There was another reason that made them settle in Siberia, however: the local teacher-training school had opened a department for foreign languages, and there was a need for instructors. The school gave Olga Shilina a room in the dormitory, so they decided to go no further, and settled in Krasnoyarsk. That fall Nikolai's mother turned thirty years old.

Anyone who has journeyed on the Yenisei knows the enchantment of its power and beauty. The Yenisei made an unforgettable impression on me, at any rate, when I was a student. I remember the roar it gave out in springtime as it surged toward the ocean, and how it would burst through fields of ice and beat on the sheer cliffs that rose above it toward the heavens. Behind those cliffs stretched an endless expanse of densely-forested hills – the taiga. The chain of hills disappeared beyond the horizon, and the further north one went, the farther apart the Yenisei's banks were, as the river grew ever wider.

Krasnoyarsk was set in a valley split in half by the river. On holidays, a platform would be set up for the authorities on a bumpy stretch of waste ground in the middle of the city, between the stately building of the regional Party committee and the central park, and processions of the local population would be arranged, as a sign of unity and mutual esteem.

In those days, the main square was bordered by perfectly straight streets and sturdy stone buildings that had been built before the Revolution and during the years of industrialization. One had only to step a block away, though, to find oneself suddenly in a dreary Siberian trading post: unpaved streets full of puddles and potholes, with only the occasional passerby, gloomy houses darkened by time and made from logs as thick as a man's outstretched arms, high fences, heavy gates, and tightly closed window shutters. The roads were lined by shallow ditches overgrown with weeds. Once darkness fell, the streets were abandoned; the local inhabitants would not even stick their noses out of their gates, as old Siberian memories had led them to fear ill-intentioned men. The little town of Krasny Yar that had once stood here had long been known as a place for marauders. Initially it was famous for Cossacks and seekers of fortune, while later on, forced laborers were settled there in large numbers, and the local transfer facility for prisoners was known across the country. Across the river Kacha, a sheer-faced mountain loomed over the city. For the edification of the townspeople, the cliff had been crowned with a shrine to St. Paraskeva, a solitary roof directed toward the heavens like a pointing finger.

After Germany, it was hard for the pilot to get used to the Arctic. This routine transfer from one place of assignment to another was more like exile: sad, melancholy Russia. After Europe, how horrible it is, ladies and gentlemen, to end up in the wild depths of Russia. The officers in the garrison, family men and bachelors alike, made no effort to hide the fact that they were living out of their suitcases. They found the place disorderly, and that dispirited them; no one wanted to settle in for long. Everyone seemed to be at a loss, as if caught unprepared by bad weather. Their aim seemed to be to wait out their time in the far north as if it were a downpour of rain or a blizzard – soon it would pass, and then they could go home. Even the locals who were born there lived in a fashion that seemed temporary, as if they might be ready to leave the next day.

The polar night fell on the garrison like an impenetrable wall. In the darkness, the fierce arctic wind would blow from the sea for weeks and bury the runway in snow. The soldiers on the airfield maintenance team would spend days clearing the concrete. They used special machines to melt the snow and ice, the nozzles of their flamethrowers roaring with hellish fire day and night.

As the polar night drew to its close, the local population waited impatiently for the sun. At the appointed hour, the edge of the sun emerged over the horizon and bathed the tundra in a faint copper light. The people of the settlement rejoiced at the light, and their rejoicing was genuine – but what did their eyes, which had grown so weary of the darkness, see? Besides the local countryside, the stony mounds and tundra, their view was not a pleasant one: shabby and squalid buildings with damp visible on the walls, steel drums strewn all around, black oil slicks, the dead earth stained with oil and diesel fuel, and trash heaps that had accumulated over many years.

Nikolai Shilin's flights mainly took him over the sea near the Norwegian border. As soon as a pair of patrolling Soviet fighters appeared over the neutral waters of Varangerfjord, where lay the picturesque Norwegian town of Kirkenes, the Norwegians would come to meet them. The Norwegians would never act aggressively, but would go through friendly maneuvers, though they would stay close and show that they were watching.

Sometimes the Soviet fighters would set off for the north from the Rybachy Peninsula, where the skies were often swept by American spy planes taking off from the NATO bases in Scandinavia. The American planes would generally fly along the border at a considerable height, observing and listening in on the wide territory to the south of their course. Naturally, the ports, aerodromes, movements of ships, garrisons, docks, and submarine bases held their constant attention and interested them greatly. However, it was impossible to chase the Americans off while they were over international waters, let alone shoot them down. All one could do was give them a few minor hassles, putting a spoke in their wheels in whatever ways the Soviet pilots could come up with.

Usually the Soviet fighters would approach the large American spy plane so closely that one wrong move and an aerial collision would result. The Soviet pilots' trick was coming as close as possible and flying right alongside in order to play on the nerves of the foreign pilots and their crews. The dozens of on-board electronic surveillance operators would abandon their control panels and monitors and gaze out the windows, wondering what the Russians were up to, for the Communists seemed to be totally out of control. Some would shake with fear, and everyone knows that a poor mental state makes for an unproductive worker; it is hard to do your job when you are constantly under the gun.

Sometimes the Soviet fighters would fly around the American planes in an annoying dance, like the mosquitoes that plague the tundra in the summertime. The fighters would suddenly pop up on one side, then on the other, or fly at close quarters in order to cut the spy planes off, for the latter were slow to maneuver.

In this endless quarrel, however, some tears fell unseen. With each new model of spy plane, the Americans could fly higher and higher. The Soviet interceptors struggled to rise into the stratosphere, since at that altitude their engines would stall. Their on-board gear was made lighter, therefore, in whatever way possible, including removing the outboard fuel tanks, which naturally had the downside of making their flight time shorter.

On top of that, to rise to the stratosphere, pilots had to replace their ordinary comfortable flight suits with special garb that would ensure their safety at high altitudes with full pressurization. This clothing made it harder for them to move around; it was very uncomfortable, and obstructed their vision, making it harder to fly the planes. Fighter pilots tried, as a result, to use these high-altitude suits as seldom as possible, and that made it difficult in practice for them to intercept foreign planes at high altitude.

The most recent spy-plane models proved a hard nut to crack for the Soviet fighters. The Americans could stroll around the stratosphere unhindered; they could even go right into Soviet airspace without any consequences. Old hands in Soviet air defense recalled, like a bad dream, something that had befallen them long ago: in the mid-1950s an American spy plane had taken off from Norway, flown over the Baltics, Belarus, and Ukraine, and landed at an air base in Turkey. While it was in the air, the Soviets had tracked it and shot at it, but they just could not reach it: it made a clear mockery of the USSR's capabilities. Soviet air defense felt completely humiliated, and generals tumbled from their posts like ripe pears. Senior leadership pushed aircraft engineers to use their brains and come up with new technology quickly, but such a thing simply could not be forced. Air defense, accepting their powerlessness, developed surface-to-air missiles instead and gradually mastered this new technology. Soon the Americans no longer felt safe in the stratosphere.

Meanwhile, in the skies above Northern Europe, as well as in Germany, there was never a dull moment. Besides interception flights or routine patrols, Shilin occasionally had to accompany Soviet aerial reconnaissance when the so-called Tupolevs – heavy long-distance bombers equipped with electronic equipment – would set off toward foreign bases and required fighter cover. The spy planes would generally take off as a group of three, and the fighters would fly in two by two from other airfields and catch up with them while they were over neutral waters.

Naturally, the Soviets would be picked up by foreign radar operators, who stood watch around the clock, and foreign interceptors would accompany them for their entire journey, handing off responsibility to their counterparts as each zone was crossed. As the Tupolevs traversed Cape Nordkinn and banked to go around the continent from the north, NATO personnel would immediately try to guess where they were headed, whether south toward the Norwegian Sea, the British Isles, or the Baltic coast, or west toward Iceland. In any case, they were closely monitored, and NATO fighters would maintain a parallel course, sometimes coming very close to them and deftly maneuvering. It was clear that the NATO personnel had received first-rate training. The Americans, incidentally, came to intercept them more frequently than others, and they were not easy to shake off. The Soviet pilots had to keep their eyes open.

However, just as the pike serves to prevent the smaller fish from growing complacent, the escorting fighters would not allow the interceptors to move around freely when the latter sought to hassle the reconnaissance planes. It was an exciting game, a real dogfight, albeit without a shot being fired. The large, heavy reconnaissance planes remained unfazed and calmly held their course, and the nimble fighters swept from side to side around them at lighting speed.

Normally these flights passed off without incident. When the interceptors noticed the escorting fighters, they would meekly keep to one side or even fly alongside the Soviets like an honor guard. Air defense would usually start to get nervous around the Lofoten Islands, in the vicinity of which were some military bases, ports, airfields, and direction-finding stations, and where NATO ships plowed up and down the sea. What really annoyed air defense, however, was when the hatches at the bottom of the Soviet spy planes were flung open, which meant that they were engaging in aerial photography. The American pilots would sometimes riskily dive under the belly of a spy plane to block the lenses, and then the escorting Soviet fighters would rush to the rescue and drive the insolent foreigners off, like dogs chasing strays from their turf.

Suitcase in hand, the pilot slowly walked down the forest road. The snow-covered forest stood motionless in its winter sleep, but the sounds of birds pointed to the imminent arrival of spring. Buntings gave out a lively trill, and to a keen ear it sounded like the very changing of the seasons. A woodpecker naggingly attacked a dry pine tree, the sound hammering the surrounding silence. The little drummer seemed to be telling its mate that it was high time now to start a nest, while at the same time it unequivocally staked out its territory against its rivals.

═══ ═ **4** ═ ═══

The letter to General Headquarters was handed over by the American embassy shortly after New Year. Stalin, however, had learned of the letter earlier. Molotov had told him over the telephone that for several days now the American ambassador W. Averell Harriman had been pushing for a meeting.

"What does he want?" Stalin asked with a frown. He was annoyed by the weather with its mud and slush, by waking up late in the day, by a general tiredness, and by the perennial expectation of bad news. He did not like it at all when business that required calm, careful thinking had to be settled right there and then. After sleepless nights, Stalin got up only slowly and with effort, and he felt overwhelmed and stressed, overcome by dark thoughts. Only late in the evening would his disgust with life melt away, and as night fell he would shake off his stupor and gloominess and rediscover his strength. His thoughts took on a clarity no longer clouded by sleep, and everything seemed to be illuminated in a steady bright light. There was no point denying it: the whole country knew that the Great Leader was a night owl.

Indeed, only at night could the Great Leader feel capable, think clearly, and make decisions. Efforts were made not to wake him during the day, except in cases of urgent need. In the middle of the night he could call or summon any officials, generals, or ministers in order to ask questions or convince himself once more of their devotion and attentiveness, and he would get very upset if someone was not reachable. The Great Leader's vast memory, comparable to Hitler's in its sharpness and power, firmly held onto any inappropriate remark, sidelong glance, blunder, reservation, or oversight, so that he could take his revenge when circumstances allowed. With time, all officials across the country came to demand that their subordinates be constantly available during the night; they all had to be on hand so that they could immediately answer any question that suddenly arose.

Reluctantly, but out of a desire to save their lives, millions of officials, major and minor, adopted a night-time lifestyle, all because the Great Leader was a night owl: they would all fall asleep as morning came, come late to the office, and work hard until dawn. No one dared even draw attention to themselves, let alone object to these demands. The windows of ministries, departments, and various government officials shone all night long, for the big boss might call at any moment. Toward morning the Great Leader would take off his soft Caucasian boots and lie down on a couch covered with a worn rug. Now all the myriad officials across the entire country could breathe freely, catch some sleep, and see their families.

Molotov, just like the others, was afraid of this gloomy, cantankerous, and vindictive man of the Caucasus, but today the need was so great and urgent that the People's Commissar for Foreign Affairs risked telephoning at an inconvenient hour.

"What does he want?" asked Joseph Stalin in a hoarse, unhappy voice, one tinged with a distinct Georgian accent.

Molotov was one of the few who had addressed Stalin on a first-name basis since their younger days. The Great Leader called his old companion-in-arms "Iron Arse" for his great strength and perseverance. By 1944, Stalin was making requests of the other Allies less and less often; for the most part, it was the Allies who were asking him for something. And he now he felt able to express his dissatisfaction to the Allies, unlike in the first years of the war, when it was inevitably Stalin doing the asking. They would come to him with requests that could sometimes be quite burdensome, and Stalin would remain silent in order to signal his disapproval. Today he sensed that a new request was looming, one that might get in the way of his plans, create unnecessary hassles, and prove to be a real headache.

The letter was delivered to Myasnitskaya, where Supreme High Command General Headquarters was located in a fine mansion with a mezzanine. Before the Revolution, the home had belonged to a prominent merchant, the tea king Soldatenkov. The grounds stretched as far as the two neighboring streets. Inside, the house featured wood trim, and the walls and ceiling were decorated with intricate patterns. One room deep within the house was fitted out in the Mauritanian style, with golden patterns and intricate Arabic ornaments, as if it were not a room at all but a painted box.

From the cellar of the Headquarters building, an underground passageway led to the bomb shelter by the neighboring air defense building; Air Defense was in turn connected via a further passageway to the Kirovskaya metro station. A guard was posted under the low vestibule in order to ensure that no metro passengers would start heading the wrong way. Stalin was afraid of aerial attacks, and so he chose precisely this way of reaching a celebratory gathering in November 1941, when the Germans were drawing close to Moscow. On the eve of the anniversary of the Revolution, the Great Leader left the building that housed Headquarters, entered the metro, and took it as far as Mayakovskaya station, but naturally he made his journey in a separate carriage from others, and he did not have to pay his fare.

By early 1944, the front had been pushed back to Western Ukraine, and was moving even further back by the day. Stalin was no longer afraid of aerial attack, and the need to move about underground vanished. Thereafter, the Great Leader did not use the metropolitan railway again.

As he had predicted, Roosevelt's letter contained a request for help. The request was not quite an ordinary one, and it brought certain difficulties, but as Stalin thought about it, it did offer some benefit and merited further consideration. Stalin brought the matter to his chiefs of staff; he wanted to hear from his men, and as they spoke, he smoked his pipe and paced quietly around the room. The matter concerned bombing Germany.

Roosevelt wrote that the bases for the B-17 Flying Fortress and B-24 Liberator planes of the Americans' 15th and 8th Air Force were located in Italy and England, and therefore the escorting F-5 Lightning and P-51 Mustang fighters would not have enough fuel for the return journey. The solution Roosevelt proposed was that after bombing Germany, the bombers, along with the escorting fighters, would cross the Eastern Front and land at the Soviet air bases near Poltava, where they could take on fresh ammunition and fuel, and the crews could rest. The bombers would then head back. On the return journey, they could bomb Germany once more, and they would have sufficient fuel to reach their bases in Italy and England.

Yes, the request from the American president was fraught with difficulties, but at Soviet headquarters everyone agreed on one thing: it was worth a try, and if the Allies were being slow to make their landing in Normandy, at least the Soviets could get this out of them. Besides bombing in the west, the Americans could begin bombing targets in the east as well, along the front and behind German lines. The chiefs of staff made their decision quickly, in mere days. Before February was out, Stalin had signaled to Roosevelt his agreement and the Soviets got to work. Air force generals, supply personnel, and military engineers rushed to Ukraine.

The Soviets provided three air bases for the Allies: the heavy bombers could be based near Poltava, and the fighters could use Mirgorod and Piryatin. By March, construction was underway day and night. By spring the rudimentary airfields built on unpaved ground had disappeared, replaced by runways and taxiways made from steel plates. The Americans had delivered these by steamer to Russia's Arctic ports, and American fuel and personnel had arrived in Ukraine by way of Iran. The Red Army's construction brigades swiftly set up entire little communities for the air bases: barracks, storehouses, field hospitals, and mess halls for thousands of men.

From the very beginning, the Allies had agreed on total secrecy. The code name Frantic Joe was assigned to the operation. All documents relating to it were classified Top Secret, and even the radio operators maintained total broadcast silence in order to avoid any suspicion. Nadezhda Peka, the head of the radio station at the Poltava air base, received an order to seal up the transmitter. The air base was guarded around the clock by special units, and air defense was provided by anti-aircraft units and a fighter division.

The Americans' first flight was scheduled for June 2. The nights were now short – darkness was falling later and dawn arriving earlier, so the flights were carefully planned to take place only under cover of darkness. On the night between the first and second of June, 130 B-17 Flying Fortress strategic bombers from the 15th Air Force took off from their base in Foggia in south-east Italy and set a course for the north-east. Seventy P-51 Mustang fighters, designed by North American Aviation, provided cover for this aerial armada from all sides.

The targets had been chosen in advance. The Americans had intended to bomb German aircraft factories near Riga and in Poland, as well as Romanian and Hungarian air bases, but Soviet command had suggested concentrating the blow on south-eastern Europe in order to not draw the Germans' attention to the central part of the front, where Operation Bagration was being prepared: a powerful surge into Belarus.

In the bomber's cockpit, Lieutenant Steven Creighton sat on the right in the copilot's chair. All four motors were humming in unison, and the Flying Fortress was holding its position in the formation. If the group of 130 huge bombers inspired fear during the daytime, at night in the pitch-black darkness these planes were simply terrifying.

The crew dozed. The evening before, they had all gone for a drink in a small Italian restaurant on a quiet street in Foggia. The restaurant owner had obtained a small cask of tart Italian wine from a nearby village, and now the crew had to pay for their evening of drinking and lack of sleep with a general feeling of lethargy and drowsiness.

Lieutenant Creighton had been flying over Europe for six months by this time, and he considered himself an experienced pilot – especially considering that many had been shot down in that time, and many others had been taken prisoner. After college, Creighton had attended flight school and graduated in late 1944, but before he was sent to the war in Europe, he managed to pay a visit to his hometown of San Francisco in order to say goodbye to his parents.

Over Germany they were met with a dense barrage of anti-aircraft fire. As always, German fighters took off to meet them. It was never the case that all bombers made it back to base. Indeed, over the six months that Creighton had been flying, their losses had been considerable, and on any flight the same could happen to him, though at the age of twenty-two it was hard for him to believe that he might die. In wartime everyone hopes to survive, and people who have been lucky so far believe that they are somehow special.

In the mess hall a crew would all sit together at the same table. When a table was unoccupied, that meant that a plane had been shot down and the crew had not come back. In the mess hall everyone could immediately notice a loss, and the obvious gap was painful to see. The grief and sadness was multiplied when many gaps appeared at the tables after a sortie. Everyone could still remember the crew that had been lost, their faces, and the way they talked and laughed, and now their table was empty, their comrades could not believe it, simply could not accept it.

Any table in the mess hall could end up empty after the next sortie. It was as if someone was eagerly pursuing the men dining there and eliminating them one by one, erasing them from among the living – a cruel hunt, a deadly game. Yes, the game would get whatever crew drew the wrong lot: a nearby table, one further away, on the right, on the left: bad luck, you're out. There were some sorties after which tables stood drastically empty, as if a plague had swept through the mess hall overnight. New planes would then arrive, new crews would sit down at the tables that had stood empty, and the deadly game continued.

On the night of June 2, the Flying Fortresses from the 15th Air Force took off from their base in Foggia, Italy and set a course for the northeast. Each bomber carried eight tons of bombs, and thirteen on-board machine guns provided protection in every direction. Through the cockpit window Lieutenant Creighton could see scattered clouds and starry sky, and the bomber formation in the moonlight was an enchanting sight. The same could be seen by the pilot in the left chair, Major Eddington, the crew's commander. However, it was the gunner who could boast the best view; his round glass bubble with a swiveling gun rose from the cabin behind the pilots' backs and was directed toward the rear.

The seventy P-51 Mustang fighters escorting the group of bombers kept alongside them on a parallel course, ready at any moment to enter into battle with the enemy's fighters. The paired large-caliber machine guns on the wings could provide a dense barrage of covering fire for the Flying Fortresses.

The aerial armada entered Yugoslavia under total darkness. Not a single light burned below along the mountain roads and in the villages. Only here and there in the forest meadows one saw a solitary fire, beside which perhaps resistance fighters and shepherds were warming themselves.

The first target on their itinerary was a large railway junction in eastern Hungary, the town of Debrecen. The formation dropped its bombs and continued onward, and over Romania it split into two: one set of planes would head north to Dej, while the others would go south to Cluj. On their maps both points were indicated as large way stations, where railway branches met from various directions, and along the railway sidings were gathered a multitude of troops and supplies. Here tanker cars came from the oil-processing plants in Ploesti, and here the Germans supplied the Eastern Front with everything it needed.

Over their target, the Flying Fortresses were met with heavy anti-aircraft fire. From the cabin it seemed that the entire sky was lighting up with explosions. Lieutenant Creighton could not believe his eyes when the plane ahead of his suddenly turned into a fireball and broke up into thousands of pieces.

"My God!", moaned Eddington, though he was battle-hardened and, one would assume, had got used to everything. The major cringed, shook his head in despair, and groaned as if he was tormented by unbearable pain. He was: the pain tore at his heart and grief clouded his mind; he could say nothing.

These feelings were shared by John Pash, the commander of the next Flying Fortress in the formation. The plane that had exploded from the direct hit had been part of their squadron; its crew were friends and neighbors to them, they had shared a barracks, eaten at adjoining tables in the mess hall, played basketball together. Steven Creighton had known each of them well, and now they were gone; they had disappeared completely in literally the blink of an eye, and all that was left of them were innumerable flaming fragments raining down. Yet nothing could be done, and both John Pash and Andrew Eddington gritted their teeth and maintained their common course. The group of bombers held its formation and tore on ahead as if they had not noticed the loss. All that remained was to hope that they themselves would make it out with their lives.

Now it seemed as if it might be their turn. Pash and Eddington's crews noticed the explosions coming closer, surrounding the planes on all sides, and there was nowhere to run – it was a sheer wall of fire without a crack in it, and the heavy thundering shook their wings and fuselages. To copilot Creighton, the heavy bomber seemed like a frail boat in a raging sea. The gunner prayed, and the pilot with a grimace held the controls. The crew of ten men were resigned to their fates. The plane, though, without breaking formation, mysteriously managed to keep flying and, against all understanding, it stubbornly kept its place in the group.

Looking at things honestly, what depended on them, how could they have influenced anything? If they were hit, the only thing they could do was say goodbye to one another, but it was their common lot and they could not run or shy away from it. Even their division commander General Ira C. Eaker, flying in the flagship, was in the same position, and could not hope for anything different from the rest.

Then it fell quiet. The fiery explosions dwindled, and the impenetrable darkness was filled only by the vast sky. It seemed that they had made it out of the danger, and now there was clear weather everywhere; the threat had given way to serenity. They all supposed that they had now crossed the front lines.

"We're out of it," Major Andrew Eddington said numbly. The first pilot had suffered more than the rest of them: while the barrage had lasted, he had kept the plane on course and now he was drenched in sweat as if he had carried the plane himself.

"You just rest now, Commander," Lieutenant Creighton said, and took the controls. The first pilot nodded, and limped out of the cabin to catch his breath and swallow some hot coffee from a thermos.

As they approached Poltava, the weather was overcast and a light rain fell. A dull day dawned, gray, with low clouds and limited visibility. The escorting fighters left the bomber group and headed for their air bases at Piryatin and Mirgorod. The inclement weather made the first landing of the heavy Flying Fortresses unusually difficult. The difficulty was compounded by the radio silence observed by the ground and all the crews. In the area of the Poltava special air base, the ground command positions and the radio operators aboard the aircraft refrained from broadcasting, so that the Germans would not pick up on their communications.

However, all the crews, General Ira C. Eaker's entire squadron of planes, worked skillfully. As they approached the air base, each crew correctly executed their maneuvers, approached, and landed smoothly and precisely, as set out in their instructions.

For the Allies, their Soviet hosts had laid out a triumphant welcome. The sound of a marching band boomed, and an honor guard had assembled at the edge of the airfield. The place was swarming with generals and colonels, a grandstanding crowd who posed as if they were participating in a performance and everyone had a leading role. Shortly afterward the American crews formed ranks, the brass band played the national anthems of both countries, the generals gave speeches, and the honor guard passed solemnly by. Ambassador W. Averell Harriman gave a speech on behalf of the Americans. He handed General Perminov, commander of the 169th Special-Purpose Air Base, a letter from President Roosevelt and a decoration for his services. The ambassador was accompanied by the American generals Walsh and Dean, by liaison officers, and by boxes full of whiskey and canned meat that the Russian soldiers nicknamed a "second front", and which made life brighter.

Air force generals from the Soviet side had flown in for the celebration, as well as political officers and secret service employees who would henceforth closely observe the personnel from both countries. The Red Army supply officers had worked hard on their part and brought in vodka, caviar, and salted fish.

The initial results of the operation were summarized right away. Five Mustang fighters had had to return to their base in Italy, while another fighter had disappeared and no one knew what had become of it. The losses included one Flying Fortress, the very one which had exploded after a direct hit over Romania. These were in fact insignificant losses for such a major operation, and the generals could look forward to commendations. They really did have something to be proud of, for a single plane shot down was undoubtedly a success, and many could expect promotions. Yet had not Lieutenant Creighton known each of the fallen, every one of them by name? Had he not lived with them and had they not flown side by side?

Nevertheless, military statistics works with large numbers and it cares little about individuals. The losses that are totaled up become nameless, for otherwise it would be impossible for men to fight. The Americans and Soviets agreed to hold a festive dinner that evening, and in the meantime the crews were taken to have breakfast. The waitresses and cooks in the mess halls were running around frantically in order to comply with the strict instructions they had received, and in accordance with their own sense of responsibility. Not to mention the caution that everyone in close contact with foreigners had to maintain and display.

The Allies amazed their hosts at the very start of the meal. This was because when it came to serving food, the American army, unlike its Soviet counterpart, made no distinction based on a soldier's rank and duties. A private, sergeant, officer, or general ate the same chow.

Naturally, the hosts from the country of universal brotherhood and equality saw this as a violation of military subordination, a mockery of all decency, a laxness, foolishness, and something harmful. They even saw a threat in this American custom, because surely their own men would start asking for the same thing.

The Soviets therefore considered that it would be appropriate to have General Eaker, the commander of the air group, and the senior command eat separately from the rest, in another room, with food of a higher quality. This was the way things were supposed to work in the country of socialism; this was how everyone there had been raised. They had the Soviet officers eat separately from the generals, and the junior personnel – sergeants and corporals – would eat separately from the officers. Everyone would be in their right place.

The Americans merely stared as the mess hall staff explained all of this to them. They could not understand what the Soviets wanted from them. To the Soviets, the Americans seemed dullards, imbeciles. The Americans, for their part, simply could not understand that an army could feed its men according to their rank, and there was no way for the Soviets to get through to their counterparts. The Americans initially blamed the lack of understanding on the interpreter, and when they finally understood what the problem was, they scowled and flat-out refused.

"In the air, sergeants and generals are both running the same risks," one of the Americans explained to the Russians, who simply could not manage to come to this simple conclusion themselves.

In its history, mankind has accumulated vast stores of stupidity, but Soviet command was completely unaware that American sergeants and officers in their units eat the same food. Why, though, would it be otherwise, when the Germans do not care what rank their enemy is, shooting them all out of the air regardless?

Naturally, the Soviets held firm to their opinion, but stayed quiet for the time being so that the triumphant atmosphere and picture of mutual cooperation would not be ruined. The excessive and completely inappropriate democracy of these allies really annoyed the Soviet commanders, but they closed their eyes to it in the hope that these disagreements would be settled, and everything would proceed as had been established in the nation of total happiness and equal rights, where everyone knew their place and received what had been set out according to their individual rank and function.

— 5 —

I arrived at work at Division X that morning. Before breakfast at the employees' cafeteria, I had managed to do my ten kilometers on skis, which I did every day, and I barely found a moment to rest, change my clothes, and catch my breath. At weekends I would do distances that were twice or three times longer, and also three times a week I would visit the gym and lift weights or hit a punching bag.

It was the fifth year since I had been conscripted into the army. Before that, I had spent several years working in a small rural clinic straight after graduating from medical school in Riga. I admit that I had thought myself unlucky with my assignment compared to my classmates, who went on to advanced studies or got jobs in clinics in Riga. However, by a twist of fate, the recruitment board, on a request from the Ministry of Defense, sent me to Moscow, where they assigned me a place of service. Through the same mischievous workings of fate I ended up in Division X, a military research center lost among the forests outside Moscow – a closed facility and one whose very existence was kept secret.

In the waiting room, Captain Shilin showed his documents and reported that he had arrived at Division X. At a cursory glance, he did not seem to be in any ill health, and frankly speaking, the captain did not need any treatment at all. His sealed medical records spoke of almost nothing; he seemed to be a healthy man. However, Shilin had been ordered to undergo an examination and a course of treatment. Naturally, one could not question or refuse orders – that is the entire essence of military subordination. Therefore, he had no choice: whether he wanted it or not, he had to receive treatment.

In the clinic, the pilot immediately opened his suitcase and withdrew a mouthpiece resembling a bird's bill, a slender reed, and a lacquered wooden pipe with a round bulb at the end; from these items a musical instrument was formed that anyone could readily recognize as a clarinet. The pilot blew into it, and this resulted in a hoarse honking sound, as if the instrument had a throat complaint. After the journey and the change in temperature, he had to test the clarinet out in each of its four octaves. The lower register produced a dark, nocturnal tone, a gloomy dawn, slow in coming and an overcast day when drowsiness and melancholy steal up undetected. The upper register was piercing and expressive: a scorching sun, bright and shining in flashes through the foliage, a glare on the water, boundless spaces and a clear sky…

The clarinet now coughed no more; it had found its voice. Its sound flowed like molten amber, a full stream of honey. It oozed with a thick, transparent resin, before splashing into sonorous drops, like glass smashed into smithereens. For some odd reason, the instrument had a rare property: it could alter time and warp space at will. Time moved forward, turned around, and went backward. Time froze in place, stopped, or jumped into a gallop like a frisky, pure-blooded horse. Space was bent; it took on a curvature: what seemed to be at an unimaginable distance suddenly turned out to be so close that you could reach out and touch it. It was as if the instrument directly expressed our existence in a fickle time and curved space, though no one had previously noticed either such a fickleness or curvature. That slice of space and time that is given to us from above and marked by our existence, strikes us as unchanging, stable, and direct.

At the appointed time, Captain Shilin appeared at the door of my office and reported that he had arrived, firmly maintaining the professional bearing and posture appropriate for an officer aware of his worth. One cannot deny that army pilots are a race apart. "You are experiencing some health problem?" I asked.

"Yes, sir!" the pilot said, with a soldierly bearing.

"What is it, then?"

"I am a foolish man," the disciplined officer reported curtly.

This – an ability to laugh at oneself – was a rare trait for the army, and it attested to an unusual mind. Clearly there was nothing for the attending physician to do other than to show some interest and ask what the ailment was exactly. The patient did not shy away from answering; he spoke openly about the matter in all its finer details.

In military aviation, certain commandments have long been honored which one cannot ignore and which should not be violated lightly. If a cow is wandering on an airfield, you should go around it from the back; if it is a horse, from the front; keep your a distance from the regiment commander; and avoid the medics at all cost and do not let them even notice you.

"I was stupid and I broke the last commandment," the officer admitted in a sorrowful and even contrite tone.

Friendly relationships, as no one would deny, always imply trust, and thus they represent a threat and a danger: a trusting person is always a vulnerable one. That is how the pilot fell victim to friendship with the regiment's doctor. As their friendship deepened, they sometimes allowed themselves meals together, lighthearted celebrations, even the occasional wild picnic. On one occasion, the pilot let his guard down, and under the strong influence of alcohol he admitted that he had from time to time entertained a vague notion. Very occasionally, he said, once in a great while, he felt that he did not belong in his native land, his regiment, his garrison. He felt like a fish out of water. An outsider of some kind, a stranger.

Of course, he was a Russian pilot, Captain Nikolai Shilin – who else could he be? Yet every so often, in confused dreams in his sleep, or in heavy drinking, he felt like he was someone else, someone from far away, where the customs are different and the people speak a different language.

"You're obviously overdoing it, my friend. You should go get some treatment," his friend advised him, and as the regiment's doctor he sent Shilin to us, to the research center, or to be more precise, Division X. To be even more precise, we were engaged not so much in treatment as in research into somewhat dubious and unusual topics.

I have never believed in the work of demons, though there is a lot of shamanism about. My responsibility was to study this patient in accordance with our own program, and his case frankly baffled me. Even my more experienced colleagues had never encountered anything quite like it. Although vague references to something that might be it could be found in the scholarly literature, the probability seemed low, right on the margin of statistical error. The following day, I plunged this strange patient into a hypnosis so deep that his reflexes abated, and he turned stiff – cataleptic, even – as if his body were made from wax. After the session the patient would forget the whole thing, every detail, and even the very fact that it had happened: complete amnesia, a tabula rasa. I would remember, though, and I was completely stunned when from his deep sleep, the patient reported that he was an American pilot, and named the wing in which he served.

These results were more than strange. In the Soviet Union's air force, there is no such division as a "wing". Those exist only in the United States, and correspond approximately to an air regiment in the Soviet system. I need hardly tell you that this information shook me, and I did not know what to think.

Our examination could detect no physical disorders. No pathology, no abnormalities were found in his organs or tissues. His mental state appeared to be stable. As far as the air wing went, an explanation was found: all of our pilots who had encountered Americans in the skies were familiar with how our opponents' air force was structured. In the pilot's deep sleep, this detail had risen from his unconscious to the surface.

In any event, I decided not to do anything with the weird things I had heard, so that the man's life would not be ruined. A man might say one foolish thing and have it seized on by some silly personnel officer who exaggerates it, turns it inside out, and ends up completely destroying the person and his service record, no matter how ridiculous the thing might seem. Especially considering that our pilot could not possibly be American. How could he be? He could not be American and that is that. It was all nonsense, a load of rubbish, ridiculous and shameless fabrication. Who cares what fantasies and nightmares each of us bears within? Is it worth raking over old ashes, digging deep into one's past?

Just to be safe, I encoded the information and tightly sealed it up inside the patient's subconscious so that it would not burst out again in the future. A person's life, as we all know, stands at the tip of a needle, the needle is inside an egg, the egg inside a bird, the bird inside a hare, the hare inside a chest, which in turn hangs on chains from an oak tree, and the oak tree grows on a mountain in a faraway land…

So the pilot returned without fuss to his unit, without any further consequences or complications. I only advised him that he hold his tongue and not share any of his feelings of doubt with anyone. This advice was particularly helpful for that era, for after all, we were still living under the Soviet regime.

The pilot's unease somehow resolved itself, which often happens with those successful people who seem immune from circumstances. One way or another, the next rotation of personnel came, and the captain left for his next assignment, in the Russian Far East.

The Burevestnik airfield on Iturup in the South Kuril Islands had been built while it was under Japanese control. The runway stretched from the depths of the island toward the shore and ended two hundred feet from the water. By the time a plane had gained altitude and retracted its landing gear, it was already over the ocean. Close to the islands of Japan, this island bordering on the Vries Strait in the north and separated from Kunashir Island in the south by the Catherine Strait had been well-maintained and a comfortable enough place to live. On Kasatka Bay the Japanese had built a large pier and made the bay deeper so that it could accommodate larger vessels. On the other side of the bay lay a fine settlement, connected to the pier and the airfield by a railway running along the shore. A shuttle train with cargo and passengers would make its away along the rails and back again, livening up the landscape as it went. At the heart of the island, over the airfield, the Japanese had erected cozy barracks for the garrison; a cable car ran up there from the shore.

Of course, once the Red Army seized the island, they could not bear such bourgeois comforts. The first thing the Soviet military engineers did was demolish the pier, the railway, and the cable car. After the army of the victors had made life on the island totally unbearable, it then turned to grappling with the difficulties that Iturup presented and settling it anew.

The garrison, consisting of infantry and air regiments, was located in the settlement of Gorny, named after the wide plateau where the Japanese forces had been based. The Japanese, familiar with local natural conditions, had built all their residential and other buildings in the hills, out of the reach of the gigantic ocean waves of a tsunami.

A bumpy, potholed road ran from the shore up to the elevated plateau, switchbacking among the hills. After they demolished the cable car, the victors relied on automobiles, but they did not bother to build a decent road, and let us be honest, they were incapable of doing so. Bad roads were an age-old custom in Russia, just like fools and rampant thievery.

These brave souls who trusted in their cars cursed their fate as they made their way along the road. It took nearly an hour to cover the distance, and the car would moan, creak, and shudder so violently that the passengers thought it would soon fall to pieces. Many preferred to take a shortcut and go on foot. This shorter way was essentially a mountain path that snaked up the forested slopes. The local Asian spruce and Sakhalin fir coexisted here with twisted Japanese pines, birch, and an undergrowth of wild Kurilian bamboo.

Just as he had in East Germany and in the north of Europe, Shilin came face to face with the Americans in the skies of the Russian Far East. He had come a huge distance, to the very ends of the earth (it was not for nothing that the cape protruding into the ocean was called World's End), and still he again encountered the ubiquitous Yankees.

Like an unavoidable nuisance, every time you turned around, there they were! The Americans had, after all, named the entire planet their sphere of interest, and their appetite was unabated.

The American planes would usually take off from the Misawa Air Base on Hokkaido and patrol the Izmena Strait, south of Kunashir Island, then passing over the Sea of Okhotsk near Sakhalin and Kamchatka, or flying over the ocean along the Greater Kuril Chain. The USSR's territory was guarded by the Soviet Air Force and the Far Eastern Air Defense District, and a network of ground radar stations covered the mainland and the islands. The Soviet navy kept watch over the Sea of Japan and Sea of Okhotsk, and patrolled the Pacific Ocean.

Day and night, Soviet airspace was guarded by air regiments along a huge span from the South Kurils to northern Chukotka, taking in the island of Iturup, where the old airfield had been given the new name Kasatka, the Sakhalin Island airfields of Sokol and Smirny, the air bases in Kamchatka and on the Komandorski Islands, Providence Bay, and the area around Anadyr. From April to October, at nine o'clock in the morning, pilots would start the day watch. The night watch began at nine o'clock in the evening. In winter the day watch would begin one hour after dawn and end one hour before twilight, when the night-time boys would replace their daytime counterparts.

After Iturup, Shilin was transferred to Sovetskaya Gavan. By that time, the pilot had become the commander of a squadron; I would ask about him when business took me to the Far East. At that time, Division X was studying (among other things) the mental stability of air force personnel under conditions of military confrontation – the Cold War was still ongoing. The USSR planned for everything. One of my patients, the commander of a tank battalion, had written a thesis on a then-relevant subject when he was at the academy: the forcing of the Seine River at Paris.

I would recall certain patients from time to time. Certain oddities had stuck in my mind, quirks exhibited by certain patients, phenomena for which an explanation had not been found. My colleagues and I would immerse ourselves in speculation and rack our brains seeking answers.

From our first meeting, the pilot Nikolai Shilin had occupied my mind for all those years. It was so odd that this officer from the land of victorious socialism, a military pilot to boot, secretly felt that he was really an American. From what our mutual acquaintances said, he was serving impeccably, without any scandal, and he was eventually promoted to major. Discreetly and carefully, so that I would not cause him any harm, I made inquiries. No one said a single word that would suggest he was experiencing difficulties; clearly his treatment had gone well and my medical advice had proved useful. After visiting Division X, Shilin seemed to have held his tongue; he had not said a thing to anyone else, entrusting his musings and doubts only to his clarinet. After all, there is nothing wrong with a person playing an instrument in his free time, even if he is a Soviet officer.

Once, in the guest quarters of a military garrison on the Pacific coast, I heard a familiar clarinet. The sound penetrated through the walls, and I recalled at once who the player was, and what instrument he played, with its natural harmony, its lowered thirds and sevenths, like in old-time jazz. The clarinet roamed freely through tonalities, moving over certain intervals, and it demonstrated an unexpected property: wood and brass are usually transposed in symphony orchestras.

The clarinet's wacky and restless syncope was unsettling. The sound swept through space like a dry leaf in the fall wind. Its glissandi brought to mind being on a gigantic swing, sledding down a mountain, or riding an amusement-park ride – that moment when you are in free fall and your heart stops. In the clarinet's improvisation, one could not help but imagine the flight of a fighter plane, a cascade of maneuvers, sweeping movements, incredible aerobatics. The plane soared up, dead straight, into the sky and then turned wildly, performing one trick after another: looping the loop and doing barrel rolls… And swooping to attack, an insane dive, the blood rushing to his head so that he grew faint, an immense weight pressing down on him that might break his back at any moment.

But now comes a pause, a relief, the gentle murmur of a stream; the sound flows peacefully, and a calm descends on the heart. Under a full moon, the airplane, with a compressed and even roar, passes over the clouds, cuts through the transparent fog, its body and wings shining in the moonlight and carrying through the night a cold copper glow. The clarinet appealed to the sky in supplication, it prayed that everyone who was on a journey by land or air or sea would arrive at their destination, or to say it in the old and grandiloquent manner, wherever their path may lead.

I knocked on the door behind which the clarinet was playing with its tortured sound, and the patient gaped. It is not every day that your doctor from the secret Division X, years later, mysteriously appears on the threshold of your room in the run-down guest quarters of a military garrison. We chatted for part of the night, and the next morning we flew off to different ends of the earth.

After Shilin had done his course of rehabilitation, he shook off his awkward fantasies and was no longer visited by odd suspicions or disquieting thoughts. Judging by the results, the therapy and encoding had done their job: his mind had achieved a harmony with his body, keeping his unconscious under strict control on a short, tight leash. After all, what complaints could he really have anyway, when everyone was fine and in good health? Major Shilin no longer felt like a foreigner in his own country – he forgot all about it, shrugged off all his doubts and uncertainties, and boldly moved on, shoulder to shoulder with his mighty country.

From a medical perspective these were all encouraging results – full remission and an optimistic prognosis. We could be content with how things had turned out, and we could look forward only to victories. Arise and sing, nothing stands in our way on land or sea, from Moscow to the British seas the Red Army is the strongest of all…

Only in rare dreams after grueling night flights, skirmishes with American planes, military anxieties and sleepless watches, when fatigue set in like a heavy weight upon him and his mind grew clouded – only then out of the darkness, out of the black abyss, did unfamiliar faces come to him and, like shadows, mysterious others speaking in a foreign language. For some unknown reason, in his sleep the pilot could understand their speech, but when he awoke, he remembered their language no more, and he could make nothing of his dreams; no explanation came to him. Sensibly, he kept silent about it – he uttered not a peep, firmly holding his tongue.

And why should he try to ferret out the truth, leaving no stone unturned, as if it is always better to know the truth? Sometimes the truth can catch a person off guard, destroy them completely, while a lie – let us be honest here – can save a person, push the danger away.

One might doubt that and think it a completely backward and reactionary position to take, but there is a lot to be said for it, as Shilin's case demonstrates. You will hear the idea condemned and vilified, as Maxim Gorky, the bard of the oppressed classes, did in his play *The Lower Depths*, but no matter how much you try, you cannot get away from the facts, they beat at the door and speak for themselves: sometimes lies can do a person good.

Let us do without any lies or pretense. As a doctor, I did not deceive the patient. I did not lead anyone astray, I merely shrugged uncertainly, and my conclusions, which incidentally I did not find entirely convincing, I kept to myself. I kept silent, one might say, in order to avoid making a mistake. There was an obvious danger of that, one must admit.

And the fact is that I had examined Shilin thoroughly and still the picture had become no clearer. The pilot did not appear to be hiding anything – from what I could see, he himself remained in the dark. I could not detect any malingering, at any rate. I believe that truth serum used in spycraft – barbiturates, say, or sodium pentothal, or hyoscine extracted from nightshade or henbane – would not have brought any results. Using the powerful substance SP-117, consisting of a dose and antidote developed at the KGB's Laboratory No. 30 on Akademik Vargi Street in Moscow, would have put the patient's health at risk – it is too much of a shock to the body, and not everyone can withstand it.

In general, the drug remains banned, but the special services employ it in extreme cases if they need to turn someone into a zombie, or make them act in an unseemly way, or start talking without restraint. They do it in such a way that the person remembers nothing afterward. At the same time, truth serum gives nothing on its own, it means nothing. What can you find out if the patient actually has nothing to hide, if there are no skeletons in his closet? Struggle as much as you please, but it is futile, a waste of time of time and energy.

After I returned from my trip, I sent off yet another inquiry, but the answer told me nothing new. I already knew that the patient had been born in a labor camp where his mother had been sentenced. As for the rest of his life story – no mystery there. However, the situation seemed too mysterious and extraordinary for me simply to send his case history off to the archives and forget about it, just to get the whole thing off my shoulders and breathe easily. My thoughts came back to him again and again. I ruminated on the results of my research, and questions kept insistently flooding into my mind.

Once, when I was on duty at Division X, working heroically all night, an idea suddenly came to me, a whisper in my ear. My attention was drawn to a minor detail: the pilot's surname was his mother's maiden name. Something lay behind that, but what exactly, I could not figure out.

— 6 —

From the first day of Operation Frantic Joe until its end, Soviet counter-intelligence and the military's Chief Political Administration ordered military interpreters to be present at breakfast, lunch, and dinner in case the USSR's allies decided to chat with the Soviet personnel serving them. An interpreter was to report every word to the higher-ups, as well as what the Americans were saying among themselves.

The crews were assigned to mess halls by squadron. Each crew had its own table, and three tables represented, just as in the sky, one wing. Even the commander of the air group, Lieutenant General Ira C. Eaker, would come in from a sortie and eat breakfast with a crew in which the gunner or radio operator was a mere sergeant. To the complete astonishment of their hosts, general and sergeant sat at a single table.

As it turned out, however, that was not the only surprise that the Americans had in store for their allies in the war. Once all the foreign air force men had taken their places in the mess hall, they did something else that left the Soviet leadership, and especially the political officers, amazed. The food was already there on the tables, but none of the Americans touched it. The Soviet officers were baffled.

"What is it? What's wrong with them?" the anxious Soviet colonels and generals whispered among themselves as they nodded toward the Americans.

The Soviet commander of this special air base, General Perminov, shook his head and said darkly to his personal interpreter Vladimir Stankevich, "Go figure out what's going on. Why aren't they eating?"

The Americans were acting strangely: they had all fallen silent and were sitting still as if they were waiting for something, perhaps an order, a set time, a certain sign. Who knew? Suddenly, at the table of the flagship crew, the air group's commander Lieutenant General Ira C. Eaker, a tall and gray-haired man with a face that was rough yet noble, stood up. Immediately the entire place froze, such a silence falling that one could hear a fly beating against the flypaper. The silence was shattered by a foreboding buzz, as if in the skies above the air base a German Henkel was flying, for the engine of that aerial reconnaissance plane gave off the same sound.

The American general bowed his head and piously placed his hands on his breast. All the crews, the entire mess hall, adopted the same pose. The Americans all sat with their heads down, as if someone had given them an order, but not a sound had been heard. In the stillness General Eaker began to recite something in a clear voice.

The interpreter listened to him intently, and then said blankly, "They're praying."

"What?! Are you kidding me?" the colonel answered, taken aback. The most senior Communist Party official present was shaking his head disapprovingly; he simply could not believe that anyone took religion seriously. The Party and the Great Leader himself had already resolved these matters long ago, and it was odd that the Allies still did not know.

Needless to say, the Red Army commanders and political officers present in the mess hall were dumbfounded, and it took some time for them to regain their composure. What they were witnessing now was something that had long been banished from their country. The Soviet hosts, who had been taught for over two decades since the Revolution that religion is the opium of the people, assumed that they were being deliberately mocked; the events in the mess hall were hard to understand otherwise. As the Communists saw it, these military officers and their general, even if they were ideologically backward, could not have been led so astray. The Soviet commanders were perplexed, but they kept silent to avoid offending their allies. They merely looked at one another with condescending glances, smiled wryly, and shrugged their shoulders, like adults watching children at play. For them, Communists and vehement atheists, they felt awkward in the presence of these Americans, as if these allies were breaching decorum and acting contrary to common sense.

The American general gave thanks to God, and the crews together praised the Lord that they were still alive. They had run a deadly risk, they had experienced fear, they had looked death in the eye, but they had made it through their trials, reached their destination, and landed safely. The Almighty had taken them under His protection, and they were beseeching Him to continue to protect them.

"Grant us, O Lord, the strength to walk this path. Help us, Lord. Save us and keep us," the tall and gray-haired general recited humbly, with the crews repeating after him.

They prayed for those who had been shot down that they might survive, they prayed for God to save them and to ease the plight of those taken captive, to heal the wounded and to make the sick well again. They prayed for those who had perished, that their souls might rest in peace.

This was a special prayer for long-haul military planes, one that had first been uttered by a famous American preacher who had held a service when the 15th Air Force was first taking off to fly over Europe. All that night the reverend had prayed on the airfield of the base in Foggia until the planes made it back. Since then, the prayer had been said by all crews who had the good fortune to make it home. They prayed to God for protection, so that everyone would land safely – to land safely, that is all they asked.

Again, each man knew that next time someone would not be so lucky. Indeed, some of them would die, for there is no war without death, and losses happen on every flight, but today they had survived, praise God. That morning, after their night raid, all the American crews recited the words of the prayer after the general. With heads bent over the tables, they silently moved their lips – it was a strange scene, like a voiceless choir.

General Perminov and the officers and Communist Party officials were confused, and stayed silent. The lives of Soviets were very different from those of Americans, and it was hard to figure these allies out. There had been no prayers said in the military for long years, so long that they had been forgotten. The regime denied God, though the Great Leader had once been a seminarian and he had recited prayers that might illuminate the soul. Now the country denied even the existence of a soul.

By that time, the overwhelming majority of Russia's people felt no need to pray. It was considered a ridiculous superstition. The Bolsheviks had tried to burn religious sentiment out of the population with a red-hot iron, and therefore the group prayer of the American crews struck their Soviet allies as something absurd, a silly whim that had to be endured until it was over.

After the prayer, the Americans seemed to snap out of it, and they fell to eating. The mess hall grew lively, a buzz arose with the sound of plates and laughter, and the laughter was exaggerated, as always, after the terrifying experience these men had survived and their return to their ordinary routine. The previous night, which had been so full of danger, was still clear in their minds, still close to them, still as it were breathing down their necks. However, the memory of it gradually faded, melting away in the daylight, along with the agonizing fear. Among the chorus of voices and the loud outbursts of laughter, the nightmares of the previous night were forgotten – though they would rear their heads again a day or two later.

Suddenly the mess hall filled with an enthusiastic whoop. The American crews craned their necks to look, and then stared slack jawed, forgetting all about their food. The diners sat completely frozen as if a bomb had gone off in the room.

It was easy to see why. Coming through the door of the mess hall were young ladies in officers' uniforms, like a ballet troupe in military costume. It was a gaggle of military interpreters, all junior lieutenants with perfect bearing, golden epaulets with a single star on their shoulders, slender waists encircled by leather belts, and boots polished so brightly they gleamed like chrome. These young ladies gracefully spread out across the mess hall, sparking excitement among the Americans.

Not long ago these junior lieutenants had been students at the Moscow Institute of Foreign Languages. They had graduated from school before the war, then entered the Institute when the war was already underway. Obviously, during a war with Germany, the German language was most in demand, and the "English people", as these students were known in the Institute, were nearly forgotten about. They had studied for three years, passed exams, and gone on to a fourth year, their last, when suddenly a need for them had arisen at the front. Within a single day the entire class was mobilized into the army.

The language students did their military basic training in just a week, and then they spent another week practicing their English on military topics. The young ladies were swiftly commissioned junior lieutenants and sent off to active duty in Ukraine. Almost all of them were Muscovites. They were delicate ladies, and nearly all of them looked as if they had been born with a silver spoon in their mouths. This was understandable, as in those years it was mainly the daughters of the intelligentsia – coddled things – who studied foreign languages, and certainly not the girls of the working class or peasantry.

Meanwhile, the commanding ranks in the army at that time were made up of extremely uncouth, rude bumpkins, and there was a reason for this: back in the prewar years, Stalin had eliminated practically everyone of aristocratic family from the army – all of the officers appointed in the Tsarist era and leaders from the educated class – anyone, in fact, who actually knew anything about military matters. The Great Leader deliberately did away with the graduates of the academies, until the army took on the purity that he sought. He then filled the gaps by promoting hordes of illiterate men from among the lowest ranks, men who just yesterday had been farmers and workers, and they were given only a hasty and cursory training. The army's acute need for commanding officers brought in a flood of these freshly-baked personnel, a gray and faceless crowd, but one representing a class that the Party and the Great Leader liked.

For this reason, the lady interpreters were a strange sight among the ordinary Red Army officers. They were not like the regular officers; they were outsiders with genteel manners from the not-so-long-ago past that were in complete contrast to the simple folk. Even the Russian speech of these junior lieutenants seemed to challenge the Soviet realities and the army environment: it evoked the Arbat, Ostozhye, Molchanovka – downtown Moscow, Bely Gorod, the surrounding boulevards. After all, on the other side of the Garden Ring, and definitely once you are across the Kamer-Kollezhsky rampart, people talk differently, and a keen ear can immediately spot an outsider.

In short, the young interpreters were attractive – which had been the intention of those choosing them – and their military uniforms, as usual, emphasized their female beauty. It is no secret that a uniform looks good on a woman; it goes well with her face and utterly transforms her. To keep up appearances in front of the allies, the Red Army had not skimped on new gabardine blouses for the junior lieutenants – oh! What slender waists, with an officer's leather belt around them! The narrow skirts cut from fine cloth clung tight to their hips and barely covered their knees; their shiny black boots were tight around their legs. The men, who had grown hungry for female company during their time in the army, felt a burning excitement, even a touch of awe. Their blood grew hot, they felt an uncontrollable exhilaration and boundless courage.

These women in officers' dress really did bring to mind a staged spectacle. It is not for nothing that dancers in a cabaret sometimes dress in uniform: long legs in boots are a real marvel. Naturally, the officers, Russian and American alike, could not tear their eyes away from this gaggle of junior lieutenants. Moreover, in spite of the young interpreters' uniforms and epaulets, they were still a group of former students, sweet young ladies who brought with them a whiff of home, the warmth of family life, cozy peacetime existence, dances on Saturdays, fun parties, shy embraces, and tranquility…

Breakfast had hardly begun when Lieutenant Steven Creighton set eyes on the interpreter. Junior Lieutenant Shilina had just started walking toward the table where the copilot's crew was seated, and he noticed her when she was still some way off. He felt as if someone had struck him a blow, as if an arrow had pierced his heart. He sat completely still, as if turned to stone. The junior lieutenant had made an indelible impression on the American at first sight.

So it happens. Rarely, but it does happen. A spark, a brief click of something into place, a bolt of lightning, an electrical charge. The young lady had not had quite the same impact on the other men; no, this was a choice made on high, and Lieutenant Creighton knew right away that she was the one. This was the woman of his dreams, and their star-crossed match was final and irrevocable, not subject to appeal.

She had just walked over to his table and was still in the dark about it; she did not even suspect that anything had happened. Creighton, however, knew that he had been waiting for her all this time, that other girls had been merely a harbinger of her, that he had been searching for her everywhere he looked. Now nothing depended on the two of them, he felt. All that remained was to humbly yield to fate.

One cannot deny that Junior Lieutenant Shilina was a fine woman. The Flying Fortresses' pilots, navigators, mechanics, gunners, and radio operators would agree, but they did not think the other lady interpreters any less fine. She could not have been called a legendary beauty; that would be going too far. She did have blonde hair, a shapely figure, and gray eyes, and she moved elegantly on her slender legs, but there was something else about her that is not often found in young ladies, let alone beautiful ones: intelligence in her eyes.

The interpreters at the air base spread out to mingle with the crews. The young ladies acquainted themselves with the men they were tasked to work with, walking from table to table like nurses in a kindergarten. Among the junior lieutenants one could notice a few undeniable beauties, and the bomber crews stared wildly, their eyes roaming from one to another. A few American counter-intelligence officers grew suspicious, assuming that the Soviets had intentionally chosen beautiful women to serve as interpreters, so that they could seduce the aviators and make them lower their guard.

In any event, Junior Lieutenant Shilina had pierced the American copilot's heart at his first sight of her. It is not given to us here on earth to second-guess what is woven above: little depends on us; it is heaven that determines when two lives intersect. For Lieutenant Creighton it was as if everything else in the mess hall had faded, retreated far away. The young lady walked up to his table while the copilot sat frozen, neither moving or speaking, unable take his eyes off her. She drew nearer and he looked at her in expectation, and who knew how long this would last for: an instant, an hour, a year, or all eternity.

The junior lieutenant came up to the table, smiled, and introduced herself. "I'm Olga." She learned who each member of the crew was, asked them what they might need, and said that they could turn to her if any problem arose.

The crew, laughing and joking, barraged her with questions, some of which she would not stoop to answer. "Are you married?" "You got a boyfriend?" Lieutenant Creighton, however, held his tongue, and did not say a word.

The interpreter was surprised, taken aback even, by his intent gaze. His silence said more than any words. The crew noticed that something was up; they traded glances, and were astonished that their copilot had been completely knocked off his feet, swept away by this Russian interpreter. If they had wanted to, these jokesters could have counted down like a boxing referee declaring a knockout, and some wondered when the lieutenant was going to snap out of it, or if he was going to remain forever in a daze like that. The men could, of course, have had some fun as his expense – they were used to ragging each other when it came to women – but now they felt something was going on and they bit their tongues.

As a result, the first minute of the American and the interpreter's acquaintance was an unusually quiet one: no one said anything, and no sound at all could be heard, near or far. Just an instant before, the mess hall had been loud, with a roar like that in a train station. Even now the crews continued to talk among themselves and a light hubbub hung over the tables, but for the lieutenant and the interpreter a mysterious stillness had set in. They heard nothing around them, as if someone had turned down the volume on the world, as if they had lost their hearing in the wake of an explosion. Some people who have had the good fortune to meet their soulmates have experienced a sudden muteness, loss of hearing, bodily paralysis, a complete mental shutdown. It was obvious that love had struck them without warning, like a burst of thunder in a clear sky, and it had utterly stunned them.

In short, Creighton and Shilina had forgotten themselves. They noticed no one around them and barely remembered who and where they were. The crew quietly stared at the pair. The men seemed to feel ashamed at having to witness this. They realized that there was no place for a third party here, and if they could not hide, then they should at least keep silent.

The translator, with some effort, shook off her amazement and then shyly moved on to another table. The lieutenant awoke from his daze and once more heard voices around him and the hubbub of the mess hall. Regaining his composure, he started eating. The crew pretended that nothing had happened and greedily got down to satisfying their hunger. After all, it was breakfast time, and the food was good.

After breakfast, the crews went to get some sleep. They had spent all the previous night in the air trying to survive the barrage of gunfire, and no one had had a wink of sleep. The excitement that the Americans had felt after their landing had gradually abated and the mess hall had left them tired. Many of them were starting to drift off. Now they could think of only one thing: getting to their beds and falling asleep.

How unfortunate it is when the intentions of hosts clash with the plans of their guests. The Soviets had obviously gone to great trouble for their allies, and had even prepared a screening of a musical comedy and a big concert. The Allies nonetheless had to let their hosts down. The men slept soundly, and many of them even missed lunch. The air base commanders and political officers were naturally disappointed, but they shrugged it off. If only they had known how much disappointment and discontent was still to come, and what hardships were in store for them.

═══ 7 ═══

Thus the little boy had been born and raised with his mother's maiden name. This was an intriguing matter and demanded explanation. Nonetheless, as Nikolai Shilin came of age, he did not ask his mother about it. Nowadays, children seldom bear their mother's maiden name; it is something encountered only once in a while. However, after the war, one constantly came across children with such names. The "Father" field on forms was usually just struck out with a dash, and this said it all: their father was nowhere around.

I must admit, as a doctor I was burning with curiosity. I had always remembered my patients well and worried about them, for I was the one on whom their well-being depended. Moreover, I tried to shield them from any attacks, pain, mistakes, or adversity. Even years later they might turn to me again at any minute – how could it be otherwise, if one had touched their lives like that? Thus the military pilot Nikolai Shilin often troubled me. His diagnosis remained a great mystery, and though questions piled up, I did not know the answers to them. Despite the chronic lack of time that I faced amid all my everyday obligations, my thoughts would occasionally go back to those mysterious symptoms of his, but I could not find any reasonable explanation for them. His case held some scientific interest, in our division at least. No one had ever witnessed a similar phenomenon.

Our research at Division X was going quite well. Our doctors delved deep into the human subconscious, carrying out renovations in the cellars and lower stories of the mind, and if they so desired, they could correct a patient's personality, remove any painful complexes, and eliminate the excessive self-reflection that acts like a heavy burden, so detrimental to a soldier's military service.

Some danger did lie in this; minor and improbable though it may be, a doctor has to look out for these things. Suppose that in early childhood, or even earlier in the embryonic state, a person had received a certain conditioning, a strong experience that had remained hidden deep in his subconscious. And suppose that now I gave him a new conditioning, something encoded firmly in his subconscious. Let us go further with this… Suppose that one conditioning contradicted the other, and even canceled it out completely. Naturally, between these centers of concentration in the brain, a collision will occur, and a disharmony will arise in the patient's mind – goodness, the consequences are difficult to predict. Such a cognitive dissonance might lead to somatic disorders, even psychosis. A person certainly does not need that.

In any event, this chance meeting of two men traveling on business turned out to be most welcome. In the guest quarters of the garrison we spent a part of the night talking. We spoke of how in Germany, in Northern Europe, the Americans behaved recklessly, even in a bullying way. They were literally on the rampage. Quite often they would feign an attack, set a course directly toward a Soviet plane, and only at the last moment would they turn aside. At this time, there were still pilots who had been through the Korean War, where they had met Americans in the skies day after day, and nearly every encounter had meant an aerial battle. The Korean War was no game – after these encounters one pilot, either ours or the Americans', would not return home.

Officially, the military action against North Korea as an aggressor nation was waged by the United Nations. Many countries joined the UN coalition, though the actual fighting was done mainly by the Americans. Their air force represented one of the strike forces, although pilots from multiple nations took part. On the North Korean side, the war in the skies was actually waged by the USSR's 64th Fighter Aviation Corps. The most experienced and bravest men were sent to Korea. Thousands of men passed through the 64th over the years of the war, dozens of divisions – a huge crowd of men, who experienced for themselves what it really meant to fight aerial battles against the best pilots from a number of countries.

The commander of the regiment in which Shilin was presently serving had shot down nine American planes in his six and a half months in Korea. Nikolai listed for me the aircraft models, as if he had fought each of them himself: F-86 Sabre, F-84 Thunderjet, F-80 Shooting Star, and Gloster Meteor. Now this same colonel was training a new generation of aviators, and after each flight he mercilessly went over what they had done wrong.

"It's kill or be killed, there's no other choice!" the colonel would exhort his pilots.

   

Kill or be killed is the law of war. The colonel was responsible for each of his men, and for that reason he taught his regiment day by day to fight. In fighter aviation it had long been known that the students of poor teachers do not return from battle. In Korea, Shilin's regiment commander had flown a MiG-15 with Korean insignia and he had led a squadron. In the skies they had most often encountered the then-new American F-86 Sabre planes. By the time I ran into Shilin in the Far East, the Soviet military's main plane was already the MiG-21, which had proven itself in the skies above Vietnam, and some pilots had already moved on to the MiG-23. Soviet pilots were now opposed by the legendary F-4 Phantom and, naturally, no one could expect an easy victory in an aerial confrontation. Therefore, the colonel was tough on his regiment; he wanted his pilots to make it out of any fight alive and back to their bases.

The pilot's mother had previously lived in Krasnoyarsk, where she taught English at a teacher-training school, in the city center on Mira Avenue. She no longer lived in a dormitory; the city authorities had given her a room in a log house behind the city's theater. The house stood on a quiet, green lane, from which a neighboring street led to the Yenisei embankment and a wide view of the river and the riverside hills.

Shilin visited his mother each year. Krasnoyarsk had grown dramatically. A great deal of new construction had taken place, and the city no longer looked like a backwater. The house in which his mother lived was a stone's throw from a forestry school, an officer's barracks, two cinemas, and the regional library. Set among the old riverside streets, the river terminal now looked like a real palace, with a spire rising high over the wide granite embankment that was home to the old steamboat *St. Nicholas*. The steamboat had been settled here for a reason: at the beginning of the century the great leader of the world proletariat and supposedly underprivileged peasant Vladimir Lenin had sailed off to exile on this very steamer, and under "Social Class" he had set down, for the ages, "Of the nobility".

By a quirk of fate, just a short time before, the same steamboat had carried the tsarevich, the heir to the Russian throne, who would soon become Tsar Nicholas II. Oh Lord, what coincidences happen by Your will, for Kerensky too, the head of the Provisional Government that the Bolsheviks eventually overthrew, had studied at the very same gymnasium as Vladimir Lenin.

Indeed, the two men were from the same provincial capital of Simbirsk; as children they had walked the same streets and lived near each other, and they met at the homes of mutual acquaintances. Their families knew each other well – brothers, sisters, mothers, and their teacher fathers were all buddies. Both of the two elder men had blazed brilliant careers, going from teachers to headmasters, then to state councilors, a rank that give them the right to pass their aristocratic status down to their heirs. The heirs eagerly accepted this; neither of them refused or scorned it – on the contrary, they sought it and appreciated it. Even the mother to the future leader of the nation, Maria Blank, daughter of a doctor and a baptized Jew, who rose to the rank of court councilor, petitioned, on the death of her husband, for aristocratic status to be confirmed for her and her children, and this was granted through a special imperial decree. In short, the men's fathers did not even think about rebelling, but rather they diligently and painstakingly rose from the lower classes to the aristocracy.

Usually the pilot would come to Krasnoyarsk in the summertime. His mother prepared for his arrival and waited. She was a slight-looking woman, but quick, hardy, and with lively eyes, and her appearance hardly revealed her age; her ease and lightheartedness made her resemble a girl. Only a slight trace of long-ago suffering that would flash across her features hinted at how much she had been through and endured. Only a keen eye could recognize such a bitter past in her, however, and most people lacked that.

Shilin's mother was an active woman. She woke up early in the morning, did exercises, and took cold showers. On Sundays she might do some skiing, and in the summers she would go off on hikes with a backpack. She read a great deal – books and magazines from the regional library located nearby, originally a gift to the city from the educated merchant Yudin. Since pre-revolutionary times it had been named the Yudin Library, and during the Revolution some Americans had purchased its collection and moved it to the United States. Rumors circulated that the collection had filled two steamboats, but a few items had been left behind and served as the seed for the new regional library.

Homemaking had little attraction for his mother, and she paid little attention to chores. She attended concerts, and seemed to lead a completely satisfying life. It would have been a sin to grumble and complain. Yet her life harbored a secret, one that no one knew, even her son, though he was an observant young man and could detect the long-ago suffering in her features.

Throughout the years, whenever Shilin found an opportunity to do so, he tried to ask his mother about the past. He would cleverly steer a conversation this way and that, but he could never expect a clear answer; however much he tried, he never succeeded. Though a friendly and joking woman, she would nonetheless close up completely. She barely talked about her past; she waved it away, and it was as if every word about it had to be pulled out of her with tweezers. Often she would change the subject to something else, and sometimes she seemed to disappear completely; she would turn numb, and then he could not get another word out of her no matter how hard he tried. Something weighed on her, something from the past, like a mysterious torment that bent her toward the ground and left her hunched. Unlike most former front-line soldiers, his mother never talked about the war. She never met with any of the people she had served with, she did not go looking for former comrades, and if anyone wrote to her, she would not answer. The war years, it seemed, were shut out behind a massive wall, cast away into a pitch-black darkness bereft of memory, a forbidden zone wrapped in impenetrable fog. His mother insistently held on to her secret, as if she had taken a vow of silence, and she kept it unshakably and unbendingly.

In childhood and as a young man, Nikolai occasionally asked about his father. His father was dead now, and that was all that Shilin managed to find out. His father had also been a pilot, but he was shot down – once he never came back, and that was all there was to it. All Nikolai had to do was ask about his father and his mother's eyes would darken, and an icy grief would spread over her face. His mother would suddenly become a stranger to him, unapproachable, even inimical, and she would immediately hurry away as if the two of them had only met in passing and more urgent matters awaited her elsewhere.

The pilot cannot be said to have lost interest in his father once he grew older. Shilin felt an odd and painful embarrassment in front of his mother. His interest in his father seemed inappropriate, as if he was breaching some unspoken agreement. He felt as if he was not allowed even to hint at the matter, let alone ask about it straight out.

After the pilot came of age, he never stepped over that line. Only once did he casually ask why back at the labor camp, which he remembered well, he had been called "the American". His mother, to his great surprise, laughed and said that sometimes nicknames do not have any explanation. The pilot fell silent, as if he were satisfied with that answer, but he could tell from his mother's voice that she was only dissimulating, and he dared not push the matter.

I would hear word from him every once in a while. He would send me greetings through comrades of his that doctors and commanders had referred to Division X. Later I lost track of him for a while. He wound up in Vietnam, where he served as a military advisor. That war proved to be a nightmare, endless carnage. The Americans' B-52 bombers, a new generation of Flying Fortress, would fly in ranks of several squadrons – countless numbers of planes; the skies grew crowded with them. Day after day the Americans systematically bombed Vietnam, pounding it square meter by square meter. In carpet bombing no one tried to hit their targets precisely; bombs were simply dropped in large bunches, like a farmer sowing his field. The planet shuddered from the heavy explosions, and it almost seemed like the earth would be torn asunder.

The Vietnamese airfield where Shilin served was located to the north of Haiphong, toward the Chinese border and near the Red River delta. The river took its name from its muddy brown waters that carried clay swept from the riverbanks. The river was lined with mangroves and bamboo. The Vietnamese knew how to disguise their airfields: command positions, stores, and workshops were carefully hidden underground – try as you might, you would never spot them from above. From the river it seemed like the village had been swallowed up by the thick vegetation, its ramshackle houses with walls of rice straw and reeds nestling among *hoa giấy* – paper trees. Their thick crowns of bright green leaves would admit no sunlight and were decked with colorful flowers that looked artificial. Even if one touched these flowers it was hard to tell them from paper, as if someone had neatly cut gay little bells from violet, lilac, and pink paper.

On the slopes of the foothills, beech and chestnut groves grew. The farmers' homes and outbuildings were shrouded by *tho-na* bushes like puffy green clouds, and a spreading *champa* tree with beautiful white flowers could hide a whole company of soldiers under its branches. The Russian military advisors liked most of all the *me* tree, thick as five men's arms. The shade of a *me* could accommodate an entire village along with the regiment based in it. I myself, when traveling on Division X business, often sat in the blessed shade of a *me*, *champa*, or *hoa giấy* when a torturous heat fell upon the earth at midday.

The pilot was teaching the Vietnamese to fly. The tiny Vietnamese looked like children alongside him. Even the senior officers seemed like adolescents. However, the pilot did not go easy on them. He drove them hard, just as he had been driven by his colonel, the regiment commander who had been through the Korean War.

The Vietnamese were sinewy and tough men, but they lacked the physical strength to handle the stresses inherent in aerial warfare. Initially they suffered huge losses, the Americans shooting them down like ducks on a small pond. The military advisors became convinced that the Vietnamese could not master complex technology at all, and that they were not capable of flying at high speeds. One Soviet general suggested that we needed to do the flying ourselves over Vietnam, just as we had done over Korea. In addition, the new supersonic F-4 Phantom easily outpaced our MiG-17 and MiG-19 planes that still flew below the sound barrier.

The military advisors often noted in their reports that even the best Vietnamese pilots were finding it hard to get used to the supersonic MiG-21. The Orient, with its inclination toward nirvana and contemplation, just could not manage with quickly-changing circumstances – the speed of sound seemed to be an unbreakable barrier for the Vietnamese pilots. Every day from morning till night Shilin drilled his students in simple fundamentals – pilotage, maneuvers, tactics – but the Vietnamese could not get to grips with aerial combat: before they could even blink, the enemy was already on their tail.

For Shilin, it was unbearable to be stuck on the ground, waiting. The Vietnamese would take off in their planes and disappear beyond the horizon. The guidance operators gave them a bearing and altitude, and now the only thing connecting the pilots with the ground was a thin voice coming through a headset. The roar of the engines would briefly hang in the air, then fade away, and all that remained was to wait patiently. Shilin was always anxious with this waiting. It was a weight on his chest; time seemed to slow to a crawl. He sat in anguish, sweat running down his back. Following an age-old habit of pilots left behind on the ground, he would glance at his watch: how much fuel was in the tanks? Meanwhile one thought nagged at his mind: who will come back, and who will not?

In the skies someone's fate was decided every day. On some, fortune would smile and grant them a reprieve, while others perished as if they had been struck off a list. As the pilot listened to the voices and sounds of aerial battles in the headphones, he was upset that he could not just climb into a cockpit himself and take off. Instead of waiting in uncertainty, it would have been easier, without further ado, to fight the Americans himself.

In inclement weather, when rain was pouring down, the war in the skies paused. The pilot would sit alone under a *hoa giấy* tree, the crown of which served perfectly as a roof or canopy. In the sound of the rain his clarinet lamented bitterly its wait for those who were away on their missions. The Vietnamese listened from afar; they kept a respectful distance and did not dare approach when the Russian pilot – the Teacher – was drawing those strange sounds out of his clarinet. Buddhists at heart, though on the outside they were loyal followers of Ho Chi Minh, the Vietnamese could guess at a secret in the eerie music that was unfamiliar to foreigners: nirvana, karma, meditation, samsara. For those who considered themselves Catholics, the music seemed like a Catholic mass, a humble prayer directed toward the heavens.

Rain, and moreover a tropical downpour, was a fine accompaniment, like an organ, choir, or large orchestra. When it rained he could imagine that peacetime had come, that there was no more war, or even that it had never happened at all. He could dream and fantasize, and all that remained was to sigh with relief.

The rain ended, however, and the war picked up again. The pilot was again raring to take off into the skies; it would have been so much easier than sitting around on the ground. He dreamed of encountering a Phantom, one on one, without anything getting in his way, on a free hunt. He felt a huge temptation to clash with the Americans himself, especially with the famous pilots Ritchie or DeBellevue from the 555th Tactical Fighter Squadron, who across all Vietnam were said to be invincible aces and often shot the Vietnamese down a flying target.

Shilin was ready to take off at any minute and start fighting – silently, without any radio communication at all, so that he would not bother the diplomats who were just so much hot air, going on and on about whether the Russians were taking direct part in the war or not. He would not broadcast a word in his native language, not a peep. He could even do so without profanity, though that was a huge and daunting challenge. Without being able to rely on swear words, a Russian man might break down and lose his bearings.

Shilin's mind painted vivid pictures of aerial combat, but then he would snap out of it and come back to reality once the Vietnamese pilots had returned to their base. One of them was always missing.

Still, he saw to the task he had been assigned. The mysterious Vietnamese, who resembled diligent schoolchildren, beamed with happiness when they shot down their first Phantom. In time this became a routine matter and everyone grew used to it, the Vietnamese included. He had not come here in vain, it seemed; he really had managed to teach them something.

The pilot often reflected on just how long he had been fighting the Americans, though in all these years he had never fired a shot at them personally. Oh, those Americans, those cowboys with smiles always on their faces, those brash fellows who had grown up used to always winning. Always first in everything; no one ever wanted to come in second – you could never make or convince them to do that. Arrogant bullies, each and every one of them wanted to be on a pedestal. By a long-established tradition, the Americans cannot ever just leave well alone. They stick their noses everywhere, entering wholly uninvited. They look down on the world from their height, and really believe that no one could manage without them, as if everyone needed them, as if they would bring everyone a happiness and peace so long awaited.

Deep down, however, Shilin was troubled by a persistent sense of doubt. Year after year he had encountered the Americans in the skies, opposed them the best he could, tried to tame them. In various parts of the world he had taken off in his plane to meet them, stop them, impede them, get in their way.

Everyone had their own job to do. He tried never to lose face. Still, he wondered if this was really what he had been born to do: to challenge the Americans, to oppose them everywhere their paths and his crossed. Was this his only destiny? Shilin looked back on all the years that he had been flying, and it seemed that he had come into the world only for that: to wrestle with the Americans over and over, make them turn tail, and if necessary, shoot them down. A year later he was transferred to the Caucasus.

$$=== \quad 8 \quad ===$$

From 42nd Street we drove past Grand Central Station and then headed south. Manhattan, as evening came, was lit up, the neon signs giving the streets a festive appearance. Light-flooded Park Avenue shone with its shop displays and mirrors, the countless windows everywhere like stars. We saw the mansard-roofed towers of the Waldorf Astoria lit from below, the towering Pan Am Building that resembled the waves of the sea. We saw a forest of rooftops that floated in the reddening light of the sunset and reached for the golden clouds.

The car had hardly moved from its parking place when the colonel began his story. I listened to him attentively as we glided along the streets, as if the image and the sound – the view out the window and the colonel's voice – merged into one. If I want to recall the details of his story many years later, I have only to take the same route from the Yale Club hotel to the airport. Incidentally, the indigenous peoples of South America used smells as a way of recording things. Each smell was kept in its own tightly-plugged little jug, each jug representing a certain event. If someone in the tribe wished to recall something, the plug was removed from the jug and the contents sniffed. The smell would then, at that later date, bring the long-ago event back to their minds. In the same way, after many years spent at home, the signs and the shop windows I glimpsed on the road have helped me recall the colonel's tale, and not just the words but also his intonation, silences, sighs, and facial expressions.

The car turned south-east onto Delancey Street, passed a riverside park, and then drove onto the Williamsburg Bridge over the East River. Other boroughs of New York came rushing toward us, with the countless lights of Queens on the left and Brooklyn on the right. We caught a glimpse of Wallabout Bay nearby, home of Brooklyn Navy Yard. Further south on the shore of the East River were the Brooklyn Heights, the foot of which was crowded with docks and ships awaiting repair. As we crossed the bridge, we had only to look back to gain an incredible view of Manhattan by evening: a sea of lights in the mists of twilight. Brightly colored advertisements flickered among these lights, and the glass-faced buildings towered into the skies like gigantic aquariums.

I must admit, I found this vista fascinating. The whole East River was speckled with vessels moving up and down it: ferries, barges, small craft, tugboats… Their lights shone and were reflected in the water; green and white fires floated weightlessly through the darkness. Floating restaurants and pleasure boats were brightly lit and decorated with lamps of various colors. Along the piers on the other shore, large ocean liners stood like multistory islands. New York undeniably offered a greater diversity than any other city on the planet. Everything that existed anywhere in the world was here, united in a single whole called New York, the Big Apple.

Unimaginably vast, colorful, booming, and frantic, New York at that time nonetheless remained a sleepy and cozy place. Deep within the labyrinth of the city, a certain provinciality persisted that was typical of small, quiet towns. At any time New York remained open and accessible to anyone, but it was subject to no one. In the final account it remained beyond comprehension, inexplicable. It struck me as a kind of UFO, mysterious and enigmatic, flying through space toward who knows where.

The river was festooned up and down its course with illuminated bridges, their reflections flickering and rippling on the surface of the East River. Traffic moved over the bridges and the riverside highways in streams of light that flowed down onto the neighboring streets and spread toward the outskirts. From this abundance of lights and cars, it was hard to believe that there could be any dark corners left, any untrodden places or pristine nature.

"Cindy, you're about to hear something you have no idea of," Colonel Creighton warned his daughter. "I hope you'll be understanding."

Cindy laughed. "Daddy, what is it?" she said, eyes charmingly wide in the rear-view mirror. "We don't know about it? You've been keeping secrets from us?"

"It happened a long, long time ago," the colonel said with sadness. "I thought it had all ended back then and there wouldn't be any continuation to the story. I thought too much time had passed since then."

The colonel was clearly upset. I listened in silence, only occasionally seeking clarification of the date of an event, the month or the year. We were speeding along in the general flow of traffic, the entire highway a blaze of headlights and red brake lights. A similar picture could be observed from the other highways; from a distance it looked as if the cars with their shining lights were flying over the earth in the twilight.

The colonel's voice was dull, cracked. Sometimes it dwindled to a hoarse whisper, and rather than hearing the words I had to guess at them. It was a sad story. From time to time the colonel would fall silent, his heart gripped by sorrow, and he had to wait for the feeling to pass.

What had happened to him was hard to believe, yet I had the strange feeling that I had long known of the things he was recounting. Strange as it might be, the colonel's story had been present in my own life, only slumbering somewhere deep down, and now it suddenly awoke. The more he talked, the stronger this feeling within me grew, though I can tell you with certainty that I had known nothing before.

The flow of traffic grew sometimes denser, sometimes sparser. Our highway would descend to ground level or, conversely, ascend to a concrete overpass on the same level as the signs and advertisements on the roofs of buildings. We flew past countless windows, with their hints at the lives of others. Without slowing its speed, our car swept through the old community of Williamsburg, once settled by Jews and Puerto Ricans, and onward toward Queens in the south-east. Unexpected things arose from unexpected places.

Cindy, who had been driving in silence, suddenly slowed down and merged into the right lane. With a frown, as if holding back her emotions, she said, "Dad, I can't drive. I'm going to cry."

"Well, what can I do, sweetie?" the colonel said, clearly at a loss.

"If it's OK, let's stop somewhere," she suggested. "We still have time."

The colonel looked around helplessly, uncertain what to do. I felt sorry for him.

"It's no problem, we can talk in the airport," I intervened. "It really is hard for Cindy to drive while you're telling your story, that's obvious. I don't think I could drive either."

"Thank you, sir." Cindy acknowledged me with a glance in the rear-view mirror. I could tell that our driver was experiencing strong emotions.

We drove on for some time without speaking, then a comment was passed on the traffic jams, and soon our conversation turned to the sights of New York. The colonel and his daughter asked me about Moscow, and did not believe me when I said that the streets of the capital were strangers to traffic congestion. In those years it was hard even to buy a car – by no means could everyone get one.

Cindy then turned right. We were headed south, toward Jamaica Bay, a highly sought-after neighborhood for locals as it offered a break from all the bustle and was a wildlife refuge for migratory birds. Birds really did love the bay, and I myself would have happily spent some time there to unwind – am I not a migratory bird myself? Wandering all over the planet, flying in and flying out, hardly able to catch my breath before the trumpet sounded and I was back on the road again, without ever being able to refuse or delay. I had only to listen to my inner voice and I could seek refuge in some heavenly silence among the chirping of birds. Our road did not lead us there, however; fate was sending us in another direction.

The John F. Kennedy International Airport occupies a wide patch of barren land at the tip of Long Island, between a huge racetrack and Jamaica Bay to the south. On the other side of a long sandy spit, the Atlantic Ocean stretches all the way to Europe. As we discussed current politics and complained about the politicians taking advantage of the situation, Cindy turned east and we exited onto the road leading to the airport.

"Daddy, are you flying with that Korean airline again?" Cindy asked.

"Yes, that's right, Korean Airlines."

The colonel's son Michael, a military pilot who served in Japan and was headed back to Misawa Air Base after his leave, would go with his father on the same flight to Seoul. Michael was coming to the airport in a taxi by himself. I had not attached any importance to the colonel's words when he told his daughter that Michael was bringing the tickets, but Cindy had grimaced at the news, as if this business with the tickets surprised and annoyed her.

Our car entered the road going around the airport. In front of us drove a shuttle bus that connected the airline terminals, collecting and discharging passengers flying in or heading off somewhere. Around the clock, the terminal was bustling like any train station, but during the day it was especially stunning. It was crawling with buses and innumerable taxis, every parking lot crammed with cars, crowds of hurrying people carrying suitcases or pushing baggage trolleys, the unceasing roar of planes landing or taking off every single minute. Toward evening this feverish activity diminished somewhat, though Kennedy International Airport never sees any calm. Even at night it lives in a sleepless whirl, with bright lights shining everywhere and the terminals and hangers lit up like daytime.

Our car slowly made its way along the road that ringed the airport. Cindy glanced up at the names of the terminals until she noticed the bright red initials "AA" of American Airlines, whose terminal was also used by Korean Airlines. It was warm, overcast, and drops of rain were falling intermittently. The myriad lights were reflected on the wet asphalt. The three of us walked through the glass façade of the terminal. The colonel looked for flight KAL-007 on the schedule board, but check-in had not started yet. His flight was set for midnight.

"Michael's not here yet," Cindy smirked. "He's always late."

The colonel reassured her. "Don't you make fun of him. We've still got enough time, he'll make it."

"You shouldn't have left the tickets with him," Cindy reproached her father.

We sat in the departures hall. The colonel collected his thoughts and continued his story. Above our heads a chime would occasionally ring, followed by a woman's voice making announcements. The colonel spoke slowly and was clearly making an effort to maintain his composure. Cindy listened without saying anything and tears sometimes appeared in her eyes, while I wondered how these long-ago events were already familiar to me. I knew of them; I simply had never recalled them. They were stored in the cellars of my mind, in a dark closet among the cobwebs and assorted junk, behind a wall.

The boredom typical of all terminals reigned around us. People dozed, lazily slouched around the hall, or sat on chairs, reading, sipping a drink or snacking as is done in all airports and train stations everywhere. Others stood at the payphones making calls to some place or another all over the world.

Meanwhile, certain phenomena that no one had yet imagined were secretly preparing to manifest themselves. An apprehension brushed against my consciousness. I felt a vague anxiety, a premonition coming over me, though I did not know what had caused it and to what it portended. However, our intuition generally does not lead us astray. Our forebodings do not trick us; they rarely visit us without good reason. Usually real events and concrete causes lie behind them – the intentions and machinations of others send out a signal ahead of time.

In most cases a person does not notice the warning, for the ability to hear this soundless signal is not granted to everyone. Now I clearly perceived some kind of danger, as if there was an electrical charge around me that signaled alarm. I do not know if anyone else felt uneasy, but as a doctor I have sometimes made a diagnosis purely on the basis of my intuition, without any obvious reasons for it; in my work, intuition plays an important role.

   

Initially I tried to ignore these heavy forebodings, to drive them away – everything is fine, there is no reason for concern, no cause for alarm. However, I could not shift the mysterious apprehension that I was feeling. Invisible trumpets were sounding the alarms and bells were ringing out soundlessly.

Colonel Creighton was continuing to tell his story, and during these minutes a towing vehicle was pulling up to the American Airlines terminal, and behind a Boeing 747 bearing the emblem of Korean Airlines on its tail came a flying crane. Mechanics examined the plane while a technician loaded cassettes into the so-called black boxes, which were in fact armored containers painted bright orange. On board the Boeing they were installed in the left side of the airplane's tail section, over the niche where passengers could hang their coats and next to the tail section's toilet.

These round containers fashioned from heat-resistant steel were installed on airplanes for a reason that, whether we like it or not, must be faced: accidents happen. The black boxes would remain intact under any circumstances, whether it be an explosion, a fire, or even being sunk beneath the sea at a great depth, and they help experts piece together what happened. A mechanism in one container recorded the readings from the on-board instruments, such as the flight speed, altitude, course, the position of the ailerons, and other indicators, over twenty-five hours. The tape recorder in the other black box recorded everything said in the cockpit; its cassette tape ran on a loop, meaning that one could reconstruct what the crew had been talking about for the last half hour. Both black boxes were also equipped with a battery-powered beacon that would activate after a crash, with enough charge for thirty days. For a whole month this beacon would emit a radio signal that could be used to locate the black box. Sometimes a black box has been found at the bottom of the ocean; they have been lifted from a depth of four kilometers.

According to rumors passed between aviation experts, this Boeing 747, being used for Korean Airlines Flight 007 on the route New York–Anchorage–Seoul, had secretly been fitted with a third box. Were the rumor true, one could only wonder about the purpose of this third box. All kinds of rumors fly around, though, too many to count.

Incidentally, in Korean Airlines' technical service logs, it was recorded that this particular Boeing had undergone inspections twice that August, within the same week of August 10 to 16. At first glance, this might seem innocent enough, nothing amiss. However, a closer look at the inspection records revealed something strange about the dates. Over the first ten days of that month, the company had carried out no inspections. Then two inspections had been made within six days, and after that, the aircraft had not been inspected at all during the last two weeks of August. One might reasonably think that something here was not right, to say the least.

Many people may boast of being in the loop, but few actually caught the rumor that on August 11 at 10:30 a.m. this same Boeing 747 with tail number HL7442 supposedly arrived at Andrews Air Force Base near Washington DC, home to the blue-and-white presidential airliner Boeing 747-200 with the call sign Air Force One, a veritable flying White House. Since 1972, seven American presidents, beginning with Richard Nixon, had flown on the same Boeing 747, until the American air force eventually ordered a new plane for Bill Clinton. The presidential Boeing 747 was a technical marvel, a well-nigh perfect machine. Its designers had paid attention to every little detail, even situations that could hardly be considered likely. The plane's in-flight refueling system allowed it to remain aloft for a week or more, as long as anyone could practically want or need. The on-board equipment could maintain communications with any point on the globe, with both ordinary and encrypted links. One had only to climb on board (though few have ever had the privilege) to catch sight immediately of dozens of television screens and what seemed to be hundreds of telephones, including highly secure satellite phones. The plane was equipped with a wide array of weaponry that kept it completely safe, even from missile attack or anti-aircraft fire. On the president's airliner, the on-board electronic center was located in the Boeing's hump, where a salon or bar was found on ordinary passenger models. In addition, the Boeing 747-200 was equipped with an emergency escape pod, which could be ejected from the plane with the president inside if necessary. Every flight of Air Force One, it must be noted, was considered a serious military operation and elaborately planned in advance, and technical maintenance provided at Andrews Air Force Base by the 89th Airlift Wing would prepare the airliner for its journeys.

It was at this very same Andrews Air Force Base, as confidential sources would have it, that the Korean Airlines' Boeing 747 landed on August 11. During its flight, it had supposedly been accompanied by an RC-135 Cobra electronic reconnaissance plane, a detail that would make one wonder. As soon as the 747 landed, a tow vehicle waiting on the runway led it to an inconspicuous building designated 1752 at the far end of the airfield.

One can only imagine that there was something to hide here. That summer, Andrews Air Force Base command had granted use of building 1752 to a private company known as E-Systems, which produced electronic equipment and was known to be a contractor for the CIA and the Department of Defense. E-Systems was headquartered in Dallas, Texas. The Korean Airlines plane, to the astonishment of the 89th Airlift Wing, occupied that remote patch of the base for more than three days, but even the base's security was ordered to keep away from the mysterious airliner. All this time, according to intelligence reports, E-Systems experts were at work on the plane under conditions of total secrecy. It must be said, though, that intelligence has not been able to verify these reports.

An informant reported that on the evening of August 14, the Boeing took off from Andrews Air Force Base accompanied, as it had been three days before, by an RC-135 Cobra reconnaissance plane. The special security measures astonished even the base's command. No one knew the plane's route or where it would land.

According to public sources, the Korean Boeing 747 had been built in 1973 for the German airline Lufthansa. The plane had flown for Lufthansa for six years, after which it had been bought by Korean Airlines and was now in its fourth year of service there. All in all, Korean Airlines' actions would make an inquisitive researcher wonder. Four years earlier it had nearly lost a Boeing 707 passenger plane in northern Europe when, either by accident or intentionally, it had strayed off course and passed over Soviet military installations housed in northern ports. In the skies above the Kola Peninsula, the airliner had been intercepted by Soviet fighters, but fortunately no shots were fired and tragedy was averted. Air defense had worked smoothly then, the fighters forcing the Boeing to land at a military airfield. Shortly thereafter, the plane and its passengers were allowed to go home. The Korean pilots claimed that they had simply strayed off course.

I learned these details only much later. We, meanwhile, were sitting in the departures hall of JFK Airport. Check-in had not yet started, and we still had enough time to finish our discussion. Cindy was listening closely to her father's words, but she was also worried about her brother. I noticed that she kept glancing at the terminal entrance. Michael still had not arrived, and her worries only grew. Even though the airport was packed, her striking features stood out from the crowd, and many men stared at her.

I should mention that the younger Cindy and the older Michael were children from different marriages. The colonel had been married twice, though both marriages had ended in divorce. He had divorced his first wife Tracy, an air force sergeant at the Foggia base in Italy, rather quickly. They married soon after the war, but it was a banal story: they simply had irreconcilable differences, neither the first such couple nor the last, and neither regretted the divorce. Michael was still small when their marriage ended. The marriage had been a brief one, and fortunately there was no painful process of dividing up their property.

Steven Creighton was in no hurry to get married again. He chose his next wife on apparently reasonable grounds, after long and sober deliberation. Susan had seemed like a smart and attractive person, but in reality there was a worm in the apple. Creighton discovered that while he was off fighting the Communists, his wife had found herself another man. This, too, was nothing new; it is something that has been happening as long as men have been going off to war. In the absence of a deep love, a woman might be expected to prefer a wealthy businessman with a sedentary life to a pilot roaming from one war to another, a pilot who was moreover risking his life day in and day out.

The second divorce happened quickly, easily, and painlessly. Susan lived with her new husband in Atlanta, Georgia, while Steven Creighton remained a single man.

═══ **9** ═══

After Vietnam, the pilot ended up in the Caucasus. After the Arctic, the Kuril Islands, and the war in the jungle, Shilin thought the Caucasus was heaven on earth: the promised land, a gift.

He patrolled the Caucasus near Turkey. Turkish and American fighters prowled the area along the border, too. Often the pilot would take off on a paired patrol whenever an American RC-135 Cobra electronic reconnaissance plane took off from a Turkish air base and headed toward the border – a frequent occurrence, practically routine. The planes, divided by the invisible and conditional line of the border, would fly on their parallel courses over the mountainous terrain. Below them was a series of ridges and gorges, forested hilltops in burned brown and yellow, cliffs, and wrinkled gullies resembling frozen lava. To the left and right of his course through the Lesser Caucasus range, he could see plowed valleys, sloping ridges with vineyards, and pasture land and alpine meadows, while far off the glaciers and snow-covered peaks of the Greater Caucasus towered to incredible heights.

In both Turkey and Iran, the border lay among the mountains, soaring, dropping and twisting like a mountain river. Just as he had in the Arctic, in the Middle East, over the neutral waters of the Black Sea, the pilot often encountered the Americans. Below him lay a blue-green expanse that seemed, from that height, to extend in all directions. The border was marked only on maps; pilots had to rely on prompting from navigators on the ground.

International waters began twelve nautical miles from shore. Sometimes fishing vessels or pleasure boats would illegally enter the USSR's territorial waters, but more common intruders were foreign submarines, military vessels, and reconnaissance planes under fighter escorts.

On serene days, when the sun shone bright on the sea and mountains, a pilot could make out from his altitude the coastal shoals, the stony beds of rivers now run dry, the slopes of the hills streaked with man-made terraces, and gloomy wild ravines cutting through the mountains. The strip of land between the mountains and the coast was cramped with tourist resorts and towns, the sight of which recalled halcyon hot days, the merry Black Sea summer, the provincial luxury of military rest and recreation facilities with their sweet idleness. Days lazing on the beach in the hot sun, evening dances, officers flirting incessantly with the gals, fleeting romances, the alluring smell of wine in barrels and meat sizzling on grills – a carefree life in the heat, which from a distance seems like a frenetic vacation, a dizzying celebration, rest for the soul.

The fighter planes flew at high speed over the edge of the sea. The coast, caressed by the warm tide, lay below the pilot like a relief map: a familiar picture of bays, capes, concrete breakwaters, piers, small boats slowly moving near the shore, and larger vessels heading out to sea, looking from high up like children's boats among the vastness.

Shilin liked his solitary night flights. When the sea and the mountains were submerged in darkness, the coastal region was brightly lit up – a dazzling strip beneath him in the thick black southern night. At supersonic speed, the fighter flew headlong into the darkness. The thin strip of the coastal region shone with myriad lights while the night reigned all around, and only the dim fires of the scattered mountain settlements or the lights of ships hinted that life was going on in other places. The instruments of his cockpit shone before him. Their cold, faint illumination barely reached his face, while right next to him, above his head and beyond the transparent light of his cockpit, the stars twinkled in the sky in their countless numbers, looking as if he could just reach out his hand and touch them.

He had only to look down, and the bright glow of the coastal region would bring certain thoughts to mind. There were no words for those breathtaking evenings in the south, the bustle and music of the countless eateries, the smell of grilled meat, night-blooming flowers, coffee and magnolias, crowds strolling along the shore, the clatter of women's high heels… So many charming faces, slender legs, captivating eyes – a dazzling parade, an endless procession of beauties. Goodness, what radiance and splendor! It made your head spin, got your blood pumping, sent your gaze wandering and you could not stop it.

Every year, Soviet air force pilots had mandatory rest and recreation. They had to go whether they wanted to or not – the military does not wait for its soldiers to agree and it does not ask what they want. Over the years, soldiers had come to like the Black Sea coast. The military's recreation facilities were mainly located along the shore, with gazebos, palms, tropical flowers, white statues, and the warm sea… From the first day soldiers, whether bachelors or already married, would be waiting keenly and eagerly for romance to blossom.

It is incredible how overwhelmed Soviet people are by emotion once we are in the south. Our thoughts wander, our heads spin. If a person observes himself carefully, he will notice how his chest grows tight in anticipation of an encounter. His heart will ache and his eyes roam in search of that someone special. But how can he choose, how can he take his pick if there is so much to choose from? Of course, the surrounding environment makes it easy to enter into a romantic mood, for how could it be otherwise if the twilight is imbued with the smell of the sea, and distant music reaches you from a small orchestra playing in the orchard among the green trees? Later, as the year moves into winter, you often look back on the splashing of the fountains, the dances, the old tangos, the smooth voice of a saxophone, the weeping violins; and then, later at night when the light dims, the heated whispering in the alleys, the long, drawn-out moans of lovemaking, fleeting footsteps, and the elusive laughter of a woman.

American RC-135 reconnaissance planes appeared over the mountains out of the Ararat Valley and leisurely, hour after hour, swept the skies along the border, as if they were diligently burning through the contents of their fuel tanks. The land border between the countries in the Caucasus twisted and wound with abandon through the mountains between the Caspian and the Black Sea. On the photographs taken by the interceptors, American planes often appeared against the backdrop of the snow-white peaks of Mount Ararat, the legendary two-headed mountain, which the Armenians had long known as Masis.

Sometimes an RC-135 would cross over the border, but more often a fast and highly maneuverable F-4 Phantom would violate Soviet airspace to vacuum up codes and radar frequencies while an RC-135 accompanied it on the other side of the border. Usually they got their way: across the entire Trans-Caucasian region, from Batumi to Lankaran, air bases would sound the alarm, broadcast frequencies would erupt in tumult, radars would search the skies with especial fervor, and fighters would take off on intercept courses.

The intruding plane would ordinarily leave, but it sometimes happened that it was cut off from the border and forced to land. Old hands in Soviet air defense recalled a long-ago occasion when an American pilot had gone on the rampage, as if he did not believe that he could be shot down, and when he finally could believe it, it was too late: the only thing left for this stubborn pilot to do was to eject. For a long time afterward, Soviet search teams found fragments of his plane in the narrow gorges and alpine forests.

On the slopes of the Armenian mountain Ararat, which now fell on the Turkish side of the border according to the will of the Bolsheviks, the Americans had built an electronic monitoring station, and not just anywhere, but right where Noah and his ark had landed. The giant silver dishes of their parabolic antennas looked rather out of place in these Biblical mountains. The pilot often thought about how these two events, separated by such long a span of time, interrelated with each other. To a keen eye, an inscrutable link between eras and events would sometimes be revealed, a hidden secret between the power of ordinary minds. Thus now the gray head of Ararat linked the Ark, the universal flood, radar antennas, and the powerful motion of the airplanes that tore at supersonic speeds through the sky over the sacred mountain.

It felt good to serve in the Caucasus. The south of the USSR usually changed people's way of looking at things; this warm region lifted one's mood. Life here was notable for its festiveness and it passed like a carnival, in an easy doze, in drunken imbibing, in a blaze, with a dash of insanity to it, and as if everything was a joke, not completely serious: let us have a good time now and we will get to work later. It always seemed to him that his stay in the south did not form part of his allotted time on earth, but instead represented something extra. How uncomfortable he felt when his losses were revealed to him; while he had lived in the south, so much time and so many opportunities had passed by that could never be brought back. A bitter regret ate at him, as often happens when one experiences a loss, proving once again that after the party comes the hangover. A delayed sense of regret gnawed at him, pangs of guilt ate at him for his careless idleness – a perennial feature of the south. In the north you are constantly waiting for something: a change, spring, a letter, summertime weather, going off to somewhere else… We spend all our lives wandering between north and south, between eager expectation and anguish at what we have lost.

The zone that Shilin patrolled began over Soviet waters in the Black Sea and proceeded south of the Çoruh River. The Çoruh was a stubborn, tenacious river which flowed through a valley amid the mountainous terrain, and only near its mouth did it cross the Soviet border at Adjara, thereafter splitting into a delta and falling into the Black Sea near Batumi. A paired patrol would proceed along the east side of the Turkish border, and in mere minutes reach the spurs of the Lesser Caucasus, south of the

Greater Caucasus range, where they would turn south-east and then, more sharply, toward the south. The planes would pass at great speed over the scorched Armenian highlands with their volcanic and wrinkled terrain, and then they would fly to the west of Mount Aragats and reach the Iranian border east of snow-capped Mount Ararat, where they turned back. Here the borders of three countries met. Sometimes the pilots were assigned to patrol the Iranian border, and then their fighters would fly further, all the way to the Talysh Mountains. The planes would land at the Lankaran airfield, and after refueling they would head back.

In clear weather, the dry land and sea were there to see, and above them a wide-open space was revealed: the entire Caucasus region was visible, a stunning vista that always took pilots by surprise. On one side of their course, the horizon in the distance lay along the sea, and the curvature of the planet was clearly visible. The fleeting change of colors far off at sea was an enchanting sight. On the other side of their course, the forested hills and picturesque valleys came in green bunches. Like a zipper, the plane seemed to part the surrounding space or bring it back together again, and white vapor trailed behind it like a woolen thread behind a thin needle. Once this stitch through the sky had been made, the thread would lose its tightness, leaving light little clouds behind.

He flew over Colchis at the lower Enguri and Rioni rivers, where the impassable marshes, completely choked with reeds, looked from above like mowed lawns. At their edges the marshes were bordered by a relict population of bearded alder trees, over which a vine-choked forest of elms rose. Among the elms were rare oaks, hornbeam, and beech with dense ferns. Black forest covered a vast expanse, a gloomy expanse of spruce and fir along with an underbrush of blackberry and clematis that was well-nigh impassable. The tree trunks were wrapped in thick ivy, sarsaparilla, and other vines from the *Aralia* and *Smilax* families. It seemed a veritable jungle. This murky, wet, sunless, and stifling subtropical forest enveloped the swamps of the river's floodplains.

A similar picture could be seen in Lankaran, where the Kyzylgach swamp was completely covered in sedge, milfoils, and a kind of water chestnut that the locals called *chilim*.

I had already had opportunities to visit the Black Sea coast, but I had never been anywhere else in the Caucasus; my work had never brought me to the Transcaucasian Military District. At Division X I called the fighter regiment where Shilin was serving and we arranged a meeting. Like an old hand at the Caucasus he already knew a suitable place: Lake Sevan. When traveling on business, I usually flew in order to save time – if Division X was sending a team with research equipment, we were given a military transport plane. This time, however, I chose to go by train and see the Caucasus up close.

Armenia's southern border runs along a stony steppe valley, surrounded by bare cliffs and hills of yellow tufa limestone. Behind these stretch the weathered, cracked mountains, consisting of a volcanic pumice that is overgrown with bushes and wiry grass. The Moscow–Yerevan train made its leisurely way along an imposing barrier; the border was close here, and the embankment on which the railroad was laid was bordered by barbed wire and plowed earth, where the authorities could check for footprints. Border guards with machine guns hung out of the train's doors and walked through the carriages to ensure that none of the passengers would make a break for it and try to cross into Turkey, something that happened nearly every year.

Two Americans, an elderly couple, were traveling in the compartment next to mine. The man's parents had been Armenians, and after the massacres at the hands of the Turks, they had emigrated to America, where the man was born. My fellow passenger did not speak Armenian, however. He knew only a handful of words and phrases passed down from his late parents. Back in his youth, his parents had extracted a promise from him that he would someday visit the old country, the very same place where they had been born, had met, married, and lived happily until they had emigrated.

He was already completely American, of course. He had made a successful career for himself, made his fortune, and married a woman whose American roots went far back; his children and grandchildren were American, too. His family lived as people live in America, but he had felt something drawing him to Armenia all his life, and he remembered the promise that he had made to his parents. When he retired from his job that spring, he decided that it was time, and his wife supported him. In September they flew to Moscow and boarded the train. For hours we talked and looked out of the window. He was reluctant even to go to sleep.

The Turkish side was no different from ours: dry, stony steppe, wild grasslands, scraggly thorn bushes. The mere thought that across that barbed wire and plowed earth a foreign land began gave the landscape a special meaning and significance. A wind from Turkey shook the long grass, lifted dust, and gradually eroded the long-extinct volcanoes. The fine dust billowed over the steppe and accumulated on the tightly-closed windows of the train carriages, the dust of ages, time itself flowing through a metaphorical hourglass. Perhaps on this train I was traveling through the centuries and millennia, for outside the window the legendary country of Urartu gradually unfolded, the sunny birthplace of the first gods.

A sudden blow struck the dry valley like a cannon going off, like an unexpected burst of thunder from a clear sky, and it nearly shattered the train's windows. Two fighter planes swept over the train. In an instant they had broken the sound barrier, and it was as if the thunderclap had split the sky asunder and dropped debris down onto the earth. The planes soared off and disappeared in the blink of an eye. The sound tried to catch up with them, but it lagged behind, withered and died.

During the years when the pilot was serving in the Caucasus, we met twice: in Armenia on Lake Sevan, and in the south of Abkhazia near Sukhumi. Our first meeting happened on an island, or rather on a peninsula, because at times Lake Sevan's waters grow shallow and the lake bottom is revealed so that the island is linked to the shore by a sandy, stony strip.

The island was home to a leisure facility for the Union of Writers, and nearby, among the heather, juniper, and rosehip, I discovered the ruins of an early Christian monastery and an ancient royal palace. The monastery and palace had stood there on the island for one and a half millennia, but the Soviet regime had no tolerance for them. In the era of Stalin and the five-year plans, the palace and monastery were plundered for building stones, and from them the Union of Writers' home had been built, in the stillness of the island, at the edge of a cliff.

From a distance, the Union of Writers' home resembled an artillery bunker. Its massive walls of poured concrete suggested reliable, allaround defense, as if its architects had wanted to show genuine talent in building fortifications. I was troubled, tormented, and plagued by one question, however: how could creative figures live here, how could they manage to write anything, how could poems and prose come to them? If they knew what stones had been used to erect this refuge, built for them to come and seek inspiration, they would hardly be able to let out a croak, let alone produce fine literature!

At the train station in Yerevan, I said goodbye to the Americans before they were driven off by an interpreter from Intourist. We did not exchange addresses and telephone numbers, as it was clear that we would never meet again, but I always regret having to part with good people. As we were saying goodbye, the American mentioned that he would cast a handful of Armenian earth over his parents' grave, just as he had promised, for there was no one else who could do it.

The Akhtamar regional train set off for Sevan from the Yerevan station, and I had only to go from one platform to another. The train took its name from an island on Lake Van, a place that for a long time had belonged to Armenia, before Western Armenia, with Mount Ararat and Lake Van, were seized by the Ottoman Empire. Russian forces liberated the territory, and it became part of Russia. Pushkin described this war in *A Journey to Arzrum*. The Russian army proved victorious, but suffered significant losses in the mountains. After the Revolution, Lenin's regime gave the territory to Atatürk; the Bolsheviks were trying to win over the Young Turks, who had just perpetrated a mass slaughter of Armenians. An honest look at the matter would show that the Bolsheviks were willing to give up everything, if it would only help keep them in power.

The regional train, with its engine powered by overhead electrical lines, struggled up the mountains and arrived in the small town of Sevan, the regional capital, which stood twenty kilometers from the lake. An hour later, as if the train needed time to catch its breath after the effort, it slowly made its way toward the lake, and there, shuddered to a stop on the shore near the pier, settling straight into tranquil coexistence with local pleasure craft and steamboats. The train station was surrounded by little eateries where one could try the famous Sevan trout, a fish found nowhere else on earth. Two old churches stood prominently on the high cliffs over the lake, dark silhouettes with pointed roofs that cut sharply into the bright emptiness of the sky.

I walked up a mountain path to one of the churches. It had been built from natural stone. Both inside and outside the coarse stone had resisted any decoration. Inside the church it seemed impossible to think about any earthly matters; all of one's thoughts were directed toward heaven. On the wall next to the altar, where in a Russian church one would expect icons, stood only a white linen scroll with the divine visage painted in cinnabar. Wherever the stone laid down by ancient master craftsmen protruded, countless small candles had been set. Clearly a large number of worshipers came to services and each left their candle behind.

Fortunately, I was the only person in the church. It was just after midday as I peeked in. There was not a soul in the vast, gloomy space. Naturally, there was no electricity here, so that the cunning and craftiness of man would not barge in and defile the house of God. Weak daylight came through narrow openings high up on the walls, and the dim beams fell into a pitch-dark blackness. It was hard to call this church a building per se; it seemed more like the mountain air surrounded by a wall, the sky encased in stone. The only earthly sound was the whistling of the wind, capricious like the leaves of fall when they fly through the air. It sounded like a bizarre melody that I had heard at times before, in different parts of the world. In spite of that, the silence gradually grew stronger, distinct and almost palpable. In the brief pauses between the gusts of wind, indistinct sounds came from the church's gloom: woeful moaning, great sighs, the rustling of fabric, a human voice that was unintelligible. The heavy muttering dwindled to a whisper, which in turn gradually diminished, faded, died away.

I looked more closely and saw a man lying face down. He had spread out his arms and pressed his face to the ground, prostrate like a monk, up against the altar where the white cloth hung with its image of Jesus painted with cinnabar. This worshiper had been almost invisible: it was very dark in the church and he wore black clothing, and he was down on the ground. Who knows what he was praying, but it was strange that he had come to the church in the middle of the day, outside any set time. Usually services were held in the church on Sundays and holidays. I supposed that the man preferred a day without services so that he could meet God on his own. Clearly some need had brought him here; he was uttering unknown words in a barely audible voice, with heavy sighs and tortured groans punctuated by hoarse silences. Sometimes the worshiper would whisper something, and the wind would seem to repeat it after him, the same humble supplication made with two voices.

I do not know what prayer he was directing toward heaven; he spoke quietly and in a foreign language. Something familiar, however, was revealed to me in the wind's curious refrain and in the man's heavy, unfamiliar muttering. It suggested a prayer that had once been sung long ago by a clarinet: give me the strength, Lord, to go on; guide me, Lord, on my path…

Shilin arrived in Sevan a day later. We spoke on the telephone beforehand. That same morning, a Sunday, people arrived on the island from all over Armenia, city folk and rural people alike, and the crowds swelled. An Armenian holiday was being celebrated, and in various places drummers beat their drums and zurna players' cheeks puffed as they blew into their instruments and produced sinuous oriental melodies. An endless service was held in the church, where the guttural voices of priests soared over the heads of the large throng.

The Armenians follow the Gregorian faith. They were one of the first nations to adopt Christianity, a whole twenty years before it was made the official religion of the Holy Roman Empire. In the late third century and early fourth, the people had sided with the bishop Gregory, who claimed that Jesus had been both divine and human, but that his divine nature had swallowed up his human nature, the latter dissolving in the former like salt in water.

I had unexpectedly arrived among bizarre festivities, in which early Christianity was mixed with ancient pagan rites. Below the church, on the slopes of the hill, pagans in times long past had set up a round altar made from crudely worked stone. Here they slaughtered rams and chickens, and the blood ran thickly down a stone drain into a granite well hollowed out of the rocks. After the pagans had made their sacrifices, they dipped their fingers in the blood and wiped it on their faces: on their foreheads, cheeks, and chins for good luck, as an elderly Armenian explained to the pilot and me.

This tradition from pagan Armenia had survived into the modern era: all along the shore and on the slopes, sacrificial bonfires burned, and the wind brought a smell of smoke and grilled meat. According to an age-old ritual, worshipers were obliged not only to attend the church service, light a candle, sacrifice an animal and bite into the sacrificial meat themselves, they were also to share what they had with passersby. Foreigners, wayfarers, and strangers were to be invited to the fire, given food and drink, and engaged in conversation.

It appeared that the pilot and I were doomed. We were the only outsiders on the island, and moreover we had come all the way from Russia. We were fated that day to suffer death at the hands of the merciless Armenians, sentenced to a cruel death by means of bountiful food and drink. We could not take a single step without people on every side urging us to join them. Fires burned everywhere among the rocks and the vegetation of the lakeside, and the worshipers were munching on the meat of sacrificed animals and drinking their homemade wine from wineskins and other vessels. Once they saw us, they immediately leaped to their feet and insistently invited us. They all competed in pulling us toward their respective fires.

To be frank, the food brought us quickly to bursting point, and we had soon had more than enough to drink, and yet we found ourselves unable to turn fresh invitations down. The Armenians could not imagine that anyone would violate the old tradition and ruin the holiday by refusing what they offered. They simply did not accept that a person's capacity for food and drink was limited.

Soon we realized that we would not get out of there alive. The pilot saved us: he started playing a zurna. A musician from a small band of performers loaned him his instrument. As soon as Shilin began to play, all the other zurnas that had been calling out from the various bonfires felt silent.

If one looks for its relatives among the instrument family, the zurna is a sister to the oboe and a cousin of the clarinet. While the pilot played, the worshipers looked on him as a priest giving a sermon: the zurna's voice ascended to the heavens, twisting and sweeping through the mountain air over the rocks and the water. The zurna admitted forthrightly that we all have a hard lot in life, and that we have pursued that lot, stumbled, walked until our feet bled, and carried our cross; our bodies had been cut by thorns and sharp stones. We might become despondent and lose faith in our ability to keep going, but the zurna believed, and urged us onward, and we steeled ourselves and overcame our grief. Each of us realized that no other path was provided to us than the present one, and so the only thing left was to walk onward and endure.

Hardly breathing, the crowd listened to Shilin play. Everyone understood the moans and cries that came from the zurna. The Armenians had walked a tragic road. How much strength had it taken to endure persecution and oppression, how many victims had had to suffer as the nation defended itself. Many other peoples have disappeared over the millennia – they have collapsed, faded away, sunk into oblivion, become utterly forgotten.

When the zurna fell silent, the crowd joined it, dumbstruck.

"It's a good instrument," the pilot said as he handed the instrument back to its owner.

"Yes, it is, *varpet*," said the musician, deeply moved and calling Shilin by the Armenian word for "master". "I'll be honest, I did not expect that from a Russian! You're a real *varpet*! Thank you!"

"Thank you," Shilin replied. "It was your zurna."

"Of course, you're right," the musician laughed. "The instrument played all on its own!"

"I just helped it a bit," the pilot said.

The crowd silently parted for Shilin and me. I had a feeling that we were in a scene from antiquity, one of Biblical grandeur and operatic theatricality. A choir of many voices was quite possibly about to ring out. It could hardly be otherwise, when sacrificial bonfires were burning over the wide expanse of the water, columns of smoke were rising on the precipitous lakeshore, a bloody altar could be glimpsed among the heather-covered rocks, and a diverse throng of people was lining the stony slopes.

The army had seen no point in trying to hide their presence. In order for me to examine this flight crew according to Division X's program, they had rented the local leisure facility for an entire month and had the equipment used in our division delivered to these delightful mountains. The leisure facility itself stood on the shore of Lake Sevan. Shilin and I stayed in neighboring rooms. I examined him along with other pilots from various regiments. The pilot confirmed what I had already known: from time to time he dreamed that he was actually a foreigner, and this went on year after year. Nikolai felt that his "self" continued somewhere beyond the horizon, on the other side of some unknown boundary. It was as if a part of his existence was hidden, not only from others, but even from himself – there was an aspect of him that reason and common sense could not fathom.

Since Shilin and I had last seen each other, he had married. At the garrison Shilin was now raising a son named Pavel who had such big cheeks that his father nicknamed him Hamster: even when he had his back to you, you could see his cheeks sticking out.

Exactly as before, the pilot continued to encounter the Americans in the skies. After Vietnam he could barely stand their antics. It was as if they were testing Shilin's patience, teasing him for their own amusement, and he often felt a burning desire to get back at them. He had to resist the urge to disobey his orders and shoot off a rocket. He even confessed to me that he sometimes feared for himself, that he might lose control and do it.

I led the pilot in a course of relaxation. He calmed down and regained his composure, but to tell the truth, even I felt annoyed when I read the summaries from the border. For example, ships from the United States Sixth Fleet, based in the Mediterranean, had come through the Dardanelles and Bosporus, cut across the Black Sea, and rushed right through our territorial waters.

Every year Shilin used three weeks from his large forty-five-day leave to visit his mother in Krasnoyarsk. Sometimes he took his son with him, and as Pavel grew up, Shilin often caught his mother staring at the boy. She studied him attentively, as if she was trying to recognize in him someone known only to her.

In all those years, the pilot's wife had only once ventured a visit with her husband to her mother-in-law. Marina came from the south, and she preferred resorts and the big city, and she let it be known that she had little desire to spend her vacation time on trips to Siberia. Just imagine her mood when she found out that her husband was being transferred from the Caucasus to Sakhalin Island.

═══ 10 ═══

Colonel Creighton continued to tell his complicated story from the distant past. Sometimes he fell silent as bitter emotions surged and he closed his eyes as if in pain. His daughter Cindy listened to her father without saying anything. She would sigh heavily and, unable to control herself, frequently shed a tear. The overcast weather on the Atlantic coast that day matched the mood. Outside the glass façade of the terminal it was raining, the drops falling on the windows all evening long as if nature was sympathizing with Colonel Creighton and was struck with the same grief. Life at JFK went on as usual, though, notwithstanding the inclement weather of that late August. Planes took off and landed as they should, and the airport functioned without a hitch.

Crowds of passengers kept moving about the planet, taking off and landing, in spite of the rain and the dark night. The airport control tower worked smoothly, tracking flights like clockwork; the personnel on duty kept the situation under control. There was not even the slightest hint of danger. Calm and composure reigned everywhere, and the bustle in the terminal was merely the ordinary state of things. Life went on peacefully, wholly predictably, and conditions were normal, with no unexpected developments or misfortunes. One could not complain or grumble, and no one did. The passengers and airport personnel saw no cause for concern. No one expected things to take a turn for the worse, let alone lead to a disaster.

Nevertheless, in spite of the general positive state of things, in spite of people's confidence and serene state of mind, and also in spite of common sense, I suddenly felt as if clouds were gathering somewhere. There was nothing I could do yet; looming beyond the horizon was the outline of something, no more, but I already sensed approaching misfortune. I had a vague presentiment of it.

I feel no need to expend excessive energy demonstrating that my feelings were correct, but I assure you, somewhere in the far distance an unknown threat was growing, one that I still could not grasp. To be honest, though, I was also beset by doubt. I needed to pay close attention and attempt to pierce through the fog, but the inner voice remained silent, and the message became no clearer. As time went by, though, the signal grew stronger. There really *was* a threat, I believed, though I did not know the cause of it. A doctor often makes a diagnosis intuitively, following a hunch, even without any clear symptoms and when the illness has still not shown itself – the latent period, as doctors call it. Now I was racking my brain searching for proof.

At Division X we had studied in depth noetic symptoms, the science of premonitions, presentiments, and the foreseeing of events: a science that concerns itself with the intuitive consciousness, and which seeks out patterns and determines their nature.

Of course, at that time I did not connect my premonition with the heightened state of readiness of the electronic surveillance groups at certain American air force bases. I did not suspect anything of that then; only much later did I learn of it. But on that rainy evening in late August, when midnight was approaching and passengers were waiting to check in for Korean Airlines flight 007, flying New York–Anchorage–Seoul, I sat in the JFK Airport departures hall listening to the American colonel Steven Creighton, and suddenly felt ill at ease. A mysterious threat loomed over the man I was speaking with and flickered at the margins of my awareness, but it never grew into a clear notion that would demand action, concrete steps. An inexplicable threat, out there somewhere. Questions naturally arose in my mind to which I awaited answers.

We already knew by then about biolocation and noetics, to which premonitions are linked. If I could only explain what I was feeling, flight KAL-007 would be canceled, but how could I express my fears, how could I insist that they cancel the flight, if I had no proof? Apart from my foreboding, I could not see any convincing reasons, and I had no sound arguments to offer. If I told people what I was feeling, they would simply laugh at me.

Colonel Creighton reached the end of his story and then, dispirited, he fell silent. Cindy wiped the tears from her eyes. I wrestled with my thoughts. I had to say something now; the colonel was waiting. There was a reason I had accompanied him to the airport, after all.

"I'll try to help you if you like," I offered. "I'm not at all sure I can do anything, but I'll try. No guarantee, of course."

"Of course no guarantee." The colonel smiled sadly. "I'd be grateful if you could just try. Maybe we'll be lucky."

   

"I'll make inquiries in Moscow. At least I know where to start."

"Really?!" the colonel exclaimed, as if he could not believe it. "Well, God bless you. I hope it works out."

I was not just saying that. I really did think that I could help him. The vague thoughts emerging from the black depths of my subconscious and swirling around my head gradually grew clearer and took shape, becoming matters I had to reflect on. In their wake came an uncertain hope that flickered like moonlight on a river by evening.

For some strange reason, the events that Colonel Creighton had recounted were somehow already known to me. Though it was hard to believe, I seemed to have heard about them a long time ago, in their general outline, though I felt sure that no one had ever told me the story, no one had given me the details. It seemed like someone had walled up and sealed the past, but it was mysteriously connected with the apprehension that was presently eating at me.

"You really should not fly to Seoul," I told the colonel in an uncertain voice. I still did not know how to explain to him the reason why.

"You mean cancel my ticket?!" the colonel exclaimed. "What are you talking about? It's an official trip. I've been invited as a Korean War veteran!"

Cindy raised an eyebrow. "What a strange thing to suggest!" She stared at me, concerned, and shook her head.

"There'll be a big celebration. It's the thirtieth anniversary," said the colonel.

"I've got a bad feeling about this," I said, without going into detail.

"Yes, well my son needs to get back to his unit. His leave is up."

"It would be better to put this off," I advised him, as if we were talking about a short outing.

"Can you tell us anything specific, sir?" Cindy asked in a polite tone. I saw discontent in her face but, like a well-mannered person, she maintained her composure. For my part, I can only add that she was becoming no less attractive. On the contrary, the attraction I felt for her was growing steadily.

"No, I can't. It's just a feeling I have."

"But why?!" the colonel said, looking at me intently.

He and his daughter probably took the view that I had gone mad. To them I was merely talking rubbish, and that in turn meant that the promises I had made to him probably seemed wasted words as well. The colonel stared at me as if trying to determine whether I was still in my right mind.

"Why?" Cindy repeated after her father. Her inquiring glance set my blood pumping and my head spinning.

"I told you, I just have a bad feeling about it."

"And that's all?" the colonel asked with a certain annoyance.

"But surely you understand that's not enough to cancel the trip," Cindy told me, in the tone one used to speak to someone with a serious illness. "My father has been looking forward to it for a whole year."

The colonel flashed a wry grin. "A bad feeling about it!"

"Sometimes they're right." That was the only thing I had to say to the Americans. After all, what else could I have said?

"Often?" Cindy asked in a mocking tone.

"Sometimes. I try to listen to my bad feelings about things, so that I don't regret it later."

"Look here, sir," the colonel said with a flash of temper. "There are hundreds of passengers here, more, probably, and they've all got their own feelings about things. That's no reason to give up my ticket."

The colonel was right, of course. What could I say to that?

"Imagine what would happen if all of them started saying what they had bad feelings about," Cindy said, like a kindly doctor to a silly, obstinate patient.

"Yes, of course," I said to appease them. I realized that I could not reveal my thought processes to them.

"I've been looking forward to this trip for a while now. Getting ready for it," the colonel tried to explain. "I'm a guest of South Korea. The government there sent me an official invitation because I'm a Korean War veteran. They've paid for my ticket and booked an expensive hotel for me. I've got to show up. How can I let them down?"

"You could change your itinerary," I suggested weakly.

"But what for?"

"So that you don't put yourself at risk."

"Risk? Seriously? Well, prove it then."

"You yourself asked me for help. You said that you were trusting me."

"Goodness!" The colonel was exasperated. "I was talking about something completely different! That was forty years ago. It happened in '44, during World War II. And now you're talking about a flight to Korea. What do they have to do with each other?"

"There is a connection", I said curtly. I realized what a burden I was putting on them with my inexplicable behavior. "My advice to you is to change your itinerary."

Like all pilots, the colonel was a superstitious man. My words sowed some doubt in his mind. He thought it over and was clearly undecided, but he needed proof.

He looked at me. "Do you seriously think there is some connection…" he began, then trailed off.

I said nothing, only nodded. My silence impressed him more than any words could do. Creighton was torn by doubt and obviously did not know what to do. He was unsure whether to heed my advice, to shrug it off, or to hope that things would just work out for the best. Tempting fate was nothing new for him, and he was prepared to do it again. Ultimately, his luck had never let him down; he had gone through so many wars and yet survived.

"I don't want anything bad to happen to you." That was the only thing I could say. I could not tell him that in a secret unit known as Division X, alongside modern medical practices I also worked with biolocation and noetic sciences, and I studied premonitions and presentiments.

To begin with, these sciences had amounted to little more than walking around in various places with a branch taken from a vine. Back in ancient times, skilled people would use a forked stick to find water and ore under the earth. A person would walk around a site holding the stick, and at certain points the stick would bend toward the side or even turn the person around to direct him toward an underground stream or spring, a vein of ore, catacombs, old buildings, or treasure. Later, instead of a stick they began employing a wire frame or a weighted pendulum. Using these tools, skilled people would find not only water or things that might be mined, but they could also detect where underground communication lines or electrical cables had been breached, or where men lay buried after an avalanche or earthquake.

"Something is keeping Michael," the colonel said, worried.

"Where is he?" Cindy shook her head disapprovingly and cast a glance at the terminal entrance. "Why did you leave the tickets with him?"

Our experience at Division X showed us that biolocation is capable of determining pathogenic zones, harmful to health, in any room or location, and of finding geological faults radiating harmful energy toward the surface. Such energy had a detrimental effect on living organisms, with the apparent exception of cats. For some inexplicable reason, the radiation from fault lines seemed positively beneficial to cats.

In our division, military engineers, doctors, and psychologists dealt with biolocation and noetic sciences. Their work was done in the greatest secrecy. All the experiments, theoretical studies, and equipment that we developed were kept firmly under wraps. One of our lines of research was remote viewing. Division X operators would work at a considerable distance, sometimes hundreds of miles away, and yet they could find people and things in the mountains and in the taiga.

We gradually accumulated experience. An operator would think of certain questions or say them aloud, and the movements of the wire frame or the pendulum would give an answer. This is how the flight of distant aircraft could be determined, their speed, altitude, remaining fuel, and landing time. Some operators at Division X possessed pronounced extrasensory abilities and did not even need a pendulum. For them, their own hands were enough. Some knew that contact had been established if they felt an unusual lightness in their hand; others felt their palms go cold, and a third group could perceive things with the back of their necks.

With time, the sensitivity of the operators at Division X increased markedly. They became able to detect harmful impurities in liquids and foodstuffs, and reveal interactions between medicines and foods and the effects of various chemical substances on individual people.

Over the millennia, countless people have been poisoned by drugs and other harmful substances, intentionally or otherwise. Some have poisoned themselves, on purpose or by mistake. If doctors had only understood biolocation, if they could just have picked up the signal in advance, then they might have saved those doomed people from death. This works the other way round as well. For example, Rasputin was completely immune to cyanide, which is lethal for most people. When Prince Felix Yusupov, the State Duma deputy Purishkevich, Dr Lazobert, Grand Duke Dmitri, and other conspirators decided to poison Rasputin, the victim astonished the men by happily eating the poisoned cakes and drinking down the Madeira wine. The secret was that the stomach of this "holy man" naturally produced an antidote. If the conspirators had employed biolocation, they would have known in advance about this peculiarity of the royal family's favorite, and they would probably have chosen some other way of murdering him. In 1916, however, no one had any idea about biolocation, though many were inclined to mysticism and the occult, especially among the aristocracy. Biolocation, it should be said, has nothing to do with mysticism and the occult. It is firmly based in fact.

In Division X we dedicated a great deal of attention to intuition. In order to explain this phenomenon, our researchers came up with the idea of an "informational field", which in their theory supposedly surrounds the planet, much as the ozone layer does. A trained operator could pick up on this information like a sensitive instrument.

Meanwhile, the passengers and the people accompanying them in the American Airlines departures hall were listening for the PA announcement so that they would not miss check-in for the flight. I still hoped to dissuade Steven Creighton from getting on the plane. To aid my cause, I mentioned the famous case when Wolf Messing, who performed psychic experiments, warned Stalin to not let his son Vasily fly with an air force crew to a football match. The Great Leader forbade his son to fly and thus saved his life.

"What happened to the crew?" Creighton asked, as would anyone.

"The plane crashed and the crew died."

"If Stalin believed what this psychic told him, why didn't he save the others, too?" the colonel immediately countered. His question was a completely reasonable one. I explained that Stalin was not thinking about them; it was only his own son that he cared about. Perhaps he wanted to test the physic, to see whether he was mistaken in his prediction or not.

"But people died!" the colonel replied, vexed.

"No one denies that," I said. I did not get into explaining that the Great Leader generally did not care about other human beings – he hardly thought about them at all. Our Great Leader and Teacher did not even go to his own mother's funeral; he merely sent a wreath.

I tried once more to coax the colonel. "Take another flight."

He shook his head to signal that it was impossible. Why should he do so anyway, if there was no convincing argument for it?

"In any case, thank you for your concern," the colonel said, and smiled. "I appreciate it. I realize your intentions are good. I look forward to hearing from you once you get to Moscow. I hope things work out."

"You know, if you get on that plane now, that will be the end of the story you told me."

"Well, what can you do? That's fate!" The colonel threw up his hands. "We can only trust in the Lord! Right now I'm more interested in what's going on with my son. Check-in is about to start, and he's got the tickets."

It was clear that the American had made his decision and that I could now do nothing to help him. That was the choice he had made.

═══ 11 ═══

The skies over southern Sakhalin, the Sea of Okhotsk, and the border with Japan were covered by two regiments of fighter-interceptors. One regiment was based north of the 49th parallel at the Smirnykh air base and the other at the Sokol airport at the south of the island. After the hot and lively Caucasus, Sakhalin Island felt like going back to the grind after a wild party. The countryside was truly striking – the forested hills, ravines, and streams recalled the Caucasus – but Shilin's wife suffered. She had grown up in a festive Black Sea resort town, and for her this distant island in the cold Sea of Okhotsk was like exile and hard labor at the end of the world. Their garrison looked like all the other garrisons they were assigned to. As with everywhere else, there was an endless wait here for accommodation; only senior officers with families were given their own apartments. Younger personnel could wait for years; bachelors had to make do with a dormitory bed, and junior personnel with families lived in cramped communal apartments. Russia is a merry country.

Shilin had the good fortune to be given an apartment, the explanation being simple enough: he was now one rank short of colonel and was second in command of the regiment. Nevertheless, his wife despaired when she saw the empty apartment for the first time: two rooms with peeling wallpaper, wooden floors with cracked paint, rusted pipes, patches of moisture in the corners, and a smell of rot and desolation. Renovating the apartment did not make it any more attractive; it had the character of a mere temporary shelter, a place to serve out their sentence.

Everyone in the regiment lived as if they had never unpacked their suitcases. They were all simply waiting for their next transfer. The former tenant of the Shilins' apartment had just left for the mainland. A look around the garrison showed sad cinder-block houses, barren waste ground, trash heaps at the edges of the settlement, and a few charred huts that remained from olden times. The pilot was not a spoiled man from the big city, but he too felt moments of despair. A car passing by on the street and raising a thick cloud of dust made him feel that he was in some dismal place in the middle of nowhere.

They arrived from the Caucasus when summer was still in full swing, but it was easy to imagine what mud and slush awaited them in late fall or early spring. At first his wife remained silent and submissive, but it was hard for her; she would sigh heavily and was not her ordinary self. For Shilin, her silence was worse than if she had openly reproached him. He felt remorse, as if he could have done something to change things but had failed and now she had to suffer because of him. On the other hand, she had known what she was getting into when she married him; a military man has to obey orders. No one had forced her to do this; she had made her own choice. A wife had to stick by her man and follow him, as the thread follows the needle. She did not nag and torment him, but the light in her eyes dimmed, and she faded before his very eyes. The pilot even thought about sending her to live with her parents in the Caucasus.

Sakhalin, not unexpectedly, had a smaller population than other places. Life on the island was incomparably worse than on the mainland. The island had long served as a place of forced labor. Everyone simply waited for their time here to end – the prisoners, their guards, the wardens and officials – this was not a place where anyone wanted to settle permanently. In Shilin's aviation regiment and all across the base, people waited for years for their transfers, sometimes without even unpacking their bags. They simply endured and suffered while they waited to be rotated out. The only thing their families could talk about, think about, was moving on, going back to the mainland.

For Shilin, such a transitory existence was nothing new. Sakhalin was no worse for him than the Arctic had been, or the Kuril Islands. His regiment was based in the settlement of Sokol near the regional capital of Yuzhno-Sakhalinsk. The south of Sakhalin had previously belonged to Japan, and back then the local inhabitants – Japanese and Ainu – had made a passable life for themselves on the island, building roads and setting up businesses just like in Japan, or anywhere else in the world where people live settled lives and did not intend to move on.

After the war, the south of the island became part of Russia, and gradually became unrecognizable. It was as if someone had intentionally destroyed the settled life there, doing away with all the homes, farms, roads, shops, and village facilities, leaving the people to grapple with hardship and simple survival, as if any leisure time and fun would be bad for them.

Shilin's base was near the Sokol settlement. His fighter regiment used the runway at Yuzhno-Sakhalinsk's civil aviation airfield. Local airlines connected the island to the mainland across the Tatar Strait. The long runway accommodated large planes flying to and from Moscow, and fighter planes used the same runway to take off and intercept any American planes that entered Soviet airspace.

In the Caucasus the pilot had learned to fly new models of planes, but on Sakhalin it seemed as if time had stood still: here, the air force used the old Su-15 and MiG-23 planes. These frankly could not compete with American technology: the Americans' atomic-powered aircraft carriers brought hundreds of cutting-edge aircraft to the Pacific Ocean, right at the USSR's borders. Each aircraft carrier hosted eighty planes of various types, as well as six Sea King helicopters for anti-submarine warfare. Sixty of the aircraft consisted of Hornet fighter planes, F-14 Tomcat fighters, and Intruder attack aircraft, while the balance was made up of ten anti-submarine Vikings, five early-warning Hawkeyes, and five electronic-warfare Prowlers. It was easy to see how just three aircraft carriers close to the Soviet Union's borders could send a massive armada into the air.

In addition, from the coast of Chukotka in the north to the border with Japan in the south, the skies were swept day and night by RC-135 Cobra reconnaissance planes, by SR-70 Orion strategic reconnaissance aircraft that could ascend to the stratosphere, and by gigantic E-3As equipped with AWACS early-warning systems. It was these planes that violated Russia's airspace the most.

In the south, the Americans worked from the Misawa Air Base on the Japanese island of Hokkaido, where a secret electronic surveillance group kept a constant watch on the Sea of Japan, the Sea of Okhotsk, and the straits, coasts, and installations deep within mainland Russia. From Misawa, the Americans would make reconnaissance flights along Primorsky Krai, Sakhalin, and the southern Kuril Islands. In the north, the American Eleventh Air Force operated from bases in Alaska, and at Elmendorf Air Force Base there was another secret group for electronic surveillance.

In the Pacific, American reconnaissance planes took off from airfields in the Aleutian Islands. The Americans had a keen interest in Kamchatka, where the Soviet navy had bases for nuclear submarines with long-range missiles on board. An American group of three aircraft carriers and escorting vessels regularly sailed along the Komandorski Islands, and planes regularly took off from the aircraft carriers and flew near Kamchatka and the northern Kuril Islands. In short, the American's giant network of aerial surveillance, stretching over thousands of kilometers, kept Soviet air defense busy. The hundreds of American planes based on land or aircraft carriers were opposed by Soviet fighter-interceptor divisions and air defense units. These had to confront the Americans along every inch of the border. Nikolai Shilin did his duty to the best of his mental and physical ability, and not out of fear but out of his sense of duty. He did not hide behind others' backs, nor he did pretend to be better than he was.

Sometimes Shilin would look back on the places he had served: East Germany, the Arctic, the Kuril Islands, Vietnam, the Caucasus, and now Sakhalin. The pilot had lived the life of a nomad: dormitories, a garrison's guest quarters, countless temporary shelters, communal kitchens, rented apartments. His hair was already beginning to turn gray; he was now in his forties, and he wanted to rest, but his life was spent constantly on the move. He had no corner to call home, no permanent roof over his head. His native country made many promises; it claimed that a joyous future was coming, and that life would be wonderful, but so far all it had given Shilin was trips to the ends of the earth, a very modest contentment, the dreariness of distant garrisons, and a constant sense of risk and danger breathing down his neck. He bounced around the world and opposed the Americans wherever he could, whether close to Russia or far away, as if he had been born only for that.

Following a longstanding tradition in Russia, new technology took a long time in coming to the east. Senior officials in the Ministry of Defense were certain that the western borders of the USSR faced a greater danger than its eastern ones, and therefore the latest generation of planes would be supplied first to the European part of the country, and only later appear in the east.

When the pilot arrived on Sakhalin Island, only a small number of aviation personnel from his regiment were present at the base. That summer his regiment was transitioning to new technology, and one squadron had gone off to a training center while others were given leave on doctors' orders. This meant that Shilin had to do a great deal of flying from the moment he arrived; stints on duty would follow one after another. In addition, as second in command of the regiment, he was responsible for its military readiness, and he often took off as the leader of a pair of planes in order to train one of the junior pilots.

Shilin had enjoyed the natural countryside of the Kuril Islands, which was wild and untouched like almost nowhere else on earth. Sakhalin resembled the southern Kurils: densely forested hills of Sakhalin pine and Jezo spruce, while the lowlands were covered with taiga consisting of larches, Manchurian cedar, and Korean pine. South of the Sokol settlement, as far as the La Pérouse Strait, one found mixed forests wrapped in vines – ash-trees, oaks, and Japanese chestnuts with an undergrowth of bamboo. To the north, the hills were covered with Labrador tea, hawthorn, birch, and Siberian dwarf pine. Further north still, things changed dramatically and started to resemble the Arctic landscape with its marshes and tundra: moss, barren ground, and bogs, with trees few and far between, and frail.

Many of Shilin's regiment were passionate about hunting, which was understandable inasmuch as hunting is a popular pastime for soldiers posted in remote places. In season, they would head north in a helicopter to where the hunting was good: places where the dense forests were sparsely-populated, meaning that there were few other hunters and plenty of wild animals.

Not many of these men had been interested in hunting before they arrived on Sakhalin. They took to hunting on the island just to brighten their lives and ward off the blues. The pilot, however, did not develop a fondness for it, though his comrades often urged him to try. He felt that hunting was murder, and their helicopter and military rifles equipped with optical sights meant that the animals did not stand a chance.

Sometimes Shilin would go fishing. The island's population would wait impatiently for July, which was spawning season for salmon. The fish would head upriver from the ocean and the water seethed with an unbelievable number of humpback, chinook, and dog salmon. For the bears too, waiting at shallow points along the river, the fishing was good.

The island looked especially attractive from above. A pilot had only to take off in his plane to catch a view of two ridges, overgrown with vegetation and towering along the western and eastern shores. These two mountain ranges, wrapped in taiga, fringed the island on two sides, like a living green wall, and extended for hundreds of miles from north to south, divided by the Tym and Poronai rivers. These rivers were fed by streams that wound down from the mountains through gorges and waterfalls, but even at twice the speed of sound, the eye could see, along the slopes and in the river valley, flat patches of green, which the locals had called *elanya*, from time immemorial. Over the time since the Russians had first come to the island, indigenous words such as these had become firmly rooted in the speech of the soldiers posted there as well as in that of the local communities.

Shilin's flights rarely took him over dry land, however. Most often the order "To the sea!" came through his headphones – a navigator on the ground would set a course, bearing, and altitude for him. They often patrolled over the Sea of Okhotsk and the Sea of Japan, where American reconnaissance places, Cobras and Orions, would constantly and uninterruptedly buzz along the border. An astonishingly large number of E-3A strategic reconnaissance planes, equipped with AWACS early warning systems, had started to appear in the skies. From a high vantage point, these systems swept the land for thousands of kilometers around, and could pick up not only every rocket being fired, or plane taking off, but also every telephone conversation.

Soviet fighters were often scrambled to intercept American planes – whether from nuclear-powered aircraft carriers or the Misawa Air Base – that seemed hell-bent on violating Soviet airspace, or were in fact violating it. Naturally, a great nation could not tolerate such a threat; it could not meekly accept another country's impudence. The Russians had no choice but to force the trespasser to land at a Soviet airfield, and anyone ignoring the command was to be shot down. They spoke softly but carried a big stick.

Just as in Germany, here too the Americans often came on air and rudely interrupted the Soviet pilots' radio communications with the ground. Every time Shilin heard an unfamiliar voice coming through his headphones, he grew annoyed, as anyone would if a random stranger suddenly appeared on your channel, your frequency. The Americans' accents usually gave them away, but sometimes the voice spoke excellent, clean Russian, and it was clear that the Americans had found someone from a Russian immigrant family to do the talking.

As the Soviet pilots went further from their own airfields, one air traffic station would pass them over to another. The ground operators changed and the pilots did not recognize their voices. The Americans often took advantage of that. They would pretend to be one of the air-traffic controllers and give a false course, in the hope of leading the Soviet fighter away from the area it was patrolling. Occasionally they succeeded in sowing confusion. Junior pilots in the Soviet teams could be unsure as to which voices they should be taking notice of, and sometimes the Americans expressly tried to imitate the voices of operators and send a Soviet plane into their zone. The Soviets were forced to adopt a rule that each pilot would communicate only with a navigator whose voice he recognized.

All in all, stints on duty were rarely quiet; over the course of a year, the watches spent without alarms ringing and pilots taking off to intercept could be counted on one's fingers. For months on end, the Americans played on the Soviets' nerves without allowing the latter a moment's rest, and sometimes the pilots on duty had to take off and land multiple times. The country at large did not know it, but there were nights on the eastern border when the pilots on watch ended up spending more time in the air than on the ground. For days on end, airfields sounded the alarm at short intervals, and with the frequent taking off and landing pilots had no time even to eat or catch their breath. As soon as a plane landed and the ground crew had refilled its tanks, the pilot would have to take off again.

Often pilots were assigned to provide the Americans with a close escort. The Soviet interceptor would match speed with the American reconnaissance plane, stick close to it, and try to get in its way until it returned to its base. The Americans were equipped with excellent equipment for electronic surveillance, and on board their planes dozens of technicians swept over the land and air, picking up every breath and every step. As in other places where Shilin had served, a fighter had only to approach one of the massive and unwieldy reconnaissance planes for the technicians' worried faces to appear in the windows. Often they were white faces, sometimes black, only occasionally swarthy Latino faces, and more rarely still Asian faces with their characteristic slanting eyes – Japanese, Korean, Chinese; America was a country of immigrants.

The reconnaissance plane's crew would of course have noticed the fighter long before it caught up with them, but it is one thing to see a blip on a radar screen, and something else entirely when a fighter plane is sticking to you, darting around you so close that you can almost reach out and touch it. Close up, the air-to-air missiles hanging from the fighter's wings were visible, and one of them alone would destroy a large target. The fighter was also equipped with a cannon, capable of rapidly firing off hundreds of armor-piercing rounds that would go right through the reconnaissance plane's fuselage. The fighter itself, though a miracle of technology and human ingenuity, moved like a frenzied dog on the prowl, with hostile maneuvers and a shark-like outline. It had a fearsome agility, and one wondered what the next target for its missiles and gunfire would be.

Some faces at the reconnaissance plane's windows looked familiar; Shilin had already seen them before on various occasions. The Americans knew him, too; they could recognize his plane's registration number. Usually they would smile and wave a hand in greeting like an old friend, though some on board looked at him with uncertainty or even dread, as if they were not sure what to expect. If the fighter passed too close in front the reconnaissance plane's nose, cutting it off in a seemingly reckless manner, the Americans became visibly nervous. The threat was clear, and the danger level had risen drastically: one wrong move, and you were dead. Everyone was aware that they were taking a big risk, that their lives hung by a thread. Some of them could not resist raising a middle finger at the Soviet pilot.

Sometimes this encounter in the skies turned into a real circus act. A black face, resembling an African mask, would appear at the reconnaissance plane's window: shiny skin, a wide grin, snow-white teeth. It was as if Louis Armstrong, the great trumpeter nicknamed Satchmo because of his "satchel mouth", was rolling his eyes in the window. The black clown would make faces, and his dazzling smile would hang in the air over the sea, far from land. It was as if the plane might fly on and the smile remain in the empty air, like the Cheshire cat's grin.

The jovial black man would cordially invite Shilin over for a cup of coffee; he always had a steaming cup in his hand. Each time, Shilin would feel the heat and bitter taste of good coffee in his mouth, the strong smell would fill his cockpit, and the plane would drag the aroma in its wake like a vapor trail. While the fighter was maintaining its close course, the black jester would laugh uncontrollably, his mouth gaping soundlessly in the window. It was like a scene at a Brazilian carnival, as he made merry and grinned from ear to ear.

Usually only certain ground stations kept watch over the skies, with the rest of the entire gigantic network of air defense on hold, in hibernation. The radar kept silent, so that they would not unnecessarily reveal their codes and frequencies. If they were to spring into life, the Americans would immediately determine their technical specifications. American electronic reconnaissance was obsessed with forcing the stations to activate, and the planes flying along the border thought up various clever ways to awaken the network. For them, the confrontations in the sky were clearly a sort of sport, a thrill, a competitive match, a duel, an exhausting rivalry with no holds barred. Like in a fight without any rules, each side was eager to win at any cost, though so far no shots had been fired. The Americans were bent on always being the winner; they tried to score the goal, come in first, and beat everyone else. For the American crews, the reconnaissance flights were a sort of match that they just had to win.

The large reconnaissance planes ran rampant, as if daring the Soviets to fight back. They would never let up and constantly kept Soviet air defense busy: all the base commanders, tracking stations, radar operators, airfield crews, and most of all the pilots, who were literally seething with anger. Even Lieutenant Colonel Shilin, a mild-mannered man with strong nerves, became annoyed, or sometimes infuriated. There were times when it seemed that he would lose his composure, and bloodshed would ensue.

Usually the Americans employed a distinctive maneuver that the Soviet fighter regiments called a *vosmyorka*: as the reconnaissance aircraft flew along the border, it would draw a figure of eight in the sky, and then it would suddenly change course and appear to be on the brink of violating Soviet airspace. At the last minute, the plane would turn aside, bank, and then repeat the maneuver. This would go on for hours, days, sometimes weeks and months. The American reconnaissance planes tirelessly hovered in the air, along the invisible line marking Soviet airspace, like a huge and annoying fly buzzing on a windowpane.

A man needed incredible patience and strong nerves to avoid responding. Some hotheads would have liked to teach the Americans a lesson, and were tempted to dismiss notions of international law, diplomacy, and other silly trifles, and give their foes a good thrashing.

They resisted the urge, gritting their teeth, and controlled themselves. The radar remained dormant and offered meager rewards for the Americans' electronic surveillance. The sensitive equipment on the reconnaissance planes picked up only routine news from deep within the adjacent region. Still, a diligent farmer appreciates even small gains, and the Americans kept their activity up, like chickens pecking at grain.

If, however, the silence stretched on for too long, the Americans would intentionally exacerbate the situation for the sake of their electronic surveillance. The operation would be coordinated with the movement of a spy satellite. When the satellite passed over the relevant area, ships would approach the USSR's territorial waters and reconnaissance planes would appear in the sky: one of them would cross into Soviet airspace while others patrolled in its vicinity, registering the activities of the Soviet anti-aircraft defense, or planning to breach a neighboring area.

Needless to say, sirens would go off across the entire Russian Far East. At the airfields, the alarm would be sounded and bases would be struck with panic, with men shouting like madmen and feverishly trying to cope with all the confusion – something very common in Russia. Fighter planes took off, and the radios and telephones were busy as commanders growled and swore and demanded reports on the situation. The whole thing was a buzz of activity. The fighter regiments found themselves caught in a downpour of orders, many of which were absurd and left the staff scratching their heads and wondering how to carry them out. They had to accept that even a ridiculous order had been given for a particular reason.

After Lieutenant Viktor Belenko defected to Japan in his new MiG-25, top brass had ordered that the fuel tanks of all planes be filled only halfway, so that pilots would have enough fuel only to return to their own bases. The generals in their meeting rooms intended that a Soviet pilot making a bid to escape would not have enough fuel to reach foreign territory. From then on, the distance and flight times of the fighter interceptors were determined, not by mission requirements, but by the desire to ensure that pilots would come back, as stipulated and prescribed in this oh so smart order.

The result was that pilots became concerned first and foremost not with planes violating Soviet airspace, not with their missions, and not with the targets that they were supposed to intercept, but with the fuel remaining in their tanks. They would glance repeatedly at their fuel gauges to make sure they turned back in time. It sometimes happened that the fighters chasing an intruder reached the limits of their flight and abandoned the pursuit, since otherwise they would be unable to make it back.

It must be said that Shilin was disturbed by this new order. He and the regiment's commander made painstaking calculations and announced to the crews that if a fight broke out above the Kuril Islands, there would not be enough fuel to get back to Sakhalin. In other words, a pilot's only choice would be to fly the plane over the nearest dry land, where he would eject and ditch his perfectly good plane.

"It's bullshit!" Shilin concluded, unafraid to state his opinion. The distance that planes could fly, before needing to turn back, had been thought up by a few eggheads in a spacious office, where real-world limitations did not apply. The requirement to defend the border, naturally enough, remained in place. Air defense found itself between a rock and a hard place, and the crews had to deal with uncertainty day in and day out.

On the one hand, they were firmly ordered not to respond to provocation, to keep calm and not get into a fight – a dog fight would only result in an international incident and do harm to their country. On the other hand, they certainly could not let a foreign plane trespass over the border. Top brass saw letting an American reconnaissance plane into Soviet airspace as an unspeakable act, one that could not be forgiven. It was in fact not forgiven, and negligent personnel could look forward to charges and a court martial. In short, the Soviet aviators were in a real catch-22. The paradox would make a pilot's head spin.

Day and night, over the border of Soviet airspace, a relentless game of cat and mouse was played out. The two countries tested each other and set traps. An outside observer, unaware of the intricacies of the two countries' relations, might assume that these were two jokers playing pranks on each other, and it was merely empty space that they were vying for. In fact, everything came down a line drawn on a map, an invisible boundary marked in the sky. Some people were driven to cross it, others objected and tried to prevent them. Each side seemed to be testing the other's strength.

Incidents when Soviet airspace was violated usually brought about an official inquiry, whether at the level of the regiment, the division, or the district. Sometimes, though, a special commission was sent, from Moscow all the way east to the ends of the earth, demanding an explanation. What could you do though, if the causes lay in a country's own deeply-rooted characteristics? In Russia, seeking causes is a pointless undertaking; one can only muse on the mysterious Russian character, the inscrutable Russian soul. Most often the cause would lie in a perennial slovenliness: men overslept, fell asleep at the wheel, dropped the ball, put their foot in it, or made fools of themselves. You want some other explanation?

Usually drunkenness was at fault, or perhaps a pounding hangover led a man to press the wrong button, or someone's fingers slipped, or they were looking the wrong way, or there was a mechanical issue; the list goes on. It really came down to the boundless sloppiness of many citizens of this great country, a feature encoded in the Russians' genes and about which nothing could be done, however hard one tried.

In any event, when a major violation of Russian airspace occurred, someone would end up falling into the Americans' trap: overworked personnel at a station would activate their radar, which was just what the Americans wanted – and had been confident of achieving. The equipment on board their electronic surveillance planes would record the technical specifications of the station. This represented a serious failure for Soviet air defense, who would now have to change the programs, codes, and frequencies. To reconfigure all this cost a great deal of time and money, and in the meantime there would be a gaping hole in the country's defense of its airspace.

More often, however, an American reconnaissance plane would prove unsuccessful and simply turn around. The Americans handled such failures easily and did not go into hysterics; it was just part of the game. Meanwhile, on the Soviet side, any such event took the Russians by complete surprise, like lightning from a clear sky. Like it or not, rare misfortunes, Zulu invasions, or the birth of a two-headed calf, do happen, contrary to all expectation and even the tiniest suspicion.

Unsurprisingly, everyone would be horrified at this unexpected occurrence, and would start looking for someone to blame. The supposed guilty party was generally everyone else, not oneself: firefighters blamed plumbers, plumbers pointed the finger at miners or archaeologists, these worthy folk in turn harbored suspicions toward astronomers and veterinarians, and so on and so forth, in a circle that left no one out.

After every violation of Soviet airspace, the Far Eastern Air Defense District resembled a trampled anthill. It suddenly awoke from slumber and its tracking stations combed the skies with radar. The Americans would record these signals, and the trespassing plane would dart back toward neutral territory at full speed. The American planes' fighter escort was ready to intervene if Soviet pilots threatened the trespasser.

Shilin soon became used to this. The Americans occasionally changed their tactics, and used any opportunity to penetrate Soviet airspace. They were often assisted in this by the weather. On both sides, meteorological data was gathered by planes, ships, and a network of ground based meteorological stations, but for some reason the Americans' weather forecasting was much more accurate than the Soviets'.

Many of the Soviet interceptors – Shilin included – were truly amazed at how favorable Sakhalin Island's climate was to American reconnaissance operations. One could not help thinking that the weather in Russia's Far East was working directly for the Americans.

The Americans generally proved lucky with fog. Day after day, fog would rise up over the sea, crawl toward the coast, and cover Sakhalin in an impenetrable veil. The Americans' planes could then violate Soviet airspace and fly at their leisure through the fog over the straits and bays, recording the signals from the ground stations that were searching for the reconnoiters and trying to scramble their fighters to intercept. When the sun came out, the fog would retreat to the sea and the Americans would depart with it until they were over neutral waters, where no one could pursue them. According to the rules, a foreign plane caught over a country's territory should be escorted to an airfield and forced to land, and any pilot who disobeyed could be shot down. Indeed, sometimes they were forced to land, but more often the Soviets let them go, and only very rarely did they shoot them down. Both sides tended to observe an unspoken agreement. The Americans knew that violence shown toward them would only play into their hands, while the Soviets preferred to hold off so that the international press would not depict them as merciless killers.

The new MiG and Su fighters, it must be said, were in no way inferior to the Americans' planes, and even surpassed them in many respects. Pilot training in both armies was roughly on the same level, but the American pilots flew more often because they did not have to save fuel, while Soviet aviation in those years was facing a fuel shortage. In the USA, even reservists and the National Guard could fly for more hours than military pilots in Soviet regiments. But Shilin was especially dismayed by the state of the fleet of planes: in accordance with age-old tradition in his country, the technical quality of production was poor. Half of a division's planes would have to be written off and consigned to scrap, while many planes from the remaining half often stood idle awaiting repair and servicing. Only a small number of planes remained actively available, though the regiment's reports to their superiors painted a rosy picture to avoid causing trouble for the regimental commander.

One cannot fly far on a report, however rosy it might be; what you say about your capabilities will not help you keep up with the Americans. On several occasions, Shilin had observed passengers at Sakhalin Island's Sokol airport stop, just as they were about to board a Tu-154 for the mainland, and stare curiously at the ranks of fighter planes lined up on the tarmac. They would slow their steps, crane their necks to look, and could not tear their eyes away. To an observer, these planes looked like perfect arrows in a stretched bowstring, like fierce birds about to launch into flight. The way the fighters were lined up in exact ranks made a powerful impression, and inspired observers to feel pride in their country. None of the passengers knew, or even suspected, that this was all just for show. Most of these fighters simply remained rooted to the spot, never leaving their places, let alone taking off into the sky. These were hardly planes any more; they had turned into fancy decorations, and they might as well have been sent away for scrap and melted down.

Even the airworthy planes would occasionally crash, and a pilot was fortunate if he managed to eject in time. Not everyone was lucky however, and some pilots did not survive. Each flight could be a man's last. This was a truth known to every pilot, and something their wives were even more conscious of, so that women sat restlessly until their husbands returned home.

Year after year, while the Soviet empire lived on, military pilots flew less and less often, though it was a hard-and-fast rule that the less pilots fly, the more they crash. Nothing in these years disproved this rule.

## ══ 12 ══

That evening, at the seven new mess halls that had been built for the American crews, the air base commander General Perminov had arranged a joint dinner, which soon turned into a lively party. The Soviet hosts had laid the tables with a considerable amount of alcohol, while on their part the Americans treated their allies to whiskey, and a large number of women suddenly appeared in the hall. Needless to say, this meeting of countries soon lost any strict and formal character, and set protocol was replaced by lively flirting. The Americans were unaware that the Communist Party officials at the base had intentionally selected a group of females from the engineering and medical battalions according to their appearance and ideological qualities, and had instructed them on how to behave at the tables. It was important that they should not drink much, taking only small sips, that they should say little and mainly listen, and that they should smile and pretend that life in the USSR was nothing but happy. Let the foreigners look at them with envy and regret that they had not had the fortune of being born in a socialist reality. The officials explained to the ladies that the Party and the Great Leader were showing great trust in them, and insistently reminded them to be careful, in such severe a tone that the women were shaking in their boots. After their ideological instruction, the young ladies were given new uniforms, makeup, and lipstick, ordered to behave, and relieved from any other duties for half the day.

In those days, the Communist Party officials at the front, the army's counter-intelligence service SMERSH, and all kinds of other special departments, had an unprecedented workload. Though the Americans were in an alliance with the USSR, they were still representatives of the capitalist world and thus still enemies of socialism. For this reason, all Party officials, counter-intelligence officers, secret agents, and informants were given strict orders to avoid drunkenness, to maintain a relaxed but alert bearing, and to keep constant watch on the Americans and anyone who talked to them.

Naturally, their American counterparts did not arrive half-asleep either. Before leaving for the dinner, the squadrons were given a preliminary briefing, and crews urged to keep on the alert. Historical necessity and a common foe had made the Soviets allies, but they still retained all the wiles and plotting so typical of Communists. They could recruit you before you knew it; they could turn you into a Communist in the blink of an eye.

Things being as they were in those years, this was the first time that most Soviet citizens had ever laid eyes on a foreigner. In spite of the order to behave freely and naturally, the Soviet personnel, unsurprisingly, closed up and became timid, wary, and clearly worried. For them, the Americans were like arrivals from another planet. Everything about them was different: their uniforms, faces, manners, language… They looked at their allies as if they were aliens – they were interesting and exotic, but who knew what they were actually thinking? Drinking together, however, brought everyone closer, and the mistrust and fear faded away. After the first shots, the two sides' tongues were loosened and the strict instructions they had received were somewhat forgotten. The presence of the young women, too, imbued the dinner with a certain lively quality.

The mess hall was now tightly packed and there was a loud hubbub. The two sides were forced to communicate with gestures. The Russians were beleaguering the Americans with questions about where they were all originally from, but they raised their voices as if they were trying to get through to deaf people. They shouted words that seemed so simple to them, like something everyone ought to be able to understand. It has long been a saying that a Russian has no idea that there are people out there who do not understand his language.

The interpreters were in great demand this evening. Before the dinner, several bottles of the perfume Krasnaya Moskva, "Red Moscow", had been handed out to them; ironically, this perfume brand had been known before the Revolution as "The Empress' Bouquet". It was with an overwhelming scent in their wake that the lady lieutenants were dashing around the mess hall and responding to calls to help the people at the tables. Only at the table with the generals was there an experienced interpreter sent from Moscow.

It quickly became stuffy in the hall. Indeed, after a while it was impossible to breathe. The windows, which looked out onto a bright June evening, had to be opened. Outside, a sleepy rural calm reigned, and it was hard to believe that somewhere out there a war was raging with all the attendant bloodshed. The multilingual hubbub among the tables carried out of the window and filled the air base, newly-built by the Red Army for Operation Frantic. In a very short time, new residential quarters, warehouses, mess halls, a hospital, baths, laundry facilities, workshops, fuel stations, and bomb shelters had popped up here in the heart of the countryside, as if by magic. This small town was surrounded by a security perimeter consisting of barbed wire and checkpoints, camouflaged machine-gun posts, and anti-aircraft defense in case the base was attacked from above.

This was the place that Gogol had hymned, the Poltava Governorate, a magical land. The whole world knew it from Gogol's life and works: Mirgorod, Sorochintsy, Dikanka! Not long before, vast herds of cattle had been driven over the dusty roads here. Fish and salt were transported from Crimea in wagon trains, and short, stocky teamsters with bowl haircuts and baggy trousers drove on the oxen dragging the squeaking carts.

At night, according to the writer's imagination, the villages, farmsteads, and surrounding forests were inhabited by dark forces: goblins, nixes, and cunning demons worked their mischief. From nightfall until cockcrow, under the moonlight, innocent people were led astray by charming witches. Nymphs sported on the waters and riverbanks, and over dark pools they waited for an unwary traveler to pass by.

That was in Gogol, however. Now, the local airfield held hundreds of American planes, the place was covered by armed sentries, and the silence of the wondrous nights here was broken by a hubbub in many languages.

The men had reached an agreement easily, as if it had come down from above: the Russians would drink whiskey and the Americans vodka. The tables, too, soon became mixed: the Russian hosts would grab their American allies by the arm and lead them to their tables. The Americans subsequently got drunk out of their minds; they did not have the Russian habit of pacing their drinking and controlling themselves, especially since the Americans' hosts were intentionally trying to make their guests drink themselves insensate.

The boozing had just started when bomber copilot Creighton again spotted the interpreter from that morning. The two young officers – Creighton and the interpreter – were still unaware that most people are unlucky in love. Sad though it might be, fortune rarely smiles on a person, though everyone hopes for it, even expects it. The world is so big, and there are so many of us, that two right people might never meet; they just pass each other by. Yes, you are unlikely to be found worthy of this honor; you are unlikely ever to be in the right place at the right time. One can regret this and feel sorry for oneself, but fate rarely brings the gift of love. Love is decided on high, and when you encounter it, you recognize it instantly.

Lieutenant Creighton decided not to drink. He wanted to avoid drunkenness, though his Russian neighbors at the table were trying hard to make him drink. In a chorus they insisted, but the lieutenant did not indulge beyond the occasional sip. All his thoughts were on her. Rather, only one thought was on his mind, and the vodka being proffered meant nothing.

The lieutenant sat silent, motionless, and he waited patiently. At times like this, everything happens of its own accord: what has been fated will happen, and what has been decided on high will come to pass. Creighton had only to wait and put his trust in destiny. However, like any real American, Creighton could not just let this opportunity go by. His neighbors at the table eventually called the interpreter over so that they could figure out what was going on with the lieutenant.

"Ask this ally of ours why he's not drinking," a Soviet pilot asked her shakily. The man was unused to drinking from a whiskey glass and now the alcohol consumption had gone to his head. "He doesn't like vodka?"

"They are asking you why you are not drinking, sir," the interpreter said. She was still oblivious to what fate had in store for her.

The American lieutenant remained stiff, just as he had that morning when they had first met. He said nothing, but he did not take his eyes off the interpreter. This silence lasted for an eternity; the noise around them abated, and the two of them seemed to remain alone in space, as if a thick wall separated them from the rest of the mess hall. The voices of others, their laughter and ruckus, did not reach them. They were alone on earth, the two of them together.

"We need to talk in private," the American suddenly blurted out.

The interpreter knew that this would be impossible – it was forbidden, out of the question. In her country, people were supposed to avoid foreigners, hold firm to their Soviet ideals, follow the Great Leader's commandments, remain vigilant, and keep the class struggle in mind. The regime assumed that any foreigner was a threat, and if the foreigner did not offer any clear grounds for such an assumption, that merely meant that he knew how to dissemble, and his real intentions naturally had to be exposed as quickly as possible.

In addition, the Soviet regime, the dear Great Leader, and the Party felt a keen jealousy about a USSR citizen's relationship with a foreigner. The authorities saw such connections as a mortal sin. There was no worse crime than to fall in love with a foreigner: it represented a real fall, a heinous betrayal of the country, like spying or sabotage, and it deserved contempt and ruthless condemnation.

As often happens, help came unexpectedly. A neighbor at Creighton's table, a tubby aviation engineer, was now quite drunk, but he still managed to get the hint, and so he moved to the side to free a seat for the young lady. "Sit down, lieutenant," the officer offered, with the drunken cordiality typical of fat people. "None of us can talk English, so you translate for us."

The interpreter accepted the aviation engineer's kind gesture and sat down opposite Creighton. This was simply her job; it was not a love affair, and no one would reproach her for it, let alone condemn her. They sat facing each other, the American and the interpreter. A lively party was going on around them, and the multilingual hubbub sounded like the squawking of birds.

What could the lieutenant say? That he had been waiting for her his whole life? That he had seen her in his dreams? Or that it was nice to meet her and he hoped to get to know her better? Would they ever even meet again? There was a war going on. And what was in store for them, anyway? They did not have much time, and both of them knew it. Life in wartime changes quickly; no one is capable of doing anything about it. Any order could part them forever, and not just an order. The unpredictable course of events in wartime could dash any plans to pieces. In peacetime, things do not always work out as one hopes, so how could they in wartime? Let us not prevaricate here, for everyone knows – and whoever does not know will find out – that the laws of peacetime are void in war. Time there is fleeting, and one's everyday existence is subject to the whims of chance. The future is unpredictable, and events rush toward you at an ever-faster pace. Even your very life is hanging by a thread, and you never know what is in store for you.

It is obvious that in wartime no one has any idea of what will happen the next moment, the next hour, the next day.  It makes no sense to think further ahead: today we are alive and tomorrow we may be dead. A man vanishes, goes up in a puff of smoke, and he will be remembered for only a short while by the people who knew him. It is therefore senseless to make plans in wartime, to try to foresee anything. One can only hope and wait, wait and hope; what other choice does one have? Though in their dreams, of course, everyone imagines what peacetime after the war's end will be like.

As part of their preparations for welcoming the Americans, the Soviets had arranged a special concert. A song-and-dance ensemble had been ferried quickly round to the base, and a troupe of musicians had flown in from Moscow along with generals Grendal, Slavin, and Levandovich. The concert organizers were keen to put on some jazz – the Soviet hosts wanted to surprise their guests.

A mixed bunch of jazz musicians was assembled, but they were very nervous of performing. They had been hounded year after year in the Soviet regime's long battle with jazz, and now fear struck their hearts as Party officials assigned them the task of playing real American jazz. The musicians listened to their instructions in disbelief; they suspected that they were being set up, so that later they could be accused of having corrupt morals and toadying to the Americans.

The Americans enthusiastically greeted the Soviet troupe, who danced the Russian *pereplyas*, the Georgian *lezginka* sword-dance, and the Ukrainian *gopak*, all in national dress. The guests rewarded this with great applause, but they were especially delighted by the jazz. This had been announced as a surprise. The lights in the hall dimmed, everyone grew quiet, and no one knew what was going to happen. In the darkness a piano began to play, backed by a guitar, and a double-bass set the rhythm. Then a saxophone entered with its purring sound, and a trumpet rang out. The Americans sat dumbstruck until they realized what was going on, and then the hall erupted in a deafening roar of approval. Whooping and whistling came from the various corners of the mess hall.

The Soviet hosts were taken aback – they were not used to such a display of emotions. The whistling especially distressed the hosts – they thought that their guests were outraged. What else could it mean if they were screaming, hooting, and hollering? The Soviets assumed, of course, that some sort of blunder had been made, a real international incident. Many on the Soviet side lost heart, fearing that judgment day was not far off. The Great Leader was quick to punish; he had a heavy hand, and everyone knew he had a temper.

Naturally, the generals and Party officials started cursing whoever had come up with the idea of playing American jazz. The highest ranking of the commanders there, Lieutenant General Grendal, leaned over in the darkness toward the American seated next to him, General Dean, and through an interpreter he asked, "What's going on? They don't like the music?"

"On the contrary, they love it. That's just how they show their approval. Thank you, you have given us a real treat."

The Soviet officers and generals felt as if a heavy weight had been lifted from their hearts, and they sighed in relief, though they still found it hard to believe that things had really worked out. They looked around in astonishment at their guests' unbridled enthusiasm. Whistling and whooping at a concert was something new for these Soviet people; the hosts were bewildered by such freely-expressed emotions.

Meanwhile, no one had any inkling of something else that was happening in the darkness, something running in a rather different direction to the general course of events – the dinner, the concert, Operation Frantic, World War II. When the lights went out, the American took advantage of the darkness and grasped the interpreter by the hand and told her that he would like to hold it forever. A moment passed, after which the junior lieutenant carefully withdrew her hand and said nothing in response. Though everyone there that evening was being kept under constant surveillance, the incident went unnoticed in the darkness.

This is a good time to note that Steven Creighton had been diligently studying music since he was a child. In his home, it was the tradition that every member of the family played an instrument, sometimes even two or three. His family loved to make music, and they played in groups and individually at weekends and at family gatherings, and sometimes they were invited to perform in public.

As often happens, all the children in the family took after their parents and were extremely musical. Over time, a *bona fide* orchestra came into being. Creighton played the piano well, and also the saxophone, but he especially loved his flute and was hardly ever parted from it. Even during the war, he took his flute with him on every flight, and if his Flying Fortress had been shot down, the flute would have shared the same fate as the plane's copilot and its entire crew.

Creighton played for his own enjoyment whenever he found a spare moment, but he readily performed for audiences, and never shied away when people asked him. He had played to his fellow students at flight school, at officers' parties, and to the crews at various squadron or wing events. He also played at social functions and get-togethers where jazz aficionados held jam sessions. The musicians would quickly form an ensemble and improvise on a given theme. The players would provide backing for one other, and each performed his solo to this group accompaniment so that he could strut his stuff. In just this way, jazz is played all round the world.

 

That night, the Russians had thought theirs was a jazz concert, but in reality the musicians were simply playing some American tunes popular before the war. The commander of Creighton's Flying Fortress squadron came up to his table and relayed a request from the air group's commander Lieutenant General Eaker that Creighton play something. Creighton had left his flute in his lodgings, but a musician in the Soviet ensemble offered Creighton his saxophone. Creighton spent a couple of minutes getting familiar with the instrument and testing it out in its different registers.

"You're the only one I'll be playing for," he told the interpreter, to her astonishment, when the time came for the two of them to walk up and join the ensemble. The hall welcomed them with applause.

The junior lieutenant was not used to being the center of attention and she shrank away, overcome. The American pilot would not be dissuaded though: he took her by the hand and, amid applause, led her to the open space where the ensemble was waiting. Creighton had the interpreter tell the musicians what key to play in, and he asked that the drums, guitar, and double-bass provide rhythm and accompaniment. The musicians asked the American what he was going to play, and his answer astounded them.

"I don't even know myself yet. We'll start playing and see what happens."

The ensemble players were all amazed at this, and assumed that something had been lost in translation, but Creighton explained that he was not going to rely on any sheet music. Rather, he would improvise according to his mood. These musicians, for their part, were used to having to obtain official approval for every song in their repertoire, and improvisation was simply not something they did. It was a taken as gospel in the Soviet arts world that if a musician plays jazz one day, he will betray his country the next.

The lieutenant tried out a few notes, roaming up and down the saxophone's register, then he thought for a moment and began to play. The saxophone emitted a few hoarse cries, as if it was sighing bitterly, and the hubbub in the hall died down. The bomber crews heard something familiar in what Creighton was playing; it had a whiff of peacetime about it, when they had all felt a hundred years younger and they all believed in the American dream.

After standing there without playing for a while, the ensemble musicians decided that it would not do any harm to accompany him. The double-bass and guitar played rhythm, and the drummer kept time by gently beating a cymbal. The lieutenant took the crews back to the great melodies that America had heard before the war. Even the pilot himself was transported to familiar territory by his own playing, recalling forgotten details of the not-so-distant past. Yachts in San Francisco Bay enlivened the city landscape; a weekend sailboat outing promised amorous adventures. A light breeze bore the boats away from the shore. Tennis balls beat on the court at the club… The smell of fish, seaweed, sapwood trees and beachfront restaurants hovered over the docks, where city folk and tourists would feed the seals, and it floated along the steep streets and green hills. Peacetime, blessed peacetime.

The bomber crews found themselves easily letting go of their cares and remembering the prewar years, even though the war had brought them far away to a Russian air base. The saxophone reminded them vividly of the old times. How much a man's heart aches when he looks back from the midst of war! In Creighton's melody, the past was sunny... Then, all of a sudden, anxiety set in. The instrument's breathing turned hoarse, heavy, and hacking. The saxophone gasped, moaned, and its sound plunged to its lower register.

Lieutenant Creighton had played the flute after every flight. His flute knew, just as he himself did, what goes on in the night skies, when fire is spewing up from the earth and the enemy has set its sights on its target. The bomber shudders as it flies along and seems to draw the shells toward itself – any one of them could hit its mark. You feel weak and defenseless, and the only thing left to do is to pray for salvation, if you can only remember the words to do so.

The crews knew well what Creighton's playing was all about – they had seen it, they had suffered it. The saxophone prayed for them, it implored the Almighty to bring everyone home safe. They were sowing death themselves, but there was no other way to defeat evil. The saxophone bemoaned this cursed slaughter, and its sound become heavy, gloomy, and rasping. It spoke of pain and torment, because when a man has no escape from suffering, he is always miserable.

Soon, however, the sound moved again into a light, clear refrain. It flowed like a cold mountain stream, and the melody offered up shining drops that splashed in the sun, and these bright flashes in turn gave way to scintillations. The saxophone moved higher and higher, as if it was soaring weightlessly into its upper register where it produced a cool whistle almost bereft of timbre. Creighton had forgotten all about his audience and blew powerfully into the sax's mouthpiece; his lungs worked like a bellows. This was a technique that musicians call over-blowing, where the extreme air pressure makes the instrument's sound jump by an octave or a twelfth and it reaches the limits of its capabilities with a piercing sharpness. A hope blazed in the sky, blindingly bright. It augured happiness and freedom, and this was something worth suffering, fighting, and carrying one's cross for.

Everything eventually comes to an end. The saxophone gave its last sigh. The hall sat there silent, momentarily at a loss, but then erupted into whistling and whooping. The lieutenant bowed and lifted a hand to ask for quiet. "I dedicate this music to our interpreter Olga," he declared to all present, as his countrymen applauded.

The Communist Party officials in the hall were taken aback and sat silently at the tables, their faces clearly showing upset. For them it was unthinkable that a musical performance could be dedicated to anyone besides Comrade Stalin, the Great Teacher and Leader. The officers were at a loss and glanced around at each other – some were imagining what terrible fate awaited them for permitting such an oversight.

Now, however, the military wind band suddenly struck up "Glory, Glory, Hallelujah", and the Americans leaped up from their tables and sang along in a thunderous chorus. All the crews sang with great enthusiasm. Ahead of them waited only more flights, sleepless nights, a barrage of anti-aircraft fire, vicious attacks by German fighters, death or capture – whatever each man's destiny might be. Those fresh dangers were still a way off, though, somewhere out there on the horizon. In the meantime, the party continued, the alcohol flowed like a river, and everyone rejoiced and made merry. The musicians played loudly, and the alcohol-fueled bomber crews sang themselves hoarse.

After the party, when everyone was properly liquored up, the fun spilled out onto the streets. The allies staggered around the air base, professed their brotherhood, bawled songs, and drank together from the same bottles in circles. They were all managing to communicate now without interpreters; there was less need for translation. The circumstances lent support to the old ideals: having come together at the call of Karl Marx, the drunkards and boozers of all countries easily united and understood one another perfectly.

Amid the ruckus on the street, the ensemble suddenly started playing. Everyone stood still and listened in disbelief, but then they livened up; how truly lucky they were! Just look, ladies and gentlemen, at this dancing, the embraces, the innocent mischief and sporting! One might think, what was so special about it? An old tango, a familiar melody in duple time with familiar steps... But why does one's heart ache and the blood stir? The Russians and the Americans recalled happy prewar times with a piercing clarity, that peaceful and undisturbed time with its evening languor, a moonlit park, a dance floor, the lilac blooming, women's eyes gleaming and an overpowering fragrance of perfume that made one's head spin.

The Flying Fortress airmen quickly took hold of various ladies from the air base's engineering battalion, or from the communications, medical, or laundry personnel, brought in especially to greet the allies. Steven Creighton took no part in this race to find a girl. He searched for the interpreter among the crowd and found her assisting two senior officers, Russian and American, who wanted to discuss the details of a night-time bombing run.

Lieutenant Creighton could not wait however. He casually saluted the American officer and said, "Sorry, sir, but the general urgently needs someone to translate." Then, without any ceremony, he led the interpreter away from the two officers, who were clearly unhappy.

"Where is the general?" the interpreter asked in astonishment when they were a little way away.

"I'm the general," declared the lieutenant, without a trace of embarrassment.

"You're tricking me?" the interpreter asked.

"Not at all. First of all, I'm going to be a general someday. Secondly, if they need somebody to translate, they can find another interpreter. I need you."

She felt embarrassed and at a loss for words. No one had ever said anything like this to her before. It is always an event for a woman when a man acknowledges her, and especially for a young woman who is hearing such acknowledgment for the first time in her life. Imagine what a big event it was for this young lady when it was a foreigner acknowledging her, an American pilot, like some fairy-tale prince who had come from far away on his magic carpet, all the way from the incredible city of San Francisco.

The interpreter naturally could not believe this. She assumed that she had simply misunderstood his strange California accent. After all, even people born and raised in the USA find it difficult to understand Californians when they speak quickly; it sounds to them as if the person is saying something with a hot potato in his mouth.

Junior Lieutenant Shilina could hardly believe that a California, with San Francisco in it, even existed somewhere out there. I myself found it hard to believe for a long time, until I eventually went there – ah, San

   

Francisco, California, green hills over a bay, like a magical dream that leaves you speechless!

It was no wonder that Olga felt like this, because she had graduated from high school shortly before the war broke out. By the time she entered the institute for foreign languages, the war was already raging. She had only recently taken her third-year exams, and been called up into the army right after the spring semester ended, a month before.

Of course she had no way of knowing how to talk with a man – how could she have known? In high school, one of the boys had sometimes walked with her, but because of the war, the students at the institute for foreign languages were mainly young ladies – her class had consisted of a dozen students who had been schoolgirls just yesterday. There was one lone male among them, but he was in chronically bad health and ineligible for military service.

Like many women at that time, Junior Lieutenant Shilina was twenty years old and had no experience of a man's kiss. This was something she shared with a whole generation of girls caught up in the war: the boys her age had gone off to the front having neither kissed nor been kissed, and nearly all of them perished there.

Hard as it was to believe, the interpreter had never met a foreigner before the allies arrived at the air base. The American lieutenant Creighton was the first she had ever laid eyes on. Though the Americans were not very different from ordinary people on the outside, they seemed more relaxed, spontaneous. They moved more easily. Ultimately they stood apart from the interpreter's countrymen, the way free people stand apart from prisoners. Even the American military uniform was better – it hung well on the men, its cut and the quality of its sewing were a sight to behold. Next to the Americans' uniforms, the Red Army's uniform seemed clumsy; it was like a rudimentary old stool next to fine bentwood furniture. Plus, to Soviet forces far behind the front lines, any foreign uniform was something unusual, and the novelty of it made people's heads spin.

When the American invited her to dance, the interpreter's hands turned ice-cold from fright. She did not dare refuse him, or perhaps she did not even realize what was happening; she remained silent and moved tensely, as if it were not she who was dancing. If someone back home, whether at the Institute for Foreign Languages or a random passerby, had told her that she would soon be dancing with an American officer, a pilot from San Francisco, she would think it some kind of joke, someone making fun of her, just words. It seemed so improbable that she could hardly believe it even while it was happening.

But the musicians played on, their old tango carrying in the twilight, and their hearts grew tender; it became as if they really were dancing together in an innocent embrace, hand in hand… They felt butterflies in their stomach, their hearts pounded, and they breathed heavily. There was no one around, or at least they did not notice anyone. All the other people present had become mere shadows, and only a single couple remained in the empty space: him and her.

The junior lieutenant danced in a daze, like Cinderella with the prince at the ball. She really was overcome by fear: the clock would strike midnight, the enchantment would be lifted, all the celebration would end, and everything would disappear, fly away, turn to smoke. For his part, the American was now more timid than he was in the skies over his target amid a barrage of anti-aircraft fire. One might have thought that he was dancing with an enchanted princess from across the sea, and a single misstep would break the spell and the princess would disappear forever.

Steven Creighton really liked this girl. He *loved* her, he had fallen head over heels, and now he forgot himself completely. When a person is in love, sometimes a dance is not just a dance but a magical road, a divine flight, and the couple moves together without even feeling their feet under them.

"You dance really well," said the lieutenant, complimenting her after a long silence, but his voice was uncertain; he was confused and tongue-tied.

"The last time I danced was three years ago, when I finished school," the interpreter admitted.

The lieutenant nodded. "At your graduation party."

"And you played well," Olga said, complimenting him on the concert he had just given them.

"I was playing just for you." The American brushed his lips against her hand, as was done in his home country.

This might have seemed nothing special, a man kissing a woman's hand. It was an old custom, one that had persisted over the centuries. Junior Lieutenant Shilina, however, suddenly started. A blush came over her face and she teetered on her feet.

I can attest – and I call the entire nation as my witness – that from the time of the Revolution, to kiss a woman's hand in the land of workers and peasants was considered an obscene liberty, a breach of hygiene, trampling on Communist ideals, a marker of foreign influence and filthy alien views. It represented complete defiance of the dictatorship of the proletariat. For many years now the regime had declared such ordinary human behaviors to represent bourgeois thinking. They were stigmatized and condemned until such alien mores withered completely, disappeared altogether.

In short, before the war, the bulk of the USSR's population saw kissing a woman's hand as a preposterous and harmful custom that spread disease. Among other things, with the arrival of the workers' and peasants' regime, whole new horizons had opened for Soviet women, and they enjoyed unlimited opportunities: working with jackhammers, shovels, pickaxes, saws, axes, and crowbars – occupations where one does not kiss hands.

After the tango, the musicians struck up a foxtrot and the crowd grew excited and abandoned themselves to dancing. The dancers joyfully pranced, sported, sweated, showed off each in their own way, and beat their heels on the earth, raising a cloud of dust over the crowd. Without saying a word to each other, the lieutenant and the interpreter slowly walked off, away from the noisy throng, away from the boisterous merrymaking, the deafening music, and the shaking ground. As they went further from the party, they gradually merged with the darkness, and then the lieutenant cautiously took the interpreter by the hand. This time, however, she accepted this gesture and did not shy away. The two of them silently and timidly walked in the semi-darkness like children – a boy and a girl in officers' uniforms, children playing at war.

They were children, in fact. In peacetime their lives had just started, they still had everything in front of them. Granted, children grow up fast in wartime, but now the American and the interpreter had forgotten all about the war. In some wonderful and mysterious way, the war suddenly vanished, disappeared, fell into oblivion. In its place, the pilot and the interpreter discovered around them the southern night, and the warm rain which had drizzled since that morning and then abated toward evening, the clouds clearing away. The moon rose and shone its vast light across the heavens and over the earth. In the bright moonlight, stars were sparsely scattered. A great silence and stillness settled everywhere, as if the entire world had gone numb in the moonlight – a boundless night-time space over which the moon had cast a spell.

It was the magical Ukrainian night that had so bewitched Gogol. In the distance, beyond a small copse, huddled a few thatched cottages, built from wattle and daub. In the village of Rybnitsa next to the air base, among the squat houses with their low straw roofs, poplar trees grew tall and slender, towering upward toward the sky like minarets. A light breeze in the air above them made the treetops sway, and the couple needed only to lift their gaze upward to see the moon slowly swaying with the poplars, a shining pendulum dispassionately measuring out the time. The American and the interpreter, hand in hand, wandered slowly past the houses and the dense trees. He told her about San Francisco, and she told him about Moscow.

Friday, June 3 was coming to an end. The war had gone on now for nearly three years. No one knew when it would end. On the night of June 5, 1944, from Sunday into Monday morning, the American planes would fly back. The Allies had planned Operation Frantic Joe as a series of shuttle flights over Germany across the front line. Twice a week the skies above Europe would shudder with the roar of engines as the Americans' 8th Air Force and 15th subjected the Third Reich and its allies to massive carpet bombing – hundreds of planes, an American-sized force.

Meanwhile pilot Steven Creighton and interpreter Olga Shilina strolled serenely in the night. They had forgotten about the war. Neither knew what lay ahead of them, what their future would hold, and neither he nor she thought about it. The flight schedule gave them only two days, Saturday and Sunday, and it was unclear whether they would ever meet again. Indeed, no one could tell whether they would ever see each other again, but it is always like that in war: any meeting could be the last. War, war…

═══ 13 ═══

The hypothesis of an informational field in biolocation, which explains one's noetic premonitions of impending events, supposes that around the Earth there is an accumulation of energy in the form of a vast sphere – a special energy layer similar to the ionosphere. According to the field theory, that ring contains a complete account of the status of the biosphere, its past, present, and future.

Here it is worth pausing for thought... We know from traditional physics that any object, any artificial or natural substance, by virtue of its being made up of atoms and molecules, is subject to fluctuations, and as a result of this it emits waves and energy quanta. This emitted energy passes through space, filling it with information and creating an ionic field. This very idea suggests that a trained operator might be capable of connecting to the energy field and reading the information therein. Of course, these would be very rough, approximate readings, without the finer details.

Researchers at Division X had been devoting ever more attention to intuitive biolocation. They expanded their experiments to search for people, animals, and objects at a distance. The geographical territory over which they carried out these searches widened constantly. The most capable operators from among our physicians made remote diagnoses for patients they could not see and did not even know. One of our operators made a precise determination of a specific patient's state, his blood chemistry and other values, and his receptivity to medication.

It bears mentioning that Division X neurophysicians found two areas of the human body that played a special role: the solar plexus and the pineal gland. In anatomy, the solar plexus is the receptor center of the vagus nerve, the main pillar of the vegetative parasympathetic nervous system which automatically, at an unconscious level, regulates the body's activity. Doctors are fond of saying that "the night-time is where the vagus nerve reigns". That is, when a person is sleeping and his cerebral cortex becomes inactive, the body's functions are overseen by the vagus nerve, and therefore most medical emergencies happen at night, such as heart attacks, strokes, various paroxysms; the list goes on.

In our neurophysicians' experience, the solar plexus is capable of finely reacting to signals from natural physical poles. Some operators intentionally involved the solar plexus in their searches when carrying out field assays. Here I cannot help but remember an unlettered peasant who could locate water. He said, "I can catch the scent of it with my insides."

From scientific journals we know that the American neurophysician Edith Jurka registered a noticeable change in the electrical activity of the brain during dowsing sessions. I do not know who was actually the first to make this discovery, but Division X's biolocation lab found a similar result. In addition, when we made a synchronous EEG recording of the electrical activity of our operators' brain hemispheres while they were practicing biolocation, we found changes in consciousness that were similar to those of yogis in deep meditation.

We also obtained curious results from an EKG. In experiments, an operator was shown alternately lovely landscape pictures and photos of car accidents. We know that a person will perceive these two kinds of images differently; the curves on the EKG will differ markedly. What is interesting, however, is that the heart activity as recorded by the EKG showed the corresponding peaks occurring *before* the picture was displayed, as if it could foresee which picture would be shown next.

A chime sounded over the loudspeakers at the American Airlines terminal, and check-in was announced for flight KAL-007 from New York to Seoul via Anchorage. From various parts of the departures hall, passengers started toward the counter. As if on cue, the three of us – Colonel Creighton, his daughter Cindy, and I – stared at them, as if we knew something about them that they themselves did not know, could not know. Whether one wanted to believe it or not, they were in danger. I was sure of it.

Soon, a large crowd had gathered at the check-in counter. The line consisted mainly of Asians: Koreans, Japanese, Chinese, and I spotted some swarthy Filipinos and Malaysians; but there were also white people – Americans and Europeans. In addition to the adults, I counted some two dozen children of various ages. The colonel's son Michael still had not turned up. His father and sister were visibly nervous and often glanced at the entrance to the terminal. If it were not for his son, the colonel would already be standing in the line of passengers at the check-in counter, but now he had no choice but to wait patiently.

Cindy turned to me defiantly and pointed toward the line. "Do you want to tell me they're all doomed?" she asked in a critical tone. Even angry she was no less attractive; indeed I found her dazzling.

"They're in danger," I answered curtly, aware that I had no way to prove the matter.

"Just being alive is dangerous!" Cindy snorted. "How can you claim that something is going to happen to those people? How do you know? Who can predict the future?"

Obviously, I could not tell this American about our secret research at Division X. The work of our biolocation lab included, among other things, clairvoyance. It also sought to explain premonitions, and it was developing a scientific mechanism for making predictions. In our experiments, the inner concentration of operators reached the level of meditation. We registered a drastic drop in heart rate, their blood pressure fell, their breathing slowed, and there was reduced gas exchange in respiration. As we gained experience, the percentage of events foreseen was constantly growing, and we felt that we were groping toward certain regular laws. Whether from the overall energy field surrounding the planet's biosphere, or from a cosmic space that contained the matrix of the future, or in some other way, our operators received, in their state of meditation, a signal. The main difficulty lay in noticing it, focusing on it, gaining a tighter grasp on it, and unraveling what it meant.

The noetic theory of intuition is, I must say, out of proportion with actual practice. A great many reliable cases have been recorded, but no explanation for them has yet been found. One hypothesis is linked with the theory of a chronal field. A chronon, according to the theory of Albert Veinik, is a very tiny particle, much smaller than an electron. Physics categorizes this class of particles among the leptons. Calculations show the presence of positive and negative chronons; their charge is determined by their spin. The theory is that chronons carry information about the past, present, and future, and in doing so create an overall chronal field that contains comprehensive information about the universe. A trained operator, capable of tuning into the chronal field's frequency, can obtain specific information from any segment of time.

Theoretically, all physical, chemical, and biological processes are accompanied by the emission of chronons. The main source of them is space, in particular the sun, though streams of chronons also come from deep within the Earth, especially from places where there are geological faults and concentrations of magma. One of the properties of the chronal field is that it appears when an object moves, rotates, or vibrates.

Light, for example, is accompanied by a stream of chronons captured by quanta. Any source of light thus serves as a chronal generator.

Similarly to light, an electrical current, a magnetic field, X-rays, and infrared and ultraviolet radiation are all capable of generating a chronal envelope. This property is also seen in the transmission of information, which has been dubbed "imprinting". Of course, any living creature participates, by emitting a stream of chronons, in the creation of the general chronal field, where, consequently, complete information about the Earth's biosphere is located. In other words, a human being – along with other organisms – is a source of, participant in, and consumer of the overall chronal field. A good operator is capable of extracting the required information from the field. For our part, we at Division X had developed a method that no one else in the world knew about; other scientists could only guess at it.

Medicine has long known of special features of the human body in the form of energy lines, sometimes called body meridians. They form chronal canals. Chronons emitted by biologically active points, which have been known since ancient times in Chinese *zhēncì* therapy or acupuncture, move along these channels. Of course, the chronons emitted by biologically active points of the human body pass into the overall chronal field and thus contribute to it information about the given organism. In other words, the Earth's energetic chronosphere contains complete information about each and every one of us.

The main chronogenerator in human beings is the brain, and the main channel by which chronons are emitted – besides the biologically active points – are a person's eyes. In this way, a person's gaze has real force and is capable of a range of phenomena, from physical to informational. At least, in Division X we often saw for ourselves that a trained person is capable of using his or her gaze to influence the course of an experiment, including the vital processes of organisms as expressed in analyses, instrumental studies, and laboratory tests.

At the Division X laboratory we determined that geometric figures of various configurations are capable of capturing chronal emissions even directly from space. The most powerful chronal accumulator is a pyramid whose sides are oriented toward the light and along the planet's magnetic lines. Of all geometric constructions, the pyramid most completely accepts chronal streams and accumulates them, and it basically establishes a link with the general field of the universe.

Experiments in Division X determined that the accuracy of clairvoyance and the prediction of future events is increased when a pyramid is included in the experiment. The results grew stronger the closer the experiment got to a pyramid. The maximum outcome was observed on a plane intersecting the axis of the pyramid at a point one-third of the way up from the base. The next strongest point in terms of chronal emissions was the tip of the pyramid, and then the edges at the sides and at the base follow with diminished effect.

In their experience in clairvoyance and predicting future events, Division X operators found that they obtained the best results at the first point on the pyramid. I must admit that all of us came running up to gawk at razor blades becoming sharper with no external intervention, water in bottles turning to ice, and living tissue becoming mummified without rotting or decomposing. Patients' wounds, including gunshot wounds, were quickly healed by primary intention. Diseases that had been rampant went into full remission, and noticeable improvements were made in the patients' functional state, especially their memory, reaction speed, acumen, and thought processes.

Unfortunately, on that night in late August I could not disclose our findings to the Americans as check-in for flight KAL-007 New York–Anchorage–Seoul went on around us. Who would have even believed me, anyway?

"If I were you," I suggested to the colonel, "I would give up on those tickets."

"Michael's got the tickets," said Cindy. "I'd very much like to know where he's got to with them."

"I'd be late arriving in Korea," Colonel Creighton said pensively.

"That son of yours has always been a goofball," Cindy complained to her father. "Now he's completely lost it with that floozy from New Jersey."

"Tell your son that the forecast looks bad," I advised the American, without any particular hope that they would agree. "He's a pilot, he'll understand. At least you can change your tickets."

"Doesn't it seem to you like… If I give up these tickets, it wouldn't be fair on the other passengers," said Colonel Creighton. "It wouldn't be fair. I would be saving my own skin but leaving everyone else at the mercy of fate."

"You could warn the others…"

"What?!" Cindy exclaimed. "Are we going to announce it over the radio or something? Can you imagine what would happen? And what would we say, anyway? That some guy from Russia has a bad feeling about things?"

"That's why I've only told you two so far."

"Well, thanks a lot!" Cindy retorted. "We really appreciate it."

The colonel frowned in disgust. "I'm not used to acting like a rat escaping a sinking ship. I've never hidden behind other peoples' backs. Let's say you're right and something does happen to the plane. Let's just suppose. And I listen to you, and out of all the passengers, only my son and I are saved. How will that make us look?" He then answered his own question, "We'll look like real good guys then!"

The feeling of alarm that had hitherto be coming intermittently suddenly became more distinct and pointed to a real and present danger. I sensed that the restless cries of a clarinet were coming from far away and growing ever stronger. Was I really the only person who could hear it?

"Tell me, colonel," I glanced at the slender black case that the American held in his arms. "You play the flute…"

"Not just the flute. The piano and the saxophone as well… Yes, I play sometimes. I've already told you that."

"We all play instruments, our entire family," Cindy said with a certain defiance. "What does it matter?"

"You must have a good ear for music." I said. "Do you hear anything now?"

They stopped, and listened closely. I could see from their faces that they were straining to hear. They squinted, and their gazes became impenetrable. It was as if all the sounds that existed in the world had suddenly come rushing in, and the American and his daughter were listening intently to try and recognize them. The colonel stood next to me but now seemed far away, and even Cindy looked concerned as her father gave himself completely over to listening. Did the Americans not hear the clear signal that was ringing the alarm across the whole earth?

The passengers nonchalantly proceeded through check-in. The sound of a clarinet was coming from some unimaginable distance to warn us, bitterly moaning as if it knew what lay ahead.

"If you like, I'm prepared to tell the airline representative about my concerns," I said to the father and daughter. "It's your decision…"

They exchanged glances and remained motionless. So far, there had only been a few words of doubt exchanged, but now the matter was taking a serious turn, and the course of events demanded action.

"Let's go," Cindy declared suddenly and unexpectedly, and set off resolutely for the check-in counter. I followed her.

When we reached the counter, Cindy said something quickly to a Korean woman in a Korean Airlines uniform. The woman nodded, and then by telephone she called someone to the counter. We were obliged to wait.

From our position a little way apart, we surveyed the crowd. The passengers were paying no attention to us. One after another they placed their tickets on the counter and handed over their luggage to be tagged and placed on the conveyor belt. With a clumsy shaking motion the suitcases trundled off toward the next section.

"There are a lot of young people," Cindy noted as she looked at the various faces in line.

"Schoolchildren and university students, of course," I said. "The school year starts soon."

"Oh, yeah, I completely forgot! Their summer break is over."

The crowd at the check-in counter quickly thinned as the passengers hurried off to board the plane. While Cindy and I talked, we looked at the old men and women, the young ladies, adolescents, little children with their parents, self-confident businessmen and serious-looking ladies, couples of various ages… I caught sight of a group of tourists sticking closely to their tour guide. The guide held a colorful flag over his head and purposefully cut through the crowd. The tourists hurried after him like chicks following a mother hen.

The thought came into my mind that this motley crowd of passengers resembled some kind of carnival of nations. I mused that if someone wanted to survey all peoples and tribes at once, there would be no better place to do so than a New York City airport. What a variety of facial features, eyes, skin colors and shades, what a mixture of languages and accents!

I shared my thoughts with the lovely Cindy, and she looked at me with sincere amazement.

"So you're not just a doctor," she said, "you're a philosopher too!"

Right before my eyes, something like a small-scale Tower of Babel was being played out. It was hard to imagine what a variety of thoughts these myriad passengers carried within them, all the different opinions, worldviews, love stories, mathematical formulas, secret passions, guilty consciences, hopes, ambitious plans, financial calculations, memories, mad designs, riddles, joys and sorrows, desires and secrets that make up our lives.

"Will all that really meet an untimely end?" I said to Cindy, but she did not respond. She just looked silently out at the people, as if she sought some hidden answer in their eyes. She searched, waited, and hoped that fate would be kindly disposed and that things would work out for the best.

Behind the check-in counter a door opened to admit a weary Korean of inscrutable age, neither an old man nor a young one. I must say that I have always found it difficult to determine Asian people's age, as one finds little emotion on their faces besides their polite and ritualistic smiles.

The female airline employee indicated Cindy to the man with a curt, professional gesture that testified to good training. Cindy asked if she was speaking to a manager of the airline, and when the man said yes, she suggested that he hear me out. "This guy wants to tell you something important."

I immediately told the man that the circumstances were unfavorable for this flight and I advised him to delay the journey. "It is not worth risking it," I said without any hope of success.

"Terrorism?" the Korean asked in a curt, businesslike manner, but I simply shrugged my shoulders. Within his company he was responsible for safety, and he continued to question me like someone who knew his job well. "Taking hostages? A bomb on board? Is someone making demands? Is there a problem with the plane? Risk of a crash? Bad weather along the way?" To each of these questions I shrugged and shook my head. Finally, he asked, "Do you have any real proof?"

"Just a bad feeling about it," I said. "My intuition."

"Are you flying?"

"My American friends are flying. I am advising them to cancel their plans."

"But you must understand, we can't cancel a flight just like that. There have to be serious grounds for it. Otherwise the airline will suffer losses."

"But if something happens, won't there be losses then?" I asked.

"Why would something happen?"

"I told you, I have a bad feeling about it."

"That's not enough."

"It would be best not to risk it."

"You mean cancel the flight?"

"At least ask the passengers. Let whoever wants to get on the plane do so. People should have a choice. Let them decide. Give them the opportunity."

The Korean thought about this. I could see what a burden I had put on him. The flight could not be canceled as there was simply no concrete basis on which to do so – a passing stranger's bad feeling was hardly persuasive. Even so, it was a hard task to bear responsibility for the lives of others.

He remained silent and deep in thought for a while. The poor man was pale from the stress and stood motionless, frozen, numb. His impassive features were like a mask. Several times he tried to say something but then cut himself short without managing to utter a word. Finally, he reached a decision. "I am going to report this to my superior," the Korean said quietly. "For our part, we have already carefully inspected the plane."

"Will you warn the passengers?" I asked, though I already knew that the airline would never agree to it.

"We cannot do that," he said firmly and then added, "No one would allow it."

Cindy had remained silent so far, but now she spoke up. "Just try," she told the intractable Korean. Perhaps she was already inclined to think that my arguments were worth heeding. The matter had become serious.

"If you wish, you can speak with the captain," our interlocutor unexpectedly offered. Cindy and I both nodded to express that of course we would like that.

At my request, Cindy approached her father. I wanted him, as a pilot, to be present when we talked to the captain. Colonel Creighton quickly came up to us. He looked concerned, often glancing at the entrance to the terminal, and he restlessly surveyed the departures hall. For some mysterious reason the colonel's son had still not arrived, and he was the one with the tickets.

The Korean took us to an office, the windows of which looked out onto the runway. The walls were hung with Korean Airlines posters and a wall calendar with the company's flying-crane logo. The bird, its wings outstretched in flight, was set against a circle in the background that might have represented a rising sun.

Through the window we saw a huge Boeing parked outside the terminal. Alongside it, the vehicles and luggage carts on the tarmac looked like small fry, unworthy of any attention.

The colonel nodded toward the plane. "A jumbo!" he said, calling it by the nickname known among pilots and aviation fans. In Africa the natives and visiting hunters had called elephants the same thing.

Even from a distance, the Boeing 747 was an awesome sight only a few other planes could compete with. It was painted in two colors, with the upper half of the fuselage white and the lower half, belly, and front part of the tail dark. The sheer size of the plane was immensely impressive. The tail displayed the plane's registration number in white on a dark background: HL7442. Like all Boeings with their hallmark "hump", the plane resembled a whale splayed out on the tarmac.

We waited a short while, and then the captain appeared at the entrance to the office. He was a slim Korean in a Korean Airlines uniform consisting of a single-breasted suit and a white shirt and tie. Like all employees of the airline, he wore a brooch in the shape of eagle wings on his breast. Shiny captain's stripes – one wide, one narrow – were sewn onto the cuffs of his jacket. Atop the captain's head was a uniform cap with a sharply upturned crown, a large cockade, and a fancy lacquered peak.

Before he introduced himself, the captain took a careful look at the colonel and me. As this silence stretched out, I assumed that he was sizing up the men he was going to speak with.

"You wanted to see me, sir?" the captain asked in a reserved and pointedly dry fashion.

The American told the captain that he was Air Force colonel Steven Creighton and I was a doctor from Russia, and then he immediately got down to business: it was nearing midnight, and the plane was scheduled to take off soon, so time was of the essence. After the captain had heard me out, he remained inscrutably silent, but I could see a flicker of annoyance on his face. He unhappily pursed his lips, as if we were lecturing him about something objectionable.

"Do you have any proof of this?" the captain asked coldly, though right from the beginning I had warned him that I was only basing it on my intuition. He stared at me waiting for an answer. I shook my head and caught a glimpse of relief in his eyes: he untensed and adopted a more relaxed stance. Of course, he maintained control over himself, but it is hard to fool an experienced doctor: I could see how much he would enjoy telling us to get lost if I did not present any proof for my claims.

"Are you flying?" the captain asked. I again shook my head to signal that I was not.

The colonel spoke up. "I'm flying. My son and I are flying. I am a pilot, too."

"I cannot do anything about this," the captain said, rather like an offended old lady. It was obvious that he was still annoyed that he had been brought here for something so silly.

"Sir, don't you feel something yourself?" the colonel asked.

"The plane is in working order," the Korean answered, stony-faced.

"I meant something else," the colonel frowned. "Pilots sometimes have a premonition of things. I know it myself. Back in '44 our plane was shot down by the Germans. The day before that flight I had a bad feeling about it. I was young, like you are."

"I am 47 years old," the captain said coldly.

"Really?!" The colonel was amazed. "I would have never guessed. Have you been flying for a long time?"

"I was a military pilot. Korean air force officer. I have flown for 10,700 hours," the captain replied, reciting mechanically.

"Oh," the colonel said, "then you are an experienced pilot and you understand what I'm talking about. It's not my place to lecture you."

"You are worried for no reason, gentlemen," the captain said to reassure us, though he remained cool. His manner of speaking was purely businesslike. "The crew will take your comments into account. I will tell the other pilots and they will pay special attention."

We felt as if we were standing in the office of some petty bureaucrat. The colonel was disappointed that he had not managed to explain things in his own words, pilot to pilot.

Whether the Korean was merely leading us on is hard to say. If he knew about the Boeing's earlier flight to Andrews Air Force Base near Washington, where expert electronic technicians, from the Texas company E-Systems, had spent three days working on the plane, he would naturally know what kind of flight this would turn out to be. Perhaps that is why the captain acted in such a closed manner; my worries would only cloud the picture and get in the way of their plans.

"Sorry, gentlemen, but I must go." With an icy politeness and Asian ceremoniousness, the Korean bowed and then left for the airplane.

All these years later, after countless investigations and trials, no one knows whether that Korean airline played any part in the game of intelligence gathering. Seven and a half years later, in May 1991, an American court of appeals reviewing the case ruled that the plane's crew had been guilty of criminal negligence. One can only guess at how the captain and the airline would have acted if they had known what the outcome would be. Maybe they were simply being used, and the unsuspecting passengers and crew were tricked for the sake of a higher goal.

The colonel and I returned to the departures hall. Cindy was nervously pacing beside the check-in counter and occasionally glancing at the entrance to the terminal.

"He's still not here!" an upset Cindy shouted to her father when we were still some distance from her.

The colonel nodded in understanding, as if this did not come as any news to him. "Something is going on," he muttered as we walked. He looked around distractedly, without seeming to notice anything. I saw that he was listening to his inner voice, to his thoughts. For a doctor from Division X, it was not hard to see that. And of course, he was listening across space, as if tuning into the world. Operators at Division X were in a similar state when they established contact with the ionosphere as it emitted its uninterrupted stream of chronons, constantly adding content to the informational field.

"I just can't imagine where he's disappeared to!" Cindy exclaimed as we joined her.

The colonel did not respond, and generally seemed oblivious to us. He did not look at us or say a word. With an absent look in his eyes, he was humming something indistinctly under his breath, and he appeared no longer surprised by what was happening. What was happening seemed to be no longer dependent on the wishes of people but subject to the playfulness of chance and the whims of fate. "Something is going on," he said pensively to no one in particular. He was in a meek stupor, a state I had not seen him in before.

Now we could only wait, resignedly giving ourselves up to events. Everything in the world went at its own pace, the wheels of time ground on continuously, and no one was capable of stopping their movement.

Something was indeed going on in the world, but we could not influence it. Layers of air were moving, the direction of the wind was shifting, an electrical charge was gathering in the atmosphere, ready to burst in a thunderstorm. Certain events, in accordance the inscrutable laws of nature, were approaching with a cold, hard inevitability. They were drawing nearer inexorably and ever faster.

The colonel and I stepped outside and stood under the awning above the entrance. A huge neon sign with the AA logo of American Airlines blazed on the outside of the terminal. The sign splashed its red light over the terminal's glass façade, the wet asphalt, the shiny cars, and the faces of the passersby, making everything appear to be drenched in blood.

From time to time, a taxi would sharply pull up to the entrance. Passengers, running late, would rush through the door and run the length of the concourse looking for their check-in counter, though it often transpired that they did not know where exactly they were running to.

"Dad, what's going on? Where could he have disappeared to?" Cindy asked her father anxiously. She was seriously upset at her brother, as if now it counted for nothing that he was a military aviator, a fighter pilot, an Air Force major. All that mattered now was that he had irresponsibly arrived late for his flight, and he had let his father down.

Colonel Creighton did not respond. He was still distracted, strangely detached, as if he now realized the uselessness of doing anything. Apparently the American was convinced that everything had already been decided, the choice had been made, events had been set in motion and could not be changed, and there was no way he could act on them or influence them. Since any actions would be pointless, any attempts useless, there was no reason to make any kind of fuss. As we say in Russia, you cannot defeat a cudgel with the butt of an ax – sometimes people must simply accept the limitations of their abilities.

Cindy drew closer to her father, looked him in the eye, and quietly said, "Dad, what's happening? Do you know something?"

Her father clearly did not hear her. He seemed to have sunk into a lethargic sleep, though his eyes remained open.

This annoyed Cindy. "Dad!" she said, as if trying to wake him, "What should I do?"

In a flash the colonel came to, as if coming back down from a mountaintop. "Just calm down," he said. "Nothing depends on us any more."

Cindy looked at him in astonishment. She fell silent, an unspoken question hanging on her lips. We returned to the departures hall. The loudspeaker announced boarding for the flight. The crowd proceeded along the corridor and disappeared down the long escalator carrying them to the gate.

The three of us stood and watched them go. One by one the passengers sailed down the escalator and vanished. One by one, one by one… I observed each of them attentively, as if each of them was departing forever. We watched them off. All the passengers were still alive, at least for the time being.

Shortly afterward the loudspeaker announced that boarding had finished. A powerful towing vehicle pulled the airplane onto the taxiway. It was clear now that the Creightons, father and son, would not be flying today. From the observation deck looking out over the airfield, we watched the tug release its towing line, turn around, and drive off. We heard the roar as the airplane started its engines. The Boeing set off and moved slowly to the runway, where it readied itself for take-off, remaining still for a moment, as if it were deep in thought, brooding on something.

At exactly this moment, a taxi sped along the airport's service road and came up to the American Airlines terminal. The taxi door slammed loudly and a tall, lean man with the same bearing as the colonel burst into the departures hall. This late passenger came running, nearly flying, across the hall with a remarkable agility, in spite of being weighed down by a suitcase and a travel bag. He ran as if he was hoping for a miracle, though it was obvious that it was all pointless, in vain, for he would not make his plane and nothing could stop it now.

The man reached the check-in counter and stopped with a pained look on his face: the lights had already gone out, his flight number had disappeared from the big board, and the check-in agents had left. The passenger looked around in disappointment and only now noticed Cindy, who had been standing silent and motionless to the side and watching her brother. Her look was one of bitter reproach, but she did not say anything or make any gesture to chide him.

"I got stuck in traffic!" her brother cried in a voice that was winded and not quite his own, as if the fact of a traffic jam could change anything now. He turned his head from side to side searching for someone, and, trying to catch his breath, said raggedly, "Where's Dad? Did he get on the plane?"

Cindy did not say a word. She merely shook her head and started for the stairs leading up to the observation deck. Her brother followed her, still out of breath. They reached the observation deck just as the engine turbines of the Boeing out on the runway howled and the plane set off, gathering speed. Deep in thought just as before, and never taking his eyes off the 747, Colonel Creighton watched the plane as it launched itself into the sky like a big rocket. It was clear to the others around him that the colonel was enchanted, mesmerized, by the swift movement of the plane.

Brother and sister walked across the observation deck toward their father. He glanced toward them briefly but said nothing, as if he were hardly aware of them at all. His gaze was fixed on the Boeing rushing headlong toward the sky, and he lifted his eyes upward to follow it. After the jumbo had gained altitude, it withdrew its landing gear and moved away from the airport, so that it could then make a turn and proceed on its set course.

"Dad, I got caught in a traffic jam! I was stuck in traffic!" Michael whined, like a child who knows that he has done something bad. He was clearly taken aback by his father's calm composure and silence. His father did not even try to blame or reproach him.

"It doesn't matter now," the colonel remarked calmly and then looked at me as if to say, you got what you wanted, I didn't get on the plane. The only thing that Creighton said aloud, however, was, "Now we just have to wait."

     

I have often asked myself whether we could have done anything to change things. Hardly. We could have gone on trying to make the plane turn back, but we would not have found anyone willing to listen to us. Of course, if the president of the United States had taken it into his mind to intervene, his subordinates could have carried out his order and canceled their plot, given up on it, reversed their decision. However, perhaps they would have found a hundred reasons not to carry out the order. Moreover, perhaps the president would not have thought to intervene at all.

Fateful events generally have a mysterious property to them: they are thought up by completely ordinary people, but then no one, even the most powerful, can stop them. And those who set events in motion tend to lose control of them. Events often seem to have a life of their own, but they can take on a disastrous and destructive power.

Sometimes the course of events calls to mind an avalanche rolling down a mountainside. Yes, some person or another was capable of giving it a first push. It might have been started by someone or something of little significance, but after that the avalanche is subject to no one. No one can hold fateful events back, and, as with natural disasters, no one can say or do anything to oppose them. The consequences are often unpredictable and they can boomerang back on whoever thought up the whole thing and set it in motion.

The plane disappeared into the night sky. For some time yet we could clearly hear the roar of its engines. Its illuminated windows hung in the darkness and its beacon lights blinked steadily. The roar dwindled away, but the lights continued to shine soundlessly, and it seemed as if they would hang in the sky until dawn. Then in an instant, they too disappeared, but we continued to stand there silently and stare out at where the plane had gone. Neither we nor anyone else in the world knew how the next day of the plane's flight would turn out, the night on which August became September. We remained in a strange daze, as if we had all been concussed together, and a rare feeling of desolation and overwhelming weakness took hold of us as we looked out at the night. We had only enough strength left to return, tired and silent, to New York.

On Sunday the bombers were refueled and loaded with new bombs. Each plane received eight tons of bombs along with ammunition for the thirteen machine guns on board. The night before, a long convoy of trucks and fuel tankers had trundled from the warehouses to the air base on the outskirts of Poltava. During Sunday, the Flying Fortress crews studied their flight assignments and the navigators charted their routes and targets. On the way back to Italy, the aerial armada was to bomb the Romanian port of Galati. It was considered a sea port, though it was in fact located on the Danube River. Although Galati was separated from the sea by two hundred kilometers, heavy-laden ocean vessels could easily sail up the Danube without obstacle.

Railway lines converged on the city from various directions. Galati was considered a major center for transshipments, and it also boasted a dry dock at which naval ships were repaired. Galati was an enticing target for the Soviet forces attacking Romania, and so the Allies decided to bomb Galati together. None of the men had yet taken part in joint raids, so they had to establish a rapport in a very short time – a sizable challenge, given that the operation was to involve hundreds of planes and they had only two days to prepare.

The commanders of the crews, wings, and squadrons, the staff officers and intelligence personnel gathered in the mess hall, where they pored over maps and aerial photography. A Soviet general, at the Americans' request, gave some information about the Germans' aviation and anti-aircraft defense in the region that was to be bombed. Planning officers described each target that they had marked for bombing.

Needless to say, the staffs of the two countries worked day and night. The officers ate and slept in snatches, while the interpreters worked themselves to exhaustion, no prospect of rest in sight even when they were practically falling asleep on their feet. In the time remaining before departure, the Soviets and Americans had to agree, come hell or high water, on their targets and routes – a grueling effort, one must admit. The two sides' staff officers examined every figure and discussed the route and the populated areas along the way. The debate was lively, and it has to be said that the interests of the two countries often failed to coincide. Red Army command wanted to run tactical missions, namely bombing communications infrastructure and the enemy's supplies, while the Americans stuck to their strategic plans and insisted on striking deep behind the enemy lines and bombing large cities.

Working feverishly, practically all the men chain-smoked, though the Americans smoked light cigarettes and the Russians preferred strong blends. Some of the Russians rolled pungent cigarettes from strong tobacco, while others preferred the wild tobacco *Nicotiana rustica* that stung one's throat mercilessly and left the Americans, who were unused to it, coughing and hacking. It was an era when no anti-tobacco campaigns had yet been conceived, and a cloud of smoke hung over the room so thick you could cut it with a knife. The uniforms of the Soviet officers took up the smell of this noxious smoke, while some of the Americans, mainly generals and colonels, freely puffed on cigars that gave off an aroma like honey. This might have seemed no problem, but the female interpreters, who were delicate creatures, were literally suffocating in the clouds of smoke that grew ever thicker and stung their young eyes. In spite of this, the windows were never opened, for security's sake: strict instructions had come down, saying that enemy plots were afoot and spies were lying in wait to steal the allies' military secrets. As everyone knows, it is better to be safe than sorry.

Each side insisted their plan was the best, and put forward innumerable arguments as to why some target or another should be bombed. The interpreters talked themselves hoarse and their tongues tied themselves in knots; they looked as if they were going to pass out from exhaustion at any moment.

At the end of the week, the weather cleared up. The sun grew warmer, and the only reminder of the recent prolonged rains were some distant peals of thunder from beyond the horizon, which was now shimmering from the heat. The airstrips and runways, which had been lined with metal plates, mercilessly heated the air and sent it upward, where it took on a quality like liquid glass, through which shapes and outlines became distorted.

The junior officers and sergeants from the Flying Fortress crews had taken off their jackets and were lying in the thick grass on either side of an airfield covered with potholes from the constant traffic. Here and there, pairs of crewmen in leather mitts were tossing and catching baseballs, while others played with bats and balls. Still others preferred to play the outlandish American version of football, and were running around with a ball shaped like a melon and tackling one another, snatching the ball away greedily and endlessly tussling over it like children.

The lieutenant liked sport himself, and would normally have been up for running with a football, playing baseball, or, of course, merely lazing on the grass in the sun. Since that morning, however, he had been distracted by a single thought, one that had taken firm hold of his mind and would not let go. It was the interpreter, needless to say, of whom the copilot Steven Creighton was so constantly thinking. He loitered endlessly outside the officers' mess, where the allies sat in a cloud of smoke and coordinated their plans before the next flight, hoping to find the interpreter. After the meeting, the Soviet and American officers poured out of the mess hall's doors in a wet, steaming mass, and behind them Creighton caught sight of the junior lieutenant's cap and blonde hair. The senior officers, however, did not immediately disperse, continuing instead their long, drawn-out conversations, which meant that the translators were still required. The interpreter was so tired that she could hardly stand.

Creighton immediately concocted a plan. He cut through the crowd and invited the Soviet officers, on behalf of his crew, to come aboard his Flying Fortress. The generals had discussed the possibility of such an invitation the day before, and the crews had received permission in principle, though everyone was told to be vigilant and keep their eyes open. Now here was Lieutenant Creighton urging them to come and have a look. The Soviet officers standing nearby readily followed the American as he started for the airfield – they were an eager crowd of carefree men who thought that they were in for a treat. Naturally, Junior Lieutenant Shilina was among them, for how could this friendly interaction between the allies go off successfully without a translator?

Everything proceeded quite naturally. Even these men, used to being wary, did not know what was happening; no one suspected any tricks. Along the way, Lieutenant Steven Creighton vividly explained the technical features of his Flying Fortress, falling in step, of course, with the interpreter, and sticking close to her. She faithfully translated all his enthusiastic observations and the many questions and answers that flowed from them.

On board the Flying Fortress, the crew offered their guests whiskey, rum, and brandy. The Soviets drifted through the enormous plane with drinks in hand. They examined the plane's equipment and its weaponry, and they took turns sitting at the controls in the cockpit, naturally not forgetting to drink from their bottles of foreign booze. The Soviets were now becoming quite tipsy, wandering around or drifting off, and the crew thought to lead their guests toward the rear of the plane. Soon both sides were quite drunk and there was naturally less need for an interpreter. The guests and their hosts talked a blue streak in slurred voices, but everything proceeded just fine without translation, for as has long been known, people can understand any language when they are drunk.

A while later, the guests and crew, on unsteady feet, came down from the plane for some fresh air and settled on the grass with the wing serving as shade. The diplomatic reception had now become a picnic. The lieutenant finally found himself alone with the interpreter in the plane's cockpit. He lifted his hand toward the switch for the battery-operated on-board radio, and searched up and down the dial until he found a Polish broadcast: a languid tango from the prewar era, played by a clarinet, violin, and accordion.

"Let's drink a toast!" The American copilot filled two cups, ordinarily used by the crew for drinking coffee during their flights, and broke a bar of chocolate into pieces.

The junior lieutenant had to stop herself from automatically translating the toast into Russian. She had grown so used to providing simultaneous translation that it took her a second to realize that the American was addressing her. They drank the contents of their cups and nibbled at the dark chocolate, and the lieutenant showed her photos of his parents: good-natured, smiling people standing in a garden in bloom.

"They'll like you," Lieutenant Creighton assured the interpreter.

"Why do you think that?" Olga asked.

"I'm sure of it. They'll like you."

"How do you know?"

"I know! If *I* like you, they'll like you even more. It couldn't be anyhow else."

The American copilot told her how happy he was to have met her, and that if he could only see her again, in spite of the war, everything would work out and they would be together.

"If it weren't for the war," Lieutenant Creighton said, "I would have never met you."

"We have a saying that a person would not be fortunate if he had not been helped by misfortune."

After a brief silence, Steven Creighton gathered the courage to ask Olga if she would let him have a photo of her.

"I want to always have you here beside me when I'm flying," the American explained. Olga did not have any photos with her, though, so Creighton offered to have her picture taken. The crew's radioman had been a photographer before the war and always had his camera with him. Without any trouble at all they could get a photo to remember the occasion.

Lieutenant Creighton grew excited, and declared that he had been dreaming of someone like her his entire life. The interpreter listened to him with her head bent, her cheeks burning hot from embarrassment. She was not a particularly shy person, but no man had ever professed his love to her before. Now, in the cockpit of an American bomber, she was caught off guard by Creighton's confession – what woman would have been able to maintain calm breathing, tranquil pulse, and composure under these circumstances? Creighton, hoping to win her heart, offered her his love and the city of San Francisco; the lieutenant was prepared to take her away with him.

Steven Creighton was acting on the basis of striking while the iron is hot. Perhaps we should blame that on the war, bearing in mind how unpredictable life in wartime is and how quickly things can change. In the depths of her heart, Junior Lieutenant Shilina knew that there was no hope for them, that her motherland would never allow it, that it was completely unthinkable. But who among us has not, at nineteen years old, longed for some happiness that could never be realized? Who has not indulged in mad dreams? Romantic music was coming from the speakers: a prewar Polish tango, a golden-voiced tenor, the sound of longing. The aching melody touched their hearts and awakened amorous feelings… and then a sudden sense of alarm came upon them. Their heads were spinning.

The interpreter did not know what to do, how she should act. She was seized by doubt; cold fear settled on her, and her shoulders were gripped by an icy chill. What should she say? She knew what kind of country she lived in, and she could easily imagine what was in store for her, what punishment awaited her. The junior lieutenant remembered all too well the strict instructions that her superiors had given her, and she had not forgotten the admonitions of junior and senior officers, up and down the chain of command. But how can you resist when you hear for the first time that someone is in love with you? Moreover, this was not just anyone, but a foreigner, an American pilot in an unfamiliar uniform, a fairy-tale prince who had swooped down from the heavens. Tell us, if you would be so kind, how a girl could resist? Even the environment in which this was happening was delightfully implausible: the cockpit of an American plane. Maybe the time had come for her to forget her strict orders and to give up arguing with the American. In the end, that is what happened.

Have there been many girls who first heard a man confess his love and offer her his hand in the cockpit of a strategic bomber? The two had now set off on a great journey, a flight that they would take together. The lieutenant and the interpreter sat in the pilots' chairs, and the cramped cabin of the Flying Fortress suddenly seemed to be their secret refuge, like a closed arbor in a garden or an abandoned building where lovers met, hidden from the gaze of others. Time seemed to have slipped strangely off its rails and was running now in quite some other way. The war was no more; things were changing for the better. Ah, life moves in peculiar zigzags, and the twists and turns of fate boggle the mind.

There is something strangely unsettling about planes, one will agree, by taking people out of their ordinary state. They strip people of their usual composure and call them far away, to mist-covered lands where everything is different, everything is a dream, an ethereal reality, a river of milk and honey.

It was like being in an enchanted sleep. Junior Lieutenant Shilina was well aware that she was not sleeping, but how could she believe it? What was happening was too much for her mind to grasp. The handsome American pilot had declared his love for her, he had asked her to be his wife, and he was promising to take her to the amazing city of San Francisco. How could this be anything but a dream?

She knew that they would come looking for her. She could not stay on board the plane, and certainly not alone with an American. Every second that she remained there represented a danger; she could be denounced to the authorities, even though she was only doing her duty. She also understood that there was a continual need for translation at the air base. She might suddenly have to assist with negotiations, she might be called to the Communist Party office, or have to help the air base's command. Wretched though it was, she should get up immediately and walk out, get up and prudently cut their time short, get up and walk out, resolutely tear herself away… but for some inexplicable reason she continued to sit there.

It is easy to sympathize with her. The junior lieutenant was confused, and lost for words. She was unable to move a muscle. She was like a little girl who had got lost in the forest. In spite of her fears, though, in spite of the danger, in spite of cold common sense, a mad thought flared up inside her like a flame in the wind: let it happen, come what may!

The interpreter was surprised at herself. Hitherto, she had thought that she was not capable of going crazy, of falling head over heels in love. The junior lieutenant had received plenty of attention from men: beautiful ladies are rare in the army. This war had brought together large crowds of men, and they would constantly circle round her, showing their interest. She, though, had only just entered active service in the army, and she remained on her guard, as a sensible and decent girl from a good family should.

Junior Lieutenant Shilina was a serious and prudent young lady. Fiery impulses and unbridled affairs had always been foreign to her upstanding Muscovite family, all down the generations. No one had ever burned with fierce passion, no one had lost their self-control. No one in her family had ever experienced an all-consuming love.

Reckless actions are usually a characteristic of people who live by their hearts rather than their minds. The interpreter was clearly of the latter persuasion. She had a natural restraint and a cool head, and showed no inclination toward the fevers and confusion of love. She had tucked away in her memory something her mother had said when she was leaving for the front: "A man will spend time with one girl, but he'll end up marrying another." Even without that, at nineteen years old she was smart enough to know that a girl should not waste her energy on frivolous flings. All around her, flirting was rife; officers were recklessly pursuing the fleeting romances of the front lines. She, though, had no desire to become someone's temporary wartime girlfriend.

The interpreter could not rule out the possibility that the American already had a girl waiting for him somewhere, in America, maybe, or Italy, or who knows where. She was right; her female intuition had not let her down. In San Francisco, Creighton had gone out with a girl from his class, though they had restricted themselves to a few shy kisses – it was an innocent fling, a school crush. In college, he was introduced to the ways of love by a pert classmate who dragged him into her bed after a party. At flight school he gained further experience: dances were held that drew crowds of local girls from the nearby town, and they would often stay in the barracks until morning.

After the Allies had arrived in Italy, Creighton sometimes spent time with a simple waitress from a nearby trattoria. Moreover, there was pretty Sergeant Tracy who had many suitors but liked him the best.

 

Right now, though, he felt that there was no one else in the world. He saw himself as being free as a bird. He forgot all about his fleeting romances. Those transient girlfriends disappeared from his mind, swept off into the far distance and out of sight. Now there was no one else, he was sure. Lieutenant Creighton was no different from any other man. He had always looked forward to finding true love one day. He hoped he would meet the right girl and that he would be able to spot her among the crowd. Now his inner voice told him that she was the one. To his own surprise, Creighton accepted this without a moment's hesitation – but a man always recognizes his other half, the only one for him, the girl he was destined to meet. Naturally, the lieutenant was afraid to touch Olga. She was different, not like the other girls, and Creighton feared offending, insulting, or scaring her. He dreaded destroying his fragile dream and shattering his hope by making an awkward move. It is always like this when a man finds true love: his soul freezes with the fear of losing her.

"I must go now," the junior lieutenant forced herself to say, though she was worried that he would object and not let her leave.

Creighton, however, merely sighed and meekly gave in. Her wishes were his command. Meanwhile, the American crew and their Soviet guests were loudly and drunkenly cavorting on the grass under the wing, or muttering away about who knew what. Their goodbyes were protracted. They had all had more than enough to drink by this time, but they kept at it, slowly passing the bottles around. The allies were all giving one another friendly pats on the back and shoulders and were unable to quieten down. They sang loud songs and danced like fools, with comical gestures and grotesque faces. General Nathan F. Twining, commander of the American 15th Air Force, had been quite right when he had ordered that crates of liquor be supplied to the Foggia air base in addition to ammunition. They would help establish, the general said, a mutual understanding with the Russians.

As the interpreter and the pilot came down the ramp, they found themselves caught in a whirlwind of drunkenness. No one seemed to have noticed their absence. In a large bunch of people having a good time, it is impossible to keep track of what everyone is up to. After the allies had emptied all the bottles, they started taking photos. They squeezed tightly together smiling into the lens, and gave no thought as to what the future might hold for them.

No one knew what the future held. The war would go on for another year – an eternity, though one brief moment within it would suffice to get a man killed. Of course, many of them did not survive: they were burned alive, blown to smithereens in the sky, they perished in a foreign land, they disappeared without a trace; but they still look out at us from the photographs as they were then, young, smiling, and alive.

Amid the drunken commotion, the radio operator took the lieutenant and interpreter's photo. He photographed the lieutenant and interpreter together and separately and, generous soul that he was, he took plenty of shots. As the crew and their guests said goodbye, they drank the last of the liquor, draining the bottles to the last drop, for leaving even one drop at the bottom of a bottle was always considered uncouth behavior and a breach of tradition, not to mention contrary to good sense. The Russians and the Americans have similar habits and temperament when it comes to the sport of drinking, and anyone who breached this tradition would be dishonoring the two great nations.

In any event, both the hosts and the guests were dead drunk; the men could hardly put two words together. With noticeable difficulty, the allies rose to their feet and slowly staggered down the airfield toward the base, unsteady on their feet, like wounded soldiers coming back from the field of battle.

The return flight was scheduled for the night of June 6, overnight Sunday and into the Monday. No one among the Flying Fortress crews knew that this date would go down in military history. Toward evening the crews snatched some sleep and sobered up. Calmness and composure returned to their faces. Some fell into deep thought, as if they were worried about the ultimate fate of their souls. Dinner in the mess hall began with a prayer before their flight. The Americans asked the Almighty to have mercy on them during their journey. The Flying Fortress crewmen, together and separately, begged the Lord to give them the strength to make it back, to protect and keep them.

Junior Lieutenant Shilina caught herself wanting to join the crews in prayer, and only with some effort did she refrain. It was obvious that if she had decided to pray with the Americans, she would not get away with it; someone would denounce her to the authorities before she even had time to blink. The urge was strong, though; she wanted to join the crew in placing her hands together and appealing to an unknown and omnipotent power for help and protection.

Like everyone else of her age in their godless country, the interpreter lived without religion. No one in her family went to church; no one even prayed, except for her grandmother. The interpreter looked around the crowded room, and the realization hit her that the next time the Americans flew in, some of the tables would be empty.

Of course, the interpreter wanted everyone to survive, but she knew that this was impossible and that many would die. She did not know that top brass had already planned for losses in their elaborate calculations. They had compared potential losses with the projected results of the bombing campaign to decide whether it was worthwhile. After all, such an aerial armada could lose up to a quarter of its planes and crew in a single sortie. The military's calculations contained a bitter but inevitable truth: air force personnel would have to be replaced two or three times over during the war, for few would escape the carnage. That was the whole reason why there was an aviation industry and flight schools: so that they could constantly churn out new men and planes in order to make up for the losses. As the interpreter looked at the praying men, she thought how sad it was, and more than sad, to meet people, to become used to having them around, only for them to vanish forever without a trace.

After dinner, the interpreter disappeared without Lieutenant Creighton noticing. He had no idea where to look for her. A few had seen her leave, but no one knew where she had gone. He was consumed by the thought that he would never see her again: his heart contracted painfully, and he became terribly afraid. In the past, the American pilot had always found it easy to break up with girls, but now he only had to think that he might never see her again and it was as if a cold wind was blowing into his face and a bottomless void had opened beneath his feet. He was tormented by the idea of being parted from her; even to imagine losing her was more than he could bear.

The American set off at once to find her. He did not think about the danger – that asking about her could land both of them in trouble. The lieutenant, like a little child, simply could not control himself. He kept thinking about how he was going to fly off that night without saying goodbye and that he would suffer, lying awake at night, until he saw her again. Creighton was restless, there was no use denying it. He decided that he had to see her again whatever it took; he wanted to meet her whatever the cost. If anyone had tried to warn him and reason with him, Steven Creighton would not have listened; it would have all gone in one ear and out the other. Any arguments, no matter how solid, any efforts or good intentions would be in vain, pointless, a waste of time and energy. Burning with impatience, Steven looked feverishly for her everywhere, but his search was fruitless. He rushed around the base searching the barracks, the mess halls, the warehouses, and the workshops, but the interpreter was nowhere to be found. Out of desperation he was nearly ready to go to the base's duty station and have the interpreter called in.

It was now sunset. The evening was warm and languid in the way that rural backwaters often are. Lively voices, laughter, the sound of radios, strummed guitars and phonograph records issued from the open windows of the buildings. It was all so peaceful that you could not tell there was a war going on. After a long search, the lieutenant finally found the female barracks, a long two-story building that had been hastily erected on the edge of the settlement. Linen hung drying on clotheslines in the yard, and young women were everywhere in evidence, in a number that surprised the lieutenant. Many were in military uniform, while others had apparently come back from duty and changed into summer dresses that made them seem like colorful fluttering butterflies. The American did not know, of course, that during Operation Frantic these barracks hosted women from the engineering battalion, from communications, from the laundry detachment, and from medical.

As soon as the lieutenant appeared at the barracks in his dashing uniform, there descended on him a veritable cascade of unrestrained and unfeigned attention. A sassy bunch of young ladies crowded at the windows to look out at him, whispering to each other, giggling coquettishly, winking at him and laughing loudly, though they had repeatedly been given strict instructions by Communist Party officials and heard stern admonishments from SMERSH.

"*Amerikanets! Eh, krasivy oficer!*" they eagerly called out to him, teasing him. When he asked about an interpreter named Olga, no one understood him – no one spoke English.

The American, at a loss, towered over this mob of young Russian ladies who, in spite of all the warnings they had received from their superiors, approached him without any fear and crowded around him. He looked around helplessly and muttered that he was looking for an interpreter named Olga, but then he fell silent and looked the crowd over, searching among this bunch of strangers for the only Russian girl he knew. The young ladies realized that something was up, and although there were many of them, it suddenly became very quiet. They stood still in a circle around him, and in the silence they stared at him.

This strange scene took place just as evening was falling, as the setting sun touched the horizon and its burning copper light caught the barracks' windows. After its initial boisterousness, the crowd had suddenly quietened down; the girls gazed at the man curiously and without saying a word, as if they had guessed that it was a matter of love and had lost the urge to tease him. What can I say, they all longed for love; every one of these lovely young women pined for it, and really it was no laughing matter. Some of them clearly felt sorry for this foreigner and envied the unknown woman he was searching for, which was also reason not to laugh.

It is easy to understand how these girls felt. The war had doomed many of them to a life of solitude; they could not marry because there were simply not enough men. By the terrible laws of war, the male population had thinned out – a bitter fate, but who could do anything about it? The war had taken away the men who were meant for them, and now these girls each seemed to be wondering what they could look forward to; a moment had come for each of them to reflect and listen to her inner voice. The girls were deep in thought and waiting for something, as if they had all asked a question and hoped now to get an answer.

While the crowd stood mute and transfixed, one of the older women in a military tunic was inspired to ask the American, in Russian, "That Olga of yours, is she an officer?" So that the American would understand, she clapped her shoulder where she wore the epaulet of a sergeant. "*Oficer?*"

"Yes, an officer, an officer!" the American responded and eagerly nodded his head.

The sergeant gave a wave of her hands. "There are no officers here," she said in Russian.

A younger lady in a colorful printed-cotton dress intervened. "The officers live somewhere else," she said in Russian and pointed into the distance, behind the houses at the other end of the street. "Go over there and ask."

The buildings of the base took up a wide swath of territory next to the airfield. Here had stood residential buildings and offices which had been destroyed by the Germans during their retreat. At the beginning of Operation Frantic, the ruins of these older buildings had been restored and rebuilt for military use in short order, and many brand-new facilities had been erected. That so much had been achieved in so short a time caused general amazement. Behind the spartan barracks towered a residential building, containing a hundred apartments for officers. The seven spacious mess halls here could feed a thousand people at one time, and twenty buildings were dedicated to the army medics.

The lieutenant wandered through a maze of baths, laundry facilities, and workshops. Warehouses, garages and hangers hulked over waste ground. In the distance, on the other side of a barbed wire fence, glimpses could be caught of the roofs of the old village of Rybnitsa that had stood here since time immemorial.

Right from the planning stage, the Americans, prudent old bores that they were, had insisted on the construction of numerous bomb shelters: the safety of their personnel was of paramount importance to the Americans – a concern not shared by the Soviets. It was always possible that in spite of all the precautions that would be taken, the radio silence and the strict secrecy, the Germans might track the bomber fleets as they crossed the front and sooner or later discover the air base. Once aerial reconnaissance had confirmed the existence of the base, the Germans would naturally try to bomb it. Thus, roofed dugouts and bomb shelters were found around the base at every step, and even outside the base in the neighboring forests and on the outskirts of the village of Rybnitsa.

As the lieutenant walked around the base settlement, he encountered a large number of his compatriots. The blacks among the Americans attracted the Soviet troops' particular attention and warmth of feeling, for black people in rural Russia were like an exotic wonder from distant lands. These poor men, oppressed and despised, were almost like the Soviet peasants and proletarians, their kin in terms of class.

Creighton stared in surprise as American officers, corporals, and sergeants scurried about. Jeeps with American registrations occasionally pulled up at the headquarters, and American technicians, mechanics, engineers, and ammunition and equipment specialists teemed around the bombers on the airfield like ants – their total numbers were over a thousand men.

The lieutenant knew America's capabilities, of course, its superior technology, but when he saw the scale of Operation Frantic with his own eyes on the Soviet air base, he was deeply impressed. The airfield's old unpaved runway had always turned to mud in the spring and was thus unsuitable for heavy bombers, but the Americans had paved it with steel plates brought in via Iran, and these provided a firm surface for the planes during take-off and landing. Each plate had actually been laid by women from the Soviets' engineering battalion, who exceeded their daily targets and even outdid American productivity.

The Americans had moved navigational equipment, generators, and radio units here by air from England, where the 8th Air Force was stationed. This equipment was subsequently given to the Red Army under the lend-lease agreement so that it would not have to be taken back.

America, of course, was no stranger to large-scale endeavors. Gawping and marveling could wait, and Creighton went on searching for Olga the interpreter, though in vain, without success. His remaining time was slipping away catastrophically; mere hours remained until his departure.

=== **15** ===

The pilot often thought about his country. When he was on watch duty, he had plenty of time to think, and he would reflect with sadness on Russia, the country he had served loyally for so many years now. In spite of his love for his motherland, Russia was a source of pain and disappointment. It was marked by such absurdity and, with rare exceptions, the most anyone could expect was a life that was far from enviable, even if they lived honestly off the fruits of their own labor. Russia was very wealthy compared to many other countries, but still it walked a road ridden with potholes and bumps, stumbling at every step as if incurably ill. Russia seemed somehow to have bad roads in its very blood; every step along them was a hard one.

Shilin's heart ached constantly. Year after year, life in Russia went on as it always did, at best vague, and usually clueless. Shilin observed a few sensible developments on a strictly limited scale, but for the most part confusion reigned. The common life and the lives of individuals proceeded in a completely ridiculous fashion, senseless and empty, all askew, out of place, haphazard, as if the country were doomed forever to ruinous chaos and eternal troubles.

His land had one particularly strange and mysterious personality trait. Russia had given birth to an unusual number of glittering talents, but the regime had no use for them. These talented folk could not find a place for themselves in their homeland and so, feeling unwanted, they left, to bring glory to other countries. However, nature abhors a vacuum. Plenty of shrewd and light-fingered blockheads entered the corridors of power. They grew in numbers and, finding themselves in the right place at the right time, and, without being too clever about it, they simply grasped at power.

The pilot was often told that Russia had its own special path, and he tried to figure out where exactly it was leading. For some reason, Russia's specialness always led it astray. Other countries glided down smooth

  

and well-trodden roads, guided by common sense, but Russia rejected those paths. It even rejected common sense itself. It dragged itself,
panting, through a pathless series of swamps and abysses, convinced
that this was a special course meant for it alone and unfathomable to
anyone else.

The pilot sided not with Gogol and his image of the winged troika,
but rather with Chaadayev, who remarked that Russia shows the rest
of the world the path it should *not* take. It diligently and enthusiastically laid a path to points that everyone could expect to be a dead end,
and where everyone would be risking their necks, sinking into a bog,
or drowning. Of its own will, Russia deliberately drifted with unusual
enthusiasm into the swamp, and then painfully struggled and thrashed
about trying to get out and back onto the right road. It seemed to use its
own fate as a warning to other nations.

"What an unfortunate country," the pilot reflected with sadness. His
heart ached with love for it, but he felt anger, and fury too. The country
was so grotesque, mad, confused. It toiled so hard, scraping its elbows
until they bled; it turned itself inside out, tormenting itself as if it were
its own enemy.

And what luck his country had had with its rulers! Russia resembled
a nature reserve where some malevolent external figure had gathered
all manner of mediocrities and set them in charge, had brought fools
and imbeciles to run the country, to manage, command, oversee, and
supervise it.

Idiocy in Shilin's native land had thrived. It was a country where
each year brought a rich harvest of stupidity. For that reason, now and
again people would complain aloud, "A country of fools! A country of
fools!" Naturally, everyone thought that they were real geniuses and the
general stupidity did not extend to them. In other words, they were a
chip off a different block, and they had ended up in a country of fools
only by accident, inadvertently, due to some devilish mix-up. As the
poet Pushkin used to say, the devil had had a hand in their being born
there, or they were just unlucky. No one doubted that they themselves
were excluded from the general foolishness; everyone else was doomed
to suffer from it.

The irony was, though, that their own opinions about rampant idiocy were wholly applicable to themselves as well. They simply did not
realize it, or suspect it. They saw the mote in another's eye more readily
than the beam in their own. As soon as one took a closer look at them
and got to know them better, they turned out to be exactly the same

as those whom they haughtily judged to be fools. To be frank, Russia's congenital stupidity had never known any limit. It was like a natural disaster, a volcanic eruption, earthquake, or epidemic striking the whole massive country. It seemed as if Russia had been cursed from time immemorial, as if a mass plague of stupidity had been sent down upon it as punishment for sins.

The pilot knew that there were plenty of sensible people in Russia, but for some reason they never managed to change anything. Russia's current life and its future development was decided mainly by stupid men. Here, common sense and any rational order or natural course of things reached an inexplicable dead end. They gave way to nonsense and absurdity, and often ended in thievery, trickery, and blood.

Shilin could only marvel at the patience of his countrymen. When he observed everyday life in Russia, he thought of how accustomed Russians had become to stagnation, grievances and adversity, and how they went on finding a way to survive, eking out a meager existence. Russia, showing extraordinary natural wisdom, humbly carried its cross and naively hoped for a miracle.

Shilin often reflected on these matters when he was on watch duty, and usually at night. If the alarm did not sound and planes did not take off to intercept, the pilots on duty generally had nothing to worry about once darkness fell. No one hassled them over some petty matter. Shilin could focus on his own thoughts, on things that he could never contemplate during the daytime. His watch duty was like a break, however short, from ordinary routine and society.

When the pilot came on night duty, he felt like he was getting away from life's enervating busyness. The everyday faded away into silence, into a sterile void from which, as if from far away, a picture of real life was revealed to him as it never was by day.

From the total peace and quiet of the little building for pilots on duty, a building resembling a monk's cell, which stood alone on the airfield beside the concrete strip of the runway, the pilot could get a clear image of his own existence against the backdrop of life in Russia. He closely scrutinized it and drew comparisons.

When Shilin's orders were to spend the night sitting in the cockpit of his fighter plane, fully equipped and ready to go at a moment's notice, the boundless expanse of the world opened up to him, as did the flow of time that carried people and things along in its wake. The pilot was no longer so young that he did not look back, into the past. His highly retentive memory swiftly took him back to years gone by, to places where he had once served. And it was always the same. He had always taken off into the sky in order to meet the Americans. It was a game of cat and mouse that never ended, an ineluctable fate, as if he had been born only to oppose them.

On Sakhalin the pilot was usually put on night duty. In the fighter regiments, night duty was given to an elite, a chosen few, while the rest served during the bright hours of daytime. It was generally the most experienced and skilled pilots who qualified for night-time fighting, men capable of flying solely by their instruments, in the pitch dark, when you could not tell where the ground was, nor the sky, nor what kind of target you had in your sights.

In the summer, from April until October, the night pilots of Shilin's fighter regiment, based at the Sokol air base near Yuzhno-Sakhalinsk, arrived on duty one hour before nightfall and were relieved at nine o'clock in the morning. In winter their shift finished an hour after dawn. At night, as they waited for the alarm to sound, their vision grew mysteriously clearer, their sight was sharpened. A feeling of enlightenment came over them, along with a much-sought-after clarity and firm determination that they had lacked during the day.

Sometimes Shilin was assigned to stand watch during the day. The mad rush of daytime and the endless hassles brought by his superiors made him anxious and unhappy. It all interfered, preventing him from putting his thoughts in order. On night duty he could sit in peace and think.

His son grew into a stubborn, willful, independent, and secretive young man. From infancy, almost before he could walk, he seemed to need no one. He kept everyone at a distance, including his parents.

The company of other children his own age did not interest him. He was content to be all by himself, and though he would play soccer with the other boys, he was quiet and never got into scuffles. As soon as the game was over, he walked off the field.

Shilin's son never took part in the larks and monkeyshines of the local gang. The other boys showed him no particular friendship, but they did tolerate him: he was the best at soccer of any of them. He outdid everyone else in everything: solving math problems, playing soccer, doing gymnastics or pull-ups – whatever it was, little Pavel inevitably came in first, pushing himself to his limits to be the best.

If Shilin's son got into a fight, he knew how to defend himself. He never acted aggressively toward others, never threatened anyone or intentionally got into scrapes, but he refused just to accept someone else's ill-treatment of him. He never tried to slip away out of a fight, but rather stood his ground and fought to the end. His confidence and cold determination astounded the other boys, even the older and stronger ones among them. With time they began to grow wary of him, and in their community he was one of the few whom the local punks never touched.

The pilot thought about what caused his son always to be the best, as if he had that trait in his blood. When Shilin observed his son, he was surprised, because it was not the Russian way to win by one's wits or skill. More often, people resorted to trickery, they tried to cheat.

Pavel lived quietly, he tried always to be first, and, though he apparently did not realize it himself, he meticulously planned what kind of life he would live. He did not rely on mere luck or good fortune, and he did not expect help from anyone else. He gritted his teeth and fought his own battles alone; he counted only on himself. His father sought a reason for this, racking his brains to find an explanation, and he often thought about his forebears. Besides his mother, the pilot did not know any of his family, and he could only guess at what traits he had inherited from his ancestors and passed down to his son.

Who knew what was encoded in their genes? By this time, the country of victorious socialism no longer considered genetic science to be corruption introduced by the world's imperialist powers. The Soviet authorities, eyes lowered in shame, had finally recognized that genes governed the way in which natural characteristics were passed down from generation to generation. True, Nikolai Shilin had no idea about his paternal ancestry – he did not even know who his father was – but there was some dogged and overwhelming force, elusive and subject to no one, that went far back in time and had firmly guided him through life. That force had been passed down to Pavel too. It could not be quashed or even argued with. A voice, silent but commanding, was now guiding the boy, showing him the way, and instructing him day by day – an invisible drive from his ancestors that was making him what he was.

The pilot had no idea who had come before himself and his son, from whom they were descended, whose traits they had inherited. Shilin's mother had never let her son or grandson into the secret, and so they lived in ignorance, but their blood was clearly hinting at something. After the pilot became our patient at Division X, he often bombarded me with questions. He was keenly interested in genetics, heredity. He would ask which inherited traits were subject to mutation over time, and which were stable and remained unchanged for a long time.

What could I tell him? I knew his ancestry only along his maternal line. I had to explain to him how genes worked, what the structure of DNA was. I talked of the right-hand and left-hand spirals, where personal traits were encoded down the ages.

"Does that mean that everything is predetermined?" the pilot asked, grinning ruefully. "It's not worth trying to fight it?"

"It is worth it," I answered, to reassure him and cheer him up. "First of all, mutations happen generation by generation. Inherited features do change. And circumstances have an effect. Every union of two people has its own features."

No one in the family noticed when exactly the boy began to show musical abilities. Shilin's son went to a program at the base's social club where an officer's wife taught music notation, solfeggio, and choral singing. Later, the boy taught himself, without help, to play the guitar, and once, when Shilin was coming home from his shift, he heard awkward honking from a clarinet. The sound was of someone feeling his way uncertainly in the dark: the boy was secretly learning to play his father's instrument.

The pilot rarely played music at home. In his wife's disapproving silence he could sense a distinct reproach. He was quick to acknowledge that she was right. She already had to suffer the remoteness and misery of Sakhalin, and a clarinet at home on top of that would be too much.

Sometimes the pilot took his clarinet with him on duty. He would play at times when he was at Readiness Level Two or Three, and not expected to take off at a moment's notice. The instrument, without him intending it, expressed anxiety, as if it was afraid of something, as if at any moment someone might interrupt it and force it to be silent. It was not because the clarinet had lost its voice or its musicality, though, nor was it that the leaden Sea of Okhotsk was depressing. For some time now a sense of gloom and worry had settled over Shilin's home, and it was eating at his heart the way the salty waters of the sea eat at the metal hulls of ships.

The second-floor apartment where Shilin's family lived was a spartan one and forever imbued with a thick smell of washing, sour cabbage, bleach, rancid oil, old rags, dullness and desolation. The paint was peeling in the corners, and through the apartment's walls they could hear the voices of neighbors, children crying, random crashes, clattering dishes, couples' quarrels, the moans of lovemaking, music, sleepy muttering, or drunken swearing. This conglomerate of sounds hung like a cloud over the Shilins' home. Even if it happened to abate for a moment, the harsh creak of the stairs or floorboards would sound from somewhere in the building and assault the ears.

His wife had fallen into a depressed silence, sighing heavily, and it was obvious how much life at the base oppressed her. For her, Sakhalin Island was simply incompatible with life. Like everyone in Sakhalin who had wound up there against their will, his wife dreamed of moving back to the mainland.

As had happened before, the pilot occasionally felt as if he were someone else, though he still could not figure out who. In the oblivion of sleep, in his dreams, and in the momentary confusion of waking, when he was no longer sleeping but not yet fully conscious, he vaguely imagined unfamiliar people, strange others, mysterious visitors, but who they were and where they came from, he could not figure out, no matter how hard he tried. Shilin sometimes, suddenly and inexplicably, felt that he was an outsider, an uninvited guest who had been away in distant regions and had unexpectedly appeared at the door.

Like an unidentified flying object, someone now and again appeared on the edges of his awareness, an indistinct presence looming somewhere in the dark shadows beyond the spotlight. The pilot knew it was pointless to think about this, for he would find no answers or explanations.

After Shilin received the order to transfer to Sakhalin, his entire family went to visit his mother in Krasnoyarsk. He found the city considerably changed; it had grown, and many new houses had been built. His mother had been given an apartment of her own in a new neighborhood on the other side of the river. A long, wide avenue named in honor of the local newspaper *Krasnoyarsk Worker* cut through the valley between the Yenisei River and the mountain ridge. His mother was older now, but she kept her spirits up. She would keenly recall her parents, though she instantly clammed up as soon as Nikolai turned the conversation around to his father. He had only to hint at the subject and his mother's gaze would become impenetrable. Again, for the umpteenth time, the pilot heard what he had often heard in childhood and knew well: his father had died toward the end of the war; he had never returned from a sortie.

"But usually a person leaves things behind. Letters, photographs…" Shilin insisted without any particular hope. "People don't disappear completely without a trace. Have you really not kept anything of his?"

"No," his mother said frostily, and shrugged her bony shoulders.

"I'd like to see a photo, at least. What did he look like?"

"Just look in the mirror. Same face."

"Did you ever meet anyone from my father's family?"

"How could I? We met at the front."

Professor Shilin, his mother's father, had been versed in linguistics, and had foolishly become involved when Stalin made some confused claims on the subject. Though Stalin's education extended no further than a stint in a seminary, he had insisted on writing an article in *Pravda* in order to lecture academics and the entire populace on "language as a means of communication". At an academic council meeting, Shilin's grandfather made a sarcastic remark about Stalin's article. Look at this, his grandfather said, the author's based his article on that pre-revolution high school textbook of Kudryavsky's. Though it was true, informers among them took the remark as mocking Stalin, and it was enough to have Shilin's grandfather summoned to Lubyanka Prison that night "for a meeting with linguists there". This scholarly disagreement turned out to be too much for Professor Shilin, and he died soon after. His wife, Nikolai's grandmother, was deported by these same linguistics experts to a labor camp, and she never returned. A senior official from the Lubyanka Prison took over the elder Shilins' Moscow apartment, with its exquisite old furniture and vast library; he was a great lover of antiques and Russian literature.

Nikolai's mother refused to move to Moscow. She was aghast at the idea of having to pester people to get her way. Strong-minded, independent people in Russia are often reluctant to engage with the authorities. Nikolai repeatedly told his mother that she should go back to Moscow, especially now that her parents had been rehabilitated, but she waved his suggestion away, pleading poor health, though in fact she continued to hike with a backpack, spend nights in a tent, and bathe in cold water as she had always done. And also as she had always done, she avoided any discussion of Nikolai's father and the story of Nikolai's birth. Like a miner with a sixth sense for trouble ahead, his mother could smell danger and deftly parry those forbidden subjects. Nevertheless, the pilot often noticed her staring at her grandson's face, as if she was searching there for some likeness to a person she had once known, in long-ago times. His mother took every opportunity to glance at the boy and, it seemed, to compare his features with those of someone she remembered.

Before they left for Sakhalin Island, the pilot took his son out to the taiga. It was late May, and the taiga was abloom with rhododendrons that were purplish-pink on the hills and white in the wet valleys. They had set off toward evening, and it was growing cold as they stopped in a simple hut at the foot of the rocks to spend the night. Stacks of chopped wood were piled around the hut. They found the doors unlocked and inside there was firewood, tea, salt, pasta, and canned foods, left by a previous traveler. This was an age-old custom in the deep forests of Siberia: every man of the taiga staying in a hut would leave some of his supplies behind, and he would chop firewood before he left, so that subsequent visitors could come in from the road and warm themselves, rest, and eat.

The boy quickly mastered the customs of the taiga. Before they left, he dragged a dry fallen trunk under the roof, and inside the hut he left matches, a packet of tea, some sugar, and buckwheat. Beyond the dirt road that had been cut through the taiga and was muddy at this time of year, the Stolby nature reserve began. The Stolby reserve was a legendary place, inspiring awe in those tourists, rock climbers, and nature lovers who knew of it. Sheer cliffs rose high above the trees and from a distance looked like gigantic statues set among the taiga. As far as the eye could see, the steepling cliffs towered above the hills and hollows, as if they were propping up the sky, and they extended beyond the horizon. A high pass above the reserve revealed a boundless country of forest. The tall rocks among the taiga and on the hilltops resembled giant castles of old, with walls and towers so impregnable that only a madman would venture to storm them.

Of course, getting to the tops of these rocks was a dangerous under-taking. Only an experienced climber could handle such verticals and make his way up the sheer walls. Shilin, however, had spent his child-hood in Krasnoyarsk and was just such a climber. He had explored all over the Stolby reserve and knew every wall like the back of his hand. For his son, Shilin chose an easier rock face, but even this could be climbed only by those who could suppress their very real fear.

The boy handled himself unusually well, without any of the undue fuss typical of novice climbers. He would move slowly and deliberately before setting his foot down or grabbing a handhold. His father could nevertheless see that Pavel was afraid. As they gained height, the boy became suffused with fear, and he made each new move with difficulty. His face was pale and he was dripping with sweat. His strength began to fade, and he had to gather himself before moving past a crack or a ledge. Naturally, Nikolai made sure the boy was safe. They were high up now, and the wall towered above them and plunged below them. Now every-thing depended on a person's character: whether to continue climbing, or to descend.

"If you want, we can go back down," the pilot said, as if the thought had just occurred to him.

The boy frowned. "No."

Pavel stubbornly scrambled up, silent and with his jaw clenched tight. With furrowed brow, he concentrated on the rock face, searching for the next foothold or handhold. Sometimes he simply had to cling to the rough granite and wait before he could move on; even experienced rock climbers have to battle fear, and Pavel was still a novice, so the experience was even more unsettling for him. His father followed, slightly below and ready at any moment to come to his son's aid, but the boy rejected any attempt to help, as if that would somehow be shameful.

"I can do it myself," he would say quietly, but it was clear how challenging the rock was for him, and how much effort he was making to overcome his fear.

Once they reached the top, the boy wearily dropped onto the sun-warmed stone and lay there, exhausted, like a warrior after a battle. He shook off the last of his fear and regained his composure. From the summit, a boundless stretch of Siberia opened up before them. Their granite rock soared up into the sky like a massive cathedral. The trees below seemed no more than matchsticks. It was hard to believe that people were capable of ascending that steep wall, but ascend it they did.

Of course the pilot often saw the ground from great heights. When the weather allowed it, the vastness of the earth was revealed to Shilin, but it was the first time the boy had ever seen such an incredible expanse on all sides. From the clifftop, the taiga looked like a shaggy carpet that stretched as far as the horizon, and in breaks in this carpet other high rocks towered into the sky.

"You did a great job," the pilot said. The boy made no reply, but was clearly pleased. It was easy to understand why. He had experienced fear, but had tamed it; he had conquered himself and the rock, and now he swelled with pride. Shilin was just as happy. His son would often have to face fear in his life, but today the boy had proven himself, and Shilin could trust that he would do so in the future.

They went back down by a different route, a mountain trail through an overgrown fissure that split the rock from foot to summit. It was the first time the boy had ever been in the taiga and he was stunned by its size and the noises that the trees made. The thick forest extended infinitely around them and, like a great big organ, it spoke in different voices. Everywhere, he heard odd rustling, squeaking, and the crackling of branches. The sounds floated weightlessly past them and faded away.

The boy listened intently and looked around, as if he expected to meet someone there.

It was late May, and in secluded pockets of the forest, female deer were giving birth to their young. The boy was amazed to discover the antlers of a buck. They had been cast off the previous fall, soon after the rutting season, when the young and old bucks vied with one another for the females, blood flowing down over their eyes. They would drive the females from the herd and mercilessly chase them through the taiga. Over the long winter and spring they would grow new antlers, and in the summer the antlers would harden. The next fall, when a new rutting season began, with its mating games and battles for females, the bucks would be freshly equipped. Any animal in the taiga, even wolves and bears, knew that it was best to steer clear of the deer during rutting season.

While they spent these days in the taiga, the pilot told his son about life in the outdoors. The boy listened attentively. Shilin hoped that his son's genuine interest meant that he would remember his father's words and, one day, pass them down to his own children. The pilot regretted that he had never known his own father. He carried sadness always with him in his heart, and now he felt that he had to give everything he knew to his son, so that the thread of family and time would never be broken like that again.

On the way back, the boy turned around at the mountain pass and took a parting look at the taiga. A dark-green sea of fir, spruce and cedar flooded the vast valley and rustled in the light wind from the Yenisei, but it yielded, powerless, whenever it ran into the foot of a massive rock. The boy carefully studied the boundless taiga landscape as if he badly wanted to remember it, to carry it with him and preserve it. The pilot hoped that his son would never forget these days spent in the taiga, because a man can never forget his first rock climb, any more than he can forget his first love.

In early June the pilot was transferred to a new place of duty on Sakhalin Island. His regiment was facing an acute shortage of personnel: one squadron had left for a training center so that its pilots could master the new MiG-29 and MiG-31 planes, and all over the base people were heading off on their summer vacations.

All the same, the portion of the Soviet border assigned to Shilin's regiment still needed to be guarded. No one cared if the regiment was experiencing a personnel shortage. Trying to explain the situation was pointless. A lax state of readiness at the border would only play into the hands of the Americans. In fact, it was as if they had been waiting for just that, for their flight activity had sharply increased. Day and night, Orion, Cobra, and E-3A reconnaissance planes prowled along the border, and here and there they tried to break through. Often the Americans violated USSR airspace outright and teased the Soviets, played on their rivals' nerves, and Soviet air defense had to scramble fighters to intercept the intruders.

For many weeks now, the border had been buzzing with non-stop frantic activity. At the Soviet bases, alarms were sounded one after another, and the harried pilots gloomily muttered to each other that it was time to shoot the Americans down…

It often happened that just when Shilin's fighter regiment managed to cover one hole in its airspace, the Americans quickly punched another hole somewhere else. The American reconnaissance planes had only to cross the border and the entire Soviet chain of command would be shaking their fists and screaming for the negligent personnel to be punished swiftly and severely.

For months now, Shilin's regiment had been the subject of commissions and hearings. None of them wanted to delve into the facts, though, and search out the reasons for what was happening. Each successive commission would berate the local command, and excoriations and thrashings would then come raining down on the base personnel. In short, the pilots were in a feverish state, the regimental and divisional commanders were constantly getting an earful, and since the situation on the border was growing worse by the day, everyone was expecting new punishments and changes of personnel.

Thus the summer passed. After each inquiry, the men in Shilin's regiment would grind their teeth in frustration. The crews of the American reconnaissance planes noted in their reports that the Soviet pilots were now behaving very recklessly in the air. Flying had become dangerous.

The end of August offered fine weather. The concrete runway absorbed and radiated heat. The sun was so hot that one would never think fall was around the corner. Yet fall arrived, and Shilin's son had to go back to school the morning after the summer break ended.

One hour before twilight, the pilot arrived on duty. He was expected to remain at Readiness Level 3, which meant that after the evening news on television he could doze for a while.

═══ 16 ═══

Lieutenant Steven Creighton walked frantically around the base looking inside the HQ and the operations room. No one had any idea where the Russian interpreters lived. One wise-guy American advised him to try General Kessler or Colonel Paul T. Cullen, who would probably know.

"Who are they?" asked Lieutenant Creighton, but the joker had already disappeared with a grin on his face, and only later did Creighton learn that General Alfred A. Kessler was the US commander of the Poltava Air Base, and Colonel Cullen was his deputy. Both were infamous for their tempers, and they rode the junior officers hard. The staff officer who had advised Creighton to ask them was playing a trick on him. "I'd have been in for it good and proper," Creighton thought later when he realized what a trap he might have walked into.

Shortly afterward, Lieutenant Creighton came across some members of his own squadron, and one Captain John Pash smiled and waved Creighton in the right direction.

The interpreters lived in a small brick house built long before the war. It had been renovated before the Americans arrived. Besides the young lady interpreters, it also accommodated older women, military doctors. When the American saw it, he thought it would be fine just to walk in. However, some girls washing linen outside stopped him and said that male personnel were forbidden from entering. Without their uniforms, these interpreters in their light printed-cotton dresses seemed even younger, and it was hard to believe that these girls doing their washing were officers. The place seemed more like a kindergarten.

While her friends were washing clothes outside the window, Junior Lieutenant Shilina was lying on her army cot, in a bad mood and not thinking at all about any kind of date. It was easy to understand her surprise when the American suddenly turned up.

The interpreter faced a dilemma. She was a smart young lady and under no illusions. She was well aware that any female at the front would become an object of attention, like a military target that must be attacked. Front-line romances did not evidence a large variety in the tactics employed: suitors would generally go right in for a direct attack, a headlong storming of the fortified position. Only much more rarely would they employ a flank attack, one requiring time and deftness, and hardly ever would they carry out a prolonged siege. After all, war was not a favorable environment for any sustained relationship. What love or constancy could there be in an army at war?

In any event, the junior lieutenant found herself a constant object of male attention day after day. It was no wonder, for even older ladies, the military doctors past forty, received that kind of attention, so naturally a young and attractive girl would too.

Men would immediately notice Shilina's pure skin, her eyes that were gray with a tinge of green, her mane of blonde hair, but she lacked the conversational ease and way with words of the more flirtatious girls. She was a pensive type, preferring to read and listen more than to speak. The interpreter was distrustful of superficial judgments and overhasty opinions, and this made it hard for her to socialize with other people, so she often spent time alone – something that has always been the fate of people who think a great deal.

There was a reason why the junior lieutenant was feeling sad after dinner. Before their departure, the Americans had performed a ceremony of farewell – a ritual. This was something that Soviet pilots did not do. After a group prayer, they forgave one another their trespasses, asked forgiveness from those they had offended, and vowed not to offend anyone in the future. Before the flight everyone bathed and put on fresh clothes.

It was a strange sight: living people preparing, calmly and collectedly, to die. Their faces took on a detached look; the fact that death might be right around the corner left its mark. For the interpreter, this confrontation with the potential loss of men, the knowledge that casualties would come, was her first hands-on experience of war. Olga had known that people die in war, but until now she had been living in Moscow and events had happened far away, to people she did not know. Now she had come face to face with the war and its fatal consequences. Men were really dying, and not somewhere at the ends of the earth, but right here, and it did not involve some faceless individual, but real people she had met and spoken with. These men were still alive, standing next to her, but they were already absent in a way, having crossed the line into real danger. The junior lieutenant shuddered, feeling herself on the edge of the abyss of war and afraid to peer into it.

In wartime, people doubtless get used to losses over time, they grow a thick skin. For the time being, however, Junior Lieutenant Shilina was still tender, anxious, her thoughts full of bitterness and pain. She thought that perhaps it was best, therefore, to get some sleep, especially considering how little she had slept lately. She went to bed, but sleep never came, and sadness continued to eat at her.

Meanwhile, outside her window in the yard, her friend Kapitolina, herself an interpreter and junior lieutenant, stood looking at the American disapprovingly. She shook the suds off her hands and stood resolutely in Creighton's way, as if to say, "Over my dead body."

The two young ladies had been friends all their lives. Kapitolina loved Olga and had a maternal concern for her, though they were the same age. Since birth they had lived in the same apartment building, though on different floors. They had even been born at the same maternity hospitality, just a few weeks apart. For ten years they sat in the same row at school, and after graduation they went on to study together at the Institute for Foreign Languages. The two friends were called up into the army together, assigned to the same unit, and lodged in the same room – a rare fortune when war usually tears people apart.

The two interpreters' parents continued to be neighbors. They were naturally happy that their daughters had been lucky enough to stay together in the midst of all this upheaval. They really might have parted for good otherwise, for it is so easy to lose someone in wartime. Parents and daughters exchanged letters; each of them had long been thought of as a second daughter by the other family.

They really were like sisters, and they kept no secrets from one another. Sometimes Olga felt that her friend's affection was stifling, for the simple reason that Kapitolina's devotion to her knew no bounds. A person had only to get close to Olga and say a few words and Kapitolina would butt in – she was always looking out for her friend's safety. Kapitolina generally became annoyed if anyone showed an interest in her friend, and she would swiftly intervene, as if she had vowed to guard and protect Olga.

Even before the war, Kapitolina had felt that Olga did not need anyone else besides her. Kapitolina did not let anyone else into their friendship, and she would drive newcomers away, as if Olga belonged to her alone. She maintained a vigilant watch over her friend. Every opinion she stated categorically, as if she already knew the truth, and for all occasions she had a ready-made answer. She had the enviable trait of never being in doubt about anything. No one could ever convince her that she was wrong.

Now Kapitolina was shaking the soapsuds from her hands and standing resolutely to block Creighton's path. She appeared ready for mortal combat, even if it meant sacrificing herself.

The lieutenant greeted her and asked "Where's Olga? Can I see her?"

"Who are you?" Olga's friend said coldly. "I do not know you."

"Does it matter?" the American said, flashing an ingratiating smile. "The important that is that Olga knows me."

"Does she really?" Olga's friend's lip curled unpleasantly, and she stared at him intently.

From the very beginning, Kapitolina had taken a dislike to Steven Creighton. She would have been similarly suspicious of any suitor of Olga's, but there was an additional reason for her hostility to him: Kapitolina did not like foreigners. She had never had the opportunity to meet any before, but the newspapers wrote about how sneaky they were, how they would pretend to be friendly and disinterested, but in reality they had some hidden agenda. In her opinion, all foreigners were cunning and crafty, and she was not going to welcome them. Even the Americans, in spite of being allies in the war, made her suspicious: the capitalists had to be confronted, the class struggle was still going on.

In short, Kapitolina saw in the American lieutenant not just a pesky suitor, but a suspicious foreigner, a cunning pretender who, under his smile, was secretly plotting. Inside Kapitolina's mind an alarm was going off and the vigilant girl had to rise to the challenge.

"What do you need from Olga?" Kapitolina asked icily, ready to stand her ground and, if necessary, fight to the death. She looked quite ready to sacrifice herself, to plug any gap even if she had to use her own dead body for it. "What do you want?"

"Are you her secretary, miss?"

This question offended the young lady. "I am not a secretary, sir! I'm her friend!"

"Well, miss, that is a great honor," the American said in a conciliatory tone. "I beg your pardon, but I need to see Olga."

"Why?" Kapitolina asked bluntly.

Creighton was taken aback at the young lady's lack of ceremony. It was the first time he had ever visited Russia, and he had not yet become used to negotiating the obstacle that a girl's stubborn friends represented. He paused, and thought for a moment as he looked upon this spiteful young woman who seemed perfectly ready to give her life to protect her friend.

"Maybe I can just go inside?" he asked and tried to go round her, but without success, as Kapitolina was blocking the door with her bosom.

He took a look and estimated its size; the barrier appeared insurmountable.

"No!" Kapitolina said categorically, and then added with exaggerated pride, "No man has ever entered here!"

"I see. It's a girl's only space, no men allowed. Could you maybe call her, then?"

"She's sleeping," her friend retorted. "It's been a difficult day for her. I would only wake her for a serious reason. She's sleeping, do you understand?"

"I understand but… I would like… It's very important. Olga has been working with our crew…" He continued to try to persuade her, but she remained unbending.

"We are all working! Each interpreter has her crew!"

Some crew had really lucked out by being assigned this one, Creighton thought to himself. Then he said aloud, "We're leaving today, flying out…"

"Everyone's leaving. What about it! It's late now, why do you need her?"

"The crew would like to say goodbye…"

"Don't make me laugh! The crew are also sleeping before they fly."

"Listen, my dear," Creighton started, but he was not permitted to finish his statement.

"I am not your dear!" his roadblock said with indignation. "Don't you dare call me that."

"OK, I won't. You are not my dear. Still, listen to me. I might never see her again. I wanted to get her address."

"Her address?!" Kapitolina was shocked. "You can't write to her, it's not allowed!"

"Not allowed?" he muttered. He stared at the woman stupidly, and then tried to press on nonetheless. "What, the mail system doesn't work?"

"The mail system works, but you are a foreigner. You should instead speak to the responsible authorities."

Kapitolina had decisively parried all of his attempts. Did he really have no choice now but to turn back and leave with his tail between his legs? Creighton was uncertain how to act, but his opponent suddenly wasted her advantage and undermined her own success by going too far.

"You don't have any reason to write to her," the woman said in a lecturing tone, feeling now that her victory over him was assured. "There's no reason why you should see her."

   

These were reckless words. The lieutenant became angry, but he managed his anger, training himself right there and then to handle and focus it. "Listen to me, dammit! This is none of your business. Let her decide, let her tell me herself, and you keep your nose out of it!"

"What?!" Kapitolina stared at him, slack-jawed, her shock stripping her of any ability to form English sentences.

"You heard me!"

"How dare you! I… You… I will report this…" she stuttered.

The lieutenant cut her off, "Shut up and get lost! Better finish your laundry."

Kapitolina, dumbfounded for a moment, could only open and close her mouth, like a fish dragged out of the water. Then she screamed furiously, "You should be ashamed! I'll tell my commanding officer about this!"

"Tell whoever you want, but if you don't get out of my way, I'll throw you into your own washtub!"

Olga now looked out the window to see what was going on. "Wait, I'm coming out!" she said.

Her friend only waved her away and shouted in Russian, "Don't come out! Just close the window. You've already gone to bed!" Creighton could not understand the words but he got the gist and stepped aside to wait.

Olga disappeared from the window. Clearly she had gone to dress and fix her hair. Kapitolina was shouting heated words toward the open window, and though Creighton did not understand her Russian, he assumed that this dame was angry that Olga was coming out to see him.

He guessed correctly, for Kapitolina was admonishing her friend without letup. "I'm trying to protect you, and now you've ruined everything! Don't you dare come out. It's an American, you understand? Don't come out, do you hear me? If you come out, they'll all start coming around here! Just stay there, and let me deal with him! These Americans think they can just barge in anywhere! Don't even think about coming out. Just stay there!"

Olga came out all the same. Instead of her officer's uniform she was wearing a printed-cotton summer dress with little flowers on it, and she had replaced her boots with light shoes. She had combed her blonde hair neatly, and Creighton noticed a light scent of perfume.

"What are you all dressed up for?" her friend exploded. "I defend her, idiot that I am, I try to let her get some sleep, and what does she do? Don't you have any self-respect? If I were you, I'd tell him to get lost!"

"Calm down, Kapitolina," Olga tried to reason with her. "There's no reason to shout."

"No reason? I know what I'm talking about. It's OK for him, he'll just fly out of here. You're the one who'll suffer!"

"How will I suffer? What for? I am the interpreter responsible for his crew. What if they have questions or problems? I have to do my job…"

"Do your job?! Now? Come on Olga, he's come to see you. He came for you personally. Look at him, those shameless eyes! He's a filthy type!"

Olga drew close to Kapitolina, looked her in the eye, and said quietly, "Why are you being like this? You don't even know him."

"I don't need to. Just look at him! He's trying to trick you. Foreigners are all the same. Ask him what he wants. Don't even think of going off anywhere. I'm right here beside you."

Olga did not seem to hear Kapitolina's words. She slowly walked off to where the lieutenant was waiting for her, and then the two of them disappeared around the corner of the building.

Another interpreter outside doing laundry laughed and said, "So, Kapitolina, your friend didn't listen to you? You always act like you're her boss."

"She's going to regret this!" Kapitolina answered, and then picked up the wet linen and began to pound it on the washboard.

Olga and the lieutenant crossed the street, walked along the dusty road, and came out in a picturesque and deserted area, where military engineers had created dugouts to serve as bomb shelters. It was summer and they were now overgrown with weeds. A thin twilight was coming in from the east, while the last smoldering remains of sunset lingered in the west.

"I didn't want to make a scene," Creighton said. "But she started screaming like a crazy woman."

"Kapitolina's a good friend and someone I trust," Olga replied.

"She was guarding you like you were her property."

"She thought she was protecting me."

"Yes, I noticed. She's so devoted to you she's ready to kill everyone around you."

"And me, too," Olga smiled.

"Have you known her for a long time?"

"For as long as I can remember. We grew up in the same building."

"Well, I think she's just jealous of you. She acts like she knows what you need better than you do."

"Kapitolina is a very protective friend."

"Over-protective, though. Do you not think so?"

"There came a time when she decided that I was her responsibility."

"I don't think Kapitolina and I are going to hit it off, somehow. She won't let you see anyone. Or anyone see you."

"I'm a big girl now."

"She doesn't agree, I'm afraid."

The first stars had appeared in the dark sky. The surrounding forest was wrapped in twilight, as if in muslin or light smoke. A bright evening soundlessly crept over the now-hushed earth and passed into deep night. The interpreter and the American pilot sat on a log at the edge of a hollow overgrown with willow herbs. Distant sounds could barely reach them here; everything was muffled in the thick grass. They had left the war behind them and remembered it only vaguely like a fading dream.

"Are you flying out soon?" Olga asked.

Creighton nodded. "We all muster at one a.m."

"I heard that the crews sleep before they fly out."

"That's right, everyone else is sleeping now. They have to get some rest before spending all night in the plane."

"What about you?"

"I don't feel like sleeping. I'm breaking the rules, of course, but I couldn't leave without saying goodbye to you first. Who knows what's going to happen."

"Are you scared?" she looked at him with alarm.

"The first time was scary, but then I got used to it. It's like tossing a coin. Some people are lucky and some aren't… But everyone hopes. The people who got shot down hoped as well."

Olga shook her head. "That's terrible! How can you live if nothing is under your control?"

"You just have to accept it. But you know, the war feels a lot easier if you've got someone waiting for you."

"Is that important for you?"

"It's important for everyone. If you've got people waiting for you, it's much easier. You feel like someone is watching over you. You feel like you'll make it." The pilot touched a slender crimson stalk. "What are these flowers called?"

"I don't know what they're called in English. We call them *kirpey*. Village people call it *ivan-chay*."

"Why is it called that?"

"People make tea from the leaves. During the famine, this plant saved a lot of people."

"Do you really have famine in Russia? I thought you had plenty of grain. How did this plant save people?"

"Peasants dried it and then they made flour from it and baked bread. Instead of wheat."

"From grass? First time I've ever heard something like that. Where did you learn about that? Have you lived in the countryside?"

"My grandmother told me. My parents used to send me to her in the summer. This grass also heals the earth after fire. Probably what happened here was there was a battle, and everything burned. Now *kirpey* has grown here."

"That's amazing! Not many people in America know about nature. Only the Indians."

Meanwhile, twilight was spreading across the earth and flooding the hollow where they were sitting. Thick brushwood grew around them, indistinct in the gloom. It seemed that night was lurking in the dense thicket and furtively filling up the surroundings.

"Look, Olga… I know what you probably think of me," Creighton said after they had sat quietly for a while.

"What?"

"That I'm not a serious guy. That I'm looking for an easy fling. I flew in here, then I'm leaving, and in the meantime I just wanted to have some fun because I'm bored."

"Not at all," Olga replied.

"That's probably what your friend thinks. But she's wrong, I can assure you. I would be so happy if you waited for me. I'm saying that honestly. I don't know if I'll make it back here. That's not something I can control, but I want you to believe me. If you don't believe me, I won't bother you any more."

Olga was slow in answering, as if she first had to think carefully and maybe even gather her strength. No man had ever said such words to her. She felt afraid, as if a bottomless void had opened in front of her. At her nineteen years of age she still did not know the tricks that women use, the pretending and playing hard to get – the things that come naturally to most women. For her, it was not proving easy to overcome the invisible wall inside her and give a clear yes-or-no answer. By the time she did answer, the American believed that it would never come.

"I believe you," she said.

"And you'll wait for me?"

This question stunned her. She looked around in bewilderment, as if she was hoping that someone would come to her rescue, or as if she were being watched and overheard, and a look of fear flashed across her face. She looked from side to side, uncertain, almost as if she was being pursued and was watching out for her pursuers. Then she gave a faint nod, and remained with her head lowered as if she was afraid of letting him see her eyes.

She really was afraid. She was afraid of her own shadow and ready to hide, or to run off as fast as she could without caring where. It was easy to understand her feelings. Life in the USSR was not at all like life in America. Everything was different. For years, the regime had claimed that foreigners were cunning foes, capable of the greatest villainy, and that one could expect from them only grief and evil plots. Soviet propaganda had relentlessly hammered this idea into their heads, and had achieved its goal: many really believed it, and those who did not believe kept their mouths shut. With time, the country's authorities at all levels came to adopt the view that knowing foreigners, or hobnobbing with them, was something only traitors would do. Falling in love with a foreigner represented the basest betrayal of one's country; it was comparable to spying or sabotage, and was punished severely. One could not expect any mercy.

A look back at history would reveal that from the first years of Soviet rule, the authorities had been distrustful of foreigners and suspected them of mortal sins. In the years of Stalin this distrust had given way to sullen hostility or outright hate, and one would have to be foolhardy indeed to socialize with a foreigner. Olga was well aware of all these prohibitions and strict demands. Now, however, she suddenly forgot all about them. The rules and admonishments vanished from her mind and disappeared without a trace. She was gripped instead by fear and shame, as if she were doing something unworthy, something for which her compatriots would condemn her and nail her to a pillory.

The American lieutenant suddenly stood up and took her in his arms. He kissed her gently, but she hung limply, as if her strength had left her. She seemed to have grown so weak that her legs would not hold her up, and it was hard for her even to think.

"I have to go now," she blurted out, but Creighton took her by the hand and pulled her back like a child.

Olga followed him stiffly. As they walked, they both felt a sense of sorrow and regret, because they would now have to part, whether temporarily or forever. Neither Creighton nor Olga knew what would come next. It was completely uncertain whether they would meet again, and they felt a mixture of weak hope and alarm.

They made their way through the darkness back toward the road. In the open space, the twilight had not yet grown thick. Before they stepped out of the total darkness, the interpreter suddenly grabbed the lieutenant's hand. He turned, and she threw her arms around him and pressed her face to his chest, as if seeking protection. They stood motionlessly, breathlessly, among the willow herbs, an indistinct dark patch resembling a tree or bush. Creighton felt her shoulders tremble. He carefully turned her face toward his and was amazed to find it wet with tears.

"What's wrong?" he asked, but no answer came. The distant lights were reflected in the interpreter's wet eyes. He kissed her, and dried the salty flow of tears with his lips.

Creighton knew that they had no more time. His crew was waiting, and soon the Americans would muster for their flight. Still, he dragged out this goodbye, and, if he could have done so, he would have delayed his departure until the morning. What had happened had left him stunned, and he could not bring himself to part with the interpreter. He knew this parting was inescapable and could be neither delayed nor put off, but how could he leave this woman, who had sought his protection and trusted in him, without a backward glance? Sadness and bitterness ate at his heart.

She knew that she could not, must not, hold him back, but she lacked the strength to take her arms from around him, and she sobbed inconsolably like a child. Her shoulders trembled as if the summer around them had turned bitter cold. Somewhere far off, lights were moving and the sound of motors reached them faintly. Sometimes a car would pass them on the road and its dim headlights would briefly pull grass or bushes out of the darkness. The two figures stood in the shadows of the trees, unseen from the road. Were anyone to come along, whether someone hot on their trail or a random passerby, he would have seen no one. The outburst of madness known as the war hung over their heads, surrounding them on all sides, leaving no room to breathe. The war forcefully intruded on their thoughts and insistently demanded attention, as if they had been sentenced to suffer it and there was no right of appeal.

Neither of them could deny that there was a war going on. The war dictated its own terms. At the same time, the interpreter and the pilot were very aware that if it had not been for the war, they would have never met. The war was the cause, their meeting was its consequence, and they could not have had the latter without the former. Day comes after night, night follows day, one flows from the other, and such consequences follow causes like a thread follows a needle. In peacetime, fate would have never brought them together at all, but the war had arranged their meeting at the right time, in the right place. Still, for the moment, the interpreter and pilot tried to forget all about this.

Time was slipping by. The crews were already assembling. The lieutenant and interpreter both knew that the American would be in trouble if he were late, but they were unable to part from each other.

Olga eventually had her fill of crying. She sighed deeply and wiped away her tears. She kissed Creighton and gently pulled away from him. "You must go. I will wait for you."

He resigned himself to leaving, hard though it was. What choice did he have? He steeled himself, then dashed away at full speed. By midnight the crews were sitting in their planes and starting their engines, and soon afterward they began to take off. After initial maneuvers, the Flying Fortresses assembled into their usual formation and set a course for Romania. Each bomber was loaded, as usual, with eight tons of bombs. They were already flying west when the Mustang fighters arrived from the Mirgorod and Piryatin airfields to provide cover. Near the border, the American formation was joined by Soviet Pe-2 and A-20 bombers, which had been manufactured by the American company Douglas, brought to Fairbanks, Alaska and then gifted to the USSR, and finally flown by Soviet pilots all the way across the country to the front.

After coming together near the front lines, the Soviet and American bombers flew in a single formation toward Galati. None of the crew members knew that at this time, at the other end of Europe, hundreds of heavy strategic bombers based in the British Isles were heading to bomb the Atlantic Wall, Germany's fortifications in northern France. The Allies had long since drawn up plans for landing parties, under the code name Operation Overlord. Amphibious assault vessels were already moving across the English Channel and, under cover of darkness, landing on the sandy beaches of Normandy.

The crew of Creighton's bomber formation would only hear this news the following day, after they had landed at their respective bases: the Americans in the Italian town of Foggia and the Soviets in southern Ukraine behind the front line. Or rather, only those who had been fortunate to make it the whole way would hear the news. On this night, German anti-aircraft fire on the Eastern Front was exceptionally heavy, and moreover, hundreds of the enemy's fighters arrived to intercept the bombers. Though the American and Soviet aerial armada succeeded in bombing its targets in Romania, the Allies' losses were considerable. Many planes fell out of the formation and the bombers' ranks thinned noticeably.

## 17

Returning to Manhattan from JFK Airport took less time than the journey there. Traffic on the roads had diminished by this late hour and there were no longer any traffic jams. We arrived back in the city quickly and without hassle. From the airport, Cindy drove us down Conduit Avenue until we reached Fulton Street, which cuts across Brooklyn, and then we headed west. At the intersection with Lafayette Street we had to negotiate an intricate series of exits and on-ramps to reach the highway over the Brooklyn Bridge.

From the bridge we had a vast view of Manhattan, though at night it was not as attractive and energetic as it had been during the day or evening. The waterfront glowed dimly, the stone warehouses and docks had blackened, and the houses along the bank stared, sullen and blind, out of their black windows. Across the East River, south of the bridge, the lights of an old seaport shone. There, on Pier 17, protruding over the river, a long glass pavilion gleamed, and behind it some old steamboats that had found their eternal resting place there.

At first glance, by night the city seemed dead. The streetlights and the glow from the shop windows illuminated sidewalks now empty of people, and it was hard for me to understand why electricity should be brought to these streets if there was no one around. Among the garbage cans in secluded corners and alleyways, indistinct figures wrapped in rags – homeless people – dozed on pieces of cardboard against the walls. The best places were located next to the vents from underground ventilation shafts, from which a stream of warm air would issue. Occasional taxis passed us, and from time to time we heard a siren wailing from behind the buildings, and a police car would appear, with its colorful flashing lights giving the night a festive quality.

Cindy lived in Greenwich Village. We came down from the bridge, passed City Hall, made our way around Chinatown, then turned north through Soho and crossed Spring Street. Unlike the deserted and barren city streets we had seen before, Greenwich Village was a hive of activity. Crowds of people teemed outside the neighborhood's clubs and theaters. Its cozy restaurants were brightly lit. The shops and souvenir stands were full to bursting, and a hubbub in many languages hung over the bars and cafes.

A sense of unbridled fun reigned in Greenwich Village. It was a real melting pot of languages and colors on a postage stamp of land; one might think that all peoples and nations had been gathered here. A carefree crowd moved past the lovely old buildings, and their conversation and laughter bounced off the glass of the windows and shop displays.

At this late hour, Greenwich Village was a sight to behold. Street musicians played at every step, so that one tune would give way to another, or rather they merged into a loud cacophony that flooded the neighborhood. Everywhere you looked, there were people celebrating the last night of the summer with abandon.

Washington Square was especially incandescent. Bands played on the grass beneath the trees as listeners danced and laughed themselves silly. Everywhere I saw smiling people. One might think that Washington Square was always home to such a carnival.

After the dry and business-like environment of the airport and the joyless, deserted districts we had passed through before, I was bowled over by Greenwich Village. No one here seemed to give a thought to any sadness or grief, they were free of the cares that other people might have. True, fun and sorrow are often close companions, weddings and funerals are neighbors everywhere, and it would be silly to deny that. But none of the revelers in Greenwich Village felt, as I did, a heavy presentiment, they did not notice the threatening signs. No one even suspected what was looming over the horizon. No one shared the heavy and oppressive expectation of the terrible events that we would soon face.

It often happens like that. We sometimes give in to celebration and merriment, and we forget about the pains of others. As we live in the carefree moment, we do not want to think about what might be happening to less fortunate people somewhere out there, yet happiness and misfortune always coexist in the world.

A boisterous crowd moved along the small streets surrounding Washington Square. Our car, driven by Cindy, had slowed to a crawl and could barely get through this unbelievable mass of people. Our car was besieged by drunken revelers, a motley collection of young actors, poets, artists, models, and the visiting tourists who spent whole days in the local bars. Mainly, though, the throng consisted of students having a traditional bash to end their summer vacations. We were their prisoners as they cavorted around us. It was easy to understand how the students felt, for this was the last night of summer, and their long break was over. Everyone was eager to have a last taste of freedom and paint the town red.

As we made our way through the crowd, we found ourselves at the intersection of West Street and the Avenue of the Americas. We drove past the venerable old Jefferson Market Library with its marvelous red-brick tower. By way of Cornelia Street and Leroy Street we reached Saint Luke's Place, which had long been a place of magnificent homes for the wealthy, set among leafy plane trees.

Cindy lived on MacDougal Street behind the wonderful Provincetown Playhouse, which dated from when Greenwich Village really was a village. Even now, on weekdays, Greenwich Village continues to resemble a quiet, provincial town somewhere in America, and one would hardly suspect that the sleepless and buzzing Broadway was just a stone's throw away.

Cindy's spacious apartment had the air of an artist's studio, a resemblance made stronger by its oriel windows. The living room had a fireplace, a bar, and a couple of low sofas and armchairs. After all the stress of the day, we collapsed onto the chairs and stared at the television screen. Cindy turned the channel to CNN, and just to make sure, she turned on the radio as well. Then she offered us a drink to unwind and pass the time. We none of us said anything for a while; it was obvious that each of us was waiting for news. As we listened to the newsreader, we became tense and held our breath, expecting to be told of horror and tragedy.

All this waiting made us weary. At times it seemed impossible to bear it, that this was the worst thing in the world – just waiting minute by minute for bad news to come in. In our minds we vividly imagined the newsreader cutting himself off mid-sentence and then, in a quite different tone of voice, announcing some ghastly tragedy. We were all expecting such news, and we were ready for it, but we still knew that it would come like a sudden and painful blow. It is a bad business, waiting to learn of misfortune.

The television news ended without even a hint of disaster, and Cindy quickly cooked dinner. After we had eaten, we passed the time with the same oppressive feeling of waiting. We drank gin and tonic, watched television, and listened to the radio. All remained quiet in the world, the ongoing war in Afghanistan aside. It was an exceptionally peaceful night –

    

at any rate, no suffering befell any airplane passengers. There had been no crashes, all scheduled flights had proceeded normally. Everyone who took off had landed safely, and we could only be happy for them.

In fact, it was almost as if all newsreaders on every television and radio channel had secretly agreed to talk only of things entirely mundane; they yammered on incessantly. We listened to every news bulletin with our hearts fluttering, trying to make sense of what we were being told.

Cindy eventually grew tired of waiting and worrying, and decided to get some sleep. It had been a nerve-wracking day, but before she retired to her bedroom, she called the airport to ask about Korean Airlines Flight 007. They told her that all was well, the plane was still en route from New York to Anchorage, and on time.

"Maybe your intuition led you astray," Cindy smirked.

"I would be happy if that were the case," I answered, completely sincere. As God was my witness, I was not just saying that to her. If I had been wrong, then all the passengers and crew would make it out alive. If I were right, however, it meant that people would die.

Cindy went to her room, but the rest of us felt unable to go to bed. Michael, the colonel's son, was guilty at having made his father miss the plane. In order to chase away his remorse, he poured himself a whiskey on the rocks, but he simply drank it down hurriedly and refilled his glass. He went at a real gallop, opening up a lead of several lengths, so to speak, over the colonel and me, and of course, ended up drinking too much.

Now rather tipsy, Michael decided to ask me what countries I had traveled in. He livened up when he heard that I had served in Russia's Far East, in the same general area where he now flew. The major turned the conversation to how often he encountered Soviet MiG and Su planes in the skies – he only had to take off and there they were. Michael even knew many of our pilots by name.

The aerial reconnaissance wing, in which the major commanded a fighter squadron, was based at Misawa, in the northeast of the island of Hokkaido, and its work was targeted toward the Sea of Japan, Sea of Okhotsk, Sakhalin, and the Kuril Islands, as well as the Soviet navy's activities in the Pacific north of Japan. The wing had a broad swath of the Russian Far East under its purview. On a daily basis, the major and the men in his squadron carried out low-level flights over Russian naval ships and commercial vessels, they provided cover for American electronic-surveillance planes, and sometimes they themselves would violate Russian airspace so that the reconnaissance planes could intercept Soviet radar signals.

From our side, fighters usually took off from bases close to Vladivostok and Nakhodka. There were, however, also fighter regiments on Sakhalin Island and the southern Kurils. Each regiment had its own assigned area, and whoever was closest to the intruders would take off to intercept them. In terms of the number of planes, a Soviet air regiment was approximately equal to an American wing, though its serviceable planes were always many fewer than needed. The Soviets had to make do with what they had.

After receiving word from the tracking stations, the officers on duty at the Far Eastern Air Defense District's headquarters would decide which regiment was closest, and give the order to intercept. Michael acknowledged that skirmishes in the air happened quite often; as usual, no one on either side wanted to yield. The two countries' forces were generally evenly matched, so each side played on the nerves of the other, and it often took a great effort to be the one to pull out of a collision or to resist opening fire. I thought of how the major had probably met Nikolai Shilin, my patient from Division X, in the skies. Shilin was presently serving in the south of Sakhalin Island and flying over the La Pérouse Strait, which was just a few minutes' flight from Hokkaido, so close in fact that if a pilot so much as blinked he would find himself an unintended guest in the other country.

Shilin and the major had undoubtedly met a few times in the skies, chased each other around in the air, played games of cat and mouse, and performed feats of acrobatics together. Perhaps they had even had each other in their sights – good Lord, how small the world is!

In the middle of the night, Michael and I dozed off in the armchairs, still wearing our street clothes. No news of a plane crash had come through, and we had grown tired of waiting. None of us wanted to call the airport; that would have been a complete waste of time. If something terrible was destined to happen, it was going to happen. I do not know about the United States, but in Russia we have long known that if one expects trouble, it is better to avoid attracting its attention and then perhaps it will pass one by.

According to the schedule, the Boeing 747's flight time from New York to Anchorage was slightly short of six hours, meaning it would land at 11:30 a.m. GMT. That would be 3:30 a.m. in Alaska, 6:30 a.m. in New York, and lunchtime in Moscow. I was awoken by the voice of Colonel Creighton coming from the hallway. The major was sleeping in the armchair opposite me. The colonel was calling the airport. The person on duty told him that Flight 007 was still on schedule. The colonel got through to Korean Airlines, asked a series of questions, and received answers to them.

Colonel Creighton found no reason for concern. He hung up and came back into the room. I closed my eyes and feigned sleep. The colonel had half a mind to curse me for making everyone worry needlessly. However, the man was a pilot and he knew that as long as the plane was still in the air it was better to keep quiet and avoid tempting fate. Still, Colonel Creighton was certain that I had raised the alarm for nothing.

Michael lazily stretched and opened his eyes. "Dad, any news?" he asked.

In a low voice, so as to avoid waking me, the colonel told his son that the Boeing was holding a steady course, all three of the plane's inertial navigation systems and the on-board weather radar were functioning correctly, ground stations were constantly tracking the plane, and the crew were maintaining regular communications with them.

"They say there's no cause for concern," the colonel said. I sensed disapproving glances directed at me; father and son Creighton were clearly annoyed at me for the needless panic.

"Who is this guy anyway?" Michael asked in a less than friendly tone. "How did we get stuck with him?"

"He's from Russia. We met randomly at the hotel when we were having breakfast."

"Why did he come with you to the airport?"

"I asked him to. I needed him to come."

"Dad, seriously?"

I did not want to deceive them and eavesdrop on their conversation, so I was forced to yawn, open my eyes, and pretend that I was waking up. "I'm a doctor, a medical doctor," I told the major. "Among other things, I study people's intuition, the way they seem to foresee certain events."

Naturally, I did not go into how in Division X I studied the intuition of military pilots and had gathered a vast amount of data on noetic symptoms. Statistics had shown that pilots with acute intuition manage to avoid disasters in one third of cases. That is, one third of disasters can be warded off, thanks to pilots' intuition. The percentage could go even higher, but not all pilots who sense a looming threat are able to identify the danger precisely and insist that the flight be canceled.

"I still think you were wrong about this," Colonel Creighton said to me. "Everything's going fine."

"For the time being," I said without adding anything more.

"I hope things will continue to go fine."

"God willing," I agreed.

In Hokkaido, the major lived with his wife and two children in Aomori Prefecture next to the military base. He and his family enjoyed a two-story house with three bedrooms upstairs, a living room and kitchen below, and a big lawn outside the house where his wife planted flowers. On Michael's days off they all went to visit the officers' recreation center, where they had access to a golf course, baseball field, swimming pool, children's playground, beauty salon, a gym, and a restaurant with a bowling alley. While Michael described all this, I thought about Nikolai Shilin, my patient from Division X. How different the two men's lives were, though they had identical jobs and lived near each other, divided only by the La Pérouse Strait.

Yes, they probably had encountered each other in the skies. How fortunate that they had never come to blows.

"Your pilots really know how to spoil our mood," the major complained.

"Who is spoiling whose mood?" I asked. "Are they flying over California?"

The major looked at me, unable to understand what I was getting at. Americans, I have noticed, have a hard time grasping matters of logic and objectivity.

"The Far East is part of our interests," he answered haughtily.

"The whole world is part of your interests," I said. "You come into someone else's home and complain that it's uncomfortable for you there, that the owner is not letting you relax."

The major shrugged evasively and said, "I'll let the politicians handle all that."

"Sure. In fact, I heard they've already reached an agreement."

This surprised the major. "About what?" he asked. His father, too, stared at me and waited for my explanation.

"We're going to set up our own air force bases in Mexico and Canada and carry out flights along your borders around the clock. Naturally, the agreement also involves us violating your airspace. I trust you don't have a problem with that?"

The colonel grinned and said, "I do have a problem with that."

"Just think what a mess that would make," Michael said. "I guess we'd have to bomb those bases mercilessly. You've got to teach the bad guys a lesson."

"I don't think the Canadians and Mexicans would appreciate your bombs," I said, though without much enthusiasm. I always feel that political debates are a waste of breath. One never manages to convince the other party, and all that happens is that people get upset.

"That's their business," the major said. "If they agreed to host your bases, let them deal with it. They knew what they were agreeing to. We'll help them free themselves."

Like many Americans, these two pilots were convinced that it was their divine mission to free people and bring happiness to everyone. Americans are convinced that all mankind needs their help and protection, and they claim that whoever does not agree are bad guys and should be punished.

An awkward silence hung over the living room for a time. When Americans find someone standing up to them, they are generally baffled and wonder what has happened. They are so convinced of their inability to do wrong, their uniqueness and rightness, and they are so sure that they are indispensable, that it boggles the mind. They find it unthinkable that people might really not need them, might be able to manage without them. To make things less awkward, I turned the conversation around to the men's hobbies and what their families liked to do in their spare time.

The major played golf at the club. His children were taken to school in a yellow school bus that would pick them up from home and then bring them back at a set time. Sometimes parties were held at the officers' club, but more often Michael went with his wife and kids to visit his fellow officers, or they invited guests to their own home. Occasionally these families would get in their cars and drive into the mountains or to the beach together for picnics.

"Do you like to play music?" I asked quite unexpectedly.

Michael looked at me with surprise and, then turned silently to look at his father. The colonel shook his head as if to say no, I didn't tell him, and the major turned back to me. "How did you know?" he asked.

"I was just somehow sure that you would play an instrument. A wind instrument like the clarinet, or saxophone, or flute. Maybe the bassoon or oboe…"

"You saw my flute!" The colonel became animated. "And I told you I play!"

"That's right," I agreed. "But you didn't tell me what your son plays."

"You simply guessed. If the father likes to play an instrument, then the son may well like to do so, too."

I decided not to tell them that life is subject to the law of the unity and struggle of opposites, which implies a symmetry that can be observed everywhere in space and time: day and night, plus and minus, hot and cold, yin and yang. If one pilot plays a musical instrument on one side of the La Pérouse Strait, then why shouldn't another pilot on the opposite shore play an instrument? If it were otherwise, then the world would lose its kilter, the scales would be out of balance, the clocks would be off, and history would take another course.

They looked at me as if I were a shaman throwing dust in their eyes, or a charlatan leading them a merry dance. The way a card sharp surreptitiously rigs the deck: his audience is sure they've been cheated, but the man's a master, and none of them manage to catch him in the act.

The truth was, though, they simply did not understand dialectics; they had not really internalized it. For them, Communist ideology was a riddle and an enigma, as was historical and dialectical materialism in general, political economy, and the great Marxist-Leninist teachings. That was, after all, the reason that they ate better than we did, they lived in more comfortable homes, and they were discouraged from espousing worthless dogma and chasing after chimeras.

The major smiled and asked, "Well, our psychic friend, any other guesses for us?"

"Hmm," I said. "Colonel, your son is an independent and headstrong young man. He tries to outdo everyone else. He is a diligent student and a good athlete. He is unwilling to accept help from others and he does not care what they think. He tries to accomplish everything on his own. He showed musical ability early on, and he plays a wind instrument."

After this, no one spoke for quite some time, until father and son had recovered themselves. They looked bewildered, and could not say a word.

"How do you know that?" Colonel Creighton finally asked.

I merely smiled a self-satisfied and enigmatic smile, like a fakir who had successfully performed a trick, and said nothing, so as to maintain the mystery and stoke their interest.

"Did someone tell you that?" the major asked grumpily.

"Who could have told me?"

"Well, I don't know. My dad, or maybe Cindy…" Michael had half a mind to wake his sister up and drag her into the room.

"Relax. Cindy didn't tell me anything."

"So how did you know?"

They looked at me with suspicion, and tried to understand what was going on. Both the major and the colonel were thinking of all the people they knew and hoping to find someone who could have crossed paths with me, or at least knew me slightly. The two men were patently uneasy. My guesses had left them deeply unsettled, as if I had stumbled onto some family secret that no one else knew about. Now father and son were trying to figure out what this was all about, and both were inclined to think that it augured nothing good.

"Don't worry. My conclusions were merely the result of observing you," I said in a friendly tone, so that I would not inflame their suspicions or attract their hostility.

"Are you Sherlock Holmes?" the colonel teased.

"Almost. His creator Arthur Conan Doyle was also a doctor. Observing people closely is simply something that comes with the job."

They were still struggling with doubts, however. Both of them looked at me with distrust, as if they were expecting some trick. Once a man's reputation is tarnished, it is difficult to set it right again.

Gradually, the night-time revelry on the Greenwich Village streets died down. The noise diminished, and the last people parted, each going their own way. Now it was truly the middle of the night, and a calm, as vast as a cathedral, hung over the buildings and streets. Through the window I could see the streetlights of Greenwich Village, burning without particularly illuminating anything. They made only bright pinpoints, like needles in the proverbial haystack of the darkness. The night was right outside the apartment's windows, as if one could reach out and touch it. It towered above the city, the further away, the higher. Next to the low buildings and the roofs, skyscrapers glimmered mysteriously, like the pipes of a gigantic organ silent in the darkness.

New York, or the Big Apple as its inhabitants called it, was vast, tall, and stately, but the night could envelop all of it, entire, all its skyscrapers, roads, bridges, and embankments. While I was studying this night-time scene, the colonel took his flute from its case and raised it to his lips. His fingers ran over the keys and he ran up and down an octave. A weightless, airy sound drifted over the room like down; it floated out of the window and dissipated, swaying on a branch. The colonel paused for a moment, then the flute gave a squeak like a baby crying softly. Its voice quivered, sighed, muttered, murmured, as if someone were hoarsely praying to the Almighty that every wayfarer by land, sea, or air might reach his destination safely. I seemed to catch something familiar in the melody, as if I had heard it somewhere before, so long ago that I could not remember when.

The flute anxiously appealed to the heavens, its strong voice sweeping through the room and hovering above the city. Sometimes it sank in exhaustion or, like a string with a weight tied to it, it would suddenly break off, but a faint reverberation hung in space afterward.

The colonel finished playing and put the flute back into its narrow case. "Still another three hours until the jumbo lands in Anchorage," he said. "Cindy's sleeping, and I think we should get some rest too." The colonel disappeared into another room.

The major got up and was about to leave, but then he changed his mind and stretched out on the living room sofa, as if he was afraid to leave me alone. It was understandable. After all, the sideboard held fine china, the family silver, and expensive curios. How could they leave me unattended, a stranger who had come directly from Moscow on some unknown business? If they had known the real reason that had brought me to New York, we would have never chatted at all; they would have called the police at once.

I turned off the light, lay down on the other sofa, and soon fell asleep like a man whose conscience is clear, but while I slept I could sense that the major was not sleeping: in the silence, his vigilant gaze pierced through the darkness. The sensation woke me. I opened my eyes and saw that I was right: the other man's gaze lay on my face like a heavy hand. The major was staring at me intently, as if he wanted to get into my dreams and eavesdrop on my internal monologue. When he noticed that I had woken up, he looked away and pensively studied the ceiling.

"Good morning," I said, rubbing my face with my hand. "Any news?"

"I don't know." The major seemed to be in a gloomy mood. Like an attentive sentry on guard, he had apparently not slept a wink that night. The latest news reports made no mention of any airplane disasters. Hearing the newsreader's voice coming from the television, Colonel Creighton came out in his dressing gown and stood unmoving as he listened to the news. The major picked up the phone and dialed the number of Korean Airlines.

Meanwhile, dawn came. The last day of summer drifted sleepily over New York and snuck up outside the apartment's windows. Early birds perched on the nearby trees, turtle doves cooed somewhere, and from far away, still barely audible, we heard the bustle of the streets. A fresh morning breeze blew through the blinds of the open balcony door, and we caught a whiff of the approaching fall, though it was obvious that the sun would subsequently warm the air and the Indian summer would envelope the city in heat.

The major got through to Korean Airlines and questioned them closely. He knew the Anchorage airport well, as he had been in Alaska's state capital several times. Before the colonel's son had been assigned to Misawa Air Base in Japan, when he still held the rank of captain, he had commanded a group of fighters at the base in Elmendorf near Anchorage. When his family flew south to other states they used the Anchorage airport, and the airport's runway served as a place for emergency landing, so the major knew it like the back of his hand.

The major hung up and looked around at us. "The plane has just landed in Anchorage. There's nothing to report: the passengers and crew are fine, and there were no problems. Now the plane is undergoing an inspection." He looked at me pointedly as if to ask, what do you think of that?

"There's still time," I said humbly, not wanting to ruffle anyone's feathers. "Let's talk again when it arrives in Seoul."

"Are you telling me you're still worried?" Cindy had appeared a minute before, but she was still standing in the doorway. Sleepy, and clad in a white terrycloth dressing gown, she was no less attractive than the evening before; indeed, I would say that she looked even better. "My brother's called the airline."

"It is not as if the airline would tell you about their problems." What else could I say? The alarm bells had not gone quiet; on the contrary, they were ringing loud and clear against the background noise. I sat motionless and listened more closely, trying to tune in to the signal. I was tempted simply to brush it off and forget about it, come what may. I would have readily admitted my mistake and repented of the whole thing, but how could I, when the signal was growing ever stronger and the danger was apparent, not giving me even a minute of peace?

"Fine, if you don't believe the airline, let's call the airport in Anchorage." Colonel Creighton picked up the phone and quickly got through to the airport's information desk. They confirmed what he had been told before: the flight from New York had gone smoothly, the plane was fine, the weather had been favorable, and the passengers had landed on schedule.

The colonel's call did not particularly sway my opinion. The airport's information desk would only give out good information, that much was obvious. That the flight had landed on time was, by the way, false: as I later confirmed, it arrived half an hour late.

In that sleepy northern airport, strange events happened that at the time I did not know of, and could hardly even have guessed at. I found out the details much later; for now, I simply remained tormented by anxiety. In essence, after the plane had landed at Anchorage, the crew made a note in their logbook that the on-board radio had functioned poorly. As soon as the sleepy passengers had staggered off into the transit area, technicians from the ground service came on board and set to work repairing the radio. Who knew, however, who these people really were and what kind of work they ended up doing. Whatever it was, these unknown workers opened up the equipment, painstakingly searched for the cause of the malfunction, and dug around deep in the internals while the plane was parked. It is noteworthy that the plane's departure from Anchorage was thus delayed, but no one gave a reason for the delay to the passengers.

Be that as it may, neither Korean Airlines in New York, nor the information desk at Anchorage airport had any bad news to break to us. Colonel Steven Creighton and his son Michael Creighton received entirely pleasant answers and were completely satisfied, but I remained unconvinced.

"I would like to say something to make everyone feel at ease, but forgive me, I can't," I said meekly. "I still feel the same heavy premonition, even more strongly than before. I'd love to be wrong, but the plane's still going to fly for another eight hours. If it lands safely in Seoul, we can feel relieved. I'll be happy if nothing happens."

The three of them listened to me impassively without saying a word. This was a polite and tactful family. Yet I got the impression that they genuinely hated me, for I had brought trouble to their family, brought them so much stress, and augured bad news, as if I wanted to jinx them. They nevertheless remained silent. I have always been amazed at the restraint and patience of foreigners, and this time I too was amazed.

After all, this was America, and America is not Russia, where somebody would have already lost his temper, struck the table with his fist, unleashed a torrent of profanity, and told me to go straight to hell. In America, everything was decent, reasonable, and governed by common sense; civility and tolerance reigned. Unlike Russia, America was not a difficult country to understand.

   

**18**

In Italy the lieutenant was in quite a state. The crew of his Flying Fortress had spent a sleepless night in the skies above southern Europe, before finally snatching some sleep and then setting off for all the various wine cellars and dive bars that Foggia offered. Italian wine was so cheap that the Americans felt awkward at being so rich in such a poor country. Later, having emboldened themselves with drink, the Americans roamed the narrow, medieval cobblestone streets, now deserted in the midday heat as if a plague had swept through.

The heat wore the Americans down, too. They walked around and among the old houses in search of entertainment. The stones, heated by the sun, seemed to glow red-hot, while in the enticing darkness behind the closed shutters, local life went on unknown to those outside. By evening, the heat abated, the local residents emerged from their homes to get some fresh air, and the city came to life. The Americans would usually be set upon by the local young ladies, who would each take a man off somewhere. Before the lieutenant had flown to Poltava, he had often spent time with a lively dark-haired waitress from a trattoria on the outskirts of town.

Behind the houses with their tiled roofs stretched well-kept vineyards, in places bordering on pine groves. The lieutenant's lady friend would usually take him to an abandoned sheepfold. The stony path twisted and turned among the thick evergreen shrubs, which barred the way better than any guard post could.

More often, Creighton saw a woman from his own country who held the rank of sergeant and worked as a clerk. Sergeant Tracy was held in universal esteem by the men at the base; she looked dashing in her US Army Air Force uniform. Certain of the officers were prepared to do anything for her, but Sergeant Tracy rebuffed all these suitors and remained faithful to Creighton as if she were his devoted wife. Unlike the wanton Italian girl, Tracy guarded her chastity, apparently in the hope that their relationship would not end as soon as the war did.

However, since his flight to Russia, Steven Creighton was a changed man. It was as if he had been replaced by someone completely different. Even when he was thoroughly drunk, he did not go to visit the girl from the trattoria, and he seemed to have forgotten all about Sergeant Tracy as well. Obviously, the Flying Fortress crew noticed this striking change: their copilot was lovesick like a teenager, as if he was being consumed by some mysterious illness. Every day that passed before their next flight out, Lieutenant Creighton was pining away, and it was painful for the crew to watch. He was literally lovesick, and his comrades thought that maybe they should get him to a doctor.

The Flying Fortress group of the 15th Air Force based in Italy was scheduled to make another run in several days. Normandy had seen some fierce fighting, and the Allies there, having successfully landed and established themselves, were gradually expanding their foothold. Over these days, the German forces across Europe increased their air defense and the barrage of anti-aircraft fire grew much heavier. As soon as the bombers took off, they would be met by German fighters coming at them like savage dogs unleashed, and the Allies' air forces suffered substantial losses. Hundreds of planes would set out every day, as they had always done, but not all of them would make it back to their bases.

On the night that the Americans were scheduled to make their second shuttle run, in the early morning hours, the interpreter Olga Shilina ran to the airfield. She was in a frantic state. In recent days, the staff had talked about nothing else except that the Germans would soon be exacting their revenge for the heavy bombing. According to reconnaissance and radio intercepts, the Germans' entire air force and air defense was preparing to strike. They would not allow the Allies to attack with impunity again.

Among the command at the Poltava, Mirgorod, and Piryatin airfields where the bombers and American escorting fighters would land, everyone knew what those German preparations portended. The Americans were expected to arrive by morning, but how many planes would make it in the end, how many would manage to cross the front lines, and what the losses would be, no one could tell.

The short June night was coming to an end. In the sky over the landing strip designated for the Flying Fortresses, a few pale stars still twinkled, fading toward the east, but the west was still plunged into twilight. Clumps of mist hung over the airfield.

Huddled against the cold, the interpreter waited with a heavy heart for dawn to come. The high, uncut grass at the edges of the airfield stood motionless, as if the individual blades of grass were frozen in fear and listening hard for the sounds of the new day. As was usual in this now godless country, the interpreter did not know any prayers. She did not even know how to pray, but if anyone had asked her what was troubling her, she would have realized to her astonishment that she had been silently repeating words to herself, addressed to who knows whom: let them come back safe, please don't let them be shot down!

If anyone had told the interpreter that what she was doing was praying, she would not have believed it. She was shaking, but not because of the cold pre-dawn air; she simply could not control her anxiety. From the time when the American had left, flying off in his plane, Olga had spent every day in a state of unease, and now the closer the dawn came, the more anxious and afraid she felt. Even if the junior lieutenant had stayed in her warm bed, under her blanket, the fever would not have left her: Olga knew no peace and would never have managed to fall asleep.

In short, Junior Lieutenant Shilina was unable to stay in bed; sleep never came. Occasionally she would forget it all for a moment as she lay in bed, as if she was falling into some abyss, but she would quickly come back to herself with a start and reach frantically for her watch. It was still dark outside her window when finally the waiting became unbearable. She sat up on her mattress and began to get dressed.

"What's going on?" The clear, sleepless voice of her friend came through the silence, as if Kapitolina had been standing a vigilant watch all night.

"I can't sleep," the interpreter answered, though she already knew what to expect.

"Where are you going?!" Her friend's iron voice was stern and severe, like a speaker on the radio announcing an emergency.

"I'm going out for some fresh air," the junior lieutenant explained. "It's stuffy in here."

This explanation did not get past her friend, however; Kapitolina found it preposterous. "If it's stuffy, you can open the window," she said. "It's nothing to do with fresh air. You've decided to go and meet him."

Olga said nothing. She merely continued to get dressed.

Kapitolina tore her head away from her pillow and propped herself up on an elbow. "Olga, don't you realize that you can't do this?"

"What's wrong?"

"You've completely lost your head. Snap out of it!"

"I don't understand what you're talking about," the lieutenant said cautiously, trying to avoid provoking her friend further.

It was too late, however. Kapitolina was already burning with rage. "You've got to understand! He's an American. Don't you see? An American!" She whispered these words hotly, as if accusing Creighton of a mortal sin. "How can you be so irresponsible? If it weren't for Germany, they'd be our enemies. America!" Kapitolina's nostrils flared. "You think there's something special between you? You're wrong! He doesn't really care about you. They're all like that, just looking for an easy fling! Well, who can blame them, if there are girls as stupid as you around!"

"Kapitolina, you're blowing this out of proportion. Nothing's going on."

"Nothing?! Are you blind? Well, they can't fool me. I can see everything. He'll be the ruin of you!" Kapitolina said this with an anguish in her voice, like a tragic actress.

"Kapitolina…" The junior lieutenant said reproachfully, trying to make her friend see reason.

"I know what I'm talking about! Do you want to get into trouble?"

"What trouble? Why?"

"You think they haven't noticed? Someone has probably already reported you. You need to stop before you do something foolish…" Kapitolina fell silent and breathed heavily in the darkness, as if she had run a great distance and was now winded. Finally, she said resolutely, "I'm not letting you go anywhere!"

"I can make up my own mind," countered the interpreter.

"You don't know what you're doing. I've got to save you." Kapitolina leaped up and snatched the key from the lock. She returned to her bed and wrapped herself in her blanket with her back to the wall. "If you aren't stopped, you could betray everyone!"

"Who would I betray?" Olga asked, her voice starting to quiver. She was now close to tears.

"Everyone! Me! Our country! Our whole class! Comrade Stalin! Your parents!"

"Kapitolina… We're friends…" Olga began.

Kapitolina interrupted her. "Well, thank you so much for remembering!"

"We're friends, but that doesn't mean that you can talk such nonsense. If you don't give me the key, I'm going to climb out the window."

"You're going to ruin your whole life! What would your parents say? Before we left I promised them we would always stick together. They trusted me. How can I ever look them in the eye again if they get you?"

"If who gets me?"

"If they arrest you!"

"For what? What are you talking about, Kapitolina? No one's going to complain about an interpreter meeting the crew she's assigned to. You could be doing it, too. And don't forget about our language practice: if we don't talk to them, we're not going to improve our English. We're missing the last year of our studies by being here, and we haven't ever had any actual practice with English speakers."

A silence fell over the room. Outside, dogs barked, and trucks could be heard delivering fuel and ammunition to the airfield. Kapitolina drew her hand from under the blanket and put the key on her sheet. "Wait for me. I'll get dressed," she said in an exaggeratedly firm and lecturing voice, like a schoolmarm speaking to a dull pupil.

Olga took the key, but did not wait for her friend. Opening the door, she walked out without a word and quietly closed the door behind her. She tiptoed along the hallway so as to not awaken her neighbors, went down the steps, and plunged into the early-morning fog. For a short while she could still be seen, but soon her blurry outline was lost and the night swallowed her up entirely.

The sky to the west suddenly lit up, erupting into flames: a heavy battle was going on over the front lines. The Americans had lost dozens of planes to anti-aircraft fire while the Flying Fortresses from the 15th Air Force were bombing Romania, and on top of that, the Germans had ordered their Messerschmitt fighters to take off from the airfields at the front. The German fighters fiercely darted around the bomber formation, burning with the desire to destroy it.

Fortunately for the Americans, the Germans did not succeed in destroying the whole formation. Mustang fighters provided the bombers with cover, tangling with the Messerschmitts over the front line. Nonetheless, several bombers were lost when the Mustangs began one by one to run out of fuel and drop out of the battle, heading back to their bases.

As soon as the number of fighters protecting the formation started to drop, the Messerschmitts flew in hot on the bombers' tails. The Flying Fortresses maintained their formation, and their on-board machine guns and cannons stopped the Germans from entering deep among them. The Messerschmitts could only bite into the edges of the formation. Soon, Soviet fighters too came flying in from nearby airfields to make up for the departed Mustangs. It was not long before the German fighters were driven away.

The interpreter waited, agitated, for dawn to come. Headquarters still did not know the Americans' losses, but according to reports from the front where the battle had raged, they had been significant.

Night still held sway, but dawn was quietly creeping up from the east. In the nearby woods, birds were already chirping, and cock crows could be heard from the neighboring village of Rybnitsa. The darkness above the airfield gradually paled, so slowly as to be imperceptible, as if thick ink were being diluted with water. The night slackened its grip, then let go entirely, and the rose red of dawn touched the sky in the east, dim and smoldering like an icy flame.

So began yet another day of the war. The interpreter did not know what it would bring, or whether she would see the man who had been haunting her thoughts over recent days and nights. Worst of all, naturally, was the uncertainty and waiting. It pulled at Olga's heart, and it took all her strength just to bear it. Sometimes it seemed to her that she was dreaming a strange dream, that the American had been no more than part of her dream, and that she had only to wake up and there would be no one there, just a few ghostly memories of Creighton flickering in her memory. As soon as this thought came into her mind, she felt an abyss looming before her and her world turned black.

Miserably, the junior lieutenant thought of how little depended on them, how little influence they had. Regardless of whether or not anyone was there to see it, days would give way to nights, dawns to dusks, and the sun would run its course across the sky. Birds would sing, trees would blossom or drop their leaves, and life would go on independent of human beings according to its age-old laws. If the American did not arrive today, nothing around would change, everything would stay as it was; but what about her: what would she do, how would she survive, if her waiting was in vain? That the American might not make it back safely was unbearable.

Meanwhile, the ground crew appeared at the edge of the airfield. They brought ambulances and fire trucks, lights flashing. The number of people around began to grow. Olga could hear their voices, and she vaguely glimpsed their movements in the darkness. Suddenly everyone froze, fell silent, and listened closely: in the stillness, above the murk in the west where night was still in full force, they heard a weak hum. The longer they listened, the more they were aware of it, and soon it expanded to fill the sky and the whole area around them.

The interpreter strained to catch the sound. The hum was coming from way off, further than they could see. Everyone remained quiet and motionless for a moment, and then the airfield returned to its usual state of activity. The ground crew took their places alongside the runway. A few Studebaker trucks arrived and discharged American aircraft technicians. Soon a convoy of staff jeeps pulled up at high speed and braked sharply. General Alfred Kessler, the air base's commander on the American side, got out of the first jeep. He was followed by his deputy Colonel Cullen.

While all this hustle and bustle went on, the distant hum grew closer and more distinct, like an immense weight over the earth. By this time dawn was breaking over the airfield, and the vehicles, trees and people were now clearly emerging from the darkness. Every object took on a clear shape and appearance, and the wider environs of the airbase were revealed.

The mixed crowd of Russians and Americans became excited as the day grew brighter. Their faces were all turned toward the west, and they peered into the gloom still covering the horizon. The far western end of the airfield was wrapped in a whitish mist. Meanwhile, the crowd grew tense and the interpreter's anxiety increased. The waiting was unbearable, she did not have the strength for it any more.

The rapt crowd, like a single organism with myriad eyes, stared into the west. The interpreter waited, hardly breathing, and just when it seemed that they could expect nothing but the persistent hum, a few dark dots emerged from the thick veil over the west. They cut through the far-off forests and grew closer, took on size, became clearer, and soon seemed like big birds.

The dots were soon transformed into airplanes, and then new dots appeared behind them. They had been born from the night like flies from the humid environment of a forest. The initial wave of planes was already coming in low and gradually losing altitude, and others followed them in a numberless flock. The first planes cut through the fog, emerged from it, and landed one by one. Once they reached the end of the runway, they immediately turned onto the taxiway and parked, where the technicians and mechanics awaited.

The interpreter watched this intently. Her gaze settled on every plane, followed it until the end of the runway, and then turned to the next plane, all in the hope of spotting Creighton's, though in fact the bombers were indistinguishable one from another. From the conversations in the crowd, the junior lieutenant understood that many planes were missing from the bomber group.

That was the most horrific thing. The junior lieutenant looked frantically around the airfield. New planes were emerging in a scattered formation from the gloom in the west, and though there were a lot of them, they were many fewer in number than on the first shuttle run. The only thing the crowd awaiting the planes was talking about were the losses. No one knew precise figures, of course, but a keen eye could readily spot the holes in the group. The waiting crowd added the planes up and knew they were too few. It was a wretched picture.

All they could do at first was guess at the losses from a quick look at the arrivals; after all, some of the men might have managed to parachute out and survive. The men who were definitely lost were those whose planes had exploded before the very eyes of their neighbors in the formation. Sometimes a plane could stay in the air for long enough after being hit to make an emergency landing, if the crew could only find a field, meadow, or perhaps a road.

It was a complete lottery. Sometimes a man would be fortunate, lady luck would smile on him, but generally the men on bombing runs had only a slim chance of surviving. Sooner or later they could expect to meet a tragic end. When it came to fighter planes, survival was more often in the pilots' own hands, and came down to their skills and training. For bombers, by contrast, survival was a matter of blind fate. During carpet bombing campaigns, there was little that the crew had control over. They could maintain their formation, heading, or altitude, but whether they would be hit or emerge unscathed was something that only God knew. They could only put their trust in Him.

The interpreter felt faint. The conversations of the people around her had left her numb with fear. At times she felt that she would not bear it and would collapse right then and there. The crews of the planes that had already landed were now walking toward the base, but she did not see Lieutenant Creighton anywhere among them. He was not there, he was not there! She could barely hold herself up.

From her position on the roadside, she stared intently at the Americans. The crews walked by her and her gaze passed helplessly over their faces. She did not distinguish between the crewmen, they seemed no more than an indistinct blur, every one with the same face. The strong wind from the propellers lifted dust over the earth. The dust rose up and spun in a whirlwind, blotting out the dawn and bringing tears to her eyes. The high, uncut grass to the side of the steel-plate runway was stirred, too, and the vegetation fluttered about like the waters of the sea in stormy weather.

The junior lieutenant turned her back to the wind and, hunched over, kept a grip on her skirt and her uniform cap. Soon, however, the wind slackened, and the interpreter stood up straight again and smoothed her uniform. As she turned around, she gasped: Steven Creighton was standing before her only a few steps away. It was so sudden, so unexpected, that the interpreter could only gasp wordlessly. The American looked at her without speaking, but a faint smile appeared on his lips. So it is, sometimes, when we wait for something, burning with impatience, and suddenly the wait is over and the shock of it breaks our stupor.

Olga had waited for him so long, she had been so concerned for his safety, that now she was unable to control herself: tears came to her eyes and she stood there frozen, unable to make a sound as if she had lost the ability to speak. The two of them had the sense – or good fortune – not to rush to meet each other, otherwise the heavy hand of their superiors would have come down upon them. There were too many eyes around them, American and Soviet shepherds watching keenly over their flocks so that they would not lose a single sheep to the other side. Perhaps they were already on someone's watchlist, but for the time being they were unaware of it, and their meeting seemed to be merely a chance one.

The American smiled. "How are you doing, Miss Olga?" he asked.

The interpreter smiled through her tears and sighed with relief, like a child who has suddenly had enough of crying.

She did not manage to answer him, however, for her friend Kapitolina appeared out of nowhere and stared at the two with disdain, looking from one to the other as if she had wanted to catch them in the act. "Olga," she said in a firm voice, "they're waiting for us. They told me to come and find you."

"Who told you?" the junior lieutenant asked.

"They're getting all the interpreters together for a briefing."

"What does she want?" The American winced, as if at a toothache.

"She said they're waiting for us," the junior lieutenant translated.

"Why can't she leave us alone?" Creighton looked at Kapitolina as if he found her an annoyance requiring rapid disposal.

"Where are we meeting?" Olga asked her friend.

"In the mess hall," Kapitolina answered, and then added with exaggerated emphasis, "The chief Communist Party officer has ordered this briefing." She stood her ground, clearly having no intention of leaving Olga and Creighton alone.

The other crewmen from Creighton's Flying Fortress were waiting at the roadside for their copilot. They noticed that Steven needed help, so they came over as a whole group to greet the lady interpreters. Their flight mechanic, a black man, pulled a funny face, his huge eyes with blindly bright whites seeming to take up half of his face. The crew joked in their usual way, but somehow without enthusiasm; everyone looked worn out. The past night had been an unusually challenging one and hard on everyone. Their group had suffered heavy losses, and now there was little room for fun when sleep was pulling at them and their spirits were low. The crew and the interpreters headed together for the base settlement. The black mechanic, continuing to grimace foolishly, walked behind Kapitolina and pretended to be in amorous pursuit of her.

Breakfast, as usual, began with a prayer. The crews prayed for the men who had been lost, for the repose of their souls. They also prayed for those who had been shot down but might have survived. The interpreter surveyed the vast mess hall and her heart sank: she could readily see how many tables now stood empty in the mess hall, a precise calculation of the losses that the Americans had suffered.

On the first shuttle run, each crew had occupied its own table. The crews were grouped by wings, and the big space had been packed from one wall to the other. Today the waitresses had put a white tablecloth over every table, they had set out cutlery, and provided bread, coffee or tea, but many of the tables were shockingly empty. No one came to sit at them. The missing crews were obvious at a glance.

Olga's faithful friend only added fuel to the fire. Kapitolina could not imagine what an empty table might mean and, as they walked into the mess hall, she blinked in surprise. "Why are there so many empty tables?" She stared dumbly, as if she simply could not fathom what had happened.

"Those are the tables of crews that were shot down," Olga replied. She took a close look around at the crews present, and thought about how their chairs and tables, too, might be empty after the next shuttle run. The risks that they were running were now manifest to her in the mess hall. Olga had a clear vision of Creighton's table becoming empty and it was too much to bear, and her legs grew weak under her.

During that day the American copilot and the Soviet interpreter saw each other only fleetingly, at a distance, as they each went about their business. At every moment, Olga was aware that Creighton was here at the base, and the knowledge that he was close by and safe reassured her.

After breakfast, the crews went off to get some sleep. Command spent the entire day poring over aerial photography in order to determine targets for the bombers' next journey. The interpreters, as they had been the previous week, were in heavy demand, and so Junior Lieutenant Shilina managed to meet with Lieutenant Creighton only briefly before dinner, when a break was called in the staff room.

   

By this time, the crews had snatched enough rest and the Americans were waiting for Olga outside the door to the staff room. As soon as she appeared, they smiled in greeting. Pilot Andrew Eddington, as the senior among the crew, saluted her, while Lieutenant Creighton beamed to see her. Olga, too, was unable to conceal her delight, and her happy face would have stood out in any crowd. Yet had a secret informant suspected them of anything, nothing could have been proven, for after all, dealing with the American crews was part of the interpreters' official duties.

The crew accompanied the two lovers like a retinue, but as soon as they had walked for some distance, the interpreter and copilot immediately ran off and disappeared from sight. As soon as Creighton and Olga found themselves alone, the American drew from his breast pocket the snapshots that his crew's gunner had taken the week before. He had photographed them together and separately against the background of the bomber, and he had captured them, smiling and young, enjoying a fleeting respite from the war.

"These are for you, and these are for me," Creighton, handing her some photos. He carefully put his own back into his breast pocket. "Now I'll always have you with me."

═══ 19 ═══

Cindy had time to make coffee and toast while we were waiting for the morning news. We ate breakfast, but our mood was not lightened. I felt just as guilty as before that I was ruining these people's lives. That is how things actually were: I retained some hope that Korean Airlines Flight 007 on the route New York – Anchorage – Seoul would make it safely, but I could not offer any reassurance to anyone, for I still felt the alarm being sounded across space, though no one except me could hear it.

The signal was even stronger now, which was easy to understand: my sleep had sharpened the workings of my unconscious and boosted my intuition. Operators at Division X always tried to sleep before their experiments. After my night's sleep, I was picking up increasingly strong negative signals, though I could do nothing to alter the course of events. Events were pre-determined, rolling unstoppable like a train on rails, and no one could prevent or influence them. I would have given anything to be proved wrong – it is not an enviable lot to serve as a messenger of disaster, and it is no wonder that such people were often put to death in the ancient world.

Michael suddenly spoke up. "I think our prophet friend here has led us astray."

"Why would I do that?" I asked.

"I don't know, dammit! I have no idea. But you were predicting doom in JFK, and what happened? They landed just fine in Anchorage! And now you're saying there's still time. That flight to Anchorage was a good test. The plane is in working order, the weather along the whole route is great. There are no terrorists on board. What more do you want?"

Colonel Creighton nodded. "Michael's right," he said.

"If nothing happens, then I'll be just as happy as you." That was all I could say in my own defense; I could not find any other words.

Meanwhile, something was happening in the world that none of us knew then, or even suspected. Across the Americans' entire network of electronic surveillance, led by the National Security Agency headquartered at Fort Mead in Maryland, all units were ordered to be in a state of readiness. That night, only the most experienced personnel were assigned duty at the electronic-monitoring stations in Alaska, on the nearby islands of Nunivak and Adak, and on board ships in the Pacific Ocean. At the Elmendorf, Ladd, Eielson, and Davis air force bases, in the Aleutian Islands, in South Korea, and on Hokkaido, the commanding officers and their most talented staff did not head home at the end of the day as usual, but instead telephoned their families to say they were going to be working late and did not know when they would be home.

I learned of all this much later, when we at Division X traced events back. While all this was happening on that night when August gave way to September, and summer to fall, the Boeing 747 designated as Flight KAL-007 had landed, as Major Creighton had been told by the New York and Anchorage airports, at 2:30 a.m. local time. Anchorage airport awoke from its slumber and the jumbo jet proceeded along the taxiway and pulled up outside Gate 2H. It took seven minutes for the plane to reach the gate after it had landed.

The passengers, weary after the six-hour flight from New York, made their way down the stairs and walked toward the transit hall. The two or three dozen payphones there immediately prodded the sleepy passengers into action, and they began making calls. The airport came to life, with passengers heading for the bar or jabbering into the phones. A hubbub in many languages hung like a cloud over the vast space of the terminal.

Anchorage airport was little different from other airports, in spite of its location in Alaska, in the far north, that legendary territory above the Arctic Circle with its echoes of Jack London, dogsleds, and the gold rush of a century before. The terminal building, with its transparent glass walls in a metal framework, resembled an aquarium. The building looked out on a small plaza with a parking lot; located nearby were a bus stop and taxi stand.

Inside the terminal, the transit hall's floor was covered with light carpeting. Powerful air purifiers maintained a pleasant, fresh smell. The ground floor was taken up, as usual in airports, by retail outlets. Prominent among these was a souvenir shop selling, as its sign proclaimed, "Native" Eskimo products – items made by the local indigenous peoples. This souvenir shop was the first stop for many of the passengers, and it grew crowded and noisy with a multilingual din.

On the next floor up, the airline offices were located, including that of Korean Airlines. They were reached by means of wide glass-encased elevators, an escalator, or via three staircases leading up from the ground floor. All the passengers booked on Flight KAL-007 intended to go on to Seoul, with the exception of one family of four people – two adults, two children – who quickly left the transit area. The father, a baggage handler for Alaska International Airlines, had been visiting his parents in New York with his wife and two children, and now they had to make their way from the airport to the city in the middle of the night.

My forebodings had not concerned this baggage handler and his family. Lady luck is capricious and her ways are hard to fathom. She had smiled on this man and his family, and thus they managed to make it out alive. The American congressman Larry McDonald, on the other hand, had decided to take flight KAL-007 at literally the last minute: his ticket was originally for another flight. Like Steven Creighton, the congressman had been invited to Seoul for the celebration of the thirtieth anniversary of the treaty between the USA and South Korea. McDonald was flying to Seoul from Atlanta, Georgia, but bad weather had forced his plane to land in Baltimore instead of New York, and so the congressman had missed his connection. He had been obliged to board KAL-007 instead.

I later thought about Colonel Creighton and his son Michael, about how they were fated to miss their flight. I also thought about the crew members who stayed behind in Anchorage. For the onward flight to Seoul they were replaced by another crew, who had come in from Toronto and caught three hours of sleep in the quarters of Korean Airlines. A further six Korean Airlines personnel also boarded Flight 007 in Anchorage. They were not on duty during the flight; they had been given free passage to Gimpo International Airport outside Seoul so that they would be in place to work the return flight from Seoul to New York.

In Russia we often say that a person cannot escape fate. In other words, no matter how you shuffle the deck, each person will draw the card meant for him or her. This is a question that has tormented me to this day: can we cheat fate? Is it really impossible to trick it? Surely all one would have to do would be to take a single step to the side, or arrive somewhere one minute earlier or later, and everything would turn out differently, would it not?

The passengers walked around the hall to stretch their legs; they sat in the brightly colored chairs; they passed the time at the bar; they crowded around the souvenir shops with their Eskimo wares; or they made phone calls to people all over the world, as is common in airports. Some of the people telephoning were doing so from habit – sending a quick word from the road. Others called to say they were on schedule; others again discussed important matters that could not be put off. Still others… what varied reasons people have for calling!

If someone had thought to observe this lively crowd, he might have noticed among it a solitary and somber Korean: a biophysicist and university professor from Pittsburgh who was flying to Seoul for his mother's funeral.

An hour and twenty minutes before take-off from Anchorage, the relief crew arrived at the airport on their shuttle bus. As soon as they arrived, the Korean Airlines employee responsible for liaison with air traffic control assembled everyone in the airline's office on the second floor and asked the crew to amend the programmed flight plan. The slight delay in arriving at Anchorage had not been foreseen when the plan had originally been drawn up, so a revision was required.

The crew received their orders from a tall, thin Korean man in a well-tailored company uniform. Puny and narrow-shouldered, in a fitted, single-breasted suit with a white shirt and tie, the flight's captain Chun Byung-in resembled a girl in a man's suit: a round face with delicate features, thin lips, and small dark eyes, and thick black hair neatly combed. The left side of his jacket was adorned with lace resembling outstretched eagle's wings, a round badge was pinned to his lapel, an engraved pin hung on his right breast, and his sleeves were encircled by four shiny captain's stripes.

Together with the Korean Airlines dispatcher, Captain Chun Byung-in discussed their flight assignment. Years and countless investigations later, no one knows what role Captain Chun Byung-in played in this ill-fated flight. Did he prepare for it in advance? Did he receive orders? Did he decide the finer details of the route? Was he aware of the danger, did he feel foreboding or sense the inevitable risk? We can only speculate, without expecting any answers.

Many people to this day still go over and over certain persistent questions: did Captain Chun Byung-in agree to it, or was he forced? Could he have refused, did he have any choice? Were the pilot and passengers simply being used as pawns in someone else's game?

It is hard to believe that Captain Chun Byung-in was unaware of what was going on. Others in the crew – a flight attendant, for example, or a mechanic – may well have known nothing; they would not normally be entrusted with any secrets. The pilots and navigators, on the other hand, would hardly have been kept out of the loop. It is my supposition, however, that only Chun Byung-in was in on the secret, for he was an experienced military aviator and a civilian pilot who had flown 10,620 hours. And indeed, if it had been Chun Byung-in who had flown the plane with registration HL7442 to Andrews Air Force Base outside Washington, where the Boeing spent three days being fitted out by electronic technicians from E-Systems, then he was surely aware of the plans and an active participant in them. Granted, the information concerning the plane's journey to Andrews and its overhaul by CIA and Pentagon employees only came to light later; the source of it was the first main Directorate of the KGB, that is, Soviet foreign intelligence, and it was cited by the journalist David Pearson, who was rumored to be an agent of Soviet influence. In short, the information is questionable, especially considering that Pearson vanished without a trace afterward.

As the Korean Airlines dispatcher and crew met in the airline's office on the second floor of the terminal, each person had the printout of the computer flight plan in front of them: fuel reserves, the passenger manifest, the placement of cargo on board. In winding up the meeting, the crew, the air traffic control liaison, and pilot Chun Byung-in compared their printouts of the computer-generated plan with the flight maps in order to make sure that they matched.

The onward flight was scheduled to take off at twenty minutes after noon Greenwich mean time. The jumbo jet would land in Seoul at nine o'clock in the evening Greenwich mean time, which was six o'clock in the morning in Korea. However, the computer flight plan apparently allowed for a headwind, although the wind along their route was in fact light. If the jumbo jet had flown at the speed originally calculated, it would have arrived at Seoul's Gimpo International Airport twenty seven minutes earlier. The passengers would have been met by closed doors: passport control and baggage handling at Gimpo did not begin work until six o'clock.

The air traffic control liaison and the pilot discussed this issue and decided to delay departure from Anchorage by thirty minutes. It must be noted that Captain Chun Byung-in was used to making decisions on his own. In spite of his youthful appearance, he was already forty-five years old and had spent half of his life as a military pilot, a South Korean air force officer. His round face with its delicate features always remained like a mask, and no one could work out what he was thinking, what he would say, and how he would act. To this day, no one knows what his feelings were as he boarded the flight.

There is definitely something to think about here. If the information leaked by an unknown source with the help of David Pearson and at the prompting of Soviet intelligence is actually reliable, and if Captain Chun Byung-in had flown that Boeing with tail number HL7442 to Andrews Air Force Base two weeks earlier, then it stands to reason that Chun Byung-in knew what kind of flight this was going to be. We can then further assume that the plane really was parked in a distant corner of the base, next to building 1752, under conditions of strict secrecy, and that E-Systems technicians spent over three days working on the plane on behalf of the CIA and the Pentagon.

It would have been possible, though, to carry out reconnaissance even without the passenger plane having been fitted with special surveillance equipment. It would suffice to change the route, to depart from the flight corridor assigned by air traffic control. The desired result could easily be achieved by altering the autopilot system.

Here we might recall that the on-board radio was repaired during the stop in Anchorage. The plane's departure from the standard route and violation of USSR airspace would naturally be noticed, Soviet air defense would sound the alarm, and the network of radars would spring to life and track the intruder – which was exactly what the electronic surveillance efforts were after: one then had only to gather the signals and decode them.

After the pilot and dispatcher had decided to delay departure by half an hour, they did not notify the passengers. The airline staff decided that the less the passengers knew, the better. None of the passengers paid particular attention to the delay; none seem troubled. They all peaceably waited, and only a few anxious types glanced at their watches.

As usual with international flights, the crowd of passengers in the transit area of Anchorage airport on this last night of August was diverse and colorful. Its variety was no surprise considering that fate had brought together people from sixteen nations. The dozen people flying first class kept themselves apart and did not mix with the economy passengers. An attentive eye could, however, spot the difference in the passengers' attitudes. Traveling for business had left its mark of concern or worry on the first class group, while those flying for leisure or to visit family were relaxed and carefree. They could look forward to a few days of fun and enjoyment – what more could one want?

There were two dozen or so children in the transit area, the smallest of whom were sleeping in their strollers, in baskets, or in their parents' arms. Other tots were unable to sleep, and drowsily fidgeted or wailed at high volume. The older children followed their parents as they strolled about, or chased one another high-spiritedly around the hall. The elderly passengers had grown weary from the journey and lack of sleep, and were shuffling about or had collapsed into chairs.

It was the young ladies, though, who particularly caught the eye. Naturally. A surprisingly large proportion of the two hundred passengers or more passengers on the flight turned out to be beautiful, lively young ladies. Their clean and elegant features were sight to behold, and beholding them is just what many in the hall were doing.

Their eyes shone and their cheerful, chattering voices floated weightlessly over the transit area. They giggled and furtively glanced at the men who were hanging around or sipping their beers. Anyone who did not know where he was could be forgiven for thinking that music and dancing was about to break out, so reminiscent of a festive ball was the atmosphere by night in the transit hall.

The young policeman on duty at the entrance to the terminal found his gaze wandering. A whole array of young ladies, each lovelier than the last. In the transit area. How could he stay alert at his post and guard against crime under these circumstances?

By the time boarding was announced, the passengers had recovered from the New York – Anchorage portion of their flight and were ready to move on to Seoul. Anyone who has flown knows how comforting it is to be cared for by an attentive and motherly crew. You are completely sure that nothing bad is going to happen. You have no worries, no troubles, only sweet relaxation, and you feel like a child who can trust in his family's protection. No one knew, of course, that when boarding was finally announced in Anchorage for Flight KAL-007, radio-interception posts on the Alaskan cape of Wakkanai got to work. The "ready" signal was transmitted around US Air Force units across Alaska, home to the 10th and 11th Divisions as well as various special-purpose wings and covering fighter planes. In the skies above the Pacific Ocean, RC-135 Cobra electronic-reconnaissance planes had taken off from Eareckson Air Station in the Aleutian Islands and were now roaming along the Soviet border. Eareckson was also home to a powerful early-warning radar station, one capable of handling two hundred targets at the same time over a distance of five thousand kilometers. It was this same station that tracked Gagarin's flight into space, and even intercepted the transmissions that the first cosmonaut made from his Vostok 1 capsule.

Sweeping the skies alongside the Cobras were gigantic E-3A planes equipped with AWACS early-warning systems. The shipborne radars of the American fleet in the Pacific had already switched from their passive waiting mood to actively searching. Meanwhile, the Americans' space-tracking stations were preparing to communicate with the Samos-F spy satellite that would, toward dawn, pass over the Sea of Okhotsk and Sakhalin Island. The way that the movements of the American spy satellite, the reconnaissance planes, and the ships were synchronized with the Korean airliner was, it must be added, something that was noted by all experts, and even the Americans could not deny it.

Communications between these stations and military command were encrypted, with all transmissions classified Top Secret UMBRA, the highest level of secrecy. Also classified Top Secret UMBRA were the Americans' COBRA BALL and RIVET JOINT electronic-surveillance programs intended to fully catalog Soviet military sites and systems.

Needless to say, sitting in the apartment in New York's Greenwich Village, we knew nothing of any of this, and neither did the passengers on Flight 007. No one had any idea of what was coming. What was, if we may speak in a lofty style, ripening.

The passengers on Flight 007 were still basking in a feeling of calm and safety. When they had boarded the flight in New York, they had entrusted themselves without hesitation to the crew and felt sure that no danger threatened them. In Anchorage, as soon as the loudspeaker announced boarding, none of the passengers had any worries about what the future held; they found nothing amiss. They all started, readily and trustingly, for Gate 2H, where the powerful jumbo jet awaited. As the passengers settled into their seats, the relief crew took their places in the cabin and at their posts. Along with the crew came the six other Korean Airlines employees tasked with bringing the plane back from Seoul to New York.

Now the passengers had taken their seats, and the crew had already closed the doors and bade everyone fasten their seat belts. A powerful airport tow-truck brought the plane to runway 32. This journey between the gate and the runway took seven minutes, as it had when the plane had landed in Anchorage.

It was two minutes before 1 p.m. GMT, or 4 a.m. Alaska time, when the Boeing 747 took its position on runway 32. The pilots requested permission for take-off and received it. The airport and the skies above were empty at this hour.

A minute later, the engines roared into life one after the other. First Officer Son Dong-hui, also an experienced pilot and former air force officer, engaged the engines at the captain's request and the plane began to move. It was exactly 1 p.m. GMT when the jumbo jet left the ground. The plane powerfully and steadily gained altitude. Soon a bright blip representing the plane appeared on the airport's radar screens; air traffic control had established radar contact with the Boeing.

As usual, as soon as the plane had performed its initial maneuvers and set its course, air traffic control gave the go-ahead "Fly 310", which in aviation jargon meant that the plane was assigned to fly at 31,000 feet. Flight 007, it must be said, had gone well from the very beginning, if one ignores the malfunctioning on-board radio – which had been fixed, after a fashion, in Anchorage. Now there seemed to be no problems and everyone could relax; it was just a matter of continuing to Seoul and landing there. No complications loomed, it was a routine affair. The pilots brought the jumbo jet onto its course as they were accustomed to doing, a well-traveled route that any pilot in their right mind would find hard, if not impossible, to mistake.

My visit to Cindy Creighton's apartment in Greenwich Village was still not over. I should have left long before, but I was patiently waiting with the Creightons for developments. We listened to another broadcast, which told us nothing new, and then I had a mind to call a taxi.

Cindy waved that idea away. "I'll drive you myself. I promised."

"I still need to go to my hotel."

"That's fine," she said. I thought to myself that she was a young lady who knew her own worth, but that for all her independence, her self-sufficiency, she did not suffer from arrogance.

"I'll do as I promised," I told Colonel Creighton as we said goodbye. "I'll look into your matter when I'm back in Moscow. I'm sure you'll be lucky."

"How can you know that?" he asked, unable to show complete faith in my assurances.

"I just feel it. I'm convinced. Pretty nearly convinced."

"I don't know what you mean by that. Life has constantly thrown mysteries my way." The colonel laughed and drew a few photos from his billfold. "Look."

In these old, faded photographs I saw Creighton as he had looked long ago, when he was young, in a light-brown Army Air Force uniform. With him was an attractive young lady dressed in polished boots, a dark skirt, a Soviet officer's tunic with junior lieutenant's stripes, and a leather bag slung over her shoulder. The two of them looked good against the background of an American bomber. They were smiling and carefree, as if there was no war going on at all and they were simply enjoying the happy time of budding love.

"May I take these?" I asked him uncertainly. "Photographs might make it easier for me to search."

"Yes, sure, take them," the colonel readily agreed. "I was going to tell you to take them."

In the entrance to the apartment, Cindy searched for a moment for her keys. I could hear Michael's voice coming from behind the door. He was talking to his father. "If you ask me, he's some kind of con man, though who knows what he's after. You shouldn't trust him at all."

"Who knows? We'll see," the colonel replied uncertainly.

I walked down the hallway and pressed the button for the elevator. As I stepped out of the building, the fine Greenwich Village morning was like a gift falling into my lap: fresh, quiet, sunny, with dew still on the greenery. Tall, spreading plane trees with dappled trunks had been planted along the sidewalk, and behind them rose stately buildings. Windows gleamed in the sun, and from the first, one noticed the incredible cleanliness and order of the neighborhood. It was as if someone had scrubbed MacDougal Street with soap and water: the pavement, glass, flowerbeds, the wrought-iron bars over the windows, the façades. One only had to stop, look around, and listen closely to notice how peace reigned over Greenwich Village by morning. A person would not even suspect that somewhere a bloody war was raging, in Afghanistan for example, or that people were afflicted by sorrow and woe – it was simply impossible to believe.

Elsewhere in the city, the Big Apple was as buzzing as it always was during the day. In other neighborhoods, a vague roar hung over the streets and bridges, and traffic was feverish at the intersections, tunnels, subway stations and over-crowded parking lots. In Greenwich Village, however, the authorities had insisted on quiet, and that morning no one was challenging their decree or daring to disrupt the prevailing calm. So serene was it in Greenwich Village at this hour that I was seized by the crazy belief that everything in life would work out perfectly: any adversity would crumble and disappear completely, and we could expect nothing but happy days and success forever.

As we walked out into the street, Cindy Creighton's remarkable features immediately added to the appeal of Greenwich Village, and all of New York. She started the car and we headed north, then turned east at 14th Avenue and crossed Broadway. We again headed north along Park Avenue, already humming with life. Cindy turned onto Vanderbilt Street and came to a stop outside the Yale Club hotel. I fetched my luggage from my room and paid the bill for the phone calls I had made, and then we headed for the airport by the same route we had taken the previous day.

"Will you really help my dad?" Cindy asked as she drove. She looked me in the eye, as if seeking there some reliable answer.

"I'll try," I replied, completely sincere. I honestly had no intention either of misleading them or of leaving them disappointed. "I have some ideas."

"I hope you'll be able to do something," she said, though to be honest, she said it without much confidence.

I remained silent. Since we had met, I had said so many things that were untrue. Now I just needed to hold my tongue.

I will not deny that every minute we were in the car I was aware of Cindy out of the corner of my eye, but I deliberately avoided looking at her. I was disconcerted by her long legs as she worked the pedals. Her presence alongside me set my blood pumping and I was powerless to resist. All the way to the airport I was gripped by a sense of regret, of loss: I was convinced that we would never meet again; never would we meet again.

=== **20** ===

The grove that sheltered Creighton and Olga was of the sort that Ukrainians call *hai*, a sparse oak forest with dense undergrowth and tall grass. After the hustle and bustle of the base, the silent grove was a place of refuge. As soon as the two were alone together, the lieutenant embraced the interpreter. They stood quite still, all words unnecessary. In any event, they could neither of them have spoken, such were their surging emotions.

Creighton eventually found his voice. "You were all I thought about all those days!" he confessed. "I couldn't wait to fly back here."

"I was worried sick. It was terrible! Thinking about you, up there in the sky…"

"Were you waiting for me to come back?"

"It was unbearable!"

"I'm happy to hear it."

"I never thought it would be so hard to wait."

"There is nothing more difficult. It's like time stops."

"Steve, I'm afraid for you. At the base they're saying the Germans are getting angry, they want to teach the Americans a lesson. They're only talking about losses now."

"Olga, as long as I've got you waiting for me, nothing is going to happen to me. The Germans are not going to shoot us down."

It was quiet around them. Voices could be heard faintly in the distance, and the sound of engines and car horns carried from the road, but in the grove everything was submerged in silence, lost among the trees and bushes. The setting sun, large now that it was approaching the horizon, bathed the grove in light as if all the leaves, boughs, and grass were themselves shining. At the base, the green grove was like an island of calm in the midst of all the stress. The lieutenant and interpreter had hidden themselves away from prying eyes, and did not think of the risk they were running, but in fact watchful eyes had noted their meeting and reported it. Agents working covertly among the Soviet personnel were ordered to increase their efforts, and from that moment on every step the American pilot and the Soviet interpreter took was tracked.

In any other country, two people falling in love was no one else's business, but Russia was different. The Soviet regime had always considered love for a foreigner to represent treason. The authorities had their reasons for this: love is like a separate country of its own, and two powers cannot reign in the same place.

It followed that for the same reason the Soviet regime considered a romance with a foreigner to be tantamount to sabotage or espionage. Those who dared to violate this injunction had to be secretive and ensure that no one else noticed. There was no point hoping, though, that a romance would escape the eyes of others and attract no interest, for every kiss from a foreigner and every amorous look was a hostile action: enemies were lying in wait and trying to see how they might turn a weak person to betray his or her country.

There was little time left before dinner. Soon they would have to go back, and the American was unable to fathom the reason why they each had to make their way to dinner separately. "Why do we have to hide it?" Steven Creighton said, confused.

The interpreter naturally knew why, but she was unable to get through to him. She could only patiently exhort him to be prudent, as if she was talking to a child: they could not be seen together, the Soviet authorities had forbidden such personal relationships.

"My God, Olga, why can't we be open about it?" the American objected, still unable to fully understand, no matter how hard he tried.

It is hard to explain Russian mores to a foreigner; Russia is a mysterious country if you are not Russian. It is no wonder that the poet Tyutchev claimed that Russia was impossible to grasp with one's mind. Some wise men have claimed that the mysteriousness and incomprehensibility of my beloved homeland derives from its twisted thinking, which is an inherent and inescapable characteristic of the place, like its climate, for example, or its fertile soil. One just had to accept it, whether one wanted to or not.

Of course, the American felt that something was wrong, and of course he was right. Any reasonable human being would find it impossible to accept that politics, the government authorities, or the class struggle could come between a man and a woman.

"Forgive me for asking, Olga, but is there someone else? Why can't we be seen together? Are you married?" The American asked this with a heavy heart, as if the answer would decide his entire future.

"No," the interpreter shook her head sadly. "There is no one else. And I am not married."

"Well, then, nothing else matters!" the American laughed, and sighed with relief. "Nothing else matters at all!"

Junior Lieutenant Shilina, no matter how much she wanted to, was unable to share his joy. She knew what kind of country she had been born in, what kind of country she lived in now. She tried to explain this to Creighton. "Steve, other things *do* matter. I understand how you think, but things in my country are… different. The whole country is like a single person. That is how things are. Everyone has to be like everyone else."

The American looked at her with puzzlement. "What if someone doesn't want to be like everyone else? Can't a person just be whoever he wants? Don't you have people like that?"

Olga nodded. "Sometimes you meet people like that. But they're called enemies of the people."

"So what?" Creighton asked blankly.

"They disappear."

"What?!" Steven exclaimed, unable to believe what she was saying. "What about laws, rights?"

Olga could only shrug her shoulders.

"What kind of a goddamn government is that?"

The interpreter had no answer to that question. She was not familiar with any other countries; from birth, the only form of existence she had known was everyone marching in step. Now it turned out that there was another way, too, but her world was not shattered; everything remained as it had been before: the green grove, the setting sun, the birds singing, and ants crawling through the grass.

"Olga, I understand that this is your country, but how can you live in a place like this?" Creighton asked. He was unaware that a person could lose his life over a few words, an opinion, or even for keeping silent. "Why do Russians put up with a government like that?"

"What can they do?"

"Not vote for them. Get rid of them and elect other people."

"There are no other people, and the government has no intention of going anywhere."

The American was lost in thought for a while, unable to get his head round the original and idiosyncratic nature of this foreign country. Then, in a tone of slight puzzlement, he asked, "Are you trying to tell me that the government elects itself?" He did not wait for an answer. Olga saw that their conversation had gone too far, and what answer could she give him anyway? Creighton followed his line of thinking to its end and said, "But that's illegal. These are criminals. They need to be punished."

Creighton was three years older than the interpreter. He had much more life experience, but she was struck by how naive and childlike he was now. One could only scoff at his ideas about her country, the nation where socialism was supposedly triumphant.

After dinner, a Soviet musical comedy was screened for the Americans. The film went down well, with much laughter, some of it occasionally erupting into a roar. A herd of cattle invading a seaside villa, a fight between members of an orchestra, and a jazz rehearsal under the guise of a funeral provoked wild applause. When the evening's entertainment had finished and the happy spectators were going their separate ways, Creighton and Olga slipped out into the darkness unnoticed. A secret informant lost them among the crowd – throngs of people often come in handy for those who want to slip away.

This time the pair walked further away from the airfield and the base. Before the war, this place that was now covered in ashes and overgrown with weeds had been a farm. At the beginning of the war, the farm had burned down, and the two found themselves walking past charred wattle and daub constructions with black windows that looked blindly into the darkness. This was Ukraine, the region that had so enchanted Gogol; the area around Poltava was a magical land. Under the light of the moon, the wasteland shimmered mysteriously, the willow herb bushes standing like eerie ranks of soldiers, and the interpreter felt as if an evil spirit she knew from old stories might appear out of the gloom.

Tall poplars grew in rows around the burned farm. The moon was shining brightly, and the cicadas were chirping so energetically that when they fell quiet for a moment, the silence was deafening. Around them they seemed to sense a mysterious sorcery whose power over the night would last until the first cock-crow. It was as if any moment now, magical scenes would be revealed to them under the moonlight, and fantastical creatures would appear in the dark and silence of the nighttime.

No one had passed along the country road here in some time. It was overgrown with grass and surrounded by bushes and trees. The American and the interpreter came upon a farmhouse that had been abandoned at the start of the war. Scorched trees stood like shadows in the moonlight, and the tall crane of a well seemed to be staring up at the moon. The smoke-blackened walls, which had once been whitewashed, gave off an air of desolation, a gloomy picture painted by the war. Wretched, lifeless buildings could be glimpsed among the rampant vegetation on either side of the old road.

Among the tall grass and bent willows they saw the glimmer of an overgrown pond, from which came an odor of mildew and damp earth. The edges of the pond were choked by sedge and cattails, and its surface covered by duckweed and lilypads. Only in a few spots did the water, almost black in the night-time, show through and reflect the rays of the moon. The pilot and the interpreter walked warily through this moonlit wasteland, hand in hand and listening closely. The night around them was otherworldly, something out of Gogol. In the golden moonlight they sensed a presence, as if this night-time landscape had been dreamed into being, had been conjured, was the magical creation of someone or something quite other.

The American and the interpreter walked past the pond, moving with caution as if they were seafarers alighting on a foreign shore. Smoke drifted from an obscure corner behind the burned ruins, suggesting that a fire was burning somewhere in the vicinity. A dog barked, followed immediately by the voice of a child scolding the dog, at which the barking abated. There was a rustle of leaves and the cracking of twigs underfoot, and then it grew quiet: someone had sensed danger and hidden in the hope of escaping these uninvited visitors. Judging by the untouched grass, Olga and Creighton were the first such visitors.

They made their way along a charred lath fence. Here and there, lone-standing pickets had survived the fire and were crowned with clay pots in keeping with an old Ukrainian folk custom. An inconspicuous little path brought the pair to a secluded clearing where a fire burned behind a clump of honeysuckle. The flames dimly illuminated thick weeds among which they found an old hut, slanted and full of cracks. This was an old grain storehouse, of the sort that the locals referred to as a *pelevnya* or *riga*. The American drew a flashlight from his pocket and shone it around. The place seemed to be inhabited: brushwood had been gathered and laid next to the fire, and there was an old kettle black with soot. Someone was here, secretly watching them. They could sense eyes on them, though they did not know from which direction: from the thick vegetation, from the darkness, or from the nearby hut.

Without exchanging a word, both Creighton and Olga concluded that they were being watched for sure. Indeed, they had probably been spotted from some way off, and it was quite possible that someone was waiting for the right moment to attack them. Junior Lieutenant Shilina unfastened the holster that hung from the belt around her tunic. In her girlish hands the pistol looked like something innocent, almost theatrical, as if it were not a weapon at all but a mere toy or prop. The American was surprised, but drew his own army-issue Colt from its holster and looked around in the glow of the flashlight. The scene was like a game of cowboys and Indians, but this was wartime and anything could happen; in war no one knows what might come next.

They heard a rustling – someone was moving behind the wall.

"There's someone there," the American said quietly, and swept the flashlight over the shed.

The interpreter pointed her pistol at the door. As firmly as she could, she ordered, "Come out or we'll shoot!"

The silence immediately after her order seemed complete, but then the rustling on the other side of the wall grew more distinct. Through the small gaps between the boards they glimpsed movement, and then the hinges of the door began to creak. The door slowly opened, and in the beam of the flashlight, coming out of the darkness of the doorway they saw a pale and emaciated girl, looking like a ghost, with her hands up, like an enemy soldier surrendering.

She was unimaginably thin and pale. She seemed to be glowing, so transparent and insubstantial was her body. One might have taken her for an utterly incorporeal being, an apparition garbed in sackcloth. Thin arms jutted from her ragged clothes, and thin legs, and a thin neck which looked as if it would break at the slightest pressure, or all by itself without any outside impact.

The girl, standing at the door with arms upraised to signal her surrender, stepped aside to make room for someone else. Now a frightened little boy in threadbare pants appeared alongside her. He cowered in fear as he looked at these armed intruders, and then suddenly realized that he too ought to put his hands up. The small, dark-eyed boy, covered in grime and scabs, carefully raised his arms as if to say, I surrender, I surrender, I surrender! There was no need to shoot, he was surrendering, just please let them show mercy, he was giving himself up.

The two children meekly stood with their hands up in the doorway, under the barrels of two guns. It was a picture so frightful that it would make most people's heart ache.

"Oh, God!" the interpreter said, and, trying hard not to burst into tears, swiftly returned her pistol to its holster. "Where did you come from?"

"We live here," the girl answered in a barely audible voice with a Ukrainian accent. She continued to hold her hands up.

"Alone?!" The junior lieutenant was incredulous. "Where are your parents?"

"The Germans killed them. And burned the farm down."

"Tell them to put their hands down," Creighton said quietly.

The interpreter, now agitated, rushed over to the children and grabbed them by the hands. "Put your hands down! Come on, put them down!"

The children's story was hard to believe. As she listened, the tears came, and the junior lieutenant wiped them from her eyes. She translated each statement for the American, often stopping to regain her composure. Creighton, listening, threw a piece of brushwood on the flames and then sat down next to the fire. The flames illuminated the children's faces. They looked utterly worn out, as if these children of war were old before their time.

Before the war, the boy and the girl had not known each other. The war had brought them together. The girl's family had lived on this farm for generations, while the boy was from the city. When the Germans came, the boy's parents took their children and fled from the city. The Germans were killing the Jews, but some who managed to escape and evade the Germans' cordon hoped to survive. The refugees found shelter at the farm and stayed hidden for a long time, in spite of a decree issued by the occupying German commandant that any individuals harboring Jews would be shot on the spot, and their homes burned down.

So it was. A neighbor made a report to the Germans, and a Sonderkommando came and set fire to the farmstead along with its inhabitants. The locals and the sheltering refugees alike burned to death in the blaze. The Jewish boy, the son of city folk, and the rural Ukrainian girl, the daughter of the farm's owners, had gone off a little earlier in order to pick berries. Their decision to head for the woods had saved their lives. When the children returned, they found only smoldering ashes. The smoke had choked them, and brought tears to their eyes.

The American listened to Olga's translation with a lump in his throat. He could only shake his head bitterly. He had seen fighting in the skies, but he had known nothing before about the war on the ground. The flames played on the children's faces. Honeysuckle and juniper bushes stood out in the moonlight around them. Their fire was surrounded by tall willow herbs and wild grass like a wall, and the deafening chirping of cicadas filled the dark Ukrainian night. The American and the interpreter would remember this night for many years afterward for its incredibly bright moon and incessant chorus of cicadas – an unsleeping night, a short respite in a long war.

The American asked, "How do they manage here on their own?"

The junior lieutenant was still weeping; she translated his question for the children through her tears.

In the fall of 1941 the children had had nowhere to go, just as they had nowhere to go now. They remained among the burned-out ruins. The girl became an elder sister to the boy. Potatoes stored in the cellar had saved them from starvation, and fortunately the farmers had been able to bring in their harvest that year. The children had proved lucky with milk: a goat grazing nearby had survived the fire, and the girl knew how to milk it, having been taught by her mother when she was very small.

Besides the goat, an underground cooler built by her ancestors long ago had also survived. Ice had been gathered during the cold months of the year and stored at the bottom of a deep pit, where sawdust had then been heaped over it. A row of logs topped with earth was laid over the pit, keeping it cool inside. The ice had not melted even in the summer, when the Poltava region saw sweltering heat.

Fruits and vegetables had been stored in the ice, along with jars of pickles and lard from a hog slaughtered at Christmas. The farm's reserves had lasted them a long time; the children had survived on them for two winters. For the last year, however, they had been living a precarious existence. The goat had saved their lives; they could have never survived without it.

Obtaining bread was the most difficult thing of all: the girl would wander through villages where she knew no one and beg. She went alone on these trips. The boy had remained hidden all these years, revealing himself to no one. The children dried the bread and crusts they had been given. The willow herb, that blessed plant, was also a life saver. In water, it produced a fragrant and healing infusion that has helped people survive hard times over the centuries. The old women of the village had also taught the girl how to cut the willow herbs with a scythe, and she dried the plants in the sun, ground them with a mortar and pestle, and baked little cakes that stood in for bread.

The girl spoke slowly. She was so weak that at times she fell silent. Lieutenant Creighton and the interpreter waited patiently while she rested. The children were emaciated, with ghostly faces and dull eyes. Sometimes the boy and the girl froze and listened carefully, their eyes gleaming like those of two cats as they peered into the darkness. At those moments they resembled two cornered wild animals.

The children really had turned wild. Their survival under the ruthless circumstances of the war was inexplicable. One wondered what strength had sustained these children, so tiny, helpless, and alone, at this time when human life was valued at nothing.

Sadness was painted indelibly on their faces. The war had taken away their smiles, and they repeatedly looked around, timid and wary. In spite of being filthy and hungry, they silently bore these hardships without crying or complaining. The war had taught them to remain silent and simply endure.

The children lived in perpetual fear. They were haunted by fear day by day, hour by hour. For all these years they had not known peace, they had never felt safe even for an instant. Threats seemed to loom over them, they faced danger on all sides. Every movement they made had something of a skittish animal in it, as if they were defenseless young prepared to dive into the nearest hole.

It was painful to see how afraid these two children were of people. They were constantly wary; it was clear that people alarmed them, and they were especially scared by military uniforms, as if they understood the danger that these represented. They clearly expected all manner of aggression from uniformed people: violence, cheating, dirty tricks. Even here and now at the fireside, the children looked at Creighton and Olga with suspicion, their eyes like those of ensnared animals. One could not help but think that these children were doomed forever to being afraid, mistrustful, and always expecting bad things.

"Maybe they could be taken to some kind of orphanage?" Creighton asked.

The interpreter suggested to the children that they go with her, right now, without waiting another minute.

It took a moment for the children to understand what Olga was offering them, but then they became worried and exchanged alarmed glances. The interpreter's assurances were unable to assuage their fears. They were afraid that they would be separated from each other.

"Don't be afraid, no one will lay a finger on you," Olga sought to assure them. "In the orphanage they'll give you clothing and food and you'll go to school. You can stay together, just tell them that you are brother and sister."

The children did not believe her; there was no power in this world capable of convincing them.

Meanwhile a shaggy dog emerged from the weeds. It cautiously lowered itself to the ground at the place where light and shadow merged, and looked around suspiciously, listening to the words being exchanged as if it understood what was being said.

"Is this their dog?" Creighton asked.

"It's our dog," the little girl answered after Olga had translated Creighton's question. The boy only nodded without speaking.

The dog had lived at the farm since before the war. It had quickly learned that it could not expect anything good from people in uniform: the Germans had killed dogs. This was the reason that the mutt had fled into the vegetation when the American and the interpreter appeared, and had not shown itself again until it was sure that no danger threatened.

These were not the only inhabitants of the farm to have survived the fire. A surprisingly plump cat appeared out of nowhere, approached them unceremoniously, sat next to the fire, and began to lick itself. The cat maintained a completely independent existence at the farm by catching mice and hunting for moles in the surrounding area. Mice and moles had multiplied enormously during the war, and so the cat, unlike the children and the dog, had no problem finding food.

When the dog saw that the cat was not being driven away, it stole up to the fire and lay down in its warmth. It slipped into a doze, paws outstretched. Its ears twitched while it slept, and from time to time it suddenly woke up to bite its shaggy flanks, snapping its teeth and looking for fleas. Occasionally it scratched itself furiously, almost setting its tangled fur on fire in the nearby flames.

Olga kept trying to explain to the children that it was bad for them to live alone, that they would be better off in an orphanage. The boy and the girl remained quiet and did not object, they only asked what would happen to the dog, the cat, and the goat. The interpreter could say nothing to console them, for the orphanages were located far from the front and it was unlikely that anyone would transport the children's animals along with them.

The children heard Olga out, and then refused to leave.

"We can't leave our friends," the little girl said in her thick Ukrainian accent.

Olga translated for the American.

Creighton nodded. "She's right. They have lived through so much together, they can't part with the animals."

The brushwood was burning low now, and the weak light flickered across the children's faces. Judging from how often the children scratched at themselves, they had not bathed in a long time. The filth had left their skin mangy and covered in scabs. The two clearly needed to be taken to get medical attention, or at least wash.

"We must get them a bath," Olga told Creighton. The American readily agreed, and suggested that they bring the children the next morning to the American facilities at the base, where they could bathe, get their hair cut, and see a medic.

The children turned down this suggestion sharply. The interpreter tried to persuade them, but her efforts were in vain and the children refused all her attempts. Olga and Creighton suspected that the children had some secret reason for this, but it was unclear to them why the children had suddenly been seized by a new fear. The thought of a bath frightened them for some mysterious reason, as if it represented a horrifying threat, a mortal danger. In short, for some reason or another, the prospect of bathing was causing the children real distress.

"No, lady, we won't," the young girl said and shook her head from side to side, refusing to listen to Olga's coaxing.

It took Creighton and Olga some time to understand that the Germans had lured people into mobile gas chambers on wheels, pretending that they were baths. Now the local population saw any van as a potential place of murder, and people feared them like the plague. No matter how hard the interpreter tried, she could not win the children's trust. Their animal-like fear of baths resisted every argument she made, and their anxiety could not be assuaged.

Olga's heart was seized by pity and tears came again to her eyes. "You are sick, you need to get help. Look at yourselves. If you don't have a bath, you might die," she said desperately, though she felt powerless.

"No, lady, we won't go," the girl stubbornly insisted.

The boy began to shake vehemently. "No, no, no!" he cried, spittle flying from his lips.

Olga gave up. "Fine, fine, hush now," she said, and then asked, "Do you at least have a washtub around here?"

"Yes," the girl nodded. "But we don't have any soap."

"Tomorrow I'm going to give them a bath," Olga said to Creighton.

"We can come together," Creighton suggested. "I'll get soap from the quartermaster."

"The children must see a doctor, but they're wild and afraid of everything. I don't want to scare them. When they've got used to us, I'll take them to get medical attention."

"It's a pity I didn't bring any food with me. I'll bring some tomorrow."

"That might be dangerous. We need to find out what these children can eat."

"True, I've heard that you shouldn't eat a lot after starving for a long time."

"The medics live in our building." Olga said. "I'll bring one of them here if I can." She turned to the children, "It's late now, but we'll come back tomorrow. Don't be afraid, we are your own people, we only want to help you."

"What people are you?" the girl asked timidly in her thick Ukrainian accent. "You talk in different languages."

"He's an American. An American! We're fighting together against the Germans. The Americans are helping us. He's a pilot. Don't you be afraid of him, he's a good man. He'll bring you a present. Wait for us here."

"But don't tell anyone that you found children here, or they'll arrest us," the girl pleaded.

The fire went out. The smoldering coals gave off their last heat, and streaks of blue began to appear among the red embers. The American and the interpreter set off for the base along the same route they had come by. At the bend in the path they turned around and saw that the children were still quietly staring at them, motionless.

"What are their names?" Creighton asked.

The interpreter realized with a start that she did not even know. "We'll find out tomorrow," she said, to reassure him, and herself.

=== 21 ===

The day that had just passed was marked by all the hustle and bustle typical of military units, but the moment Lieutenant Colonel Shilin began his assigned watch, it all faded away. The day vanished behind him and grew distant like a fading dream.

Combat duty demanded focus. Readiness Level One required that a pilot spend his whole shift seated in the cockpit, fully clothed in his gear and ready to take off within three minutes of the order being given. When one is assigned duty under Readiness Level One, there is nothing to do but sit and think. The cockpit took on the quality of a solitary prison cell, or perhaps something even worse. In solitary confinement one could at least move or pace around. The cockpit was like the worst kind of punishment cell, where it was impossible even to extend one's arms, and the only thing one could do was think. Granted, in the military, outside distractions were detrimental to one's duty. A soldier has to do what he is ordered to do: if he can't, he'll be instructed on how to do it, and if he doesn't want to, he'll be made to do it.

Readiness Level Two allowed pilots to spend their time in a building located on the airfield. They nonetheless had to stay clothed in their flight suit or high-altitude pressure-suit for the entire time, albeit without the sealed helmet.

Readiness Level Three meant that a pilot was practically free. He could do whatever he wanted: read, play ping-pong, watch television, shoot pool. He could sleep or lounge on the sofa, as long as he did not leave his station. Under this level of readiness, a pilot had ten minutes to get into his flight suit and take his place in the cockpit of his fighter.

It was nevertheless impossible to forget about everything; even under the relaxed conditions of Readiness Level Three, a man would feel under a certain stress. At any second the alarm might sound, and pilots on duty never knew what to expect. Who could say whether a pilot would make it back alive after answering the alarm, for if sometimes men did not come back from training flights, what might happen during a real aerial clash?

From his first days on duty, Nikolai Shilin felt that once he began his watch, he was liberated from the grind, from life's cares. The everyday routine receded, and on duty he seemed to be freed from the earth's gravity and soar up from all of the little hassles of life, into the clean and pristine atmosphere of the alpine peaks. Here, as if from a great height, a vast horizon was revealed to him, the secret meaning of things that was inaccessible at any other time.

From the quiet and solitude of the little building set apart for pilots on duty on the airfield, Shilin gained a clear view of himself, his mother, his family, his past and present, and the details of his life. The mysteries of existence were revealed to him, the flow of time, his own place in it, the distinctive features of his country, and the general course of life – here, close by him, around him, near and far. Out of the corner of his eye he caught hints of a mysterious world, among other things, an unfamiliar reality that lingered unseen at the margins of his consciousness.

Shilin was often on night duty. As an experienced fighter pilot, he had already commanded a squadron for several years now, and was an elite aviator. On Sakhalin Island he was promoted to lieutenant colonel and assigned to be deputy to the regimental commander. For nearly a year now he had worn the Sniper-Pilot badge on his chest, which testified to a high degree of mastery as a pilot. He was naturally the go-to man for night duty, for only a rare few were capable of operating under conditions of darkness and thick cloud cover when visibility was low – it was so easy then to make a wrong move. In the summer, from April to October, pilots on night watch arrived for duty an hour before twilight and were relieved at nine o'clock in the morning, while in winter they were relieved an hour after dawn. At night, waiting for the alarm to sound, Shilin's thoughts grew oddly clearer, his gaze was sharpened, and he attained an enlightenment that he lacked by day.

At Readiness Level One Shilin spent his assigned hours seated in the cockpit of his fighter, musing on the world and the fast-flowing river of time. He compared the life he lived with his plans, hopes, and dreams, and thought of his successes and failures. He was no longer a young man, who always looked intently ahead and did not reflect on the past. He would recall the places where he had served: the sea, islands, military communities, the airfields he took off from and landed on, faraway bases, the dull life of provincial locations. Only the sky allowed him to overcome the monotony of his existence; it was an endless expanse to which he was eternally drawn.

To his surprise, the same thought would always come to his mind with an unusual insistence; his whole attention would be drawn to it. It was that since the very first time he had been ordered to take to the skies, it had been to meet the Americans. It was an endless hunt, an eternal rivalry, a long and drawn-out dispute. This thought was firmly nailed into his consciousness. Sometimes Shilin felt that he had been born just to meet the Americans in the skies and resist them everywhere: here and there, today and forever.

One hour before twilight, on the last night of August and of the summer as a whole, Shilin arrived on duty exactly as usual. All summer long, the night-time assignments had been extremely stressful, especially toward late August when the Americans' Lockheed SR-70 spy planes, RC-135 RIVET JOINT surveillance aircraft, and huge E-3A reconnaissance planes equipped with AWACS systems prowled along the USSR's border without let-up. They would paint a figure of eight with their maneuvers, pretending that they were about to violate Soviet airspace, and sometimes they did violate it, darting in and out as if puncturing the border.

That midnight Shilin would greet September, and with it the fall. The days were still fine, the sun was warm, but one could already see a change in the local Sakhalin countryside. It was a pity that summer was over; a sadness hung in the warm air. Through the winter, people waited impatiently for spring, and then in spring they looked forward to summer, but Ecclesiastes was right – all the seasons turn. Now summer was passing, one in a series by which a person's whole life slipped away.

Happiness was so fleeting. Now came the heartache, the hangover; the bright lights were extinguished, the fireworks finished. The summer was remembered as a joyous time, and now regret crept into Shilin's heart that time was passing by, never to be regained, and no one could do anything about it or turn back the clock.

Fall arrived on Sakhalin at midnight. The entire territory to the west of the island could still expect some summertime, but the changing of the seasons began from the east. Now fall began its journey across the country, and it would take its first step onto the mainland from Sakhalin.

As the senior officer on duty, Shilin had been assigned watch at Readiness Level Three. He made his report to his unit's headquarters, where it was forwarded up the chain to the division and then the military district of which they were a part. In spite of all the alarms they had experienced that summer, a rare complacency had settled over the regional headquarters, units, and tracking stations in the Russian Far East. Everyone had grown weary of the alarms, the sleepless nights, the stubbornness and persistence of the repeated American sorties. They were tired of being dressed down by senior brass and of the investigations launched into every single incident. They needed a break for the sake of their mental health, and were hoping for a quiet night.

A young lieutenant was sitting in the cockpit of his MiG-23 at Readiness Level One. His colleagues were assigned Readiness Level Two and were passing the time, dressed in their high-altitude pressure suits, in the small building on the airfield. In an emergency it would only take them a minute to put their helmets on, run to their plane, and climb into the cockpit. All that was required was for Command to order them to take off.

Dinner was brought to them by the duty soldier, after which the pilots turned on the television. Shilin lay down and closed his eyes. He drifted off instantly, as if someone had turned his mind off with the flick of a switch. Shilin rarely dreamed, but lately dreams had visited him more often, and now he dreamed of a confrontation in the skies. The dream came swiftly and powerfully, like a fighter bursting out of the clouds below. The foreign plane in his dream resembled a transparent vessel, and through its glass he could see a large number of people. Even in his dream, the pilot understood clearly that if he attacked, he would shatter the glass and the passengers would die. Nevertheless, some stern and commanding voice reached him and penetrated into his consciousness like a steel blade: "Attack!" Disobeying an order like that would require great effort.

He awoke in horror, immediately recognized where he was, and sighed with relief. It was all just a dream. The pilots on duty at Readiness Level Two were watching television. Shilin, whose lower degree of readiness allowed him to pursue his own pastimes, took his clarinet and retired to the other room where he would not disturb anyone. A vague anxiety continued to weigh on him after the dream; a remnant of his fear gripped him and would not let go. The sense of unease was so hard to shake off that the only thing to do was to let out his feelings through his clarinet, and thus perhaps calm them.

At this same time, I was flying over the Atlantic to Europe, where I had urgent business. Long-distance flights are, I must say, a dull and wearying obligation – there is nothing worse than spending a lot of time waiting; you get so weary of finding ways to amuse yourself. Three hundred passengers sat patiently and meekly in their seats. I tried hard to doze off to the lulling roar of the engines, but I could not, because I kept thinking of the work I had to do over the coming days. This assignment was the reason why I had traveled to the New World, why I had roamed across the globe, for a straight line is not always the shortest distance between two points. Now the time has come to explain, without going into too much detail, the reason why I was on my way from one end of the earth to the other.

Why hide it: people work as spies. Interestingly, agents, just like everyone else, sometimes get sick and require treatment. So let's not be coy: Division X was part of the Ministry of Defense; every state institution has its own medical staff. From time to time, Soviet intelligence, whether the internal secret police or foreign intelligence, turned to us. Sometimes a diagnosis was uncertain, sometimes a prognosis was needed, and sometimes we were asked to create models of a certain patient's behavior under various circumstances. Intelligence work is generally concerned with possible consequences, and also actions that must be taken to ensure that things run smoothly.

If a person winds up in intensive care or on the operating table there is no guarantee that he will not give himself away while he's delirious or under the influence of anesthesia. He might suddenly talk in his native language, for instance, or begin recalling his youth. He might start prattling to the woman he's been married to for ten years that his real wife is waiting for him in a Moscow suburb.

It goes without saying that if the workings of the cerebral cortex are hindered, consciousness will likewise be impeded, and the subconscious will be unleashed. I have often witnessed a patient produce a ceaseless and uncontrollable stream of words at the moment when he gradually awakes from anesthesia or is lying in a feverish state. Naturally, Soviet intelligence could not run any such risks.

Sometimes – not very often, but it happens – prolonged stress leads to changes in a person's character, his personality. Put simply, he goes nuts, and his superiors have no idea what the agent might do and where he might go. Sometimes an embedded spy might capriciously drop out of the game, spurn any communication, or avoid meeting his handlers. In the worst case, he might become a double agent. I remember one such fellow who became a successful entrepreneur in Latin America. He was, of course, helped out with some starting capital, and opened a small business. He had no special hope that it would be a success; he was content with the idea of simply making ends meet. However, he was a savvy businessman, and in time he grew very rich indeed.

In spycraft, an agent's funds are very important, inasmuch as a network of spies is often discovered by tracing the source of income. Foreign counterintelligence will sooner or later look into where money is coming from. Intelligence agencies therefore prefer their spies to become embedded in the local business environment and make good money, so that they can pay their own costs and recruit on their own. Now imagine a wealthy businessman who has a big house with a swimming pool and tennis court, several cars, a yacht moored at the marina, a trophy wife from a prominent family; a man whose children are studying at elite schools and bound for Oxford or Harvard, and the family spends its time exclusively among the cream of society.

Such was this man. Several times a year, the family went to the world's best resorts to unwind, where the husband and father was able conveniently to slip away from his luxury hotel and secretly meet unknown people. However, from time to time, whether intentionally or involuntarily, the now-successful Latin American businessman recalled his tiny one-room apartment back in Moscow, located on the fifth floor of a Khrushchev-era housing block without an elevator, where he had lived with his wife Albina, a homely teacher at an elementary school. His Russian wife, it must be noted, was still living in that same apartment, raising their son, and patiently awaiting her husband's return from his long assignment. To be fair, the wife was receiving her husband's officer-rank salary, but she knew nothing about the life he is living abroad. Nostalgia is a powerful factor, of course, but where is the man's real home, where should his troubled soul find rest?

After a decade of reliable service, the experienced spy suddenly went somewhat off the rails, saying that he was tired of his job, and could his handlers please not bother him. He went on an indefinite leave of absence, planning to live thenceforth as a private individual. This news naturally came as a surprise to his superiors. They tried to reason with the stubborn argent. In reply, he insisted that he would not collaborate with any foreign government, but begged them to leave him alone. He said that if they kept bothering him, he would be unable to vouch for the consequences. It would not have been particularly difficult for his superiors to bring him to heel, but in espionage no one doubted that the man, aware of his own agency's ways, had prepared some insurance for himself in the event that they might try to do so. They understood that the man would not give up just like that, and if they insisted, and threatened him, he could create problems for them.

At first they tried to be friendly with him, thinking that maybe he would change his mind. Unlike most defectors, the number of which reached four hundred in those years, he had chosen an odd way to behave. He did not go into hiding and sink without a trace. No, he continued to live the same way as before and show himself in public. But his superiors had only to approach him – on his morning jog, in a restaurant, or in a parking lot – and he would begin to goose-step and blare out a marching song. He sang exclusively in Russian, with a stately bearing and bold expression on his face. He straightened his shoulders, thrust his chest out, and swung his arms like a soldier on parade. His superiors were at a loss as to whether he was truly mad, or whether he was merely putting on an act to scare off anyone who might be sent to him. In any case, his couriers and the men sent to negotiate with him would immediately get the hell out of there, lest they aroused suspicion and fell into the hands of foreign counterintelligence.

The agency in question was unable to cope on its own, and so the only thing left was to call in Division X. We were tasked with determining the man's condition, making a diagnosis, and reporting our conclusions and the prognosis. We could not call the patient in for an examination, of course, and the scanty accounts from people who had seen him did not make things any clearer. It was known, however, that the agent occasionally visited New York on business, and August would be a convenient time to catch him.

Fortunately, I did not have to smuggle myself from one country to the other. It so happened that the Yale School of Medicine, in the town of New Haven north-east of New York, was holding an international conference on a subject that interested me. I went there as a completely legal participant at the conference. I would return home through New York, and as a participant in a conference at Yale University, I would be allowed to check into the Yale Club hotel.

I met the agent in New York's Central Park. I had called him earlier and said that I was a doctor, that I had arrived in the country in a completely legal fashion, and that he should not be afraid of me. In addition, I assured him that it was not worth trying to scare me, and it would be best if we met for a nice chat to clarify some matters.

He was silent for a moment, and then asked, "You're a doctor and I'm the patient? You intend to examine me?"

"I'm staying at the Yale Club hotel at 50 Vanderbilt Avenue. You can drop by here whenever it's convenient for you."

"No," the man laughed. "You might chloroform me and stuff me into a suitcase."

"A small carry-on is the only luggage I have."

"You could stuff me in there in pieces. I know how you people operate."

"I'm just a doctor. You can check, if you like."

"Of course I'll check." He thought for a moment, and then suddenly agreed. "Maybe you're right. We should meet. We need to get everything clear between us."

We arranged to meet by a pond in Central Park. I walked there from my hotel along Madison Avenue. It was easy to find the pond, in the south-east of the park, along Fifth Avenue. A few minutes still remained before the agreed time, so I sat down on a bench and waited. Tall buildings loomed on the other side of the trees. The cityscape was lively and cars sped along, but here by the pond, a person immediately felt a sense of peace. Birds sang and the noise of the city hardly reached me.

Some time later, at the agreed time, the agent appeared from the depths of the park. He had obviously arrived earlier in order to scout out the location and ensure that he was not being followed – the first commandment of a spy. Moreover, he did not fully trust me, and was worried that someone else might have come along with me. I cannot rule out the possibility that we really were being watched, as Soviet intelligence hardly trusted things to proceed of their own accord. If they were observing us, it would have to be at a great distance using binoculars. I did not spot anyone, at any rate, though I had the feeling that we were indeed being watched.

Experts at Division X usually traced the feeling of being watched to the pineal gland, which is wrapped in mysterious tissue. This tiny formation, only a few millimeters across, is located in the forebrain and produces the biologically active substance melatonin, which influences the hormones produced by the adrenal cortex. Those hormones, in turn, regulate the metabolism. Some researchers believe that the pineal gland is a place where energy is gathered in the brain; energy coming from outside is transmitted either through the eyes or through the foramen magnum opening on the rear of the skull. Anatomically, the latter feature resembles an eye socket and is linked with the legendary concept of the "third eye", which may have been a real feature at the back of the skull earlier in animal evolution, but gradually became a vestigial trait.

The pituitary gland is horizontally directed precisely toward the foramen magnum; it is as if the pineal gland is looking backward. Here it is worth mentioning that next to the pineal gland, a mysterious formation known as the parietal eye is located. Anatomically, this consists of two structures known as the retina and the lens. We have no knowledge of the parietal eye's functions, but the heightened sensitivity of the backs of our necks to the gaze of another may possibly be connected with the pineal gland and parietal eye.

The agent appeared from behind a tree and walked slowly down the footpath toward me. I recognized him from afar from the photographs I had been shown in Moscow. From East Drive, which sliced through the park, came the sound of hoofbeats as a horse-drawn cart slowly hauled its load of tourists toward the Victorian Garden and on to the Columbus and Walter Scott monuments.

I was sitting on the nominated bench waiting patiently for the agent to approach. His behavior, however, was strange, testimony once more to his vivid imagination. When he was still thirty or forty paces from the bench, he stopped, proudly straightened his back, and threw back his head, so that he seemed to grow taller. He took exaggerated steps, lifting his knees high, then opened his mouth wide and broke into song as he marched:

> Stalin is our military glory,
> Stalin is our spirit of youth,
> With song, onward through battle and victory,
> Our nation follows after Stalin.

I was expecting a surprise like that; Soviet intelligence had familiarized me with the reports of his handlers, and judging from an analysis of the man's personality, he may well have been trying to scare away anyone who might seek contact and trouble him. In short, I was ready for any turn of events, but I still involuntarily looked around. Whether you want to or not, you find yourself wondering if anyone else is looking or listening, and of course whether the police or FBI might show an interest in this spectacle. Needless to say, I felt it best to avoid any scandal.

Our worries were for nothing, however. No one saw us; perhaps no one at all saw this man walking strangely along the footpath. Besides, New York has already seen everything and it would be impossible to surprise it. The Big Apple was full of crazy people, and Central Park was a favorite haunt of theirs, so who would be surprised to encounter a crazy in Central Park right now?

With fire and steel
Our tanks set off on their fearsome way,
When Comrade Stalin sends us off to fight,
And the First Marshal leads us into battle.

How he marched! He seemed overwhelmed with joy, overcome by happiness. His face had lit up and his eyes shone. He strained his throat in exaltation, lifting each leg in perfect time to the rhythm of one! one! one-two-three!

It was a strange scene taking place now in Manhattan: a victory parade, a song, impressive legwork. Still, no one took any notice. The occasional passersby were indifferent. Behind the trees on East Drive hooves clopped, and along with the horse-drawn carts, cyclists and roller skaters glided along, as if in a dream, against the backdrop of skyscrapers. In short, New York showed no interest in us, and no one besides myself was concerned with this smartass spy. I was the only person in the entire city who was appreciating his inventiveness, though I did not believe there was anything wrong with his mental state – one cannot trick a man with my experience. After I had watched him for a bit, I felt he was trying too hard, overplaying his hand. The expression in his eyes, as if he could see Stalin right there on the tribune, was impossible to take seriously.

I got up and made my way toward him, to cut his parade off in mid-march. Up close, his pretense was obvious. The patient was a good actor, and had control over himself and his behavior. He was drenched with sweat from the exertion – but his eyes occasionally darted toward either side – he was keeping a lookout. One could only conclude that he was trying hard to convince others that he was a raving lunatic, a now-useless man, and it would be wisest to let him go in peace before he made trouble for others.

A doctor with a certain training and experience is capable of detecting fakery; it is hard to fool an expert. Little things gave the man's pretense away: subtle contractions of the muscles, his facial expressions, a mild tremor, throbbing of the blood vessels, sweat, smell, breathing, vibration of the voice, features of his gait, his pupils and the movements of his eyes. Wolf Messing had possessed a similar gift, and at Division X we had studied his abilities, and our findings, classified Secret, were still kept in our archives.

I looked the man in the eye. "That's enough, Anton Viktorovich," I said, trying to reason with him. "Give it up, you don't fool me. No reason to pretend. I'm a doctor, after all."

   

"Surprising but true – you really are a doctor and you really were at the conference in Yale," the spy said. "How did you guess I'd be coming to New York?"

"We were lucky. It didn't take you long to find out about me, either, Anton Viktorovich," I said, praising him for his efficiency.

He smiled. "I too am a man not without options." He said it would be more congenial if I would call him simply Antonio, as his Latin American wife and his friends knew him. He looked like a real Latino, a swarthy black-haired man with skin naturally olive and tanned. He had an easy-going bearing, spoke pure Russian albeit with a distinct accent, and I praised his excellent mimicry, for he had adapted so well to his place of assignment that one could not tell where he was originally from.

With a movement that was second nature to me as a doctor, I grabbed his wrist. "If you'll allow me…" I took his pulse and looked at his pupils. Antonio did not object. He clearly saw that I represented no harm to him.

His pulse was even, calm, but rather slow. I could identify a clear case of bradycardia, which was understandable: the patient was physically fit, and a fit heart beats more slowly. However, going now by Eastern medicine, the pulse at his index and middle fingers and pinky suggested a light mania or psychosis. Well, a man who wants to play the spy game understands that he must think about the consequences; there is a price to pay for everything. But he knew how to maintain control over himself.

"Am I going to live?" he asked with a faint smile while I was checking his pulse and other signs.

"Maybe you understand better now that I'm not an agent of Soviet intelligence," I replied.

He nodded in understanding. "Very subtle. Are you trying to tell me my life isn't worth a dime?"

"Your words, not mine."

"I'm just tired, fed up of everything. I want a break."

"You could have them recall you to the USSR so that you can get some rest. You could go to a good resort."

"What, you mean to a prison camp?"

"You're being dramatic."

"No, doctor, I am not. Back in Moscow they haven't even given my family a better apartment."

"That has nothing to do with me. My only task is to determine whether the patient is sick or healthy."

"Doctor, I've been slaving away for them for ten years now. I want to live my own life. Go tell them I'm a reasonable man. I'm not going to betray anyone. No one's rumbled me yet, and I won't raise any suspicions. If they leave me in peace, no one's going to get hurt. I just want them to leave me alone. But if anything happens to me or my family, they're in for such a world of pain. They have no idea."

From his words, I assumed that he had put some embarrassing information in an envelope and entrusted it to a notary. In the event that he vanished, the notary would be authorized to hand it over to the press. That is, merely making the absconder disappear, as a few generals and colonels in Soviet intelligence had proposed as a way of teaching others a lesson, might well cause more problems than it solved. Better therefore to not lay a finger on him as long as he remained quiet.

"You should let sleeping dogs lie," he said as we parted.

"What about your family?" I asked out of simple curiosity.

"It hurts," my patient acknowledged. "But I've got a family here, too. I'll find some way to help them. In any event, they won't go without: I'll buy them a new home."

My thoughts nagged at me as I and the other passengers flew over the Atlantic between America and Europe. I had business in Italy, too, just as I had in New York: several members of our European network of spies had gathered in Italy for medical attention. They worked in different countries, but had fallen ill and needed treatment, and for obvious reasons could not go to local doctors. According to the usual way of doing things, Soviet intelligence had sent them to Italy, where I could meet with them and decide what must be done next: either have them brought back home, or let them stay in the country where they were working. This assignment of mine proved to be conveniently timed, during the Venice Film Festival. It had opened on September 1 and thousands of people had headed for that magical city from every corner of the world. It was not hard to avoid suspicion at a big event like that. After all, we might just all happen to like movies.

I was no longer thinking about my assignment, however. As we flew over the Atlantic, I felt an overwhelming anxiety come over the world and burn itself into my consciousness, a presentiment of tragedy. As time went on, this field of energy grew stronger, and the signal became clearer. An unstoppable danger was rushing toward the world, a threat loomed ever closer. At this same time, on the other side of the planet, the Korean Airlines jumbo was continuing its flight over the Pacific Ocean and approaching the shores of Kamchatka.

=== **22** ===

By the time Olga arrived back at her quarters, everyone was already asleep. The floorboards gently creaked in the corridor as the junior lieutenant carefully tiptoed over them, hoping that no one would notice. As soon as she opened the door to her room, however, the stern voice of her friend rang out in the dark:

"Where have you been?"

"I went for a walk. Why aren't you asleep?"

"Like you even have to ask! It's because of you. How am I supposed to sleep?"

"Has something happened?"

Kapitolina was indignant. "Ha, you act like innocence itself, like nothing was the matter!"

The interpreter quickly undressed, and without even turning the light on, lay down on her bed. She thought that if she just went to bed, her friend would calm down and let her be. This was not the case, however. Kapitolina went on haranguing her.

"Don't act like you don't know what I'm talking about."

Olga realized that she was in for a long and tiresome lecture, and the thought made her cringe.

"You were with him!" said her friend accusingly, apparently quite free of any doubt on the subject. "I warned you, and you just brushed it off. You didn't care. That American matters more to you than your friend."

What could Olga answer to that? If she agreed, it would only inflame Kapitolina's wrath, but if she denied it, she would be stooping to a lie. The interpreter said nothing. In the silence she could hear water dripping from the faucet in the kitchen.

"You thought I was just hassling you for no reason," Kapitolina went on with the same level of indignation. "You didn't listen to me. Like you're a free spirit and I'm a bore and a grump."

"No, Kapitolina, come now," Olga protested. "This is silly. I haven't…" But she felt embarrassed, because her friend was telling the truth.

"You thought, 'I know best!'" Kapitolina snapped, and Olga could see the angry gesture she made in the dark. "You acted like a complete fool. I told you he's an American, he's only looking for a fling."

"Kapitolina, you're wrong," Olga objected, though she had promised herself not to get into an argument. "He's not like that. You don't know him at all."

"They're all the same!" Kapitolina muttered furiously, and if it were not the middle of the night she would probably have shouted it. "Americans! They're just looking for an easy lay. They're messing with our girls' heads, the gullible little fools! And you're one too! I never expected that from you." Kapitolina suddenly fell silent, breathing heavily. When she spoke again her voice sounded cracked and distinctly bitter, "You had it coming, my friend."

Olga sat up in her bed, fearful. The darkness could not hide her alarm. She realized that something had happened, but she could not bring herself to ask what.

"I warned you," her friend said darkly.

"Kapitolina, don't do this to me," the interpreter begged, though she already knew that her friend would first cut into her as if with a rusty saw, and only then get to the point.

"Of course, I have no right to talk about it," Kapitolina went on. "But they called me to the Communist Party office. They asked about you. I didn't say anything bad, you understand, but I'm afraid it didn't help. They know everything. About you, and about that American of yours."

The junior lieutenant's heart was gripped by terror and her voice failed her. There had been talk among her family before the war about arrests, and many of her family's acquaintances had been taken away. She knew that there did not even have to be a reason for it, that it made no sense to try to prove one's innocence, because no one would listen. A person would vanish, and everyone around would pretend that nothing had happened. Some people, in order to try to pre-empt their own arrest, would hasten to denounce someone they knew.

The interpreter was at a total loss. "What should I do?" she asked, like a little girl who was going to be punished.

"It's a bit late now!" her friend snapped, then stopped. "I think it would be best if you went yourself."

"Went where?"

"To the Party office."

"Why?!"

"You can explain, and tell them you're sorry."

"Sorry about what?"

"Well, for letting your guard down. You made a mistake, but you admit it. You're sorry and are prepared to make it up to them. That's what people usually do."

"But that would mean admitting I'm guilty."

"That's right. You're guilty."

"Guilty of what? What have I done to anyone?"

"You know the answer to that yourself. Was an American flirting with you? He was. Did you report it? No. What if he was ordered to do it? Maybe he's a spy?"

"Kapitolina, get serious. How could he be a spy?"

"Have you forgotten? They warned us: foreign intelligence will lie in wait and try to make us weak, try to infiltrate our ranks."

"It's not like that at all!" the interpreter protested. "He's the copilot, a member of the team. He's risking his life with everyone else. No, he's not a spy."

"How do you know? How can you prove it?"

"I'm sure of it!"

"She's sure of it! How can you be sure about those Americans? Right now they're our allies, but what about later, after all this is over?" Kapitolina started passionately, then her tone became more formal. "As you wish, Olga, but I can't understand you. You don't seem able to stand back and get this in perspective. How can you be so politically short-sighted?"

The two Soviet interpreters sat wrapped in their blankets on their beds, facing each other. Their eyes gleamed in the darkness, and it was obvious that neither of the young ladies would get any sleep that night.

Olga was afraid, of course she was. More than afraid: an unaccountable terror stabbed her through, blotting out all thoughts and freezing her deep inside. She had never thought about it before, but now she understood the infinite weakness of an individual human being against the crushing power of the Soviet regime.

It seemed to her that the regime was like a thick wall looming over the people. Like any reasonable person, Olga knew that words were useless against this wall, that there was no trying to negotiate with it or argue against it. It was pointless, there was no use even thinking about it. For the first time in her life, Olga thought about the mindless, faceless, and harsh oppression that the regime practiced, its ruthless power, and she felt small and helpless before it.

There was no going back, however. Olga listened to her inner feelings and knew that she was not going anywhere. Reporting on her own mistakes and denouncing the American pilot would be unthinkable. No matter what, she would not turn her back on him. She would face any fear, suffer all manner of threats and accusations, but she would not give in and admit guilt. No one would force her to repent of what she had done. She could not sacrifice her love to save herself, otherwise her remorse would kill her. The unjust prohibition of their love was against her own spirit.

As soon as Olga came to this realization, it became easier for her to breathe. She shook off her fear and her voice grew stronger. "I'm not going anywhere," she said as calmly as she could, as if to show that she had thought this through, made her decision, and was not going back on it.

Kapitolina was taken aback. "What?!" She had thought that she had managed to get through to her friend, but now she stared at Olga through the darkness as if seeing her for the first time. "Olga, they'll arrest you," was all she could say, though the warning sounded helpless and her voice had lost its accusatory and ardent tone.

"Whatever will be will be," Olga sighed. Now she seemed somehow detached from the matter, as if she thought nothing of the looming danger and trusted instead in divine providence. Now there was no need to stress or exert effort; the only thing left to do was to be resigned to fate and wait.

In the morning, at first light, the interpreter left her sleeping friend and quietly slipped out of the room. She walked down the corridor and knocked at the door of two neighbors who were doctors. One of the women was on duty at the medical station, but the other opened the door. Olga launched into a rapid and confused account of the children from the previous day, as if she was afraid that she would not have time to explain.

Major Sofia Margolina nodded in understanding. "It's a common story. Children of war," she said. "Malnutrition, protein deficiency, trophic ulcers, pediculosis. They need to be examined."

The doctor got dressed, and then she and Olga set off for the burned farm. Outside the air was fresh, and the surroundings were peaceful and deserted. Mist hung over the damp hollows and they saw the nearby bushes and trees as through a veil. Willow herbs grew like countless soldiers in ranks. Slender poplars were just visible through the fog.

"I'd forgotten all about it, but there's that story by Gogol… this place is just like it," the doctor said in astonishment. Her voice hung in the stillness like a shapeless object, but rather than melt away or fade, it continued to hang there in the fog.

In the pre-dawn light, the ruined farm was a wretched place. The charred, ramshackle buildings were a depressing sight, and the black holes of their windows could strip a person of all hope.

"Are there really people living there?" the major asked, astounded, seeing the burned logs, the trees, and the scattered ashes.

The junior lieutenant told her more of the story, and the doctor suggested that the children be sent to an orphanage. As they walked, the major and the interpreter discussed what they should do if the children refused to go. If the children felt threatened, they might run away and begin to wander the region, and any attempt to remove them by force would mean worse hardships than the ones they were already enduring. The two women would have to act cautiously.

Olga and Sofia passed the burned farmhouse and entered the yard. The ramshackle barn seemed to float in the white fog, like a boat moored in tranquil waters and lightly swaying in the wind. The door creaked as the interpreter opened it. In the depths of the barn, dimly lit by the entering daylight, the women saw a strange picture: the boy and the girl were sleeping on a decaying mattress under a threadbare blanket, while the cat and dog lay at their feet. The foursome had made a rudimentary shelter from the war. The dog lifted its head and whimpered in warning.

The doctor and the interpreter silently stared at the children from the threshold. Their brunette and blond heads were side by side; the children slept huddled tightly against each other as they had grown used to doing in the three years that they had been living together alone.

"Incredible!" the doctor said. Tears came to her eyes. During the course of the war she had seen everything, and thought that nothing could surprise her. Children, a boy and girl, sleeping side by side… nothing remarkable… but the major, an experienced military doctor, could not stop herself from shedding a tear. She pulled herself together, wiped away her tears, and announced in a bright voice, "The little things are sleeping! Come on, children, time to wake up. The doctor is here!"

The boy and the girl awoke in a fright and leaped up, their features distorted by fear.

"It's all right, it's me!" said Olga, hastening to comfort them. "Don't be afraid, the doctor and I have just come to visit you." She tried to put on a smile to relieve their fear.

The doctor had already carefully undressed the children and begun examining them when a faint noise was heard from over near the burned-out farmhouse. The dog whimpered vigilantly, but did not start barking. The junior lieutenant looked through a crack in the wall: a tall man was coming down the path to the barn in the fog, stepping over the wild grass. As he drew closer, the male figure's features became more distinct, and the interpreter recognized the American.

The junior lieutenant opened the door and stood on the threshold, watching the American approach. The thought suddenly came to her that if she had Creighton, there was nothing to fear. She realized that she needed no one else but him.

Dawn was gradually and quietly spreading over the farm and through the fog. Fog lay over the overgrown pond, a promise of fine weather by noon, while the thick dew promised a rich harvest in the fall. Closer to the barn, wild rose bloomed majestically, clover shone white on the pasture where the goat grazed, and Olga caught a glimpse of the golden petals of *Melampyrum nemorosum*, the plant which Russians knew as "Ivan-and-Maria". The morning gradually grew brighter, and birdsong came from the dense foliage. Such peace reigned over their surroundings that they could hardly believe there was a war going on, a war where men were writhing in agony and explosions were shaking the earth.

Steven Creighton had brought a heavy box with food in it: chocolate, condensed milk, tinned meat, sardines, cookies, powdered eggs. A separate packet contained a bar of soap whose fragrance trailed behind Creighton like a cloud. The junior lieutenant introduced the American to the doctor.

Major Sofia Margolina was taken aback, but she contained her surprise and took a serious look at the foodstuffs. "The children are starving," she said. "They have been eating a meager diet with little protein or vitamins. They need to eat frequent meals, but in small portions. But first of all, they need a haircut and a bath."

The major suggested bringing a cart so that the children could be transported to the base hospital, where the nurses would do what was necessary. The children refused point-blank, for they were unwilling to abandon the dog and the cat. The doctor said that the animals could be taken too, but the children would not agree even to this. They did not want to leave; it was as if something was keeping them there and would not let them go. At every one of the major's suggestions and promises, the children shook their heads and bluntly said, "No!", as if this was the only word that they had learned how to say.

After long attempts to coax the boy and the girl, the adults gave up. They decided not to move the children until the children had grown more used to them; they could wait a day or two. The doctor promised to bring them medications, ointments to treat their sores. The children looked wary as she said this; they clearly guessed what they were in for.

Creighton had already lit the fire, filled the teapot with water from the well, and set it to boil. They gave the children a bite to eat, but the doctor ordered that most of the food be taken back, because otherwise the starving children might gorge on it and die. The boy and the girl had to be gradually nursed back to a normal diet over several days.

The doctor promised to return, and then left for the base hospital. Olga, too, had urgent business and would have to head back very soon. Meanwhile, the sun had come up and the fog had thinned, gathering itself into bundles and then melting away to reveal a wide open view of the surrounding landscape. The air shook off the remnants of the night-time chill, and grew warmer. The timid morning was becoming a fine day before their very eyes.

This June day was lush with greenery, and pleasing to the eye, and yet it contained more than enough sadness and gloomy thoughts. The interpreter's face showed visible worry. For her, spies seemed to lurk behind every tree and bush. She was sure that she was being watched, and she could not help but look around warily.

"Olga, what's wrong? Are you OK?" Creighton said when he noticed that she did not feel at ease.

The junior lieutenant had not intended to tell him anything. She had never liked putting her worries onto other people. Now, however, he stood there silently looking at her and awaiting her answer, and she thought that she could trust him. She recounted everything that had passed between her and her friend the night before.

Creighton listened to her, and quietly thought the matter over. He then shook his head as if he had answered his own question and made a choice. "I'll take you away from here," he said calmly, without any hesitation. It was clear that the American would do what he had decided to do.

He had already said, a week before when they had first met, that he would like to take her away. Back then it was just words, a fleeting whim, but now he spoke with certainty, as if he was not asking for her agreement but assumed she had already given it.

The interpreter was at a loss. It is not easy for a person to make up their mind when events take such a sudden turn; it is difficult to change one's life completely just like that, to undergo such a death and rebirth. Olga was bound by a thousand threads to the country where she had been born and raised. Here everything was known to her, familiar, even the regime. At least she knew what to expect from it. How could she tear herself away from all that at a stroke? How could she live, knowing that she would never again see her parents, friends, her childhood home, the places dear to her heart?

It was well-known that under the Soviet regime, fleeing the country meant a living death. It would be impossible to send letters, to telephone, or to visit those left behind. The regime kept a vigilant guard over its citizens like a savage chained dog, watching them day and night. Those who had managed to escape the USSR were left with only their memories.

The American's determination stunned Olga. No one else she knew could suggest changing his or her life so abruptly. The thought was foreign to her, too, but the words had been said, a line had been drawn that divided life into what had been and what was to come.

"But I… No, I can't give you a quick answer… It's impossible…" she stammered. "How can you…"

Yet she seemed to know the answer already. Creighton answered calmly, "It's really very simple. I asked myself, could I live without you? Could I turn my back on you? No, I can't. That's all. They won't let us be together here."

"No, they won't." The interpreter nodded sadly in agreement.

"So, we have to solve that. Are you ready? I'm ready."

Silently she traveled the same path as he had: she asked herself a question and received an answer. But when one thinks about what is going to happen, what huge changes are on the horizon, what choices have to be made, it chills the heart. The interpreter thought hard about her fate. It would be the fate of any of her compatriots under similar circumstances: in the blink of an eye a person could make himself an outcast, a traitor, be subject to a smear campaign, and crushed to bits.

In addition, Olga did not realise that if she flew away with the American, she would become a deserter. She was nineteen years of age, young and inexperienced. But this was the army, in wartime; orders were strict. According to the regulations concerning deserters, being absent from one's place of duty for more than two hours meant a court martial.

"We should separate now," said Creighton, taking the initiative. "We'll meet in the mess hall."

A few minutes earlier, the American had been puzzled by Olga's wariness, and her fear that they were being watched. Now, as a military man, he had quickly assimilated the need to employ subterfuge, and he took measures so that no one would catch them. Creighton seemed to have immediately taken upon himself responsibility for what she had confided in him, and he wanted to protect her.

They walked away in separate directions, but after a few steps the American turned around and quietly said, "Olga, don't tell your friend anything."

The interpreter said nothing, but raised an eyebrow, as if to ask: why not?

"And don't show her the photos of us. She'll report them," Creighton said without the least doubt. Olga reflected miserably that he was right, of course. She would have never entertained the thought before, but now Olga was unable to vouch for her friend.

The path led Junior Lieutenant Shilina through the vegetation toward the base. Dew glittered in the sun, and she saw bunches of lilac among the wild grass and thistle. In the damp hollow, modest globeflower was blooming. Willow herbs had grown rampantly on the burned ground and flooded the area like a shaggy carpet, as if the ground had burst into purple flames. It was the season when summer still lay ahead, and fall was so far beyond the horizon that it seemed like it might never come at all. We all love the warmth of June. Summer comes carelessly and merrily over the region, soothes our hearts and delights our eyes. But right now, the interpreter was thinking of something else.

The American command had scheduled a bombing run for the next night. At breakfast, among all the hubbub, Creighton and Olga managed to exchange a few words.

"I've got a plan. The crew will help us," Creighton said. "Let's meet and we'll talk about it."

They agreed to meet at the burned-down farm. Olga could not believe that she might actually manage to flee the USSR, abandon her old life completely, part with the existence she had always known, turn her back on everything around her. The junior lieutenant would have happily remained in her country, if only the government had been different; if only it did not persecute people for natural demonstrations of their humanity. But there could be no other government. The USSR savagely ripped lives apart; individual human beings meant nothing to it, whether they be parents, children, families, men or women. It cared nothing for the population.

As Olga was walking out of the mess hall, she was swiftly intercepted by Kapitolina, who put on an air of concern and zeal, as if she were risking her own life and sacrificing everything to warn and protect her friend.

"Olga, where did you disappear to? I woke up in the morning, and you were gone."

"Why stay in bed? I didn't get any sleep anyway."

"Strange. Where were you?"

"I went for a walk. Did they order you to follow me?"

"You're crazy! What are you saying?!"

"You seem really interested in everything."

"Of course I am. Aren't we friends? I'm worried about you. You're digging a hole for yourself."

"Excuse me, but I'm busy. My crews are waiting for me."

"I've got things to do, too. But unlike you, I think about my friends. Olga, there's still time to set everything right. Just go to the Communist Party office before they have to call you in. Later it will be too late."

"I'm not going anywhere," Olga said. "I'm not guilty of anything, and I have nothing to apologize for!" Then she went down the steps of the porch.

"You'll regret this!" were Kapitolina's last words as Olga walked away.

After breakfast, there was painstaking, detailed work to be done at the base. Photographs taken during aerial reconnaissance were hung on the wall. Soviet and American officers were verifying them against their maps and designating targets to be bombed. The commanders and navigators of the bomber crews noted the coordinates and direction on their clipboards. Afterward, Creighton and Olga, as they had agreed, made their way to the farm, but they each went separately and took a roundabout way, so that they would not attract attention. To their astonishment, the children were gone: the boy and the girl had vanished and did not respond to their calls. The dog was gone, too; it must have left with the children.

The junior lieutenant and the American began to search for the pair. They looked all over the burned farmhouse and the vicinity, but they could not find the children. Of all the farm's inhabitants, only the cat dozed in the sun and showed no desire to run away.

"Where could they have gone off to?" said Creighton, casting worried glances at the surroundings.

The interpreter was herself deeply worried, but she was amazed and touched by the American's concern. Why would he care about two foreign children, why would he take their lives upon himself?

The truth was that thousands of people, including children, had perished at the hands of American pilots during the war. Carpet bombing had wiped whole cities off the face of the earth. The pilots tried not to think about the victims, and they reassured themselves with the thought that bombing might hasten the end of the war. This was cold comfort, however, when after each bombing run only ruins and piles of dead bodies remained on the ground, casualties beyond number. Was Steven Creighton feeling guilty, and trying in part to redeem himself, or was there another reason? Deep down, Olga hoped that the American was not capable of looking coldly on as people suffered, and that he felt others' pain as he did his own.

Suddenly the dog came into view. It burst out of the foliage, glanced at the visitors, and worriedly retreated the way it had come. Behind the barn there was a barely trod path snaking through the uncut grass. Creighton motioned to Olga to remain silent, and beckoned her to come with him. They followed the dog through the waste ground and a thicket of willow herbs, and arrived at a ridge looking out on an overgrown depression that smelled of damp earth and decay.

They came to the edge of a grove of burned and broken trees where the ground was littered with spent shells. It was an ugly sight: the aftermath of fighting. Among the nettle and burdock they recognized collapsed trenches and destroyed dugouts. The earth was torn up and strewn with bits of iron, splintered boards, and posts from which barbed wire hung. Their eyes fell on helmets which were crushed or shot through and lying scattered among the weeds.

A destroyed German tank stood in the midst of this battle-scarred landscape, the barrel of its gun tilting limply toward the ground. This beaten and burned machine looked in its frozen state like a sort of memorial, the apotheosis of war. At the edge of a sandy crater, they found an overturned German machine gun. Its tripod, wrecked in an explosion, jutted from the ground like a broken skeleton. Judging from this location, heavy fighting had taken place here; strewn everywhere were heaps of weaponry. Along the line of defense, among the craters, trenches and barbed wire, one could recognize positions that had been destroyed.

Fighting in this region had flared up in September of the previous year, when the Steppe Front, led by the Soviet marshal Ivan Konev, had pushed down from Kharkov to Poltava. The German Army Group South, under the command of Field Marshal Erich von Manstein, had been based in Poltava. In anticipation of the Soviet advance, the Germans had seriously dug in with their race's stereotypical thoroughness: military engineers erected massive fortifications, dug anti-tank moats, and laid mines. Manstein ordered his forces to fight to the last man and to turn this flourishing region into a burned wasteland.

That is precisely what happened. The previous fall, before the rains came, it was a place of smoking buildings and smoldering orchards and groves. Only in the winter did the earth seem to catch its breath again, and in the spring it erupted with weeds: sow thistles, couch grass, jimsonweed, and henbane, but primarily nettle, burdock, and orache. These wild plants had taken easily to the burned earth and now covered the scraps of metal and human remains, so that in time no one would recognize those whom the earth had swallowed up here.

To one side of the battlefield, a few destroyed peasant huts stood bleakly. Their empty black windows stared at the American and the interpreter, and one could guess at the death and ruin inside them. No one had come this way for a long time now. There was not a soul for a long distance around, and so silent and deserted was this place that one felt that human beings had abandoned it forever.

The dog disappeared into a clump of blackthorn on a small hill. Ample trees stood on the slope among a dense undergrowth of hazel and elderberry. The scent of juniper in the air hinted that rain might come, its fragrance wafting across the surrounding area. At the foot of the slope, among the junipers, the American and the interpreter discovered a dugout that was still intact. They entered among the bushes, trying not to make a sound. Judging from its appearance, the dugout had been built by the Germans and cleverly hidden on the slope: a roof consisting of three logs had been laid over it, and a narrow opening led to the shelter within. The dugout must have been built in the winter, for there was a chimney leading to the outside.

In the stillness, the American and the interpreter heard something, something jingling, a knocking. Next to the dugout, fallen trees lay on the ground. In the fall, when fighting had raged here, an artillery shell had hit the slope and left a large crater strewn with fragments of trees and bushes. The mysterious sounds were coming from there. Creighton drew his Colt pistol and put a finger to his lips to warn Olga to remain silent. The interpreter in turn drew her pistol from its holster. Together the two quietly crept along, ready for any surprise, any turn of events such as can happen in wartime.

═══ **23** ═══

From New York I flew to Venice, where my patients were waiting for me. According to the plan that Soviet intelligence had prepared, I was to fly into Venice's Marco Polo Airport on September 1, for the opening of the film festival. After I took off from JFK Airport in New York, my plane spent several hours over the ocean by night, steadily traversing space to the sleepy hum of the engines. Outside the window was an impenetrable darkness, as if curtains had been drawn over the world, and only the light of the engine exhaust and the stars in the sky above us lent some depth to the night. I had crossed the Atlantic on several occasions in all kinds of weather, fair and foul, on commercial vessels and passenger liners. A ship rocks ceaselessly, and one sails along day and night with seemingly no end to the journey. The view quickly becomes boring, a dull and wearying scene: empty water as far as the eye can see without a single tree, bush, sail, or smokestack. One has nothing to look at, and the endless expanse stretches from horizon to horizon, the water swelling and falling back like the breathing of a living being. To be fair, the scene is sometimes made more lively by a sudden fountain of water and the humped back of a whale, like a submarine. After several days of sailing, at the midpoint between continents, the Azores become visible in the distance, looking initially like other ships heading the opposite way.

Now, as I flew from America to Europe, I vividly imagined the boundless expanse of air and water below me, the desolate plain of the sea, on which would be floating the occasional ghostly lights of trans-Atlantic ships.

A man bound for Venice is impatient to reach it; he counts the days and hours left. He has a foretaste of the pleasures there that he has been dreaming about his entire life. It is an awe-inspiring city, one that alarms and inspires alike. It is no accident that the poet Joseph Brodsky called Venice his favorite place on earth; his thoughts constantly turned to it, and he visited it every winter for Christmas.

However, Venice barely entered my head at this moment. My thoughts turned to it only in the rare moments when I could manage to ignore the anxiety I was feeling. We were flying over the Atlantic Ocean, and most of the passengers were sleeping. I tried to fall asleep myself, but I could not. Restless thoughts overcame me, sweeping me off to the other side of the world. For the whole of my journey, I was tormented by uncertainty, for the alarm that had come upon me in New York had not left me even for an instant. In the world something was invisibly coming to fruition. I could sense its approach, and events were moving ever faster. I did not know the exact details, but it was connected with the Korean plane whose departure from New York the previous evening I had tried to forestall.

At this same time, on the other side of the world – on Sakhalin Island, to be precise – someone was playing a clarinet softly. Its weak sound, for some odd reason, easily passed through the walls, flew weightlessly across the airfield, and, like a radio signal, radiated through space. On the other side of the world, anyone could pick up on it, provided they knew how to tune into that frequency. That is clearly why I was feeling restless and anxious that night. The clarinet was communicating an alarm across the world, depriving me of peace and preventing me from sleeping.

After Shilin had played for a while, he put the clarinet back in its leather case and rejoined the pilots assigned Readiness Level Two. They were still watching television. The television news was informing them that their native USSR was flourishing, and that life there was marked by a prosperity that was the envy of all the world. However, if one would only listen to what was going on or take a look around, the shock would be staggering. Alas, most people remained unaware… Yet if there was such abundance and good fortune in the Soviet Union, if there was everything one could hope for and more, then why didn't a single one of us ordinary people ever seem to have enough?

Soviets as individuals for the most part trudged along complaining about their lot and, with rare exceptions, cursing the authorities and incessantly complaining about the country's leadership. However, when these same people came together, they smiled cheerfully and on command they formed ranks and marched in step. The complaining stopped, and instead their faces shone with joy, their eyes lighting up with contentment. Their compatriots would gush with excitement whenever they saw one of the country's great leaders in person. This was the deep mystery of Russia that foreigners could never figure out.

After the television news, Shilin fell asleep again, following the old military wisdom that one should seize any opportunity to sleep.

He awoke toward dawn, feeling as if someone had shaken him. A weighty silence hung over the airfield, the nearby settlement of Sokol, the whole of South Sakhalin, the islands in the Sea of Okhotsk, and the entire world. The silence was heavy and oppressive and seemed portentous, as if it had been fashioned on high as a sign of ruinous change.

Shilin listened closely. There was not a sound to be heard, but somewhere in the world something was happening. And when we came to face the consequences of it, it would already be too late to change anything: the night could not be wound back, nor could things be restored to what they were. Mankind has still not invented the time machine. Later, the pilot and I made a joint effort to trace events back in time step by step, to connect our disparate thoughts into a single chain. Both of us were tormented incessantly by a single question: what happened on that night from August to September, from summer to fall, in that unforgettable year?

If memory serves, the Boeing 747 belonging to Korean Airlines and flying from New York to Seoul left Anchorage, Alaska thirty minutes late. An airport vehicle towed the plane from gate 2H to runway 32, a process which took seven minutes. The plane stood still for a moment at the beginning of the runway, and as soon as the crew had received permission from air traffic control, the plane took off.

We know that at 1 p.m. GMT, 4 a.m. Alaska time, the plane left the ground, performed its initial maneuvers, set a course along the J501 flight corridor, and gradually gained height as normal. It took around half an hour to reach cruising altitude. Air traffic control then directed the plane to airway P20, which had been calculated by computer and appeared on all maps. The jumbo jet entered onto this course.

While the plane was climbing, air traffic control at Anchorage airport maintained radio contact with the crew. By all indicators, things on board were fine, more than fine. The engines and instruments were working correctly, the plane was steadily holding its course like a train on rails. The pilots reported that all was running normally, and air traffic control confirmed the message as is customary in aviation.

Soon after air traffic control had received the crew's report, it called "Fly-310", which in civil aviation parlance means fly at 31,000 feet. The crew immediately ascended to the assigned altitude, and flew on in strict accordance with the plan without any difficulties. It must be added that the American tracking stations monitoring local airspace maintained routine radar contact with the Korean airliner. On the screens of various institutions – the Navy, electronic surveillance, the Air Force, and civil aviation – a blip denoting the plane moved along.

While the Korean airliner was over the Pacific Ocean and heading south, its Captain Chun Byung-in regularly radioed air traffic control with details of the plane's heading, speed, altitude, and conditions on board. Even the most meticulous fault-finder would detect no deviation from the plan: the situation on board was fine, and all the passengers were sure, completely certain, that they would soon land in Seoul.

Yet they never landed in Seoul. For some strange reason, the plane's autopilot was connected not to the integrated navigation system, but only to the magnetic compass, which erroneously indicated a heading of 245 degrees. The jumbo jet deviated from the appointed direction, and in the forty-ninth minute of its flight it headed twelve miles off course. One can only wonder why air traffic control did not tell the crew that they had made such an obvious error. And of course, no one can tell us whether Captain Chun Byung-in was aware of it. Perhaps he continued to think that he was flying the plane toward Seoul, that is, he had simply got lost. It is equally possible that he intentionally changed course and knew where he was flying. Experts, at any rate, consider that Chun Byung-in was too experienced a pilot to lose his way.

We are left to puzzle over these events and do our best to piece them together, which we later did at Division X. It is hard to tell whether the crew knew about the route change. First Officer Son Dong-hui, for example. He was also an experienced military pilot and had held the rank of lieutenant colonel. But the captain surely knew what he was doing and where he was taking the plane. If Chun Byung-in had flown that Boeing to Andrews Air Force Base near Washington D.C. three weeks before, there would of course be no doubt that he knew what he was involved in and what course he was flying. One cannot, however, put too much stock in that rumor, which was spread by the journalist David Pearson, reputedly a Soviet agent.

The captain surely had a clear idea of the plane's true course; he must have prepared in advance and then strictly followed his instructions. It is most unlikely, though, that we shall ever know who gave him those instructions. He was well aware of the risk he was putting everyone through, both the passengers and the crew. At Division X we managed to obtain from Korea an account given by Chun Byung-in's wife. She claimed that her husband had been reluctant to take this flight, and had hinted at some danger associated with it. What can you say to that?

An experienced military pilot, an air force lieutenant colonel with an enormous number of hours in the cockpit, unable to conceal the fear he felt before a seemingly ordinary, routine flight. He had clearly been informed of the details and did not want to fly. Be all that as it may, one thing is quite clear: after half an hour, the plane was a long way off the airway P-20 assigned to it.

Later, we received at Division X flight charts with a detailed chronological breakdown. I diligently compared my forebodings on the same night to the times specified on the chart. After the airliner took off, it swiftly turned 12 degrees to the right of its intended direction, and this strange maneuver and deviation from the set course corresponded to a sharpening of my own presentiments. The figures clearly showed that the Korean plane's movements in the skies, its inexplicable change of heading, its departure from its intended flight corridor, and the risks taken by the pilot corresponded exactly to my own feelings of anxiety, right down to the minute.

Shilin was experiencing similar feelings as he stood his night watch at the Sokol airfield in the south of Sakhalin Island. As I did, the pilot later traced his feelings minute by minute. Later still, we compared accounts, and they corresponded in their details, in the times, and in their sharpness, and amplitude; we felt all the same things exactly. Like two sensitive seismometers placed at an enormous distance from one another, we both registered the events in the night-time skies in the same way – from evening until morning neither he nor I felt at ease.

Whatever the case, at 4:59 a.m. local time, operators at the Kamchatka radar station detected a large target on their screens. It was moving over the ocean from north to south along the east coast of Kamchatka, but it did not attract any special attention from the monitoring stations. At all those stations, the radar operators, the officers on duty, and the shift commanders decided that the target was simply an American RC-135 Cobra reconnaissance aircraft, as those planes prowled the neutral airspace along the Soviet border day and night.

Kamchatka, incidentally, was a place the Americans were constantly interested in. The peninsula, like a shield held up at a distance from one's body, served as defense for the mainland. It was no coincidence that the Americans' nuclear-powered aircraft carriers and escorting vessels often came into the vicinity of Kamchatka and the Commander Islands. Planes would take off from the aircraft carriers along with E-2 Hawkeye airborne early warning aircraft; five such planes were based on every aircraft carrier.

After the planes had taken off from the aircraft carrier, they would fly toward Kamchatka, but once they were within a whisker of Soviet airspace they would usually turn back. These maneuvers performed by the Americans' ships and planes naturally annoyed the Soviets, and at times the American fleet would find itself surrounded by Soviet nuclear-powered submarines. The Americans' reconnaissance planes were intercepted by Soviet fighters and closely tailed. The interceptors would fly dangerously close or try to cut the American planes off.

With time, such playing on the nerves of the other became an ordinary and habitual thing for both sides. For that reason, one more target on Soviet radar screens did not represent a cause for alarm. Everyone was sure that it was an American reconnaissance plane that would approach and then depart. No one had any doubt about that.

As far as doubt goes, Russia for centuries has been renowned as a deeply conservative country where the force of habit rules. Where else on earth can one find such an inclination to lazy thinking? This is why any unusual turn of events or unexpected news always takes us by surprise. As the old Russian saying goes, a peasant will not cross himself until thunder strikes.

Soon the radar screens showed a second target approaching the first. In the air defense personnel's logs, this new target was noted down under code 6065. This second target did not especially trouble the Soviets either, because American reconnaissance aircraft often approached Soviet airspace. We later learned that an RC-135 Cobra did in fact approach the Korean airliner: the two blips on the screen merged into one. One might ask why a reconnaissance plane would want to approach a passenger aircraft. Might it have been to fool the opponent's air defense? The personnel on duty at the monitoring stations and at Command assumed that a tanker aircraft was refueling the reconnaissance plane.

Both targets came together, as ordinarily happened during aerial refueling, and for a time they flew the same tack before separating and going their own ways. The Soviet side expected that target 6065, which they took to be a tanker aircraft, would move north toward Alaska and the Aleutian Islands, which was where such planes usually went. In fact, target 6065 flew south. The personnel at Soviet monitoring stations were puzzled by this: something that came from the north should return to the north, but for some strange reason it was flying south. Nevertheless, this strange behavior was not a cause for great concern either: let it fly south if it wants, as long as it does not violate Soviet airspace.

Target 6065 flew south over international waters. Soon, however, radar operators noted that the target was steadily turning right, toward the west and therefore the Soviet border. They now paid great attention, and frankly they hoped that the American was only feigning an intrusion in order to scare them, and it would actually just change its mind and depart.

At 5:25 a.m. local time, the target came right up to the border with Soviet airspace. Much later, when Shilin came to Division X for examination, we listened to the radio-interception transcripts that we had managed to get hold of. From the transcripts we learned that American air traffic controllers in Alaska were aware of the Korean plane's deviation from airway P-20, even though it was meant to follow that route toward Seoul.

Yes, with hand on heart I can attest that the Americans were clearly aware of where the plane was going. They even tried to alert the crew: air traffic control quickly radioed the pilots to tell them the plane's real coordinates and they sternly warned it that the Soviet border was close by and the crew was running a great risk.

A strange picture emerged. As we listened to these radio transcripts again and again, the pilot and I discerned a clear pattern: if American air traffic control alerted the airliner's crew to the plane's coordinates, but the plane kept on its same course, that must mean that the crew had a different assignment. That is, the crew was strictly following orders that they had been given before the flight – or which they had received when they were already airborne. If air traffic control back in Anchorage had noticed the error but failed to provide the crew with the right coordinates, the question arises: why did they behave like this? Someone must have forbidden them to correct the error, but who?

If I had to guess, I would assume that it was someone powerful, someone who was particularly interested in the plane crossing into Soviet airspace and flying over Soviet territory. That therefore means there was a conspiracy, a dirty game, a set-up with fatal consequences.

According to US Federal Aviation Administration internal regulations, all of air traffic control's communications with plane crews and among themselves must be recorded on tape. The transcript of the Alaskan air traffic control's communications with the plane lasted only 15 seconds, but the picture that emerges is completely clear.

If the Soviet monitoring personnel had had the chance to listen in to Alaskan air traffic control, they would have been shocked by the panic that erupted there. Granted, the quality of the recording is quite bad, full of noise and static. Perhaps some clever people from American intelligence meddled with the tape. After all, people in the know at Division X told me that tape recordings of our pilots' conversations in the air were re-recorded to the accompaniment of electric razors.

In any case, the voices of Anchorage air traffic control are totally clear:

"Uh, guys, you've got someone there rushing right at Russian airspace."

"You're kidding me!"

"Someone needs to warn him."

"You should have said so right away instead of waiting."

"I can't believe it… Radio him his coordinates."

The bewilderment of American air traffic control is understandable. They couldn't imagine how a Boeing 747 passenger airliner, one of the most hi-tech planes in the world, could deviate so far from its assigned route. The Boeing 747's navigation system had three backups. The on-board instruments continually obtained via satellite the plane's coordinates, accurate down to one meter. In addition, the plane was equipped with three inertial navigation systems, on-board radar, and computers. Besides all that, the flight was tracked by ground stations from which it was impossible to hide.

There was, however, another factor that baffled American air traffic control. The US Air Force had established a two-hundred-mile buffer zone alongside the Soviet border that was off limits to passenger planes. The Alaskan division of North American Aerospace Defense Command, located at Elmendorf Air Force Base, carefully monitored the zone to ensure that this prohibition was respected. In order to fly in that buffer zone, a pilot would require special permission from the Air Force. By the time Alaskan air traffic control noticed that the Korean airliner was drawing close to the Soviet border, it had already flown through the buffer zone for two hundred nautical miles. For some mysterious reason, not a single American monitoring station, nor a single air defense, navy, or electronic surveillance installation – not one! – told the Korean airliner that it was running a deadly risk.

All of this is even stranger when you consider that everyone at these installations was clearly aware of the coordinates of this buffer zone and the line behind which Soviet air defense could shoot aircraft down without warning. It remains unclear whether this was a case of criminal negligence on the part of these installations, or whether the Americans intentionally and deliberately kept silent so that the Korean plane would remain bound for the USSR.

   

Either way, the Soviet side was not especially troubled by this target approaching its airspace. Everyone had long since grown used to American reconnaissance planes and had no doubt that this one, too, would approach and then turn around and leave. Nevertheless, this time the target did not turn around. It stubbornly maintained its course toward Soviet airspace, and after eight minutes, at 5:33 a.m. local time, it violated that airspace. The personnel on duty in Kamchatka were ready to order fighters to intercept the target, when suddenly the target disappeared from their screens. No one knew what had happened. It was so unexpected that at the monitoring stations and among Soviet command everyone stood slack-jawed: nothing like this had ever happened before.

I have said it before, but I must mention again a peculiar trait of my country: we are always taken by surprise. At Division X, I spent some time studying chance events: disasters and accidents whose laws were still unknown to anyone. Odd though it may sound, my country is distinguished, at one and the same time, by resourcefulness and folk wisdom and an unusual gullibility, shortsightedness, and utter laziness.

Yes: an eternal peculiarity of the Russian people is that whatever happens, no one was expecting it. No matter how hard we try, whenever winter comes, or snow or rain falls, or a rich harvest comes in, it is always a complete surprise for us Russians. It is an inescapable law; it is what it is.

However, we were later forbidden to study the operation of chance, the reasons for chance events, and their nature. Since then, little has changed in our national character. As they always have done, planes crash, submarines founder, mines collapse, weapons arsenals explode, and we have as many road accidents as the Turks and Arabs. It has long been known that something breaks at the point where it is most fragile. However, higher command ordered us at Division X to cease this line of investigation: one of the country's senior authorities had expressed unhappiness at it.

The disappearance of target 6065 from radar screens shocked the officers on duty and their subordinates. Everyone kept staring at the screens in astonishment, deliberating on what they should do, but the target did not reappear. It had vanished completely without a trace. After a brief moment of numb bewilderment, a wild commotion arose. The monitoring stations, command points, and higher brass began calling each other like mad. The personnel on duty at Kamchatka air defense decided that their equipment must have malfunctioned, and with great alarm they began telephoning every installation.

To the senior officers' great surprise, the equipment had been oper-ating correctly. The personnel on duty had also kept a more or less sober watch, which was a great achievement in itself and certainly called for medals and commendations. However, while the duty personnel were consulting with the monitoring stations, time was being wasted and no one was sending a patrol to the border. The chance to intercept was lost.

To be honest, Russians cannot be bothered to measure time down to the second; we know nothing of the stopwatch. In my country, we prefer to measure time by means of the wall calendar or, even worse, the sun. After some reflection, therefore, the operational duty officer decided to soothe his own conscience by sounding the alarm, though he opted for the training alarm rather than combat. In other words his innate wisdom prompted him to pretend to have a real zeal for work while trying not to annoy, hurt or offend anyone. He ordered a couple of fighter-interceptors to take off, but their pilots were left without any accurate guidance from ground control. Searching for a strange plane in the night sky over the ocean is like trying to catch a black cat in a dark room.

The fighters looked around the ocean for a while and then turned around and headed back home. Unlike Europe, where there is a foreign border everywhere you turn, the Russian Far East was renowned for its spaciousness: there was plenty of room to move around in. The fighters burned their fuel doing not very much and then returned to base. When the pilots landed, their fuel tanks were empty, which proved how dili-gently they had conducted their search.

Naturally, all these flights and maneuvers in the skies were under-taken just to put on a front. In other words, the personnel on duty had ordered planes to intercept just to show that they were doing something, while the fighter pilots had pretended to be searching just to show that they were also doing something. The fighters were still airborne when target 6065 suddenly reappeared on radar screens, which came as a shock to everyone. It had been gone for thirteen minutes and in that time it had managed to fly a great distance into the country from the border, which is understandable considering that the airliner's speed was 600 miles per hour.

One can only wonder at why the target had disappeared from the radar. In any event, after thirteen minutes, target 6065 suddenly came over the Kronotsky Nature Reserve in Kamchatka's southeast, where the peninsula's shore curves in a small bay. The intruder flew over forests of Erman's birch, groves of relic firs, over towering hills and snowy volca-nic peaks, and over valleys with geysers where steam hissed from cracks in the rocks and jets of hot water issued from openings in the ground known as fumaroles. Everywhere the smell of sulfur erupted from the depths, as if from hell itself.

The airliner flew past the ridged cone of the towering Kronotsky Volcano, crowned by a deep and sheer-walled crater which was plugged by cooled lava and ice. To the west of the volcano, in a vast hollow in the rock that geologists call a caldera, was Lake Kronotsky, looking as big as the sea and indescribably beautiful among the mountains. The passengers on the Korean airliner had no idea where their plane was taking them, though, and most of them were sleeping. The crew made radio contact at the set times.

At the Soviet monitoring posts and command centers, everyone was astounded to watch this target behave so oddly, so mindlessly. Instead of quickly exiting from Soviet airspace, retreating at full speed, it foolhardily continued on its course. The officers on duty had never seen anything like this before, and were unsure how to act.

By this time, the first pair of fighters sent out had almost no fuel left in their tanks; they were running on fumes and had no choice now but to return to base. The duty officer ordered a second pair of fighters to take off to intercept, but again it was impossible for them to reach the target. Behind the chain of tall volcanoes the radar signal weakened, which was understandable, but nothing could be done about it. The fighter pilots were operating blind and so they naturally failed to find anyone.

In my country, notoriously, something always prevents us from seeing anything through properly. The weather interferes, the climate, the wind. This time it was the mountainous nature of the terrain that hindered the search. Yet if it had not been the mountains, some other excuse would have been found: the men's low salaries, for example, or the lightly overcast conditions, or high inflation. In extreme cases, one might blame the intrigues and machinations of Freemasons, or yet another wedding celebration going on at the garrison that was distracting the regiment's personnel. One way or the other, the two pairs of fighters were unable to locate and intercept the target.

Naturally, this represented a failure, an adverse combination of circumstances, bad luck, dashed hopes. When there is a failure, there is always a need to blame someone for it, and it was clear that the same would apply in this case. The officers and generals realized that they were in for a world of pain if the target escaped them. Everyone serving in the region knew that they could expect severe reprimands or, worse still, demotion. For a military man, death would be a kinder fate.

In fear of such retribution, the officer on duty woke the commander of the Pacific Fleet in Vladivostok and got him out of bed. Admiral Sidorov arrived at fleet headquarters, where officers had quickly set up a command center. Also woken up was General Tretyak, commander of the Far Eastern Military District in Khabarovsk. General Tretyak had served in the army for many years now; he had vast experience and would be able to advise on this case.

Across the entire Russian Far East, from Kamchatka to Vladivostok, the military was baffled by their target's senseless and odd behavior. Everyone was sure that the target would turn south toward the Kuril Islands and the Pacific Ocean and leave Soviet airspace. The call to arms was sounded at the base on the Kuril Islands and the personnel there awaited the target. However, the cunning target once again dashed the expectations of the army, the navy, and air defense. It flew past the western shore of the Kamchatka Peninsula and continued over the Sea of Okhotsk. Soviet top brass and base commanders were dumbfounded. Defying all laws of military science, the target kept stubbornly flying toward danger. It foolhardily continued on its westward course, as if it intended to cross the whole country, reach Moscow, and then leave the USSR for Europe.

Only on the third try did they manage to locate the foreign plane. God loves a trinity of events in Russia, and even in old Russian tales things come together only the third time around. Otherwise the country would not be Russia at all but a completely different one.

When the third pair of fighters had taken off from their Kamchatka air base, they finally located the target and managed to tail it. By this time, the target was flying over the neutral waters of the Sea of Okhotsk. Regulations stipulated that in international airspace an intercepting fighter could come no closer to a foreign plane than fifty kilometers. However, when one examines the present episode closely, one's attention is drawn to a peculiar fact: none of the pilots, nor the monitoring stations on the ground, nor headquarters, attempted to determine the foreign airplane's type and to whom it belonged. No one tried to reach it over the radio on the international aviation frequency 121.5 MHz, no one warned it of danger, no one notified American air traffic control or the American military.

Later the Soviet generals muttered some excuses, claiming that they had bent over backward to contact the plane's crew on the 121.5 MHz frequency, but there is no proof of that: no one heard these transmissions, though many stations in various countries were listening.

   

Oh, I have known some generals in my day. I have seen and heard enough to not fall for those claims. It was the rule that as soon as someone broadcast over the international aviation frequency 121.5 MHz, all other channels would be muted; that frequency was considered the most important. However, there were generals who constantly complained about adverse circumstances. "Ah, force majeure," they would say...

A few years after the incident with the Korean airliner, the 19-year-old German amateur pilot Mathias Rust crossed into Soviet airspace in his small Cessna plane, flew all the way to Moscow undetected, and landed right next to Red Square and the Kremlin. For Soviet air defense, Rust's plane proved a very challenging target: it flew too low and too slowly, and moreover the Cessna was so small that radar did not pick it up. In addition, Rust made his flight by day, which was unthinkable for Soviet air defense; surely a foreign adversary would wait until nightfall. No one expected the enemy to arrive by day.

Rust broke the rules, and that greatly offended the generals. Moreover, no one noticed him. Some suspect that Rust even stopped to refuel somewhere along the way, though no one knows where. He landed, took on fuel, and then continued his flight, just like a regular bus, and the only odd thing is that he did not pick up anyone else along the way and kindly take them as far as the next village. He might have even made some money from a hitchhiker that way and covered his fuel costs. Apparently the man was afraid of highway patrol or, in accordance with his German sense of fairness and dislike of corruption, he did not want to pay them any bribes.

Compared with Rust's small Cessna, target 6065 was moving too high and too fast; it was flying by night and in the dark when everything looks alike and nothing can be distinguished from anything else. Moreover, the Boeing 747 was a large plane, and from a distance it resembled an aerial reconnaissance aircraft; even a trained eye would not be able to tell the difference right away.

Frankly, target 6065 had cunningly broken all the rules. It shamelessly flouted all expectations and refused to move in the direction expected of it. No one had any idea of what was going on. In other words, just like the naive Mathias Rust, target 6065 was not really suitable for Soviet air defense. The generals should have made it clear beforehand what kind of targets they preferred to deal with. For air defense, it would have been a lot more convenient if the intruder had simply notified them in good time of its intentions, the where, when, who, and how of it.

In the small building for duty officers at Sakhalin Island's Sokol airfield, Nikolai Shilin woke up in the middle of the night, as if someone had nudged him or called his name loudly. He clearly felt the presence of someone or something else, though there was no one next to him, only the night outside the windowpane.

The last night of August harbored a threat somewhere in its dark vastness, though it was unclear to Shilin whether this danger was looming nearby, right outside the window, or far off at a great distance. Far from fading away with his dream, Shilin's sense of unease grew into a clear sense of alarm. The pilot naturally had no idea of what was going on, though distress weighed on him and immediately banished all thought of sleep.

Shilin, as the senior officer on duty, decided to make some rounds and ensure that a good and alert watch was being kept, but before he could set off, the phone suddenly rang in the next room. The phone was picked up by a captain, who had been napping in a comfortable chair, clad in his flight suit at Readiness Level Two. After listening to the voice at the other end of the line, the captain stood in bewilderment for a moment, apparently trying to pull himself together.

He turned to Shilin. "Lieutenant Colonel, you are now at Readiness Level One," he said, as if he was unsure that he had understood everything correctly.

In fact, both men had a reason to be perplexed: the order had disturbed the established routine. There was currently another pilot at Readiness Level One seated in his fighter's cockpit and ready for take-off. He had just come on duty and would be relieved in another hour. They could only wonder why command had assigned Lieutenant Colonel Shilin such an unusual state of readiness.

Orders are orders, however, and not subject to debate. Shilin had grown comfortable with Readiness Level One since his days in flight school. To test military readiness, Soviet air defense sometimes launched a test target and sounded the alarm to go and intercept it.

It took ten minutes for a pilot on duty to make the shift from Readiness Level Three to Readiness Level One. In what was now second nature to him, Shilin pulled on his high-altitude flight suit, stepped into his tall boots, and put his helmet on as he walked out of the door. While he was getting ready, the airfield personnel brought his plane out. Before the regulation ten minutes were up, Shilin had already entered the cockpit of his fighter, switched his radio on, and reported that he was ready for take-off. Command confirmed that he was now at Readiness Level One and ordered him to wait.

—— **24** ——

The American and the interpreter stopped dead in their tracks. A German soldier was sitting on a fallen tree trunk at the edge of the dugout, holding a pot in his hands. He had cooked himself something and was slurping it up. In the stillness they could clearly hear his spoon scrape against the pot. The boy and the girl were seated beside him, attentively watching him eat.

Creighton and Olga could not believe what they were seeing. The scene was unreal. The pale, blond, emaciated German was eating with great concentration, thoughtfully gazing at each spoonful as he brought it to his mouth. His torn uniform hung threadbare on his body, and through the holes his blindingly pale skin gleamed. A reddish beard covered his face. The German moved with effort, as if each motion hurt him, and his dull gaze remained fixed on the pot.

Creighton watched until he was satisfied that there was no one else around. He readied his Colt pistol and motioned to the interpreter that she should not move from where she was, only wait. With pistol in hand, the American stepped out of the bushes into the open, and slowly drew close to the German and the children, intently focused like a hunter and ready to shoot at any moment.

The children noticed the lieutenant first and froze in fear, afraid even to breathe. They watched, quivering, as the American drew closer, and it was obvious how scared they were, for they made not a sound.

*"Hände hoch!"* Creighton said softly, calmly, and with restraint. One might have thought that it sounded less like a command than a friendly request.

The German had just scooped up another spoonful and was unwilling to leave it unfinished; he clearly figured that it might be his last. He brought the spoon to his mouth, swallowed the food, and then placed the pot on the ground, carefully, so as to avoid spilling its contents. Only then did he rise to his feet and raise his hands. Behind him the children, too, stood up and raised their hands high, trying hard to show that they had no weapons and were putting up no resistance.

"Children, put your hands down!" cried Olga, unable to contain herself. She stepped out of her sheltered spot and led the children aside.

The American, keeping his pistol at the ready, patted the German down and ensured that he was not hiding any weapon on him. When Olga reached them, the German was still standing there. His mien was dispassionate, and he looked straight ahead as if he were not seeing anyone.

"You can sit down," said the interpreter, who had studied German as her second language at an institute in Moscow.

The German sat down obediently, though he did not dare return to his meal. Olga told him that he could do so, however, so he picked the pot up and began eating again. The American pilot and Soviet junior lieutenant sat on a fallen log facing him.

The girl's tale was quickly told, to the point, and also hard to believe, though it is well known that in war anything can happen. Fighting around the air base had raged the previous fall in the middle of September, when Soviet forces were liberating Poltava. The Germans had found a village that had been destroyed at the beginning of the fighting and holed up there. Most of the village's inhabitants had abandoned it back in the summer of 1941, leaving with the retreating Soviet troops or fleeing into the forest. Just a few elderly people had continued to live a miserable existence among the ashes.

In September 1943, when the fiercest fighting had occurred, the place had emptied out completely. The Germans gave up their position after suffering heavy losses, and the front was quickly rolled back toward the west. During the Germans' retreat, the corporal whom Olga and Creighton had now met came under heavy fire. An artillery shell exploded nearby, leaving him wounded and concussed. He lost consciousness, and it took a long time for him to come to, but when he did, he was all on his own: the German forces had retreated across the Vorskla river and on further, toward the Dnieper.

In addition to his concussion, the corporal had lost his hearing. He could not even hear the din of shellfire. Deaf, mute, and bloody, he had lain on his back, gazing blindly at the sky. The earth absorbed the blood from his wounds and gradually turned moist, as it might in drizzling rain. When the German soldier came to, he was still unable to stand up, so he crawled, dragging his wounded leg behind him. Sometimes he again lost consciousness and lay in a daze, but then he would once more come to and crawl onward, breathing noisily from the effort. When his strength was finally exhausted, he lay still with his face to the ground. He was wheezing deeply, stirring up the dust around his face, and his dry throat was starting to itch.

The German was still in a daze when the children found him. After the battle, they had wandered among the destroyed machines, trenches, and dugouts in search of food, matches, kerosene, clothing – everything they needed to stay alive. They spotted the German but thought he was dead, and gave his body a wide berth. At that moment, he moaned in pain, lifted his head from the ground with a great effort, and begged them, "*Wasser! Wasser!*" He thought he was shouting, but in fact his throat had seized up and no words at all escaped his lips. The corporal, like a fish hauled onto dry land, could only soundlessly open and close his mouth.

The children stood a little way away from him, watching him timidly, ready to run away and hide at any moment. The German soldier rolled in the dust, but no matter how hard he tried, he was unable to stand up. Even the grime and filth could not hide how pale his face was.

He was an enemy to them, of course. He had come to this place with the war and had dispossessed the locals of their land, burned down their houses, killed people, and executed the two children's parents. They ought to have feared this man and run away from him.

The children were terrified by the Germans. Over the course of the war, they had grown accustomed to thinking of Germans as vicious and cruel, invaders with no sense of mercy who should be shown no mercy in their turn. For the children, the Germans were like mindless automatons, monstrous machines that knew no human language and were capable only of killing. The children's fear ascribed to the Germans unlimited power and superhuman strength. The Germans, they believed, did not feel pain, were incapable of growing tired or showing leniency, and it was useless to beg them for anything.

Now, however, a German soldier was right there in front of them, writhing in pain, dripping with blood, groaning pitifully, unable to rise to his feet, and weeping at his own impotence. The only thing he could do was pathetically wallow in the dust. The children suddenly saw in this wounded and prostrate soldier a helpless human being, not a killing machine at all but someone who suffered the way all people do, someone who felt pain and was in need of mercy, assistance, and relief just like anyone else.

The children watched the German from a distance for a while, and finally took pity on him. They filled his canteen with water and carefully placed it on the ground beside him. The corporal swallowed some of the water, but his strength again failed him and he dropped the canteen. The boy picked it up and set it upright again – he was still too young to rage at the loss of his parents. Life returned to the German's face, which was wet with sweat and tears and stained with soot, dirt, and gunpowder. His weeping, sore eyes looked out at the children from the blackness of his face. He grimaced from pain, and the children were aware that he was weak and unable to do them any harm.

The German tried to sit up, but he lacked the strength for it, and the children helped him. He sat there, propping himself up with his hands and gathering his strength. Then he drank the rest of the water, and with a clumsy motion undid his belt and fashioned a makeshift tourniquet around his leg to stop the bleeding. He tried to take his battered boots off, but he could not, for he did not have the strength. He gave up, motioning to the children to help him. The boy and girl together used their four hands to pull his boots off. The German howled in pain and fell backward, his eyes wild. Eventually he regained his composure, examined his wounds, and realized that he had been lucky: the shell fragment that had hit him had not been flying too powerfully through the air, and his boot had softened the blow. With great effort, he took his tight uniform and his undershirt off, and with gestures he showed the children where the wound needed to be bandaged.

The children conferred with each other and then headed to the burned village to draw water from the well there. The girl washed the soldier's wound, and placed on it blades of plantains[1] that were growing right there, and then she bandaged the wound with the soldier's undershirt. After drinking more water and resting for a while, the German began to feel better. His wound was no longer bleeding and the pain had subsided, but he was still dizzy from loss of blood, and his concussion had left him with a torturous ringing in his ears. The corporal was barely able to sit up and he wanted to sleep, though as an experienced soldier he knew he should not stay in such an open place for long. He had to find shelter where he could lie down. He gestured to the children that he needed a stick that might serve as a crutch. The boy hunted around and found a stake a hand's breadth in size. The soldier nodded approvingly. What a smart Jewish boy, he thought to himself – and was at once taken aback by the wonder of it all, for how could any Jews be left here?

This was not a time for Nazi race ideology, however. He had to survive, and a Jew could help him do that. The German held up two fingers

---

1    This plant should not be confused with the banana-like vegetable of the same name.

    

to the boy, who then brought him one more stick, and now the soldier could move about, albeit on one leg. The children helped him stand up, and the corporal awkwardly hobbled on the two sticks with his wounded leg lifted off the ground. The children followed after the German, the girl carrying his canteen and the boy his ragged boot. This little train of three people gradually proceeded along the destroyed positions until it reached a dugout that remained intact.

The German rested for a moment, and then with an effort he made his way down the steps, just boards laid over the bare earth. Inside, the dugout was dry and dark, dimly lit by daylight from the open entrance. The children remained at the threshold, unwilling to descend into the shelter. The dugout's walls had been neatly lined with boards, and the children caught sight of a wooden table, a cot next to the wall, and a wrought-iron field stove. The German army had placed this equipment here during the harsh first winter. The stove's chimney passed through the dugout wall to the outside.

The German collapsed onto the cot. With his hands, he pulled his wounded leg up, and undid his belt. Exhausted from the effort, he lay there, lifeless and quiet. Neither the corporal himself nor the children knew whether he had passed out or merely fallen asleep. When the German came to, a carbide lamp had been set on the table and lit, and the children were sitting nearby. They had already started the stove, boiled up some water in a military-issue pot, and brought some simple food from their own meager reserves.

As hard as it was to believe, the children had nursed this German soldier that whole fall. The soldier's poor diet slowed the healing of his wound, and he was unable to walk. The shell fragment had cut through his Achilles tendon, and even after the wound had healed, the soldier had a pronounced limp.

The German's hearing and ability to speak gradually came back to him, and he recovered from his concussion. For nine months – through fall, winter, and spring – the children had visited the German to bring him water and wood, and to share their meager food with him. He never asked them about their parents, for he knew there was a reason that these children were living alone.

In the breast pocket of his uniform, the corporal kept a worn and creased photograph of two children, a boy and a girl, who were smiling and squinting in the sun. The snapshot had been taken before the war, and behind the children it showed a small town with sleepy, narrow streets and gingerbread houses which evoked an earlier era of peace and plenty. The corporal muttered something in German, repeating the word "*Kinder*", and tears came to his eyes.

For four years now, the German soldier had not seen his children. They must be all grown up by now, he thought. He did not know what had become of them. His town had been heavily bombed and he had not received word from home for a long time.

"We did a bombing run over that town," Creighton gloomily remarked to the interpreter.

Ever since the nearby airfield had been set up as an American base for shuttle runs, the German had hardly left the dugout, except when he was forced to. The children secretly kept him supplied with food, though they realized that sooner or later he would be discovered and there would be trouble.

When the girl finished her story, everyone stood there without saying a word. The American and the interpreter understood now why the children had refused to leave for the orphanage, or to go to the base hospital as the doctor had suggested: they could not abandon the German; he might not survive without them.

"What a strange war," Creighton mused, after Olga had finished interpreting. "The Germans killed their parents, but the children saved this German. I bombed his town and maybe his family died. Now you and I have to help all three of them."

Junior Lieutenant Shilina nodded in agreement. "Everything in the world is connected," she said.

The children watched anxiously as Creighton and Olga spoke to each other in English. It confused them to listen to this unknown language. "Don't tell anyone what you have seen," the little girl said in her strong Ukrainian accent. "They might kill him."

The interpreter was taken aback. "We don't kill prisoners," she said. "They'll take him to the hospital and do an operation so that he can walk again."

"We're afraid," the boy said in the same Ukrainian as the girl. Before the war, his family, like most Jews in Ukraine, had spoken Russian. Over the three years that the two children had lived together, the boy had shifted to the rough mixture of Russian and Ukrainian common among simple people in the region. It was this mixture of Russian and Ukrainian that Gogol's characters had spoken.

"Don't worry, no one will hurt him," Olga explained. "The doctors will treat his injury."

   

The children, unable to trust Olga's words, remained afraid. They stared anxiously at these newcomers as if trying to guess their intentions. They were afraid that the German would be taken away, or even executed on the spot, just as the Germans did with those they disliked for whatever reason.

"Don't tell anyone!" the girl repeated.

It was inconceivable that these children were fighting for the life of a German. He was one of those who had killed their parents, left them destitute and alone, and brought them such grief, but now they were worried that someone would hurt him or kill him. By all rights they should have felt a burning hatred against any German soldier, an unquenchable desire for revenge, but instead they were worried that he might come to harm.

The whole time the children had been telling their story, the German had said nothing. He had long since finished eating, after which he had cleaned his spoon with a little sand and placed it in his pocket: a spoon is a handy thing to have even as a prisoner of war. The corporal could guess what would happen to him: officers would escort him to the local commandant, and then he would be sent far away from the front to a Soviet POW camp. He was afraid, however, that during the interrogation at the commandant's office he would be beaten and tortured, just as his fellow Germans had tortured and beaten their prisoners. Or they might just shoot him outright, to avoid the bother of escorting him to a prison camp.

Yet these two foreign officers did not take him away; they merely stood there for some time in silence, and then suddenly walked off. The corporal was unaware that Creighton and Olga felt sorry for the children and did not want to frighten them again. He assumed that the two officers would send a patrol to arrest him, some sort of nasty police detachment, as the Germans had used on the front.

The American and the interpreter walked, hand in hand, along the green valley, surrounded by its picturesque hillocks. Oddly, they had already nearly forgotten about the German, and even about the surveillance they might be under from their respective countries. They thought nothing of eyes watching them, as if no danger threatened them and this fine day promised a life unclouded by troubles.

It was June, and the year was in full flush. The young summer was ablaze with flowers: endless clear days, short and half-lit nights, the singing of nightingales. It was a season when, in peacetime, loves are often kindled. Indeed, June was a month of hope, when summer had just started and fall was still far off, seemingly a whole lifetime away.

On the way back to the base, Creighton told Olga how he planned to take her away. She neither agreed to his plan nor objected. She was at a loss for words, and only looked around blindly as if unable to see anything.

The American lieutenant was adamant that helping her escape the USSR was the only way to save their relationship. "Olga," he said, "I know it's hard for you to decide, but I feel responsible for you. Just try to understand me here. In Italy, I was constantly worried about whether I'd ever see you again. I need to have you next to me, safe and sound. In the army they might transfer you somewhere else, and then what would I do? Everything could change in an instant. The politicians or the generals will think of something, they might change our route, or assign us different bases, or call off these shuttle runs completely, and what happens then? I might lose you. And now you're saying they might arrest you. What are we going to do, just wait for them to come and take you away? Sit meekly doing nothing? I can't do that!"

"And if I agree?" Olga asked numbly, as if gripped by cold. Her heart froze when she thought about what was ahead of her.

He was right, of course. She could see no other way out. The weather was warm and sunny, the countryside all around them was peaceful, and it might have seemed like the only thing left to do was to live and rejoice in life's blessings. But she could sense some kind of hostile presence around her. A vague danger loomed everywhere; it touched her face, and from all sides came an icy wind that cut through her.

"If you agree," Creighton said, "then I'll get you aboard my plane, we'll cross the front, and I'll set you up in Italy, in Foggia. You'll be safe there."

"The front is moving," Olga replied. "You might be transferred somewhere else."

"Then I'll send you to my parents in San Francisco. I'll get there myself eventually. This war won't last more than another year."

She nodded to show she understood, but in her thoughts she was far away, somewhere no one could reach her. Her escape from the USSR would have repercussions for her parents, she was aware of that, and she feared for them. Before the war, people often repeated the Great Leader's words, "A son should not answer for his father." If the Great Leader was speaking the truth, then that gave hope to Olga that her parents would not answer for their daughter. Deep in her heart, however, she knew that it was foolish to hope like that, for those words were a lie. She wanted to believe in justice, though, whatever rational thought might suggest to the contrary.

     

If I make this bed, Olga thought, then I will have to lie in it. She knew what she was getting herself into, but if everything worked out, then she and Creighton would be happy. But if not… She did not pursue this thought to its end; the implications were obvious.

Olga made no reply for a while, and then suddenly said aloud in Russian, "*Chemu byt', togo ne minovat'.*"

"What's that?" Creighton replied, not understanding her. "What did you say?"

"I do not know what I can expect," Olga said, and gave him an uncertain smile. "You are my only hope now."

Her smile was joyless, tinged with palpable sadness. The young lady's face shone in the sun, and a strand of light blonde hair lay over her forehead. Lieutenant Creighton looked at Olga and felt her confusion and vulnerability. Yet in her weakness there was a subtle charm the like of which he had not met before. The copilot thought how lucky he was, for he might well have never met her. Now that he had, it meant that things would turn out alright, for it was far easier for lovers to pass by without meeting than to come face to face with each other.

══ 25 ══

In the fighter cockpit, time passed slowly. Distant voices spoke on the radio, barely audible in Shilin's headset. Shilin was not listening closely, anyway. He preferred to save his energy for flying. Across heaven and earth it was still dark. The pilot glanced at his dimly-lit watch: it was now 5 a.m.

Oddly, while Shilin sat there in the fighter cockpit, Command showed no sign of life. In spite of his being assigned Readiness Level One, no one contacted him. It was as if they had forgotten all about him. He started to think that nothing would happen, that there would be no sudden order to take off.

This sometimes happened: the alarm would be sounded and a pilot assigned to wait for take-off at a moment's notice, but then the alarm would be called off, only for it to sound again, and then again be called off. Pilots on duty would spend all night in feverish anticipation, only for nothing to happen. The oddity this time, though, was that time was passing, Shilin was sitting in his cockpit at Readiness Level One waiting for the order to take off, but no order was forthcoming – and yet no one had called off the alarm.

The pilots on duty had no idea what was going on. As usual, the monitoring stations, command positions, and top brass did not bother to keep the pilots informed of events. Pilots were given a target, a bearing, an altitude, and they simply had to fly their planes. Only later would they learn any details from their command or from the findings of various commissions, but more often from idle gossip in their units, and rumors, of which, as we know, the world is full.

The fighter stood there on the airfield at the start of the runaway, though at Readiness Level One there was little that still bound the pilot to the ground. In the cramped cockpit, under the sleek glass, he was all but cut off from the outside world. The earth was now far away from him, even though his plane had not budged from its spot on the runway, and only the distant voices in his headphones served as a fine thread connecting him to reality.

Meanwhile, time passed, the minutes slipping by one after another, and no order came. The pilot made guesses at what might be happening, what the snag was. The anxiety that he had been feeling all night now grew stronger and weighed on him, like the ache of an old wound. This was no mere exercise, Shilin was sure of that. Long experience led him to suspect that some big military operation was underway, some bloody clash had been sparked off somewhere and things had taken a sharp turn for the worse. No one was filling him in on the details, though. Soviet air defense in its entirety remained mute and paralyzed. Something strange was happening out there this night.

The pilots were not the only ones who were puzzled. All the officers and generals and the monitoring stations were also in the dark. Commanders and subordinates alike were baffled, as if they had been assigned an unsolvable problem.

At this time, target 6065 was stubbornly maintaining its south-west heading over the neutral waters of the Sea of Okhotsk. Neither the Soviet pilots at the Kamchatka, Sakhalin, and Kuril Islands airfields, nor the crew of the Korean 747, and certainly not the airliner's passengers, were aware of how alarmed Soviet air defense was across the Russian Far East. The personnel on duty and their commanders awoken in the middle of the night were frantically hurling questions at one another, but no one had any idea what to do. Everywhere the military was at a loss, if not in a state of outright panic. They dared not lose the target, but they were afraid to shoot it down. They knew that if they made a mistake, heads would roll and they would never hear the end of it.

Everyone knew the Ministry of Defense regulations that during daytime hours and in conditions of good visibility, it was strictly forbidden to open fire on passenger planes and training aircraft. The same regulations ordered that fighter pilots must guide such planes to a forced landing. However, at night and in conditions of poor visibility, any plane violating Soviet airspace should be shot down. This was a strange regulation, pure madness. At night, in the darkness, in cloud cover or fog, it would be easier for a passenger plane to stray from its course than during the day under good visibility. Where is the logic here, I ask you? And should the passengers really be the ones to pay the piper?

Meanwhile, the minutes were slipping by, and the night with it, and target 6065 maintained its south-westerly course. Soviet officers and generals jabbered frantically to each other over the communications links. And yet no one, not a single person, bothered to find out what exactly target 6065 was. Everyone was firmly convinced that it was an American spy plane, and the thought that it might be a civilian airliner did not enter anyone's mind. Every one of these men was concerned only about the consequences for him of this airspace violation, and none of them asked themselves the obvious question of who was flying the plane.

Our doctors at Division X, working day and night with patients as they did, came to the conclusion that the army had, at some historical point, ceased to think. More specifically, it had been weaned off thinking. If anyone had simply thought about what target 6065 was exactly, it would have been the simplest thing in the world to go onto the international aviation frequency and ask the plane's crew or the air traffic control stations on the ground – Anchorage for example. Yet no one thought to do this. No one thought very hard about anything at all.

There was another way to determine who the target was. Soviet air force command could order its pilots to fly up to the target and take a good look at it – any pilot could do that. But no such order was given; air force command did not even think of it. Everyone already assumed that the target was an American RC-135 Cobra reconnaissance plane, a sneaky intruder, a hostile agent. No one on duty had any doubt of this, and so they took no pains to make sure. That is, a strong belief had already formed in their heads; a fixation, as psychologists call it. Another way of describing it would be that their mental capabilities had suffered a sharp decline. Bureaucratic dementia or state stupidity, simply put.

From the cockpit of his fighter, Shilin saw that the ground crew was readying a second plane, a Su-15 that was, moreover, equipped with auxiliary fuel tanks. Events had clearly taken a serious turn, but no one in the whole world yet knew what was coming. Well, top brass at the National Security Agency (Fort Mead, Maryland) had probably tumbled to it, but there was no hope of them ever admitting it.

Nothing was inevitable as yet, nothing was unstoppable; there was still time to turn back. No one thought about this, though, because for them it was a foregone conclusion. Things were inexorably and inevitably approaching that fateful line beyond which nothing could be changed.

As Shilin sat in his fighter cockpit, he naturally could not know that Soviet radars had lost the target over the Sea of Okhotsk, but that the Sakhalin radar station had picked it up again. Target 6065 continued to move south-west toward the Soviet border; by all indications, it had no intention of turning back, and judging from its present speed, it would soon violate Soviet airspace again. From the Smirnykh airfield, located near the 50th parallel that divided Sakhalin Island in two, command ordered a new pair of fighters to take off, the fourth pair in just two hours.

It was still dark across heaven and earth. Night reigned over the ocean; it was that time when there was no indication, not even the faintest hope, that dawn would ever come. Sometimes, as we all know, moments come in life when it seems as if the darkness of the night has set in forever. To come to the point: the fighters were unable to locate the target quickly. The guidance crew on the ground worked ineptly, unable to determine its exact coordinates – all their efforts and their training were of little use. It took a long time, but fighter planes eventually did locate the target. Even so, they dared not approach it, since the target was by this time in neutral airspace over the Sea of Okhotsk, and the Soviets were afraid of sparking an international incident.

In all countries, fighter pilots on interception flights were expected to be able to identify foreign planes from a distance, at first sight. This was a core requirement of the job and not subject to dispute. In other words, if a pilot was unable to recognize a plane in the sky, it was better that he stay on the ground. Such a pilot was not cut out for the job.

Be that as it may, on this occasion, the fighters simply circled the target helplessly at a considerable distance and then, unable to identify it, turned to head back to base. Experience tells you that if things do not come together smoothly at the beginning, then one can expect only trouble to follow. This was already the fourth pair of fighters to be sent up. On the way back, the pilots suffered a rather bad few minutes. They were running out of fuel, and fog had covered the airfield from which they had set out and where they now needed to land. All ways round, the outlook was grim.

Their commanders on Sakhalin ordered the planes to proceed south instead and land at the civil aviation facility in Sokol, where Nikolai Shilin was seated in his fighter's cockpit at Readiness Level One. Shilin himself had spent much time studying the outlines and configurations of various planes, so that he could recognize them in the skies if necessary. The walls of air force pilots' classrooms and duty stations were decorated with pictures of airplanes, civil and military alike. Shilin had carefully studied these so that he could instantly recall them. When he was on night duty, in any weather conditions and at any distance, he would try to determine a plane's type and the country to which it belonged. In time, a quick glance was all he needed to be able to identify a plane, even at a considerable distance and in poor visibility. This was one of the reasons why he had been assigned duty as a night-time sniper pilot, whose number could be counted on the fingers of one hand across the USSR. Not that it mattered. Russia, as a rule, and with few exceptions, is a country ruled by non-achievers: it is they who decide the mores, rules, and laws, and impose them on the whole country.

In the fighter cockpit, time dragged on. Shilin spent such a long time waiting with nothing happening that he assumed they had forgotten all about him. He remained in contact with command over the radio, but no one called him, and were it not for the distant voices in his head-phones, he might have assumed that communications had been cut off entirely.

The anxiety that had come upon him earlier in the evening grew stronger as the night went by. It weighed on him and would not let go. Shilin had a longstanding habit, whenever he felt concerned or restless, of trying to get some sleep. It was like a prudent defense mechanism for his mind and body. It was well-known that good soldiers try to take advantage of any opportunity to rest; they can get some shuteye even in the brief pauses between shooting. Shilin leaned back in the cockpit, and was very nearly asleep when the voice of the duty officer suddenly came over his headphones:

"Five Zero Three, this is Zero Nine…"

The practice was that air bases used identifiers consisting of two numbers, while each individual pilot's call sign consisted of three.

Shilin came to with a start and shook off his fatigue. "Zero Nine, this is Five Zero Three, I read you."

"Five Zero Three, you are ordered to take off."

"I read you, ordered to take off," Shilin repeated in accordance with the eternal ritual. Pilots were obliged to repeat their orders back for them to take force, a rule that they colloquially referred to as "giving Command a receipt".

Shilin flicked the switch on the right of his instrument panel to pow-er his engines, and then moved the throttle from the stop position so that fuel would flow from the tanks to the engines. With his right hand, the pilot pressed the ignition. The engines roared and the plane came to life. With a quick motion, Shilin activated all on-board systems and equipment; the electrical power was the last to come on.

The technical personnel on the airfield were already awaiting their orders. Shilin shook his hand in a distinct motion like that of a fluttering bird to signify "remove the safeties". With well-trained movements, a technician pulled the safeties out of the launchers for Shilin's on-board missiles, holding them up one by one so that the pilot could see them. In response, Shilin nodded and raised a hand, and then immediately notified command. "Zero Nine, this is Five Zero Three. I am taxiing for take-off."

Shilin placed his feet on the pedals and used them to work the plane's wheel mechanism. His plane moved slowly along the taxiway toward the runway. After taxiing, the plane stopped at the beginning of the long concrete strip. An observer could sense in the temporarily immobile machine an immense power, a tense waiting, like a runner kneeling at the starting line. The pilot notified command that he was now ready for take-off.

By this time, the red light at the edge of the runway had turned green, and command now gave him his assignment: "Five Zero Three, maintain a course for the ocean, altitude eight thousand meters!"

Shilin repeated the order back and then pressed the button on the left of his panel to extend the flaps for take-off. He quickly glanced at his instruments to ensure that all systems were operating correctly, and only then did he push his control level all the way and switch his engines to full speed. All that remained was to obtain permission from Command.

"Zero Nine, this is Five Zero Three, requesting permission for take-off."

After receiving a response from Command, the pilot undid the safety clip on the engine lever, set it to afterburner position, and then immediately released the brakes. The plane started from its place and began to move more swiftly with each second. Shilin closely observed the plane's motion, and when his speed reached two hundred kilometers per hour he pulled the control stick toward him. With great sensitivity, the fighter responded to his motions, increasing its lift and raising its nose.

It was still dark. Two rows of lights on either side of the runway, stretching into the distance, showed him the way. The fighter's own navigation lights, too, were now lit. Before the plane actually lifted off, Shilin activated his forward lamps, and their bright light lit up the concrete slipping under the fighter's wheels. From air base command, the fighter moving in the darkness looked like a huge lighted artillery shell being shot into the night.

At a speed of three hundred kilometers per hour, the plane lifted free of the runway. The pilot pulled a lever on the left of his instrument panel in order to retract the landing gear, and then performed a maneuver to enter on his assigned course. Shilin had already come a long way from the airfield. He was intently focused on flying, and unaware that in a few minutes another Su-15 fighter would be taking off on a different course. Command had evidently decided that sending pairs of fighters to intercept in tandem had not worked, and these next two fighters would go their own separate ways.

The latest fighter was the tenth to be sent on an intercept course in the last two hours. That's right; ten aircraft had taken off to confront the mysterious target.

Truth to tell, from the very beginning, an apparently ordinary flight had acquired strange and inexplicable properties. An implausible set of circumstances, extremely inauspicious and outright mystical, had come together. One could be forgiven for concluding that even if every one of the USSR's squadrons, regiments, divisions, and corps had taken off into the sky that night, most likely none of them would have been able to make contact with the stubbornly unyielding target. No; destiny had decreed that no one would recognize the target as an ordinary passenger airliner making a regular journey along a well-known route. An inexplicable jinx hung over the Korean plane that night, and even now, many years later, no one has been able to explain it.

After Shilin's fighter had taken off, his own regiment handed him over to the ground control covering the whole region, located some six hundred kilometers from Shilin's airfield. Shilin maintained radio contact on channel three, which pilots used for communicating among themselves and with the ground.

The command at Shilin's air base, it must be added, were not involved in guiding him toward the target. Once Shilin was outside the immediate area, guidance was provided by other command positions, and each would eventually pass the fighter over to its neighbor. As Shilin flew on, the call signs of the ground stations changed as well, and they now used words instead of numbers. Airfields were designated by fixed call signs, such as Bronya, but the call signs of long-range navigation stations were changed every three months: *Vodoley, Igrok, Kulon*[2]... These names were arbitrary and not based on any particular system. The military simply thought them up, and the only requirement was that they be short and easy to make out over the radio. It was easy to imagine headquarters writhing in creative agony.

At the very end of August, the Sea of Okhotsk was enjoying calm, settled weather. At night, bright lights were reflected in the black water,

---

2  Aquarius, Player, Pendant.

   

and along Sakhalin Island's coastal waters, crabber and seiner vessels were hauling in their catches. This, the last night of summer and the first night of fall, proved unusually clear, and through the transparent window of his cockpit Shilin could clearly see stars overhead and the flashing lights of ships far below.

After eight minutes of flying time, the silence was broken by the ground control station responsible for this area. "Five Zero Three, this is Deputat. Maintain a course for the ocean. The target is ahead of you, it is an intruder. Maintain a course to meet it."

"Roger," Shilin replied, then fell silent, awaiting further orders.

No further orders came, however. Instead, ground control told Shilin that for some strange reason their forward radar was inoperative.

Naturally, it was an awkward situation, but in Russia it would have been strange if all systems were actually operating correctly. If they were, then it would not have been Russia but some completely different country. Under the Soviet regime, planes and helicopters often crashed, instruments malfunctioned, ammunition stores exploded, submarines foundered, fuel tanks ignited, men on watch duty got drunk and opened fire, while generals went hunting for wolves and deer from military helicopters and used soldiers' labor to build their summer homes. In short, there was never a dull moment in the Soviet army.

Frankly, every Russian already knows that instruments, mechanisms, machines and devices of all kinds often go haywire in our climate. Everyone has grown used to breakdowns, accidents, shipwrecks, and disasters. So common are they that people are amazed when something goes off without a hitch; it seems like a violation of the prevailing norm.

Sad though it may be, Russia is a wacky country. Each of us seems to have two good hands, and a head on his shoulders, yet nothing ever comes together correctly, and even if it does work out, it only does so haphazardly and with great difficulty.

The present occasion was no exception. "Five Zero Three," said the station Deputat, "radar in the forward hemisphere is not operational. We will guide you using rear radar."

Shilin was tempted to express his opinion of the situation aloud with a torrent of profanity, but he knew that other ears were listening to his transmissions, and so he had to hold his tongue. He banked sharply and entered on a reverse course, as the ground-control station guided his plane toward the target and at the right altitude.

Shilin's fighter completed its turn and raced to catch up with the target. At high speed, the interceptor passed over the coastal region and flew headlong toward the north-west and the intruder. The skies above the sea were clear, and only a few light clouds hung ahead of him along his course. Shilin was not thinking about how his encounter with the other plane would turn out; he did not speculate, but kept his eyes fixed on the horizon. He felt ready for any turn of events… but then he caught sight of the target and could not believe his eyes: far ahead of him, almost at the limits of his sight, were flashing navigation lights. They clearly showed, without a shadow of a doubt, that this was a passenger plane. A red light burned steadily on the left wing and a green light on the right, while the aft light was white. In addition, a white strobe flashed on the left wing and a red beacon on the tail.

Shilin was taken aback, even dumbfounded. This was hard to credit: aerial reconnaissance planes would fly over foreign territory without these navigation lights on. He felt that he had to report this immediately to Command. "We've got a big 'un here," he radioed. He described the target's heading and speed, and then he loudly stated, so that the ground station would clearly understand, "It's flying with its lights flashing!"

Nevertheless, the fact that it was a large plane with its navigation lights on made no impression on ground control, and did not attract especial interest among higher command. They were all quite convinced that they were dealing with a spy plane, and obviously the lights were merely being used to camouflage it. Everyone knows that spies are a crafty sort – they have even been known to put reindeer hooves under their boots in order to cross the border undetected. The famed border guard Nikita Karatsupa and his dog Ingus had caught a great many of them back in the 1930s.

Indeed, the scene had a truly mystical quality. The plane's steady, intractable, unshakable forward movement was charged with a peculiar sense of predestination. Just as fateful was the fact that no one had managed to identify it all night long.

The plane seemed to have come out of nowhere and was flying toward who knew where. One might have thought that there was no one on board at all, neither passengers nor crew, that this huge empty jumbo jet, like a *Flying Dutchman* with its navigation lights eternally lit, was on some endless voyage across the skies. The thought unexpectedly came to Shilin that the plane had been flying for years now over the earth without ever landing – it was a ghost plane, a flying mirage.

The huge plane with its navigation lights on was moving at an altitude of ten thousand meters with a cruising speed of one thousand kilometers per hour. As Shilin approached it, he could make out its dim windows; clearly the lights were on low in the plane's cabin, as is usually the case when passengers are sleeping. Shilin could even see a logo, a flying crane, on the plane's tail. If this logo was for real, then the plane belonged to the Korean airline whose flight corridor R-20 ran five hundred kilometers away to the east, over the sea. Shilin could hardly believe his eyes. Heavens, he thought, how did it get here?

Civil aviation routes were located far from the Soviet border. It was hard to believe that a passenger plane, with its triplicate satellite, inertial, and magnetic navigation systems, could be so inept as to stray so far off course. In the clear sky there was nowhere to get lost and fall off the beaten track. That meant that it could only be a foreign spy plane using the lights and logo of a passenger airliner.

With a motion that was unthinking and second nature after years of service as a fighter pilot, Shilin activated his plane's on-board radar, which functioned as a sight for his weaponry. Lights came on right away to indicate that his missiles were now guided. The intruder had nowhere to run; it was flying right in Shilin's electronic sights and its life hung by a thread. Shilin only had to press a button, and in the blink of an eye his missiles would hit their target.

Nevertheless, the pilot had never stopped feeling troubled. His doubts remained; he was not fully convinced, and he hesitated. After all, civil aviation planes had sometimes strayed off course for one reason or another. Shilin had only to admit the thought that this might be a passenger plane for his heart to freeze. He did not have it in him to become a murderer. This thought brushed against his consciousness and burned him with an unexpected intensity. Indeed, if he pushed the button now, there would be no going back, these people could not be saved, the sentence would be carried out and it would never be subject to any appeal.

Now the decision came down to him alone. If this was a spy plane, then it ought to be shot down – it would get its just deserts. But if it were a passenger plane, then only a single instant stood between now and massive loss of life.

Just think, a quick, barely noticeable flick of Shilin's finger could easily shatter the world – for anyone on that plane, the one and only world they knew. If Shilin pressed the button, an instant later those people, strangers to him, would perish, be lost without a trace, tumble into the black abyss of the night. As his fighter plane shot through the night at incredible speed, the pilot was suddenly overcome by a thought inappropriate for a military man: no one had given him unlimited power over other human beings. Hard on the heels of this first thought came another: he had no right to decide so recklessly whether others would live or die.

These thoughts tumbled through his mind, but there was little time to reflect on them, nor was the cockpit of a fighter-interceptor a suitable venue for it. Yet the feeling that he was a pilot and not the Almighty, and therefore he could not punish or forgive so categorically, remained lodged like a splinter in his brain. Such musings might be expected to get in the way of the performance of one's military duties, but independent of this feeling and even in spite of it, the pilot confidently performed all maneuvers, his many years of training showing their worth; his reliable internal autopilot. The fighter was moving much faster than the target, so Shilin had to match its speed as best he could and keep at a distance from it while he awaited orders from the ground.

"Deputat, this is Five Zero Three. I have intercepted the target and am now on its tail. It is a passenger plane, what are my orders?"

The voice from the ground with the call sign Deputat was acting rather strangely, however. It seemed unfazed by Shilin's announcement that the target was a passenger plane. Instead, ground control began insistently to ask what course the intruder was maintaining, its bearing and altitude. Shilin repeated that the plane had its navigation lights on and that it was a passenger plane.

Not for the first time that night, ground radars had lost track of the target. No signals were being received, for some strange reason, and all the planes that had been sent up toward the target now disappeared from the radar operators' screens. The first night of fall was not a very smooth one for air defense. The ground stations, now blind, had repeatedly to ask the pilots what they could see and where the target was located. Fortunately, radio communication was still operational.

For a while, four planes were airborne in the night skies above the Sea of Okhotsk: three Su-15 interceptors and one MiG-23 fighter. Two of the Su-15s had come from the Smirnykh air base along the 50th parallel, while the other two planes – which included Shilin's – had taken off from the Sokol airport at the south of Sakhalin Island. Although the target had already violated Soviet airspace once, in the area of Kamchatka, it was now no longer permissible to open fire. The plane was approaching the Soviet border once more, but as long as it was over neutral waters, the fighters could only accompany it.

Meanwhile, the operators at the ground stations were still looking at empty screens. The voices guiding the fighters were baffled by what was going on, and they could only radio the pilots with a torrent of questions. Things turned chaotic as the four pilots spoke among themselves on channel three while also maintaining their links with the ground. Radio communications over the Sea of Okhotsk came to resemble the din of a noisy bar.

Later, we at Division X studied the actions of the pilots who took off to intercept. We were provided with tablets showing flight assignments, and we received charts and maps from the United States and Japan, where they were used as official documents supplied by electronic-surveillance stations. The devices had recorded, and the plotting boards confirmed, that the intercepting fighters were moving at high speeds and with sharp changes in altitude and rapid changes of course, as if they were engaged in aerial warfare. They were flying at top speed across the sky. One can imagine what the personnel at the command posts and headquarters felt when the ground stations suddenly went blind. The officers and generals looked at each other in confusion; none of them knew what was going on in the skies above and what action should be taken. Once again, they could distinctly hear the nails being pounded into their own metaphorical coffins when word of their failure spread. They clearly understood that if they let this target slip away, tomorrow they would be buried alive, crucified, and burned at the stake. No one had any doubt that punishment would come down on them swiftly and definitively, and with no objective investigation having taken place. The best way out of this was to die a brave death at their posts.

=== **26** ===

Toward evening, Junior Lieutenant Shilina and the doctor Sofia Margolina convinced the children to go with them to the base hospital. First, however, they had to promise that after a bath, the children would be able to return to their home. It took a long time to win the children over. They looked at the women warily and shook their heads uncertainly. Major Margolina frowned and threw up her hands, unable to figure out why these foundling children should be so incorrigible and what it was that they wanted. The American and the interpreter, however, had guessed at the real reason: the children were worried about abandoning the German to the whims of fate; they realized that he would not be able to survive on his own.

All through the previous fall, winter, and spring, the children had taken care of the German corporal. He had grown used to them, and waited day by day for them to come, unable to manage without them. Like all children, they needed adults around, but besides the German there was no one left, and the children took it on themselves to care for him. If they no longer visited the dugout, there would be no one to feed the corporal or be company for him, and he would assume that the children had abandoned him. The children were furthermore worried that the German would leave the dugout, be spotted, and be killed. In short, they were afraid for him and knew that he was done for without them; and this was the whole secret behind their odd behavior.

Against the shining white surfaces of the base hospital, the boy and girl looked especially filthy, emaciated, and sickly. The staff instantly appreciated what hunger and hardship the children had faced. Everyone was eager to wash them, feed them, and show them some affection. As soon as the children appeared on the threshold, before they could even step inside, they were surrounded by nurses, doctors, and orderlies. Some of the staff gasped, screamed, or even burst into tears. The women gathered around the children and shooed them forward, clucking their tongues like mother hens accompanying their chicks.

     

It was easy to understand the medical personnel. The young women among them had joined the war effort when they were little more than girls. They had grown up during the war, and the sight of these children awakened their maternal instincts. Others had children of their own whom they had not seen for a long time, having been forced to entrust them to the care of a grandmother, and now they saw their own children in these little orphans and were overcome by tears. It was obvious that a great deal of tenderness had accumulated inside them during the war and not found an outlet, and now they lavished it on the children. They carefully and affectionately removed their clothes, and once disrobed, the children looked like real starvelings, all skin and bone, and the sight was hard to bear. Their dirty skin was covered with festering sores and scabs, and it was easy to see how much they had suffered. The women were horrified, their emotions clearly showing on their faces. Some of them began to cry, and one elderly orderly let out a great moan, though she had seen everything in this war and one might think it impossible to faze her.

All the staff on duty took pains to show the children affection. Amid the general commotion, Major Margolina ordered that the children be bathed. At that, utter pandemonium broke out. All the nurses and orderlies were eager to take part in bathing the children – something they had done long ago, in peacetime, before the war. Each of the women wanted to show that she knew better how to do it, as if she had been bathing kids her whole life.

A typically Russian outcry erupted, and a quarrel broke out like in the kitchen of a communal apartment. The women began pushing and shoving in order to get ahead of one another. Emotions were running high, and they had apparently forgotten about anyone else. The American watched, confused and unable to understand what all the commotion was about. The interpreter felt embarrassed for the entire Russian people.

"What's going on? Why are they shouting?" Lieutenant Creighton asked Olga. "Are they upset about something?"

"They want to bathe the children," Olga explained.

Creighton was still unable to understand. "Why are they fighting, then?"

"Each of them wants to do it herself, with her own hands."

The American watched the agitated crowd keenly in the hope of gaining an insight into the mysterious Russian soul. At college, Steven Creighton had read Tolstoy and Dostoevsky, but this was the first time that he had seen the Russian people up close, with his own eyes. The

Russians really were bizarre people, or at least strange. The more close-ly Creighton observed them, the more astonished and confused he be-came. Major Margolina was shouting at her subordinates, and only with difficulty could she get the women to quiet down.

Once silence had been established, the doctor scolded them and promised reprimands if they did not calm down. "Are you in the army or not?" she asked, her face a mask of severity.

Major Margolina had a daughter of her own growing up far from the front. She had not seen her daughter since the beginning of the war, and she was not averse to the idea of bathing the children herself. The medi-cal personnel stood back, disappointed, and some even complained that it was unfair, but the major raised her voice and shut the women up. She looked round the crowd and selected two experienced orderlies who were usually tasked with bathing seriously wounded men. These wom-en put on their oilcloth aprons and led the children to the bath, where they fell to washing them with especial care. The other women huddled in the hallway outside the door, unwilling to disperse. It was only with difficulty that the major sent them back to their various duties.

Meanwhile, the American and the interpreter stepped outside. In the general commotion, no one paid any attention to them. Creighton quietly told Olga that he had arranged matters with his crew and, if she was ready, they would fly off that night.

"What?!" Olga replied, and then lowered her voice. "Tonight?"

"If we've made up our minds, it's better to do it now."

"But so soon… I'm not ready. Please wait a little bit."

"Olga, you've got to understand, we can't put this off, otherwise it might be too late. There are rumors going around that we're going to be transferred. Plus, you said yourself that if you wait any longer, they're going to arrest you."

"No, they won't. What for?"

"Didn't your friend tell you?"

"Kapitolina was just trying to scare me. She wants to separate us. Why would they arrest me?"

"She's helping them in all this. It's all her doing."

"Come on, you're being unfair to her. She wouldn't do something like that."

"You want to make sure of that?" Creighton looked deep into her eyes. "Are we really going to wait and see?"

Olga fell silent and wrestled with her thoughts. She was riven by doubt. She found it very difficult to think that there was no way back, that everything had been decided, that she had burned her bridges and now had to make her escape. And not just sometime in the future but now, tonight, in just a few hours' time. Just thinking about fleeing the USSR gripped her with a cold fear. Her heart alternately stopped and pounded frantically, and she found it hard to breathe.

"Please understand… I thought we had more time, we would do it later. I'm not ready now. I'm really scared…" Olga said haltingly. "I can't just abandon everything and leave. It's too hard for me. I have to get used to the idea first."

It was easy to understand the way she felt. We are all afraid of making big changes; of completely altering our lives. We try to dismiss those thoughts, and even if we really can't avoid it, we still try to put it off. Important decisions that cannot be postponed require courage; they seem a challenge to our very existence. Even easygoing sorts need time to think things over before they can accept that something really is necessary, before they can be sure that there really is no other way.

At the same time, Lieutenant Creighton was right about the need to escape. As a nation of immigrants, Americans related quite easily to the need to move towns and countries. They were rarely if ever burdened by an attachment to a particular place. He felt truly sorry for Olga. He realized how hard this was for her, how afraid she was of making the change. He knew that she was deeply torn, and he could clearly understand her pain and fear. However, like a surgeon, he could not let emotions get in the way if he was going to save her.

"Olga, right now is a good time," Creighton tried to explain to her. "They still haven't got you. Later it will be too late. Everything could change, literally in a flash."

She knew that he was right. If they had decided to do this, then they could not wait for a better moment. She had to make her escape that night, or give up on the idea altogether. She was no longer able to give the idea up, though. If they were already planning to arrest her, should she really just wait resignedly, meekly extending her neck in anticipation of the falling axe? Creighton, as if he had guessed at what she was thinking, asked her if she was not going to at least try to evade her persecutors and save herself.

This is how human beings are: we try to find a reason not to go through with a plan; we invent a reason outright and simply say not now, not today, later, some other time.

"What about the children?" Olga suddenly asked. "What will happen to them?"

"We've done everything we could. The doctor will take care of them," Creighton replied. "The major will see to them better than we could."

"The children don't trust her. The major said she would send them to an orphanage. She doesn't know about the German."

"What could you do to help them?" Creighton asked wearily, as if realizing his own helplessness.

"I'll look after the children. If they run away, they'll die. I'll talk to them, they trust me. The German will become a prisoner of war, and the children will go to the orphanage."

"How much time do you need?"

"Two or three days. That will be enough."

The American bowed his head, deeply troubled. This was not for the best; her answer and his decision were not in accord. It was clear from the gloomy expression on his face that he did not agree with her. He shook his head and asked morosely, as if he felt a heavy weight descend upon him, "Next time, then?"

"Yes, yes, next time," Olga nodded. This seemed to her a good way of proceeding: today she would stay behind and he would depart without her, and in the meantime she would get ready and grow more used to the idea of leaving.

Olga felt guilty at her own indecisiveness, though, so she firmly promised the American that at the next opportunity they would fly off together. She promised this to him and felt convinced of it herself. The truth was, however, that she was relieved. She did not have to leave there and then; she was delaying her escape, giving herself time to catch her breath, and feel a little relief. Like anyone to whom some great life drama beckoned, she was nagged by a single thought that pulsed inside her brain: not today. Any other time, just not now.

The matronly orderlies brought the children back from the bath, wrapped in sheets. Women ran up from all over the field hospital and surrounded the children, squealing as if in unison, "What clean little darlings we are now!" The children stood there in their makeshift garments and looked on impassively. The bath had made them sleepy; they yawned, and their eyelids drooped. They were not left to go to sleep, however. Major Margolina appeared. She drove the onlookers away, and then, with the help of the nurses, started treating the children's sores. Then the children were dressed in some army clothes: clean white shirts that reached below the girl's knees and right down to the boy's feet.

"Olga, we're making a big mistake," Creighton said with a degree of ominousness. "You need to leave today. There might not be a next time."

"No, no, I can't today! I'm not ready," Olga said, flustered. She felt an alternating chill and fever of anxiety. "Next time, I promise you! It will only be a few days. What could change? You will come back, won't you?"

Creighton sighed heavily. "I don't know."

"Of course you'll come back! By then the children will be taken care of. I'll feel better, and you will too."

The American listened, but then shook his head gloomily. "I'm worried about you," he said, trying to keep his voice calm. "But I can't force you. It's your decision."

He fell silent, not even attempting to repeat his arguments. Common sense told him that it was not up to him whether or not he would come back safe next time. Our human experience tells us that things change, that neither individuals nor even whole nations can rely on things staying the same. Neither the American nor the Soviet interpreter could claim that fortune was on their side. Their luck seemed to be highly uncertain, and things might change overnight. The natural course of events might end up taking a sharp turn and result in a disaster for them both. Both Creighton and Olga knew how little hope meant, for regardless of what they hoped, they were not in control of events. The American copilot might be shot down, his wing might be transferred to a different air base and different route, while the interpreter – even if she avoided arrest – might be sent elsewhere. All of us are subject to the whims of fate and must navigate all of life's obstacles, unaware of what lies ahead of us.

Meanwhile, the children had been given semolina to eat and sweetened tea to drink, and then they were put to bed in an empty room in the hospital. They put up some feeble resistance, as they wanted to go back to the farm, but Olga and an orderly named Marina Kovaleva convinced them to stay in the hospital until the next day. The children instantly fell asleep side by side on beds made with clean sheets. For the first time in the three years since they had been orphaned, the children slept in a civilized environment, just as they had done before the war. Major Margolina showed some sympathy to the staff on duty, and allowed them to take turns quietly looking in from the doorway.

The women crowded in the doorway and stood still, as if they were gathered for a group portrait that would capture them forever. As the women stood in the doorway, they recalled peacetime, their homes and families. They forgot about the war and they hoped, hoped, hoped that victory would come soon and life would resume; it was only a matter of waiting patiently. This was how Olga and Creighton remembered the children and the hospital staff. They never saw them again; fate never brought them together again.

Now came the most difficult part: Creighton and Olga had to go their separate ways so that they would not attract suspicion. To their surprise, Major Sofia Margolina was strangely anxious to accompany them. The three of them walked out into the yard of the hospital and stopped under the trees. It was now late in the day and the sunset had faded, but it was still light outside and twilight loomed in the peaceful stillness. Far off in the vegetation, nightingales echoed each other's songs. The birds' whistling, trilling and clicking sounds carried over the wide space.

"Is he flying out today?" the doctor asked, referring to the American lieutenant.

"Yes, he's leaving tonight," Olga replied.

"We've got an electric stove in reception," the major began, but cut herself off. Then she flashed a timid smile. "If you like, I can make you some tea."

"Let me ask him," Junior Lieutenant Shilina said, and interpreted the major's invitation for the American.

Creighton readily accepted. "*Da*," he said. "*Khorosho, spasibo,*" thus managing to use in one go almost all the Russian words he knew.

"That's great!" Major Margolina praised him. "His Russian is excellent."

The hospital's reception was located in a different wing of the building. The doctor led them down a dark and deserted corridor and opened a door with her key. Darkness had not yet fallen outside the window of the office, but little light entered through the window, and the room was almost completely dark. Nevertheless, the doctor's first action was to draw the curtains.

"Oh, I almost forgot!" the major suddenly exclaimed. "I still need to make my rounds!" She stuck the key in the lock and then walked off, waving goodbye. "Have a good flight!" In the silence, they heard her footsteps sounding in the corridor, and then a door squeaking far off.

Hard as it was to believe, this was the first time since the American and the interpreter had met that they had been left alone together in a room. For the first time, fortune had smiled on them and given them a refuge and a roof over their heads. They were astonished at the unexpectedness of it all, and looked around in bewilderment, unable to understand what had happened. The major had clearly been aware of their romance, but until this moment had not revealed her knowledge of it.

   

A roof over their heads and a key for the door. Such was the perennial concern of lovers, whether in America or in Russia. Or in any country, for that matter. And if two people managed to obtain those things, then they were truly lucky. Olga and Creighton stood there for a moment without speaking, and then the American tenderly embraced the interpreter and brushed his lips across her face. Olga herself had spent so long waiting for this moment, dreaming of it. The pair stood still in a long and drawn-out kiss. Olga felt breathless, her pulse raced and her heart pounded, and her head spun. Their kiss contained the quiet pleasure of togetherness, as well as the uncertainty and sadness of not knowing what was in store for them both. It was easy to understand how they felt.

The circumstances in which the interpreter Olga Shilina and copilot Steven Creighton found themselves contained a distinct bitterness. They had to be cautious and keep their affair secret. Danger loomed everywhere, a threat hung over them, and at any moment they might be found out, condemned, and branded for their crime. Yet as we all know, forbidden fruit is the sweetest, and a secret affair has an especial appeal and a burning passion to it. Lovers who are forced to keep their love hidden experience much stronger feelings than those whose passion faces no obstacles. In a forbidden affair, one values every moment, the time spent together is worth its weight in gold, and the lovers cannot wait until they are able to be alone with each other for at least a brief moment.

This hospital room proved a perfect example of such an instance. The interpreter and the American sat down on the narrow bed that had been made with fresh linen.

Creighton looked into the interpreter's eyes. "Olga, I don't know what's going to happen next," he quietly said. "But I want you to know that I love you, and I want you to be my wife."

"Yes," the junior lieutenant nodded timidly. "Of course I'll be your wife. And you will be my husband."

He carefully undid the metal buttons on the collar of her tunic. Olga helped him in this, and with her own hands she undid her leather officer's belt. The interpreter knew that her friends would condemn her for his, and so would all her comrades, superiors and Communist Party officials, the staff officers and quartermasters, the navy, air force, and infantry, and the Great Leader himself. Furthermore, the overwhelming majority of her fellow Russians, the whole nation, would hate her for behaving so immodestly with a foreign officer.

In those years, a relationship with a foreigner was equal to treason, a shock to the country's very foundations. Both the authorities and the people, it must be said, thought alike in this regard. But what else was she to do? Every time she met the American she spent the rest of the day thinking about nothing but him. In her thoughts, her whole future was bound up only with him, and she could not bear the thought that they might be destined to be apart. How would she go on living? How would she bear her cross?

The interpreter knew for sure that he was the man she had been waiting for. He was the man of her girlhood dreams, and she needed no one else. The thought did not even enter her mind that this American might only be attracted to her out of boredom, that he had entered into an affair there on the front line only out of idle curiosity, and he was merely taking advantage of the circumstances to have a good time. No, Junior Lieutenant Shilina trusted in Creighton without a moment's hesitation. She knew that he was not deceiving her.

However, on this occasion, fate had other plans in store. The telephone suddenly rang, a sharp, jarring sound that caught them by surprise. The interpreter looked angrily at the black office telephone as if it were a living creature. She waited for it to stop, but the infuriating little beast kept up its torturous ringing and demanded an answer.

The ringing stopped for a moment. The two thought that the phone had called off its evil pursuit of them, but this was not to be: once more it erupted into an angry ringing that refused to stop. The phone, in short, seemed out to get them. It was hard not to pick it up and answer. The sound seemed to pin Olga to the bed with its piercing sound, and she did not know what to do. Maybe someone was trying to warn them, or someone had telephoned this room in search of the doctor, or there was some other reason for it. Regardless, Olga felt deeply afraid.

"We've completely lost our minds," Olga said. She turned cold and, as if sobering up, pushed Creighton away and buttoned up her tunic. It is true that women in love are always more cool-headed than men. "You should hurry, you're flying out soon."

"I don't want to think about that," Creighton answered. He seemed crushed. "Do we really have to say goodbye? Olga, darling, maybe we can leave together after all? It's not too late."

She shook her head sadly. "No, my dear," she said, and put her belt back around her waist. "We have already decided everything. Next time."

They heard footsteps coming down the corridor, then someone cautiously knocked at the door. "Olga, it's me," came the whispering voice of Major Margolina. "They're looking for you."

     

Olga turned the key in the lock and opened the door. The doctor was standing at the threshold.

"The Communist Party officials called and asked about you," said Major Margolina. She sounded distinctly alarmed.

"What do they want?" Olga asked. She felt a cold, empty feeling inside, and her legs were weak with fear.

"They asked where you were. Only you… I said you were somewhere around, and that I could go and look for you. They said they'd call back. Say goodbye to him, he needs to go now." The doctor then delicately shut the door.

Olga embraced Creighton and kissed him. "Time for you to go. I'll wait for you. We'll see each other again soon."

Olga did not tell him that they were looking for her. She felt sorry for the American, and she had decided that if they were going to arrest her, it was better that he did not know about it. She did not want him to be upset. The major told Olga to wait there while she led the American away through the quarantine ward, which was empty for the moment, but which in accordance with hygiene regulations had its own separate exit.

After Creighton had left, the interpreter and the major set off together for their lodgings. Olga repeatedly glanced around nervously; she felt pursued by an unknown fear. All the way back to her quarters she sensed that she was being followed, watched from all sides.

"Olga, calm down. It's just your imagination," the major said, trying to reason with the interpreter, but without success. Olga continued to look back, as if some intent gaze was burning into her back.

Along the way they encountered other soldiers and officers, and in each chance person met, Olga suspected a spy who had been assigned to watch her. At times she felt that she might never make it home, that she would be arrested there on the road. She looked back with regret on her refusal to fly out that night. Steven had been right, there might never be a suitable moment again, and she could only be sorry that she had let the opportunity slip by.

All of us experience similar feelings. When you think about who exactly you have antagonized, what power now stands against you, you feel weak and alone, like a lone blade of grass in a cold wind. For many Russians, the regime seemed like a merciless and hungry beast that could not be mollified and was incapable of forgiving. Up against that mindless and severe regime, a human being feels helpless, abandoned, overcome by horror, and is tempted to flee from the eyes of others, or simply collapse and pull a blanket over his head.

In Russia, individuals generally felt intimidated by the authorities. That is why, when people noticed they were being watched or suspected that they would be accused of something, they would do inexplicable, strange, silly things, or they would immediately make a run for it. During the war years, a person's life was not worth even a kopeck. It was therefore understandable that the interpreter was now literally shaking with fear. It was only with Creighton that Olga had felt secure, as if he was capable of protecting her. With him, things seemed calm and reliable. If she could only be with him again, her fears would fly away. She would feel confident again that everything would turn out fine, and perhaps the devil was not as fearsome as he had been made out to be.

Once back at their lodgings, Major Margolina invited Olga in for tea and tried to calm her and assuage her sadness. They spent some time in gossip and idle conversation. The major remarked that American men were much nicer than Russians.

"Of course you can have your fling," she said. "I understand you, Olga, I really do. No matter what anyone might say, there's nothing shameful in that. And they are gallant men, not like ours at all. Civilized people. Compared to them, our boys seem uncouth, childish. What could you expect, though? It used to be that officers came from the aristocracy, they had been brought up differently. But these modern ones… What do they know? Let alone about manners. I'm even a little jealous of you, you'll have something to look back on. Is this the first time you've ever been in love?"

"Yes," Olga nodded. "The first time."

"Great! Your first love, and he's so romantic! It's just a shame that sooner or later he has to leave. But people in love have to live in the moment. Just a brief instant and then it's over. You're still young…"

"I think this will be forever," the interpreter said.

"Who knows. Everyone thinks that. Well, if God wills it… But be careful. If they ask, deny everything. No flings, no romances, just purely professional contacts. Do you have to work with the American crews?"

"Yes, I do."

"That's good. It means that you are just doing your duty, and I can back you up. The children are a sufficient argument. The two of you decided to save them."

"Thank you," came Olga's whisper. Tears had returned to her eyes. "Sofia, I am very afraid."

"Of course you are! They are adult men and yet they don't know how to act. Those old wolves are always so fretful. And they have to deal with sweet little girls like you. They'll offer you a chance to confess everything, they'll say that for you it would be better to just accept a reprimand. Don't you give in, though. You stand your ground. Can they prove anything? Though they don't necessarily need any proof. That's how they operate, without needing any proof. But just keep one thing in mind: you maintained a professional relationship with the Americans, nothing more."

They drank tea in the twilight without turning the light on. Fresh air blew in from the open window, carrying with it a scent of night-blooming flowers and greenery. Outside the neighboring barracks, someone was playing an accordion. In the evenings there was dancing in the street, and the mood became loud and festive. Lively voices, music, and women's laughter reached Olga and Major Margolina from far off. The party was already in full swing. Here, though, in the solitude, cicadas chirped in the stillness, and life seemed to be passing by on the other side. It was sad, it made the heart ache, and it was hard not to feel sorry for oneself.

When Olga returned to her room, her friend was sleeping, but Kapitolina immediately awoke and wasted no time in questioning Olga. "Did you see him off?"

"I was with the doctors," Olga replied.

"Are you ill?"

"We were drinking tea."

"Why didn't you invite me? You're there drinking tea with them, and I'm here all on my own."

"Sofia Margolina invited me."

"Olga, I don't get you. It's like you're deliberately ignoring me. And now you're talking to me in this weird way, like we're strangers."

"Just remember our Communist Party officials, then, and how they always bring people close together."

"You talk like I should feel guilty about something. This is all your own doing. I warned you. They were asking about you at the office today, by the way."

"How do you know?"

"I was there and I overheard what they were saying. You've got some explaining to do."

"Fine," said Olga. She undressed and went to bed.

Junior Lieutenant Shilina thought back over the day. It was hard to believe that it had all been real, and not a dream. If someone had told her earlier that she was capable of falling head over heels in love and completely forgetting everything else, she would have said no, impossible! She had never been driven by burning desire and turbulent passions. She was more inclined to follow her mind than her heart. Had she been deceiving everyone, deceiving even herself, the whole time? She was suddenly unsure of her ability to reflect on things with a sober, cool head. The day that she had just spent suggested that her uncertainty was justified.

Olga had already come to link all thoughts of the future with the American. Before meeting him, she had seen her life as something dull and routine – though she had not experienced any anxieties or worries either, whereas now she found herself worried and afraid day by day and hour by hour. Nevertheless, no matter what, the interpreter knew that she would readily choose her present worries over her former feeling of calm.

A heavy roar now reached her quarters from the direction of the airfield. The junior lieutenant realized that the bomber planes had started their engines. The roar increased and filled the entire surrounding area, then grew to such a degree that it utterly drowned out all other sounds.

In her thoughts, the interpreter kept saying to some unknown listener out there, "Just let him get there safely. Just let him come back here safely…" She was unaware of whom exactly she was addressing and, having been brought up under a godless regime, she did not even think about who it was. Something had changed within her, though, since the time she had witnessed the American crews at prayer. The more time went on, the more she was conscious of that change in herself, as if those prayers that others had made were now having their effect on her, too. Even an impenitent sinner may address a clumsy prayer to God when the need comes.

"You know, Olga…" her friend suddenly said to her in the darkness. "I even thought you might fly away with him tonight."

"With who? Fly where?" Olga asked. She was feigning tiredness, but she felt a chill come over her.

She suddenly felt that she was standing on the edge of an abyss. A bottomless void yawned before her feet. Her friend ignored her questions, left them unanswered, as if they required no response and there was no use wasting her breath.

"Flying away with that American…" Kapitolina said, continuing to think aloud. "That would be a huge mistake. The biggest mistake of your life. You know I could never allow you to do that."

"Kapitolina, what are you talking about?" Olga said with a pretense of weariness and fatigue. "You're being silly."

"As your friend, I bear some responsibility for you. Would I really let you suffer for the rest of your life?"

"Kapitolina, I want to sleep!" Olga snapped, as if she were experiencing relentless torment and wanted to show that she was begging for mercy: as if she was saying that she had no strength for such silly fantasies, especially at such a late hour when she was dead tired.

"You wouldn't just be a deserter," Kapitolina said, only more feebly and sleepily than before. She fell silent, as if she had said everything that needed to be said, and she could fall asleep with her conscience clear.

Olga, however, could not sleep a wink. Her friend's words had set her heart pounding with horror and all but leaping out of her chest. The void at her feet had not disappeared; no, it was only growing clearer, closer, vaster, and terror gripped her.

The next morning, Junior Lieutenant Shilina was called to the Communist Party office. A captain there demanded an explanation, promising that there would be trouble, and vowing that she would rot in jail for it. The interpreter was then taken to Command, where a colonel gave her a grave look and asked, darkly:

"Well, what is it then?"

"I don't understand what's going on," Olga shrugged innocently. "The comrade captain yelled at me about something, but he wouldn't say what."

The colonel opened the folder in front of him and gloomily leafed through its scanty contents: he had nothing to go on but idle gossip and speculation. Among the piles of more important things that he had to see to, he really had no time to deal with these silly Moscow girls who had no understanding of military discipline and the concept of remaining vigilant.

"Fine, you are dismissed," the colonel said with annoyance, and waved her away, as if she had been the one who pressed for a meeting and now he was refusing and hoping to avoid her. As usual with commanding officers, the colonel could not deny himself the pleasure of adding a final threat: "You watch out now. If anything happens, you'll be sorry! I will rip that officer's insignia off with my own bare hands!"

What weighed most heavily on the interpreter now was the thought that she now longer had any choice: they would not leave her alone, so whether she liked it or not, she should leave with the American. She had at least had some kind of choice before, and had decided for herself what to do. Now she could not even choose. She was shocked, though, that her friend had guessed she might fly away with Creighton. Had she really acted so irresponsibly and, frankly, so stupidly, and given herself away?

In general, it was hard to keep military secrets – a challenge that Communist Party officials and secret army divisions were facing now for the first time in this war. The arrival of a large number of female personnel meant a lot of headaches: love was blossoming at the air base. Around the clock, in any weather, regardless of the barometer and the direction of the wind, love was in the air for officers and rank and file alike; personnel at the base were abandoning themselves entirely to flirting. This was hardly a surprise, though. In an army at war there is a surplus of unsatisfied desires, and it is a crying shame to not seize the opportunity when good fortune comes calling. Female company – happiness has arrived – seize the moment!

At first, Communist Party officials looked indulgently upon this unbridled flirting. They did not particularly care when the fires of love were kindled between two of their own. One cannot fight natural instincts, and mentally and physically a person needs normal sexual relations. However, as soon as the USSR's allies landed at the air base, Communist Party officials found that their task had become a lot harder. Now they had to ensure that individuals' longings did not proceed in a suspicious and harmful direction. Secret informants were set to work. Military duty is, it must be admitted, not an easy job. How were they to defend the virtue, ideological convictions and values of their compatriots from the wiles of these foreigners? How could they protect the naive and simple-minded female sex from such cunning seducers? In other words, the air base personnel needed to be guarded from harmful foreign influences. The senior Communist Party official at the base would be held personally responsible for any lost sheep.

The staff at the Communist Party office complained about it being summer. If Operation Frantic had taken place in the winter, things would have been a lot easier for the authorities: it is less work to keep an eye on lovers in the cold and frost. Granted, lovers are a remarkably crafty species, well able to arrange their rendezvous in winter too; but in the summer, the whole of nature is inclined toward love and contributes to its various manifestations. To their bitter disappointment, Party officials discovered first-hand how difficult it was to keep a tight rein on the army in summer.

How could you ever keep an eye on them all if thousands of men and women came together at one time in one place, and they were surrounded by the tender month of June with its warm nights, secluded groves, and tall grass? Gogol's native land lay bathed in warm languor, it lusted with desires, and longed impatiently to satisfy them.

Radar operators swept the skies over the Sea of Okhotsk, but they were unable to locate their target. It seemed to have disappeared entirely, vanished without a trace. They found themselves wondering if the fighters sent in to intercept the target had already shot it down without a second thought. And if there was no longer any target, there was no longer any problem, so why keep talking about it?

There were various reasons why it might have disappeared. Perhaps one of the pilots had lost his temper and, completely fed up with this impudent intruder, had decided to teach it a lesson. Nor could one could rule out the prospect that the target itself had pulled some clever move and disappeared on its own, which sometimes happens with aircraft.

There was no shortage of possible explanations. All versions were plausible and credible, but none of the Soviet ground personnel bothered to determine for certain what had happened. Moreover, their own fighters sent in to intercept had disappeared from their radar screens – a puzzle for everyone at the tracking stations and command positions. In all of our lives there are moments when we strive, we keep trying, we flap our wings, we make an effort, but to no avail, we merely tear ourselves to pieces. Even the powerful ground station with the call sign Karnaval, which kept watch over the Pacific Ocean and the countries of the Pacific Rim, was unable to locate the target in spite of its painstaking, almost superhuman efforts. The officers on duty there could only shrug helplessly and mutter a few pathetic words to justify themselves.

Thus, as it has been said before, the skies above the Sea of Okhotsk and Sakhalin Island were filled with nervous radio chatter. An outside observer listening in on these transmissions would have assumed that a heated quarrel was playing out on channel three. Everyone involved – pilots, ground control, and commanders – competed in trying to shout louder than everyone else. The commotion resembled a Central Asian bazaar. Amid all this confusion, Shilin stubbornly tried to get through to the ground station that was guiding him:

"Deputat, this is Five Zero Three. Its navigation lights are on, its strobe lights are flashing! Establish communication with it. Establish communication with the civilian plane!"

Nevertheless, his words seemed to fall on deaf ears. The station he was addressing simply ignored him. Meanwhile, American and Japanese electronic-surveillance stations were listening in on these transmissions on channel three. They would later make available a tape recording that would vex any listener to the point of erupting into profanity. What a sorry excuse for an aerial interception this was if such confusion reigned. We later listened to this recording at Division X, and some gritted their teeth in anger: how easily we Soviets had made fools of ourselves!

After a while, though, target 6065 suddenly reappeared on radar screens of its own accord and, imperturbable as before, continued to move south-west. The crew of the foreign plane seemed to have no idea of what was going on around them, whether in the skies or on the radio waves. It flew on, impassive as if it were sleepwalking, without changing course, and one felt there was no power in the world capable of getting through to it. Stubbornly yet serenely, the target maintained its course for the border with Soviet airspace. One found oneself musing on the peculiar thought that there was no one at all on board, and the plane was flying on autopilot.

The scene brought a chill to the heart. There was still time to fix everything; the stranger was still flying over neutral waters. A few kilometers remained before the Soviet border, the zone stretching twelve nautical miles out that was forbidden to foreign planes and vessels. If any of the senior command took it into their heads to question whether this really was a spy plane, if they just thought for one minute, then it would still be possible to save all these people. Yet there was no one around who was capable of entertaining doubt or engaging in reasonable reflection. The personnel at the command positions and monitoring stations were thinking mainly about what would happen to them if they let an intruder through.

Sakhalin was close by. The island seemed to rise up out of the ocean like a gigantic whale, a mythical beast that bore on its back mountains, forests, towns and villages. The ground radar stations suddenly regained their sight just as they had earlier gone suddenly blind. Blips appeared on their radar screens that denoted the target and, sweeping around the target at greater or lesser distances, the fighters that had been sent to intercept it. Just as before, every screen showed the same picture: a foreign plane stubbornly and recklessly moving toward the Soviet border, as if it were steered by a cold-blooded and suicidal pilot who was bent this day on dying.

When we at Division X examined the records of the actions taken by our pilots, we found that the interceptor with the call sign 503 had come closest to the target. Neither fighter 121, fighter 805, nor 163 had been able to get such a close look at the target as 503. As Shilin studied it, he was struck by its dimensions: it was larger than any plane he was familiar with. Even the Il-76 intercontinental airliner was no match for this target's size, and the only planes that resembled the intruder were huge military transports.

From a distance, the intruder looked like the Soviet Tu-16 strategic bomber, but once Shilin got a closer look he decided that the stubborn target was probably a Boeing, based on the huge, seemingly bloated body of the plane, its sleek and wide surfaces, its angular tail rising high above the fuselage, the bull-like hump that swelled over the cockpit, its short, dark tail, and its round, snub nose.

The alien plane really did seem humpbacked, and Shilin thought of it as the humpback plane. The intruder's shape recalled a whale, much as did Sakhalin Island as drawn on a physical map. In the dark sky, this large whale bore itself along confidently at a dizzying altitude. On it, the navigation lights of a passenger plane shone; a white strobe flashed on the body and a red beacon at the tail. The lit windows of the plane were a long line along its body. All this pointed to a passenger airliner making a scheduled flight to its destination. Yet an aerial reconnaissance plane might also turn its navigation lights on, or flash its beacons, and a spy plane with a large number of crew and electronic-surveillance technicians on board might have the same row of lit windows.

Shilin was seized by doubt. If ground control had not reported so confidently that he was looking at an RC-135 Cobra spy plane, he would have certainly taken this mysterious aircraft as a passenger plane on an ordinary scheduled flight. But how could a passenger plane be here? The closest airliner route passed far to the east, five hundred kilometers away.

Shilin stared intently at the strange intruder. It gave off an air of peace and security, untroubled calm, and confidence. Behind its dimly lit windows he could guess at rows of seats and dozing passengers in them, sleepy voices, the quiet conversations of night owls. Reason suggested that the intruder was an ordinary airliner, with the only extraordinary thing being that it was five hundred kilometers off the closest route used by planes going to and from Japan and Korea. This was too great a deviation for anyone to believe in error or coincidence.

All these musings counted for nothing, however, for after a period of silence, ground control said in a clear, curt voice, like an officer leading men on parade, "Five Zero Three, the target has breached Soviet airspace. You are hereby ordered to destroy the target."

These words could be interpreted in one way only: as an order that was to be followed, and that meant that people would die. When we later listened to the tape recording at Division X and reconstructed the course of events that night minute by minute, everyone froze at hearing these words spoken by ground control. Before that, it had been a mere game, in which one could take a guess at the plane's identity, debate the matter with others, or construct theories; but now that these words had been uttered, the die was cast. An order was an order, and now it was time to set everything else aside and forget about it.

I can imagine how the operators at the electronic surveillance stations in Alaska and Japan must have gasped when they overheard this transmission. They knew Russian, and were probably just as struck as we were at Division X. Those operators naturally were unaware of the real background to these events. When American intelligence had planned this operation, its analysts and technicians believed they had thought of every detail and left no room for any mistakes. They naturally counted on this game being played according to their rules, where all the details had been taken into account and all fitted neatly together.

Plans and calculations, of course, are one thing, but real life is something else entirely. A game often does not depend on the players; it gets out of their control and takes an unexpected turn. It is completely understandable that the American operators at the ground stations became worried when they overheard the order to destroy the target.

Shilin pulled his thrust lever to boost his fighter's engines. Indicators blinked to show that the target was in his sights. Now the on-board radar guiding his missiles was locked on the foreign plane. Everything was ready, and the only thing remaining was to press the button, the simplest thing in the world.

During these seconds, however, doubts arose unbidden in the pilot's mind. He had felt before that he held the lives of other people in his hands. This time the feeling grew even stronger and dominated his thinking, nagging at him like an old wound that would not heal. Shilin could think only of how, if he pushed the button, the intruder was done for.

All he had to do was to push the button and the missiles could no longer be stopped or called back. There is no way to wind back time like film in a projector; events proceed only in one direction, and the dead cannot be resurrected. Later, one would be left to regret and mourn what had taken place, to reproach oneself for being rash and overhasty. Shilin's feelings grew stronger and more distinct. He knew he was not sure that this was a spy plane in front of him. It might be a transport plane, for example, with a peaceful cargo on board, perhaps a civilian rescue plane, or a flying meteorological station, or a passenger airliner, or something else.

According to military discipline and Shilin's training, the order had to be carried out immediately and unquestioningly. Yet riven by doubt, the pilot hesitated, delaying for a moment as if he were waiting for something. His state of mind clearly showed how harmful extraneous thoughts could be when a soldier was on duty.

While the pilot was still hesitating, the navigator's voice was suddenly heard again over the radio, this time frantic and agitated:

"Five Zero Three, stand by! The order to destroy the target has been overruled."

The lieutenant down at ground control was clearly frightened that his initial order might have already been carried out and the missile delivered to its target. He consequently rushed, the poor man, to issue a new order. "Five Zero Three, match altitude with the target and force it to land."

With an effort, Shilin found his breath again. Cold sweat was running down his back and perspiration had broken out on his forehead. He might have been struck dead by the transmission, such was his reaction to it. A chill seized his heart and fear stabbed him like a knife. He thought of how he could so easily have pressed the button already, an eternity ago.

Yes, he might well have carried out the order. The death sentence. The circumstances vividly resembled an execution suddenly interrupted by a reprieve, blessed news delivered in haste and handed over to the executioner. Shilin felt unwell, sick at heart. There was a painful tightness in his throat and chest. The pilot had never had any complaints about his health, and frequent physicals had never identified any problems. Now he was queasy, almost to the point of vomiting. What if that stranger so carelessly traversing the night sky really was a passenger plane that had gone off course? And he, a sniper pilot and an expert in aerial warfare, had destroyed it with an air-to-air missile and killed hundreds of people? All it took was to press the button.

Such thoughts could drive a man crazy. The pilot had himself taken overnight flights right across the Soviet Union on the airline Aeroflot. Row after row of passengers sleeping in their seats in the half-lit cabin. Outside the plane, the murk and cold of night, and the plane swiftly bearing all these peoples' colorful dreams through the night at a dizzying altitude. For a brief moment, Shilin imagined traveling to visit his mother in a plane that was suddenly designated a military target. This was a frightful image; of course it was. Mortal danger blowing like a bitter wind straight in your face.

Meanwhile, down below on the ground, hopeless confusion reigned. One might think that air defense on this fight night of fall was suffering strange mood swings. None of the staff officers at the units and monitoring stations, none of the navigators and operators, no one of whatever rank, whether senior or junior, had any idea what was going on. Expectations strengthened and slackened, hopes swelled and vanished, and the sense of unease and feverish anxiety grew.

Figuratively speaking, communications links between members of the Soviet military glowed red hot during these hours. The senior commanders who had to make the decisions suddenly grew scared of their own orders, became self-conscious, hesitated, changed their minds, became confused, or wavered. Contradictory orders which canceled one another out came rolling down the long chain of command, leaving everyone in their path in alternating states of hot fever and cold chills.

Later, when I studied the course of events at Division X, I followed the whole chain from the regiment up to the Ministry of Defense and, of course, the other way around, so that I could determine who issued the final, definitive order. The ground control station with the call sign Deputat, the regimental command, the division, the air defense district, the whole military region and its commander General Tretyak, Minister of Defense Ustinov… The senior generals prattled to one another and deferred to the decision of the USSR's senior communist, known in the terminology of that era as the General Secretary. For Yuri Andropov, however, just as for those overseas who had plotted their deadly adventure, the lives of others meant nothing and were merely bargaining chips in a vast political game.

By the fall of 1983, Andropov was terminally ill. The kidney problems he had long suffered had taken a serious turn and resulted in total renal failure. Toxins could no longer be purged from his body, and they remained in his blood, gradually poisoning him day by day.

At weekends, the General Secretary would check in to the Kremlin Hospital for dialysis. This was the only way to keep him alive. A state-of-the-art imported dialysis machine of the sort that otherwise could not be found in Russia at this time purified the general secretary's blood at the weekend so that he could go on living a tolerable life for the next week, until the following weekend.

Andropov had his own quarters at the hospital, a suite of three furnished rooms with a treatment room kept completely sterile. During his stay, Andropov would read, accept visitors, write poems about nature, and listen to music – his favorite tunes being old American jazz. It must be admitted that for a KGB general and the General Secretary of the Communist Party, Andropov was a man of fairly refined tastes.

Nevertheless, Andropov's condition continued to decline. The toxic compounds that his kidneys could not purge from his blood took up residence in his body's tissues and organs and destroyed them. His body gradually broke down day by day, hour by hour, until the point was reached when it might utterly fail him at any moment. He was approaching the time when he might enter into a coma and his body would be so poisoned with toxins that he could no longer survive. This was a man with one foot in the grave, and yet he had the power to decide if people far away, strangers to him, would live or die.

Meanwhile, Shilin was thinking about how he was going to execute his new orders. Unlike the previous order to destroy the intruder, the command now given to him was to force the target to land. The indicator lights for his missiles went out, which meant that the on-board radar system had released the target from its fix and turned off guidance for the missiles. The pilot increased thrust to the engines and approached the strange plane from below. The fighter matched speed with the forward speed of the intruder and flashed its lights to attract the other pilots' attention. However, the strange plane stubbornly maintained its course, completely unperturbed. It maintained its cruising speed, and it seemed to notice nothing amiss, or at least to pretend that it did not notice. Shilin reported his maneuvers to the ground, and after the personnel there had discussed the matter, he received a recommendation:

"Fire a warning burst."

Shilin knew that opening fire would do no good. It would merely be an empty gesture, but he carried out the order nonetheless. His plane's thirteen-millimeter rapid-fire canon shot off four rounds, and so two hundred shells were lost forever in the darkness. This was frankly a waste. Firing off tracer rounds that glowed in the dark would have made sense, but no one would notice the armor-piercing shells that Shilin had just released, meaning that he had expended all four cannon rounds in vain. With the usual carelessness of the Soviet military, however, his plane had not been supplied with any other ammunition.

They flew side by side: the huge jumbo jet and the light-winged swift that was Shilin's fighter. The interceptor frantically swept around the imperturbable giant, but no good came of it, for the strange plane paid him no attention. The huge airliner, accompanied by the fighter, kept charging on, like an elephant accompanied by a gnat.

Around this same time, I was arriving at Venice's Marco Polo Airport, which is located some ten kilometers north of the city on the Viale Galileo Galilei. This came as no joy, however: the anxiety I had felt before now grew noticeably stronger, the signals being sent out across the world taking on a painfully acute quality. It seemed as if any minute now the worst possible news would arrive, and the world would be shattered by the tragic events that loomed on this first day of fall. According to my presentiments, many people were in deadly danger.

Be that as it may, my painful forebodings did not release me from my duty. I had never been to Venice before, but I had studied my route beforehand. To avoid wasting time, I had taken my small travel bag as a carry-on when boarding the plane in New York, and so I did not have to wait for any luggage upon arrival in Venice. I was among the first to reach passport control and customs on the first floor of the arrivals terminal, and I passed through without incident.

I recalled the route I had studied in advance, and turned left after exiting the terminal. A ten minute walk brought me to the Alilaguna pier, a stop for the convenient ferry known as a vaporetto that traveled around Venice's islands. I needed to reach the island of Lido, where the film festival had opened and my hotel awaited. From the pier, the vaporetto took a course to the left, slowly traversed the open water of the lagoon, and entered the channel running along the island of Murano, where boats, gondolas and small barges swayed along the embankment with its narrow pedestrian walkways. Here colorful old stone buildings were huddled, two or three stories tall and with brick roofs. Murano had been home to glassblowers since time immemorial, forced by the city authorities to resettle here lest they started a fire. I liked these houses, both all of them together and each one in itself. Each one was attractive, and I fancied I would enjoy living in any one of them. At the very least, I would have liked to go in and have a look around.

Ah, it seemed as if there was no reason whatsoever to be sad, that one could just enjoy life, give in to the moment, and take in everything around oneself. What else was there to dream about when here was Venice, open before me, a magical reality, a delightful scene, a dream come true. And what was there to be sad about, when I had a once-in-a-lifetime chance, thanks to my job, to come to this paradise. After all, I had a job to do, but I should enjoy myself as well.

In spite of this, all this way on the vaporetto through the lagoon and the canals, I was not so much thinking about the incredible Venice scenery as listening to the signals coming across space. My ill forebodings had not left my mind, and my anxiety had increased considerably. Fear came flying toward me across a vast distance, and now it was tormenting me.

I naturally had no idea that at this same time, two aircraft, a gigantic jumbo jet and a military fighter plane, were flying side by side over the town of Okhotsk, Cape Patience, and the tiny island of Tuleny with seals lounging on its rocks. The planes cut across the island and approached the western coast of Sakhalin near the towns of Nevelsk and Gornozavodsk. Indeed, I had no idea of any of this. I did not even suspect it, but I felt uneasy. I felt an urge to telephone Colonel Creighton or his daughter Cindy in New York and ask whether there was any news, whether they had heard anything, but I was worried that they had already forgotten about it, that I was now out of sight and thus out of mind.

Shilin, meanwhile, had fired off his warning burst and was flashing his lights once more. It seemed that the pilots of the strange plane had now noticed him: the intruder reduced its speed, but this appeared to be a deliberate maneuver, because the intercepting fighter was incapable of flying at such low speed – it would have put Shilin's plane in a corkscrew spin downward. The speeds acceptable for a fighter jet are much higher than for a large plane. In other words, if the intruder reduced its speed, the fighter would not be able to remain alongside it and would be forced to pull ahead of the target.

This was evidently just what the pilots of the other plane were counting on. The western coast of Sakhalin Island was rising up before them, and twelve nautical miles out from it lay the boundary with Soviet territory. A few more minutes of flight time, and the plane would escape back into neutral airspace, and then the Soviets could do nothing other than make a complaint.

Shilin peered into the periscope which afforded him a rear view. It was now light in the east; the first day of fall was already arriving. No one in the world had any idea what this day would bring. The horizon was tinged with the red of dawn, and the sky above it recalled the waters of the sea when lit by the sun – a light green with a bluish touch. The higher one looked in the sky, however, the darker its blue, and eventually it lost all color and turned murky. Shilin had only to look up to see the darkness already disappearing above his cockpit; the stars were fading, but toward the west – where the foreign plane was bound – the night still maintained an unshakable reign, and an impenetrable darkness lay ahead on the planes' joint course.

To his surprise, through his periscope Shilin caught sight of another fighter maintaining a parallel course, though far behind and barely distinguishable against the background of the dawning sky. This was a Su-15 with the call sign 805. Before take-off it had been equipped with auxiliary fuel tanks, which would prolong its flight time but reduce its speed. This fighter hung behind them like a dog that had been unable to keep up with the pack, but was now in chase of its prey and running headlong for it.

Is this really a passenger plane, Shilin thought as he looked at the foreign plane, and how did get here? He was amazed by how strangely the plane was behaving, for it held firm to its course from the north-east to the south-west, ignored the fighter's maneuvers, and did not seem to bat an eyelid. Its windows were dimly lit, its navigation lights shone brightly, its beacons flashed in their clockwork rhythm, and the plane maintained its steady forward movement like a train on rails.

Even if the intruder were some kind of spy plane, it looked just like a civilian airliner. It flew just as a passenger plane would, calmly and confidently. It had the lights of a passenger plane and its behavior was in no way different from an airliner and not at all typical of reconnaissance aircraft. Over foreign territory, spy planes usually took a very cautious tack, like a thief in the night. The crews of spy planes knew very well what would happen if their plane were spotted in foreign airspace, and so they would turn tail and try to slip away without a trace. This plane, however, was definitely a civilian aircraft.

In short, the intruder was flying on without any fear or hesitation, as if the pilots had already known in advance that nothing bad was going to happen. They seemed to feel fully entitled to do so and at no risk. Judging by the way the plane was moving, they were convinced of their safety and untouchability. The only planes that would fly like that are civilian airliners, the lords of the sky, with whom no one would try to interfere, and of whom no one would even be suspicious.

Shilin hesitated, plagued with doubts. Was this a reconnaissance aircraft, or a passenger plane? A thought suddenly came into his mind, one that was somewhat strange and out of place for a Russian fighter pilot: might it not be better to let a spy plane go than accidentally shoot down a passenger jet? This was an extremely unusual kind of thinking, completely shocking. From its very first days in power, the Soviet regime had insistently taught the country always to act firmly against any perceived opponent, in order to strike fear into everyone else. In other words, let us kill hundreds of random bystanders in case the enemy is hiding among them. Enemies, as everyone knew, could not be allowed to get away at any cost. Naturally, the Land of Soviets had no fondness for the bourgeois ideal that it would be better to let ten criminals go free than to convict an innocent man.

However, the foreign plane's maneuver to slow down left Shilin baffled. If Shilin decided to match speed with the other plane, his fighter would go into a corkscrew spin, steadily losing altitude. A fighter was unable to remain airborne at low speeds, just as a bicycle keeps its balance only as long as it continues to move forward. Put simply, a fighter cannot fly slowly.

Shilin had no choice other than to reduce his speed to the lowest possible limit, four hundred kilometers per hour. However, the foreign plane, too, slowed down, and Shilin's fighter overtook it and lost height. Judging by the intruder's maneuver, it wanted just to slip away now that the boundary of Soviet airspace was only a stone's throw away. Perhaps it would have reached neutral airspace and got away safely, but fate suddenly took a turn in the opposite direction: down on the ground, plans changed once more. The airwaves lit up with new orders.

=== **28** ===

Toward morning, fatigue clawed at the Great Leader. For a while he resisted it, tried to overcome it. Stalin knew that if he lay down, his insomnia would prove too strong and would torment him. Worn out by the struggle within him, he eventually resigned himself to lying down on the sofa with its old, threadbare upholstery. Stalin did not bother undressing. He removed only his shoes, the *ichigi* boots popular in his native Caucasus which he wore at his nearby dacha in Kuntsevo, where he liked to live nearly year-round.

Sleep did not come, however. The leader of the Soviet Union was overrun by endless cares and concerns swarming around him in a cloud. No one could help him and take part of this heavy burden from him. Stalin did not know whom he could trust. He could not find any dependable people around him; perhaps there were none. He certainly trusted no one; he suspected everyone of plots overt or covert, and if a person did not stand out in any way, that most likely meant that he was secretly plotting. These restless thoughts plagued Stalin's brain and held sleep at bay. Sometimes he was so beset with suspicions that he would lock himself in his office and cook his own meals on an electric stove so that no one could poison him. Though every one of the sciences was subject to the Great Leader, he would still read textbooks to refresh his already deep knowledge; he was adept in biology and physics and familiar with linguistics. None of it helped him find peace with himself, though. He was beset by periods of depression. The neurologist Bekhterev had made a diagnosis of manic depression, and this diagnosis and Stalin's paranoia cost that great scientist his life. Everyone around Stalin was well aware that their leader forgot nothing and would never forgive even the smallest slight.

As dawn came, fresh air blew in through the open window, bringing with it a scent of cut hay and moist earth. Stalin's dacha stood on its lonesome not far from the village of Davydkovo, among dense groves and picturesque green hills. The dacha was connected to the Kremlin by a tunnel, a whole subway line built for a single person. A comfortable carriage waited below ground for Stalin's use, but he preferred to avoid the tunnel and go by car instead – even though he was in constant fear for his life, and fretful that someone would attempt to assassinate him. The head of Stalin's bodyguard, General Vlasik, had set up checkpoints along the entire road running from Kuntsevo to the Kremlin.

It was easy to understand why Stalin preferred to travel by automobile. This proud man of the Caucasus found the idea of heading underground demeaning. Why should he cower like a mole? Was he really to behave like an outcast in his own country? After all, the people at the Kremlin and the heads of every state institution knew him simply as the Boss. Granted, the forced laborers in the countless Gulag workshops called the country's leader by a strange nickname, Minai, while the camp bosses used among themselves the insulting sobriquet Pocky. That was fair, as Stalin's face really did bear the scars of smallpox.

Going underground in order to reach the Kremlin, his dacha, or General Headquarters felt like something shameful. He had already had enough of it in 1941, when he had taken refuge in the General Headquarters air raid shelter on Myasnitskaya Street. An underground passageway led from the cellar of the mansion, which in imperial times had belonged to the merchant Soldatenkov, to the air raid shelter used by senior military officials in the neighboring building. This shelter was in turn connected deep underground with the Kirovskaya metro station.

In November 1941, Stalin had made his way from General Headquarters to the Mayakovskaya metro station, where he gave a speech in honor of the anniversary of the October Revolution, and then he returned the same way. He was forced to do this at his bodyguard's urging; safety concerns had obliged him to crawl underground. The point was, though, that at that time the Germans were approaching Moscow. Why should he do it now, in June 1944, when the front had been pushed back far to the west and was retreating even further by the day?

Stalin had longed for some time now to get a good night's sleep, but he never managed to do so. Every night he struggled with insomnia, but he never seemed to be able to overcome it, and the effort left him exhausted. Toward morning he would drift off, catching a few brief moments of sleep. He would toss and turn restlessly, coughing hoarsely and breathing heavily, and often he would wake up in a cold sweat and in the grip of fear. Fear pursued him all night long as it would an inveterate sinner; it ate at him. The man they called the Father of Nations festered with a vague sense of foreboding. He was afraid like any mere mortal, driven mad by fear, and he knew clearly what guilt he bore.

When he drifted off, nightmares would haunt him, and when he came to, it took him a long time to catch his breath again, his heart pounding frantically and seeming ready to leap out of his chest. His face contorted in a grimace, Stalin tried to shift this immense weight from his chest, but it remained, and he felt as if he were being buried alive.

By midday or a little later, when the day was in full swing and the rest of the country had long since been up, Stalin awoke with great effort, but he spent a long time lying there, morose and unmoving, overcome by feelings of frustration and discontent. Not even successes on the war front could lighten his spiteful state of mind.

No one dared disturb the Great Leader in the morning. People waited outside his door, and until he appeared all business was on hold. His secretary, bodyguard, and assistants were afraid to wake him. They would listen carefully for any movement behind the wall before they disturbed him.

When Stalin woke up, he experienced a disgust with life. Life held no appeal for him. He was utterly worn out, and the feeling of total exhaustion only accumulated day after day. Only with effort could he get up, and he moved slowly and clumsily. His staff and bodyguard observed his snail-paced movement and waited patiently for the Boss to regain his composure. Even fine days seemed like inclement weather to Stalin, and his gloom and fatigue were like an iron fetter wrapped about his body and mind. His sharp dislike for other human beings led him to scowl in disgust. He did not want to see anyone, and he suffered from attacks of unprovoked anger that would come upon him like bowel spasms.

Oh, yes, the Great Leader knew what other human beings were worth, the same human beings who idolized him. He thought about his fellow Communists with contempt: mediocrities swarmed around him, cowardly small fry who fed themselves at his trough.

His comrades in arms were worthless. Those who had actually commanded respect, Stalin had already had killed or sent off to the camps. That had made things no easier. He had no one to relieve him of his burden, and how could he walk away if the people and the nation were hanging on his shoulders like heavy chains that did not allow him to breathe.

It was in such low spirits that Stalin would get to work. He spent a large part of the time ill at ease; the victories announced in communiques from his generals gave him no pleasure, nor did any of the flattery and adulation that he received. Granted, he was no longer able to avoid those things. Earlier, when he had been doing whatever it took to consolidate his hold on power, such things had warmed his heart and boosted his spirits, had given this failed seminarian a sense of importance, but with time they meant ever less to him. He had turned cold inside, though he remained relentlessly vigilant and if anyone faltered in their devotion to him, his vengeance would be severe indeed, like a dagger thrust home by a highlander of the Caucasus. The Great Leader knew no mercy.

Lately Stalin's allies had often annoyed him. There was a strange lack of clarity in the USSR's relations with them which Stalin could not bear. The Allies burdened him with questions and requests, and he was fed up with it, often more fed up than he was with his fellow Soviets; at least he knew how to keep them in check. These foreigners went too far; they behaved in too audacious and independent a manner. He could not detect in their faces any fear of him personally, and their arrogance was intolerable: his name and his visage sparked no fear and trembling in their hearts. He could detect humor in these foreigners' eyes, even outright mockery, as if they did not take him seriously and laughed at him, especially Churchill. With his keen sense for these things, Stalin knew that they were whispering behind his back "Uncle Joe, Uncle Joe..." They secretly mocked him and tried to get him wrapped around their fingers, so that he, the leader of nations and the guiding light of the world, would dance to their tune.

It sometimes seemed as if they had no idea of what kind of a man Stalin was, that they did not know their own place. He was tempted to teach them all a lesson, knock them off their pedestals, give them a fright, so that they would know who was boss over one-sixth of this world's surface. That would not have been difficult to do, for after all the Allies occasionally came crawling to him. Without his help, they might well have drowned in their own blood on the Western Front.

Stalin had contradictory feelings about the Western Front. The Allies had spent a long time waiting as the Germans bled the Soviet army dry, and had only opened their other front when it was clear that Stalin could manage without them – they were frightened at the thought that they had come too late to divvy up the spoils.

Nevertheless, Stalin had forced them to come to terms with their own position. Stalin enjoyed exacting vengeance. He would grin under his heavy mustache, puffing on his pipe filled with tobacco taken from Herzegovina Flor cigarettes. Let them have a taste for themselves of what war was really like. And as the old Russian saying goes, even a mangy sheep will provide at least some useful wool. At the same time, he felt jealousy at how easily the Allies were winning the victory now, as if this were no war at all but a walk in the park. When they managed to breach the Atlantic Wall, as the Germans called their system of fortifications on the Normandy coast, Stalin had sent Roosevelt and Churchill a congratulatory telegram, but he still felt that the other Allies did not really know how to fight.

In any event, Stalin had been forced to come to their rescue several times. When times were tough, the USA and Britain turned to him for assistance with tears in their eyes, and they asked him to help make things easier for them when the Germans had them surrounded. The Allies would usually request that he strike a blow on the Eastern Front, so that part of the German army would have to be transferred from the west to the east.

Frankly, he had often been tempted at those times to teach them a real lesson. He would remain silent in the face of their desperate pleas. He would reproach them for their inappropriate actions, try to knock some sense into them so that they would know how to behave in the future. Yet ultimately, he never did refuse to help. Joseph Stalin wanted to appear all-powerful in the Allies' eyes: let them know that for him, there was no such thing as an unfulfilled wish, that he was completely capable of handling any task and could overcome any difficulties. In his own country he had long since been likened unto a living god, and he would enjoy it if people outside Russia also believed in his divinity. After yet another request from the West, Stalin would change his plans and speed up the military operations that he had already planned in advance. At his order, General Headquarters would hurriedly redraw their forces and send the army into the attack without having made the necessary preparations, though it was obvious that the Soviet forces would suffer excessive casualties. But what did losses mean to Stalin? When he issued an order, he never thought about the price that had to be paid. The lives of others meant nothing to him. Such small trifles did not get through to the Great Leader.

Deep down inside, Stalin knew why in his sleep he was tormented by nightmares, though it was hard for him to admit it to himself. To admit why he was choked with fear at night, or why he awoke each morning with a heavy heart and even at midday still felt ill at ease. Three years ago, his only friend, the only like-minded person in Europe, in the whole wide world, had turned against him. Stalin had rated Hitler a lot more highly than he had the British and French leaders, who were just a lot of hot air.

Back then, just as it was today, it had been a warm June night, the shortest night of the year. No one would ever understand how much Stalin had suffered then. And the main reason for his pain was not that war had come to the USSR, but rather that he, who was so sagacious and shrewd, had been tricked. He had not believed in the deception that many people had been warning him about. It shamed him to recall how sore at heart he had been on that night. Oh, Hitler, Hitler, dear Adolf, the leader of the German people just as he, Stalin, was the leader of the Russians, had proved such a wily neighbor. The bitter truth lay in the fact that Stalin had trusted him. Hitler was the only person Stalin had ever trusted. At this same time three years ago, Hitler's betrayal had been unbearable. His friend had secretly been manipulating Stalin as if the latter were a mere child.

Before the war, Stalin had imprisoned many of his compatriots – diplomats, intelligence officers, soldiers – who had tried to warn him about Hitler. And what of the German communists and social democrats who had taken refuge in the USSR? They too had warned of war, but Stalin had simply considered them provocateurs who were trying to stir up trouble between him and his friend Hitler. They were prostitutes, vile traitors. Even after the war had already been raging for some time – a year or two into it – there were still prisoners in the camps who were serving their sentences for the peculiar crime of "anti-German sentiment".

The prisoners are not the only examples. There are others just as good. When Stalin was notified in the early morning of June 22 that the Germans had launched an attack on the USSR, he could not believe it. He gave orders that the USSR should continue fulfilling its export contracts with Germany. Luftwaffe planes were already bombing Kiev, Minsk, and other cities, but shipments of oil, steel, and grain were still flowing in the opposite direction toward Germany. Utter absurdity.

Three years previously, Stalin had been deeply hurt at being treated like this. His friend's betrayal had come as a crushing blow. So shocked and disappointed was Stalin that he collapsed to the floor. He drank heavily and moaned like a bull cooped up in a cramped stall and aware that slaughter was imminent. He could only mutter indistinctly, as if he had lost the power of human speech overnight.

Over those first days of the war, no one knew what to do. Only the day before, the Soviet army had paraded triumphantly. They had sung that they were up to any challenge that might come – tank operators had a song that went "When Comrade Stalin sends us off to battle…" Everyone believed the words that "from the taiga to the English Channel, the Red Army is the strongest of all". But these illusions were all shattered on June 22, 1941.

While the man they nicknamed Minai was wallowing on his threadbare carpet, moaning indistinctly in a drunken stupor, women were weeping across the entire country and crowds were huddling by the loudspeakers. Stalin's fellow communists were at a total loss, his staff looked on shyly, and his bodyguards whispered among themselves. The Great Leader had shut himself up inside his room and left everyone else to their own devices.

Soon rumors spread that Stalin was living in seclusion at his dacha. He had shut the door tight, disconnected his telephone, and was not admitting any visitors. People were afraid to gossip much about it, but they could sense how much inner pain Stalin felt from his good friend's transformation into a vile foe. It was fortunate that Stalin had not simply lost his mind entirely in those first minutes after word of the attack came in. According to witnesses, Stalin listened to the news with disbelief, his legs gave out under him, and his heavy body fell to the floor. Minai sank like a stone and lay there crushingly disappointed, disconsolate. His sallow, pockmarked face was distorted by grief.

Stalin was honestly unable to understand what had happened. After all, he and Hitler had been on the same page, they had told the League of Nations and the pesky European states to get lost, they had shaken hands, signed joint treaties – both public and secret – had drunk champagne, exchanged compliments and smiles. What more could a person ask for? They had redrawn borders to their mutual benefit, assigned territory to one or other of them. They had sent greetings, congratulatory messages, heartfelt wishes, and were thrilled to be dividing the world between them. What scores did friends have that needed to be settled? German pilots of the Luftwaffe came to the USSR to train at Lipetsk, they were fed and lodged and not charged a penny for it. General Heinz Guderian's tank personnel learned to shoot at bases in Belarus.

What about the joint maneuvers in the western military districts? What about the joint parades at the training centers? The Germans and Russians had marched together, in a single rank, saluted one another, proudly flaunted their soldierly bearing, and the two sides' commanders had drunk vodka and schnapps together. Plus, in its propaganda, in its work with the masses, and its battle with its political opponents, the Nazi Party was following in the wake of the Bolsheviks. They had studied Stalin's experiences and, one must admit, done well. The pupils had quashed resistance no worse than their teachers had, though they could not outdo them; they turned out to be too weak for it.

Stalin simply could not understand such treachery. He himself knew how to manipulate others, and when it came to cunning he was unrivaled. Even Lenin, for all that that man had been crafty and cunning, underestimated the man from the Caucasus, and when he realized his mistake, it was too late: Stalin had him locked up at his dacha in Gorky and assigned guards and informants to keep watch over him. Stalin had outplayed Trotsky, Bukharin, and the whole pack of so-called Old Bolsheviks, too, as if they were all mere children. Hitler's betrayal, though, was something inexplicable for Stalin, when after all the two men had been a team and worked together for mutual benefit. If they were united, no one would dare oppose them, and the two of them together would have Britain, America, and everyone else on their knees. And Stalin, whose distrust and suspicion of others was common knowledge, had trusted Hitler. A man who trusted no one had, damn him, trusted Hitler.

Once the war started, Stalin felt as if he was hostage to it. He realized that he had miscalculated, committed a blunder, and as everyone knows, the losers are thrown out with the trash – if they are lucky. If they are not, they are slaughtered on the spot. He, the unquestioned leader, the highest authority, a man so great that he was nearly a god, was now sweating, deathly afraid that a reckoning had come. After all, there had been the earlier student plots, and the Old Bolsheviks had hatched their conspiracies, and the Red Army generals at their dachas and on their maneuvers had carried out discussions as to how they might remove Stalin from power. A general, one of the Kremlin commandants, was prepared to go with a platoon to seize the usurper and have him shot on the spot. Fortunately, at the last minute the conspirators were exposed, though it was a shame that some of them managed to get away.

Now it had turned out that he had made a mistake with regard to Hitler, Minai was afraid and trembling, drenched in a cold sweat at the thought that a reckoning had come. He knew that he would pay with his life. In his drunken stupor on the threadbare old carpet, he imagined that men would come for him shortly, accuse him of treason, of being complicit with the enemy, of espionage. In search of evidence they would torture him just as he had tortured others, and in the end they would mercilessly slay him just as he had slain others.

At moments of clarity, when Stalin came to from this week-long binge and sobered up a little, he would listen nervously to the sounds around him and think that he heard footsteps. He was prepared to leave, disappear, step down from power, just as long as he could make it out with his life and be left alone.

While the Great Leader was going through this spiritual crisis, Molotov addressed the nation on the radio and urged everyone to strengthen the nation's defense, rally their resources, and strike back at the Germans. Stalin meanwhile was nowhere to be seen; all he wanted to do was hide in some secluded place and not make a sound. He longed to disappear into a cave and live an inconspicuous life where no one would bother him, recognize him, or address him. Now, at the start of the war, he suddenly realized just how much the USSR and its people were like iron chains around him, an unbearable burden that would break his back.

In his drunken stupor on the floor, he seemed to have reverted to the boy they called Soso, the young seminary student Jughashvili, a hungry, scrawny and pimply young man who was, due to his negligence in his studies, kicked out of the seminary and forced to remain only half-educated for the rest of his life. For this reason he had always felt a hatred for learned people, the educated and smart, for each of them seemed to represent a reproach for his own life.

One could understand this, even sympathize. He was a school dropout, the dubious son of an alcoholic shoemaker named Beso. The father was subject to fits of violent rage and, some rumors have it, was ultimately killed by his son. Well, what are rumors worth. In Gori, according to local reports, Stalin was known as a bastard child. Those reports claim that the beautiful Keke, the mother of the future all-time genius, found some comfort and consolation for her abusive marriage on the side.

Many people felt sorry for him. He was a dirty urchin who would wander around the shops and market stalls in search of some meager sustenance. At some places he was given food out of pity, while elsewhere he was driven away, and in yet other places people would steal from him or even beat him to a bloody pulp if he did not manage to get away quickly.

Yes, Soso Jughashvili, a scrawny and defenseless youth who was met with insults everywhere and might have perished from hunger and neglect, had suddenly risen to the throne. The former seminary student and outcast was nevertheless perpetually seized by fear. Just like a street urchin, he worried that at any minute a watchman or the real owners would appear at the door, and then he would be lucky to get away with just a thrashing before being driven off. He might suffer much worse, and so he ought to make a run for it now before they caught him and beat him up.

With time, Joseph Jughashvili's authority over Russia came to exceed even the former tsar's. No one can deny that. It was not for nothing that the ninety-year-old actress Yablochkova, when Stalin was conferring on her a state honor, addressed him in a senile fashion as "Your Imperial Majesty". However, like any thief or impostor, Soso was tormented by perpetual fear and doubt: a twist of fate had unjustly elevated him to an incredible height, but the higher he climbed, the harder he might fall.

Goodness, could anyone grasp just how great was the loneliness and trepidation of a little urchin who had suddenly ended up at the very top! This all-powerful ruler apparently lacked confidence in his position and felt that his authority was shaky. Due to that uncertainty, he had time and time again spilled Russians' blood so that he could convince himself that his rule was secure, but his main aim was always to instill fear in others. The cycles of bloodshed among the population were a symptom of the paranoia which Joseph had suffered since his boyhood, and which grew worse year by year. In later years this paranoia was joined by manic depression. Uncertainty and doubt ate at the Great Leader like rust, poisoning him, stripping him of any peace, and driving away all sleep. Chronic insomnia gradually wore him out over the years and gave birth to a pathological malice.

One has only to think of how over all the years that Stalin ruled the Kremlin and the nation, he felt that sooner or later someone would appear and claim that Stalin had usurped his place, or someone else would come along and decide that he wanted that place for himself. It was clear, completely obvious, that even if Stalin were not killed – and there was little hope of that – he would be kicked out. The only thing left would be to go back to Georgia, again wander through the bazaars in search of sustenance, hang around the stalls, just as he had done long ago when they called him Soso.

But where could he run to, where could he hide? The country was decked with countless portraits of him, busts and statues. Everywhere every citizen, young and old alike, recognized his face. Yes, he ought to have thought about all this earlier, before he had gone so far. Could it be that he would not now make it out alive, that he would be unable to defend himself? After all, his pal Adolf had learned from him how to smash his friends and enemies. Whether one wanted to believe it or not, it was the truth that the German dictator had intently studied Stalin's experience in securing his power, and this schooling had proved useful.

He and Adolf had both lived similar lives. Both had showed an artistic inclination early on: Hitler painted, while Stalin wrote poetry. Their abilities proved mediocre, however, and neither of them found recognition. When Hitler was a young man and still known as Schicklgruber, he was turned down by the Academy of Fine Arts and, apprentice painter that he was, had to paint fences instead. Stalin, then known as Jughashvili, published doggerel on themes drawn from nature in local Georgian newspapers under the *nom de plume* Sozeli or Soselo, diminutive forms of his nickname Soso. He was not accepted by the circle of Georgian poets, however – which rebounded on them later; the insult he had felt cost all of them their lives.

Both Joseph and Adolf drank heavily from the time they were young men; they remained poorly educated; both went hungry; both hated their fathers – shoemakers and drunkards who beat their sons mercilessly; both suffered from an irrepressible vanity; and both longed for glory and recognition and made plans to achieve it. Sadly, if they had only been given some ability, if nature had endowed them with talent, then the world might have had an artist and a poet instead, and history would have taken a different course. Perhaps it would have been better if Adolf Schicklgruber had been accepted into the Academy of Fine Arts, and Joseph Jughashvili had gained recognition as a poet; the world would have paid – you would agree – a much lower price.

Instead, we are left to lament that both of them were met with rejection on account of their mediocre abilities, and both had to make their mark on the world in a different, roundabout way. Both satisfied their extraordinary vanity, pride, and ambition and proved themselves with an approach that was already tried and tested: through bloodshed. Oddly enough, the two men were both foreigners who came to the fore in neighboring countries. Hitler was an Austrian in Germany, and Jughashvili a Georgian in Russia. Indeed, they each contrived an extraordinary ascent, outdoing everyone around them in cunning and trickery, and establishing a grip on their respective countries. It took Hitler two years to lay waste to Europe, and the Georgian admired the Austrian as a kindred spirit. It was no accident that they struck up a good rapport; both foresaw a long road ahead together. But now Stalin's friend had betrayed him, shot him in the back, and he simply could not figure out the reason for it.

Since then, exactly three years had passed. Day after day had gone by, night after night – how fantastical life is! It might seem high time for Stalin to forget about that confusion and turmoil, but it refused to be forgotten; it remained lodged in his memory and tormented him. His memory had always been a source of pride for him, and now with distinct clarity it reminded him of the man he himself – the USSR's leader, teacher, and commander-in-chief – had been three years ago on the first day of the war. Every year on June 22 those memories came flooding back involuntarily, like a painful seizure, and they left him bitterly distraught.

Stalin would always pull himself together and regain his composure by the end of the following week. In the meantime, the nation waited, meek and perplexed. The Great Leader received every report mistrustfully; he would look around questioningly and rest his eyes, yellow like an owl's, on his confused staff. Though none of them said it out loud, they knew their boss was doomed to suffer for every remaining hour of this, the shortest night of the year. The vivid memories of that first night of the war came back and he felt as if they were burning him alive. On this night every year, a deep black hatred would gather within him, and Stalin gnashed his teeth and flew into a blind rage.

Now the same June night had come, June 22. It was obvious what a state the Great Leader would be in. He could not sleep all night, plagued by memories that vividly painted a picture of events three years before. However, toward morning General Headquarters received a report which pushed Stalin's memories into the background somewhat, and greatly annoyed him: the previous evening, the Germans had bombed the air base in Poltava, which the Americans had been using for their long-distance bombing runs across Europe.

It had been a huge effort for the Soviet army to build up and equip the air bases at Poltava, Mirgorod, and Piryatin, and it had required a great deal of energy and ingenuity on the part of the Soviet army. So many new buildings had been erected, steel-plated runways had been installed for the heavy bombers, and now everything had gone up in smoke due to the Americans' stupidity.

The report spoke of the destruction and loss of personnel, and of how the runways were no longer usable. Oddly enough, Stalin's annoyance was combined with a certain contentment. He read the report once more, and a wry smile came over his lips under that renowned mustache of his: the Americans had shown again that they were careless idiots, total fools, incapable of doing the simplest things.

A week before the shortest night of the year, on June 15, two American F-5 Lightning fighters had taken off from an air base in England. Each plane was carrying photographs and charts of military targets that were to be bombed. These materials were obviously of great importance. They were meant to be given to the bomber crews doing shuttle runs, with each crew receiving one of the charts.

In order to achieve maximum precision, the Allies had spent a long time carrying out aerial reconnaissance and taking photographs. Experts meticulously examined the photos and added the coordinates of the various targets. Routes were carefully planned for the planes to follow on their bombing runs. To avoid any accidents, a complete set of these materials was dispatched on each of the F-5 fighters, in the hope that at least one of them would make it safely to its destination.

After the fighters took off from their base in England, they flew over the English Channel unhindered, passed the Western Front over northern France, and then they crossed the whole of Europe from west to east. The fighters were flown by pilots John Hoover and Ralph D. Kendall. In order to make it easier for the pilots to cross the Eastern Front, Soviet command had cleared out an air corridor in advance over western Ukraine near the provincial capital of Radekhov, located forty kilometers northwest of the old town of Brody, first mentioned in twelfth-century sources.

Hoover and Kendall were experienced pilots, having already flown all over Europe. However, the American fighters did not appear over Radekhov at the appointed time, and no one knew where to look for them. It later transpired that Hoover had gone three hundred kilometers off course and crossed the front line to the north over Belarus, where naturally no one was expecting him. The American plane was attacked by Soviet fighters north of the town of Mozyr and his plane suffered a hit. The American was forced to land near the village of Saltykovo, some twelve kilometers west of the city of Rechytsa, whereupon a report was made to headquarters.

The American pilots were both lucky to make it out alive that day. After Kendall lost his companion, he descended in order to compare his map with the landscape below. His fighter came under anti-aircraft fire and he was forced to land outside the village of Bobrovichy, to the rear of the Soviet lines. One can imagine how astonished the Red Army were to see him. The American's arrival was a huge surprise for the soldiers and their commanders and caused great commotion. As Stalin read the report, he scowled and smiled in turn: the Allies had really screwed up this time. This left the USSR's commander-in-chief feeling very satisfied; once again he was convinced of the inability of the Allies to wage war properly.

The planes, after a brief overhaul, were sent on to Poltava, but the military misadventures did not end there. On the contrary, they had only just begun. When the Germans observed the movements of the two F-5 Lightning fighters, they suspected that something was afoot. American planes were paying visits to the Eastern Front much too often. German top brass dished out an earful to their intelligence services, who then began to search diligently to discover where the Americans were flying in from, where they were landing, and why they were making these journeys.

The Germans' search dragged on, but it was the Americans themselves who finally gave them the answers they were looking for. The Americans had been careless with their military secrets, preferring to rely instead on their power and strength. Stalin complained to his men about how scatterbrained the Allies were.

The Allies' secret was discovered after American Flying Fortresses made yet another shuttle bombing run over Berlin. This bombing happened to take place on the third anniversary of Germany's initial invasion of the USSR, and were to serve as a reminder to the Germans of who were to blame for the war and what revenge they could expect for it. It was a way of teaching the Germans a lesson, a just punishment, and a public lashing for the sins they had committed.

On June 21, 1944, without any attempt to conceal themselves, one hundred and fifty P-51 Flying Fortresses and six dozen escorting Mustang fighters appeared over Berlin in broad daylight, shortly after midday. This daytime attack, visible to the whole city, was a way of mocking the Germans. The Americans were openly demonstrating their strength and their scorn for their foe. Hitler raised hell with Goering for the Luftwaffe's inability to defend the capital. The Fuhrer was right; this was all too much. An upset Goering sent up every available fighter plane, but it was too late: the Flying Fortresses had already dropped all their bombs on Germany.

The whole spectacle seemed like the end of the world, pure apocalypse. Fighting broke out over Berlin, fighter planes swept from horizon to horizon and the sky lit up with fire. Bombs burst across the entire city, their explosions shaking the earth with a deafening sound, and houses collapsed. After each explosion, clumps of smoke and thick dust were thrown up over the roofs of buildings, windows shook, and black clouds covered the city. A shower of stones, splintered wood, metal shards, and dust and ash came down like rain on the streets of Berlin.

After the attack, those Germans who had survived were unable to recognize their own city. It was a wasteland of ruins, stone fragments, and craters. All Berlin was strewn with broken brick, twisted metal, piles of debris over which soot and shredded foliage floated. Countless fires raged across the city, and ambulances swept through the smoking ruins. Rescue crews teemed among the destruction, but was there anyone left to rescue?

After the Americans had carried out their bombing, they behaved quite strangely. Instead of heading back the way they came, the planes maintained their stubborn course toward the east, far from their bases. The Third Reich's air defense was immensely surprised: where could the Americans possibly be headed? The American bombers later crossed the Eastern Front, and at four o'clock in the afternoon they approached Poltava.

The American bomber armada was usually met at the air base by crowds of people. This time it was a baking hot day. The air above the steel-plated runway and taxiways shimmered. As the planes approached, a brass band struck up a loud march. The large crowd shuffled restlessly and peered nervously at the empty horizon. As before, they first heard the roar of engines, then a few dark and indistinct spots appeared far off, growing in size and taking on shape as they came nearer. A hub-bub broke out among the crowd, people waved in greeting, but as they watched, worry appeared on their faces. They were all troubled by the same question: who had made it safely this time?

The huge planes with their roaring engines came into land. The stretch of uncut grass to the side of the runway shook under the strong wind generated by the planes' propellers. The crowd gasped and moaned, for even to an untrained eye it was clear what damage the aerial armada had suffered. The Germans had been unable to prevent the bombing, but their Messerschmitt fighters had set upon the American fleet and picked off the Flying Fortresses at the edges.

The American bombers had flown in formation in ranks of three planes. Now some of those ranks were reduced to two planes or even one. The crowd could see these gaps in the formation; the empty spaces were glaring, an eloquent statement of the losses the Americans had suffered.

The interpreter, overcome by fear, stood there with bated breath. She did not have the strength to wait any longer. Next to Olga stood Kapito-lina, who glanced at her friend and saw that she was upset, but this time held her tongue. What use was there saying anything when Olga was this frantic with worry? Any reasonable person would try to feign indif-ference, pretend to be calm and composed, but Olga lacked the strength to put on such an act. Mind you, how could any person, however reasonable he or she was, remain indifferent to this game where winning or losing meant life or death?

General Kressler, the air base commander on the American side, and his deputy Colonel Cullen met each crew. Even from a distance one could see how these two men saluted the crews and shook their hands. This solemn and ceremonious ritual took place in spite of any losses that the crews might have suffered. Kapitolina was the first to notice the American whom she so despised: the lieutenant and his entire crew of ten men were, like the other crews, walking along the runway. The copilot was scanning the vicinity and clearly looking for someone. Kapitolina naturally knew who it was whom he sought, but she pretended that she had noticed nothing and only glanced at her friend without a word.

Ever since the American's departure, Olga had regretted not leaving with him. Firstly, they would not have had to part and they could have spent the past several days together instead. Secondly, she would have been able to put all her fear at escaping the USSR behind her. Creighton had been right, of course: she should have made up her mind the week before, but she had not wanted to take the risk, and Creighton had flown off without her. She had spent all these last days waiting for him to return and reproaching herself for her indecision. She vowed to herself that if they met again, she would be more receptive to his prodding and not say a word against it. "Just let him come back, just let him come back!" Olga kept repeating to herself, as if chanting a spell.

As she regretted her decision to remain behind, Olga was still oblivious to the fact that fleeing from the USSR would make her a deserter, as it would any military officer. The law, and being brought before a court martial, did not enter her mind.

Amid the roar of engines, the two Soviet interpreters battled through the crowd of onlookers toward the American crews. Familiar faces became a blur for Olga; she was hardly able to recognize anyone through the tears in her eyes. When she finally caught sight of the American, she was barely able to refrain from crying out. She felt as if she might faint or the spot or dash headlong toward him. She did well: she maintained control of herself; there were too many eyes watching her.

Her caution was understandable. Since the supposed people's regime had assumed power, the population had always had to be careful. People felt that they had to hide what they thought, hold their tongues; there was only one man in the whole country who was permitted to display his feelings and air his opinions publicly. The regime kept a vigilant watch on the level and degree of the population's love for Comrade Stalin. Across the entire gigantic nation, people competed to show who could express their devotion more loudly and more exuberantly.

Yet in people's personal lives, showing emotion in public was a faux pas. And love for a foreigner was something completely obscene. Showing love for a foreigner meant that one was publicly defying and mocking the Soviet regime.

Among the crowd and the flow of people, with the roar of engines in the background, Steven Creighton and Olga Shilina stood motionless and silent. Kapitolina caught Olga's eye and understood what was going on without any need for Olga to explain.

The crowd swelled around them and the strong wind whipped up the grass. They were surrounded by the faces of strangers, and the scene was loud and festive. The American and the interpreter looked at each other in silence, neither moving a muscle lest they reveal their feelings to the people around them. If only people knew what a struggle it was for them to remain so restrained!

Meanwhile, all the Flying Fortresses had landed, but no one had yet noticed that a German Heinkel He 111 reconnaissance plane had followed the bomber formation at a distance. This plane had taken off from a German air base as the Americans finished bombing Berlin and headed toward the Eastern Front, and had tailed the bomber formation in order to find out where the Americans landed.

The Germans watched as the last of the American bombers landed. An alarm was sounded, and a pair of Soviet fighters took off, but the German spy plane hid itself among the clouds and the Soviets were unable to catch up with it.

# 29

Shilin was sure he had misheard when some time later the voice from ground control repeated its earlier command:

"Destroy the target!"

Events took on the quality of a dream. An irksome, recurring dream that ineluctably haunts a person. The firm voice from the radio, just like in a dream, was drilling into his ears the same words, as if it were not a person at the other end but a tape loop playing over and over on the airwaves.

To be exact, the order to eliminate the target had been given twice over the past twenty-seven minutes: the first time when the foreign plane had approached the island, and now as it flew away from it. The first time, the order had been immediately retracted, but the fact that it was repeated now struck Shilin as odd and unexpected. What sense did it make to open fire on a plane and shoot it down when it was already flying away?

The Soviet commanders – we must be honest here – were apparently at a loss and did not know what to do. They were looking for some kind of solution and were obviously baffled. But neither the pilot nor the station guiding him nor the higher-ups knew who had issued this order. Later, when we retraced these events at Division X, we followed the whole chain of command upward and ended at Minister of Defense Ustinov. By all indications, it was he who had given the order to destroy the foreign plane.

The story does not end there, however. Later, by a strange twist of events, we found ourselves a witness. According to his account, the chain of command that the order had followed from Moscow to Sakhalin did not end with the Minister of Defense. Ultimately, the last link in the chain was Andropov.

The General Secretary was lying in hospital, hooked up to an IV, when Ustinov notified him that the foreign plane was continuing on its course. After breaching Soviet airspace for the first time along the east coast of Kamchatka, the plane had flown another two and a half thousand kilometers to the south-west and was now flying over Sakhalin island and toward the Soviet border once more. By all indications, it was prepared to cross the border with Soviet airspace for a fourth time.

The Minister of Defense was convinced that they were dealing with a spy plane. The closest route used by passenger planes was a whole five hundred kilometers away. Naturally, a passenger airliner with its complex navigation systems and experienced pilots would never go that far off course. While Andropov listened to the Minister of Defense, he drowsily watched as drops of solution dripped through the IV tube and into his veins. Andropov could not have known, of course, that the rate at which these drops fell was exactly the same as that of the blinking lights on the foreign plane. In other words, the General Secretary's medication was hitting his body in the same rhythm as a plane's beacons.

No one in the world noticed this whimsical coincidence; it was something that struck me only later when we analyzed these events at Division X. If we acknowledge that chance does not exist, that there is no such thing, then chance resemblances appear instead to be the workings of natural laws. The slowly dying General Secretary was invisibly but tightly bound to those people flying in the night sky on the other side of the world.

"Yuri, what should we do?" Ustinov asked.

"You can't force it to land?" Andropov asked, with his perennially gloomy tone.

"We tried. It won't respond."

"Try once more…"

"Yuri, it's flying away. Away!" Unease, even upset, could be heard in the Minister of Defense's voice.

"If it is," Andropov sighed, "you'd better shoot it down."

Thus the fate of others was decided. A terminally ill man hooked up to an IV with almost no time left to live made the final decision. If we think about these causes and effects, one thing stands out: none of the responsible people at the tracking stations, regional command, or the Ministry of Defense along the whole long chain of command up to the General Secretary's hospital bed – no one! – thought about what might lie behind that standard piece of military terminology, "target".

Meanwhile, Nikolai Shilin was racked with doubt. The foreign plane had a distinctly large body; hundreds of passengers could fit inside it. As Shilin thought about those people, he was troubled. They were flying in the sights of a guided missile launcher, and it would only take the push of a button for all of them to die. The foreign plane continued to fly through the pre-dawn murk and flash its beacon lights rhythmically. Shilin thought about how, if this target was a passenger plane, an order to destroy it meant that many people would die, and it was obvious that if there were the slightest doubt, the order should not be carried out.

Yet drawing such conclusions is something that only other countries thought appropriate. Russia was not ruled by good sense, and through-out the ages it had been the custom to seize all kinds of people, just so that the guilty would not go unpunished. Obviously, the more random people on the street that you put in jail, the higher the odds that there will be some evildoers among them. If the innocent have to suffer, well, you cannot make an omelet without breaking a few eggs. For centuries, the lives of individual people had been considered insignificant, and Russia's rulers developed a well-ingrained habit of treating everyone as if they were inveterate criminals. According to the old Russian saying: evil is like coal – even if it doesn't burn, it still leaves you blackened.

Meanwhile, target 6065 was already approaching the western edge of the island and was about to pass over it. Good sense would suggest that the plane be allowed to depart, with good wishes for its onward journey. Yes, they had screwed up this time, but they just needed to be smarter in future. And can a person really make good his own incom-petence by taking away someone else's life?

If Shilin were to utter these thoughts aloud, they would hardly be shared by others in his regiment. At best he would be met with puzzle-ment, and at worst would be called to a hearing and Communist Par-ty officials would go to work on him. They might even dishonorably discharge him from the army for questioning orders. Shilin kept these opinions to himself, and they went no further than the cramped cabin of his fighter plane.

The tracking stations meanwhile had their hands full. The blip de-noting target 6065 showed on their radar screens, with the blips of four fighter-interceptors close behind it. One can imagine how these men were holding their breath as they waited for the target's fate to be decid-ed. If the target got away, heads would roll, but if the pilot executed his orders, then everything would be all right; no one condemns the victors.

Shilin again cast an eye over the foreign plane. Its windows were glowing dimly in a long ellipse around its vast fuselage. For the entire time that the Soviet fighters had been accompanying it, it had never once altered its course, flying steadily on toward the Sea of Japan. Shilin knew from his many years of experience patrolling the Soviet border that reconnaissance planes did not act like that. Spy planes often changed course, executed clever maneuvers, drew figures of eight horizontally, and were ready to retreat from the Soviet border at any moment. Target 6065, on the other hand, stubbornly maintained the same heading, as if it were capable of nothing else, as if that one course had been assigned to it now and forever.

Yes, something here was not right. No one could see why the plane was taking this particular course. From the time that it had first been spotted on its approach to the eastern shore of Kamchatka, the intruder had flown for two and a half hours along a heading of 240 degrees toward the south-west, as if it were being towed on an invisible line.

"Five Zero Three, do you read me? Destroy the target!" came the angry voice of the ground control with the call sign Deputat. The officer was no longer able to control himself and was now shouting into the radio. "Quickly, it's getting away! Quickly!"

Why don't you all get lost, Shilin thought to himself, as if an angry crowd were swarming around him. He looked at the strange plane and tried to urge it on with his thoughts. The intruder had already crossed the coastal strip and was flying now over the Soviet Union's territorial waters that stretched for twelve nautical miles before the border with neutral airspace. Shilin turned his fighter around and maneuvered from one side of the intruder to the other. The strange plane continued to fly straight ahead like an enormous whale.

Meanwhile Deputat was frantically announcing the intruder's heading and altitude. Shilin, though, his eyes focused on the plane, merely answered, "I can't see it!"

In response, a whole chorus of voices erupted on the radio. The pilots of the other fighters shouted over each other that they could see the target. When I later listened to the recording at Division X, these transmissions sounded like a crowd on market day. Everyone was trying to shout louder than everyone else, and one might have assumed that there was a heated argument going on over the airwaves. Amid this noise and confusion, Deputat frantically repeated the order to destroy the target.

"I can't see it!" Shilin cried, as he looked at the strange plane and thought to himself, come on, get out of here now.

Now that dawn was close, visibility had improved markedly. The foreign plane could be clearly seen. Its navigational lights illuminated its bloated body and vast wings. The flashing strobe beacons took turns in pulling the rear of the plane and its tail out of the twilight. As Shilin looked closely, he noticed that the plane's body was painted in two colors, the upper light and the lower dark. Shilin could make out text, still illegible, that stretched across the body of the plane: dark letters on a light background.

Meanwhile, Deputat was asking again and again what was going on.

"I can't see it," Shilin repeated, trying to play for time in order to give the strange plane a chance to make it out of Soviet airspace.

All these planes were flying at high speed, but time dragged unusually slowly. The intruder seemed simply to hang there in the air, though it only had a short distance to go now before it crossed the Soviet border.

"Five Zero Three, report your position!" the ground station ordered.

At this moment, Shilin's instruments showed a heading of 240 and an azimuth of 45, while the other interceptors were flying at various altitudes and at distances of seven, twenty five, and sixty kilometers away. Some time after this, I listened to the radio transmissions at Division X and compared the pilots' remarks to the flight records of each of these planes.

"I just can't see it!" Shilin cried once more, and then he heard ground control order the other fighter, with call sign Eight Zero Five, toward the target.

Shilin was at a loss as to what he should do now, and he was deeply afraid for the strange plane. He knew that his silence could not save it. Eight Zero Five confirmed the order to destroy the target and began to maneuver to get the intruder in its sights.

Needless to say, all of us sometimes find ourselves in situations where it is hard to say yes or no. It makes us desperate to stay silent and wash our hands of the matter. Sometimes silence is itself akin to taking action, tantamount to a refusal, when someone is demanding that their orders be heeded and executed. At other times, however, by remaining silent and trying to wash one's hands of the matter, one becomes an accomplice, like the Roman governor Pontius Pilate. The pilot suddenly realized that, if he remained silent now, he would never be able to forgive himself. For the rest of his life, he would reproach and blame himself for it.

"Eight Zero Five," Shilin addressed his neighbor, "this is Five Zero Three. You've got a passenger jet in front of you!" The other plane was flying at an altitude two kilometers lower and was presently seven kilometers away from the target. Shilin's voice sounded awfully weak in his own ears, and he thought no one would hear it or pay it any attention. "Eight Zero Five," Shilin said again, straining his voice and trying to overcome the general commotion on the airwaves. "Do not attack the target, it's a passenger plane!"

No one paid any attention to his words, neither the ground nor the other fighter planes in the air. The intruder had already come right up to the Soviet border and now it only had to cross it. Later, when Shilin visited Division X, I asked him if he had had any hope that the others would listen to him.

"I did," he nodded meekly. "I wanted to save that plane."

To tell the truth, Shilin in those minutes was not completely sure what the strange plane was, whether it was a spy plane or a passenger jet. However, he felt sure that if there were any doubt at all, the plane should not be shot down. Strangely, no one ever mentioned Shilin in what followed. He disappeared from the story completely. He played no role in the subsequent reports and investigations, his name and his call sign were never brought up, and no one ever made reference to him, as if the man had never existed at all. Nevertheless, at the local air force bases, word of his actions spread widely. It was said that a certain pilot had refused to shoot the foreign plane down. Some people laughed at him, others respected him for it. Still others condemned him for failing to obey the command, for what kind of army was it if soldiers could ignore their orders? Some felt a dislike for Shilin, as happens when everyone else has got themselves into a mess and one person has managed to stay out of it. We were all in the shit, they thought, and this guy came out snow white.

Yet unbelievable though it might be, Shilin was completely absent from all of the investigations that various countries carried out subsequently. On their big charts, the monitoring stations designated three fighters with call signs One Two One, One Six Three, and Eight Zero Five, though air defense had sent up four planes to intercept: three Su-15s and one MiG-23 – one pair from Smirnykh air base and another pair from Sokol Air Base.

Lieutenant Colonel Shilin disappeared utterly from the record. In time, the talk about him locally turned into a legend that existed completely on its own, separately from how things had really been. The local commanders and top brass all maintained silence in concert. Someone spread a rumor that the pilot had long been unwell, and what could you expect from a mentally ill man?

Indeed, it was a typical scenario for Russia, where a man who dares to question authority risks being called a madman, and is lucky if he does not end up rotting in jail. The lot of any close acquaintances of the madman was likely to be similarly wretched, for their reliability might be called into question. This was apparently the reason why Shilin was shunned in his regiment and in the community in which he lived. Later, when the buzz around him had died down, he was quietly examined by local doctors and then sent to us at Division X. This all happened much later, however, and for now the foreign plane was still soaring through the sky over the USSR's territorial waters off the western coast of Sakhalin.

It was difficult to believe that there really were people aboard the plane. The gigantic aircraft with its lights shining in the pre-dawn sky made a peculiar impression, and from afar Shilin was enchanted by its air of mystery, by the notion that it was hardly there. The foreign plane seemed wrapped in soundlessness. The plane was clearly visible: its lines, its dimensions and shape, the windows running along its side. Yet along with that, there was something unreal and inexplicable about it, a cold detachment, as if it were not a plane with passengers and crew aboard at all but an apparition floating in space. Like the *Flying Dutchman* borne along at full sail and yet with no one at the helm, the strange plane was like a ghost that might disappear, melt away in the blink of an eye, without leaving a trace behind in the sky.

However, the plane that Soviet radars had picked up off Kamchatka long before and which was being tracked as target 6065 was none other than the Korean Airlines Boeing 747 flying on Flight 007 from New York to Seoul. By a curious coincidence, I myself had seen it off at New York's JFK Airport. The plane had reached Alaska without a hitch, and after its stop in Anchorage it continued on toward Seoul as usual.

The airliner's passengers naturally had no idea what a commotion was going on around them across thousands of miles. For them, the plane was a temporary home that they could trust in. Dim lights shone in the cabin, and the passengers were lulled by the hum of the engines. Among the snores one caught the sound of children crying or throwing a tantrum, sleepy muttering, people talking in low voices. There was no cause for alarm. The plane was flying steadily on autopilot, and in the cockpit the crew chatted among themselves and radioed at the set times. In the alcoves between sections of the cabin, the flight attendants passed the time in conversation or listened to music on headphones, and a few were napping on the unoccupied seats at the rear of the plane, ready at any moment to jump up and answer a call.

In short, all the passengers felt safe and none of them suspected the danger they were in. They had no inkling that a manhunt had been going on for three hours now, that air force jets were tailing their plane through the sky like fierce dogs around a large prey, trying to get it in their sights.

One shudders to think about it. In spite of its huge size, the airliner was a fragile little vessel lost in the vast space, a tiny boat in the boundless sky. Only a thin metal tube separated the passengers from the cold and the darkness outside. The jumbo jet bore through this icy abyss the dreams and snoring of people who were unaware that their lives hung by a thread. For the last three hours the airwaves had been filled with stern voices, and radar signals had spread out across space as antennas swept the skies. At the monitoring stations and command positions, military personnel maintained a sleepless and feverish vigil. Alarms were ringing across the Russian Far East and fighters were flying in to intercept the intruder.

We still remember, though much time has passed since then. With each year that goes by, events recede ever farther, but every year on the first night of fall I travel with those passengers on their final journey. At the very end of the night, just before daybreak, we all fly together over the sleepy ocean, all of us invisible inside the plane. Far below, the Sea of Okhotsk restlessly tosses and turns, a gray, featureless plain, its waters the color of lead.

The passengers, settled in their seats, had willingly and readily put themselves in the crew's hands. They were happy to trust in the pilots' skill and in good fortune. On overnight flights even travelers who suffer from insomnia drift off to sleep, and their sleep is especially deep at that hour near the night's end. According to folk wisdom, people are visited by prophetic dreams toward dawn.

For already the umpteenth year now I have wandered in my mind down that narrow aisle between the seats. I have looked again and again at the faces of the sleeping passengers – they are still alive, there is still a chance to save them. The passengers on board include a number of prominent men in the very prime of their life: Han-Tae Park, a forty-year-old electronics engineer from Pennsylvania, Stanley Dorman of Long Island, Chung Soo Yoo, a chemistry professor at the University of Pittsburgh, and many, many others sleep in their seats as I walk sadly among them.

Good Lord, how many beautiful women! There is Becky Scruton from Connecticut, probably having dreams about her children, two-year-old Alicia and five-year-old Todd. There sleeps the bright-eyed Kathy Spier, a fashion designer and company director from New York.

  

There is Sarah Draughn, a smiling twenty-year-old college student from Massachusetts. There is the dazzling Hiroko Stevens, also from Massachusetts, the town of Somerville to be precise, where she was survived by her loving husband William. Sadly, all of them on this night were target 6065.

Later, at Division X, Shilin took from me the list of passengers and the photographs of them. He spent two days looking over them in a silence broken only occasionally by a painful sigh and the words, "If I had known… If I had known." He reproached himself for doing so little to save them, and grieved over these passengers inconsolably.

Goodness, what peace reigned over the Sea of Okhotsk! The huge plane and its pursuers roared across the sky, but as often happens at fateful moments, it is the deafening silence that one remembers. It hung over the land, sea, and sky, and seemed unshakable. One might think that the entire planet had frozen and was waiting with bated breath.

"Destroy the target!" came the voice of ground control once more, flung out across the whole wide world over the airwaves.

Like Shilin's MiG-23, the Su-15 fighter with the call sign Eight Zero Five was following the foreign plane toward the edge of Soviet airspace. The position of the fighter at that point was recorded by the monitoring station on the ground: Eight Zero Five was seven kilometers from the target and two kilometers below it. It was obvious that it was incapable of carrying out the order from there. The fighter's on-board radar would not intersect with the target, and thus would not be able to establish a lock on it in order to guide its missiles. In short, Eight Zero Five was simply unable to destroy the target.

Be that as it may, once the Su-15's pilot received the order from the ground, he started thinking about how he could execute it. He was not used to questioning orders – once he had received them, it was his task to carry them out. The Su-15 pilot even wondered if he should ram his plane into the intruder. In any event, Eight Zero Five began quickly searching for a way to maneuver into position. The fighter's position gave it little chance of success; he would not be able to match altitude with the foreign plane, and now the border of Soviet airspace was only a stone's throw away.

The Su-15 pilot thought for a moment and then did the first thing that came into his head: he activated his afterburner to boost his speed. The plane seemed to rear up, and it thrust its nose upward like a speedboat in the water. Pilot Eight Zero Five did not expect much from this maneuver, however, for his position was a hopeless one. Mainly to soothe his own conscience, he activated the on-board radar linked to his guided-missile system. He increased his speed further and pulled the controls toward him. The plane jumped up with its nose pointed straight toward the intruder.

God's ways are mysterious. For some strange, inexplicable, and unbelievable reason, the Su-15's missiles immediately launched, which meant only one thing: the radar had locked onto its target. This was so unexpected that the Su-15 pilot could not believe his eyes. This could only be the hand of fate at work. Perhaps the stars on that first night of fall were against the Korean airliner. A whole chain of unlikely events had occurred, and the last decided the airliner's fate.

The first missile was fired off at a distance of five kilometers, and it was followed an instant later by a second. There was no power in the world capable of stopping those missiles. Even if one could appeal to all-powerful gods, they would hardly be able to save the airliner. One thing might help: the flares deployed by some planes in order to send heat-seeking missiles off course. However, these flares were only used in military aviation, and a passenger airliner would not be equipped with them.

Shilin watched in anguish as the tragic events unfolded. The first missile hit the rear of the foreign plane: he could clearly see flames engulf the tail. The second missile hit an engine and took half the wing with it. The navigational lights were extinguished before Shilin's very eyes. The plane's nose plunged and it began to lose altitude.

Strangely, ground control remembered Shilin now, at the last moment:

"Five Zero Three, report!" the voice suddenly called.

"I am witnessing an aerial confrontation!" Shilin answered.

"I don't understand, repeat."

"I am witnessing an aerial confrontation!"

Shilin could hardly believe his ears as ground control suddenly directed him to observe the target. It assigned Shilin a heading, and added that the target was already dropping in altitude.

"Five Zero Three!" came the voice from the radio. "The target is descending. The target's altitude is five thousand meters."

"I can't see it," Shilin replied and this time he was telling the truth: the foreign plane had disappeared.

Shilin scanned the entire space in front of him, but he could not find the intruder, though the sky was already beginning to brighten. The space below him, however, was still untouched by dawn. A mist hung over the sea, and the foreign plane had vanished into it without a trace.

  

Shilin reduced his speed and turned his plane around in order to hover around the place where the intruder had disappeared. The moment the missile struck the plane, all the passengers woke up, but they did not immediately realize what had happened to them. They naturally had no idea of what was going on. Soon, however, everyone aboard understood that they were falling – falling! falling! falling! – and the situation was already hopeless.

The airliner's plunge lasted ten minutes. Every moment of the fall was one moment less to live, and death approached inexorably and ineluctably. Ten endlessly long yet unbearably fleeting minutes. Now it was too late for anyone to help them; they could only spend those ten minutes meekly awaiting the inevitable end. This was freedom, complete freedom, unlimited freedom. They were still alive, but nothing connected them any longer with the living: they were in freefall, on the last flight of their lives.

As the Boeing 747 fell, it lost speed, but through inertia it continued its forward course. It crossed the end of Soviet airspace and went on falling over the neutral territory that it had been so desperate to reach. It had been too late in reaching it however, and this was a situation in which the price to pay for tardiness was death. If the order to attack had only been delayed, or if the pilot responsible had only hesitated, everyone on board the airliner could have been saved, but alas it was not meant to be.

Much later, Shilin and I spoke at length about whether it might have been possible to save the Korean plane. It might have been shot down even earlier, over Kamchatka or Sakhalin, but it ultimately fell over international waters, outside Soviet territory. However, for those who hunted for the airliner, as well as for those who had sent it along this fatal route, it was merely a target.

Goodness, how can one comprehend what happened on board the plane in those last moments? Can one even imagine what the passengers must have experienced and how they behaved? It is heart-wrenching even to think about those final ten minutes. The fear and despair inherent in this story chills you to the bone, the anguish cuts right through you. These people must have meekly and submissively prayed as they awaited the end; the end of the first night of fall was marked by such anguish. Lord, how should we speak to You, where can we find the words? Have you really abandoned Your people, Lord?!

Sunrise approached, and the pre-dawn darkness gradually gave way, and ultimately vanished entirely, revealing empty space hung with sparse and transparent fog. Below, through the fog, a gloomy gray expanse appeared, of water of the color of lead, a depressing sight to behold.

What inexpressible sorrow lay in that scene, what pain and grief! Those who have sailed the cold ocean know what a grim expanse it can be. Yet some people are drawn to it, forever captivated by it and, when they have to leave it, they dream of returning to it.

The airliner dropped like a stone through the fog and finally crashed into the tranquil ocean, rending its waters and sending spray flying. The plane shattered into bits as if it were made of glass. The fragments sent ripples through the water and sank, and the waves from the impact ultimately crashed onto the rocky Moneron Island nearby.

Around this time, I was flying from America to Europe. A signal from unimaginably far off cut through to me, striking me like a bolt of lightning. I was pierced through by a sense of tragedy. I sensed that something had happened that was now irreparable, and that all hope had vanished without a trace.

━━ **30** ━━

As soon as the Flying Fortresses had landed, their crews came into the mess hall, and one could then clearly see the toll their latest bombing run had taken: the room had never been so empty. It was as if a plague had passed through the mess hall. The empty tables were a glaring sight and painful to look upon.

Olga noticed unfamiliar faces at many tables: new crewmen had replaced the ones who had perished on earlier runs. The squadrons had taken on fresh personnel in Italy; new crews had filled the empty tables in the mess hall at the air base near Foggia. Some of these newcomers had in fact been particularly unfortunate and been shot down on their very first flight. Such was the luck of the draw. According to military statistics, bomber crews saw a complete turnover every two months. It all came down to fate, and no one could know beforehand who would lose and who lady luck would smile on. The wheel of fortune turned continuously, the thresher of war operated ceaselessly and without mercy. No one needed to say anything; the empty tables said it all.

After landing, the American crews prayed in the mess hall before eating. As usual, they remembered those who had perished, then they prayed to the Almighty to help those whose planes had been shot down, and finally they gave thanks that they had made it out alive, and they asked God to keep them safe in the future.

From an initial glance, it appeared that the mess hall had emptied out by a quarter or perhaps a third. Here and now one could observe the deadly game of roulette with especial clarity. The empty tables, decked with white tablecloths, stood out sharply in the mess hall. With no people at them, the tables and chairs had a deserted air about them; one could even imagine them being anxious at the loss.

Before dinner that evening, Olga and Creighton were both busy and managed to exchange only a few words. They found no opportunity all day to be alone together; there were always other people around, numerous other eyes and ears. Dinner passed in a gloomy, quiet atmosphere as the crews kept silent and each crewman privately struggled with the heavy burden of the casualties the fleet had suffered. Moreover, everyone was anxious about what tomorrow might bring, what lessons the Germans had learned from these night-time bombing runs; the American crews were due to fly back the following night.

Meanwhile, things were happening in that theater of the war of which the Allies still had little inkling. Late in the day, near sunset, another German reconnaissance plane appeared in the skies over the Mirgorod Air Base near Poltava. It flew at a high altitude and stayed hidden. As the American crews were eating dinner, the spy plane performed the maneuvers typically associated with aerial photography. The setting sun flooded the vast air base and the ample number of bombers that it now hosted. The Flying Fortresses were all right there in plain sight. The Americans had been careless, and had not bothered to camouflage the bombers, or even to disperse them to different holding places. The planes were arrayed one alongside the other, almost wing to wing.

It took some time before anyone noticed the Germans. The alarm was eventually sounded and fighters took off, but they failed to intercept the spy plane. Now the arrival of German bombers was inevitable; it was obvious that revenge for bombing the German capital was looming. Junior Lieutenant Shilina was writing up her report on her work with the American crews when General Perminov, the Soviet commander of the base, ordered air defense to be on the alert. Perminov advised the Americans to move their planes to auxiliary air bases in the region that had not yet been discovered by German reconnaissance.

The Americans, with their natural frivolity, gave this suggestion no heed. It seemed to fall on deaf ears. It was mainly to show that they were at least doing something that the base personnel began spreading the planes out more widely across the airfield, but the Americans limited their actions merely to this, and simply hoped that disaster would pass them by.

Toward twilight, Olga and Creighton met on the waste ground outside the base. It took a long time for darkness to fall on this long June day, and this shortest night of the year remained palely lit. Fog hung in clumps over the damp hollows. The trees and willow herb bushes were reflected in the pond. As soon as they met, the American lieutenant and the Soviet interpreter forgot all about the danger. They rushed to embrace each other and were breathless from emotion. They stood there quite still for what must have been a minute or two, though who knows, no one was counting the time. They were surrounded by total silence, wilderness and desolation. The place smelled of damp, mud, wet wood and grass.

The American was first to break the silence. "God, I'm so happy! For some reason I thought I'd never see you again!"

"Me too," Olga confessed.

"Tomorrow?" Creighton asked without the need to say a single word more.

Olga immediately understood what he was referring to and she nodded meekly. "Tomorrow." Over the days since Creighton had left, Olga had grown so distraught that she no longer hesitated. She only repeated, "Tomorrow."

What relief they felt at having both made up their minds. Now they no longer had to struggle; it was as if a stone had been lifted from their shoulders and they were seeing clearly now: there was no going back. In an instant the war vanished, receded utterly. Creighton kissed the interpreter. They were seized by feelings of tenderness which came over them like the ocean waves. They were breathless, barely able to rise to the surface, and when they did, they struggled to breathe, like people winded from running a long race.

When they had said goodbye to each other three days before, it had seemed that an eternity would pass before they saw each other again. All the time, Creighton and Olga had been worn down by longing; they waited impatiently to meet once more, anxiously anticipating being together again. Now they joined hands and set off for the burned-down farm, and the sudden flood of their emotions sent them hopping and skipping down the path like children. They really were little more than children, and it was the war that had made them grow up. Now, when no one could see them, the interpreter briefly felt as if she was as free as a bird, and she was unaware that, far away, the Great Leader was thinking about her and maintaining a sleepless watch, like a goblin that works his trickery by night.

The dark and threatening Georgian thought about everyone: how each one should live, with whom they were permitted to fall in love, what they were allowed to say, what they should do and how they should do it. If he learned of some shenanigans on the part of a Moscow girl who had lost her head, who had forgotten all about the Great Leader and his commandments and fallen head over heels in love with an American (a temporary ally in the war effort, but an enemy to Communism), then the great teacher and eternal leader of the Soviet people would scowl and, with the bent-palm gesture that people of the Caucasus were fond of, motion to do away with her. Stalin had been angered and annoyed even by his own daughter. He often grew indignant that, whoever she might have got involved with, she had not found anyone better than that hack screenwriter, who moreover was a Jew. Even though the exceptionally talented Kapler had no thirst for power, the discontented Father of Nations had put the impudent suitor behind bars nevertheless – let him see what happens if he tries to convert someone's daughter to his faith.

"Do you know what day it is today?" Olga asked.

"What day is it today?" Creighton replied.

"Three years ago today the war started. It was the shortest night of the year."

"Oh, yeah. The summer solstice."

Stalin was thinking about the same thing that same night. The shortest night of the year brought memories back to him, painting a picture that the Great Leader tried in vain to forget. Meanwhile, Creighton and Olga found no one at the burned-down farm. Only the eyes of the cat gleamed eerily in the depths of the hut.

"Where are the kids?" Creighton asked.

"Perhaps they went to visit the German," Olga replied. She looked around but found no one. Even the dog, who usually was inseparable from the children, was nowhere to be seen.

On each of the previous days, Olga had visited the children, given them food, and taken them to the base hospital. They were already less malnourished, their sores had been treated, and they were cleaner and stronger. Olga shuddered to think what would happen to them once she was no longer around. Major Margolina from the base hospital intended to send them one of these days to an orphanage.

The burned-down farm was like an uninhabited island in the middle of the dark ocean. Creighton and Olga grew worried as they looked around. They stood still, listening closely, troubled by a distinct foreboding. From all indications, the shortest night of the year was no different from any other – it was an ordinary June night. Yet as soon as they fell silent, looked around, and listened to the sounds around them, the night took on an eerie and mysterious quality.

This night was like those remarkable Ukrainian nights that had so enchanted Gogol, when the air is still and filled with moonlight as a well is filled with clear water. In the silence, one senses some mysterious unease; it leaves people unable to sleep, and they can only wait to find out what ethereal things might happen in such a place as this. These are nights when people are afraid to turn around and look behind them. Cold, staring eyes seem to look out at you, evil spirits lurk – as Gogol was their witness! – and lie in wait for people in secluded places. Who would doubt that remarkable things would happen at this hour on this, the shortest night of the year?

While Creighton and Olga were wandering around the destroyed farm, base headquarters received word from Kiev that a German bomber formation was now flying south. Nevertheless, no one had any idea where they were flying to, and everyone hoped that they would pass the Poltava region by. The base was ordered to stand ready in case. The fighter pilots on night duty hastened to their aircraft, and technicians checked the planes' fuel tanks and ammunition. Creighton and Olga knew nothing of the Germans' approach, however. They had left the war far behind, a world away. The two lovers did not even think about it or remember it.

Hand in hand, Creighton and Olga walked to the edge of the battle-scarred grove, occasionally stopping to embrace and make up for the days that they had been separated. From time to time, Olga looked around attentively, as if she were looking for the children, but in fact the reason lay in something else: Olga was saying farewell to her native country. Tomorrow she would fly away and find herself in a foreign land, and there would apparently be no way back. She stared at her surroundings, hoping to retain the memory of the overgrown pond, the deserted farm, the picturesque grove, the sloping meadow, the hollow, and the forest beyond. She wanted to carry all this with her and keep it with her forever.

Just as a man who has received a long sentence tries to breathe in as much freedom as he can before his imprisonment, the interpreter on the eve of her escape tried to take in as much as she could of her surroundings so that it would last her in the future. She would have loved most of all to wander now through Moscow, say goodbye to her parents, visit the places she had loved since childhood.

The German soldier was standing at the entrance to the dugout. A stream ran with a barely audible gurgling along the bottom of the nearby ravine. Sometimes a light breeze shook the trees and the murmur of the water merged with the rustling of the leaves. As Creighton and Olga came closer, the German corporal stood motionless and stared straight ahead; he did not turn his head or seem to hear their approach. He apparently had not heard their footsteps, or he was deep in thought and did not want to be distracted. A fire burned in a sandy pit next to the dugout's entrance, the pale light of its flames flickering on the soldier's face. The scene was marked by a certain theatricality, as if the German were playing a major role on a stage set.

What was he thinking about? Was he reflecting on the war, was he transported away from the Ukrainian forest to Germany and revisiting his home and family, or was he thinking about deep universal things and soaring high in the clouds? Perhaps he was thinking about his present urgent concerns, such as whether he was eating enough, whether his bowels were functioning properly, how he was tormented by itching, and how nice it would be to wash with soap and hot water…

They reached the edge of the area where the firelight gave way to the darkness of the night. "Where are the children?" Olga asked in German.

"They were here," the soldier answered blankly. "They left not long ago."

"Where did they go?"

"I don't know?"

"What did they say?"

"We didn't talk. I ate and then they left. The food has got better these last days."

"I see… They got food from the base and shared it with you. A German soldier saved by Russian children."

"The boy is a Jew," the German tried to correct her. He clearly appreciated precision and could not tolerate such an error. Order above all.

"You Germans killed their parents," the interpreter reminded him sternly.

"That's war," the German answered blankly, as if that said it all.

"War is for soldiers," Olga countered, annoyed. "These children's parents were not soldiers fighting in the war. They were killed."

"Maybe they were being punished?"

"Punished?" Olga was outraged. "They were burned alive!"

"That is regrettable, but there must have been a reason for it. No one is punished for no reason."

"What reason? What reason could there possibly be?"

"Perhaps these people broke the rules."

"The rules?" Olga was now furious. "What rules? The Sonderkommando would have burned the children alive, too, if they had found them."

"War has its own laws."

"Burning people alive, that's in the rules? Their children saved your life!"

"The children showed mercy. I was wounded."

"You only understand mercy when you are the recipient. I don't think you have ever saved anyone."

"I'm a soldier, I follow orders," the German answered robotically, as if reciting.

Olga translated the gist of their conversation for Creighton, and the American cast a deprecating look at the German. "Ask him what he plans to do now," Creighton said. "If they take the children somewhere else, he's not going to survive without them."

Olga translated Creighton's question, but the German only shrugged his shoulders.

Creighton needed no translation to understand the German's gesture. He frowned and said, "The children went hungry themselves, but they fed him."

"The situation is difficult for everyone now," the German said calmly.

"Let him go to a POW camp," Creighton suggested.

The German thought differently, however. "A prisoner of war camp? With these Russians? They will shoot me."

"We do not shoot prisoners!" Olga objected, indignant.

The German fell silent. It was obvious that he did not agree with these two intruders on his domain, but out of a sense of self-preservation he felt compelled to be quiet. He could see that the man and the woman were angry, but he did not understand the reason why. He felt that he had explained everything clearly and convincingly, and could not figure out why they had become so upset. No, it was better to keep silent, though he was sure that his perspective was a just one – there was nothing that he personally ought to be reproached for, at least.

Olga and Creighton left the German by the fire and headed for the base. They walked over the meadow where the Germans had dug in at their fortifications a year before. The path wound among the destroyed trenches, pillboxes, and machine-gun nests. Suddenly they caught the sound of engines far off. The sound gradually grew louder. Airplanes appeared out of the west, and then flames erupted in the night sky and cast a deadly light over the surrounding area.

The leading wave of Luftwaffe aircraft had dropped illumination bombs on parachutes. The planes then performed maneuvers that took them over the area and allowed them to scout it out. They discovered beneath them the airfield, which was presently hosting row upon row of Flying Fortresses. In the vicinity of the airfield were storehouses, hangars, and barracks. Several minutes later, as the alarm was sounded across the base, fighters from the Soviet air-defense regiment were sent up, but only the pilots who were then on duty took off. For some inexplicable reason, the rest of the regiment hesitated; the alarm, as was usually the case in Russia, had caught everyone by surprise.

Meanwhile a heavy buzzing was coming from the northwest. It quickly increased in volume and came closer, filling the skies and pressing on the earth like a leaden weight. The buzzing was soon revealed to be a formation of German Junkers and Heinkel bombers, and these got down to savagely bombing the air base. They came in from an altitude of three thousand meters in groups of six to eight planes. The first bombs fell on the runways and thus an entire regiment of Soviet fighters guarding the air base was left grounded. The Germans dropped their bombs judiciously; as spy planes had carried out aerial photography earlier, the German bomber crews were working from prepared charts where each target had been precisely noted.

The airfield was dotted with explosions from one end to the other, and the surrounding areas as well. The aviation fuel-storage facilities caught fire almost immediately. Incendiary bombs fell on them, sending flames surging into the sky like a volcanic eruption. An intolerable heat swept over the vast space of the air base, and it became as bright outside as during the day. Across the airfield, planes exploded or were consumed by flames. The hot air carried clouds of debris which then rained down.

Meanwhile, the base's air defense lay idle. As soon as the aerial attack began, a bomb had hit the command position that directed the base's anti-aircraft fire. The individual gunners were no longer receiving any direction, and so they could only fight back against the German bombers with ineffective, scattered volleys. The Germans succeeded in bombing the fortified storehouses where the Flying Fortresses' ammunition and bombs were kept, and a deafening explosion rocked the area and blew the neighboring buildings to pieces, as if a fiery tornado had passed through the airfield.

The Germans knew what they were doing. As soon as one group of bombers departed, another group arrived in its stead without even the slightest pause. This left the Soviets and Americans at a total loss. From above, fragmentation and incendiary bombs fell in a continuous torrent, and the planes also dropped mines and gasoline mixtures to fuel the flames. Scattered Flying Fortresses burned across the airfield, their metal frames now twisted and melting in the conflagration. Hot incendiary mixtures flowed in streams over the earth like lava. A fiery whirlwind swept across the airbase and its surroundings.

It was hell on earth. Creighton and Olga ran under the rain of fire in search of shelter. The explosions seemed to follow them closely, right on their heels. In short order, the American pilot and Soviet interpreter's faces were blackened with soot, their skin begrimed and scorched by cinders, and they became well-nigh unrecognizable. Explosions followed one after another. The base's numerous workshops, barracks, and warehouses were ablaze. The fuel pumps and trucks burned. The fire spread to the neighboring forest. One might have thought that the red sky had descended to cover the earth in a huge inferno.

Creighton grabbed Olga by the hand and led her away. She had no idea where to run to; danger seemed to lurk in every direction. A tree had caught fire, and fell onto their path, looking like a radiant cloud, and embers flew everywhere and stung their faces. Choking from the smoke, the two of them dropped into a deep crater to seek refuge. There were people at the bottom of it, strangers to Olga and the American. It was dangerous to remain in this open crater, though; bombs were exploding close by, and myriad fragments were cutting through the air above their heads, and the acrid smoke stung their eyes.

After waiting out another series of bombs, Creighton and Olga dashed from the crater and ran, looking frantically around them for some kind of shelter. They crouched as low to the ground as possible, barely able to make their way among the raging fires. They stumbled, fell, and then ran on again with every last bit of strength they had. An unbearable heat assailed their faces and it seemed as if any minute now they too would catch fire and burn alive as they ran. At times they collapsed, totally winded, but then got back up and continued onward. They choked, unable to breathe, on the air that was full of embers and soot.

Making one final effort, Creighton and Olga were dashing toward a bomb shelter when a bomb fell on its camouflaged log roof. It was a direct hit; no one inside could possibly have survived. With a preternatural power, the explosion sent a whole mountain of earth up into the air. Logs, boards, and human bodies went flying in every direction.

The shockwave from the explosion lifted Creighton and Olga and flung them down onto the scorched grass. Stones and dry earth came raining down from above. Burning trees were hit by a surge of air, and their branches cracked. The two of them lay there, deafened, confused, and covered in dust, amid the smoking rubble. Their initial thought was that they would never be able to stand up again, but Olga slowly and numbly lifted her head and tried to look around.

Everything suddenly went very quiet; all sound died out entirely. The whole area, for as far as she could see, was a wretched sight, a disaster that could never be set right: burning ruins, airplanes reduced to skeletons, charred human remains. In the light cast by the flames, among the smoldering branches an ant could be seen scurrying frantically, as if stumbling. Usually ants sleep at night, but this madness had awakened them, fire pouring down from the sky instead of rain. The lone ant fled headlong, the poor creature quite unable to fathom what had happened to the world it was used to, nor where its anthill had disappeared to. Olga made an effort to sit up, supporting herself on her hands, and then, shaking, she cried without tears.

"I can't bear it …. It's awful…" she repeated again and again in despair. She did not even have the strength left to shed tears. She merely rocked back and forth and moaned in agony, as if she had lost all conscious control over herself.

Creighton shook his head and tried to come back to his senses. He rubbed at his eyes and face, brushed the dirt from his hair, and made sure that he really had made it out alive: his hands obeyed him, he could move his legs, his brain apparently still worked. He got up, walked over to Olga, and lifted her up, but she was unable to stand. Her legs gave way and she slumped to the ground.

"*Nyet*…" She shook her head wearily, as if even that required great effort. She went on mumbling in Russian, like a person half-awake. "*Nyet*… I don't want to. Leave me alone. You don't need to…"

As she was speaking Russian, Creighton would have understood nothing of what she was saying, but in fact he was unable even to hear Olga's words. Olga seemed to him to be moving her lips soundlessly. Creighton gathered his strength and lifted the young lady up. He pressed her against him, stroked her hair and said something, but he was unable to get through to her. Still holding her, Creighton tried to start walking, but Olga could barely move, her legs would not support her. The American knew that they stood no chance in such an open place: they would burn, or be hit by an explosion or flying rubble. He picked Olga up and carried her in the hope that they could find some kind of shelter. Explosions continued to go off, dust swirled around them, and burning trees were collapsing. Creighton did not know in which direction they should go. The area was covered in thick smoke.

With Olga in his arms, Creighton made his way forward, gasping, almost dropping from fatigue. His mouth was dry and sweat ran into his eyes. He stumbled repeatedly; with each step he took, he thought he would fall and be unable to get up again. His legs held out long enough to get them to an old trench. At least this is some kind of shelter, he thought.

Meanwhile Olga had come back to her senses. "I can walk on my own," she said.

Creighton gently set her down on the floor of the trench. They spent a moment there catching their breath, and then they slowly walked on, Creighton leading and Olga behind him. The line of trenches stretched endlessly, often taking sharp turns, as was traditional in the building of such fortifications. The Germans' bombing raid continued. Wave after wave of planes came in, and they were clearly intent on reducing the air base to its very foundations, burning it to the ground.

In the open space beyond the trench, bombs were still going off, and in a fiery whirlwind, metal shards, stones, blazing fragments, and clods of earth came raining down. Death lay in wait at every step.

Finally one of the trench lines arrived at an empty dugout. Wooden steps led deep below and into a mysterious darkness, though the flames raging outside cast an uncertain light through the narrow doorway and into the space within. The door, clad in old tin plating, creaked on a single hinge, seeming to call them and invite them to enter. They did so, closed the door tightly behind them, and carefully stepped down the stairs into the impenetrable darkness. It was cool down here, and much quieter. To Creighton and Olga, plunging into this silence was like entering deep water, though the muffled sound of the explosions still reached them from far away. Creighton took out his flashlight. Its beam fell on a bed rudely fashioned from boards, and a bare wooden table on which a candle stood.

"It's like a hotel. A real fancy hotel!" Creighton exclaimed and then struck a match to light the candle.

The dugout had the air of a cellar. It smelled of damp, abandonment, rotten wood. The candle dimly illuminated the walls and showed them to be scarred by mildew and moss. Olga fell exhausted onto the bed. She ran her hand over her hair, which was now smeared with soot and matted from filth and sweat. She tried to shake off the dust and dirt, and then drew a comb from her uniform tunic's breast pocket and spent a long time combing her hair, strand by strand, with great effort.

Creighton brushed the dust from his uniform. "I've never seen a better hotel," he remarked. "I ought to order in dinner for two with champagne."

"I would prefer a bath first," Olga said.

"And I'll buy flowers," Creighton replied.

They sat there on the bed and listened. The explosions continued, sometimes closer, sometimes farther away. Through the cracks in the log roof above them, earth periodically rained down in thin streams like sand in an hourglass.

"Listen up, mister copilot." Olga suddenly addressed Creighton in a voice that had to be obeyed, stern as if giving a command. "Come to me."

Creighton obeyed her order without saying a word in reply. He embraced her and kissed her, his hand stroking her cheek.

"Yes," Olga said quietly but without any hesitation, as if she had already thought this over, made her decision, and there was no going back now. "Yes." She undid the leather belt of her officer's uniform and set it down on the bed beside her. "Yes," she nodded earnestly as she undid the metal buttons on her tunic.

The time has come to talk about the ways and whims of love. We all know that this strange and inexplicable phenomenon does not obey any rules, it is not bound by any laws. Love cannot be controlled. For some people it is calm and merriment that inclines them toward lovemaking, while for others it might be the raging elements, like a tornado for example, or an exploding volcano, as if those were the raging manifestations of a person's own inner emotions. For certain types, it is fear that especially arouses them, moments when their blood seems to turn cold and their heart skips a beat. There is no sense arguing about it; only love is capable of defeating horror, only love has the power to overcome fear. If one traces these things to their roots, fear and the natural elements are similar phenomena. At Division X I have had patients who were greatly aroused by danger. It made adrenaline surge through their blood, and it made for romantic encounters full of unbridled, fiery passion.

Be that as it may, on this shortest night of 1944 on the planet Earth, there was now one maiden less and one woman more. The Great Leader and Teacher of the Soviet people, he who was so well aware of everything going on in the world, missed this momentous event. He knew nothing of it, had no inkling of it, and hardly suspected it. No one reported it to him, though Stalin did receive a report of the Germans' bombing raid. The reports that came in from the front listed in detail what losses had been suffered in terms of personnel and war material, but no one mentioned the loss of a young lady's innocence. One must assume that the generals either ascribed no importance to this fact, or they were simply unaware of it. The Communist Party officials, as they often did, missed this secret coming together; it escaped their notice. We can only guess at which of the avalanche of happenings is more important; who knows at the time how significant this or that event might prove to be in the course of time, what consequences it might have for the nation.

The Germans bombed the base for two hours, and that is how long Creighton and Olga's rendezvous lasted. How strange life is that this great misfortune for everyone became for Creighton and Olga a surging happiness, of the sort that neither of them had ever experienced in their lives. They were two people and yet joined into one, and no one was tracking them now, no one was getting in their way. For a time they had been left in peace, the two of them alone. What more could they dream of?

Granted, that night they had come close to death. Many people had not survived. The American and the interpreter would later be troubled by the thought that the bombing was the price they had to pay for their coming together, for their moment of happiness. It was an exorbitant price that they paid in full.

However, they still had no idea just how much they would have to pay in the future. As sometimes happens, they spent the rest of their lives paying for it.

═══ 31 ═══

Soon after Murano, the island of Lido, which divides the Venice Lagoon from the sea, hove into view off the port side of my vaporetto. The vessel reduced its speed and came up to the jetty, shuddering against the lines pulling it in, as if it wanted to break free and head back out on its own.

Lido is a narrow island, only a few hundred meters across. Even someone not fond of walking would find crossing it no trouble. The still water of the lagoon gave off a faintly stagnant smell, but as soon as I had stepped ashore, my face was caressed by a fresh sea breeze: the Adriatic coast was so close that I could almost reach out and touch it. It took only a few minutes of brisk walking to reach the Cappello Hotel, a modest but wholly satisfactory three-star establishment.

The architect had made very skillful use of this plot of land right on the bank of the canal. It had clearly not been the easiest of jobs. The canal flowed along the hotel's rear wall, and on two sides the building butted up against the walls of the neighboring properties. In order to extract the maximum benefit from the site and to fit more rooms into the building, the architect had been forced to bend the building's out-lines at various angles and deftly squeeze it into the cramped, crowded plot. I walked in to find a modest reception. There was hardly room in the small space, reminiscent of a compact car, for the heavyset recep-tionist. He towered over the dark wooden counter like a giant who had been compelled to dwell in a cave. Behind him there was a radio qui-etly broadcasting the news. The burly receptionist was listening close-ly, his head bowed as if to hear it better, as if he were afraid to miss a single word. He nevertheless greeted me with an officious smile when he heard the bell ring and saw me standing on the threshold with my travel bag in hand. Indeed, his well-developed business instinct sprang to life – the hotel was happy to have a customer. All the same, he con-tinued to stand and listen to the news, unable to tear himself away. To my astonishment, the cordial smile disappeared from his face as soon as I placed my passport on the counter. His mood immediately turned dour; he frowned, and looked at me with suspicion, as if to say that I was unwelcome. Moreover, he had closed up, the spark in his eyes was gone, and there was a strained look on his face, as if he sensed danger and was prepared to repel it. Nevertheless, he checked my reservation, and with exaggerated formality handed me the registration form to fill in. I did so. Without looking at me, and with a rude gesture and a loud clatter, he threw my room key down on the counter. The key hung from a large wooden pendant on which my room number was written. The wooden pendant resembled the wooden mallet that we in Russia use for mashing potatoes. The heavyset clerk then turned his back to me, and I understood that I had fallen from his grace and had turned out to be an unwanted guest in his establishment.

In the dim depths of the hotel, the narrow, winding corridor followed a meandering path, changing direction, apparently, to follow the lines of the building. My room proved to be perfectly adequate. The window looked out onto the canal, along which boats were making their way. The room lacked a television, but on the table next to the wide bed I found a radio with ten channels to choose from. However, I decided not to follow the receptionist in listening to the morning news, hurrying instead to find some breakfast.

I was lucky with my neighbors on this floor. A group from the Union of Cinematographers had arrived, about thirty people altogether, and some of the actors I already knew by sight. In the restaurant I had the good fortune to be at the same table as the actor Alexander Zbruyev, the Saint Petersburg documentary film director Aron Kanevsky (an extraordinarily witty fellow, by the way), and Volodya Savitsky, who was a major figure on the production side of Soviet cinema. Sitting across the table from us was the actor Valery Nosik, a man who was perennially sad and introverted, invariably pensive and taciturn.

In stark contrast to Nosik, the young film critics and cinema buffs around us chattered incessantly. They immediately set upon the directors and cinematographers, and were dazzled by the beautiful actresses whose attention they strove to attract and with whom they flirted. In short, the hotel was full of creative figures and resembled a lively picnic. I started talking to my neighbors at the table, and we quickly found common ground and formed a group in and out of which I found myself dipping. Naturally, no one knew what had brought me here, where I had come from, or how it was that I was here at all. Of course, I had no intention of being open about these matters.

I must say that the festival happened at exactly the right time. Not that coincidence was at work here. When Soviet intelligence had planned the operation, they deliberately scheduled it for September 1, at the same time as the Venice Film Festival. The bustling crowds of people and the general level of excitement greatly helped the mission for which I had left New York not for the USSR and Division X, but rather for this festival in magical Venice. What a great opportunity it was for me!

The Lido is famous for its beach. Its wide sandy shore stretches along the Adriatic on the outer side of the island. From the Cappello Hotel I walked down a side street until I reached the broad, waterside Avenue D'Annunzio. From there I crossed the intersection with the island's major thoroughfare Gran Viale Santa Maria Elisabetta, and continued along Marconi Avenue to the Hotel Excelsior, where the festival's organizers based themselves each year. A mob of festival attendees strolled lazily along the promenade, swarming outside the bars and street cafes, of which the most crowded of all was the Lion. The excitement here was in full swing, the very embodiment of the *dolce far niente* of this upscale destination.

A steady breeze blew in from the Adriatic, ruffling the colorful flags flying over the Palazzo del Cinema and the entrance to the legendary five-star Hotel des Bains. The latter had served as the setting for Thomas Mann's story *Death in Venice*, and it always hosted famous film stars during the festival. I must admit that I found the Hotel des Bains rather ordinary, a humble Art Nouveau building from the Mussolini era. The wind caressed the wide coastal avenue of Marconi, worried at the white canvas beach huts at the waterside, swirled over the vast open-air Arena cinema, and beat in vain against the dreary concrete walls of the casino – a building resembling a bunker designed to withstand a long siege. The casino's exterior was not remotely beautiful, its architecture more repellent than inviting. Not that playing at the tables, placing bets, trying my luck, or generally gambling my life away were in my current plans.

Everywhere on Lido hung posters advertising the violinist Yehudi Menuhin, who had come to Venice to give a performance. The elderly, gray-haired musician wore a checkered black and white shirt and looked out from the poster with a restrained, somewhat ironic smile. Lido's beaches today were unusually empty, although with films being shown at five different locations from morning until late in the evening, who would think about sunbathing or going for a swim? I thought it might be enjoyable to jog my usual distance of ten kilometers along the beach – wherever I find myself, I regularly go for a run. Just at the moment, however, I could not even allow myself a visit to the pool or the gym, let alone some boxing practice. All my thoughts were focused on the upcoming meeting scheduled for me by Soviet intelligence. We had to maintain strict secrecy and stay on our guard.

Even from afar, the Hotel Excelsior drew attention to itself. With its white and pink façade of sculpted stone and its recessed windows and wide domes more typical of mosques, it resembled a medieval fortress from the Arab world. This was no wonder, for it had been built with a Moorish theme especially for Arab sheikhs. It was even fitted out with towers in the style of minarets. It stood like a daunting ark on the narrow strip of land between the Venetian Lagoon and the Adriatic Sea.

The spacious hall on the hotel's first floor, which was presently hosting the festival's press center, was packed, and a hubbub in many languages swirled around the heads of the crowd, filling the vast space from wall to wall. Young ladies were sitting at tables in the depths of the room and registering the arriving journalists. A plain, short-haired girl who knew Russian registered me, with obvious distaste, as the supposed representative of a provincial film club on the outskirts of Moscow. Her assistant sullenly thrust a heap of promotional materials at me: film synopses and screening times at the five different venues. By and large, if I were actually under surveillance, my watchers would be puzzled, for this object of suspicion was behaving in an entirely innocent fashion.

To my surprise, I found that these girls from the press center, just like the receptionist at the Cappello Hotel, were hostile toward me for some strange reason. Their facial expressions were sour, and they were not especially keen to do their jobs, as if dealing with me was repulsive and something they were simply being forced to do.

A stranger turned to me and asked, "Excuse me, who are you representing here?" He was a tall Russian with a noble but rather battered face.

"Myself," I answered wearily. I was not willing to explain who I was and where I had come from to someone I had only just met.

The man turned out to be Oleg Bitov, a special correspondent for the Russian magazine *Literaturnaya Gazeta*. He was the brother of Andrei Bitov, the famous writer from Saint Petersburg, then still known as Leningrad. Right then, on September 1 just after we ran into each other in the film festival's press center, the journalist was asking me to help him out. He wanted me to let him know if I saw or heard anything interesting during the festival. We both noted the hostility shown toward us by the girls at the press center. They flashed welcoming smiles to everyone else and were keen to assist them, but when it came time to deal with us, they turned cold and made gestures of evident distaste. I again recalled the receptionist at the Cappello Hotel, and I sensed that something was amiss, because ordinarily Russians were treated kindly in Italy. The Italians apparently knew something that we did not.

Hostility from an outsider swiftly brings two people from the same country together, and Bitov suggested we meet for a cup of tea and a chat. He was staying at the Biasutti, which astonished me, as that hotel was considered one of the most pricey on Lido, and how had a mere press correspondent obtained such luxury?

This new acquaintance came in handy, inasmuch as Soviet intelligence had strongly recommended that I speak with a large number of people. I was to make conversation on any subject, chatter away, ask questions, or even just exchange a couple of words with other people in passing, all to lead any foreign intelligence astray. Granted, I had no sense that I was being followed, but I did the best I could to fool any watchers that there might be.

After taking my leave of the journalist in the press center, I walked down the wide marble staircase along which bright carnations had been planted, and headed for the beach, where stood row after row of little beach huts, reminiscent of steppe nomads' yurts. I walked along the surf and out onto a wooden pier jutting into the sea, trying to kill time before my first scheduled meeting. Sometimes, in order to carry out all the silly instructions meant to throw foreign watchers off the scent, I asked others on the beach what time it was, whether the water was warm, or how deep it was.

My first meeting was set for the Park Hotel restaurant. I had studied the way there beforehand: from the Santa Maria Elisabetta landing a waterbus left every ten minutes for the San Marco, Rialto, and Piazzale Roma landings. There were few other passengers. A graceful young lady fluttered in front of me on the deck. I was unable to see her face but I was dazzled by her legs, which were remarkably long and slender, as is common among the ladies of Venice. The sun was already high in the sky, and a warm wind was blowing in from the lagoon and whipping up the waves. The boat rocked from side to side, and from its deck I caught a breathtaking view of the lagoon and all of Venice.

I went straight to the boat's stern and took a seat. As we sailed along, I greedily devoured the scenery. I wanted to record this magical picture firmly in my memory, and carry it with me everywhere. In the hazy distance, palaces, cathedrals, towers, and domes rose up, all looking as if they were made from muslin. The old buildings on the island of San Giorgio Maggiore were enchanting even at this distance, and the tallest of them all was Andrea Palladio's bell tower, looking like a finger pointed at the sky. Farther away I caught sight of Giudecca island. There was the Punta della Dogana, and next to it the church of Santa Maria della Salute. The young lady I had noticed even as we were embarking on Lido was sitting in front of me and bent over a book. Her thick hair fell down and obscured her face from me. We entered the waters of San Marco and gained an impressive view of the Piazzetta, the tall bell tower, the Doge's Palace, the famous winged lion sculpture that was the symbol of the city, the Biblioteca Marciana, and the incredibly rich and elaborate Byzantine architecture of St. Mark's Basilica, dedicated to Venice's patron saint. Dozens of moored gondolas were rocking alongside the landing, protected from rain by blue tarpaulins. A few gondolas were gliding over the turbid green water of the Grand Canal. I had known these views from countless illustrations, yet I was still amazed and unable to get enough of them. I simply could not believe that this was no dream, that I really was here. I forgot about the young lady in front of me for a time. I was occupied by other things, you see, especially as I could not see her face.

The waterbus slowed in preparation for making its landing as we steadily approached the Riva degli Schiavoni pier. I realized that it was my stop now, and so I rose from my seat. The girl remained hunched over her book, and the wind from the lagoon lightly rustled her hair. From time to time, she smoothed her hair with her slender hand, and I caught sight of an expensive ring on her finger. I glanced over her shoulder at the book and read the first sentence my eye lighted upon: "You lose women the same way you lose a battalion…", it said in English. The sentence sounded somehow familiar. The waterbus rocked wildly from side to side, and it was hard to keep my eyes on the page. I stared more intently, and read the words, "I have lost three battalions in my life and three women and now I have a fourth, the loveliest, and where the hell does it end?"

I knew this book. In it Richard Cantwell, a colonel in the American infantry, takes a short leave of absence and travels to Venice in the wintertime, where he hunts duck in the lagoon's marshes and visits the last of his loves, a nineteen-year-old beauty named Renata, who came from a rich and prominent Venetian family. The author even mentions in passing that ducks had flown in from Russia for the winter.

The book abounded with vivid descriptions of Venice, hunting, fine food and wine, and there were some great love scenes. The author knew a lot about all these things himself. I had read the book in my youth and been captivated by it; it seemed to paint a real man's life. Hemingway wrote this novel soon after the war, echoes of which can be found on many of its pages.

"*Across the River and Into the Trees,*" I said aloud in English, and then hastened to disembark. The waterbus had made its landing, and the sailor on duty was now tying the end of the boat's line around a bollard. That done, he opened the gate on the gunwale. I dashed away, desperate not to arrive late for the meeting. If I had not been obliged to be there, if Soviet intelligence had not carefully planned this whole operation in advance, then I might have lingered on the boat longer. Perhaps I would have even traveled on further, as far as that young lady's stop, so that I could at least get a good look at her.

On the Riva degli Schiavoni jetty, gondoliers waited for passengers. They wore striped shirts, and the ends of the colorful ribbons on their flat straw boater hats fluttered in the wind from the lagoon. Their little boats, moored to poles, restlessly rocked in the little waves lapping along the shore. The gondolas had sharp prows and were bent upward at either end. The protrusion jutting upward from the bow resembled a rhinoceros' horn. The boats bobbed up and down incessantly in the wind. The sun and reflections off the water played on their black lacquered sides.

Tourists were everywhere around me. They were enjoying themselves in the Bella Vista bar, whose gelateria drew passersby to its vast selection of ice cream in every color of the rainbow. Also crowded was the neat Ponte della Pietà street cafe with its red tablecloths and wicker chairs the color of fresh foliage.

I did not immediately set off on the route that Soviet intelligence had planned for me. Instead, I walked across the Ponte della Paglia bridge that traverses the Rio di Palazzo canal behind the Doge's Palace. The Piazzetta San Marco greeted me with a din in every conceivable language. The square was packed with visitors from every country, along with the local pigeons. At every step I passed tourists taking snapshots and loudly shouting to one another. The pigeons got in my way, then timidly waddled away or fluttered to another spot and perched there. Sometimes, a whole crowd of pigeons would take off for no apparent reason and fly to the other end of the square, and the beating of so many wings was deafening. Though I did not want to, I had to dive into this crowd, into all this fuss and commotion. The bustling mob of tourists surrounded me and I felt overwhelmed.

Suddenly, silence seemed to fall on the square. It was as if everyone around me had stopped speaking, struck dumb, and not just the people but even the pigeons for some strange reason seemed to sense that something was up and stopped still for a moment. In the silence that had come over St. Mark's Square, I felt as if someone was calling me. No, not a sound reached me, I heard nothing, but I sensed the gaze of another on my back. It bore lightly on me like the touch of a person's palm. I even wondered if I was being tailed. That was far from impossible, and it would not have surprised me if it had indeed been the case.

The waterbus which I had taken had left its mooring. The young lady with a book in her hands was still sitting in the same place, but now she raised her head and looked at the shore, as if she was seeing someone off. Finally I saw her face and we exchanged glances. Of course she was pretty, for how could it be otherwise? I could even see in her Renata, the colonel's sweetheart from *Across the River and Into the Trees*: she had a beautiful face, intelligent eyes, a noble bearing, good breeding. Perhaps she even was the daughter of Renata, or her granddaughter; she had the same features as in my imagination. One dreams of finding one's other half out there somewhere, and now here she was, but alas, she was sailing away, and I would never meet her again.

The waterbus set a course for the Grand Canal. We continued to stare at each other, but the boat was now far off and she eventually had to turn away. We parted forever, and regret washed over me as my hopes ever to get to know her faded by the second. The boat receded, taking her with it, and my heart ached bitterly at losing her. It seemed as if she too regretted it and that disappointment showed on her face. But what could we do now? Whether we liked it or not, we would never meet again. Luck never strikes a person twice. I ought to run after her now, race headlong along the canal and take shortcuts through the small streets in order to reach the next jetty. There would be no harm in trying; the vaporetto would make several stops before the Rialto bridge at the Grand Canal and Piazzale Roma jetties.

If it had been up to me, I would have run after her. If only I did not have a job to do. My mission still awaited me and I could not ignore it. It weighed on my shoulders and seemed to grip my arms and legs like fetters. Whether I liked it or not, I was not a free man at this moment: my mission was a crushing burden. On the other hand, if it had not been for this mission, I would have never come here at all, and the magical city of Venice would have remained an unfulfilled dream.

Now I needed to think about my safety. Before I set off on the route to the Park Hotel mapped out for me by Soviet intelligence, I had to look around and ensure that I was not being followed. I slowly wandered along the embankment in no particular direction. I passed the Londra Palace Hotel, an old gray stone building with carved balconies. A plaque on the wall stated that in December 1877 the great Russian composer Tchaikovsky had stayed here for two weeks. As I continued walking, I glanced at the Leoni bar, whose tables with their pink tablecloths and wicker chairs were tightly packed together both inside and outside under the open sky. I lingered outside the wide shop windows as if I were studying what was on offer, though I was actually observing the street behind me by means of its reflection in the glass. Everything was peaceful and untroubled. No one seemed to be following me. I passed the four-story building of the Hotel Savoia with its white balconies, and then the jetty for vaporettos bound for Murano and a mooring for water taxis. Streetlights stretched along the embankment in two long rows, like great candelabras: each had three white lamps and a purple one. I thought how nice it would be to come here at night and see the lights prettily reflected in the water.

The Riva degli Schiavoni embankment resembled a bustling marketplace. I had not expected such an agglomeration of people. Around the impressive equestrian monument to the Savoy king Victor Emmanuel II, who was triumphantly depicted with upraised sword, such a large crowd of people was moving along that I could hardly find space among them. It was approaching midday and the wide embankment was jam-packed. One after another, vaporettos came up to the jetty and discharged their passengers, and I found myself worrying that the sheer number of people would cause a stampede.

Nevertheless, in accordance with the need to maintain the secrecy of our operation, I had to examine the area around me carefully. It struck me that if I was being followed, I would not be able to see my pursuers in such a dense crowd – it would be like finding a needle in a haystack. On an empty street, or alongside a deserted canal, it would have been much easier to determine whether I was under surveillance; I could readily spot the person there. I passed the impressive white edifice of the Hotel Danieli, which offered a fine backdrop for the equestrian monument, darted through the low gateway of a neighboring yellow building, and came out on a narrow canal, where I immediately found myself face to face with a station of the carabinieri. The old building seemed to have been plunged into the canal, and the water was splashing nearly at its doors. A wooden jetty stretched along its façade, and official police boats bobbed at their moorings. A few tall and dashing carabinieri stood picturesquely on the pier in their dapper dark uniforms with red stripes, like actors on a stage set. There were other policemen there, however, who did not look so festive; they wore ordinary uniforms with dark berets and had rifles slung from their shoulders. One of the carabinieri had remained on a moored boat and was standing at the helm and fiddling with the dial on the on-board radio. This made me worried. I've had it, I thought, and I felt a cold sensation in my chest. I had not planned to run into the police.

On the other hand, if foreign intelligence had decided to keep a watch on me, they might well have assumed that I had voluntarily arrived here at this station in order to give myself up. You follow every instruction carefully, you observe all the rules, and look where you end up by pure coincidence! The quarry runs right into the hunter.

This was an overreaction on my part, however. The carabinieri paid me no attention, seeming not to notice me at all. They talked among themselves, and I slipped by them with feigned indifference. The helmsman on the boat was lazily turning the knob on the radio in search of a frequency. As he did so, I caught snippets of music, voices, and static. Suddenly he found a local station and an announcer was speaking at the typical breakneck speed of newsreaders. Like all doctors, I had studied Latin once, but I could not make out any of the words, and the announcer was speaking too quickly and excitedly. Nevertheless, from the way the carabinieri grew tense and fell silent, and then all together, as if on command, turned toward the boat in order to listen closely, I realized that something unusual had happened. This news was clearly of some extraordinary importance.

Suddenly, after the blisteringly fast and incomprehensible speech of the Italian newsreader, I heard Russian coming from the radio. Amid much crackling and background noise, a male voice was shouting "Deputat, this is Five Zero Three. Its navigation lights are on, its strobe lights are flashing!" The voice seemed familiar to me, as if I knew this person from somewhere, though I could not remember where.

Judging from the amount of background noise, this was a radio intercept, and the brief snippet was cut off as suddenly as it had begun. It was followed by more rapid speech in Italian; apparently the newsreader was discussing this news. However, I needed to make my way along the narrow Rio del Vin canal and back to the embankment from which I had come. I walked over the Ponte della Paglia that traversed the Palazzo canal and then wandered along St. Mark's Square, where the mechanical Moors appeared at the top of the Clock Tower and loudly struck noon on the big bell with their hammers. Their twelve blows resounded across the neighborhood.

The news from the radio had set me wondering. I was also feeling a little uneasy after running across the carabinieri. I still had a job to do, however, and I mentally prepared for my upcoming meeting. Once I had regained my composure, I walked around the Campanile, the high bell tower built from red brick, and crossed this remarkable square, lined as it was on all sides with unique and unforgettable buildings: the Procuratie Vecchie and Procuratie Nuove, the Clock Tower, St. Mark's Basilica built all the way back when Venice was still a Byzantine possession, and the azure Doge's Palace which resembled an exquisite handcrafted box.

Naturally I was interested in all this architecture and the way of life of the Venetians, but my first concern was for my own safety. Soviet intelligence had insisted that I thoroughly scout the area out first, and so I leisurely strolled along the covered galleries and archways crammed with restaurants and souvenir shops. There was a whole array of street cafes, with hundreds of small round tables, and colorful metal chairs with wicker seating and advertisements for Cinzano vermouth posted on their backs. Dashing waiters slipped among these tables in their black trousers and white jackets with gold thread woven on the shoulders. Among those Venetian institutions, sheltering among the galleries under the arches, the luxurious lounges of the Caffè Florian stood out, its ambience like that of a museum. The prices here were exorbitant, but all the same I sat down on one of the heavy chairs made from oak and trimmed with leather. I drank a cup of fragrant tea, breathed in the air of the place, and imagined that I was sitting at the same table with all the people who had visited here before me.

I experienced a strange feeling in the Caffè Florian, I must confess. This was the first cafe in all Europe. Over the preceding two and a half centuries, eminent figures from many countries had sat here: Goethe, Byron, Casanova, Dickens, Hemingway himself when he was writing *Across the River and Into the Trees*. Just imagine what these walls had seen! Nevertheless, I was not thinking of this just now. I was experiencing a sensation of being watched, a feeling that some stranger was secretly spying on me. Nor could I shake the thought that something terrible had happened, some disaster, far away at the ends of the earth.

     

An echo of it reached me even here, in the Caffè Florian with its lush interior, precious furnishings, and painted ceilings.

Paintings by old masters hung on the walls of the cafe's baroque interior. Two or three tables away from me, an elderly couple were drinking coffee. The man and woman were gray-haired, so slight as to appear practically weightless, and remarkably similar to each other. They had clearly been together for a long time. They were listening with concern to a pocket radio, their wrinkled faces bent over the small round table. They had forgotten all about their coffee, which steamed on the table but was quickly going cold. They shook their heads sadly and their faces, which resembled baked apples, gradually took on mournful expressions. The news had deeply touched the old couple, I could see the pain in their eyes.

As I studied these elderly people, I recalled the receptionist at the Cappello Hotel that morning and the carabinieri on the jetty. They too had been listening to the radio and apparently heard news that had shocked them. I could guess what had happened, but I was afraid to admit it to myself, and I was in no hurry to make sure of it. I felt a sharp bitterness in my heart, though the job I had to do now was foremost in my mind and overshadowed all else.

In the Caffè Florian and on St. Mark's Square, small bands were playing old time music, and there were a few solo performers about. Their languid melodies wove through the air here in the dusky galleries.

I wandered from shop to shop, admiring the window displays of Venetian lace, gloves, gondoliers' straw hats, Murano glassware, fans, carnival masks, and women's jewelry of every kind. It was a delight for my eyes. The instructions that Soviet intelligence had given me were proving quite worthwhile after all. I diligently followed the rules of ensuring secrecy. I occasionally made small purchases, and picked up some postcards with views of Venice, without forgetting, of course, to closely examine the area around me. Like a man paranoid, I felt the eyes of every passerby on me, especially those who pointed their cameras at me. Nevertheless, I did not notice anything out of the ordinary – but I had to be completely certain. My profession is a special one, and demands thoroughness.

After duly waiting there for the proper time and having a good look at my surroundings, I set off for my meeting at the Park Hotel. Behind the archway of the Clock Tower, narrow old streets and lanes ran deep into the city. I walked past houses darkened by time that now hosted Italian and Brazilian airlines. In front of a shop with a sign reading "MURANO

GLASS", an ancient round fountain gurgled, its marble steps well worn. I was amazed at the number of bars here: they seemed to outnumber the pedestrians. My attention was drawn to the Hotel Concordia, a dreary dirty-yellow building with dull brown shutters. The building gave off an air of crime from a mile off. I walked along the Via Merzaria, passed the San Zulian church, and came out on the Rio Guerro canal which flows at a right angle into the Rio Fava canal.

It was a magical walk. The unique gray, yellow, and pink houses, adorned with fine stone carvings, were reflected picturesquely in the canals. Their ground floors of whitish stone were bleached by sea salt and covered with algae, and their marble steps and thresholds, worn down by centuries of footsteps, ended in the turbid green water. The sunlight played on their walls. Every house was distinct, unique, and every one of them was striking. I would have liked to linger in front of each of them, without checking the time, without looking away, without even breathing. On any other occasion I would have done just that – I would have taken the time to admire them. Now, however, I had the long-appointed meeting hanging over me.

Soviet intelligence had instructed me to orientate myself using the San Bartolomeo church. It was only a stone's throw from the Rialto bridge, hanging so marvelously over the Grand Canal. My eyes widened in delight at the Rialto market stretching along either side of the bridge, and abounding with cheese shops and haberdasheries. Nevertheless, I pressed straight on without loitering, though one can imagine how much effort and self-control this required.

On the other side of the Rialto bridge, my route took me along the canals, passing church after church, from one bridge to another. First I passed the San Silvestro church, then San Polo, followed by the red brick Gothic basilica of Santa Maria Gloriosa dei Frari. Then came the tall and majestic Renaissance church of San Rocco, adorned with myriad sculptures. A little while later, on the other side of the Muneghete canal, I found the San Nicola church, a monumental and awe-inspiring building in the late Romanesque style. Nearby, on the other side of the Rio dei Tolentini canal, I finally caught sight of the Park Hotel.

══ 32 ══

The aerial bombardment lasted a little over two hours, but for everyone caught in it, it seemed to go on forever. At an altitude of three thousand meters, wave after wave of German Junkers and Heinkel bombers arrived and unleashed a hail of bombs, as well as rivers of incendiary fluid. The airfield and its surroundings were rocked incessantly by explosions. Fires raged, and this shortest night of the year glowed red-hot. Sometimes a pause came in the bombardment, like a fermata in a piece of music. A deafening silence then descended on the area, and one might think that the savage concert was over, that the survivors could now all make their way home. However, a new wave of bombers would then appear from over the horizon, fly unhindered over their targets, and relieve themselves of their heavy load of bombs.

For the entire duration of the attack, the American personnel at the air base and the crews of the Flying Fortresses huddled in bomb shelters. No one was willing even to look out of the door lest the consequences should prove fatal. All this time, the Soviet soldiers labored under the rain of bombs and fire, trying to save the Americans' Flying Fortresses. Some of these men perished, burned alive, but they managed to drag many of the bombers to safety with the help of tractors. Dozens of Flying Fortresses were lost, but the majority of them were saved.

On the day after the bombing, a sharp disagreement broke out between the Allies, quickly turning into a heated argument. The Americans aired their complaints with regard to the Soviets. These came down to the actions of Soviet air defense, or rather the lack thereof. The Germans had been able to bomb the base freely and no one had put up any resistance.

When the Soviet command heard these complaints, they were outraged. "Just compare your losses to ours," they said. "While you were sitting pretty in the bomb shelters, we saved your planes!" The Americans, however, were astounded that the Soviets were pointing to losses as if they were a sign of military valor. The American generals and colonels retorted that the lives of its soldiers were more valuable than any hardware, and that if the base had failed to spot the Germans' approach, then they should at least have saved the personnel. It must be said that the Russian army throughout its history has thought little of losses. The rural population would quickly make up for any losses, and the Russian people's ability to replenish itself became its distinguishing trait.

Of course, compared to the Americans, the Russian soldiers had acquitted themselves gallantly during the bombardment, and they deserve eternal praise and glory. But frankly, what choice did they have, when Soviet air defense had proven so incapable, when no fighters had managed to take off against the Germans, when the anti-aircraft guns had remained idle? What was left but heroism and the willingness to run deadly risks? They knew how to march in formation accompanied by an orchestra, and how to make their way singing under bullets. They could attack tanks with cavalry, as they had done in the Kalmyk steppes: "Draw your swords and charge!" German tanks would then simply run the cavalry down with their treads, without even needing to open fire. In Russia through the ages, it has been thought that two in distress make sorrow less. But that is not the issue here.

For the two hours that the Germans' attack lasted, Creighton and Olga remained in the dugout. This shortest night of the year was a strange one of fire, explosions, and hell on earth, but also of poignant tenderness.

The Germans finally finished dropping their bombs and flew away at around three o'clock in the morning. After the attack, fires raged everywhere and the charred earth smoldered. Dozens of Flying Fortresses that had been the pride of the airfield just hours before were now reduced to mere husks of burned metal.

Creighton and Olga emerged from the dugout, and slowly made their way toward the base. The air was filled with thick soot and an acrid smell of burning. They were surrounded by smoking ruins. Dawn was near, though it seemed as if day would never come, and the night would give way only to smoke and soot. Nevertheless, it gradually grew lighter, and charred ruins emerged from the darkness like black skeletons.

The American pilot and the Soviet interpreter wandered, aghast, among the craters and burned earth. Blue flames flickered among the embers. A fickle wind blew and stirred up clouds of ashes. No one paid any attention to Creighton or Olga; perhaps the two were not even noticed at all. Rescue crews buzzed among the destruction, and medical personnel were carrying wounded men and women on stretchers. Other personnel gathered the bodies of the dead for burial, trying to maintain an air of detachment. This scene from a nightmare that was now real life played out soundlessly.

The Americans had, unlike their Soviet allies, made it out of the attack with almost no losses. Now they quickly and readily got down to dealing with the destruction. The airfield swarmed with jeeps, cranes, and tow vehicles. With the help of these machines, the Americans loaded the remains of their destroyed airplanes onto large truck beds and transported them off the air base. Those planes that could be repaired were towed into hangers, where each aircraft attracted a team of mechanics and engineers who worked with the same selfless dedication as the Soviets' socialist heroes of labor.

The Soviet generals, after their arguments and friction with the Americans, were seething with resentment. They swore and gritted their teeth in frustration at their stupid and ungrateful allies. However, nothing could be done about it now, and it was time to get down to work. Army engineers worked to dispose of the rubble, and also to disarm a host of time bombs. The Germans had dropped twenty thousand of these devices on the base and its surroundings, and they were set to explode later when the rescue teams and repair crew had got to work.

As soon as the army engineers had taken care of this unexploded ordnance, construction personnel patched up the airfield's runways and taxiways, while engineers and technicians replaced the equipment that had been destroyed. To the quartermasters' great relief, the warehouses holding spare parts – and that in a quantity of truly American proportions – had survived the bombing.

This work lasted all of that day and the following night. By the evening of the next day, planes were able to take off and land again, though around forty crews – four hundred men – were now without their aircraft and forced to return to Italy as passengers on the other planes. For Creighton and Olga, these circumstances proved very helpful; the general hustle and bustle aided their plan.

While the repair works were ongoing, the two lovers saw each other only in snatches. They could only exchange glances when they happened to pass each other. On the second day, they found time to visit the children at the burned farm which, fortunately, had been spared in the bombing. However, they did not find the children there. Only the cat sat on the threshold, like a hired guard that kept up its vigilant watch day and night.

Creighton and Olga were already familiar with the place, and so they headed for the forest, toward the old fortifications where the Germans had once dug in. The children were here; the American and the interpreter found them in the ravine. After the aerial bombardment, this place was well-nigh unrecognizable: the German planes had bombed it thoroughly. Fallen trees were strewn among the craters, and the earth was littered with splinters.

The boy and the girl were sitting on the edge of a deep crater, and next to them their shaggy dog was scratching itself. Olga and Creighton stared in astonishment, and were even unsure whether they had come to the right place: the dugout had vanished as if it had never existed. An explosion had blown its roof to smithereens. The children seemed unable to come to terms with the thought that the German soldier, whom they had nursed for so long, had died. Yet it had been a direct hit, a German bomb had fallen right onto the German dugout.

Though the war years had weaned the children from crying, for the umpteenth time already it had brought them grief. The boy and girl sat disconsolate on the edge of the crater. Creighton and Olga sat down beside them and did not speak, unable to comfort the children. The children were filled with grief as if they had lost someone close to them, yet this was hard to believe, for the soldier had been a German, one of those who had killed their parents. His death came as a sorrow for them nonetheless. Olga and Creighton were overwhelmed by the strangeness of war. The four of them sat on the edge of the crater as if they were performing a ritual together in silence. In the stillness they could even catch the sound of sand slithering down the slope.

Olga broke the silence. "Come on, kids. This was not your fault. You did everything you could for him. If he'd surrendered, he would still be alive. It was the Germans who killed him, his own side. Let's go."

Olga and Creighton led the children off toward the base hospital, and along the way they collected the cat, too. The children were followed everywhere by the dog, and so it was as a group of six that they arrived at the hospital. Its appearance had changed overnight. It was full of wounded now, and nurses and orderlies were rushing this way and that. Surgeons were constantly at the operating tables.

After a sleepless night, Major Margolina looked exhausted, but she could still expect no rest as long as operations were being scheduled one after another. "Leave the kids here," she told them. "I'll see to them later."

"What's going to happen to them?" Olga asked. She could see that the doctor had other things on her mind right now, but she could not leave without an answer.

"I'll send them away from the front line," Major Margolina replied. She was so tired that she was barely able to remain on her feet. "You see what happens? A war is no place for children. I'll have them taken to an orphanage."

"Doctor, I beg you, don't let them be separated. They are brother and sister."

"Come now, who would separate them?"

"They can only live together, the two of them. Otherwise they'll die!"

"Olga, calm down. I'll see to it. Don't be so upset. I'll write that they are brother and sister, and that they cannot be separated. If you want, you can bring them to the orphanage yourself. I'll arrange documents for you."

"Me?" Olga shook her head uncertainly. "No, I can't."

Under any other circumstances she would have happily accompanied the children away from the front, but now she was unable to do so, because a long journey in the opposite direction awaited her.

Olga took her leave of the doctor, then hugged and kissed the children. "I'll come see you later," she promised, wiping tears from her eyes. "Don't be afraid, everything is going to be all right."

She walked off, and the children remained there at the hospital entrance. The boy and the girl were so small and scrawny. Their heads had been shaved bare and they were wearing baggy clothing that was far too big for them. They were so lonely and helpless that it made Olga's heart ache. The boy held the cat, and their dog lay beside them. As Olga walked away she kept turning to look at them, and she was choked with tears.

The American was waiting for her at the crossroads where a clump of thick bushes was growing. As she walked past, Creighton called out to her from the bushes and pulled her in beside him. "Don't bring anything with you," he said. "For God's sake, don't! None of your possessions! We want everyone to think you're still here somewhere around the base. Otherwise they'll know something is up and start looking for you. It could ruin everything."

Olga nodded. "I understand," she said, to satisfy him.

However, as soon as they parted, Olga felt that there was nothing wrong with quickly running back to her quarters.

It was easy to understand her. Who among us, knowing that they were leaving forever, would be prepared to make a complete break with their past? Olga Shilina could not abandon everything that linked her to her home, her parents, her former life. She could not just forget all the years that she had lived here. Before dinner she ran back to her quarters, and fortunately found no one there. She took the photograph of her mother and father down from the wall and put it into her small officer's shoulder bag along with a volume of Pushkin and letters from her parents.

Olga's wariness told her that she needed to get out of there quickly, before anyone came. Nevertheless, she hesitated. She looked around her quarters and thought about what she should take with her. Perhaps she also simply recognized that as soon as she stepped out of the room, that would be that, and there would be no way back.

Olga finally made an effort to overcome her indecision and forced herself to leave. On the road outside their barracks, she saw Kapitolina come running up, her face red from the exertion, as if she was running late for a meeting of crucial importance.

"Olga, where have you been!?" Kapitolina clasped her hands before her as she ran. "I've been looking for you everywhere! Where have you been?! I've been so worried about you!" She was yelling, her voice ringing like brass. "Where have you been?"

"At the hospital," Olga replied.

"Talk louder, I'm half deaf!" Kapitolina shouted. "A bomb fell right next to me. I can't hear anything! Where have you been?!"

"At the hospital," Olga repeated, this time loudly. "I left the children there. Sofia Margolina is going to send them to the orphanage."

"At the hospital? That's strange. I was looking for you. I asked about you all over. You weren't wounded?"

"No. I hid when the bombs started falling."

"I thought you were dead. I was looking all over for you, but I couldn't find you anywhere."

"You know, Kapitolina…" A strange thought had come into Olga's mind, but she seemed unable to express it, or she did not dare utter it. Finally, she resolved to say it, and nodded to herself. "Kapitolina, if anything ever happens to me…"

"What?!" Her friend did not understand her and looked at her with a furrowed brow. "What are you talking about? What could happen?"

"It's just, you were worried about me…"

"Of course I was worried about you! I looked all over for you and you weren't anywhere! I thought you were dead!"

"You see…"

   

"What are you on about? I was in such a state. You weren't among the dead. You weren't among the wounded. No one had seen you, no one knew anything!"

"That's what I mean. If something ever happens to me, like today for example… Please comfort my parents. Write to them and tell them that everything's all right, that I'm still alive and well. Just don't let them worry."

"Olga, you're scaring me!"

"Just in case. I don't want my parents to be worried like that."

Dinner time had come, and the two friends set off for the mess hall. Dinner was late, however, as the Germans had bombed the food-storage facilities, and the kitchen had been suffering from a water shortage all day. While the interpreters waited for dinner, they passed the time with the Flying Fortress crews. To the discontent of the Communist Party officials, the Americans openly cursed Soviet air defense; almost fifty crews had been left without planes. Now they were forced to depart for Italy as passengers, and they found this situation humiliating.

The Americans, upset, tired after a horrible night, hungry, and forced to wait, now griped and criticized the Soviets. The most impatient of them were prepared to make a dinner of dry rations, or prepare some sandwiches and coffee with their own bare hands, and tell the Russians to take their dinner and shove it. The interpreters, uncomfortable at the bomber crews' directness, softened the translation into Russian for the Communist Party officials' sake, and sought to calm the Americans.

When dinner was ready, the Flying Fortress crews recited their customary prayer before they fell to eating. They beseeched the Almighty to watch over them on their return flight, to let them land safely and survive the journey.

As usual, Kapitolina observed this ritual from her seat in the mess hall. She had now come to accept the Americans' religiosity, but she thought it was a childish whim, a harmful habit, and an absurd and empty ritual designed to satisfy the reactionary views of the bourgeoisie. As a loyal young Communist, she could not fathom how adult people could seriously believe in God, pray, and go to church. She considered religion to be a pretense, and hypocritical, and she found it intolerable. Kapitolina was convinced that something was not right with these Americans, that they had in some way gone completely off the rails. The Americans had no idea of materialism and dialectic, they were unaware of the works of Marx, Lenin, and Stalin, and that seemed to her like complete barbarism and ignorance.

Just think, these Americans did not know the primary sources of Communism! Kapitolina looked at them the way a wise and knowledgeable teacher looks at foolish children. She firmly believed that religion was the opium of the masses, just as the Great Leader had thought. How fortunate she was to live in the country of socialism triumphant, and how scary it was to think that she might have been born instead in their notorious capitalist paradise.

Now Kapitolina wearily looked round the mess hall, and the Americans at prayer repulsed her. Like any militant atheist, she could not calmly accept people praying; her temperament simply would not allow it. Outwardly she feigned indifference, but inside she was indignant. If she had her way, they would be prohibited from showing such ignorance and obscurantism in a foreign country. Let them keep their foolishness to themselves.

"Silly people, thinking prayer will do anything for them," Kapitolina whispered to Olga in disapproval.

"They're taking such risks," Olga whispered in reply. "They have to believe it will help."

"It's just putting on a show," Kapitolina retorted emphatically, and glanced over at Creighton, who was also praying with his crew. "That American of yours is the same."

"No," Olga answered firmly. She fell silent, and did not try to explain, feeling it pointless. Nevertheless, she went on to add, "They really believe, but we simply don't understand them."

Olga's reply offended Kapitolina. Until now she had believed in her friend. She had felt sure that Olga would, sooner or later, recognize the Americans and their foreign capitalist ways for what they were. Now Kapitolina felt that her friend had deceived her, abused her trust, and abandoned the lofty ideals for which the Communist revolutionaries had shed their blood.

Kapitolina was more than offended. She was wounded to the core. She was tempted to grab Olga by the shoulders and shake her, to try and get through to her. A sense of righteous anger burned within her. No one should dare betray the sacred ideals of Communism, and Kapitolina at any rate was not going to let anyone do so, even if it was her best friend. In such a crucial matter as the class struggle, there are no friends or family, there are only two classes separated by the barricades, and each human being had to decide which side he was on. In short, Kapitolina was indignant and ready to sound the alarm.

  

The prayer came to an end and the crews began eating. Kapitolina, however, was unable to eat a bite. She realized that according to the rules of friendship, and out of loyalty to her ideals, she had to save her friend. For Olga's own good. As a simple and good-hearted young lady, Olga did not sense the danger, she was unaware of the threat that now loomed over her. She was flying, like a moth drawn to a flame, toward the false sun of their class enemies. To save her friend, Kapitolina felt ready to sacrifice even herself.

After dinner, the interpreters assisted the staff officers as the Americans and the Soviets were discussing the flight assignments and marking targets on their charts. At some point, Kapitolina lost track of Olga, and began to run around searching for her friend. She badgered everyone she met, but no one had seen her.

Olga was nowhere to be found. Kapitolina ran to the Communist Party office and the hospital, looking for her. She asked everyone along the way, but in vain. Her friend had vanished without a trace. Kapitolina could not imagine where she might have disappeared to. She ran, worried, to their quarters, but found no one there; her doctor neighbors were all working at the hospital. She sat nervously on the bed and looked distractedly around the room.

Something was wrong with their room today; something had changed, but Kapitolina could not tell what exactly it was.

She suddenly noticed the light reflecting on the opposite wall, above Olga's bed. Yes, the narrow metal bed was still there, but something was missing from the wall; an empty space there caught her eye. Kapitolina remembered that some of Olga's photos from home had been up on the wall, but now they were no longer there. Who could have taken the photos from the wall – who, if not Olga herself?

Kapitolina froze as she pieced things together. She sat motionless on the bed while the missing photographs brought her to a terrible conclusion that made her almost nauseous. She then decided that she could not simply stand idly by and watch her friend die. She had to save Olga.

There was no time to waste. Kapitolina abruptly jumped up and ran with her characteristic resoluteness to base headquarters. There was little time left before the American bombers took off. The final preparations were coming to an end on the airfield: trucks had supplied the planes with fuel, with bombs, and with ammunition for the on-board machine guns.

══ ══ 33 ══ ══

It is hard to tell if you are being followed on the street, if the person following you is capable. I have never been able to know for sure, at any rate. Perhaps I was not being followed at all, but it felt like it the whole time. Fear has big eyes. The closer I got to the place appointed for my meeting, the more I was overcome by doubt, and a spy seemed to lurk within every passerby.

The Campo dei Tolentini square in front of the San Nicolò cathedral is spacious by Venetian standards. On the bell tower side, the square borders the narrow San Teresa canal with its motorboats. A few tourists, visiting pilgrims, and locals were strolling around the church, and before I headed for the Park Hotel, I decided to have a final look around – God forbid I be tailed as I arrived there. My meeting would be of especial interest to foreign intelligence, and it would not hurt to be a little overcautious.

The square in front of the church was quite sleepy, but this was no time for me to be dozing off. I carefully studied my surroundings, my muscles tensed in concentration. A curly-haired street artist was sitting with his back to the passersby and painting Venetian scenes from memory with colored chalk. He looked hard in my direction, and I wondered in alarm if I had been found out. I quickly pulled myself together, though, realizing that this man had been sitting here all day, and saw me solely as a potential customer.

Two monks in enormous snow-white cowls floated past me. They were smiling, and there was something playful in their swift steps, as if they were yachts running at full sail. There were no grounds to suspect them of secretly watching me. The two disappeared behind the heavy doors of the cathedral, from which I caught the ethereal sound of an organ. I thought that it would not do any harm for me to take a look inside either: in spy movies, Catholic churches have occasionally been used for secret meetings and plots.

The interior of the San Nicolò church made a powerful impression on me. It had been built a very long time ago, when the Tolentini neighborhood was impoverished, a place where practically everyone was destitute. Back then, it was home to many beggars who survived solely on what they were given at the entrance to the church. The church had been renovated many times in the intervening centuries, and its central nave struck me with its lavish decoration: fine carvings, golden arches and columns, paintings on the walls and ceiling, and statues above the altar. I saw no poor folk at the entrance begging for alms, though the church continued to bear the epithet "dei Mendicoli", the church of the mendicants. Where had they all disappeared to, I wondered.

The church was deserted. Daylight flooded in through the wide windows near the ceiling, and entered more stealthily through the side galleries. As the two jolly monks entered, they became serious. They stepped toward the altar and knelt before it. The unseen organist was rehearsing a Bach chorale in preparation for mass. The sound of the organ filled the vast church, splashed against the high arches, and then suddenly plunged downward. In its lower bass registers, the organ beat against the walls like a heavy wave. Massive benches wrought from dark wood invited one to take a seat, forget about the everyday bustle, and reflect on life's vicissitudes. I sat in the last row, the music making a suitable accompaniment for my thoughts. The chorale helped sharpen my thinking, and it boosted the signals coming from far away. I suddenly understood beyond all doubt with incredible clarity that, sadly, I had not been mistaken: the terrible apprehensions that had come over me these last days and nights had been fully justified, to our common woe. I did not know the details, of course, but I felt sure that my presentiments had come to pass, that my intuition had not led me astray.

From time to time the organist paused. In the stillness, the organ pipes exhaled hoarsely, the instrument seeming to catch its breath and take fresh air into its lungs. While I sat there, no one else entered the church; it appeared that no one was obviously following me. Deep down inside, however, I had the strange feeling that someone was watching me from the side. Or perhaps the eerie emptiness of the cathedral served as an invisible antenna that picked up signals from across the earth. It seemed to me that an eternity went by, though my watch showed only a few minutes.

Outside the cathedral, nothing had changed. Exactly as before, a few tourists were taking photos in the square in front of the church. Visiting pilgrims and locals were strolling around. I did not notice anything suspicious, though I examined every face carefully.

Incidentally, it would be hard to find a better place for carrying out surveillance than one of the arched bridges over the canals. One would appear to have done no more than choose a high vantage point from which to admire the architecture or stare out at the turquoise waters, like any impressionable tourist. In reality, of course, one would be maintaining a careful watch over the area. Not to mention that one could quite justifiably keep one's eye pressed to the viewfinder of a camera.

From the crest of the bridge over the Rio Tolentini canal, the whole area opens up: the square before the Church of San Nicolò dei Mendicoli, the narrow embankment, and the canal on both sides of the bridge. The Tolentini canal here bends at a right angle before it meets the lagoon, and it was here, on a headland, that the towering Park Hotel was located. It was a modern building of seven stories, a rare phenomenon in such a traditional city. A solitary gondola rested in the placid waters near the hotel's entrance, which was hidden under an awning. The hotel's moniker was fully justified by an island of green flourishing inside the block: tall trees, trimmed hedges, flowerbeds, and a lush lawn. A shaded park behind the hotel on the opposite side overlooked the Grand Canal.

A modest staircase in burgundy tones led up to the hotel from the water, and a yellow lantern hung on the wall at the entrance. I saw no one around; the area was completely deserted. It was as if someone had sounded an alarm in advance and had everyone prudently lured away. There was not a soul in sight.

The hotel's lobby, too, stood empty, as if everyone was hiding somewhere. Only the cozy little restaurant trimmed with rough-hewn stone served as proof that the planet still harbored life. A few guests were quietly taking their luncheon and paid no attention to me. Quiet reigned over the place. I admired the intertwined roots here, dry and knotty, that preternaturally soared upward from the ground to where evergreen ivy densely covered the room. The far wall was of glass, and the shadowy vegetation of the park grew right up against it, looking from inside the restaurant like a veritable jungle. I paused at the threshold to study the people inside, and my surroundings. I cannot say that I experienced fear, but the anxiety that had smoldered within me since morning suddenly awoke and brushed against my heart. The moment of truth had come: anything at all might happen if one of us made a mistake, took a wrong step.

The man whom I was to meet was already seated at a table. I recognized him from the photographs that I had carefully studied at Division X. We exchanged the usual greetings, and I took a chair opposite him. He did not look much like a fellow Soviet at all, which was no wonder, as he had long resided abroad. Frankly, I knew nothing about him, nothing about where he was from, how he had arrived, where he worked and what his cover was. I had not been informed about these matters. For reasons of security, of course, I did not think to ask him about any of this. I was not even aware of what country he was based in, but naturally the less I knew, the better.

I supposed that this agent was of immense value to Soviet intelligence. He had undergone long and strict training and had then been sent out through a series of intermediary countries. They had spent years carefully embedding him, so as not to raise even the slightest suspicion. Ultimately they had succeeded, and he had ended up where they wanted him. He had made a career for himself, risen up through the ranks, and now he was looking forward to another promotion, a position that Soviet intelligence was keenly interested in as it would give him access to valuable information. There was only one problem, though: the position required him to take a polygraph, and if he did not, he would not be considered for the job. Such were the rules in the clandestine service where the agent was presently serving: from a certain level up, personnel were subject to strict checks that they could not refuse. Moreover, failing the lie detector test could lead to great suspicion, and then all those years of the agent's meticulous work would have been for nothing. Not to mention the serious risks he faced: being discovered, arrest, prison…

Years ago, when the agent was still in training, he had learned through careful preparation how to deceive a lie detector. That had been long ago, however, and since then new polygraph models had appeared, and methods had changed. Thus the agent urgently needed a consultation, and he had flown to Venice specially to meet me.

The round table with its cream tablecloth had been set for four people with an array of silverware and glasses. The dishes were a delight to behold: fine china with the Park Hotel restaurant's logo on them. There were plenty of empty tables in the restaurant, and we hoped that no one would think to sit at ours; the other two bentwood chairs with yellow wicker seating were unoccupied.

"Will you have something?" the agent asked me in English. He recommended something Venetian, and said that it would be his treat.

Naturally, I agreed without a moment's hesitation. When would I ever be so lucky again? Especially considering that I would not make it back in time to the Cappello Hotel on Lido, where I was entitled to the set lunch. We Soviets sent from the provinces on official business had little opportunity to visit good restaurants, let alone pay the bills in them. Our accountants objected to the prices in the capitalist world, and foreign currency had to be spent in great moderation and strictly accounted for.

The prices on the menu did not seem to bother the agent at all. Robert – that was the name he introduced himself by – ordered the *verdure fritte* and *polpette di granchio*. "Venetian cuisine is world-famous. You must try it now you've come all this way," he said like a real connoisseur, though he did not need to make any effort to convince me; he was preaching to the converted.

For the first course, instead of the usual soup we were served *risi e bisi*, that is, risotto with green peas, roasted brisket, onions and parsley, and grated parmesan sprinkled in abundance. The second course was *baccalà alla vicentina* – slow-cooked cod with tomatoes, capers, and onions.

We chatted about various things, mainly the film festival. We discussed recent films, actors and directors, and an eavesdropper would have taken us for cinephiles for whom the Venice festival was heaven on earth. We did not discuss the business that had brought us both to Venice, as the table might have had ears, or someone watching us could have easily worked out the subject and content of our conversation by reading our lips. We did not order wine either, content instead to drink only mineral water, though this came as a great surprise to our waiter: Venetian cuisine suggests certain wines from the Veneto region. Our waiter had no idea, however, what clarity of thought our job required, what effort and attentiveness. As much as we would have liked the wine, we could not take the risk.

From time to time we stepped out into the garden and took a leisurely stroll among the greenery. Once we had made certain that no one was eavesdropping, we discussed the matter for which we had met. As I learned more about the patient, I thought about how he could best beat the lie detector.

Soviet intelligence had, in creating his cover story, coached the agent in how to play his part. Professional actors and directors had been brought in to teach him how to play his role with maximum authenticity. It is well known that a good actor can completely merge with the person he is portraying. While the actor is onstage, he forgets his own self, and there is no longer a border between him and the character. Indeed, a skilled actor sincerely believes that he is the man whom he is portraying, and his behavior conforms to the role – according, that is, to Stanislavski's system.

Experts know that actors and people with strong dramatic talents, those who know how to bring a role to life and are used to producing laughter or tears on command, can be confident of beating the polygraph. If the subject of the lie detector test has the ability to inhabit his characters, then his physiological indicators – pulse, breathing, perspiration, even his galvanic skin response – will come to match the character he is portraying.

In short, the polygraph machine cannot distinguish between a convincing illusion and reality. For it, there is no distinction between an invented role and an individual's real personality. For this reason, it would be pointless to submit a psychopath with a warped perception of reality, or a pathological liar who believes his own fables, to a lie detector test. As far as the machine can tell, their fantasies and inventions are real; it will not bat an eye at them. For patients suffering from manic psychosis or schizophrenia, a lie detector test is a completely pointless idea, a waste of time and effort.

For dessert the waiter brought us *bussola*, a cake soaked in Marsala wine. We decided that the dessert would not hurt; the quantity of wine in it was meager, while some good coffee would sharpen our wits. Indeed, I must confess that the coffee and *bussola* cake raised our spirits, got our blood flowing, and imbued us with a feeling of optimism. Why argue with what the doctor prescribed? We strolled once more in the park, deep in conversation, occasionally returning to the table in order demonstratively and energetically to discuss films, and then again stepped outside to discuss our urgent matter in low voices.

"If you like, I can take the test for you," I suggested to the agent.

Robert laughed at the joke. "I wouldn't mind, but I fear the company would be opposed to it." He told me that back in the day he had been carefully trained so that his physiological indicators would remain stable under any circumstances, even in situations of great stress. This training had proved successful, for his metabolism had maintained its equilibrium under detailed polygraph tests, and his physiological reactions had remained practically unchanged. The agent had achieved good results under examination and had successfully fooled the machine. Robert had also been training himself the whole time, acquiring an excellent grasp of meditation and self-hypnosis, and moreover he had steadily distanced himself from the details and experiences of his former life.

Years had gone by, however, and he was now worried about being tested. It was my task to coax him free of his doubts, strengthen his self-confidence, and lift his spirits. The polygraph does not like winners; in the face of quick, confident answers the device starts to go haywire and its indicators become random.

As usual, the first thing I had to do was dispel any ideas he might have about the polygraph being infallible. This was a myth, invented by corporations and operators so that they could make their living. In fact, the polygraph was very unreliable in practice. The process relies on the fear it inspires in the man in the street: you can't hide anything from us, so don't even try.

Laboratory and field experiments at Division X have shown that it only makes sense to employ a polygraph in a maximum of fifty percent of cases, and even then there is no guarantee of reliability. Once one adds into the mix the kind of training Robert had undergone, the polygraph's accuracy plunges drastically. I explained my thinking to the agent and he cheered up noticeably; a weight seemed to have been lifted from him. To convince him, I mentioned a study carried out at Northwestern University in the United States which showed that if the subject is sure of his superiority, and he answers quickly, readily, and confidently, then the device loses its calibration and can only record approximate values without being able to distinguish between truth and lies.

"Those American scholars believe the polygraph is *almost* always wrong," I told the agent. "But we must take that 'almost' seriously. We can't be too careful."

"I'm ready, doctor. Just tell me how to do it. Help me, and I'll amply repay you."

Now I needed to examine the patient, learn about his medical history, and think about how to proceed. I asked if he suffered from any chronic illnesses. He complained of vegetative-vascular dystonia, which sometimes manifested itself in sudden leaps in his blood pressure, or sweating, or occasional sensitivity to ultraviolet, i.e. sun rash.

"That's great," I exclaimed. "An excellent diagnosis."

My reply astonished Robert. "What do you mean?" he asked.

I explained that his ailment was very convenient, for he would be able to take medication for it. Medication could lead the lie detector astray. Hypertension drugs, say, which would lower his blood pressure, or beta blockers that would interfere with the production of adrenaline.

   

We worked carefully. As we walked, I entered step by step into the details of the man's life. A fresh breeze from the lagoon occasionally swept over the tops of the trees, producing a whistling and rustling across the park, but among the thick bushes the wind lost some of its strength and brought a gentle coolness. Robert called the waiter over, paid our bill and left a tip, and then we went up to his hotel room to continue our consultation. His first action was to turn on a small device disguised as a camera. It showed that there were no hidden cameras or microphones in the room; no one was recording us. Once we were certain of our safety, we continued working. I suggested that he disrobe so that I could examine him.

"What if they ask if I've taken any medication?" the agent asked as he removed his clothes.

"You answer honestly 'Yes, without batting an eye.' That happens to be the truth, and that's what the polygraph will record. Your diagnosis gives you ample reason for needing medication. It'll be obvious you're taking drugs for your ailment."

I examined him closely, tested his reflexes and the twelve pairs of cranial nerves, his sensory system and skin responses. I studied his endocrine system and listened to his heart and lungs.

"Am I going to live?" Robert asked me, with a grin.

"Indeed you are," I reassured him.

"My palms are sweaty," he complained, and raised his hands to show me.

The vegetative nervous system regulates the body day and night independently of a person's consciousness. Robert's was acting up. The patient could skillfully control the functioning of the cerebral cortex and central nervous system, as he had been trained, but prolonged suppression of his instincts and desires, as well as his inability to relax, was something that acted at a subconscious level. Sublimation had led to a dysfunction of the vagus, that is, the parasympathetic nervous system, which is not subject to conscious control.

Frankly, I am opposed to artificial methods of fighting the polygraph. Supposed experts usually recommend that a person bite his tongue during the session, or press his tongue against his palate, tense his leg muscles, press his toes to the floor, or direct his eyes down toward his nose, which will supposedly help distract him from the polygraph by making him focus instead on his inner sensations. Some clever people have even suggested putting thumbtacks in one's shoes, so that the pain will confuse the lie detector. Sweating, they claim, should be prevented by using antiperspirants. All such methods are easily detected, though: mechanical tricks with the help of additional sensors, and chemicals by means of scent or color. In any case, a competent and attentive operator will suspect that the subject is trying to deceive him.

No, I prefer natural techniques, ones which can always be explained on completely ordinary grounds. At Division X we employed the "anchor method": we would train a person to reduce his latent time, or in other words, speed up his reactions. In addition, the person was taught how to switch immediately to the required psychophysiological state.

Other techniques besides these exist. Some people have used lack of sleep and physical fatigue to dull their sensory responses. If a person sleeps little but does a lot of running, swimming, chopping wood and working out, and on the eve of the polygraph test drinks a decent amount of alcohol, then he will exhibit sluggish reactions, caused by fatigue and a hangover. That will smooth the readings out, and the polygraph will prove difficult to interpret. It would not hurt to drink a liter of water just before the test, so that a burning need to run to the bathroom overshadowed all other thoughts. That would be an even better distraction than a sharp tack in one's shoes.

We discussed each method from various angles, and without the agent even noticing it, I gradually managed to instill confidence into him. His doubts and anxiety abated. I also invited him to visit me at the Cappello Hotel on Lido, so that we could conduct another session in a relaxed atmosphere and build on what we had achieved.

We thus agreed to meet on Lido. I was just about to leave when Robert said worriedly, "Doctor, I can control my breathing, but what should I do about my palms? Antiperspirant wouldn't be a good idea."

Any polygraph will generally record the subject's breathing; sensors are placed for that purpose on his chest and belly. Other sensors on his fingers determine his degree of perspiration and the electrical conductivity of the skin on his hands.

"It's not something I would usually advise," I said, "but there is a proven technique that we can use. About two hours before the test, rub some ordinary salicylic-zinc ointment onto your skin. You can buy it at any pharmacy. For a time, your galvanic skin response will remain stable and the sensors will not pick up any changes."

"What if they make me wash my hands?"

"Good point. They nearly always make the subject do that. OK. Before you apply the ointment, soak your hands in hot water. Then take a few minutes to rub the ointment in properly, so that it penetrates deep into the epidermis. Before the polygraph session, rub alcohol on your hands. That will dry the skin and clog the pores. You can then go ahead and wash your hands without any problem."

Robert was clearly impressed. "Wow, doctor, things are a lot easier with you around! Too bad I can't take you with me."

"Unfortunately that's not allowed," I said modestly, like a functionary from the lowest ranks.

"You must know how to beat any lie detector," he said, with obvious admiration and approval.

"That's my job," I replied in a casual, almost bored tone. I did not want either of us to seem arrogant, puffed up, turn up our nose, or to look down on the rest of the world.

To be honest, my skepticism with regard to the polygraph was well-founded. In the spy services of many countries, agents who have successfully passed a polygraph examination have often turned out to be up to something, or been recruited by the other side, or vanished without a trace shortly afterward, leaving the intelligence service high and dry. Yet their polygraphs had revealed no reasons for suspicion, had set off no alarm bells. On the other hand, I know plenty of cases when good agents have spent years or even decades working successfully under cover, and then suddenly they are subjected to a polygraph and they fail it, even though they have never entertained a single thought about defecting to the enemy, committing treason, or betraying anyone. Nevertheless, the machine won, and these people were no longer trusted. As a rule, I am not fond of household appliances. All those kettles, hair curlers, coffee makers, curling irons, and polygraphs, damn them all!

I headed back a different way so that I could discover more of Venice. After the Tolentini bridge I turned left toward the Calle dei Amai, which brought me to the bridge over the Muneghete canal. To my surprise, the old lanes turned out to be deserted, and there was not a soul in sight. The canals, too, were dead: along the narrow embankments various vessels – rowboats, motor boats, longboats for cargo – floated immobile and crewless in the water.

I felt a sudden desire to see another human being. The city seemed to have been emptied of people; locals and visitors alike had all gone off somewhere, vanished, or fallen into the water, as if Venice had been struck by a plague (as it had been several times in its history).

Imagine how eerie it was on Tolentini. The bustling crowd at the Riva degli Schiavoni was still fresh in my mind, as were the crowds and colorful scenes in St. Mark's Square and the plaza with the statue of Victor Emmanuel II. I had not forgotten the lively boat traffic on the Grand Canal. Yet now a strange, unreal silence reigned. My gaze wandered across the abandoned streets in search of other people. Frankly, I was taken aback. A boundless stillness hung over the side streets paved with time-worn slabs, over the canals lined with stone, over the narrow embankments, over the old buildings whose lower floors had been assailed by sea salt and algae over the centuries.

In this stillness I walked alone down the Calle dei Amai, in the neighborhood known as Santa Croce. Further down I could see the wide bridge that spanned the Muneghete canal, but it was just as deserted, as if we were on a dead star or lifeless planet. One might have assumed that people had utterly abandoned this place and life had gradually become extinct, all trace of it lost. Perhaps I was the sole survivor, the only poor fellow still alive in all of Venice. The only thing left to do was to look this way and that in hope of spotting another human being, yet there was no one around. No one appeared, and I caught no glimpse of anyone.

Suddenly in that dead stillness I heard footsteps on the other side of the bridge: someone was walking along casually in high heels. There from across the Muneghete canal, from the Sechere waterfront side and its streets Campazzo and Chiovere, someone was slowly coming toward me. Clearly someone else had, fortunately, survived in this plague-stricken district. Of course, it was a she, a mysterious and unknown lady, the very embodiment of femininity, the dream of a poet – how could it be otherwise?

Slowly, almost floating along, she came up the bridge toward me, closer and closer. It was deserted all around, deserted and silent, and we were the only people left on the earth; the silence, like that of deep space, was broken only by the loud clopping of her high heels.

Naturally our gazes met and neither of us broke off eye contact until we had passed each other. Her face seemed familiar. I realized at once that I had long known this lady, had met her somewhere, but where, when? I racked my brains trying to remember.

If I may speak frankly, she was good-looking. Though she was no longer in her youth, her eyes had retained a spark, her figure was still svelte, and her legs were long and slender. As we drew nearer at the midpoint of the bridge, she smiled at me and I felt elated, though I still could not recall who she was. In spite of my efforts, my memory was unable to place her. We drew nearer, passed each other, and then went on our separate ways, like two ships passing in the night. A few steps further on I turned around, and she did too, with a sly smile. Thus we walked, turning back to look at each other and exchange smiles, until we each reached our respective end of the bridge. It was then that I suddenly realized who she was: there on the bridge, fate had brought me face to face with the actress Monica Vitti. The peak of her stardom had long since passed, but twenty years earlier she had been known around the world for playing beautiful, smart, and disillusioned upper-class women. Now she was evidently fleeing from the bustle of the festival and enjoying some solitude. For my part, I thought about the incredible opportunities Venice brings a man.

By now the sun was setting over the city. From the Rialto waterfront a vaporetto set off down the Grand Canal toward the lagoon. The golden light of the sun still hung behind Venice's cathedrals and palaces, its light reflected in the windows and seeming to start countless fires in the green waters of the Venetian canals. The setting sun made a bright road down the wide waters of the lagoon. My head was spinning; the Venetian sunset could drive a man crazy.

I was thinking of how, if it had not been for a matter of vital importance to Soviet intelligence, I might never have come here at all. Breathtaking Venice would have remained only a dream. Thus in a way the polygraph turned out to be something useful for me; the so-called lie detector had made a positive contribution to my life and brought me some happiness.

The journey back to Lido proved to be a short one. Upon arrival at the jetty, I walked down the teeming Gran Viale Santa Maria Elisabetta, where a huge crowd strolled this way and that, and eventually I reached the Marconi waterfront. The Adriatic Sea greeted me with an evening breeze. Outside the Hotel des Bains, autograph seekers waited patiently for their next victim. The sea breeze lazily shook the flags raised there for each of the nations present at the film festival. On the open terrace of the La Pagoda restaurant, which overlooked the deserted beach of the Hotel des Bains, music was playing and the scene was loud and merry. The many guests circulated with glasses in hand. It was an obvious assumption that a cast and crew of filmmakers from some unknown country had organized a reception for their premiere. Only one solitary couple, bathrobes wrapped around them, sat at the water's edge in a romantic, downright cinematographic scene, but this only highlighted how deserted the beach was otherwise on this evening. Yet something else was happening now.

At the corner of the waterfront, I found people standing around a small convertible that looked like a racing car. It was not the car which drew their attention, however, not its sleek lines and rapacious look. The crowd was standing in silence and listening to the radio. The Italian announcer was reading the news at high speed and the crowd was listening carefully. I could see how their faces were troubled, and some even had tears in their eyes. Some shook their heads gloomily, others were upset and expressed their indignation aloud, grumbling bitterly and with clear hostility.

"Damn commies!" someone said in English. "They ought to drop the bomb on all of them!"

To be honest, I have never believed in the idea of Communism myself. I have always thought that Russia's rulers were a gang of con men and criminals. Nevertheless, it was only Party members – members of the *only* party, of course, but the country's guiding force – who could serve at Division X. There, whether one liked it or not, everyone was required to hold a Party membership card, as if that made any difference or meant anything. For my part, I resolved that I was not joining the Communist Party; let them drive me away, let them kick me out. Year by year they tried to drag me forcibly into the Party by the scruff of my neck. They firmly insisted, or they tried to coax me, win me over. They promised impressive growth in my career and promotion up the ranks, but I resisted, refused, waved them away and kept my distance as best I could.

In the end, I came up with the tactic of playing the fool, suggesting that I was a dullard who was completely unable to understand their goals and objectives. When I met with the authorities, I sincerely claimed that I was not worthy, that I was not yet ready to join their august party, but as soon as I was ready, I would rush to knock at their door. "Straightaway," I said repeatedly, seeking to reassure the Communist Party official at Division X and my other would-be benefactors who promised me a soaring career, not to mention various honors and titles.

They would doubtless have loved to get rid of this stubborn doctor with his independent spirit. I was under no illusions. The only defense I could lodge was through my work. Whether they liked it or not, I was irreplaceable in my field. Especially when it came to predicting events, foretelling what would happen. Everyone was aware that if I left, that would be the end of that. Without me there would have been wailing and gnashing of teeth. And what was interesting was that all the defectors and traitors from the ranks of these carefully vetted public servants were Party members. Believe it or not, there was no one among them who had *not* aligned with the Party.

 

Now if the people on the street listening to the news found out who I was, where I came from, and what business had brought me here, they would get their bloody revenge. I realized that they would crucify me, lynch me right there, grind me into dust and then let the wind blow the dust away. I did nothing to disclose my identity. I spoke to no one, and remained totally silent. I pretended to be a deaf mute, and not particularly bright.

The Italian newsreader fell silent for a moment. His voice gave way to the intercepted radio transmission that I had already heard that day outside the carabinieri station. Through the noise and static, the anxious voice of a pilot could be heard:

"Deputat, this is Five Zero Three. Its navigation lights are on, its strobe lights are flashing!"

This time I recognized the voice. My old patient Shilin seemed to be crying out in despair, trying to get through to someone. He kept shouting and shouting to get someone's attention. It was obvious that something grave had happened. I was not aware of the details, but a feeling of catastrophe had followed me all day.

The Italian announcer came back on. The crowd gathered there on the street around the fancy convertible listened to the radio, restless and tense. I felt the gaze of another on me, as if someone was staring at me, and as I had done earlier that day, I wondered if I were being followed.

I called to mind the rules for maintaining the secrecy of our operation, and looked in at the Hotel des Bains, where Gianni Buttafata, a columnist for the Milan weekly *L'Espresso*, was staying, along with a host of film stars. I had met Gianni six months earlier, in Moscow during the winter, at a bachelor's party at the home of the poet Rein, my long-time friend. We had chatted about this and that, and Gianni told me that if I were ever in Italy I should visit him. Now the acquaintance which we had struck up suddenly seemed rather convenient, and I decided to drop in to see him. If anyone were following me, let them go crazy pursuing the false trail that I was laying for them. I even asked in a deliberately loud and exaggerated voice at the reception for the room of *signore* Buttafata, the journalist from Milan.

The wide corridors of the hotel were a glorious sight: spacious, with huge windows, white walls and high ceilings, paintings and antiques, the old-time luxury of the early twentieth century. To my pleasant surprise, I found jolly old Gianni, stout and looking quite at home, in his room. He was seated in his braces at the table and writing an article for his magazine. Films were being screened in five different venues and he, as a film critic, was expected to visit each of them – or even to be in all five at the same time – just as war correspondents were supposed to visit the trenches on the front line.

Gianni did not seem in the least bit surprised to see me. He readily put down his pen and immediately invited me to have a drink with him in the bar. There he ordered a strong cocktail made with bourbon, and when he had been served, he leaned over and said quietly:

"Have you heard? Your people in Sakhalin shot down a Korean Boeing." He sipped at his cocktail and looked at me with curiosity, awaiting an answer. But before I could say anything, he rushed to add, with reproach, "A passenger jet!"

"I know," I answered coldly. I needed to make a short call to New York, but I did not leave my seat.

What could I tell Gianni? That I had known this would happen, that I had foreseen it? That I had seen the passengers before take-off? That the flight had been doomed? That I had tried to get it canceled? That I had wanted to save all of them? Nothing I said would mean anything now.

=== 34 ===

The sun had long since set, but it was still light outside, though not quite as bright as further north in Russia at this time. In these lands of the south, evening came earlier and faster, the light gradually faded, and the air grew thick like smoke rising from the scorched earth and turning into the mists of twilight.

Soon it was completely dark. A new moon hung over the edge of the air base. There was a murmur of vehicle engines in the darkness on the airfield. The ground was dimly lit by the trucks' headlights, shielded in accordance with the blackout rules. Jeeps and heavy Studebakers moved around the base. The personnel worked silently and deftly. Even in the dark, one could sense a distinct anxiety and tenseness. In accordance with their earlier agreement, the American and the interpreter met on the airfield away from the guard posts and sentries.

"No one saw you?" Steven Creighton asked, concern audible in his voice.

"No one, I think," Olga replied and looked around uncertainly. For a time they both stared into the darkness and listened carefully to hear if anyone else was around. There was no one there. This June night was a clear and quiet one, the first stars now twinkling in the sky. Far away on the airfield, vehicle engines hummed, the weak beams of their shielded headlights appearing and vanishing, reflecting for an instant in Olga's eyes.

Olga looked tensely around her. She seemed to glimpse vague figures in the darkness, and felt as if she were being stared at from all sides. Goodness, how scared she was! Though she did not know all the details, she had an idea of what kind of country she lived in. Fortunately, the bloody purges and savage executions of the 1930s had passed her family by, but still, only a blind person could fail to notice the fear and arbitrariness that reigned over the Soviet Union. Danger lurked everywhere, and even daring types still felt fear – how could it be otherwise if the country was ruled by a paranoid madman?

Of course the interpreter was scared; a deathly fear had entered into every cell of her body. She was tempted to give up on their plan, abandon everyone, and run back to her quarters before it was too late. And who could blame the young lady for her weakness? She was afraid that she would not hold out, that at a decisive moment she would ruin everything. Her stifling fear clouded her mind and clamped her heart in a deathly grip.

Olga Shilina was doubtless aware of just who she was up against. The American could make only a vague guess at the threat she was facing, but the interpreter knew what an inexorable and inhuman power stood against them. It was a cruel machine accustomed to crushing human beings to powder; it could not be sated, and it knew no mercy. There was no use trying to move it to pity, it could not be reasoned with.

Olga knew well whom she, a nineteen-year-old girl from Moscow, had dared try to outwit. Only a single thought flickering at the margins of her consciousness kept her there, kept her from running away without a backward glance: yes, she might be facing fear and danger, but they were momentary and fleeting, and then she would have her whole life ahead of her!

It was not too late; she could yet save herself, give up on their plan. If they arrested her now, then at least she was still not facing the wartime punishment of being shot for desertion. She would instead be subject to more ordinary disciplinary measures. However, Olga forced herself with every last bit of strength she had to see their plan through to the end. She knew that otherwise she would never forgive herself for her momentary weakness, she would regret it forever. Once the Americans had flown, then that would be that, there would be no next time.

The last fuel and supply trucks pulled away from the Flying Fortresses and drove off.

"It's time," Creighton said quietly and led her across the airfield, skirting the runway.

His plan was simple: to approach the parked Flying Fortress from the side opposite base command, at the tip of the runway. At the far end of the airfield, among the sparse trees, there stretched a barbed-wire fence dotted with guard posts.

The American and the interpreter moved quickly through the grass, which was wet from the evening's condensation. Any minute now, vehicles would arrive from the base with the Flying Fortresses' crews, and the two conspirators had to reach the plane before they did. Creighton led Olga among the parked bombers, trying to read the planes' numbers in the darkness. They walked a while until he found his plane, which fortunately had survived the Germans' night assault. His Flying Fortress was no different from all the others: rectangular windows, four engines in pairs on each wing, the cockpit rising above the body of the plane like a ship's cabin over its deck, and a turret for the crew's gunner with a machine gun directed toward the rear.

Creighton went up the metal stairs and opened a hatch at the end. Olga waited below and looked around apprehensively. It was uncomfortably warm; the steel plates of the runway had been in the sun all day and now they radiated heat. A hot wind blew against Olga's face, as if the air base bordered on a sun-blasted desert. She did not feel it, though. She was in such an anxious state that the summer evening seemed to have turned icy cold.

"Olga!" Creighton called out to her, trying to keep his voice low. He stuck his head out of the hatch and motioned to her. "Come on!"

Olga gripped the handrails and timidly made her way up the stairs. Creighton bent to help her through the hatch, and then with the beam of his flashlight he guided her down the long, wide body of the plane. They passed an ample cargo hold loaded with bombs, then a broad hatch on hinges through which the bombs were dropped, and finally they reached the tail of the plane where there were some boxes covered with a tarpaulin.

Creighton bade Olga sit on a box. "Wait here. Once we take off, I'll come for you," he promised. Then he kissed her, and left.

Olga listened to his departing footsteps. It grew quiet. Silence set in around her. She had no idea how long she would have to wait, but now it stretched ahead like an eternity. When Creighton had been with her, she could manage, even though she was not entirely confident about their plan. Once he had left, however, she felt utterly alone, like a weak and defenseless little girl who had been abandoned deep in the forest.

It was impossible to breathe inside the plane. The bomber had been parked in the sun all day long, and sitting in the tail section was like being packed in a tin can. It was unbearably stuffy, and the stale air was like hot glue around her. Again, however, Olga did not notice it; she felt a wintry chill run over her, and her teeth were chattering.

It was still not too late to turn back. If she wanted to, she could get out of the plane and head back to her quarters. Yet some inexorable force kept her rooted to the spot. She sat immobile on the box, her thoughts wandering distractedly. Among all her worries and apprehensions, one thought stood out above all others: what awaited her, what was in store for her?

Everything that had ever happened to her up to this point had seemed so ordinary and familiar. It had all been a known quantity – until she met the American. This chance encounter had changed her entire life, had transformed it utterly. Now everything was markedly different from anything Olga had known in her nineteen years. She felt that she had stepped across some sort of boundary, and a new and breathtaking reality had been revealed to her, of which she had had no inkling before, of which she had not even dared to dream.

It still had not sunk in. She was sitting on a box in the hold of an American Flying Fortress strategic bomber. Why? To what end? The fact that there was no one to answer her did not make the questions go away; in fact, they came at her with renewed force, beating on her as on a bell. How could she, a reasonable and prudent Moscow girl from a family of the intelligentsia, and not a person inclined to fanciful adventures, have ended up here? What was she hoping for?

Again and again she asked herself these questions, but she had no answers to them, and found no explanations. An inexplicable and mysterious power, one not subject to reason, had remade her life, diverted her from the expected path, and brought her here. To all her questions there was only one answer: love!

Yet for the Soviet regime, and most of her compatriots, this was no justification for what she was doing. It was not even an explanation. People would say that she was breaking a vow. The laws of wartime also applied. Wartime deserters were usually sentenced to the ultimate penalty: death. Olga Shilina's guilt was plain, though the junior lieutenant herself was hardly aware of the law, so young was she. Death, though … her fellow Soviets might judge her for what she was doing, but how could they sentence her to death for love? The hard truth was, though, that only a very few people, a tiny minority of the country, would stay away from the rush to accuse her, and only a mere handful would actively approve of her actions.

Ah, but what could anyone do in the face of destiny, so whimsical and capricious? Lieutenant Steven Creighton, an American from San Francisco, California, had fallen in love with a Russian girl at the front. Can we forget about the war, please?

People were dying en masse, countries were being overrun, villages and cities were going up in flames, blood was flowing in rivers and the sky was crashing down to the earth – could these two really not have found another time for themselves? They did not care about the war, though; they wanted to be together, and that was all. Since the creation of the world there has only been one eternal and indisputable truth: love conquers all.

The translator waited meekly for her copilot in a darkness so impenetrable, it was as if her eyes had been plucked out. She was surrounded by a heavy silence, like a stone wall with nary a crack in it. Olga lost track of time; it seemed to her that she had spent half her life sitting here in the dark. She was ready to spend the other half waiting as well, as long as the American would finally come.

After a while she heard distant sounds: knocking, footsteps, unintelligible voices. A hum outside swelled and grew stronger, and Olga realized that the Flying Fortress crews were starting their engines. Soon the hum grew into a full-fledged roar moving somewhat strangely around her, growing closer and then receding. Judging by the sound, the planes were slowly making their way to the start of the runway for take-off.

A short while later, Olga suddenly felt a shudder, as if the plane was raring to go but a strong hand was holding it in check. The plane nevertheless started moving, and carefully, as if it was in water and afraid of splashing, followed after the other planes to the start of the runway.

That's it now, Olga thought. She was weary. Their plan seemed to have succeeded, but Olga felt no elation. The long waiting and fear had drained all her strength. The engines roared, the plane shook, but Olga could not believe in the reality of what was happening. She felt like she was only passively observing events that bore no relation to her – she just happened to be there to watch. The bomber reached the end of the runway, then turned and stopped. Now the only thing left was for it to receive permission to take off, and it would soar up from the earth.

At this moment, however, Olga and Creighton's plan hit an unexpected snag. Base command was dragging its feet for some strange reason, and would not grant permission for take-off. Already more than twenty planes had taken off, and they had all received the OK instantly. This one bomber's crew was being met with silence, and was facing an unexpected delay.

The crew's commander, pilot Andrew Eddington, eventually became fed up of waiting and decided to take off regardless. "Let's go," he said. The commander was aware of the passenger they had on board, and he knew well what the crew could look forward to if the interpreter was discovered.

"Thanks, Commander," said Creighton. He had been frozen stiff with anxiety as they awaited permission to take off.

They increased power to the engines and the roar grew stronger. None of the crew were aware that right then, vehicles sent from base command were driving across the airfield at high speed. One was a small, nimble jeep carrying officers from SMERSH along with Communist Party officials, while the other was a Studebaker truck, soldiers with weapons in hand sitting on the benches on either side of the back.

The gunner was the first to notice the vehicles driving headlong down the airfield. He was seated at the machine gun in the round, transparent blister over the body of the bomber, and had the best view. "Commander, it looks like we've got company," the gunner reported, alerting the captain over the intercom. "And they're in a hurry."

"Dammit," the pilot swore and immediately released the brakes.

For an instant the bomber stood there in indecision, as if it could not believe that its path was blocked, or perhaps thinking about whether it ought to try taking off regardless. Then the plane hesitantly set off. But it was too late. The jeep tore over the grass, reached the runway, and sped headlong for the plane. The bomber had not yet gained much speed, and the jeep quickly caught up with it, pulled ahead of it, and then, with a sharp turn, stopped on the steel-plated surface to bar the plane's way.

The crew of the Flying Fortress had not expected such a turn of events. The pilot braked and the aircraft slowed, though it continued to move forward by inertia. The huge, heavy bomber bore down on the jeep; the jeep was like a tiny dog trying to stop an elephant. It was obvious that the Flying Fortress would crush the vehicle like a bug.

The men inside the jeep did not wait for that to happen. The officers burst out of the open car and dashed away to a safe distance. Then the Studebaker caught up with the jeep, and also maneuvered to block the runway. The detachment of soldiers seated in the rear of the truck hopped off and ran to the sides.

The bomber's commander swore again, but now there was nothing he could do. He activated the emergency brake. The wheels on the bomber's landing gear, held firm by the brakes, were no longer moving, but they continued to skid down the runway. The heavy bomber lumbered slowly forward, then the force of inertia turned it so that its sides faced the runway. The plane eventually came to a stop only a few steps away from the truck.

At that moment, an open jeep with American officers drove up to the Flying Fortress. One of the officers stood up in the jeep and motioned to the crew to open the bomber's door.

   

"Nothing we can do now," the commander said with sincere regret. "As God is my witness, I wanted to help."

"I'm not giving her up!" said Creighton. His tone was resolute, but at the same time he knew the game was up. His hands moved to his hip and he unfastened his holster.

"Don't be a fool," Eddington told him, and then ordered him sternly, "Give me your weapon!"

Slowly and numbly, as if in sleep, Creighton drew the pistol from his holster, but he was in no hurry to part with it.

"Steve, are you crazy?" The commander reached out his hand. "I've got a whole crew here. You want to get us all killed? Do you know what they could do to you? To her?" He took the pistol from Creighton and put it in his pocket.

Meanwhile, the soldiers had completely surrounded the bomber and were standing there with their weapons at the ready. The bomber's propellers spun weakly, no longer making any sound. Their blades, turning ever slower, swept hot air across the runway. The Soviet and American officers approached the plane and shone their flashlights on the plane's hatch.

"Do you still insist on searching the plane?" asked one of the American officers.

"Yes," his Soviet counterpart answered. "We have proof." He had ordered beforehand that the plane be searched regardless.

"Fine," the American said. "But if there's no one there, this is going to be massive."

"I don't care. I have my orders. Make them open the door."

No one opened the hatch, however. The officers waited there on the runway, craning their necks to stare up at the plane. Meanwhile, emotions were running high in the cockpit.

"I can't do it. They'll kill her!" Creighton's voice trembled, and his face was distorted in a painful grimace.

"Sit down!" the pilot ordered him harshly, and pushed Creighton back into his seat. "You'll do her no good. You'll just make it worse for her." The commander paused for a moment to assess the situation, and then he called loudly, "Crew, I need you all here!"

The crew immediately filed toward the cockpit; even the gunner hopped down from his blister. They crammed together in the small space. Eddington ordered that no one was to leave the cockpit. He nodded toward Creighton, still sitting in the copilot's seat and with his back turned to the other men. "Keep an eye on him," said Eddington.

Eddington opened the plane's hatch and stood there, bent in the dark opening. Lit by the officers' flashlights and looking like a man on a stage set, he waited for an explanation. It all looked very theatrical.

Meanwhile Olga Shilina, sitting in the dark at the plane's tail, guessed that something was up. The only thing that had remained was for the plane to speed down the runway, take off, and enter on its course. But now the bomber was now standing immobile on the runway. The shuddering had stopped, the engines had fallen silent, and that could only mean one thing: they had been prevented from taking off. An American plane had never before been stopped from taking off. Olga assumed that she was the reason.

No, she did not merely assume, she *knew* she was the reason. Their plan had failed. At the last minute, someone had caught on to what she was doing and called off the flight. A last flicker of hope remained in her heart, barely alive, that it was just a technical problem. Such a thing was not unknown. The crew would resolve it, and then they would take off. She had little faith in miracles, though: if the crew did take off now, it would be without her. She was paralyzed with fear, vividly imagining how any minute now she would be caught, insulted, sworn at, and thrown in jail. In anticipation of her imminent arrest, she shrank with horror in the dark, neither dead nor alive.

Olga did not realize that she would probably be accused of desertion and face execution. Nor was she thinking about how the vast majority of her compatriots would readily approve of such a sentence.

Goodness, how scared she was! Olga did not know what awaited her now, but she felt the danger like an icy breath on her face. The bitter cold chilled her skin and gave rise to renewed horror. Now, of course, it was already too late to go back. Now she would get all of whatever was coming to her.

The Soviet officers filed one by one up the stairs and, flashlights in hand, fell to searching the plane. They dispersed through the vast body of the aircraft. Their flashlight beams cut through the darkness, illuminating the plane's nooks and crannies and crawling along the walls in bright spots.

The officers made their way through the plane, sweeping their flashlights from side to side. They looked into the cockpit where the crew huddled as if afraid to move a muscle. There the gunner, navigator, and mechanic were using their six hands to keep Creighton in his copilot's seat. The Soviet officers then stepped warily into the bomb hold. The hundreds of bombs there, packed into containers and awaiting their time, sparked in the Soviets an irresistible desire to move on. With so many bombs around, even daring types can feel a little uneasy and want to get away. The officers began to move cautiously, constantly looking around in case – God forbid – they knocked into anything.

Olga sat frozen on the box in the tail section and held her breath. The American did not appear. She realized that she would never see him again.

Within the black belly of the Flying Fortress, Olga heard voices and footsteps. Snatches of light appeared through the darkness, and Olga could see that the lights were coming closer. An unbearable feeling of being utterly alone came over her now; there was no one who could come to her rescue, say an encouraging word, or at least cast a comforting glance at her. She was all alone in the world, alone in a bottomless black abyss.

Olga was terrified. She was doomed, and she realized clearly that great suffering was in store for her. A thought briefly flickered in her mind that she could bury herself among the boxes, cover herself with the tarpaulin, but she pushed the thought away. She was tired of hiding, and now let whatever was to happen, happen. The interpreter was not yet aware that dignity is a force that helps people survive, and those who lose it are the first to perish.

Light struck Olga's face and she squinted. A bright flashlight was shining on her out of the darkness. The officer holding it froze from the unexpectedness of it; the human shape suddenly revealed by the flashlight beam took him by surprise. A woman was shrinking helplessly from the bright light, her face drained of all color.

The officer could hardly believe his eyes, then recovered, turned, and shouted to the others, "She's here. I've found her!" Then, as if worried that he was only imagining the woman, he rushed toward her, forced her arms behind her back, and pushed her toward the plane's exit.

The interpreter took a step and then struggled against him and came to a stop. "Let go of me!" she said sternly. "I'll go myself."

"You wretch! You obstinate creature!" the officer thought, but he released her nonetheless so as not to make life any more difficult for himself. If this absconder had resisted, he would have had to forcibly drag her, and the Americans would have seen it.

Strangely, Olga felt a bitter relief, as if a weight had been lifted from her. She had grown tired of waiting, gotten fed up with being afraid, and now she reconciled herself to meeting her fate head on. The only thing left to do was to accept the inevitable with her dignity intact. Olga gave in, and a feeling of peace descended over her heart.

In Russia it has long been known that whatever happens, it is for the best. While it might seem that there is nothing worse than trial, imprisonment, and the bullying and arbitrary actions of the camp guards, Olga's arrest saved her from certain death: there is no extra parachute on a bomber for the use of passengers.

Olga was led from the plane, forced into a car, and driven off to an unknown destination. The photographs found on her person were used as evidence in the case. She was tried by court martial. Article 193 on desertion set out, according to paragraphs 7–10, the highest criminal penalty: death by firing squad with confiscation of all property. It could not have been otherwise: this was an army at war. However, the tribunal considered her pregnancy a mitigating circumstance, and she was sentenced instead to ten years in a prison camp.

Meanwhile, all the other bombers eventually took off, entered into formation, and set a course for the west. Commander Eddington asked, without special hope, for permission to take off. The entire crew went back to their places and waited in anticipation, certain that permission would be refused. Surely they would be detained there on the base and subjected to interrogation. No one had any doubt what was in store for them.

To their complete surprise, the crew was granted permission to depart. They started their engines according to the usual procedure, sped down the runway, and lifted free of the ground. After initial maneuvers they entered on their course and joined the bomber formation at the rear.

The Soviet interpreter never learned what happened to the American crewmen. Over Germany, the Flying Fortresses flew into heavy anti-aircraft fire. A shell hit the bomber's tail section and the aircraft burst into flames. The crew managed to parachute free of the plane, but they were taken prisoner. The Germans held them all in a POW camp until the war's end.

## 35

None of the Soviet film industry people yet knew of the tragic events over the Sea of Okhotsk. When I told of the destruction of the airliner at the dinner table, my neighbors were horrified, and shook their heads in concern. The news quickly spread across the room from table to table, though some, especially the young ladies, paid no attention to it. Some of these artistic types simply did not grasp what a painful incident this was, and its universal import. They were, as usual, preoccupied with themselves.

Soon, however, the entire delegation understood what it was like to be called a murderer. It was if they had personally shot down the airliner and killed innocent people. They might deny any involvement, but it had been their country's doing. People no longer welcomed the Soviet delegation. The hotel staff had previously been quite friendly, but now the concierge, the waiters and the maids turned away from the Russians. When shopkeepers recognized a Russian, they showed evident distaste, just as the girls from the festival press center had done. Whether the Russians liked it or not, they had to pay for the sins of their country, for a transgression committed by someone else; a portion of the common guilt lay on each and every one of them.

The head of the delegation was a mediocre director, known for producing lame films but a member of the Party committee at Mosfilm studios. Though he had always been a supine, sleepy type, he now raged with frustration and actually seemed to age before our very eyes, for the delegation had failed in its mission. These trusty ambassadors of Soviet culture had not brought a good and life-affirming message to the bourgeois West; they could do nothing to influence the general hostility and negative sentiments toward the USSR.

Meanwhile, airlines announced a boycott of the Soviet Union. The delegation were not sure how they would get back home. It was suggested that they drive to Yugoslavia, as planes were still flying from Belgrade to Moscow. In the end, everyone managed to get on the very last flight from Rome, and they quivered with fear for the entire time they were above Europe, wondering if anyone was going to shoot them down in revenge. When they finally landed at Moscow's Sheremetyevo airport, the applause from the passengers was louder than after a performance at the Bolshoi Theater.

After dinner at the Cappello Hotel, the others at my table invited me to a screening. At ten o'clock, the Arena open-air cinema was to show two films in competition, an Italian picture and a Bulgarian. The first was Pupi Avati's *A School Outing*. There was no Russian translation, and for my neighbors' sake I had to spend an hour and a half rendering the English subtitles into Russian. It was a hard job and very mentally taxing, but anything for friends.

When the time came for the Bulgarian film, *Hotel Central*, we simply walked out. I did not want to waste my time on it, and my neighbors agreed; we could see Bulgarian films in Moscow whenever we wanted; we did not need to come all the way to Venice just for that.

Three of us walked out: Alexander Zbruyev, the famous actor; Volodya Savitsky, the big film boss; and myself, an ordinary filmgoer and provincial doctor. A weak evening breeze came across the Palazzo del Casinò. It blew pleasantly on our faces and swirled among the festival leaflets that lay scattered on the ground. A colorful fragment of a Yehudi Menuhin bill fluttered weakly in the wind, like a military banner that had been lowered in the camp until daybreak. Outside the brightly lid Palazzo del Cinema, where the jury members watched the films in competition, a vast and diverse crowd thronged day and at night.

We walked across the square, with its scattering of trees. At the Marconi waterfront we had a view of the sea, a featureless dark plain on which ships' lights shone dimly. Far away, at the limits of our vision, a handful of islands could just be seen. On the other side of the waterfront, the brightly-illuminated Hotel Excelsior rose up over the shore like a medieval castle. Its glass-façaded restaurant, flooded with light, resembled a transparent yellow crystal or an amber box into which someone had placed the sun itself.

"I've got an invitation," Zbruyev suddenly informed us.

"Me too." Savitsky spoke up just as unexpectedly, and I immediately imagined an interesting game in which one lady invites two men into her home.

"Shall we?" Zbruyev asked, and motioned toward the enchanting hotel. "Let's go."

    

"Let's go," Savitsky readily agreed.

"Stop!" I objected, and stood rooted to the spot, forcing the others to stop. "Maybe you've been invited, but I haven't. Am I going to be an unwanted guest?"

"Don't worry, we've all been invited," Savitsky said vaguely. I gave him a look that showed that I insisted on knowing more. "I said I'd be bringing a doctor," he went on. "No one minds meeting a doctor."

"Ah, that's different," I conceded. "If only you'd warned me, I could have brought my stethoscope. Or some medicines: laxatives, expectorants, diuretics. What's the diagnosis over there?"

"Fine, fine," Zbruyev waved my joke away. "We're just popping in," he said.

I looked at my watch and saw that it was nearly midnight. "It's not too late?" I asked, like an inveterate killjoy. I was not knowledgeable about the customs prevailing among the filmmaking community and my bohemian companions.

"It's fine. In fact, it's good timing," Savitsky said. "The jury finishes at eleven. They told me to get there after eleven."

"They told me the same," Zburyev nodded. "At midnight the party's barely got started. They're waiting for us, gentlemen."

"But we're arriving empty-handed," I said, again rather getting on my friends' nerves. I felt that I was making a big fool of myself.

"Exactly, empty-handed!" the actor said, exasperated. "You'll see for yourself."

I must admit, I like pleasant surprises, fun adventures, and sudden changes for the better in the world. Let me put you out of your misery by saying right away that it was the actress Inna Churikova who had invited my dinner companions. Her husband, the director Gleb Panfilov, was on the jury of this year's festival. She had arrived with him and they were staying, as they usually did, with all the film stars at the Excelsior – what else would one expect?

Zbruyev, I should mention, had worked with Churikova in the same theater. Savitsky had known her since childhood, as they had neighboring dachas and they had gone together to the same Pioneer camp. While I had been off on my mission for Soviet intelligence, dealing with lie detectors, my dinner companions had run into Churikova at the festival and she had invited them to visit her. Now I was a sort of poor relation who had suddenly found himself in paradise.

The spacious hotel room of this cinema power couple dazzled me with its luxury. The white furniture in palace style, the jacquard fabrics and gold and porcelain furnishings had originally been intended, of course, for Arab sheikhs. The room's main attraction was its capacious refrigerator, crammed with all manner of premium spirits. The bottles were packed tightly against one another like books on a shelf, and my eyes scanned their enchanting labels. These supplies were replenished daily; as soon as one consumed the contents of a bottle, that bottle would be immediately replaced – everything on the house, of course. The festival had not failed to be generous to its jury members, I can give them that. This arsenal of liquor would have been more than enough to bring happiness to the entire Soviet delegation along with all the Russian journalists present. Once I realized how abundant and inexhaustible this supply was, I felt ashamed of my feeble proposal to bring something. I knew nothing of such bohemian circles, and I would have brought an ordinary bottle from a nearby shop.

We started with tequila. Then we moved on to whiskey and brandy, and sampled some cognac and a range of excellent Mediterranean wines. The snacks were limited to cheeses, nuts, crackers, canapes, and some salted pretzels – nothing substantial, in the European style. Our talk was mainly about the cinema, though later everyone talked about their children. Our hosts had left their son Ivan with his grandma, and now they were worried about what he was up to.

The conversation suddenly turned to the Korean airliner. Inna and Gleb had still not heard the news. The film royalty, it seemed, had spent all day in happy ignorance of it. Zbruyev and Savitsky competed to fill the couple in on what they knew, or rather what they had heard from me.

"I felt like everyone was looking at me strangely today," Panfilov said. "Now I understand why."

"I hope they don't blame you personally for what happened," I said, though without much confidence. Zbruyev and Savitsky began fervently debating whether it was really acceptable to shoot down a passenger jet, even if you were itching to do it and felt a burning need.

"How horrible!" Churikova sighed.

We finally staggered out of the hotel in the middle of the night. Although the journey back to the Cappello Hotel was only a short one, we had a hard time covering the ground. What could we do? Our ability to orientate ourselves was impaired, and we encountered difficulties at every step. The sleepy receptionist, woken by our racket, threw our keys down on the counter and muttered something malicious-sounding at us. He clearly held the view that all Russians not only turned up at random hours of the night worse the wear for drink, but also shot down airliners.

"It wasn't us who shot the plane down," I told him resolutely and in English. Then I repeated the thought in my mother tongue, "*Sbili ne my!*"

The teetering figures next to me nodded to back me up: it wasn't us, they seemed to say, it wasn't us...

"Who knows with you people', the receptionist said, his disapproval and hostility plain to see. He clearly had little love for Russians.

"I am completely against what happened!" I stated firmly, so that the Italian would understand who he was dealing with, and I explained to him thoroughly that he should not tar everyone with the same brush.

"In a state like that, anything can happen." The porter's voice carried an accusatory edge: by now the air in the hotel reception was rich with alcohol vapors.

I tried to get through to the Italian and explain the intricacies of international law and foreign policy, but the receptionist did not appreciate these efforts, and warned us that he would call the police.

"That won't be necessary," I objected, and said that I had already met the police on the street that day, and they had said nothing to me.

Our group appeared at breakfast still quite sleepy. With the exception of Aron Kanevsky, of course, as he had not gone out with us the evening before. He was a generally chipper person, and unlike the other artistic figures there he was always in a good mood. I should add that Aron was much older than the rest of us. He was a veteran of World War II and had shot some excellent documentaries, but now he was complaining that the festival left him no time to go shopping. If this error were not rectified, Kanevsky firmly stated, then once the prizes had been awarded he would have to request asylum in Italy.

After breakfast, my neighbors went off to watch films, each according to his individual tastes and interests. For my part, I did not waste any time: I was expected at the next meeting that Soviet intelligence had long since planned for me. At the hotel reception, I looked in the phone book for the San Lazzaro degli Armeni monastery and dialed the number. I said that I was a pilgrim from Russia, interested in Armenian history and culture. That was, after all, the pure and honest truth, no matter what way you looked at it.

To my surprise, the father superior sent his own personal boat to fetch me. It resembled an admiral's yacht. The boat was extremely comfortable, with lavish furnishings and fittings. I was even the sole passenger, but sadly, the journey lasted no more than five minutes. A pity, as I would have preferred to stay on such a fine boat for a round-the-world trip. In my job I had often needed to sail on various vessels across the oceans of the world.

The island of San Lazzaro is located toward the south of the Venice lagoon, next to Lido. St. Lazarus, the man whom Jesus healed and raised from the dead, was the patron saint of lepers. The island had once hosted a leper colony, hence its name. In my work I had visited the leper colony near Ventspils in Latvia, and I thought it fortunate that the colony on San Lazzaro had been shut down long ago, in the sixteenth century. Two hundred years ago an Armenian Catholic monastery of the Mekhitarist brotherhood had been founded here. The Armenians had fled from the Turks when Venice was at war with the Ottoman Empire. The monks found on this island a refuge and a shelter.

The boat, glimmering in the sun, sailed around the square-shaped island, which was lined on all sides with pink stone and surrounded by a white balustrade. An artificial harbor had been cut into the south-east end of the island, and here yachts and boats were moored. Beyond a wall of trees and shrubbery, I caught sight of whitish-pink stone buildings, two or three stories tall and with the red tiled roofs that had long been a typical feature of the Mediterranean landscape. I stood on the deck, and as the engine fell silent I sensed a peace and stillness that was unshakable and centuries old.

After the crowds, the noise, the fumes, and the general commotion of big cities, after the busy airports, painful experiences, sorrows, and heated arguments, after the wars and disagreements, the island offered consolation and reassurance for a sore heart and a hot head. The stones of this sacred place radiated a blessed warmth, and in the shade of the gardens and along the footways of the park, well-kept flower beds gave off a lovely fragrance. An unusual silence reigned all around me.

The monastery's inner courtyard, surrounded by archways, seemed to protect it from all adversity and misfortune, from intrigues, machinations, trickery, evil intentions, and hostile manifestations – it was enveloped in utter serenity. As soon as one arrived here all worries vanished, all anxious thoughts disappeared, and one was drawn to enter the concentrated silence, to plunge into a peaceful, timeless existence.

I was immediately impressed by the monastery library and its collection of paintings. In the round hall of the library with its walnut paneling, a great number of unique incunabula were kept behind glass. I thought how nice it would be to read them all from start to finish, or if life was too short for that, then at least to leaf through them. How good it would be if there were no risks or dangers in life, no bitter regrets, and we could calm our nerves and curb our passions.

Shortly after I had entered the library, a monk in a black cassock appeared. He was bald except for a few remaining hairs, his beard was gray, and he wore round spectacles. The monk's name was Friar Vartan, he was the guardian of the ancient manuscripts here, and he spoke every language imaginable. Friar Vartan had graduated long ago from a monastery seminary and had already lived and worked on this island for fifty years. From our conversation, I learned that the monastery had its own printing press, which had produced some of the best art books in the world, though the business was now struggling. The monastery lacked staff for the press, and the monks were advancing in years and dying out one by one. As a result, the press would soon have to close; it had been barely surviving for some time now, and the art books were not covering the expenses of running it.

The monastery had always provided a roof for travelers. Pilgrims and eminent men had often enjoyed its modest hospitality. Among them was Lord Byron, who studied Armenian here. I looked into his old cell where he had written poems. The second-story window looked out over the lagoon which, legend had it, the poet could easily swim across. I readily believed this, as Byron was a noted swimmer.

For some time now the monastery had served as a retreat for bigwigs from the corporate world. Secret meetings and confidential negotiations could be concluded in a low-key fashion here at the monastery, its brethren providing their wealthy guests with perfect conditions: beautiful scenery, comfort and privacy, complete confidentiality guaranteed. And safety, too, of course: thick walls, reliable security, connections with the whole world, and no spies or journalists around – what more could one want?

The agent that I was to meet had been staying at the monastery as a welcome guest. He really did have some business negotiations scheduled, and had flown in for a week. I never learned what country he was working in. I was reluctant to find out any details, according to the old principle of the less one knows, the better.

The only thing I had been told was that he needed a serious operation. The local doctors in his country of assignment were urging him to have the surgery done quickly. When Soviet intelligence learned of this, they were worried that something might happen as he was coming out of the surgery. Sometimes patients experience logorrhea, a state characterized by uncontrolled talkativeness and even speech incontinence, and then the spy might betray himself. After deep anesthesia, sensory aphasia sometimes occurs in which the patient utters words non-stop without even understanding their meaning, an uncontrollable stream of speech, a violent outpouring, verbal diarrhea.

Now it had to be decided whether Soviet intelligence should evacuate the agent to Moscow, though that was not an especially desirable option. The fears might, after all, be overblown, and there might be no real threat. The agent himself wanted to stay put. Soviet intelligence suggested that he arrange his negotiations with his business partners on the island of San Lazzaro, where I could examine him, draw my conclusions, and offer useful advice. Naturally, the agent could not turn to his own doctor in the country where he was serving covertly.

I walked around the monastery, visited the extraordinary library and rich collection of paintings, and had a look at the orientalist museum and its rather jumbled collection of ancient artifacts which the monks had gradually acquired over the centuries. Each of these monks had been experts in their respective fields, professors, doctors of theology and many other disciplines – philosophy, for example, or history, or philology – and they each knew many languages. Interestingly, among themselves they spoke the old Western Armenian dialect, which is known today in Armenia only among a handful of specialists.

I found San Lazzaro degli Armeni to be a very interesting place. I was fortunate indeed to have had the opportunity to come here. Yet as interesting as the monastery was, I had to remember that I was here as part of a covert plot, and I had to ensure my own security. I had not spotted anyone watching me; I was apparently not under surveillance. As I moved around the monastery I tried repeatedly to confirm this. There were a few people at prayer in the distance. Sometimes out of the corner of my eye I glimpsed a monk in a black cassock or a seminary student walking past, like shadows in sunny weather.

In accordance with tradition, visiting guests, even if they were bankers or industrialists, stayed in old cells with bare white walls and spartan furnishings of heavy wood: a dresser, table, and a bed over which hung a crucifix carved from rosewood. The strict regime of the monastery and the simplicity of the quarters here called for modesty and humility, so that the wealthy visitors would temper their desires, limit their habits, forget about luxuries, and perhaps turn toward the spiritual life, renouncing earthly goods, vanity, lusts, and stormy passions. True, unlike medieval cells, these lodgings did offer some amenities: a toilet, shower, bathtub, and hot and cold water for the delight of those staying here. Plus, the windows provided a view of the lagoon in all its vastness, and in the distance, between the sky and the water, the stunning city of Venice glimmered.

At the appointed hour, the agent was waiting for me in his cell. He was already advanced in years and had the look of a clerk, a bookworm, a blind mole. He was pale, with gray hair, glasses, a puny build, and pasty skin. Frankly, I could immediately tell that he was ill. He spoke Russian, though with a faint accent, and his formal and commanding attitude and old-fashioned manners led me to think that he had been born and raised in a family of Russian emigres. He must have come with the first wave of such emigrants and learned Russian firsthand from his parents. Clearly he had then been wooed, recruited by Soviet intelligence. Perhaps he had feelings of patriotism for a country he did not live in; perhaps he was a naive romantic who, to honor his forebears, had decided to selflessly lend aid to his ancestral homeland. From time to time, albeit rarely, Soviet intelligence exploited people's ideological sentiments; more often the motivation was money.

I do not think, however, that this agent lacked for anything materially. He was not interested in money, and as an already wealthy man, he could obtain whatever he wanted, and even pay for his own covert activity.

By and large, I do not think that he was spying, obtaining secrets. He was probably being used as an agent of influence, and perhaps he was financing certain efforts, such as publications in the press and television coverage, and thus creating a positive opinion among society, which is important for any country.

He introduced himself as Alexander, though that was not necessarily his real name. Initially we talked about the monastery on the island, about the Mekhitarist brotherhood and the monks. Alexander was well informed about the San Lazzaro monastery's history, and had a knowledge of religious movements. When he had learned that he could stay at the monastery, he had suggested to his foreign business partners that they hold their negotiations here. He then arrived a day early so that he could meet with me in relaxed circumstances. We chatted about the monastery's museum, library, and gallery. Alexander was so enchanted by these treasures of art that he seemed to forget about the reason for our meeting, as if we had met only to discuss such spiritual themes.

"Excuse me," I said to interrupt the agent's ecstatic monologue, "but do you talk in your sleep?"

Alexander suddenly snapped out of it. "Ah, forgive me, doctor! Please understand that I rarely meet fellow Russians, let alone art lovers. Do I talk in my sleep? Honestly, I don't know."

"Your wife has never mentioned it?"

"I must disappoint you there, doctor. We sleep separately, in different bedrooms."

"And when you were a child? Did your parents ever say anything?"

"Again, forgive me, doctor. I can't remember. It was all so long ago."

Both intelligence and counterintelligence were interested in this subject. For them it was very important whether a person talked in his sleep or not. As usual, this interest manifested in what one might call two opposite directions: some leaned toward concealment and secrecy, others toward revelation and exposure. We at Division X had not been idle, and we had studied this phenomenon ourselves, though it was an obscure subject, difficult to understand.

Talking in one's sleep, or somniloquy, is one of the parasomnia disorders. Scientists have determined that there are four phases of fast and slow sleep which alternate and each last from an hour and a half to two hours. A person usually talks during the first phase, when sleep is still shallow and the sleeper makes rapid eye movements. According to our findings, logorrhea when coming out of anesthesia is most commonly found among people who also talk in their sleep. In other words, a relationship is observed between somniloquy and post-operative logorrhea. Clearly the speech center of the brain shows increased activity at these times. Granted, only five percent of patients belong to this category, but in examining the agent I was obliged to account for even the slightest chance.

Furthermore, at Division X we found a curious phenomenon. If the patient talks in the first phase of sleep, his speech is clear and intelligible, while other sleep phases are characterized by incoherent mumbling. Moreover, somniloquy almost always reflects real events; the information spoken aloud in sleep is exclusively truthful. Our research revealed a clear inter-connection. A man might recite in his sleep a text that he had read the evening before. Sometimes a patient discussed in his sleep events that he had witnessed himself. In short, if someone had something to hide, then extreme caution was called for. That is why Soviet intelligence was concerned about the upcoming operation; they were afraid, to put it bluntly, that information might leak out uncontrolled.

Such concerns were nothing new to me. I studied the agent and put him in a trance. This hypnotic sleep revealed no signs of somniloquy. I would have liked to do an EEG and get an exact picture, but from the indirect signs it was clear that Broca's area, which is located in the frontal lobe of the left hemisphere of the brain and regulates speech, was not affected by any pathology. I hoped that the concerns of Soviet intelligence were unjustified. There was practically no risk – though frankly in medicine it is hard to be completely sure about anything: sometimes an unloaded gun goes off, sometimes a good horse stumbles.

"I think everything's fine," I told the agent. "I don't expect any undesirable consequences."

"Goodness! Really, doctor?" he said and flung his arms wide in delight. "And I won't have to go to the USSR?"

"In my opinion, that would be unnecessary."

"Splendid, doctor, just splendid! My handler was afraid that I would start talking under anesthesia and he wanted to get me out. I was so worried I couldn't sleep!"

"That's not good, because for you sleep is the prescription. You don't need to worry, but you should take some precautions. I'll give you a few recommendations."

"I'm all ears, doctor! To make it easier, can you speak into this?" He placed a small voice recorder on the table.

"No, we won't record my voice. I'll put it in writing, in my own hand."

The agent nodded his understanding and did not argue. He replaced the voice recorder with a notepad and pen. I advised him to get rid of any tension he had, forget about all his concerns, and relax fully. He should get some good sleep and go for walks in the fresh air. He should have a massage and take warm baths at night, and he should also use sedatives in small doses to balance his nervous system. As Division X has observed, a hot and stuffy room doubles the risk of somniloquy; in a cool room it is rarer that a person talks in his sleep. My main piece of advice was a secret that we at Division X had discovered.

"I don't know what you'll think about this, but there's never been a case when a person talked in his sleep after sex."

Who knows what he really thought of that, whether my words appalled him or, on the contrary, inspired him. His eyes widened in surprise and he was temporarily taken aback, but then he recovered.

"My, that's incredible! What a fine recommendation. Thank you, doctor. No one has ever given me advice quite like that." His spirits suitably lifted, Alexander gestured that I should come with him. "Doctor, would you be so kind as to have lunch with me here in the monastery's dining hall? The cuisine here is exquisite. It's like my late grandmother's cooking. She was a pureblooded Russian aristocrat and she knew how to cook. The *dolma* here is simply delicious, you won't find anything like it anywhere. And the wine cellar! The monastery's collection of wines is as fine as its collection of paintings."

I managed to resist his invitation in spite of myself. Refusing was not easy, I must admit. It took an enormous effort to force myself to head for the island's harbor instead. Alexander came along to see me off. The father superior's impressive boat was still waiting there, as if at military readiness. The sun's reflection off the water played along its sides.

"If you'll forgive me, doctor," the agent said, and then he went on somewhat uncomfortably, "This business with the plane. How could such a thing happen?"

"It happened," was my only answer. What else could I say?

"Yes, but, excuse me… there were people on that plane, ordinary passengers. They all died…"

"Yes, they died," I said with a heavy heart, and frankly I found it impossible to add anything more. The captain of the boat had started the engine and was standing at the helm while the sailor on duty unwound the mooring line from the bollard. Both looked at me expectantly, patiently waiting for me to come on board.

"What can we do, doctor," Alexander said, at a loss. He seemed uncertain of how he could bear on his own the immense weight that he felt on his soul.

"You know, while you're here, you could say a mass," I suggested.

He apparently thought he had misheard me. "A mass?" he asked, as if the meaning of the word had not gotten through to him. "In a church?"

"A mass for the dead, and yes, from a church it would reach its destination faster," I said with effort, as if I were rolling a heavy stone. "That's the only thing we can do for them."

Who knows whether the man was a believer or an atheist, but my words affected him deeply. Perhaps he had not expected to hear such a thing from me, an ambassador of a godless country. In the stillness, the boat's engine purred and its crew looked at us. A light breeze from the lagoon blew over the waters of the harbor, and the slight swell glimmered in the sun like wrinkled foil. Alexander nodded and said softly, almost under his breath, "Yes, of course… I'll say a mass, I promise. Don't worry, I'll say a mass on my behalf and yours."

With that, all my business on the island of San Lazzaro came to an end. Nothing else needed to be said. I stepped onto the boat to return to Lido. The boat moved away from the mooring and slowly set off from the harbor. My patient stood motionless on the pier, then slowly walked away, pale, confused, and not quite sure of what tomorrow might bring.

Some time later I learned at Division X that the operation had been a success. Nothing was amiss, all worries had been in vain. The patient soon recovered to the full satisfaction of doctors, myself included – after all, I had done my part to ensure that everything went without a hitch.

══ 36 ══

Things were quiet for a while. Shilin was perplexed: had he really managed to avoid any repercussions? But he already knew too well what the army was like: the generals would never forgive anyone for their own incompetence. Clouds began to gather around the pilot. Rumors reached Shilin from various sources that he was considered unwell: he had gone funny in the head and needed treatment; he ought to be committed. No one was willing to give an official order. His superiors, naturally, sought to cover their own backs, steering clear of records and papers showing what had happened and working to make sure there were no witnesses, no proof, not even a hint. It was obvious which way the wind was blowing: his commanders wanted to have this brazen pilot, who had refused to obey a direct order, sent to the loony bin. A diagnosis of insanity would mean that they could have the rebel locked up.

For those who do not know, mental hospitals in the Soviet Union were more terrible than prison. A man arrested or incarcerated could at least appeal to the law, he could hire a lawyer, and his sentence grew one day shorter every day. A patient in a mental hospital was the most defenseless creature, a person utterly without rights. He could not lodge any appeal or beg for clemency, he could only moan and hit his head against the wall. Nothing else was in his power.

After the shooting down of the Korean airliner, things did not go smoothly for Shilin. He was seen as a wise-ass, and his superiors hated him with a vengeance. The opinion of his colleagues was divided. For the most part, they condemned him, too – there were those who believed that the situation with the Korean plane had been handled correctly. Others approved of Shilin's actions, but they kept quiet so they would not bring trouble on themselves.

The army generally does not like competent officers who think carefully about their orders. Top brass prefers servile types whose sole commandment in life is that if an order comes, it must be executed. Plus, the army does not like those who stand out in any way from the ranks as a whole. Shilin's fellow pilots who had participated in intercepting the airliner were especially annoyed. They claimed that they had done everything correctly with regard to the Korean plane, yet at night they were tormented by anguish. By day that anguish turned into outright hatred for Shilin: his comrades were unable to forgive him for their own mistakes.

The pilot with the call sign Eight Zero Five, though he had carried out his orders, was no happier for it. He was called a hero and thrust onto a pedestal, but behind his back some quietly called him a murderer, and he was praised and cursed by turns. Moreover, is it easy to go on living if you know that with a single movement of your finger you killed two hundred and sixty nine souls?

At first Eight Zero Five would keep repeating, "I don't think about my orders. I just carry them out. If they tell me to jump, I ask how high. They told me to destroy the target, and that's what I did." However, he then began to claim that he had actually intended to shoot down an American plane, an electronic surveillance aircraft which had been flying alongside the Korean airliner, but their blips on the radar had merged into one. One way or another, he had shot down an American spy plane, he said, and then the Americans had shot down the Korean plane in order to push the blame onto Soviet air defense. No one ever questioned Eight Zero Five's sanity, though, because he was a man who had carried out his orders.

Shilin's comrades decided he was crazy. How could he be anything else? He had thought he was so smart, that he knew better than everyone else, and had disobeyed orders. Naturally only a nutcase would disobey an order. It was a good thing, they said, that he had not decided to abscond with his plane and land it at a foreign air base, as had already happened once before.

As everyone knows, it is pointless to fight against rumors, though if fortune smiles on a person, the rumor will die out of its own accord. Shilin followed subsequent procedures correctly, dealing with all the paperwork, but he was no longer permitted to fly: how could a mentally ill man be trusted with military equipment? The rumors spread through his garrison and his entire air base, and his reputation was tarnished among the staff officers and aviators. The role of outcast is a bitter one. Shilin's peers and neighbors eagerly sought out any oddities and quirks in Shilin's behavior, so that they could then make that circling motion with their index fingers at their temples to suggest that not all was well with this man, that he had a screw loose.

Shilin quickly assumed that he would be dismissed from the army, and he started thinking about how he could feed his family. His wife felt ashamed because of him, and he felt sorry for her: it was not easy to be the wife of a lunatic who was the subject of malicious rumors. He found it especially painful to look at his son, though. The boy felt all alone and avoided his peers. Shilin understood how much he must be suffering. There is nothing worse than a child's pain for his parents and parents' pain for their child, when nothing anyone might do will change anything.

The Korean Boeing was shot down during the night of August 31, and the school year started the next morning. The day after the incident, the boy's classmates looked at him strangely, the next day the teacher joined in, and the day after that the whole school. School is often the first inquisition we face in our lives. At school, the children of "enemies of the people" faced a great stigma, and it was demanded that they renounce and expose their parents. However, Shilin's son proved to be a tough character: if one of little Pavel's classmates said something offensive, then Pavel would immediately sock the boy in the face without wasting his breath arguing. The boy would accept insult from no one, and even his teachers were wary of upsetting him.

Shilin's son would come home from school as tense as a wound string. "Finding it hard, son?" a guilty Shilin would ask, knowing that the rumors were in full swing, tongues were wagging at the base and among his regiment. But it was not hard for Pavel in that way: Pavel was proud of his father. "You stood alone against everyone," the boy said.

The shooting down of the Korean airliner had caused a huge uproar in the international press. The whole world was talking about it, and politicians and diplomats were quick to repeat the American president's claim that the USSR was an "evil empire". From the very first day, Soviet generals closed ranks and tried to defend themselves: they were smart enough to claim that the intruder had flown off toward the Sea of Japan. Official spokesmen muttered some vague and nonsensical claims. Granted, among the general commotion and chorus of accusations, the original cause of all this was forgotten: who had sent the plane on its deadly route? As always, it was the consequences that held the chief interest rather than the causes of them. As a rule, people make no more than vague assertions or guesses as to true causes, and rarely go digging properly for the facts.

   

In turn, the Americans kept silent from their side; the NSA did not say a word. Meanwhile, journalists were insistently trying to determine who had given the final order. That order had reached the pilot with call sign Eight Zero Five, who had then shot the airliner down, and in his native land he was feted and praised for it. Strange to say however, while the regional commanders were awarded medals and given bonuses, the pilot who actually carried out the order received nothing. It was a whole year before the pilot was awarded the Order of the Red Star, and even then, the commendation stated that the award was in recognition of high marks in military and political training.

To everyone's surprise, the hubbub in the international press died down quite quickly, almost as if a gag order had been placed on the story. Journalists in various places, as if on command, shut their mouths and lost interest. Perhaps the two countries reached an agreement to keep the matter hush-hush, for their mutual benefit and in order to distance themselves from whatever missteps they had each made.

Incidentally, the generals had still not decided what to do about Shilin, whether to discharge him, demote him, or bring him before an inquiry and charge him with dereliction of duty. Rumors swirled around this pilot who had not carried out his orders and, moreover, had refused to shoot a foreign plane down. Other people were not aware of the details and did not delve into the matter, and this suited the authorities. God forbid that the details should come to light; better to wait it all out.

Be that as it may, the gossip spread through the entire army. Some hailed Shilin as a hero, others thought him a lunatic, and ultimately he was sent to us at Division X. Officially, though, the pilot himself was never mentioned after the Korean airliner was shot down. He disappeared entirely from the record, became a sort of ghost, a shadow over the whole story. The international press already had the names of the pilots who took off to intercept the intruder on that night of August 31. In the newspaper reports, ground control and monitoring station operators vied for attention, the orders issued by the generals were discussed, but Shilin was nowhere to be found, as if he had never existed.

The charts at the Japanese airspace monitoring stations showed the call signs and maneuvers of three fighters which flew toward the Korean Boeing shortly before its destruction – three! – even though it is known for certain that two pairs of fighters, *four* planes, were sent up to intercept the Korean in the skies above Sakhalin Island.

Yet regarding the fourth plane there was only silence; everyone clammed up about it. Only a vague rumor slowly spread among the garrisons, as if someone was secretly digging an underground passageway by night. Gossiping tongues claimed that of the ten pilots from Kamchatka to Sakhalin who had flown in to intercept, only one had questioned the order and refused to shoot down the unknown plane. Granted, no one knew the name of this bold individual.

As usual, with time this gossip died down and became mere myth or legend. Occasionally someone would recall the rumors from long ago, but the pilot's name passed into oblivion. If one takes an honest look at the matter, the pilot's refusal was a bold action. Anyone who thinks about defying the Soviet regime ought to remember the story of Novocherkassk. Its inhabitants, proud and headstrong, refused to be mere sheep when the regime swindled them yet again, instead they rejected stupid obedience, and rose up in revolt. Naturally the regime decided to grind these troublemakers into the dust, but the soldiers sent in refused to fire on the crowd: they disobeyed their orders. We would all like to know them by name, know them and commemorate them, but is there anyone who remembers them?

True, others were found in Novocherkassk – generals and guardsmen from the interior forces – who did carry out the order. They shot at the protesters, managing in so doing to hit chance passersby, onlookers, and children who had climbed trees to get a better view. Their machine guns covered the city in fire, bullets were flying everywhere. As a colleague of mine from Division X watched, a wayward bullet shattered the window of a barbershop and killed the customer seated there in the chair for a shave. The butchers of Novocherkassk earned no fame; indeed, they shied away from it and their names were carefully kept hidden. After all, who wants to be known as a murderer?

Shilin was still a fairly young man, only thirty eight years old. By that time, most of us have established some stability and security, and few of us have to start their lives all over again. It was clear, though, that the regime would not leave Shilin be. Once the rumors had died down, the authorities would settle their score with him. He was under no illusions in that regard.

Nikolai had been born in a prison camp, and his earliest memories went back to the age of three. His mother served her entire prison sentence to the day. No one showed her any clemency. After the famous amnesty of 1953, when many convicts were released and political prisoners were rehabilitated, she remained at the camp: her sentence was not shortened, nor was she pardoned. There is nothing strange about that, as nowhere in the world does the state have any sympathy for deserters.

   

They were released when Nikolai was ten years old. He obviously did not feel that he was guilty of anything himself. Olga Shilina naturally said nothing of her own crime, and she never told the ten-year-old boy that his mother had been court martialed for desertion. Wartime law called for the gravest punishment, death. Since his mother might easily have been shot, it was good that the tribunal had shown some mercy. The interpreter had been lucky, all things considered. She had even got off lightly.

When Shilin's mother retired, she moved back to Moscow, the city where she had been called up into the army. By law she was entitled to an apartment in the place where she was originally conscripted. Before the war, Olga had lived with her parents in a big professor's apartment on the Arbat, but now she was given a small room in a communal apartment. The authorities promised to help her with time, give her better conditions or move her somewhere else, but Shilin's mother was already content: in her old age she had returned to the city of her birth.

On his way to Division X, which was located in the outskirts of Moscow, Shilin decided to visit his mother. She guided him tirelessly around the Arbat area, along Prechistenka and Ostozhenka Street, where she had spent her childhood before being called up. She pointed out the building where she was born, and the window of her old apartment. Then she led him into the pleasant, green courtyard, where she had played as a girl in the prewar years.

"I never thought I would come back here," his mother admitted. "It feels like it wasn't me who lived here but someone else."

"Who?"

"Someone I knew a long time ago. I feel like I've missed my life. My life passed me by, and I lived someone else's."

Shilin nodded. "Yes, I know. I get the same feeling sometimes."

They sat at the edge of the courtyard, among the ivy and wild lilac, honeysuckle and jasmine. It was warm, but the sun seemed somewhat bashful now; the Indian summer was coming to an end and the cold fall rains were on the way. Old linden and maple trees towered over the bushes and were already losing their leaves. The pale leaves, in various shades, lay scattered among the grass, and the scene resembled a painter's palette. Shilin was amazed by the stillness here and the sleepy, warm calm of the place – it did not seem like Moscow at all. Moscow still made its presence known, however, by the big-city buzz on the other side of the buildings and rooftops. The din swelled and abated like steam over a hole cut into ice. Children were enjoying themselves on the courtyard's playground. The littler ones, under the watchful eyes of their mothers and grandmothers, were hard at work in the sandpit, while the older ones were darting among the trees and bushes like bright butterflies in flight.

A fat old woman was sitting nearby, at a cursory glance looking wrinkled like the cracked wooden deck of a ship. Seen more closely, she resembled a worn old monument. From time to time, the old woman turned her proud head to stare at Shilin's mother, looking hard as if trying to remember or recognize her. More often, however, she watched over the playground and, like a cavalry officer, barked commands at the children: Stand up! Sit down! Stop! Come here!

What was odd was that the old woman spoke to the children in English. In these years the kindergartens in Moscow were packed full, and so parents made efforts to hire babysitters who could look after their children while also teaching them languages and good manners.

The elderly people of the neighborhood sat among the greenery in the courtyard, trying to soak up the fall sun.

"Mom, do you not recognize anyone here?" the pilot asked as he looked at these old men and women.

His mother only shrugged.

Shilin went on, "Maybe we should go up to your old apartment?"

"Why?"

"Maybe we'll find something. Stuff left there…"

"What, and we'll go off with them?" His mother smiled.

"Letters, knickknacks, photographs… Something might have been kept."

His mother shook her head. "No, I don't want to. I ought to be careful, I don't want to get too upset."

"Don't worry, you're still a young woman."

That made his mother laugh. "Thank you for the compliment," she replied. "I still can't believe that I've come back. I just want to breathe in this Moscow air. I woke up this morning and I thought, where am I? Am I really in Moscow?! I kept worrying that they would find some mistake with my papers and send me all the way back. When they've been hammering fear into you for so many years, it's hard to get rid of it just like that."

A leaf suddenly slipped from a maple tree for no apparent reason and plunged down, but instead of falling to the ground it seemed to fly freely, soaring up and down across the yard with a light, sweeping movement. Shilin followed the leaf with his eyes until it came to rest in the grass. He was pulled away from this distraction by the feeling that someone was looking at him. The fat old woman seated nearby was staring at him intently and openly, as if trying to remember or recognize someone.

"What does she want?" the pilot muttered, annoyed. His mother did not answer, and did not look at the rude old woman. On the contrary, she looked directly away.

"Mom, did my father ever come here?" the pilot asked.

"No, never," his mother replied. Shilin felt her tense up.

"You don't want to tell me anything?"

"You already know everything." There was a distance in her voice now. In an instant a mighty wall had gone up between them.

"Mom, I think you're hiding something from me," the pilot said as gently as he could.

"Why do you think so?" Now the gates were closing and the drawbridge over the moat was being pulled up, making the fortress utterly unapproachable.

"It just seems that way," the pilot said. "I still don't know what you were sent to the prison camp for."

"I already told you, for being absent from my place of duty."

"You got ten years for that?"

His mother shrugged, and her face wore a neutral expression. "There are strict laws in wartime," she said, but then went on to add something she had never said before. "On the front, being absent for more than two hours is equivalent to desertion."

"Really?!" He shook his head disapprovingly, and then said with obvious reproach, "Was it worth risking it? Did you at least have a good reason for it?"

"To meet with your father," his mother replied harshly, even with some hostility, as if compelled to utter these words. It was the first time, it must be said, that his mother had spoken about the matter in all these years.

Shilin said nothing for a long time and sat lost in thought. It suddenly came to him that this ill-fated meeting may well have been the cause of his coming into the world. Ten years of imprisonment was the price that had to be paid for his conception, and he and his mother had paid that price in full.

"Sometimes I talk with my father in my dreams," Shilin said after a lengthy silence.

"What does he look like?" his mother asked. She was clearly astonished by his statement, and genuine interest gleamed in her eyes.

"You said that we're very alike…"

"Yes, you are," said his mother, and then immediately seemed to grow very distant, without moving from the spot. Though she continued to sit next to him, she was preoccupied by her thoughts and apparently off somewhere else, in a different and half-forgotten time long ago.

Shilin often thought about what would happen to him. It was obvious that they would never let him fly again. Sooner or later, the army would settle scores with him, and not just the army but the whole Soviet regime. He did not know what to do: go with the flow and give himself up to events, or take the risky step of alerting journalists and revealing to the world just what had really happened.

"Are you in trouble?" his mother suddenly asked. She had clearly sensed his worries and hurried to help him.

"No, it's nothing," the pilot replied dismissively, wanting to stop his mother thinking anything was amiss.

"I hope it's not affecting you," his mother said. "I mean, this awful situation."

"What awful situation?" Shilin feigned ignorance, but he already knew what she meant, and he dreaded the fact that he would now have to lie to her.

"What awful situation?! They shot down a passenger jet and now they're pretending that nothing happened. It's shameful! It's their doing, but they don't want to admit to it. Instead of saying sorry, they just lie and lie. They're covering it up." His mother scowled and shook her head in condemnation.

From the neighboring bench they suddenly heard a loud voice like a clarion:

"What have you done?! You ought to be ashamed of yourself. What a dirty child. I'm going to tell your mother! Oh yes, I'll tell her! You can't love her very much." The old woman was shaking a finger at a little girl who had decided to roll in the sandpit.

Her harsh voice carried across the entire courtyard like a loudspeaker. The woman finished scolding the girl, then let her go with a careless gesture and sat stock still in an arrogant pose, like a monument to herself.

"Mom, it's time to go," the pilot said. He helped his mother to her feet, and they slowly headed off.

The pilot walked beside his mother. He was tall, tanned, and had short-trimmed hair that was starting to turn gray. As he reached the end of the courtyard, Shilin felt the intense stare of the loud old woman.

   

Her gaze was like a heavy blow on his back; it drilled into his spine. He turned and saw that the old woman seemed to want to say something; she was steeling herself to speak, but she could not bring herself to do it. By all indications, she wanted to call out to them, but she hesitated, and did not budge from her spot. She clearly did not know where to start. Or perhaps she was not sure it was worth trying.

$$=\!=\!= \; 37 \; =\!=\!=$$

The set lunch at the Cappello Hotel where I was based did not bring me special pleasure. Day after day, the omnipresent and all-conquering pasta dominated the meals. I had eaten so much pasta now that I was afraid it was going to start coming out of my ears. I still remembered the vast menu offered at the dining hall of the San Lazzaro degli Armeni monastery, and felt a bitter regret that I had not taken advantage of the opportunity then. Obviously what was done was done, but why lie, I naturally regretted my silly refusal of the agent's invitation: one *dolma* alone would have been worth it, not to mention the cold and hot appetizers, Armenian flatbread, stewed meat and herbs, and the wine cellar – what a loss! I would probably not have turned down such an opportunity if it had not been for my upcoming meeting with Robert: business always came first.

I was waiting for Robert to arrive at the Cappello Hotel; he was due any minute now. Exhausting work awaited me. It would have been easier to dig ditches or haul stones, with the only difference being that a digger or a stonecutter could be replaced, but no one could do my work for me. Whether I liked it or not, I had to rise to the challenge.

To Robert's and my surprise, the Cappello Hotel was unusually empty at this post-luncheon hour. My neighbors at the hotel were all off watching films or seeing to duties at the festival, and so Robert and I could take care of our business undisturbed. In preparation for his polygraph examination, Robert needed to seal off his memories of the past – delete them, place a taboo over them, and banish them for a certain period. In order not to be caught out by the polygraph, the agent had temporarily to forget the man he had once been.

As one might guess, amnesia with regard to previous events would help Robert feel more secure in his current identity, should the operator ask any questions about the distant past. In that section of memory which I was helping Robert close off, there would be a black abyss that the polygraph could not penetrate – not the polygraph, the operator, a discerning doctor, nor anyone else. Except me, of course.

Thus I did my job, and hopefully I did it well. After the session, Robert had completely forgotten about the distant past, his childhood, his student years, his intelligence training, and the person he had been in those days.

The program I had put him through now meant that dissociative amnesia was blocking a vast area of his long-term memory and was firmly embedded in his cerebral cortex. I had wiped from Robert's memory long-ago events, people, and details about his personal life, but I had ensured that all acquired knowledge, skills, and capabilities were retained – it was work that demanded as much precision and care as a jeweler's, I must say.

There was no reason to be worried about the agent's identity and well-being. The amnesia would gradually weaken over time, and holes would appear in it. The agent would come to recall various events from his past, and his memory would recover little by little all on its own. In an emergency, I could unblock his memory myself without difficulty.

After our session, we drank tea and ate cakes. As I was already a seasoned business traveler, I had known to bring my own water boiler, loose tea, and strainer, and I used them in spite of the rules for fire safety and the fact that the hotel strictly forbade them. What I had to offer admittedly did not quite live up to the laws of hospitality and mutual reciprocity: Robert had treated me to some Venetian cuisine, and I feted him with a cup of tea. Say about that what you will.

Far from condemning my feeble hospitality, he set off with a spring in his step, cheerful, carefree, and wholly satisfied with his life. No uncertainties were now tormenting him, no unnecessary fears were bothering him, his worries had vanished. Only good fortune and success beckoned, and he felt his life to be unclouded and uncomplicated. He knew only the truth that the polygraph required. The agent had left his previous life in pledge to me, and I was carefully guarding it.

Robert no longer required anything from me; he had no need of a doctor. I saw him off, and he hurried away, as joyous and happy as a champion, toward the jetty. He went boldly on his way like a graduate from a provincial institution heading off to dazzle the big city.

After I had said goodbye to Robert, I went for a stroll through Lido and decided to go and see Oleg Bitov, the correspondent for *Literaturnaya Gazeta* whom I had met at the film festival's press center on the first floor of the Excelsior. I entered the Best Western Biasutti Hotel at

Via Enrico Dandolo 27 without any particular aim in mind – if I had been invited, then why not simply pay a visit? Especially considering that I still had to lay a false trail for anyone who might be watching me. If I was being followed, meeting with various people would help lead my pursuers astray.

The Biasutti Hotel occupied four buildings and was five minutes' walk from the beach. It was a comfortable, even grandiose establishment, but the outbuilding with the impressive name of Villa Ada where Bitov was staying proved to be a mere concrete box without any ornamentation or architectural interest. It was even on the other side of the street from the rest of the hotel. After a long search, I found room 57 in the basement, which made sense considering that the festival was paying for the Soviet journalists' presence. His room was locked. The head of the Soviet delegation was staying at the Otello villa nearby, but he was not in either. I could not find a doorman or receptionist; apparently there were none.

The hotel's main building resembled a typical villa in the classical Venetian style, with bay windows, balconies, and a mansard. A shaded garden stretched around the building and featured a few gazebos and flower gardens. The restaurant was located on the enclosed terrace, which was surrounded by balustrades and densely woven with ivy. I stepped inside and noted the spartan interior with coral-colored trim. At the center of the lobby stood an oval leather divan that encircled a wide column. To my surprise, the receptionist said that Bitov had not been seen around the hotel for a whole day now. I even wondered if I was the last of his compatriots to lay eyes on him.

It was a strange story; just think about it: the correspondent for a famous metropolitan newspaper, a grown man and a prominent journalist, disappears without a trace at a film festival. It was a baffling and mysterious development.

A week later the Italian police, after receiving a request from the Soviet consulate in Milan, launched a search. They searched high and low for Bitov, but never found him. His possessions and suitcase had been left behind in the hotel room; nothing was out of place, even the souvenirs and gifts which he had bought for friends and family.

It later became known that Bitov had somehow contrived to end up in England. He had supposedly been spirited away by British intelligence after being mistaken for a valuable Soviet agent, a colonel, perhaps, who possessed valuable information, someone entrusted with secrets, a trained spy. One can imagine how disappointed his abductors were to learn that they were mistaken. It is quite possible that they were after a different person entirely. One can only speculate as to who they really wanted. The question naturally and involuntarily came to mind – who were they really looking for?

A year later Bitov reappeared in Moscow. According to his account, he had been kept under guard at a London apartment belonging to British intelligence until one day he had managed to escape and reach the Soviet embassy, where he was secretly brought to the airport and flown to Moscow. I never met him again, and as to what exactly happened, the doctors at Division X never inquired. The matter seemed irrelevant to our work and held no scientific interest.

I stepped out from the Biasutti and then walked slowly past the flowers to the Via Enrico Dandolo, which runs toward the beach. It was still light out, and I had time enough before dinner so that there was no need to hurry. In fact, there was nothing left for me to do on Lido, the film festival aside. I had come at just the right time, I must admit. During film festival time, if you are not a star, an actor or a famous director, you attract no attention from anyone. No one is curious about you or pays you much heed, which is exactly what I needed.

Needless to say, during these days the hotels, clubs, screening venues, street cafes and drinking establishments were jam-packed, and there was noise and bustle everywhere. Crowds of filmgoers swarmed around the actors, and journalists were scurrying this way and that in search of something sensational to report. I naively assumed at the time that Bitov must have been running around the festival trying to sniff out interesting news.

I thought it highly convenient to be here at the festival. The hustle and bustle and the influx of guests from all over the world allowed me to be lost among the crowd, a mere extra. Anyone who arrived here on Lido during the festival was like a needle in a haystack, and it was not hard to dissolve into the teeming masses.

That's right, ladies and gentlemen, esteemed readers, that's right. Who can argue against it, refute it, or deny it? We must pay tribute to the most important of the arts – I am referring to the words of the Bolshevik leader Ulyanov, who had long before chosen Lenin as his *nom de guerre*. If it had not been for the downing of the Korean airliner, these days would have been entirely pleasant, life would have been perfect. It was not to be, though. Things did not work out. Fortune, that vile nag, galloped straight by us.

It proved impossible to forget what had happened. The passengers on that doomed plane hung over us like a cloud, seeming to breathe down our necks. For every minute of the day, day after day, those victims were ineluctably present in my thoughts; reminders of them were like the sea breezes on Lido: everywhere.

I could never manage to take ten steps without the thought rising up from my subconscious that I really ought to call New York. I should get in touch with Colonel Creighton, for example, and his daughter Cindy, hear their familiar voices, and ask how they were getting on. Deep in my heart, though, I knew that I would not call, that I would be reasonable, maintain caution, and not add to the general grief. Nevertheless, I was not willing to dismiss the idea entirely. The thought occasionally materialized, weighing on my mind, and I was forced to decide against it over and over.

And then – oh good God almighty with all His angels and prophets – I saw her. She was walking toward me down the Via Enrico Dandolo with light steps in high-heeled shoes, heading for the same Hotel Biasutti that I had just left. Had things happened just an instant earlier or later, we would have passed each other by entirely, and I would have never forgiven myself for it.

I could not believe that this encounter was real. I stood there in disbelief. We had first met by chance in New York. The following day Cindy had driven me to JFK Airport and we had said goodbye to each other, a parting which I had thought was forever. And now here we were, meeting again! Lightning rarely strikes twice, but I had been fortunate indeed.

If I was surprised, she did not seem so at all. I stopped dead in amazement while she was still a fair way off. She came closer and closer toward me, swift and slender, and there was something in her step that evoked flying, as if she did not even touch the ground as she walked. Frankly I, a grown man able to control himself and deal reasonably with his desires, became as gleeful as a child and I was unable to believe my eyes. Her sudden appearance here seemed unreal.

"Hello my dear!" she said, and kissed me, as if we had kissed often before, as if we had arranged this meeting long before, as if we often, or at least from time to time, met like this, as if she had come from just down the block and not from an ocean away.

"What are you doing here?! You said you weren't going to come!" was all I could manage. I was completely at a loss, and could only mumble. I felt in seventh heaven.

Cindy nodded. "I didn't plan to come," she said and smiled at her words. "I changed my plans on the spur of the moment. I knew I'd find you here."

   

"How? The place is packed. We might have never met at all!"

"True, we might have never met," she replied confidently, "but I was sure we would."

"I'm flying out tomorrow morning," I said in a voice laden with regret and contrition, as if I was admitting to some great crime. To be honest, I really did feel guilty, because I was powerless to do anything: my mission for Soviet intelligence was over. Invisible trumpets were sounding, the hour of my departure had come, and I had to rejoin my ranks. The marching army would not wait for anyone, and arriving late was strictly forbidden.

Cindy did not seem disappointed. She simply replied, "That's OK then. We've got heaps of time."

"Just one night," I said. Again I had to be a killjoy.

"A whole night!" Cindy corrected me, her voice cheerful and enthusiastic.

To the west, the clouds beyond the lagoon were tinted red by the setting sun. Dusk had spread over half the sky above Venice and all its domes, spires, and bell towers. The crowded beach was emptying out before our eyes. A fresh breeze from the sea drove waves toward shore, and they crashed with spray and foam and filled the air with sand, salt, the smell of seaweed… and a vague and nameless feeling of unease. I was thinking about how good it would have been to spend even just a few days on the island with this woman who had sideswiped me, driving me completely crazy, head over heels.

"Don't fret, my dear." Cindy smiled slyly. "It would have been worse if you'd already left," she added, to comfort me. Smart, beautiful women often find just the right words.

The secret behind her appearance here was simplicity itself. Cindy was a journalist covering the movie world. She wrote in-depth articles and insightful reviews, and had her own column in a magazine. Publishers often sent her to festivals, and every year she came to Venice to write about new developments in world cinema.

This year had not seemed to offer much in the way of quality productions, and so Cindy had originally decided to pass on the festival and visit Hawaii instead, or spend the fall in Miami, which were also perfectly good places to unwind.

But just as the festival was reaching its zenith, Cindy had received a call from *Premiere* magazine. They offered her the job of reporting on the jury's decisions and the awarding of the prizes. She considered turning the offer down, and might well have done so. She had forgotten all about Venice, and her thoughts had turned to other things. So it often goes: an instant later, and events would have taken another direction, but instead fortune chose to smile on us. Thinking more deeply about it, though, the important thing here was not the events themselves, but what lay concealed beneath them. Meanings and causes are usually hidden from the eye and not subject to reason.

I must admit, all the time I had been here I had been dreaming of calling Cindy in New York. I did not do so, because I wanted to maintain the secrecy of my work and I was afraid of attracting attention. Still, a man will dream. In New York I had not even told Cindy where I was going. I had buttoned my lips and clamped my tongue to my teeth to avoid saying too much. She had been unaware that I was flying to Venice. I had kept silent about my movements around the world and I had not said a word. My work forced me to be discreet.

Now I looked at her and I thought of how often I had called her, written her letters and telegrams, sent her flowers… but only in my imagination, in my own unfettered world of make-believe that knew no boundaries. And now Cindy herself had been tugged toward Venice for no apparent reason and much to her own surprise. We compared times and dates and concluded that Cindy had been drawn to Venice at those moments when I was thinking about her and wanted to call her. There had definitely been some link between us; we were on the same wavelength across the ocean in an unspoken harmony unknown to physics. I thought of the unknown capabilities of the human body, and of how nature can still surprise us. Believe it or not, make of it what you will, those times when we were joined followed one after another, as if during the festival days a stable line of communication had been established between Venice and New York: an invisible cable, wireless contact, a transatlantic signal.

Why keep fighting it? Cindy agreed to the magazine's offer. Like it or not, there is no escaping fate. If you look for a reason and think about the consequences, there are very few clear explanations to be found. Just guesses, vague forebodings and uncertain assumptions, and even they cannot be taken seriously. In the end, Cindy left for Venice, though only a few days remained until the end of the film festival.

That Cindy was staying at the Hotel Biasutti was no big mystery. Every year *Premiere* magazine booked her a comfortable room there, where she could work in peace and engage in her favorite pastimes of tennis, swimming, and horse riding. In addition, the hotel rented a private beach a five-minute walk away that was closed to everyone else, especially rabid autograph seekers and star-struck fans.

Once, when Cindy was at the Moscow Film Festival, she had to be content with the Hotel Rossiya, which resembles a large barracks, has noisy plumbing, and at night drunken bands of men wander its endless, dirty, gray-carpeted corridors, mustachioed Caucasians roam tirelessly in search of women, fights erupt and sometimes knives come out.

No, the Rossiya could not offer this young American lady a swimming pool, tennis court, golf course, or horse riding. It could only give her a tiny, miserable, smoke-stained, smelly room that looked out onto Red Square. The hotel administration evidently believed that a view of the Kremlin would make up for the lack of any other amenities; anything else a guest might ask for were merely the silly whims of the capitalist world.

I thought Cindy was lucky the Moscow Film Festival had not put her up at the "Collective Farmer's House" in Tishinsky Market, where a dozen guests are packed into a single room. The toilets are outside, behind the fence, and the gate locked at night. How could it be otherwise? Let justice prevail! No entry – so that passersby had to relieve themselves in the market, those unlucky ones whom fortune had passed by on the other side, who had found no room in the "Collective Farmer's House". Here we must give the brave and unpretentious hotel guests their due: they did not gripe or complain; they meekly accepted having to make a night-time dash to the toilet in the square, where the architect and poet Andrei Voznesensky and the sculptor Zurab Tsereteli would shortly erect their strange monument to Russian-Georgian friendship. Critics have said that the Georgian sculptor had put up a monument to the sexual potency of Caucasian men, while others have denounced the monument as a skewer with meat on it, the only thing missing being the grill.

No sense denying it: I was thinking that we might well have met earlier, had heaven allowed. It is odd that chance had not brought us together while Cindy was in Moscow. Goodness, how much of our lives is wasted, how much joy we miss out on! But why complain? We should be grateful that our paths finally crossed; better late than never. Let us praise fate and direct our gratitude to heaven.

I could hardly believe how fortune had smiled on me here on Lido. I had been brought here to pay a brief visit to the journalist Bitov so that I would then find myself in the vicinity of the Biasutti. To this very same place, fortune had then led the woman of my dreams.

We were still amazed at our chance meeting, and still somewhat shy, but we gradually relaxed as we walked down the Via Enrico Dandolo to the canal that cuts across the island from north to south. We crossed the canal and came to the Via Sandro Gallo waterfront, and slowly, as if in a dream, walked northward along the lagoon. It really was like a fantastical dream, a magical turn of events.

By now it was already growing dark, and a translucent purple haze was spreading across the sky over the lagoon and the island. In the twilight, the white and colored lights of the pleasure craft, tugboats, and waterbuses criss-crossed from one end of the water to another: a nighttime navy that knew no rules of navigation. Two miles to the west, at the far end of the lagoon, we could see the glow of Venice, a boundless sea of lights, more than anyone could ever count.

I must admit that I had finally emerged from the long days of solitude I had spent on the island, and been favored with attention. Oh happiness, to be stirred up and excited by the marvelous glitter of a woman's eyes. Now Lady Luck has finally smiled on me.

Where were we walking? If anyone had asked, we would not have known the answer. Our meeting had been so unlikely and unexpected that we were simply wandering like shell-shocked soldiers, dazed and confused.

Unlike the canals of Venice, where the stagnant water sometimes smells of decay, the air at the edge of the lagoon was pleasant, and a fresh evening breeze was blowing. Everywhere on Lido one felt this wind from the Adriatic. Southern Europeans would feel the need to put on a sweater, though it was only September – but there were none in evidence: we saw no one at all on the Via Sandro Gallo. All passersby seemed to have vanished, and we walked alone. In the twilight, Cindy's eyes reflected the shifting play of the light, though to tell the truth, the glitter of her eyes in the darkness evoked a precious jewel, a pure diamond.

"Where are headed, then?" Cindy finally asked as we came to the intersection with the Riviera San Nicolò. Here the wind was noticeably stronger, the air smelled of salt, and from the nearby restaurants we could hear Italian music, always good for setting a romantic mood.

"I thought we were just going for a walk, the first walk we've been able to take together," I explained, in what I felt was a very straightforward and direct way. I tried not to conceal anything from Cindy, although my work had taught me to be discreet and remain silent.

"No, darling," Cindy replied. "I'm an upstanding woman. I've got to be modest and think about my reputation. Although I…"

I cut her off before she could finish. "Your reputation is impeccable!" I said resolutely and categorically.

"Oh, if only it were so." She shook her head. "I should be making sure you think well of me."

   

"I already do!"

"Now I'm going to say something awful. I'm afraid you'll think … God knows what you'll think."

"I won't think ill of you. Just say it."

"We don't have time for a walk. In the morning you're flying out, and who knows when we'll meet again."

"So, what then?" I stopped and looked at her stupidly. Our walk had taken us further away from the Riviera San Nicolò. Ahead of us was the Piazza Santa Maria Elisabetta, where the windows of the Hotel Panorama and the colorful sign on its façade glowed invitingly. From here we had an even grander view of the lagoon, the islands of Giudecca and San Giorgio, and Venice further off. The three-story hotel building with yellow walls towered over the waterfront near the jetty. The heavy black shutters on the windows gave the building a rather provincial, rural appearance.

"Where are your things?" Cindy asked. "I remember that in New York you had just a small carry-on bag."

"That's right. It is at the Cappello Hotel."

"That's strange," Cindy said, surprised. "I thought I knew every hotel on Lido." It turned out that she knew only the establishments of four stars or more. Wealthy people, whether they like it or not, are forced to choose places at their own level: firstly, their status requires it; secondly, you cannot stop them from living a comfortable life; and thirdly, it is habit for them, second nature. Yet I had Cindy down as a woman who could easily live in a hut, a yurt, or a tent, and bathe in a nearby stream, cook her own food over the fire, and the mosquitoes would not bother her at all.

"My dear doctor," said Cindy, "we're grown-ups. Let's not pretend. We need to go the other way." "We can go for a walk the next time we meet. I promise."

I knew I could trust her, that she would keep her word. I did not argue with her, I simply gave in. Together we set off for the Cappello Hotel to get my bag. Without it having to be said aloud, it had been decided that I would leave for the airport tomorrow morning from the Biasutti. I didn't dare argue or object. I couldn't risk it.

The small lobby of the Cappello Hotel was crowded. My fellow Soviets from the filmmakers' delegation had gathered in reception after dinner, and the scene resembled a mutiny on a ship. Judging from the commotion, something or someone had made them all angry. The Caucasian delegation was especially upset, of whom the most fired up of all were those talented people from the Georgia Film studio. Waving their hands like ping-pong bats, they were competing in shouting at the head of the delegation, the mediocre director from Mosfilm. Enraged, they were threatening him with all manner of reprisals, all the way up to writing a letter to the Party committee. There was anger in their voices; their discontent had evidently reached boiling point already and was still growing. The heavyset receptionist leaned over the counter and listened closely, as if he was trying to figure out the reason for all the commotion.

"What's all the fuss about?" I asked my neighbors from lunch. They told me that the Georgians were upset at the schedule for the festival, which was not giving them any time to go shopping. It seemed they had the same complaint as that voiced by the director Aron Kanevsky, who had earlier suggested that he might need to seek asylum in Italy.

To be honest, the whole Soviet delegation turned out to share the Georgians' distress, though unlike the Georgians the others behaved more calmly. They kept quiet, afraid that they might bring trouble on themselves and even be struck off the list of people allowed to attend the festival next time. The Georgians, on the other hand, were fearless, and true to their type seemed to think nothing of consequences. They simply rushed into battle without caring about their own lives. As the old Latin expression goes, *aut cum scuto aut in scuto.*

This group of rebels behaved like capricious children or ancient heroes; their eyes shone with passion, and one feared that blood would be shed any moment now.

"We changed all our Soviet money and now we're not allowed to spend it!" one filmmaker from Tbilisi cried in a strong Georgian accent. At every word he swung his hand as if playing ping-pong. "Don't think you'll get away with this!"

After a while, the delegation's interpreter managed to get a word in. He said that Venice was an expensive city, the prices were horrendous, everything cost three times as much as elsewhere. It would be better, he said, for the delegation to save all its shopping for Florence, as they would be moving on to that city soon. This had been the plan all along, he said, so that the members of the delegation would not waste their money. The organizers had been selflessly looking out for them.

These words were entirely empty, but the crowd nevertheless quietened down. Everyone sighed in relief. Smiles blossomed. The mood improved at once to a level of elation. All present cheered up noticeably, their spirits rising and continuing to rise. These anxious filmmakers realized that perhaps not all was lost, that life would still go on, albeit in a different way.

Even the Georgians instantly calmed down. They realized that it was not worth venting their anger, and that it would be better just to wait and see. Hope was not dead yet; they would still get a chance to spend their lire. And if that is the case, my friends, then there is no reason for sorrow; we have the whole world in front of us.

Quicker than thinking, a dramatic change came over the Georgians: peace was re-established, their excited spirits were calmed. The men of the Caucasus are generally outgoing, and rarely hold grudges. As long as you do not impugn their honor or step on their toes, they can be perfectly friendly. Now they instantly let all their anger go; their natural affability was re-awakened, their rage disappeared. One could not have told that just a minute before, they had been seething, ready to take up arms, spill blood, and even – just think! – write a letter to the Party committee.

The Georgia Film delegation proposed to the Mosfilm party, as a sign of friendship and brotherly love, that they immediately have a drink, so that there would be no hard feelings and no one's mood need be spoiled.

To everyone's surprise a big jug of wine in wicker casing appeared out of nowhere. It had been transported straight from Georgia, and how it had made it through customs remained a mystery, but somehow it had. Naturally, no one showed particular reluctance to turn down the opportunity. Everyone rushed to get themselves a glass; there had been little wine around the hotel so far. The movie critic Cindy Creighton and I did not remain on the sidelines long; we each managed to get hold of a glass, in spite of the fact that we had not participated in the uprising and did not, strictly speaking, qualify for the treat. No one thought about this, though, for why should bosom friends, compatriots and fellow countrymen, keep accounts?

Once the Georgians had downed some wine, they warmed up, as they usually did. They became brash, swinging around the room singing together in a chorus. I do not know whether they had agreed beforehand on who would sing what part, but they sang in perfect harmony as if they had rehearsed it earlier. They sang passionately, from the heart. Could one, though, expect anything else from a Georgian? The glorious sound spilled out of the room; it raised the roof and soared high above the sinful world toward the heavens. Georgian polyphony is world-famous, and as Miss Creighton and I listened, it was as if angels were singing.

The Georgians were clearly in their element. One might think they had gathered for a feast or a village wedding in the mountains. They sang so superbly, so sincerely, that Miss Creighton and I even forgot all about our plans for a time. We had a sleepless night ahead of us: a coming together, then a farewell followed by a long period of … total uncertainty.

Meanwhile, friendships were being forged in the hotel's corridors, and the atmosphere was getting chummy. People were inviting one another to their rooms to continue the drinking. What a metamorphosis and transformation, taking place before our very eyes! The quarrel had turned into a big celebration that swept like a wave over the Cappello Hotel.

"I'm checking out now," I told the receptionist.

Like any Italian, he was very fond of singing. Indeed, he had been so touched that a tear had come to his eye, and it took a moment for him to compose himself. "Now?" he said. "But it's still evening!"

"Yes. I'm in a hurry. I can't wait."

He cast a glance at Cindy and gave a slight nod. "I understand," he said. "You're a strange people. One moment you make films and sing beautiful songs, and the next you shoot down a plane…"

What could I say to excuse myself? That it was others, not I, who had done it? That would be cold comfort. That I condemned the atrocity and regretted it? To that, some might counter that a fox would regret being caught in the henhouse. That I felt guilty and that I was sorry? That would mean nothing, because there was no going back, the victims on that plane could never be brought back. That some people shoot films, but the plane had been shot down by others, and it is just a coincidence that they all share the same planet? We know, we know, we have heard that many times before. Pontius Pilate tried to wash his hands of it all, too.

From the first day of the fall, the downing of the Korean plane had been a big subject of conversation. My fellow Soviets traveling abroad were everywhere dubbed murderers. People cursed them, as well as their country in general. They were castigated, they became outcasts. Who can bear such treatment? They, of course, had nothing to do with it, but a country's people always have to answer for the actions of their government.

I myself served this same country, and so whether I liked it or not, a portion of the blame lay on me, too. Not to mention that there were some dreadful Soviets who even said it was right to shoot the plane down. What a pity they were not on that flight themselves.

Cindy, I should say, did not say a word about the Korean airliner. I was afraid that after my grim presentiments, she and her father and her brother would be suspicious of me, as if I had known beforehand what would happen to the passengers and was therefore involved in it myself. Cindy did not broach the subject at all. Her father and brother had escaped sharing in the other passengers' fate, and the two of them were still alive: why would she pour salt into the wound? Yet those who had secretly sent the plane on its doomed route remained in the shadows; no one even mentioned them or tried to call them to account. Perhaps they even received awards and commendations. After all, their undertaking had been a success.

I took my bag from my room and said goodbye to the Cappello Hotel. We headed for the Via Enrico Dandolo, where I would spent the night at the Biasutti. Cindy's room looked directly out onto the park and the terrace. Very convenient, I must say, as I did not want to make things awkward for the hotel's receptionist or staff. Moreover, I was thinking of this young lady's reputation, and was pleased that getting into the park and climbing up onto the terrace posed no difficulty.

Her room turned out to be one of capitalist splendor. It had an air of old-time luxury, plush furniture, bronze, silk upholstery, lush curtains, lace, fancy lampshades and carpets, and damask wallpaper. Everything suggested the early twentieth century, before World War I.

As I climbed over the balustrade, I looked through the glass door into Cindy's room and saw the yellow glow of a wall light, and a floor lamp. Thoughts immediately came into my mind of an inviting shelter, a haven, a secluded refuge for two. The bed was especially impressive. Its dimensions seemed to approach those of a whole basketball court; an entire platoon could fit into it. It was so big that a person could get lost in it and never be found again. I froze now, afraid that I would forget the way back from inside that bed. How would I ever leave it again? Would I ever leave it, indeed?

No further words need to be said. We ceased from all conflicts raging on the earth, we concluded a truce, reached an agreement with whomever, for just one night. So that there would be no victims among the civilian population, so that we could avoid any losses, shell-shock, or bloodshed. For one night we established a moratorium, took a break, had a breather – just for a single night, no more.

In other words, we wanted to forget for at least one night the foolhardy generals, the politicians. We wanted governments and regimes and Division X to leave us in peace. In short, regardless of what others might think of it, the two of us walked away into the night, went underground, disappeared out of sight. We had had enough of the gossip, the conflicts, the hostilities and confrontations, enough of the threats and accusations. We refused to have any part of it. No one could dispute that love conquers all, it is the champion of the world. Love, love, O love…

In the morning I left to catch my flight to Moscow. We did not know when we would meet again, or if we would ever meet again. The airlines' general boycott of the USSR was about to come into force and I barely made the last flight out. Cindy accompanied me to Marco Polo Airport and saw me off without tears. Her red eyes, though, glittered with treachery, and she looked as if she was going to cry, but she held on. I must give her that: she controlled herself.

That night I was awoken by a clarinet. The sound was barely audible. Sometimes it grew slightly stronger, sometimes it abated. It was as if the clarinet had got lost in the dark and was wandering through the woods in search of a road.

What was driving the clarinet on? Was it bemoaning its lot, weeping over the time it had wasted? Was it complaining about its wanderings through the night? The clarinet moaned, wheezed, cried out in sudden passion, fell away again to a whisper, muttering something indistinct, like a prayer recited swiftly and in a barely audible voice.

I stepped outside and walked toward the sound. In front of me was dark forest. At first it seemed like an impenetrable wall, but as I drew closer the trees parted. Black trunks rose around me like organ pipes, and the rustle of leaves in the wind carried across the open country. It was as if the forest was accompanying the clarinet, a large orchestra to its soloist.

The pilot was playing among the trees on the edge of the ravine. He had gone off alone so that he would not wake anyone up, and now through the clarinet was expressing his sadness to the forest at night. The instrument evoked grief, the sound sweeping among the trees like a wounded bird. Who was the instrument addressing itself to, what did it hope for, what was it looking for? A solitary wayfarer, wandering exhausted in the darkness, was beseeching the Almighty – how else would he be able to make it to his destination?

Initially, the instrument seemed to have caught a cold; its sound was sickly and weak. In each of its four octaves it managed only a hesitant muttering, wheezing and coughing in its lower and upper registers. Gradually its voice grew clearer. The melancholy clarinet mused on what might lie ahead, no longer showing any trace of the hopes it had once cherished. The long downward glissandi recalled a fall into the abyss, the sort that would prompt in any listener a chill of fear and dejection. The clarinet knew no consolation, it could only groan and cry out in mourning. The sound wandered randomly from register to register. I was struck by the instrument's syncope and sharp rests. I stood there in the darkness among the trees. The pilot sensed that someone else was there, and the clarinet fell silent. On this night, the clarinet's sound had not been intended for the ears of others.

"Who's there?" Shilin asked in a low voice, as if he were afraid to wake the others up.

I walked toward the sound, no longer trying to be furtive. I cut through a spider's web, unseen in the darkness; in the fall, forest spiders spin their webs. Dry branches and twigs cracked under my feet. It was a warm, clear night, almost like a summer night, as it usually is on September 14, the feast of Saints Symeon and Martha. In Russia, sayings about the weather are linked to this day. For example, if it is sunny on St. Symeon's day, then the weather will be good all fall, or if it rains on St. Martha's day, the whole fall will be rainy. There are a great many of these sayings, too many to count. If on St. Symeon's day the wind blows from the south, the winter will be lousy; if the geese fly off on St. Symeon's day, winter will come early.

There are plenty of sayings but the most peculiar of them all is the following: you won't find any sparrows on St. Symeon's day. People say that the devil is checking them against some yardstick of his own, deciding which to take with him and which to let go. This is why there are no sparrows to be seen on St. Symeon's day: they have all flown off to Hell for roll call.

Around this time, the Indian summer comes to Russia. On the feast of Saints Symeon and Martha it is time to pay one's debts and taxes, and to fulfill one's promises and agreements. All debtors are obliged to pay their arrears, and each claim must be considered. From time immemorial, St. Symeon's day had been the last chance to show up in court. On the day of St. Symeon, people settled their debts and counted their profits and losses. The pilot and I came to some conclusions, too. It was quiet everywhere around us, though dogs were barking far off in the village beyond the forest. The wind ceased and the forest became silent, seeming to listen carefully to our words and eavesdrop on our secrets.

Shilin and I talked until morning. I learned the details of that ill-fated night. He told me of how he had hesitated when he was given the order, and how he was uncertain as to what kind of target it was that had violated Soviet airspace.

"I didn't know what it was, a passenger plane or a spy plane. But if you aren't sure, if you have doubts, then you can't just shoot it down," Shilin said. I nodded to show my full agreement.

Toward morning it became cold. A clump of mist hung over the ravine. At dawn, the forest was quiet: not the slightest breeze or rustling of trees. A vast and foreboding silence set in around us, as if important events were soon to happen, serious discussions, fateful decisions, abrupt changes.

Meanwhile, rumors were spreading throughout the Soviet army. Some called Shilin a hero, others a madman. Division X was asked to provide its findings as to whether Shilin could continue to serve. Frankly, our doctors were facing a lot of pressure, taking into account both the facts of the case and the acute needs of the regime. The commanding officers involved in the downing of the Korean plane insisted that Shilin be committed to a psychiatric hospital. In fact, the longer he could be kept there, the better; ideally he would be hospitalized indefinitely. The military wanted to put the genie back into the bottle and seal it up forever.

"Perhaps they'll reconsider?" Shilin asked, hopeful.

"Don't count on it," I told the patient, with a tone of doctorly reassurance. "What you did has a lot of people worried and lying awake at night."

"But I'll keep quiet! I won't say a word," Shilin said ardently, as if winning this argument would mean his freedom.

"People are worried about what you might do. You might suddenly tell the whole world, bring shame to the entire Soviet air force, name names. The higher-ups can't simply rely on your mood. But if you're diagnosed, well, what can anyone expect from a sick man?"

The patient looked at me with narrowed eyes. "Are you going to write that I'm mentally ill?" he asked.

"I'm going to write that you're healthy. After all, that is the simple truth."

Shilin's face lit up. "You mean I'm fine? I have no problems?"

"No, my friend. Unfortunately, that diagnosis means nothing. You're a grown man and you ought to understand: as long as you remain in the military, you're a reminder to everyone at command that they screwed up. A constant danger for them."

"What do they expect me to do? Just die? That would calm them all down."

"Perhaps… You're thinking along the right lines. A lot of people would find your death convenient. Except you, of course. There's no way you can make the generals happy. I think it would be best to hand in your resignation."

"You mean retire?!" Shilin was aghast. "At the age of thirty-eight? But I can still fly! Plus, they won't let me go. I'm the only sniper pilot in the whole division, and an expert night pilot. They won't want to lose me."

"Yes, they will. After what happened, they'll let you go. No matter how irreplaceable you might be."

The army was unusually enthusiastic to process Shilin's resignation. He was provided quickly and smoothly with a pension based on his service. He left for a region he had long dreamed of, a provincial town lost among Russia's huge spaces.

The town of Ostashkov is located on a peninsula, and on three sides is washed by Lake Seliger, a body of water seemingly as vast as the sea. On the fourth side a marshy neck of land connects the peninsula to the mainland. A railway passes across that neck of land, curving to avoid the wooded marshes and the ravines, and it allows people to travel north or south. A journey of seven hours will bring one to Moscow or Saint Petersburg, and Tver and Novgorod are even closer. The quiet streets, lined with old wood and brick houses, stretch across the city and end at the picturesque lake shore. There are houses right on the lake. One can sail right up to them, and just like in Venice, boats are moored alongside them.

The whole town is imbued with the smell of the lake: fish, tar, wet wooden docks, pure water. At every street intersection the view is expansive: as soon as the street ends, the boundless expanse of water stretches away into the distance. In the east, the lake splashes against a concrete embankment; behind the embankment, as far as the eye can see, the lake stretches away, and at the limits of one's vision, islands rise from the water, overgrown with vegetation.

There are a great many churches in Ostashkov, and if you sail a boat around the peninsula, the distant skyline is like something in a fairytale: high steeples, domes, bell towers. To the north, the embankment ends in a maze of crooked streets covered in weeds where goats graze, old boats lie abandoned, and the local mutts wander in packs on some mission of their own. The nearby harbor is crammed with vessels. Until deep into the fall, this fleet sails freely, but when winter comes it is restricted to the backwater. The city is renowned for its magnificent old parks, built back in the recesses of time. To the south of the embankment, along the lakeshore, one encounters a few dusty and unattractive streets, green lawns, and groves with spreading, tall trees.

Long ago, the Ostashkov locals dubbed the southern part of the town "America", and this nickname caught on. On Fisherman Street in America, the pilot bought an affordable house consisting of three rooms, a kitchen, and a terrace. The windows looked out onto the lake. Shilin initially spent a long time looking out of the window, unable to tear himself away: the water, the vast space, fishing boats, islands... Behind the house was a yard and a garden. At the edge of the yard stood traditional outbuildings: a woodcutting shed, a hayloft, a barn. In short, Shilin had managed to buy himself a manor, and for a steal. In those years, few buyers came to Ostashkov, and village homes frequently went up for sale: the old folks died, and their heirs, who had long left their hometown behind, saw these old houses as a burden and were keen to relieve themselves of them.

It was the Valdai region: clear lakes, sparse settlements, emptiness, boulders, forests full of mushrooms and blueberries, marshes full of cranberries, and ancient abandoned hermitages. Flood meadows and marshy lowlands stretched across the America side of town, and here there was a wide channel which connected the lake with the Volga River. If one wanted, it was possible to travel by boat from here to the north, toward the Baltic, the White Sea, and Scandinavia; or to the south, toward the Caspian, Turkmenistan, the Caucasus, even to Iran; and by means of canals, one could reach the Sea of Azov and the Black Sea.

The fishermen were more than content with Lake Seliger, however. A local pleasure boat criss-crossed the lake all day, from sunrise to sunset. In the forest on the north shore, a hardy trekker could find an inconspicuous spring, from which came a modest stream that would eventually become the mighty Volga. Even a child could step across the Volga here.

Once upon a time, Ostashkov had been a wealthy trading city. Its inhabitants produced leather goods, caught fish, and worked as blacksmiths. The local merchants, smiths, fishermen, and tanners were renowned for their wit and bravado. After the Revolution, these trades faded away. Petty government officials, as innumerable and rapacious as locusts, settled into the homes that had once belonged to the merchants. Ostashkov's industry declined, and the city became a shadow of its former self. The town became ramshackle before one's very eyes, its prosperity vanished, and after a time no trace remained of its old buzz and liveliness.

For those new to the town, especially visitors from Russia's biggest cities, Ostashkov had an air of desolation. As with many provincial towns, there was nearly nothing left to keep Ostashkov going. Everywhere, wherever one looked, one was struck by the huge number of stray dogs and cats, by the drunkards that staggered, slouched, or fell soundly asleep in the thick weeds on the roadside.

In everyday life, the people of Ostashkov spoke mainly in obscenities. It was no longer angry swearing but simply the local lingo, which the local population used unabashedly. In the town's appearance, in the faces of its inhabitants, one sensed a hopelessness and degeneration, as if Ostashkov and its inhabitants had reached the end of the line, after which nothing remained but ubiquitous deterioration, airlessness, emptiness, and ruin.

Nevertheless, Shilin liked this old town, bathed by its clear lake, though any new arrival in Ostashkov found himself immediately pursued by the smell of decay. It was a town that made one's heart ache, an unlucky Russian provincial community, a hint of a once-glorious past. One felt as if one had been suddenly transported to a bewitched place where time had stopped. At every step there was a kind of poetry that set the town apart from Russia's biggest cities with their vast populations, prosperity, and constant roar. At dawn, oars in rowlocks knocked gently in the stillness, a chain jingled faintly, water splashed quietly beneath the oars. In the thick fog, the fishing boats were indistinct black spots lying motionless on the water. On the sandy lakeshore, nets were stretched over poles and left to dry, their glass floats dimly gleaming.

In fine weather, Lake Seliger sparkled blindingly in the sunlight. Bad weather brought a gray gloom and low clouds that clung to the steeples and domes of the churches. For some time, the town had attracted artists and tourists, and visitors, charmed by the surrounding countryside, had bought up the empty houses. In season, the local history museum arranged musical evenings to which famous performers were invited. The city gained a sort of second life, and gradually recovered.

When Shilin bought his house, with it came an old boat which, like forgotten firewood, lay in the grass outside the window. Shilin daubed the old vessel with tar and caulk, and then he and his son sailed out to the islands to fish, catch crabs, or pick mushrooms. Pavel developed right away a fondness for the lake. He loved Lake Seliger in any weather, even in inclement conditions when a strong wind whipped up fierce waves. Shilin's son loved camping outdoors and eating food cooked over a campfire.

Shilin's wife, however, did not care for Ostashkov. She had been raised in a resort town in the Caucasus on the Black Sea, where in season the mood was festive and a motley crowd of people filled the streets. His wife took against Ostashkov, frowning and pursing her lips in disappointment. For her, the place was a backwater, a complete hole. One day she took their son to visit her parents and did not come back. She remained in the south, intending to spend the winter there instead.

I visited the pilot in late November, when he was already living alone. My overnight train rolled for hours through the fall scenery, winding among the forests until finally it arrived at Ostashkov around dawn. Nikolai met me at the station platform, and we made our way to America on foot. A light drizzle was falling, and the wooden houses, bare trees, outbuildings, and stacks of firewood around us dripped under the overcast skies.

"This is America!" With a motion of his hand Shilin drew my attention to the melancholy landscape of sparse groves, flooded grass, muddy roads, ramshackle fences, and wet yards.

"You're a lucky man," I said approvingly. "Congratulations!"

"What do you mean?"

"You live in America."

It was warm inside the house. Wood crackled in the stove, the windows were fogged, and outside the house Lake Seliger rippled in the rain and shuddered in the wind. Shilin really did live in America. He had spent all those years confronting the Americans in the skies just so that he could settle down in America. What tricks fate plays on us!

Meanwhile, the circle closed with no way out, and my vague guesses became firm certainties. To begin with, I had asked for the file of the military interpreter Junior Lieutenant Shilina from the archives. I requested the verdict of her tribunal, explaining that it was necessary in compiling the medical history of a patient. After all, Colonel Shilin was my patient at special Division X, and as his doctor I needed to reach my conclusions based on full and solid information. What conclusion could a doctor make if the etiology of an illness, that is, its origin and the reasons behind it, remains unclear?

Fortunately, there had recently been some changes at the Soviet archives. The staff's former strictness had been relaxed, and they were no longer so hostile and suspicious. Eventually I received permission to look into the case file, and so I went to visit Podolsk where the archive was located.

There were the usual mug shots, showing the criminal from the front and side. The junior lieutenant seemed to be quite a young lady, poetry incarnate. I noted her fine facial features and found it hard to believe that she had served as an army officer. She was purity and innocence itself. Indeed, I could understand the American pilot Steven Creighton:

no wonder this young lady had made such an impression on him. The lieutenant had decided to pursue this dream and make it a reality; not everyone gets such a chance.

I examined the other photographs in the file: Creighton and Junior Lieutenant Shilina against the background of one of the Americans' Flying Fortress bombers. These photographs must have been confiscated from the interpreter upon her arrest and entered into the file as evidence. I possessed the very same photographs myself, having received them from Colonel Creighton in New York City. In these faded and time-worn snapshots, taken by the bomber's gunner in the summer of 1944, the interpreter Olga Shilina and bomber copilot Steven Creighton remained forever young. She was nineteen years old then, he twenty-two. It cannot be denied, both he and she looked as pleased as newly-weds, and they were smiling at the camera as if they had nothing to look forward to but happiness and a wonderful, carefree existence. It should also be mentioned that they looked good against the background of the Flying Fortress.

I was delving into this case file in the archives when I suddenly received word that I was to be sent to San Francisco on an assignment. I had no objections to that at all, no complaints, and I simply accepted my orders like any disciplined officer. A voice within me told me that it was time, high time, to fulfill the promise made to Colonel Creighton in New York. But whether I liked it or not, a trip to San Francisco meant that before my departure I would have to meet with the interpreter – without fail and at once, the voice within me said.

=== 39 ===

A fresh wind from the bay swept through the waterfront streets of San Francisco and then died among the skyscrapers near the Bay Bridge connecting the city to Oakland. The tall buildings of the city's downtown business district were all packed into a narrow space not far from the port: a throng of lanes, walls, roofs, and windows soaring into the sky above the wharves, warehouses, terminals, and multistory parking garages, and of high-speed expressways and onramps on concrete supports high over the earth.

The waterfront formed a wide arc around the lower city as far as the Golden Gate Bridge. The area was heavily built up with jutting piers where local ferries, ocean liners, and pleasure boats docked. At the foot of the huge Russian Hill, fishermen's wharfs, yacht clubs, innumerable taverns, and floating restaurants filled the streets and squares with a heady smell of the ocean, the port, fried fish, and seafaring. Russian Hill's dizzying slopes resembled an amusement-park rollercoaster: cars sped up its steep inclines or plunged down, looking as if they were about to topple over.

The best form of transportation in the city was the cable car. The old wooden cars had an odd raised roof that suggested a boater. They slowly but surely made their way uphill and downhill, tirelessly hauling their passengers, mainly tourists. The small, low, snub-nosed cars had steps and handrails running all along their sides from which hung clumps of passengers. All day, day after day, the cars slid along the steep streets.

Along Hyde Street, the cable car descended to the Victoria Square on the waterfront, where an aquarium and maritime museum were located on a green expanse near Fort Mason. In the other direction, the cable car ran along California Street up to one of the city's main thoroughfares, Market Street. The straight line of Market Street divides downtown in half, and runs until Stuart Street near the port. The latter street ends at Justin Herman Plaza near the Ferry Building, a wide shopping mall set right over the water like a pier. The Ferry Building's slender clock tower even looks rather like the bell tower in St. Mark's Square in faraway Venice.

The colonel loved San Francisco. Steven Creighton generously shared this love with his guests, and insisted on showing them around and pointing out the city's traditional sights. He took me out to Sausalito in the early morning. We watched the sunrise there from a hill covered with mighty trees. A thick fog hung over the strait connecting the bay to the ocean. The fog covered the water and shore alike, enveloping the rocky island of Alcatraz with its lighthouse and old fort. The Golden Gate Bridge, its shape recalling a great harp under the firmament, was swaddled in the fog as if in gauze. Only the tips of the high pylons, painted orange vermilion like the rest of the bridge, stuck out of the white mist which bunched and swelled over the strait.

From the top of the hill, above the clouds below, we had a boundless view of the sky and the last fading stars. Far away, on the other side of the bridge, San Francisco stretched over the hills and lowlands, a fairytale city that has haunted the dreams of romantic young people around the world.

Sometimes the colonel and I went to Pier 39, near which innumerable sea lions cavorted. Pier 39 housed a collection of marvelous gray-green buildings with large glass verandas, and the area was famous for its seafood. There, we found ourselves walking right out over the sea, in a small town perched on stilts. Sea lions frolicked in the greenish water and, like tiresome beggars, sought to convince passersby to part with some of the small fish they had bought here from local fishermen.

The marina was full of white yachts, accessed along narrow piers. In the evenings, crowds of sea lions would climb up onto the gangplanks and lounge there, as their relatives had grown accustomed to doing on the rockeries of the northern seas. Sometimes the creatures would start to fight, and their alarming cries would drown out the sound of the traffic on the streets and carry along Stockton Street as far as Chinatown.

The colonel lived in Menlo Park, a southern suburb of San Francisco and a small town of its own set on a peninsula between the bay and the ocean. Here the sleepy Stone Pine Lane recalled a quiet village street, but the spacious and well-kept homes with their lawns and swimming pools showed that the inhabitants were well-off indeed.

The colonel's large, comfortable house was built from brick and granite. It had three floors, a cellar, an attic, a garage and a loft, several bedrooms each with its own bath and walk-in closet, a den, a big living room, all manner of closets and alcoves, and even a dumbwaiter that ran from the cellar to the attic.

The owner was especially proud of his kitchen. It was spacious, seemingly the size of a gym, and it recalled the kitchens in old English and Dutch homes. I found here a smoky hearth and a cast-iron stove, which in olden times had been fed with wood. On shelves hung along the wall there were antique utensils and copper and tin dishes which had been polished to a shine. The kitchen was packed with various appliances. Refrigerators and freezers stood in a little room apart, and there was a wine cellar in the basement. A wide wooden counter separated the kitchen from the dining room; the latter resembled a port tavern or a sailing-ship cabin with its oak paneling, oak-beamed ceilings, and colorful stained-glass windows.

Naturally, the colonel had no idea of Division X's existence. He did not even show an interest in why I had come to America, in the reason for my arrival in San Francisco, I have to give him that. "A scientific conference," I had told the colonel over the phone, and he had asked me nothing about it. He simply suggested that I come visit him, as old friends do.

A tacit agreement had been established between us: the reason for my arrival – my work – was not up for discussion. The details did not concern him, nor any of the people whom we knew. It was as if he and I had concluded a separate treaty, a limited convention, a special pact, and a separate peace among the general conditions of hostility and total enmity. I did not stray from this pact, unlike many of my fellow Russians who would tie themselves in knots praising their native country and political system and swearing personal fealty to the Soviet leaders. Ultimately, the colonel and I did no harm to either NATO or the Warsaw Pact. What is wrong with someone helping a fellow man who has a problem? Millions of people have wound up under the grindstone of history – who will show sympathy, who will help, who will assist? Everyone hopes for happiness, but life is not plain sailing.

Incidentally, my visit to San Francisco had a completely valid cover story. The University of California San Francisco on Parnassus Avenue boasted a lavish budget and state-of-the-art equipment and was known as one of the best medical centers in the world. It was renowned not only for its clinics and top doctors, but also for its in-depth research into biology, physiology, and related sciences. Famous Nobel laureates worked there, but in recent years research had particularly focused on human emotions and the pathogenesis of lies. This university, whose motto was

"Fiat lux" (Let there be light!), and whose mascot was a bear, just like on the California flag, had organized a conference. Division X was naturally interested; we had been studying related topics for some years now. For my part, I obviously could not turn down the opportunity to take the trip, and in addition to the general sessions I readily signed up for a seminar on the subtle motor features of the human face.

I must admit, I was especially interested in the seminar's director Paul Ekman. This professor had done an internship at the Langley Porter Neuropsychiatric Institute, and served for a period as a US Army officer where he worked in clinical psychology. Moreover, he was known as one of the leading experts on the theory of emotion, interpersonal communication, and detecting deception.

I had long wanted to meet Ekman. In studying human behavior, he had discovered a whole system of voluntary and involuntary movements. He identified a secret language of facial expressions and gestures, learned to understand this language, and arrived at a code that would allow one to identify both conscious and unconscious lies. These markers included not only blatant signs, but also small, barely noticeable indicators.

Whether for good or for ill, the professor had turned out to be a savvy businessman. He founded his own company, the Paul Ekman Group LLC, to which American intelligence, police, and the FBI turned for consultation, as well as banks, various agencies, industrial and financial corporations, politics, and rich men – everyone who needed to determine the truth and was willing to pay for it. With time, Ekman entered the ranks of the hundred most influential people on earth, and a mystical aura appeared around his name, as if it was impossible to hide anything from this man or dissemble, as if he could see right through a person, or deep inside them.

In the end, Professor Ekman did not come either to the conference or to the specialized seminar. He was too busy with other matters and unable to tear himself away from them. Years later, I learned that Ekman had moved from the Langley Porter Neuropsychiatric Institute, where he worked for over forty years, to the University of California San Francisco – the very same place where I had hoped, in vain, to meet him. Ekman made several visits to the USSR and Russia, and he even lectured for a whole month at a Russian university. But we never met; our paths never crossed. It was clearly not fated to be: on every occasion I was away somewhere else on another trip.

It is also worth mentioning that it was Ekman who inspired the television series *Lie to Me*. He was one of the scientific consultants for the show, and the main character, Dr Cal Lightman, as portrayed by Tim Roth, was based on him.

For a whole series of reasons, I arrived in San Francisco well ahead of time. First of all, I had to spend some time at the university library and familiarize myself with the latest research. There were other reasons, however: Soviet intelligence had required me to make this trip. I was not told the details beforehand. I was simply instructed to visit our consulate, where everything would be explained.

I must confess, I was lucky with my accommodation. I was lodged on the university campus near Golden Gate Park. Ever since I was a young man I have been fond of jogging, and every day I have run ten kilometers regardless of the weather, the time zone, the winds, or the mood of the place. I have gone running in all kinds of places over the years: in cities large and small, on faraway military bases, in forests, tundra, deserts, and mountains. In my work I have sometimes had to make long journeys by sea, to sail around the world, and so I would simply go for runs along the waterfronts of foreign ports, or at sea I would run my usual distance around the deck of the ship.

Thus it was glorious indeed to go for a run early in the morning in such a fabulous park. Golden Gate Park spans five kilometers from east to west. One suddenly arrives right at the shore, the wide and sandy Ocean Beach from which the open sea stretches to the horizon. The Pacific extends as far as the eye can see, and I thought of how one could sail the thousands of nautical miles to Asia without ever once encountering land.

A person can easily get out of shape on business trips, but in San Francisco I visited the swimming pool, where I would swim my usual distance of one and a half kilometers, and I also went to the university's gym where I lifted weights, hit a punching bag, jumped rope, or even entered the ring to spar with the local boxers, as I had grown used to doing at Division X.

In Golden Gate Park one is naturally drawn to reflect, to contemplate life at one's leisure. Sometimes, once in a while when I felt the need to, I would walk through the park in order to dive into its extraordinary silence. Here, far away from the hustle and bustle, I could reflect on the flow of time, try to grasp the hidden background of events, their underlying essence. The dense and secluded vegetation, the long chain of ponds, the green hills, the waterfalls and the grass all contributed to allowing me to think deeply. Once must admit that nature cleanses our minds, it takes us out of the everyday grind.

From Parnassus Avenue I would usually cross the entire park from south to north and go toward the Conservatory of Flowers, a large orangery built from white stone in a nostalgic Victorian style. If one wanted, one could look at all manner of flowers, too many to count. I was in nirvana in the Japanese Tea Garden, with its pagoda, mossy rocks, a bronze Buddha, humpback bridges of cut stone, and wonderful little houses for the tea ceremony. The place plunged me into a drowsy contemplation from which I did not want to emerge. Past the rock garden and the Temple of Music, where orchestras play in the evenings, past the Shakespeare Garden on Martin Luther King Jr Drive, past the pasture where American bison sleepily graze, I would finally arrive at the gigantic windmills that cut across the sky, like an imported slice of Dutch countryside. The mercurial scenery in the park was like a colorful planet in itself, where different nations and tribes were doomed to live side by side. Finally, the tulip garden was a comforting sight and boasted countless distinct shades, too many to find a name for all of them.

In spite of these musings, I also had to think about my mission here. The Soviet consulate was located at the top of Russian Hill in the city center, at the intersection of Green Street and Baker Street. The monumental six-story building, built of apricot-colored brick, towered, like a skyscraper, over colorful little single-family homes in a quaint Victorian style with mezzanines, bay windows, turrets, garrets, decorative balconies, and porches, all of which brought back sweet memories of a long-ago time. The consulate's façade had a marble veneer at the first floor and the building's flat roof featured add-on brick structures and antennas. An ample area around the building was girded by a metal grill fence, and security guards patrolled the perimeter to ensure that no intruders entered.

As Green Street descends Russian Hill, it runs for a long distance east toward downtown and Pier 15 at Fisherman's Wharf, while Baker Street runs down the north slope toward Marina Boulevard and the Yacht Harbor.

Enough digression. One day, as the consulate's security guard was making a routine check of the grounds, he noticed an envelope lying on the grass inside the fence. Inside the envelope was a handwritten note. Someone had flung the envelope over the fence while walking down the sidewalk past the consulate. Or perhaps the person had just quickly stuck a hand through the fence and dropped the envelope. The note's author offered valuable information and long-term collaboration. This naturally piqued the interest of Soviet intelligence, as one never knew where such an offer might lead and more information was always welcome.

Yet Soviet intelligence obviously had to be careful. They held their horses, afraid that someone might be luring them into a trap; the risk was real. The aspiring source, too, had behaved in a very deliberate and cautious manner. The note contained no details, not even the slightest hint as to his or her job, their reason for establishing contact, what the source was, or what Soviet intelligence might gain from the collaboration. The note had been written in such a way that even the author's sex was impossible to determine. The human population, as everyone knows, consists of men and women. In the event that the source's attempt to contact Soviet intelligence was discovered, knowing the person's sex would allow American investigators to reduce the number of suspects by 50%. The handwriting also gave no clue as to the author's identity; the note had been carefully written in block letters using a ruler. No individual handwriting features remained, and had this miserly missive come into the wrong person's hands, they might as well have tried to catch the wind: the author could not have been traced for love nor money.

In any event, the source said that if there was interest on the Soviet side, then an advertisement should be placed in the *San Francisco Chronicle* seeking to purchase a St. Bernard puppy.

Publishing a classified ad was easy as pie, and shortly afterward, the consulate's security found a new note lying in the grass next to the fence. The source suggested a meeting with a trustworthy individual, though the proposed arrangements were somewhat intricate. On a set day and time each week, a representative of Soviet intelligence was to sit at a certain table of the Crab House restaurant at Pier 39, Fisherman's Wharf. The representative was to come there over the course of a month, say, each Sunday, and stay there for one hour, for example from five until six, and await contact. The source could appear on any of these Sundays, or the source might never appear at all if there was any sense of danger, or if the source changed his or her mind or felt unable to trust the Russians.

Soviet intelligence was left with no choice. By and large, the person actually running the risk is the one who decides. How could the Soviets argue with these stipulations? For their part, they had diplomatic immunity and reliable cover stories, and if the worst came to the worst an agent would simply be declared persona non grata and expelled from the country. The source, on the other hand, was facing arrest and a long prison sentence if things turned sour. Not to mention that such prudence and caution was a good sign in any source.

Just to be safe, the wife of one of our diplomats was sent to make the initial contact. Her husband, an attaché at the consulate, also tagged along and remained at a distance to ensure that no harm came to his wife. People teemed like ants at Pier 39. Innumerable tourists walked along the boardwalk over the water, admiring the sea lions who spent all day lounging there. The crowd was enjoying the cafes, shops, and souvenir stands. A long line of children with their parents stretched in front of the big yellow and blue carousel which was crowned, like a Christmas tree, with a spire atop. Even the huge metal crab sculpture guarding the entrance to the pier seemed exhausted from all the tourists posing for photos in front of it.

It was cold, but the sun shone brightly. At times gusts of wind would blow in from the bay, whipping up the waves, shaking the signboards on the pier, and setting people's scarves fluttering. According to the source's terms, the meeting was to take place on the second story of the Crab House restaurant. A steep staircase resembling a ship's gangplank led up to it. The black and white interior of the restaurant was densely packed with bare rectangular tables lacking even a tablecloth and surrounded by bentwood chairs with red wicker seating. The wide windows offered an ample view of the bay and the sailboats ploughing back and forth; of the rocky island of Alcatraz and the old fort atop it; of the neighboring piers where fishing boats moored and unmoored; and of the whole Embarcadero waterfront that ran, bow-shaped, around downtown. On the other side of the restaurant, the windows looked out onto the cliffs and hills of Sausalito and the flame-colored Golden Gate Bridge which stood where sea gave way to sky.

So that the time was not completely wasted, the attaché's wife ordered the restaurant's house special, California-style clam chowder. The clams were cooked in milk with onion, potato, parsley, and celery. This hot, thick concoction was then served in a bread bowl. Americans and Europeans typically leave the bread bowl on the table after draining the soup, but visitors from Russia prefer to tear apart the empty bowl, now richly imbued with the flavor of the soup, and eat it too.

Finishing an entire serving of clam chowder is often beyond the power of a single individual, but Russians can manage it. The Soviet representative, in spite of the fact that she was a diplomat's wife, showed that she was up to the task, though it did take her the entire hour that had been appointed for making contact. She was so absorbed in this delightful soup that the hour simply flew by – a productive use of the time. She had probably forgotten all about the task she had been sent to perform. Who could maintain an interest in espionage, secret agents, and spycraft, when soup this good was on offer?

The source did not come at the first appointed time. Although the Soviet representative had a full belly, she left with nothing else to show for her waiting. Her husband observed her from a distance, but came no closer in case they were under surveillance. American law enforcement knew all the Soviet consulate staff's faces, so why do anything unusual and attract their attention?

Over the course of a month, the attaché's wife made four visits to Crab House at Pier 39, every week ordering her favorite dish, but the source never showed up, as if he was playing a game whose sole purpose was introducing Soviet intelligence to the restaurant's cuisine.

It appeared that no progress was being made, though the diplomat's wife was soon considered a loyal customer – on her third visit she was even given a discount. She noticed other regular customers of Crab House. One of them, a nondescript man with glasses, would sit next to the window at the neighboring table on the days when the attaché's wife made her visits. This other diner never seemed to notice anyone around him. He stared distractedly out of the window, looked at the ocean and, like a romantic type with his head in the clouds, he followed the fishing boats, yachts, and commercial vessels with his eyes.

To the Soviet representative's astonishment, her neighbor generally ordered Dungeness crab in garlic sauce. Daydreamer though he might be, he clearly knew about good eating, and he managed to finish his serving of crab on his own, without help. In spite of the huge servings that this regular consumer downed, he remained a pale and skinny guy – the lavish food seemed to be wasted on him. In general, he was not a naturally attractive person: the diplomat's wife noticed that he had a nervous facial tick, and he would grimace involuntarily and fidget painfully in his chair, often shaking his leg under the table as people ill at ease and lacking confidence tend to do.

In short, he was a sickly man, and off-putting. So she did not look at him and tried not to notice him. After all, there are all sorts of people out in the world, wasting their lives away and then presenting us with the bill. A countless multitude of terminally ill, poor, and mentally disabled people.

The attaché's wife simply ate her clam chowder slowly and with relish. Her husband sat nursing a cocktail at a table at the other end of the restaurant. He kept an eye on the entrance and examined each person who stepped over the threshold. From time to time he and his wife cast a glance across the entire place, and with their facial expressions they signaled that they were simply resigned to the circumstances. There was nothing to do but wait.

Eventually, however, the span of time set for making contact, one month, reached its end. The last hour of the last day went past without anyone showing up. Soviet intelligence did not mourn, tear their hair out, or sprinkle their heads with ashes, though it was of course a pity that things had not worked out.

In spite of their high hopes being dashed, the sun still shone, and a rich scent of herbs and fine cooking still came from the restaurant's kitchen. At the nearby and more distant piers alike, boats still moored and unmoored, yachts sailed across the bay, throngs of people enjoyed Pier 39. The sky did not fall, the end of the world did not come, mankind successfully continued to grow and remained on the path of progress.

When the attaché seated at the distant table saw that time was up, he picked up his cocktail and walked over to his wife. "Disappointed?" he asked, laughing, and then he grandiloquently quoted Pushkin, "'Bliss was so near, so altogether attainable!'"

"He never showed," his wife said dryly.

"I know how you feel. You waited, but alas, the meeting never happened. That's how things are sometimes."

"Maybe he might still show up?" his wife asked.

"I don't think so. He must have changed his mind. He got scared, or something happened to him. Let me just try some of your soup, at least." The attaché took the spoon from her and scooped some of the clam chowder from the bread bowl, then nodded approvingly. "It's good. You're lucky it goes on your expense account. Don't forget to keep a copy of the receipt so that you can give it to the accountant."

They spoke in Russian, and it seemed that no one else in the restaurant was concerned with them. The random visitors and regular customers, aficionados of crab dishes, were absorbed in their own tasks. Husband and wife paid the bill and were getting ready to leave when an unfamiliar voice called out:

"Excuse me, but are you looking to buy a St. Bernard puppy?"

Goodness, how they froze from the unexpectedness of it. It was the skinny man in glasses with the nervous tic who had called them. On every one of these days he had sat inconspicuously by the window, grimacing and looking distractedly out on the bay. He had not seemed to notice anything around him; he had paid the others in the restaurant no attention. He was aloof from everything else that was going on, as impassive as an item of furniture, and other people's gazes swept past him as if he were mere empty space.

Frankly speaking, we tend to avoid looking at the disabled out of embarrassment. And what kind of a secret source could he be, with his twitching lips, wild facial expressions, his leg shaking uncontrollably under the table? He grinned like a fool and muttered to himself, seemingly far away from the reality around him.

Even the attaché, who was a calm and composed man, was dumbstruck. "Yes, we want to buy. We have dreamed of a St. Bernard for a long time," he finally said after a long silence. The husband and wife, still feeling somewhat at a loss, went over to sit at the sick man's table. They could not conceal their utter astonishment and they hid their eyes from embarrassment.

"Why didn't you introduce yourself?" the attaché's wife reproached the man. "I waited and waited, but you were sitting here next to me the whole time."

"I was keeping an eye out," he said curtly. One could not argue with that. The source would reveal himself when he saw fit.

To start with, and to pique Soviet intelligence's interest, Anthony provided details of American ships' port rotation and the movements of aircraft carriers. He said that three aircraft carriers would soon arrive at Hunters Point, the naval base in southeast San Francisco, for fuel replenishment and repair.

The source made a wide gesture. "There, that's my gift to Soviet intelligence."

"Thank you very much," the attaché said courteously. "Now we must wait to confirm the information."

"I guarantee it," the new agent assured him. "You'll see for yourselves within a month."

His information was of interest, and Soviet intelligence would next have to determine how reliable it was. The attaché, though, already sensed that things would work out. "Thank you for taking the initiative. I hope that our collaboration will be of mutual benefit," he said solemnly and with as much sincerity as he could muster. He then went on to add, more simply, "We work on trust. For now we'll make an oral, gentleman's agreement. A preliminary one, you might say. We will do the formalities later."

The source nodded. "Of course, of course, I understand," he said, but it was clear that he was feeling anxious. His eye was twitching and his hands shaking; what doctors would call a tremor. His lips were twisted in a grimace, his facial features distorted.

It was understandable, though. It is not every day that a person enters one of the world's best intelligence services. An invisible fanfare sounded at this new arrival, drums beat, an honor guard marched. Still, it would still be some time before the man was officially enrolled. First, a thorough check had to be carried out.

"Tell us, Anthony, what led you to join our ranks?" the attaché asked nonchalantly, but he was in fact paying close attention to the answer. In spycraft it is extremely important to know the reason why a person would take such a step. Intelligence services really prefer adherents of a certain ideology. Those kind of people work selflessly; they are eager to join the fray of their own accord, and it is easier to establish a relationship with them, you do not have to goad them on.

As Anthony thought his answer over, he became visibly more uneasy, and his tremor grew stronger. He perhaps wished to conceal his reasons and was hesitating, but eventually he waved his hand as if to signal that he might as well say it. "They didn't appreciate me at all," he said bitterly.

In a nervous and halting account, and with a great deal of resentment, he told them how, after graduating from the Naval Academy in Annapolis, Maryland, he had served in San Diego as an analyst for the Pacific Fleet. Things had not gone well for him there, and he had been transferred to Naval Base Coronado to serve as a supply officer. Coronado is infamous in America for its high cost of living, and in turn, the amphibious installation there is famous for its detachment of Seabees, a naval construction battalion. An aerial view reveals that the barracks on the base were built in the shape of a swastika, and many have speculated about who played this trick on the US Navy and why.

The source had served without distinction at Coronado. For him this was misery, not service. He showed no zeal or enthusiasm for his work. How could a person possibly be enthusiastic about a supply post in a backwater? Anthony had tried simply to kill time, and eventually his superiors too wanted to get rid of him, or at least move him out of their sight. Now he had recently been transferred to the Hunters Point Naval Shipyard, a facility on the verge of being shut down. Drydocks were located at this shipyard for maintaining the fleet.

"I'm a naval officer. I graduated from the academy. I could have sailed the world, and they sent me to the goddamn sticks!" Anthony was so wounded that he was nearly in tears. He scowled and gritted his teeth. "Because of them, my wife left me! She thought I was a loser. She said that she didn't want to rot out here, that she deserves better. Don't I deserve better, too?!" He asserted this in a raised voice and stared intently across the table, waiting for recognition.

"You do deserve better, Anthony, you do," the attaché reassured him.

Anthony's eyes suddenly blazed with an infernal light. "But I'll show them!" He slammed his hand down on the table, which drew the attention of the other diners, some of whom turned to look at him. "They'll regret this! I could have had a shining career, but they just threw me out with the trash!"

In a voice that ranged from a shout to a whisper, Anthony claimed that he had been the best student in the academy. He had excelled in every subject, had his pick of the girls, and played football on the academy's team and broke all kinds of records. Who knows whether he was lying or not, or whether he was instead indulging in a fantasy in which he had come to believe himself. He longed to get even with those who had offended him; he threatened that he would have his cruel revenge. Resentment, jealousy, dissatisfaction and a thirst for revenge are common factors that push people to spy for a foreign country. Essentially, this man had already been recruited without Soviet intelligence having to make an effort. By and large, the attaché was pleased, yet he was also taken aback by how difficult it was to calm the bespectacled man down. Anthony was still eager to prove how smart and talented he was, and how much his colleagues, his ex-wife, and the United States Navy would lose without him. It was no easy task for the attaché and his wife to take their leave of him. He seemed in no hurry to leave, and he even suggested that they get a drink and toast their new friendship and drink to the success of their joint enterprise.

"Poor thing," the diplomat's wife said, when she and her husband had finally managed to leave Pier 39. She felt truly sorry for the new agent. "I'm worried that he drinks like a fish."

"That may well be," her husband agreed. "People like him are dangerous. They can bring a lot of problems. Unreliable assets. We ought to examine him, get him to a doctor. Is he really fit to work for us? He might be nothing but trouble."

Some time later, three aircraft carriers entered port at Hunters Point, confirming the man's information. And soon I myself arrived for the conference at the University of California San Francisco. Soviet intelligence made use of the occasion and asked me to assist them.

═══ **40** ═══

Shortly before my flight to San Francisco I met, as I indicated, with Olga Shilina, Nikolai's mother. We met on the Arbat on one windless morning in early winter. It was a weekday, but I took a day off from my duties at Division X. I had fallen asleep in fall and when I woke up it was already winter: the first snow had fallen that night. That morning I took the commuter train into Moscow and found that the snow was already melting in the streets, but a sprinkling of powder remained in the squares, on the hedges, and in the courtyards of the Arbat where the trees, which had still not dropped all their leaves, seemed to have blossomed lushly overnight, so strewn were they with snowflakes. Moist, loose snow covered the roofs and ledges of the buildings, the windowsills, benches, and trashcans. Any footprint left in the snow immediately filled with meltwater.

It was warm and cozy in the little cafe on the Arbat. Soft music came from a cassette player on the counter. Amid the calm and cleanliness of the place there was an aroma of strong coffee, pastries, and vanilla. One would be hard pressed to come up with a better meeting point here at the end of fall and beginning of winter. The vague silhouettes of passersby slid along the windows facing out onto the Arbat.

I chose a table, made my order, and then stepped outside into the street to meet Olga. She soon appeared. I saw her while she was still far off, but I could not believe my eyes. The person coming toward me down the street seemed to be a young woman: there was a spring in her step, her hair was cut short, and she had a slender figure. There was something implausible about it. Perhaps she was among those rare women for whom age is just a number and who continue to attract men's attention everywhere and always.

Frankly, one might have thought her a witch, a sorceress, an enchantress who knew the secret to everlasting youth. Some people indeed possess a magical potion that stops the passage of time or even reverses it. It was impossible to believe that her son was already nearing forty.

As she approached, I looked at her with incredulity. I even suddenly wondered if she had sent another woman in her stead. If I had not been familiar with all the details, I would have assumed that someone was playing a trick on me. One could take this woman for one of her son's girlfriends. I imagined how confused others must be when Nikolai addressed Olga in public by saying, "Mom…"

We met there on the corner in front of the entrance to the cafe. I offered her breakfast, but she was content with a cup of tea. She clearly maintained a strict regimen and did not allow herself to over-indulge in eating. So now here we were at a small table for two near the window, with its fogged glass on which we witnessed a shadow play of passersby on the Arbat.

She paid no attention to my compliments on her preternaturally youthful appearance, and simply said calmly, "You wanted to see me? I'm listening."

"Poltava," I blurted out, like a psychiatrist stating a word to hear what association his patient has with it.

"I don't follow," she replied, completely unperturbed.

"Poltava," I insistently repeated.

"That's a town in Ukraine." She honored me with a condescending smile.

"That's right," I replied, and then I tried a new tack. "Now let's try a rather odd word: ABON."

She maintained her self-control, but not enough to conceal her unease. Her face briefly showed discomfort, there was a flash of fear in her eyes, but then she immediately regained her composure.

"What does that mean?" She shrugged and feigned boredom, but she was slightly exaggerating.

"ABON, *aviatsionnaya baza osobogo naznacheniya*." Specially Designated Air-Force Base. I carefully recited each word. "If you'd like the number, I can tell you that, too. ABON 169."

"And what else?" she asked coldly, though I could see how she tensed, as if preparing herself to strike back at me.

"1944, June," I said coyly, but she remained silent and feigned a dispassionate indifference.

I imagined how the interpreter must have remained silent under interrogation. The investigators probably went crazy trying to get anything out of her. There was no power in this world that could compel her to speak.

"Poltava, ABON 169, June 1944, shuttle flights by American Flying Fortress bombers from the 15th Air Force." I began my story. From her expression I could guess at some inner turmoil, though she maintained a pretense of calm and annoyance at this person's pesky curiosity which was directed at her for reasons she simply could not understand.

I told her the story of the military interpreter, as I had heard it in New York from Colonel Steven Creighton. She listened attentively and did not interrupt me. At some points she had to make a great effort to hold back her tears. She never gave herself away, though, I must give her that, and were I not a doctor from Division X I would hardly have been able to see through her.

"Nice story," she smiled, and that was all that the listener honored the storyteller with. "Why are you telling it to me?"

"I thought it might interest you."

"Yes, it is interesting," she said in agreement, but no more.

Frankly speaking, Olga Shilina was one of those people who could not be outwitted. But sometimes it is best to act directly and try to break straight through. I served, and the ball hit the court on her side.

"You are perfectly well aware of everything I've just told you…"

"Not at all." The ball was back on my side of the court. She shrugged wearily and asked, as if with indifference, "Why do you think so?"

"I think you know."

"You are mistaken," she assured me sincerely.

"There is more to the story. Shall I go on?"

"As you like. You decide."

"Well, I would like to go on. A military tribunal, Article 193 of the Criminal Code, paragraphs seven through ten: desertion. Shall I continue?"

Poor woman! She froze, dumbstruck, and her face turned unnaturally pale. Genuine fear showed in her eyes. It was understandable: she had for so many years had to dissemble, keep silent, conceal the facts of her life, suppress her memories and keep them locked up. Now, when it had seemed like she had succeeded and her past was behind her for good, suddenly a stranger had come along who knew her secrets.

Of course she was scared – how could she not be? She made an incredible effort to get hold of herself and quash her fear, but it proved too difficult for her. She could only say, in a voice almost too low to hear:

"Who are you? What do you want?"

I did not answer her question. Instead, I said that after the interpreter was arrested, the American copilot's plane had been shot down by the

Germans on its return journey to Italy. The crew had had to bail out, and they had been taken prisoner. The copilot included. If it had not been for her arrest, the interpreter would have perished.

"Why?" she asked, unable to follow me.

"Parachutes," I replied. "They are provided for each crew member. But what about passengers?"

"Indeed," she agreed, and then she realized that she had given herself away completely.

"So, after that, don't you think that everything that happened was for the best?" I said, gently so as not to cause her any more grief.

It was painful to look at her. She suddenly realized that her arrest had saved her from certain death. Yet I could not tell her about my trip to America and my chance meeting in the elevator. The details would have to be left out: my job required that I keep silent about these things, that I hold my tongue. I saw how Olga was suddenly full of questions – first and foremost, how had I learned about these long-ago events which she had tried to forget. She decided not to ask, however, for though the Soviet regime was now in a weak state, it was still far from collapse. Flies bite most viciously in the fall before they die. Thus she was afraid, if not for herself, then for her son: scandal in the family could harm him as well.

Without saying another word, I laid out the snapshots which Colonel Creighton had given me in New York. "Just in case", he had said, to help in the search. Olga spent a long time studying the photographs, each in turn. Before my very eyes, she plunged back into the past, to forty years before, as if she had entered a time machine. Now she was back there again, young, nineteen years old, and in love.

"Is he alive?" She placed the photos back on the table.

She could not keep from asking that question. Any woman who had experienced true love would ask that, and one did not have to be a doctor at Division X to understand. All these years she had been tormented by this very question, it had eaten her alive, and the very second she was given the chance to ask, she did so. Who could blame her?

I nodded. "He's alive. I got these photos from him."

"They took mine away from me when I was arrested," she said haltingly, as if still uncertain as to whether she should talk about the matter.

I told her how after the war, the American had continued to serve in the army, and he had fought in Korea and Vietnam. He had risen to the rank of colonel, and then retired, and he now lived in San Francisco. He had two children from different marriages, a son and a daughter. The son was a military pilot who served on Hokkaido in Japan. Finally, I said that Steven Creighton had spent many years looking for her, but in vain. He was not even aware that he had a son in Russia.

Olga was quiet for a long time. It was obvious that this was difficult for her. She hesitated and wrestled with doubt. Hidden thoughts flickered across her face like the silhouettes of the passersby outside the cafe window.

"I'm still here," I reminded her of my presence. "What do you think? If I ever happen to run into him, what should I do?"

She shrugged. "Why ask me?"

"I'd like to know your opinion."

"How kind of you." She again smiled condescendingly, the way an adult smiles to a capricious child. "But if you ask me, it's best just to let everything be."

"Really? Would it not be natural to write to each other, meet…"

"Why?" she asked, as if of the two of us, she were the reasonable one. The question cut as precisely as a scalpel, but we are all wary of the surgeon's diagnosis.

"Your son has a right to know his father."

"Unfortunately, we live in a country where relationships like that can only harm him."

She trusted no one, and I could understand her. The authorities constantly treated the population in such a way that no one trusted anyone else, everyone was afraid of everyone else. What then – should she write a letter and spend the rest of her life dealing with the consequences? I could not deny that the woman was right: this is how being wise is different from merely being smart: a wise person will not even get into a situation that a smart person could find a decent way out of.

It was clear that if an American colonel suddenly appeared in a Soviet fighter pilot's family tree, the regime would inevitably take action; the relationship might lead to the Shilins being accused of fraternizing with the enemy. At this time, there was not so much as a hint that changes were on the way, that the Soviet regime would eventually collapse overnight, like a rotten tree in stormy weather.

However, that strange meeting over tea on the Arbat was useful for at least something: I knew what I should tell Colonel Creighton when I next saw him. Let sleeping dogs lie. I doubted that this answer would make him happy, but what was to be done? We are all doomed to suffer losses throughout our lives, even if other people do not mean it to happen.

It was nearly midday now, and all the remaining tables in the cafe had been taken. In the cramped space a hubbub hung over the tables and the windows had fogged up from the breath of so many people.

We walked outside onto the Arbat. I undertook to see her home. At the corner, we turned onto Starokonyushenny Lane. It had grown warmer outside, the snow had melted, and soon we came to an old Arbat courtyard, which looked like a small walled city-state of its own. Olga seemed completely at ease, and did not give herself away. Perhaps she was thinking about how she could test my knowledge; she might have come without any particular aim, out of habit, or driven by a secret yearning for consolation. There are places on earth where a person can draw new strength and be convinced that he or she had done the right thing.

The interpreter looked at the courtyard with interest, her gaze running over the windows and trees which seemed to bloom with snow. She was no longer here next to me; her mind was roaming far off, back in another time. I could tell that she was wandering now through the past.

The snowy courtyard was dotted with footprints. Children in bright colored jackets and overalls were marching submissively under the watchful eye of a fat, stern-voiced woman. Like a sergeant major, she had mustered the children into line and set them marching, and was issuing orders. Her voice thundered across the entire courtyard like the sound of a martial trumpet.

We walked past her, and it grew quiet behind us. This stillness seemed to bat against our ears: in an Arbat courtyard one enjoys a rare peace amid the noise of the world, like being high up in the mountains. In this capacious stillness, a piteous voice suddenly addressed us:

"Olga, is that you?"

I turned to see where the question had come from. Making her way toward us, pitching awkwardly from side to side in her old-fashioned rubber boots, was the trumpet-voiced old woman. As she approached, she looked at us beseechingly, as if afraid that we might drive her away.

"Olga, is that you?" the old woman repeated. The timidity she now displayed was strange; it was not clear where that sweet voice, akin to a steamboat's horn, had gone.

The pilot's mother did not reply, but she slowed and turned around. She looked at the old woman silently, and waited expressionlessly.

The old woman did not even wait for a reply. She saw Olga's face and was bemused. "Oh, I'm sorry," she said. "I thought... You come here sometimes. I had a friend once, you look a lot like her. True, that was forty years ago… you're much younger… Though some people don't show their age…" She said this haltingly, staring Olga right in the face, and then she asked timidly and uncertainly, for the third time, "Is it you, Olga? If it is, then forgive me. I wasn't thinking, I didn't want… I thought I was saving you. How could I have known what would happen? They promised me it wouldn't be like that. They tricked me… I didn't know you'd go to prison. So many years have passed and I still feel bad about it. I've regretted it all this time. I want to… Just please forgive me, if you can… But tell me, is it really you?"

"You are mistaken," the interpreter answered coolly. Her face was remarkably calm and composed, without the slightest trace of hesitation, regret, or hope.

It was clear that the old woman's memories had eaten at her. Olga walked on and the old woman, unhappy and ill at ease, stared at her as she went. One might have thought that the old woman was watching to see how Olga's small footprints in the wet snow would fill with melted water.

The old woman went miserably back the way she had come from. She moved with difficulty, as if the exchange had drained her last strength. She hobbled in the rubber boots so identified with elderly people. "Farewell, youth", they were nicknamed. The rubber boots aside, she was already well aware that her youth was now far behind her, and she could no longer hope for any positive change. The woman whom she had recognized, on the other hand, was walking comfortably further and further away, comfortably and easily storing in her memory the melted snow, the courtyard, the old house, her memories, and a fragile and timid hope, which, in spite of everything, was faintly glimmering before her.

What can I say? I was sorry. I thought I had come up with a clever way to make everyone happy, but my idea had collapsed in the blink of an eye; the soil had proved unsuitable for it. You cannot build a solid structure on mere assumptions, on hope, and without first making careful calculations; you cannot build on sand.

Naturally, I said nothing to Nikolai Shilin about my meeting with his mother. She did not give me permission to do so, and I am not accustomed to flaunting another's prohibition – my work had taught me that. It was a pity that I now had to travel to San Francisco. I had dreamed of meeting with Colonel Creighton and (I won't lie) bringing him good news, and I had been looking forward to the feeling of self-satisfaction that everything had worked out.

═══ 41 ═══

One evening Colonel Creighton invited me over. We sat at the counter dividing the kitchen from the dining room. The overhead lights were off, the counter lit instead by lamps with colored lampshades on long ropes that hung down from the ceiling. On the way from the city to Menlo Park, the colonel had stopped to buy some of the huge Pacific Ocean crabs that the locals called Dungeness. Now we were engaged in something that would baffle any onlookers: after wrapping the crabs tightly in a white cloth, we were mercilessly beating them with wooden mallets on the marble countertop. What we were doing was quite simple: we had to separate the delicious crab meat from the hard shell.

We accompanied the crabs, I concede, with a Californian white wine: Creighton's wine cellar boasted a rich collection. While we were still sober, we avoided raising any sad topics, but after the third bottle an inevitable melancholy and self-pity set in.

"It was so strange, the way we met," Colonel Creighton suddenly said. "Everyone might have still been saved back then."

"I don't think so," I replied. "We did the best we could."

"Are you trying to say they were all doomed?"

"That may well be."

"Did you know beforehand that the plane would be shot down?"

"Steve, you must be kidding! I had no idea!"

"But the whole thing was a set up."

"It was your side that set it all up. American intelligence, the NSA. They probably assumed they couldn't lose. If the plane passed over Kamchatka and Sakhalin Island, they could get all our codes and radar frequencies. It takes a long time, and a lot of work, to change them. If the plane was shot down, then we'd look like murderers to the whole world. The Evil Empire. No matter how things turned out, the USA would benefit. We were set up, and sadly we fell for it, we acted like idiots. The passengers were just a bargaining chip in all this."

"Did you really know nothing of what would happen?" the colonel asked me mistrustfully. "You were so insistent that I shouldn't get on that plane."

"As a doctor, I've studied intuition. It's one of the things I have researched. According to our statistics, a third of all airplane passengers can foresee catastrophe."

"I still feel bad. Everyone else died, but Michael and I were saved."

"That's not your fault. First of all, Michael was running late and he had the tickets. If he hadn't arrived late, you would have both got on the plane. Secondly, we tried to warn the Koreans, but they didn't want to listen to us. How could we have proved it to them?"

"Still, I feel like I could have saved them and I didn't. I just abandoned ship and let everyone else drown. But how could they shoot down an airliner?"

"Our people didn't know it was an airliner. They couldn't determine what it was. They thought it was a spy plane, like it always is. American spy planes fly in that area all the time. But it was your electronic surveillance who were responsible for this operation, like I told you. It was their doing, they planned everything."

"Who knows. But that doesn't make it any easier. People died."

"I warned you. None of you believed me."

"But how could we have believed a thing like that? When we heard the news, we were all shocked, my son and daughter and I. We figured you must have known it would happen."

"I was afraid you'd think that. But it's always like that: at first people don't believe what they're being told, then they claim the guy must have known in advance. But I didn't know, I didn't! Think about it: what could I have known? That the Korean plane would go five hundred kilometers off course? Who could have known that, besides the people who sent it?"

"Our boys deny it."

"Did you expect them to admit it? Let's assume they didn't send it that way deliberately. Let's just assume, though I don't believe it. They knew the plane was in danger, and they could have warned the crew, they could have contacted Soviet air defense to alert us, to tell us that we shouldn't harm the plane, that it had just gone off course, nothing more. But they didn't get in touch with the plane or with us. They didn't warn anyone. They kept quiet and waited to see what would happen. Personally, I'm convinced that American intelligence planned the whole thing. Unfortunately, we went for the bait. Those poor passengers…"

   

What could he say to that? A palpable sadness hung over us in the semi-darkness, and we were wrapped in a mournful stillness as in a cloud. We relived again those terrible minutes, for the umpteenth time, and we thought of how the passengers on Korean Airlines Flight 007, numb with fear, had looked death in the eye and said farewell to life.

We had been talking now for some time, but the colonel had not said a word about the request he had made of me when we met in New York. He was clearly anxious about it, afraid of being met with a refusal, of being stripped of all hope.

This old soldier, who had seen so many wars, who had put his life on the line and flirted with death on many occasions, was now afraid to ask, even to bring the matter up – he was simply scared. It is true, though, that for many people it would be better not to know anything than to hear bad news. Even Shakespeare had written on the subject. I myself was wrestling with the question of whether I should say anything, or if it would be better for me to keep silent. Who knows, perhaps the wisest position was the interpreter's, when she said that we should just let everything be.

"By the way," I said, breaking the prolonged silence, "I did look into… the thing you asked me."

"Really?!" the colonel jumped up. "God, I was afraid to even ask! Did you find her?"

"Yes, I did."

"And she's alive?!" The colonel seemed ready to ask a flood of questions, but for the moment he held his tongue and stared at me, awaiting my answer. His lips were tightly pressed together, his gaze remained fixed on me, and his expression was tense.

"She's alive," I answered.

The colonel sighed in relief. "Thank you! You can't imagine how much you've done for me!" The tension in his face gave way, his anxiety gradually abated, and he cheered up. "How is she?"

"She has had a difficult life. After her arrest she spent ten years in prison."

"Oh, Good Lord. That's inhuman! Why?"

"Desertion. Those were the laws in wartime."

I told Colonel Creighton a story about inhumanity that I had heard from an eyewitness, an army officer and commander of an artillery unit. Soviet troops were already advancing into Europe when Marshal Zhukov, the commander on the front, drove with his bodyguards and staff officers past a field hospital. On that day, Soviet forces had launched a head-on attack, sending in wave after wave of men, and the losses they had suffered were enormous. Marshal Zhukov, however, never thought about losses at all. The great commander had no sympathy for his men; human lives meant nothing to him.

Wounded men were constantly arriving at the field hospital. The hospital yard was packed with stretchers. The surgeons worked non-stop, day and night, without leaving their operating tables, but still they could not cope with the influx.

When Marshal Zhukov saw the wounded men lying on stretchers outside the hospital, he became furious and flew into an unfeigned rage. Then he announced that he would return in three hours, and if they had not operated on every single man by then, if a single stretcher remained there outside the hospital, he would have the director of the hospital shot.

The frontline commander, just as he had said, returned after three hours. By that time, nearly all the wounded had already been treated, but a few men with light injuries were still in the yard waiting their turn. When Zhukov saw them, he darkened and demanded to know why his order had not been carried out. A medical officer explained to the marshal that everyone had in fact already been operated on, but new patients had arrived in the meantime, and were constantly being admitted for their operations. Zhukov ordered that the hospital's director be brought to him, but the medical officer replied that that was not possible, as the hospital director was presently operating on a patient; in fact she had already been working for two days without a break.

"She's operating on the men with the most serious wounds, and she's been able to save a lot of them," the medical officer explained.

"She?" Marshal Zhukov scowled, and raised his eyebrows.

To his astonishment, the director of the hospital turned out to be a gentle woman, a famous Moscow surgeon, a colonel in the army, a professor, and a world-recognized expert in field surgery. She was idolized by the doctors she had trained, as well as by the patients whose lives she had saved. Some staff officers even felt emboldened to tell the marshal that the army was lucky to have such a prominent expert working there on the front, that they were fortunate to have doctors like that.

"Everyone here practically worships her," the medical officer said, and he mentioned again that the professor was presently in the operating room and could not leave her patient.

Zhukov went on scowling, and chewed his lips. His heavy jaw testified to an iron will, his imposing figure reflected his unbending character.

"I see," he nodded as if he had understood and was in full agreement, but then he went on to add, "Have her shot when she is finished with the operation."

Zhukov's retinue knew of course what kind of man the marshal was, but they still were shocked, utterly dumbstruck. They initially assumed that they had misheard his remark, that they had misunderstood him. The marshal cast a disdainful glance at his men, then turned around and curtly said over his shoulder, "My order remains unchanged."

As I told this story, Colonel Creighton listened tensely, anxious to hear what happened next. "But why?!" he said. "Did they really shoot her?"

"They did. The marshal had ordered it. So, your interpreter was very lucky. For desertion in wartime, she might well have been shot."

"That's awful!" the colonel moaned, shaking his head in disbelief.

"But they wanted to spare her child."

"Child?!" The old pilot was confused, and assumed he must have misheard me.

"When they arrested her, she was pregnant. She gave birth to the child in the prison camp. Congratulations, you have a son in Russia."

The colonel, tightly gripping the countertop, shook his head in disbelief. He was already dazed from the news that I had located the interpreter, but this new development seemed to strike him dead. Imagine hearing that you have a son you have never even suspected in a faraway country. The colonel was completely bowled over.

I told Colonel Creighton about his son. He listened without moving and without saying a word, and for a long time he remained silent. Then we talked, comparing where his various sons had found themselves at different times in their lives. Together, we worked out that both Michael and Nikolai had served in assignments near to each other at the same time. Blind fate could well have brought them together in the skies at some point.

"How awful," Colonel Creighton said dispiritedly. "They could have got into a fight. What a crazy coincidence. Can you imagine?"

"Yes, fate divided two brothers on either side of a border. That's not the worst thing, though."

"What could be worse?" the colonel asked with bitterness in his voice.

"Imagine you and your younger son flying on that Korean plane. And your elder son receiving an order to shoot the plane down, and then carrying the order out."

The colonel nodded in dismay. I could see that he was imagining the scenario in his head, and it was an utterly bleak one. May they be cursed, those who doom innocent people to die, those who encourage and show indulgence to murderers!

I told him the details of that first night of fall when the Korean airliner had been shot down. The colonel listened closely, sometimes asking questions. As a pilot, he knew well what was hidden behind my words, what their essence was. When he learned that Shilin had not carried out the order, he was unable to contain himself. "You know what, I'm proud of my boy!" he exclaimed. "I can imagine how difficult it must have been for him. That's real courage!"

While we were talking, Steven Creighton still found it difficult to get used to the fact that he had a grown son in Russia. "I just can't believe it, it's so crazy!" he said.

The American asked me about his Russian son, but there was nothing I could say to cheer him up: the son knew nothing about his father. "He already has many problems, even without you," I tried to explain, but this foreigner simply did not understand what life in the USSR was like.

"Are you telling me that my son doesn't even know who his father is?" Colonel Creighton asked.

"Of course. His mother hid it from everyone. From her son, too."

"Sure, but when the son grew up, she could have told him."

"But he'd have wanted to find you then."

"That would be only natural," the colonel agreed.

"That could have caused problems for him. Big problems."

"Why?"

"Politics. In the USSR we have a habit of thinking that a foreigner is always an enemy. It would be very dangerous for him to correspond with you or meet you. I know cases when people's lives have been destroyed. For a military man, it would mean the end of his career."

"What kind of foolishness is that?!" the colonel exclaimed.

"Do you think this happens only in my country? Think about the witch hunts in America. Do you remember Senator McCarthy?"

"I do."

"Even Charlie Chaplin had to leave your country. Every country has its own demons."

"Still, I'd like to write to him, to go visit him or invite him here… I could help him out financially."

How could I get through to the man about what kind of a country we Russians were living in then? This foreigner was incapable of understanding life in the USSR; it would forever be a mystery to him, and the words of another person would never convince him.

We were living behind the Iron Curtain then, behind a thick stone wall. Our huge country sometimes reminded us of a prison, or perhaps a psychiatric ward. How else could one understand the pointlessness and absurdity of life, how could one measure the thickness of the walls, the unending vigilance of our guards, the arbitrariness of our bureaucrats, the food shortages, the squalid conditions in our prisons, the overwhelming hopelessness, the despair, poverty, and unbearable anguish? How could one even begin to explain the stench and suffocation of our imprisonment? And ahead of me lay the task of pronouncing sentence on the American. I already knew that he would not believe it, he would be unable to accept it.

The colonel beat me to it, however. "Have you seen her?" he asked anxiously.

"We met before I came here."

Creighton looked at me with hope in his eyes, and waited for me to say more, but what could I tell him? While I hesitated, the colonel looked at me impatiently; it was obviously that he felt like shaking the news out of me.

At last I had to tell him the pure and simple truth. "Just let everything be," I said.

"What?!" the American was taken aback, sure that I was mistaken, that I had got something wrong. He frowned, and said with some annoyance, "What did you say to me?"

"Just let everything be."

"But how…?" He was unable to believe it. He scowled, looking at me in disbelief and with furrowed brow, and then stared distractedly around. "Did she tell you that herself?"

"Those were her words."

"I want to see my son!" the colonel raised his voice. "Who can stop me from doing that?"

"You must accept that she is afraid. Afraid for her son, first of all."

"I don't want to accept it," the American leaped to his feet. "I want to see them! Him! Her!"

"Just be happy that they're alive out there. You've found them, after all. You might never have found them. You might never have known anything about them. If you and I had not met like that in the elevator…" But I did not manage to complete the sentence before he interrupted me.

"But now I find them and then immediately lose them? That's unfair!"

"You can't imagine what she's been through."

"Yes I can. I was a prisoner once, too. The Germans kept us in a POW camp until the end of the war."

"She's scared. Scared that she might cause problems for her son."

"My son has a right to know his father!" the colonel insisted. "He might refuse to have anything to do with me, but let him say it, him alone. Let him decide!"

The poor American! I could understand what he was going through, but what could I do to help him? We were fated to be born as the people we were; it is difficult to deny the whims of chance.

Steven Creighton had no intention of acquiescing. He was unable simply to leave everything alone, otherwise he would not have been an American. In the New World it was ordained from the very first years of colonization that only the strongest and most determined would survive; natural selection had forged the colonel's nation. Indomitability was Americans' foremost trait; it was in their blood to fight. Steven Creighton insisted that I step into his office, where I saw on the wall the old snapshots, blown up to portrait-size: himself and her, together and separate, smiling, young, happy, still unaware of what lay ahead of them, still unfamiliar with what it was like to lose someone or something, and confident that things would work out for them.

"Look here," the colonel indicated the photographs. "I've been looking for her all these years. I've written so many requests. Now, with your help, I've found her. And now what? Are you going to destroy all hope?"

"You must be patient," I replied. That was the only advice I could give him. "Time will put everything in its right place."

"But what, no addresses, no telephone numbers, nothing?" the colonel asked.

I only shrugged and said nothing.

"But what if we have to get in touch urgently, find something out? Get hold of medicine, say…"

There was no way I could give the man hope. I could not even provide him with my own address or telephone number; I was working at Division X, after all. Nevertheless, I felt sorry for the American and I could not leave him in such a miserable state. It is difficult, if not impossible, to live without hope.

"Perhaps later. With time, I hope, things might change," I said to cheer him up. "I know how to find you."

   

"What might change?" he asked bitterly. "It might be too late then."

All of us were hoping for change, though no one knew when change might come or where it might lead us. Many did have hope, though, and some believed firmly that things would eventually change, though hardly anyone thought that the regime and the Party would collapse overnight, crumble into dust.

"This is awful," the colonel said bitterly, and then sighed heavily. "You find out you have a grown-up son out there, and that you won't ever be able to see him. How can I go on like this?"

January in San Francisco was like Indian summer in Moscow: warm, sunny days, but a sun that shone only somewhat timidly. There was a transparent stillness, and from the sycamore and pine-covered hills the inlets and bays opened out, and the picturesque blur of the distant shore, and the boundless, light expanse of the ocean.

Some days we made plans in advance, and the colonel would come for me in his car. He would show me the city and its surroundings, the famous bridges, piers, museums, and old forts. Sometimes we took the ferry to the quiet green areas outside the city, and sailed among the white, slow-moving yachts and the faster, multi-colored speedboats trailing their foam wakes behind them.

From time to time, ocean liners would soundlessly slip through the water, so big it seemed that a whole city was sailing by, maybe a city journeying from far away, or maybe the city of San Francisco itself, on a journey to visit someone in a distant land.

The city was a paradise, a dream made reality. Wherever you looked, people seemed to live content and untroubled lives. I would look around and the question would come into my mind as to why fortune had so smiled on America, while Russia was refused such blessings.

At that same time, my homeland was in the grip of a hard frost and the empty shop shelves were provoking despair. Fog hung over the snowy streets, where anxious people hurried along on their business. My fellow Soviets lived half-starved lives: day and night they worried about obtaining food, and people spent most of their time standing in bread lines. As soon as night fell, the cities emptied, as if an alarm had been sounded. Only a few ghostly shadows slipped through the cold fog, prompting passersby to feel uneasy or afraid.

The feeling that some unknown danger loomed, the prospect of an unexpected misfortune or a sudden attack from on high, was the usual state of affairs in Russia. Its population was perennially beset by anxiety; people felt uneasy and constantly expected bad news. Everyone expected nothing but wars, arrests, the evil eye, currency reforms, bad harvests, natural disasters, the whims of the regime, the greed of officialdom, technological breakdowns, the evil designs of foreigners, the plotting of external enemies... No one ever felt safe, ever felt real calm, composure, or self-confidence. Life in Russia was unsteady, shaky, shorn of any kind of stability. People expected sorrow and misfortune to come at any moment, and the reality in which they lived relentlessly reminded them never to forget, never to promise anything, and simply to wait for the blows of fate.

I can sincerely attest that a calm and steady existence in Russia was a real luxury. Everyone was just waiting for the dam to burst, for the regime to go crazy, for yet another mad leader to arise, and for a brick to fall on their heads. The place to which I now had to return – to Russia, where the chief source of interest and excitement is our daily, inexhaustible anxiety. Only there, shaking with chills and fever, can we maintain a normal existence. It is no wonder that around the world, daredevils call the deadly game with a loaded revolver and one round in the chamber "Russian roulette".

Indeed, our whole lives are a game of roulette. For us Russians, peace and calm quickly grow tiresome; we get drunk on a sense of risk, and frankly life without danger is no life at all. That is the reason why I could live only in Russia, the country which teaches the rest of the world how not to live.

═══ 42 ═══

After my visit to the Soviet consulate, the careworn, anxious resident promised to set up a meeting with the would-be agent. The attaché gave me a pager so that we could keep in touch – in those days, mobile phones were still only a twinkle in someone's eye. Pagers themselves had only just appeared, and it must be said that they proved a real boon for spycraft. Back in Russia, people still did not know about pagers, but I had seen them when a ship on which I was making a round-the-world journey stopped in Singapore for refueling.

After my morning run in Golden Gate Park, the pager beeped and an anonymous message alerted me that the meeting would take place at noon, next to the right lion on the Dragon Gate. By this time I already knew my way around San Francisco. The Dragon Gate was located at the intersection of Bush Street and Grant Avenue, and it marked the entrance to Chinatown.

The gate, built from gray stone, consisted of three archways crowned with sharp green roofs in a Chinese style. The archways on either end served for pedestrians and the central opening for cars. On either side of the gate stood goggle-eyed stone lions with open maws – angry gatekeepers, watchful guards protecting the entrance to Chinatown. Behind them, Bush Street, narrow and with low buildings, proceeded steeply up the side of Russian Hill. From afar, it looked as if it was climbing toward the very heavens. Atop the roof of the highest archway, golden dragons slithered toward one another, symbols of power, kindness, and good luck.

I had just arrived at the lion on the right side of the gate and I was standing behind a lamp post when the pager suddenly announced that the meeting would take place instead at the Oriental Pearl restaurant on Clay Street, which was located along the cable-car route following Washington and California streets.

The Oriental Pearl restaurant occupied an imposing white two-story building with mighty, fortress-like walls and small windows like those from which defending archers would shoot their arrows. One might have assumed that this was no restaurant at all but rather a medieval fort capable of withstanding bombardment, attempts to storm it, and a lengthy siege. Around it rose tall old buildings, which looked as if they had stuck close to the Oriental Pearl in the hope of protection. From here Portsmouth Square was a stone's throw away – "the heart of Chinatown" is what the local Chinese called that shaded park surrounded by skyscrapers. Nearby was the Embarcadero, which stretched in a bow shape around the waterfront, and Fisherman's Wharf.

The green signs with large Chinese characters painted in white and a smaller text in English showed that I had come to the right place. However, this was not the endpoint. The pager beeped again and moved the meeting place to the Pot Sticker restaurant. Rather annoyed, I walked up the hill in search of Waverly Place, thinking about how even a lifetime would not be enough to visit the hundreds of restaurants in Chinatown.

I got lost, I must admit. The fantastical streets with two- and three-story buildings snaked up and down the hillside and were little different from what one finds in Hong Kong, Singapore, or Malaysia. Everywhere there was an explosion of colorful signs with large Chinese characters on them, and much smaller English text. Chinese paper lanterns hung on streamers over the street. Red lanterns, bright ribbons, and canvases adorned the façades of the buildings, balconies, windows, and doors. Some buildings recalled an oriental pagoda, the eaves of their roofs turned upward in the Buddhist style, and from them the sharp claws of a dragon pointed toward the sky. Everywhere I looked, there was an unbelievable number of tiny restaurants, banks, hairdressers, greengrocers, laundries, jewelry stores, and noodle stands. Here and there, in small nooks, on the porches and terraces, men played mahjong. On the well-trimmed lawns, people of various ages, but mainly the elderly, practiced tai chi.

I eventually discovered that I had been going around in circles. Waverly Place proved to be next to Clay Street and Grant Avenue. The Pot Sticker restaurant was located in a plain-looking brick building consisting of three stories and with three windows. The little, yellowish building with balconies and lovely paper lanterns at the entrance seemed to have been squeezed with difficulty into the narrow space between its neighbors, one of which was the Lucky Dragon gift shop.

To my surprise, the interior of the restaurant was lined with wood panels, over which light-colored wallpaper with a pattern of green sprigs of mint had been laid. Over the tables, copies of ancient Chinese engravings and traditional paintings hung in wooden frames: oil paintings, ink, watercolors, and gouache on rice paper, silk, and bamboo. Now the pager again sprang into life and the message was a single word: ROSES. I did not immediately get the meaning of this, but I thought about it for a while until it dawned on me. The situation was a little ridiculous, I have to say. I walked around the restaurant studying the collection of paintings, as if I were in a museum.

It would, of course, have to be the solitary diner, a man wearing glasses and seated beneath a painting depicting a rose spray freshly cut from a bush: the leaves and flowers looked like the real thing. In the left corner of the painting, Chinese characters were set in descending columns according to the old style, presumably poetry or an old adage.

The low table was inconspicuous among the mirror-faced columns reflecting the restaurant's white tablecloths, hardwood chairs with high, carved backs, the counter where the head waiter stood, the entrance, and the street outside the window.

"Are you selling a St. Bernard puppy?" I asked with a wry smile, as if we were merely engaged in make-believe, playing spies like silly children.

"I'm selling if you're buying," the diner readily answered. His facial muscles sprang to life and his expression seemed to change wildly and randomly, but the nervous twitch looked too obvious and intentional – deliberate, if not downright artificial. Although I was in no hurry to reach my conclusion about the man.

In order to avoid attracting attention by sitting there without placing an order, I asked the waiter for green tea. The teapot was delivered to the table in a colorful knitted cover, and the teapot's fine painted porcelain was a delight to behold.

"You're a doctor, I believe," said Anthony. I merely nodded, and he immediately went on, "You intend to examine me?"

"'Examine' is too much. I want to get to know you. Do you have any health problems?"

"Doctor," he said, "the thing is, I'm constantly being transferred. Like I'm some kind of slacker or moron. But in high school and at the Naval Academy, I could always figure out problems faster than anyone else. I had a great future in front of me. I could have become an admiral…" He went on to talk with great excitement about how he had been a lady killer, he could get any girl he wanted, and how his achievements in the sphere of football were still remembered at the Naval Academy. If I wanted, he could even show me newspaper clippings.

"Alright," I agreed. "I'd like to see them."

"Sure I'll show you. I just need to find them first."

One's first impression was that this man was woven together entirely out of grievances and complexes that ate at him and never gave him a moment's rest. As he went on with his monologue, he sometimes even forgot what he was talking about, and he would sit for a moment in silence and then suddenly pull himself back together, toss one topic aside, and move on to another. His thoughts rambled wildly, zig-zagging, and he was unable to stick to the point. He would often fall silent, and then perhaps mumble a few words, and his tremor would grow stronger, and his shoulders would twitch. In short, he presented a very clear clinical picture; there was no doubt about it.

As Anthony went on, he would occasionally take off his glasses and wipe them with a handkerchief. People who are used to wearing glasses usually feel less confident without them; they squint and seem a little lost, and their gaze becomes fixed on some invisible barrier. Anthony, I noticed, appeared to be strangely relieved when he took off his glasses, as if they were a burden to him. His pupils also dilated – an involuntary reaction which happens whether a person wishes it or not, and which indicates positive feelings.

The next time he took his glasses off, I casually picked them up. "Nice glasses," I complimented him, while at the same time confirming what I already suspected: the frames held ordinary glass instead of prescription lenses. One might puzzle over this, but why waste time in speculation – I could simply ask him why. I held my tongue, though, and did not show that I was concerned. I simply handed the glasses back to him, and he put them back on, though I could see that deep down he was reluctant to do so; his body resisted. The patient could not hide this dislike, and perhaps he did not even consciously notice it. This is because the autonomic nervous system is not under conscious control; the pupils contract independently. The most important thing was to notice these reactions, as they typically last for only an instant, and notice them I did, thanks to my experience at Division X.

The man's speech would slow, growing halting, and then he would stop entirely, as if he had completely lost the thread. His thoughts tied themselves up in knots, they proceeded in spirals, he kept repeating things that he had said before. I was reminded of a saying, attributed to sages of the East, possibly even the Magi, though I think it existed even earlier, long before the Flood: say something once and I'll believe it, repeat it and I'll doubt it, and if you keep saying it, I'll know you're lying.

From the moment we met, he was extremely defensive. Like Napoleon, he would fold his arms over his chest, as if he wanted to control his shaking, and then he would place each hand on the opposite shoulder so that his crossed elbows covered his solar plexus. At times he would rub his lip or throat, stroke his forehead, or shield his eyes as if from a bright light. Sometimes he leaned over the table with his elbows resting on it. These were unconscious defensive reactions, as if he was in danger and expected attack.

"Do you like roses?" I suddenly asked.

"Roses? What do you mean, roses?" His emotional response seemed authentic – for a tiny fraction of a second his brow furrowed and then unfurrowed, but I managed to catch the reaction. Artists and photographers are well aware of the asymmetry of the human face. When emotions are feigned, that asymmetry only grows stronger. However, when feelings are sincere, there is practically no difference between the left and right halves of the face. One has only to observe carefully, to look for the tiniest changes that happen almost as fast a camera's shutter.

For my part, this was a test question to check the initial state of his face, to determine what is called his isometry. His reaction was normal. When a person is secretly afraid, for example, the wrinkles are generally shorter and cluster over the bridge of the nose, and, moreover, surprise manifests itself only in a very fleeting manner, while other emotions last longer.

Without taking my eyes off him, I nodded at the wall behind him, where the painting was hanging. Anthony turned, but he could only see the edge of the canvas, and twisting in his seat like that was uncomfortable for him. He fidgeted in his chair for a moment, but then felt he had to stand up, though he did so only reluctantly.

This was precisely what I wanted him to do. If a person says what he is really thinking, then the sensory nerves of his body send signals with certain properties; in science they are characterized as unambiguous. In these cases, the axis of the body is perfectly vertical, the person's posture is straight, without any bend or hunch. If the person's words do not reflect his actual thoughts, the sensory nerves of the body send ambiguous signals and the axis of the body becomes less straight, the contours take on a broken appearance. A similar process is observed when a person looks for support, for example, from a wall, piece of furniture, or door, or when he or she leans against a fence, tree, or pillar. Such signs are not one hundred percent reliable, but they do lead one to think. Every detail is a piece of a puzzle.

As Anthony turned toward the wall, he leaned against the column to support himself. He was completely hunched, the lines of his body were bent.

"Oh, it's just a painting, Chinese-style." He shrugged his shoulders, and I noticed his shoulders twitch convulsively. He rested both arms on the table and his hands trembled slightly. The man looked as if he would fall over any minute. There was a lack of equilibrium in his facial expression: his eyebrows twitched, his lips were twisted, his nose and neck danced wildly. Yes, there was a clear impairment in his motor skills. A certain lack of coordination in his movements – ataxia, scientists call it – would persist for long periods. At the same time, these symptoms seemed rather exaggerated to me, excessive. He appeared to be trying to lead me toward a specific diagnosis and was dropping hints, but was worried that I would not notice.

"Sit down, sit down. I imagine it's hard for you to stand there like that," I said, as if feeling sorry for him. I moved to help him, and gripped his wrists with my two hands, but I was secretly trying to apply force. Just a couple of seconds were enough to confirm my guess: to confirm it, to become certain, convinced, and confident of it.

The external symptoms that I was observing in him are usually accompanied by objective markers not under conscious control. Ataxia, cramps, tremors, and muscle fibrillation, coupled with sluggish thought, amnesia, and confabulation in which false memories arise, tend to combine with tachycardia and arrhythmia. In addition, the patient's pupils exhibit symptoms: miosis, say, or anisocoria, where the pupils are disproportionately shrunken or differ in size, and are slow to react to light. In addition, strabismus and ptosis are manifest.

This man had none of this. There was no tachycardia or arrhythmia, his pulse was even and steady, and I observed slight bradycardia – a slowed heart rate characteristic of trained athletes. His pupils responded normally, and the only symptoms present were those which a person could choose to imitate. Obviously this officer had studied symptoms and was deliberately trying to suggest a certain diagnosis. For some unknown reason he was feigning illness, trying to lead me astray. Once again, I had to ask why. Yet I remained silent this time, too, and I tried not to reveal through my words or expression the fact that I knew.

Now we could move on to further examination and diagnosis. When a person is lying, tiny and unconscious changes take place in his facial expressions, gestures, and movements. It is no secret that these changes are difficult to see; they occur only briefly, lasting a fraction of a second, and it is harder still to recognize what they mean, to decipher them. However, at Division X we had long studied this topic and made some progress. In any case, if one hones one's powers of observation, then one will be able to spot lies and trickery.

Let us start from the fact that a person who is seeking to deceive will occasionally touch his face while he is speaking, without realizing that he is doing it. He will touch his lips or his brow, stroke his cheeks or chin, or rub a finger over his ear, without even thinking about how these gestures and movements will give him away. If a person covers his mouth with his hand, and his thumb presses against his cheek, he is probably deceiving you. But an especially subtle sign of lying is touching one's nose.

Light, fast, and nearly unnoticeable stroking of the tip of the nose or the skin under it is easy to explain. The nerve endings in this region are quite sensitive. Intentional lying acts on the subcortical centers, by way of the cerebral cortex. The subcortical centers in turn, by means of the parasympathetic nervous system, act on the local nerve endings, sparking paresthesia in them at an unconscious level, i.e. a mild itching, a ticklish sensation. The liar's hand will then involuntarily move to touch his nose.

Similarly, a liar might rub his eyelid. This gesture shows a real fear of attracting suspicion, of being unmasked, and it is usually accompanied by the person directing his gaze downward.

I should say that Anthony would sometimes make such gestures and movements, in a mechanistic manner, running on autopilot, but then he would immediately check himself. Yes, he knew well how to maintain control over himself; he had clearly had good training, but in a fraction of a second I managed to detect his efforts to control himself. My experience and training at Division X came in very useful.

Close study of the subject reveals that among right-handed people it is usually gestures with the left hand that reveal they are lying, while with left-handed people it is the opposite. As is known, the left hand is controlled by the right hemisphere of the brain, which is responsible for a person's emotions, imagination, and sensory activity. In other words, the left hand, when it unconsciously executes commands from the brain, reveals what a right-handed person is really thinking.

By this time, the Pot Sticker restaurant was full of people: regular customers, lovers of Chinese cuisine, locals, and people from Chinese immigrant families. There were also some who had come here in search of the exotic – visiting tourists, foreigners, travelers, and Americans from other states – a diverse crowd dreaming of eating their fill of delicious food. A rich aroma of spices, herbs, delightful sauces, meat, and vegetables wafted across the tables and filled the room with the clinging smell of the freshly-prepared food currently being served to the diners. This establishment, I must say, was not stingy with its food: the portions were huge. The more food the better – who would argue with that?

I had done well by choosing not to order any of the food, being content instead with tea. Otherwise, the entire operation would have gone off badly. It would have been hard for me to reach a diagnosis when my whole attention was focused on my plate. The staff here spared no effort to make their diners happy. My mission would have ended in complete failure.

Instead, I had not taken my eyes off the American. He, of course, maintained a careful watch over his movements; he knew how to keep control of himself, and he feigned an array of symptoms. Not everything was in his power, however: the right hemisphere of a person's brain, which is responsible for emotions, controls the left half of the face, and so it is more difficult to conceal one's feelings there than on the right side. If a person is experiencing positive emotions, both halves of the face will show practically the same response. Negative feelings, on the other hand, will mainly be reflected in the left side of the face whether a person wants it or not. I could see that something was troubling him; a sense of unease would subtly appear in his face, though he carefully obscured it with a series of deceptive actions: coughing, wilder gestures, and much smiling.

I do not need to prove that a specialist can tell the difference between deceptive and sincere actions. If a person's emotion is real, if there is no secret attempt to deceive, then facial expressions and gestures will occur simultaneously. However, deceptive actions always start with movement in one's extremities, then the full gesture is made, followed in turn by the facial expression. Granted, the delay involved is brief, a fraction of a second, but if I could spot it, then there was nowhere for him to hide.

Anthony did try hard, I have to give him that. He had clearly prepared well, he had studied theory and gone through training, but he was unable completely to avoid giving such subtle signs. Is it possible for any human being to go against their very nature? Regardless of his intentions, his lips occasionally tensed, he raised his eyebrows slightly, his eyes grew exaggeratedly wide and remained so, he would open his mouth and delay closing it, and his lower jaw was slightly lowered. How was he to strike a balance among the muscles of his face and combine his facial expressions into a single whole?

In addition, at times he would unconsciously raise the pitch of his voice, which made the overall picture even worse. Not to mention that Anthony would often swallow, his saliva having thickened, and he drank water not because he was thirsty but rather to deal with the dry mouth that reflexively occurs when the parasympathetic nervous system is inhibited. This, in turn, pointed to the fact that he was hiding something, that he harbored certain dark designs.

The man presented a clear clinical picture, there was no doubt about it. If we recall Ekman's signs of lying, the slight changes in Anthony's facial expression confirmed that scholar's conclusions. We at Division X had been no slouches in this field ourselves, and our methods were just as good as those employed by foreigners.

By the time there was not a single free table left at the Pot Sticker, and the place was full to bursting, I no longer had any doubt about it: I was certain that Anthony was lying, trying to wrap me around his finger, though he remained on his guard and maneuvered to conceal his true thoughts and plans. To be blunt, though, this guy was small fry. He was in no position to fool Division X. He simply did not have what it took.

Now it was my turn to speak. I steered the conversation around, like a fighter pilot, and moved to make a head-on attack.

"Anthony, why are you lying to me?" I said, finally asking the question I had been dying to ask since we had met. I confess that I had wanted to ask it earlier, but I was patient, I held back, waiting instead for the right moment. I looked right into his eyes, paying full attention, so that I would not miss his reaction.

According to our observations at Division X, it is easier to lie with words than to mask the hidden processes of the autonomic nervous system, which run automatically in a self-regulating mode. They occur at a subconscious level, and regardless of his training and level of self-control, a liar will give himself away by the movement of his eyeballs. That is why I was now carefully examining Anthony's eyes in order to catch their subtle movements: left and up, and then right and down. No, something here was wrong, the reaction was a mirror image of what I expected. I thought about this for another instant, and then I asked my next question before I had even received an answer to the first.

"Anthony, are you left-handed?"

"No." He shook his head, and I saw that he was telling the truth. Well, in medicine one encounters paradoxes all the time, but I was not just going to give up. I reached a fresh conclusion immediately, and said it aloud.

"You were born left-handed but taught to use your right hand."

The man hesitated for a moment, thought the matter over, and realized that it was not worth fighting me. "How did you guess?" he replied, raising his eyebrows in surprise. "That was when I was a kid."

According to Division X's understanding, if a liar is right-handed, his eyeballs would move right and up, and then left and down. Anthony was acting like a right-handed person would. When he was a child, his parents had insisted that he use his right hand, and his brain had finally accepted it and adjusted to the new circumstances. However, deep in his subconscious he retained a memory of being left-handed, and as I questioned him, that memory was reflected in the unintentional movement of his eyes. Everything was now explained; there was no longer any mystery, all the pieces had been put into place, and I now awaited an answer to my first question.

"Why do you think I'm lying, doctor?" the American asked. He was smiling, but his smile was exaggerated, a mere pretense that was obviously forced, and wry; or, as we call it, it was asymmetrical, which once again pointed to an intent to deceive. He continued to make various gestures, expressions, and spastic movements for my sake, but he no longer seemed so determined, and his efforts weakened.

"Anthony. I've come here to attend a scientific conference. If you like, I can take you along to my seminar as an exhibit. Let the scientists there debate whether you're lying or not."

He had not expected this. Tiny wrinkles appeared for an instant on the bridge of his nose. He opened his mouth involuntarily, and sat slack-jawed. His lips tensed and his eyes widened and flashed fear – but the fear did not immediately vanish, as happens when a person is momentarily surprised or experiences only a brief shock; instead, it lingered.

"What are you talking about, doctor? I'm taking a huge risk here… I'm an officer in the United States Navy. If anyone found out that I was collaborating…" He was unable to finish, because I cut him off.

"Drop it! You're not taking any risks. Except perhaps the risk of being reprimanded by your superiors for ruining the operation."

"What operation? What superiors? What are you talking about, doctor?" His voice had risen to a higher pitch and he was struggling to regain his composure. Sweat gleamed on his upper lip. His hand began to move involuntarily toward his neck in order to unbutton his collar, then stopped. The American was still aware of the need to show the right symptoms and maintain control; he was certainly a professional.

   

"Anthony, let's make an agreement," I proposed. "I'll talk, and you'll remain silent and listen. Agreed?"

"Is that it?"

"That's it."

"An interesting proposal," he laughed, and this time it was completely sincere. I noted that the pitch of his voice had dropped, his face was not so asymmetrical, and his smile was now quite even, across either side of his face.

"And stop fidgeting like that. There's no need to put on an act."

"What do you mean?"

"You know what I mean. You act like you have ants in your pants. And take off those damned glasses. They don't exactly suit you. Especially considering the lenses are just plain glass. So, let's get down to business…" I paused, caught my breath, and then took the bull by the horns. "You were assigned to contact our consulate. Who assigned you to do that, I don't know, but it doesn't matter. I don't care who you work for. You were ordered to infiltrate our ranks. They prepared you carefully for it. They knew you would be examined…" As I spoke, I carefully studied his face and saw that my words had reached their target, and he did not bother objecting. From time to time, astonishment dimly registered on his face, then immediately vanished, melted away. He was still maintaining tight control over himself, and though he had been knocked off balance, he showed patience and a strong will.

"So," I went on, "the main thing is that you thought up a false diagnosis as a cover: alcoholism, Wernicke-Korsakoff syndrome. Your superiors thought that symptoms of alcoholism would help hide the fact that you were deceiving us. Those symptoms would serve as camouflage, a smokescreen, stop you being discovered. And an alcoholic is vulnerable and easy to control. Any intelligence agency will always try to work out why an agent has decided to collaborate with it. Alcoholism is a convenient reason. It tends not to arouse further suspicion. You created the illusion of a man with an inferiority complex, because people like that try to prove their own worth – they dream of revenge, and they're prepared to do anything. Basically you tried to make your task of infiltrating us easier."

All in all, the picture I was drawing was pretty accurate. It might have been out in a few minor details, such as between a copy and the original. Anthony listened to me carefully. Sweat had broken out on his forehead, his upper lip, and on the bridge of his nose, which suggested that inside he was feeling uncomfortable and was suppressing his feelings. His face remained an impenetrable mask, but through that mask some bewilderment nevertheless showed, as happens when a person is caught in a lie.

I could see that he was tired. After all, maintaining a pretense is a hard job, and there are limits to a person's endurance. Paul Ekman notes that a disconcerted liar is like a skier who, as he speeds downhill, has to think about every single movement he makes. It is too much for his brain, he can barely hold on, stay on his feet.

For me, the main difficulty lay in not missing anything, in maintaining full concentration, in spite of the noise in the restaurant, the rich aroma of its cooking, and the waiters darting all over the place. The establishment was teeming with activity, and only our table, which was quietly tucked away behind a column, was characterized by a quiet sense of expectation. But I could see how incredibly uncomfortable the American was, how he was taken aback. He was amazed that someone had been able to see through him. Granted, Anthony heeded my words, he ceased to feign the symptoms, he no longer twitched or grimaced, he displayed no tremors or odd facial expressions. He even took off his glasses, aware that this ruse no longer did any good.

As I reached the end of my observations, I waited to see how the patient would behave. I really ought to have simply stood up and walked out, for I had already done my job, yet professional interest and a burning curiosity kept me rooted to the spot. I wanted to know what the man was feeling. However, he remained silent, wrestling with his thoughts, and gathering his strength. On the neighboring tables, plates heaped with food steamed alluringly. I felt that I could now have a look around me.

"Perhaps we can come to an agreement." Anthony suddenly spoke up, calmly enough, after his prolonged silence.

"About what?" I asked. His words took me aback, but I maintained my composure.

"You would be very well paid."

"For what?"

"For reaching the right conclusion. Confirm my diagnosis."

"Hardly. I'm not a bureaucrat. I'm not a politician. I can't be bought. I'm not even a member of the Party."

"How can I make it worth your while?"

"I'm only a doctor. I really don't want to get tangled up in that kind of trouble."

"Then maybe we can declare a draw, doctor."

"What do you mean by that?"

"I'll leave now. I'll disappear, and you'll never hear from me again. Things didn't work out. That happens sometimes. But you keep this quiet, too. Everyone just minds their own business. So, a little deal between you and me."

"I'm afraid I must disappoint you. I do not participate in deals. I will not be part of your plot."

"That's a shame, doctor, a real shame. It's hard to make it through life if you can't make deals. I thought we could at least part on good terms."

He had, of course, a clear view of the difficulties of my life: I really did not know how to make deals. But what can I do, ladies and gentlemen, there is no use crying over spilled milk. The thought suddenly came into my head that nothing terrible would happen, that World War III would not break out, if I just gave him a chance. Ultimately, any person, even an inveterate sinner, has the right to leniency.

"Perhaps I can help you, meet you halfway," I said peaceably. He perked up, leaned forward, and seemed so elated that he nearly floated above his chair. "I'm all ears, doctor," he said. His face showed a sincere interest in what I might have to say, and his eyes shone with optimism and a zest for life.

"You've eaten, and I've drunk tea. I suggest that as the loser in our little contest, you owe me lunch. I don't want to make you spend too much, so a serving of pork would be enough."

For a moment he looked at me blankly. Then he pulled himself together, turned round in his chair, stood up, and with a click of his fingers and a brusque gesture he summoned the waitress. It would have never occurred to me now to suspect him of pretending. Anthony's behavior was natural, unfeigned, and calm, without the slightest hint of deception. I thought about what this unsavory job can turn people into. No wonder Professor Ekman claimed that love and goodness, as well as compassion, can disarm people.

Soon the establishment was full of joy, poetry and high art. A slender Chinese woman, not terribly quick to serve us but attentive, brought me an appetizer: *hong-shao* pork in sherry with ginger, broccoli in soy sauce with basil and celery, and fried rice with shrimp. Then something in the nature of soup was brought to the table: catfish in a broth with mushrooms, vegetables and chili peppers. According to the Chinese custom, the waitress brought this broth to the table boiling hot. Later appeared *xiaolongbao*, Shanghai-style steamed dumplings made from thin dough and filled with ground pork. Depending on the season, that filling might also include bamboo shoots, shrimp, or crab meat. The Chinese waitress brought these dumplings in a bamboo basket, which turned out to be a steam cooker, and I was instructed to dip the dumplings in an inky sauce as is the custom in Zhenjiang province. Finally, as the crowning touch, the main course came forth from the kitchen on an ample plate that was nearly the size of a tray: sweet-and-sour pork with vegetables. This serving would have been enough to feed an entire platoon of soldiers after a grueling march over rough terrain. Anthony wanted to order desert as well, but I turned him down on the grounds that I had come alone and had not brought any reinforcements to help me finish the meal.

After I left the Pot Sticker, I headed for the Soviet consulate on Green Street, where I wrote up my report.

"Thank you, doctor," the attaché said. "You have saved us a lot of trouble. But if this was a ruse, if he was not the person he claimed to be, then why did he spend a whole month making us wait before he revealed himself?"

"He had to prove his worth. He had to make you think he was a valuable asset, someone with access to important information. So he had to carefully maintain secrecy."

"It's a good thing you were around when we needed someone," the attaché replied, as he examined my report. He thought about my remarks for a moment, and then looked at me with evident interest. "Tell me, doctor, what do you think, perhaps we should still recruit him? As a counterintelligence agent rather than a naval officer. After all, we've got a hook to snag him on: he failed his assignment."

"That's not up to me. I'm just a doctor. You asked me for help and I gave it. I don't know how to play your complicated games."

"He might make an interesting asset," the attaché went on without seeming to hear me, indeed without seeming even to notice me. He was deep in thought, as if he was trying to remember a favorite poem or had given himself over to romantic daydreaming.

Naturally, I did not report on my culinary experiences. I did not tell Soviet intelligence about the secrets of Chinese cooking, I kept these details confidential. I simply filed away the fine menu of the Pot Sticker restaurant deep in my heart. Frankly, that treat was a reasonable reward for my valorous efforts. According to general opinion and the views of various individuals, a worker deserves his wage, and who would dispute that? Honestly, I regarded that fine meal as a just recompense, a bill put to a foreign country for my precious but wasted time.

     

The United States of America, as we know, has never had to fight a foreign adversary on its own soil. The cuisine of the Pot Sticker restaurant served as a mighty weapon capable of securing victory. I employed that weapon without the slightest remorse. For the first time, I was able single-handedly to inflict a heavy defeat on the USA on its home turf. It was a clear victory.

— **43** —

What can I say, I obviously had to stop over in New York. Where there's a will there's a way, for a start, and anyway, when love is your driver you'll climb every mountain, ford, every stream… I had been provided with a return ticket to the USSR before I left Division X, and strictly, my assignment involved a direct journey from San Francisco to Moscow, with no discretion to deviate from that route. However, I admit to being a little extravagant. I chose to change my itinerary and return to the USSR by a roundabout route, so that I could see for at least a brief while the golden-haired woman about whom I had been dreaming all these years. It is no wonder they say that a year is no time at all for true love, and no huge distance, forest, or marsh can bar one's way to it.

Since that ill-fated night when the Korean airliner met its doom, New York's Greenwich Village had hardly changed. It had been toward the end of August then, close to the start of September, Indian summer. Now January had come and, I must confess, the weather in New York was considerably different from California's. The days were fine but chilly, and rain fell in brief showers that left the city dripping. A cold, sharp wind would often blow in from the Atlantic, romping through the city streets and shamelessly sending scraps of newspaper flying along the asphalt, like a madcap child. Sometimes a wet snow fell, and the puddles in the morning were covered by a thin layer of ice, something which the people of Pskov call *stynka*. Later the ice would melt, and a chill would remain in the clear air until midday, but the tall, spreading plane trees were still green on MacDougal Street, where Cindy Creighton lived. The bare trunks, having shed their bark, stood in a row like old, time-worn marble columns. The trees stretched along the fine buildings behind the Provincetown Playhouse near St. Luke's Place.

To be honest, I was apprehensive about seeing Cindy again. Frankly, what did I have to offer this woman whom I loved besides brief, random, and furtive meetings in various corners of the world? Living under the

　　　　　　　

Soviet regime, I would scarcely be able to invite her to my apartment in the grounds of Division X. Entry to outsiders was strictly prohibited: it was a military facility that was carefully guarded and kept top secret. A high fortress-like wall surrounded the perimeter and was equipped with infrared emitters, sensors that could determine motion and the size of objects, and ultrasonic piezoelectric elements. Each evening, ferocious and vicious guard dogs were unleashed in the no-man's land beside the metal fence. Soviet citizens were not allowed to visit Division X without good reason, let alone foreigners. Furthermore, Division X employees were strictly forbidden from maintaining relationships with foreigners, and there was no hope of getting around that.

Though we could be grateful for small mercies: we managed to meet several times a year, and it was fortunate that we could do that. In summer, Cindy would usually come to the Moscow Film Festival to report on the event for a newspaper or magazine. She had completely valid grounds for making the visit: her profession brought her there. I would take a few days off from work and go to Moscow, where one of my friends had gone away for the summer and left me the keys to his apartment.

If we tried hard, we could imagine each one of these meetings as a honeymoon, a romantic getaway. No one knew about our meetings, not a single living soul. We maintained strict secrecy and were careful to leave no traces, so that we would not be spotted by anyone, and no word would slip out about our relationship. Just like the bomber copilot Steven Creighton and the interpreter Olga Shilina all those years ago, we were running a huge risk day in and day out; danger lurked at every step. It is no wonder, no wonder at all, that they say love knows no law, recognizes no authority, and will wait forever.

If the regime did catch wind of us, it would be goodbye to love and I would never see my American sweetheart again. Thus we had to hide, keeping our affair completely secret, and constantly take care to ensure that no one found out: not the regime, nor Division X, nor close friends and acquaintances, nor American and Soviet intelligence or counter-intelligence. We did not even let Colonel Creighton, Cindy's father, in on our secret – we literally did not say a word to him about it. Frankly, what could we tell him, what good news could we offer him: marriage, grandchildren for him, a home together? For better or for worse, the colonel knew nothing; he had not the slightest inkling. As long as I was working for the Soviet military, and moreover at a place like Division X, there could be no living happily ever after for us. Our lives looped in a spiral, each successive loop resembling the one before it; the fate of the children repeated the fate of their parents, and the fate of the parents predetermined the fate of their children. We did not even dare to dream of a time when we could meet openly.

No herb will cure love. During the Moscow film festival, my friend's apartment in the suburbs near a birch grove served us as a real home, a trusty shelter, a peaceful roof over our heads, a humble refuge, a reliable retreat for our secret and forbidden love. As for the future, we did not have a future together at all; that was the pure and simple truth, and we knew it. No wonder they say truth is a coarse and prickly thing, sharp like an awl; you cannot hide it away in a bag. Who could deny it, though: truth is good, but happiness is better.

Argue if you will, but I say happiness is more precious than wealth, though it is capricious: you cannot harness it to a shaft, you cannot catch it by the tail, and you cannot put a bridle on it. Frankly, happiness is a free bird which alights wherever it wishes. Of course, everyone could use a little happiness; each and every one of us needs it – but where will you find happiness enough for everyone? All that remains are phantom dreams, unsubstantiated and unfounded, unsteady illusions, baseless hopes… There is no harm in dreaming, as they say, and you cannot stop people from doing it. But as Georgy Ivanov, a poet from the first wave of Russian emigres, wrote long ago, "To the devil with dreams! Raise instead a prayer to God!"

More often, however, I was sent on assignments abroad and Cindy would drop everything and fly out from New York to meet me. Like newly-weds, we would spend a day, or two, or three, or in the best case a whole week together. On the other hand, sometimes we had only a single night: we would meet in the evening and part the next morning. We never knew where chance might take us next, where fate had in mind for our next meeting: Europe, Asia, the United States, or Canada. With her American passport the world was her oyster; Americans can go practically anywhere without a visa. Hers was a rich country of people with thick wallets, who were welcome guests elsewhere.

Very infrequently we would travel together, albeit in a peculiar way. I had long been tasked by the Soviet army and the space industry to study interpersonal relationships among crews – what makes people compatible and able to coexist. I was looking for formulas and recipes that could be used to create a harmonious team. The crews of seagoing vessels made for a convenient model: a small team serving in an enclosed space, isolated for long periods of time in a magnetic field charged with static electricity, suffering constant vibration and the constant rocking and pitching of their ship. And, of course, theirs is a monotonous existence: working dull four-hour shifts, seeing the same faces day in day out, not to mention the oppressive effects of the scenery around them: the open ocean – a boundless expanse of water without a hillock or tree in sight. These were men staring into the void and finding nothing to grab hold of, just water, water everywhere.

As Division X doctors worked with these crews, they found that three months shut up on board ship without ever entering port eventually gets to a person and leads to irreversible consequences: basically, the crew members go crazy. One patient of mine, a machinist's mate, would drag his boot by its lace behind him on the deck, walking it like a dog. But sometimes more serious complications arose. For example, under the influence of the constant low-frequency rumble of the ship in a stormy ocean, a crewman might lose his mind and step overboard.

Usually I would be sent far away, generally to the other side of the world. On board ship I was free to spend my time as I wished, and in port I could go ashore and return at my own leisure. I could even change vessels at my own discretion: I would send a radiogram beforehand, and then move from one ship to another either in foreign ports or on the open sea. I can recall rotating among a great number of types of vessel: bulk-carrier ships, tankers, roll-on-roll-off ships, container-ships…

Thus I knew the port rotations, cross-over times, and stops in advance. Cindy would get to my stop before I did and stay at a hotel right next to the port. As soon as my ship put in, I would go ashore and stay there as long as the ship remained in port. I would then have to return to the ship as it departed. I would go aboard, while Cindy would travel onward to the next port for which the ship was bound. In this way, we would roam the world together. How clever we were!

Sometimes events occurred which were completely unforeseeable and totally stunning, utterly mind-blowing, and unbelievable. The cargo ship *Yakov Bondarenko* of Black Sea Shipping slid away from Pier 36 at the port of Odessa one evening when it was already dark. At the outskirts of the port, large vessels stood with their red and white lights aglow, waiting their turn to enter. Beyond the ship's stern, on the steep coastal slopes, streetlights had been kindled in Odessa's parks from Langeron to Arkadia. The further we went out to sea, the wider our view of the city: the coast blazed with lights. From afar we could see the famous sights of Odessa: the Voronovsky lighthouse shining on the end of a bow-shaped jetty, the Potemkin Stairs leading to the Duke de Richelieu Monument, and the Morskoy Vokzal terminal building that resembled a glass box.

Late that evening a storm came in. The men at the helm witnessed a terrible scene: a powerful wave promptly lifted the mast, the forecastle, and the foremast toward the heavens, threatening to topple the ship over. Once the ship reached the highest point of the wave and passed over the foamy crest, the ship plummeted downward and was shaken by heavy blows. Tons of water came flooding over the deck and into the chain locker for the anchors. Water flooded over the battened hatches of the holds and over the lifeboats hoisted on the deck. The anchor-hawse holes and the scuppers on the ship's deck and along its sides could not cope with this torrent of water, and the flood simply swirled around the deck from side to side as if it had been poured into a big washbasin.

I must admit that seasickness usually strikes me in a peculiar way. I suddenly feel empty inside, and I am overcome by insatiable hunger which torments me incessantly and relentlessly. For this reason, in stormy weather I generally prefer to lie down and sleep through all the rocking and rolling of the ship. The next morning, I saw that the storm had abated and the sea was calm, a smooth and untroubled expanse of water without the slightest wind or ripple on the water. By this time we had already crossed the Black Sea and were nearing the coast of Turkey. The sun rose above the horizon beyond the ship's stern and painted the sea a delicate pink, filling the water with the timid light of daybreak.

Regardless of our education, we all know that it is possible to pass from the Black Sea to the Mediterranean only through the Bosporus Strait. I do not need to prove it; it is a known fact. Now, however, all I could see were hills and green groves all along the shore, and here and there, pink and yellow houses with red tiled roofs standing in small clusters on the slopes. The Turkish coastline seemed to stretch unbroken before us from one side of the ship to the other, with nary a breach or a gap in it. Yes, the Bosporus was still marked on the map, but as I looked ahead, it was hard to believe that it really existed. As I stood on the ship's bridge, I was truly afraid that the path was barred to us, that there was no way out, and the Black Sea had turned into a lake overnight. My anxiety grew; I worried that the captain was unaware of these overnight changes, and I feared that the ship might simply hit the shore as if running into a wall.

Then suddenly the coastline parted slightly, and a gap appeared in the hills and groves, growing wider by the minute. Though the appearance of the coast did not change – it remained the same hills and vegetation, the same houses with the same roofs – the land off the starboard side of the ship had oddly become Europe, and off the port side Asia. Between the Rumeli cape on the European side and the Feneri cape on the Asian side I could observe a strong current that bore our ship along the way a whirlpool draws in a piece of driftwood. Eventually we raised the Turkish flag on the foremast: a crescent moon and a star on red. A boat drew close and stuck close to the ship's side. A gray-haired pilot climbed up to guide us.

Hour after hour we passed down that narrow strait along the picturesque coasts. Green hills stretched endlessly around us, and along their slopes and atop them, cypress and the local pine grew, curved trees with flat crowns that resembled umbrellas. Among the hills there often appeared communities of two- or three-story buildings with balconies looking out onto the strait. On both sides of the strait I spotted now and again old fortress walls that had been swallowed up by the vegetation, and coastal ramparts that had once protected the entrance to Istanbul from the most dangerous of enemies: the Russian navy. Russia had long dreamed of bringing the Bosporus and Dardanelles into its empire, and if the Bolsheviks had never carried out their coup, that dream may well have been realized.

As the picturesque strait curved and occasionally shifted its direction, we ourselves were making alterations to our course practically every minute in order to remain within our narrow shipping lane. Ships came toward us from the opposite direction one after another, and boats and ferries also scurried across the strait everywhere I looked. In some places the Bosporus was literally teeming with vessels. In short, the ship's crew had to stay alert and keep a lookout. The helmsman would loudly and distinctly repeat the pilot's commands back to him. Besides the first mate, who was then on duty, all the other helmsmen were present on the bridge, and of course the captain was too.

Meanwhile, Istanbul was coming toward us, a tangle of streets running over the hillsides. Red tiled roofs rose over the slopes. Beyond the older districts, modern buildings towered as high as the tops of some of the hills. My gaze was eventually drawn to the Soviet consulate, a lovely old-style building of three stories with a frieze of carved stone, a tall annex from granite slabs and ornamental cornices. The whole territory was protected by an iron fence painted green and perched on a foundation of white stone, beyond which lay a finely-landscaped lawn. Near the consulate I saw a light-colored building with tall windows and burgundy curtains, and Soviet-made Zhiguli cars standing idle next to the gates. On the quiet waterfront, fishermen sat with their poles, and now in the early morning a few solitary customers or occasional pairs of men sat in the street cafes, few of them paying any attention to the passing ships.

With unwavering concentration, the Turkish pilot issued his commands to the helmsman. We sailed along under the grandiose bridges connecting the European and Asian sides of the city. We proceeded past the ancient sultans' palaces, past the luxurious villas with turrets on their roofs and grottoes serving as boathouses underneath, past the city's famous mosques, past the Golden Horn… Bridges spanned the bay at the Golden Horn: the Galata Bridge next to the Yeni Cami mosque and the Atatürk Bridge in the Küçük Pazar neighborhood. Küçük Pazar was home to a huge, centuries-old bazaar which sprawled unseen under its vast roof. I must say, even that portion of the bazaar which dealt exclusively in gold was much larger than Odessa's Privoz market, no offense to those born and raised in Odessa.

As we moved along the strait, seagulls whirred above our heads, clearly used to being fed by the many ships' passengers and crews. If one holds to the superstition common in the navy that seagulls are the souls of drowned sailors, then in the Bosporus they exist in a number too large to count. From loudspeakers on the high minarets, the muezzin loudly called believers to prayer, dragging out every syllable. The Bosporus gradually grew wider, and the role of the pilot became less critical. A red boat with a green deck pulled jauntily up alongside our ship, and the gray-haired Turkish pilot descended the ladder. From here, we sailed on our own, though as we were coming out of the strait near the Kadıköy cape and Haydarpaşa harbor, a gigantic tanker ship, which had foundered here many years before, jutted intimidatingly out of the water. We managed to skirt round it, and then the Sea of Marmara with its many islands lay before us. A warm sea breeze blew toward us, and to the port side we left the Princes' Islands behind.

"Thank you, one and all!" said the captain in appreciation for his crew's work in getting the vessel through the narrow strait.

Without a moment's hesitation, the helmsmen who had all worked together on this unusual shift wandered off, each to his own cabin. Only a solitary seagull that had long followed the ship continued to hang over the bow, as if it was unable to leave, as if it had become so fond of us that it could not fly away.

All day long we moved through the Sea of Marmara toward the Dardanelles. For several hours without a break I worked with crew members who were off duty. I subjected them to tests and made tables and graphs to determine the patterns in the relationships between them. I managed to study three of them: a boatswain, a radio operator, and the third machinist's mate. In each of them I sought to identify the hidden motives for his behavior. It was painstaking work; I had to delve into the details. For some time I had been carrying out experiments with homeostats, devices which determine the interactions and compatibility of people in a particular group. We had developed these devices at Division X, and had them delivered to the ship the day before it sailed.

The Dardanelles greeted us as a pitch-black expanse. In the clear, clean air, the lights of settlements shone, and between them the mountainous shores of the strait suggested emptiness and desolation. We were moving south, but northbound ships came toward us, their distinctive lights aglow: on the starboard side green, on the port side red, on the foremast white, and at the rear a white hull or stern light. The radio on our ship's bridge chattered incessantly, voices in different languages coming from the speaker. No lights were on at the ship's helm, of course, and in the semi-darkness the instruments shone dimly. The captain did not take his eyes off them, and he checked our course minute by minute, while the watch officer in the curtained-off navigational compartment painstakingly tracked the ship's course on the map and reported to the captain.

As the strait grew narrower, the atmosphere on the bridge grew more tense. The captain's voice took on a sharper quality, and the helmsman's reports became shorter and more abrupt – not a single superfluous word was said. The helmsman was naturally absorbed entirely in his task, standing stiffly and with extreme concentration, and he loudly repeated back each order he was given. Sweat gleamed on his forehead from the tension.

Believe or not, the atmosphere reminded me of a military operation. It was as if the crew had been given a military task to accomplish and they were carrying out their orders perfectly and to the letter, so that they would not later be given any grief by their superiors. Dangers occasionally still loomed in the strait. One Turkish vessel made a reckless maneuver in the shipping channel we were using, while another vessel cut across our course. Our prudent captain sent the boatswain to the windlass so that we could drop the anchor if need be. He also sent an engineer below to a place where it was possible to control the ship manually.

Near the Nara Burnu cape, the strait turns abruptly, and we had to alter our course sharply. We had to look lively about it too, because the narrowest place in the Dardanelles was coming up. In spite of his serious responsibilities, the captain was a fairly young man, thirty-seven years old, but he commanded his ship sagely and took all precautions to avoid trouble.

The narrowest point of the strait lies between Çanakkale on the Asian side and the village of Kilitbahir on the European side. On the Asian side, Cape Namazgah juts out into the strait, where the bastion of the same name and the small settlement of Hamidiye are located; the lights of the settlement sparkled in the dark water. Farther off, beyond the city of Çanakkale and high in the hills, like a bright constellation in the middle of the night sky, the cloud-wrapped village of Sarıcaeli twinkled. The air over the mountains and the sea was so clear that the lights shone through the night like precious stones laid on black velvet; sometimes it seemed that a fire was about to break out any moment. Meanwhile, the constellation of Orion hung literally right over the foremast, the seven readily visible stars that have been famous since ancient times.

Fortunately, we turned out to be the only vessel navigating the narrow strait at that time. We slipped through and re-entered the open sea. The Aegean greeted us with a fine drizzle and gentle waves.

The captain now sighed with relief and looked truly pleased at his crew's good work. I sensed how everyone else was also relieved, and the tension that had hung over the bridge as we moved through the strait now melted away. Without further ado, the captain suggested that after all the challenges and hard work it was time to unwind and relax – the crew needed a break.

A ship's captain is a tragic figure. In spite of his monarchical rule over the ship, he is doomed to stand apart from everyone else. He cannot even have a drink with anybody. On board the ship, there are strict rules of subordination that have to be observed; superiors and juniors have to keep their distance one from another. Any captain knows this simple truth. In this sense, my presence on board turned out to be useful for the captain; he could allow himself to treat me as an equal, and we often had drinks together or shared meals.

He invited me to his cabin, which consisted of several compartments: a bedroom, office, living room, and a small dining room. According to long-standing tradition, the captain was free to eat either in the mess hall with his officers or in his cabin alone or with a guest. No one ever dared to disobey him: on his ship he was king and god, and his word was law. All legal authority on board the ship was entrusted to and personified by the captain, and he was even entitled to conclude marriages. Such powers, it must be noted, were something not enjoyed even by the Soviet head of state, commander-in-chief, and General Secretary of the Communist Party.

Be that as it may, in the captain's cabin I was treated to excellent food and drink. We did not even need to wake Galina, the woman assigned to serve him according to the staffing schedule or, if you prefer naval terminology, the ship's articles. The captain and I had hit it off well, and we became fast friends.

"What are your plans in Genoa?" he asked me.

The ship would be making a brief call in the port there to unload some goods and take on others. The captain recommended that we visit a modest, centuries-old establishment that served the finest Ligurian ham and excellent Ligurian wines. According to legend, Giuseppe Garibaldi had been a frequent visitor.

Sadly, I had to turn down the captain's invitation. I explained to him in rather vague but not wholly incomprehensible terms that a woman was waiting for me in Genoa, and as we rarely got a chance to see each other, we treasured every minute we could spend together. The captain asked if it was a serious relationship, and I replied that it could not be any more serious.

"So why don't you get married, then?" he said.

"It's impossible," I replied. It was a completely honest answer, but I left out much of the detail.

The captain had a general idea that I had been sent on board this ship by the army, but he was not told anything else. He was not a complete outsider, of course, but as I had been trained to do at Division X, I held my tongue and kept my mouth shut. He seemed trustworthy enough, but I still did not disclose to him all the details. Why should he know that I served in a secret division, that I had sworn a military oath, that the woman was an American and I could not just desert the army and leave the USSR to be with her, even for the sake of love.

And of course I could not bring the woman from America to the USSR. "America? What the hell?!" my own superiors and the colonels and generals would ask. And there you had it: the terrible challenges and impossibilities that reality imposed on us. What could anyone do, ladies and gentlemen? How could anyone help this weary military man surmount the obstacles in his path? The captain thought about the matter calmly, as he thought about everything, and suddenly proposed that I bring my love on board.

"Just don't let any of the crew see you," he said, and that was the sole condition he imposed. Food would be brought to my cabin from the galley by his personal attendant Galina, who would not say a word about the matter; he would warn her beforehand about the need for secrecy.

Goodness, even in my wildest dreams I would have never imagined that things could have turned out this way. Over the next three days and nights the ship went around the boot of Italy, passed through the narrow Strait of Messina between Sicily and Calabria, and after rounding the cape we came out into the Tyrrhenian Sea. As I stood on the ship's bridge early on the morning of the fourth day, I caught a far-off glimpse of the famous medieval lighthouse of Genoa.

From the harbor and the waterfront, the city extended up the hills and resembled an amphitheater. Modern buildings crawled up the steep slopes and perched on the ledges. On the shore at the sea's edge lay the cramped lower city, a curious maze of old streets that dated from the time when the Genoans were lords of the sea. The ship slowed as it came into the city's vast port with its myriad piers where countless vessels loaded and unloaded.

Cindy was waiting for me in the Zanzibar bar, located not far from the port in an old building near a parking lot. Here the incredibly narrow Via Pre began, which sailors had nicknamed Salami Street.

Through the window of the bar I saw my young, red-headed beauty, intently reading a magazine over a cup of coffee. I was immediately led to wonder how she managed to maintain such liveliness in her face, such vitality and firmness in her body, and a clear head and a keen interest in reading after a red-eye flight across the Atlantic. How could a person look so dazzling in the early morning, when the majority of the population was still either soundly asleep or yawning languidly?

The bar was unusually empty, though it was no wonder considering the early hour. Music played quietly from speakers, old-time jazz, and the place smelled of good coffee; steam rose from Cindy's cup. It all looked like a romantic rendezvous scene from a love story, and of course it did, because that is what it really was.

A smile came easily and naturally to her face. "Hello, honey!" she said. "I've booked us a room at the Bristol."

The Bristol Palace was a very bourgeois and impressive hotel on the Via XX Settembre in the heart of the old town and right next to the port, the Piazza De Ferrari, and the Zanzibar bar. The date of September 20 meant nothing to us, but the street impressed us with its wealth and its calm and confident atmosphere. The buildings here exuded luxury, and the Bristol Palace stood out even among them with its extraordinary architecture, smart decor, and peculiar nostalgic beauty – European modernism from the late nineteenth and early twentieth centuries, with a mansard roof, balconies with elaborate wrought-iron railings, bay windows, and stucco cornices. A revolving door made from dark wood around glass invited us to enter. The hotel's interior did not disappoint us either – beige and burgundy tones, damask wallpaper, and an abundance of antique furniture. A wide winding staircase led upstairs and was covered with thick carpeting of a rich burgundy color. We had breakfast on the first floor in the glass-façaded restaurant where there was an American menu and a buffet table. We then went upstairs, where the decor of our room suggested that we were eminent and wealthy guests aware of our worth and used to subtle luxury and immense comfort.

"Your next port is Barcelona?" Cindy asked. She then reached for the phone to book herself a plane ticket, but I said that our plans had changed: the two of us would be going together to Barcelona by sea, in a single cabin. Sure, the cabin lacked fine antique furniture, but the conditions were quite tolerable: the toilet and shower were in working order, and our bunk was even equipped with a rail so that we would not roll out of bed if the ship rocked in a storm.

"Oh, sweetheart, a bunk with a rail is all I need to be completely happy!" Cindy replied sincerely. She added that she had been dreaming of such a bunk for years now and, if I was not opposed, she would stay right there in that bunk all the way to Barcelona. For my part, decent and honest man that I was, I had to warn her that I would be absent from time to time to see to my important duties, but Cindy sought firmly to persuade me that she would not leave the bunk and would patiently await my return.

After breakfast, the ship's crew was given leave to go ashore, and the crew members went mainly to the marketplace and cheap shops, to buy particular goods that were in demand back in their home port of Odessa. They were not completely free: to avoid anyone trying to flee to the West, the sailors were forbidden from walking in groups of fewer than three people, and each person was instructed to keep a close eye on the others. Be that as it may, the ship quickly emptied, and only those crew members then on duty remained behind.

From atop the ship, the captain's first mate saw us come up to the pier. He sent the sailor on watch away somewhere else, and then he himself walked ten paces away and gazed from the upper deck in the opposite direction, pretending to have a burning interest in the neighboring piers and in the old neighborhoods of Genoa where bell towers soared up to the sky. We went up the gangplank unhindered and made our way to our cabin near the stern.

"We're home," I said as I locked the cabin door behind us.

"Oh, honey, with you I feel like I'm eighteen again!" Cindy said as she looked at the cramped and narrow space where the two of us would have to live.

"Why is that?" I asked, secretly hoping that that the reason lay in my generosity of spirit, my extraordinary intelligence, or in my perfect physique. Alas, while my hopes flattered me, they were deceiving.

"Because you only have crazy experiences like this when you're young," she explained, and glanced toward the corner, across which a curtain had been drawn. "Is this the famous bunk with a rail on it?"

"Do you want to try it out?" I drew the curtain back to unveil the bed and its safety precaution.

"Yes, right away!" the American stated categorically, with a firm determination in her voice, but no sooner had we lain down when someone quietly and timidly knocked on the door.

"It's started already," I said, annoyed, and then I shouted, "Who is it?"

The only reply came in the form of hastily retreating footsteps. I opened the door to find a wicker basket full of fruit: peaches, grapes, bananas, pears, and apples. Besides the fruit, the basket contained two bottles of wine – one red, one white – several types of cheese, and salami and Parma ham. On top of that, a long and crunchy French baguette extruded from the basket, and we enjoyed breaking it in half. It was food from the captain's own private stocks, usually meant for celebrations and important guests, and we found it very welcome. Poor lovers often face hunger and a need for foodstuffs, who would deny that?

It was a real honeymoon, as if we had set off on this journey straight after getting married. We were on a cruise, with a private cabin, a little refuge for two. We completely forgot about the times we were living in, we shrugged off all the politics, told the Soviet regime and all other governments to go to hell, and tore down the barriers, obstacles, and roadblocks that got in the way of people's lives. Honestly, we did not care about them at all. They vanished, melted away, and the two of us remained alone together on a deserted island where, frankly, we were not keen for any foreign ships to visit.

## 44

I spent my summer vacation on Lake Seliger. For a whole month I camped in a tent, caught fish, gathered mushrooms, cooked food over a campfire, and ever so gradually lost the capacity of speech. The hilly island was bordered by deep water on three sides, but on the fourth a wide reach opened up. Over the summer, the grass on the island grew nearly up to my waist. My tent stood alone on a rocky, forested cape, from which I had a boundless view of the water and the distant shores.

Seagulls whirred over the island and the lake with their shrill cries. Far off in the water, a buoy swayed to mark the channel that local boats would use as they slipped past me and then disappeared beyond the horizon. I would fish on a steep bank over a backwater, or head down to a narrow, rocky gully to a sandy neck, or row some distance out on my inflatable boat and fish where the water was deeper.

Nikolai Shilin continued to live in Ostashkov. Seven years before, he had settled into a modest home on the tree-lined Fisherman's Street, which stretches along the lake, right beside the water, through the southern margin of the city, a neighborhood which had long ago been given the curious name of America. Yes, America, a Russian provincial community that served as a counterpart for the American small towns across twenty-three states that bore the name Moscow.

The pilot lived alone. All these years no one had remembered him. Moreover, we were now living in a different country. Of the country we used to live in, only memories remained. The Soviet empire had collapsed, leaving behind an aching regret in my heart, a memory of former greatness.

The pilot's wife had left him. Marina had grown up in a resort town on the Black Sea coast and she was not at all happy about the idea of living in a provincial town lost among Russia's vastness. She felt that Ostashkov was a dull backwater and she did not want to bury herself alive there. Shilin did not bother trying to hold on to her or argue, he simply let her go. They agreed that their son would live with his mother, but he would spend all of his summer school vacations with his father.

The boy waited impatiently for summer to come. Before his son's arrival, the pilot would make preparations: he would feed the fish and ready all the fishing tackle. He had his own favorite places on the lake: small creeks and channels among the countless islands, overgrown with reeds, bull rushes, mare's-tail, and water lilies. Near the shore, large schools of bream, roach, and ide were found among the aquatic vegetation.

The pilot taught his son the ways of whitefish. Among the thick vegetation he found patches of open water where crucian carp and tench could be caught. Predators – pike and perch – came into these inlets in search of young whitefish, and Shilin would catch the little fish himself to use as bait. The larger fish, however, he caught from a boat farther away where the water was deeper. The pilot knew places where, over really deep water, he could catch zander before dawn or around twilight.

The young man and his father fished together on the lake, and they kept up the house together: they did some carpentering, maintained the stove, whitewashed the walls, and painted the doors and window frames. There was a lot of work to do in the garden, the orchard, and in the greenhouses. The harvest they reaped from these was enough to last Shilin a year, and he could even sell some of it. After a while, Shilin bought a used car and overhauled its engine. The car ran well, and whenever he had the urge, Shilin would go for a drive. He seemed to have no regrets; he had made an acceptable, tolerable, and satisfactory life for himself.

Once in a while I would visit him in Ostashkov. We would go fishing together or fire up the traditional bathhouse, but more often Shilin visited Moscow to see his mother. By that time she had obtained an apartment that was small but at least her own. She gave lessons or did translations in order to supplement her pension. She had become an ardent theatergoer, and she went to concerts at the conservatory. She could hardly dream of a better life.

When we do not see children for a long time, they seem to grow up fast. Before Shilin even noticed it, his son had become a grown man: tall as a beanpole, bursting with health, and broad-shouldered. Pavel remained rather taciturn, he played sports and read a great deal, and was a pensive type. He was not close to any of his classmates, but even the worst bullies never gave him any trouble: they knew that he did not forgive insults.

The pilot took a liking to the Valdai region from the very start. In the wilderness on the shores of Lake Seliger, Shilin felt he was under reliable protection: the forest and lake soothed his anxieties, and a feeling of peace descended on him. Shilin's entire life before had been connected with technology, iron, breathtaking speed, and intricate machines, but now the pilot willingly sought a connection with the local nature. In the forest and on the lake he was in his element, just like the grass, the trees, the fish, or the animals. After the military, the pilot now enjoyed a quiet life here among this seclusion and silence. The natural world of the Valdai region gave him a sense of peacefulness, as if it were a close and good-hearted person capable of understanding and sympathizing with him.

Sometimes, though, once in a while, he would experience a strange sense of alarm; it would suddenly grab hold of him and not let go. Shilin was oddly tempted to abandon everything and rush off. At these times, the stillness around him seemed like a cruel prison from which he needed to escape. Suddenly and sharply, like an attack of angina, a mysterious fever would come over him, and he was racked with chills. A mysterious force was driving him away, to somewhere else, and he did not have the strength to oppose it. He would feel the need for big-city lights and huge crowds just as a person in a stuffy room longs for a breath of fresh air. Usually Shilin managed to take hold of himself and quash these feelings. His urge was not yet so extreme that he could not cope with it.

Sometimes, however, the feeling was unbearable. It seemed to Shilin that if he did not get out of there, his sanity would not bear it, his heart would fail him. The pilot would then hastily pack the car and speed off toward Moscow – a six-hour drive if there was no traffic. Sometimes it was enough merely to walk the Moscow streets for him to regain his composure and be ready to head back. In rare instances, he stayed in Moscow for a while longer, but he soon became fed up with the city. The noise and crowds depressed him, and from Moscow the Valdai region began to look like a paradise to which his heart was aching to return.

This is not uncommon. Many of us go through these mood swings: you are impatient to fly off somewhere, but once you arrive at your desired destination and find no happiness there and you are in a hurry to go back. All our life is a pendulum swing from one extreme to another. Our existence inevitably involves disappointment, but a change of scenery is nevertheless comforting.

After the pilot and his wife separated, he never thought about marrying again. It cannot be said that he avoided women, not at all. From time to time he might have female friends, but he did not take any of these relationships seriously, in spite of being considered a great catch for the local women there in America on the southern outskirts of Ostashkov.

Before Shilin even knew it, his son had grown up and graduated from high school. Against his mother's wishes, Pavel left home to enroll in flight school, and upon graduation he received an assignment in the Arctic region: life in this family seemed to have proceeded in a spiral and gone back round to the beginning.

One summer Olga Shilina came to visit her son in Ostashkov. We occasionally saw each other if I managed to get away from Division X for a while. During the dog days of summer, when the asphalt in Moscow melts from the heat, and it feels impossible to breathe, and the cars on the baking-hot streets seem hardly able to move through the sticky and viscous air, Lake Seliger offered coolness, space, and boundless silence. The vast expanse of water shimmered in the sun, and the green islands were reflected in the lake.

When we were away from the everyday rush, Shilin and I often talked about Pavel. The young Lieutenant Shilin lived, just as his father had, in an officers' barracks. Like his father, Pavel excelled in his regiment, but unlike his father, the young pilot rarely got to fly, as Soviet bases were now facing an acute fuel shortage. The Soviet air force's old planes often broke down, new planes had not been delivered, and the factories stood idle through lack of funds. Many of us wondered aloud when the army would decide to axe Division X: they would surely disband it and scatter its personnel to the winds. We had to count our blessings that our unit still existed at all.

But I could not believe – how could anyone believe? – that such extraordinary experts and priceless materials would go to waste: could the government really kill the goose that laid the golden egg? But Russia has often sawn off the branch it was sitting on; it has sent academics to do farm labor, used microscopes to hammer in nails, and assigned educated people the lowliest tasks.

The Russian military was experiencing unprecedented humiliation. Military personnel began to run short of food, and everyone was weary, worn down, as if they were not an army at all but a worthless rabble. Granted, in recent years, there had been a sharp fall in aerial confrontations; the Americans had cooled down, although life in the Soviet air force still followed the usual schedule of Readiness Levels One, Two, and Three, and drills. It was just that take-offs to intercept foreign planes happened much less often.

American reconnaissance planes, as before, took off from bases in Norway and prowled the neutral airspace next to the Russian border. Like his father, Lieutenant Shilin was often assigned watch duty. Though a lot had changed in Russia in the years since his father had served, the old way of doing things still applied to watch duty. At Readiness Level Three, the pilot could do whatever he wanted, as long as he remained at his station. If the order came in to change to a different readiness level, the pilot had ten minutes to get into his flight suit.

At Readiness Level Two, the pilot spent his time fully clothed in his flight suit except for his helmet. If the alarm sounded, he could then put his helmet on, climb into the cockpit of his fighter, and await the order to take off. Readiness Level One meant that he had to spend his entire watch inside the fighter cockpit. If the alarm sounded, he had three minutes to get his plane off the ground.

As his father once had, the young lieutenant patrolled the border in tandem with another aircraft. Ground control would guide him toward foreign planes, and he had to approach them and escort them. Sometimes the plotting board down on the ground would show two crossed arrows, which graphically represented an intercept.

The Norwegians often behaved calmly in the skies, even kindly. They would never go on the rampage, and when a Soviet fighter flew up to them, they would tip their wings in a sign of greeting and friendship. When Russians encountered Americans, however, anything could happen. The Americans quickly learned to recognize Pavel's tail number, and already knew him as one of the most dashing and skillful pilots. Though he was still a relatively fledgling pilot, the lieutenant had developed a taste for bravery and he readily stood up to the Americans. As soon as the Russian navy went out to sea, American spy planes were right there. They constantly buzzed around the ships like gnats. Over neutral waters, no one could do anything about them except try to follow them, drive them off, come dangerously close to them, or cut them off. But how could anyone bear their boorish behavior and their cockiness? The Americans' constant presence near our Northern Fleet and air-force bases seemed like a brazen challenge.

Indeed, they would hang around the area as if it was their own home, and track every move that the Russian military made. Only a scrawny weakling would be unable to get rid of an annoying fly – it seemed to have already covered us in bites, and now it was time to swat it, or at least drive it away.

The Russian pilots were especially fond of a maneuver that would hinder the Americans' aerial photography. As soon as an American spy plane opened the hatch on its belly in order to point its camera at the ground, Lieutenant Shilin would immediately dash toward the foreign plane, stick close to it underneath, and block the camera's view with his fighter.

This was an extremely difficult and complex maneuver, one that required exceptional skill and precision. A pilot had to get as close as possible to the spy plane, practically right up against it, and maintain a position there as long as the photography efforts lasted. Everyone was aware of how dangerous this maneuver was; the slightest mistake and a collision would result.

Usually the spy plane's crew would get nervous and begin to maneuver so as to get rid of this troublesome hanger-on. However, the fighter pilot would not be driven away so easily; he would continue to stick close to the spy plane. Ultimately, the only choice left to the spy plane was to give up and retreat.

Lieutenant Shilin was especially keen on hassling the Americans, and invented new techniques to get in their way. It was clear that his deft maneuvers left the Americans deeply angry and frustrated, and eventually their patience ran out and they decided to teach the young man a lesson.

Another routine intercept flight augured no complications, Shilin felt, but the Americans thought otherwise. As soon as the pilot covered the spy plane's camera with his fighter in the usual fashion, a set of sonobuoys dropped from the open hatch; the Americans would use these to mark a place in the water where a submarine had been spotted.

Fortunately, these sonobuoys only whizzed right past Lieutenant Shilin's fighter. If they had hit their target, he would have been forced to make an emergency landing or eject. The lieutenant's response to this came instantly, before the Americans could even blink. His fighter leaped ahead of the Americans and upward, and without hesitation he pressed the fuel-jettison button. A stream of fuel surged out of his fuel tanks and dissipated into a fine mist of kerosene. The American plane was immediately swaddled in the yellow cloud, the kerosene covered its windows, wings, and body with an oily film, and penetrated every crack. Soon the cockpit, the operators' section, the entire crew and their seats, clothing, and whizbang technology reeked like kerosene-soaked rags on an old tanker ship.

When the American crew landed at their base and the doors were opened, a stench issued forth from their plane like from a fuel drum.

   

The entire base collapsed in stitches, and from then on the plane's crew were known as "the fuel guys". This nickname stuck for a long time.

In the middle of the summer, the young lieutenant arrived in Moscow. His unit had sent him to visit a repair facility there. On his way, he spent a couple of days in Ostashkov. It happened that I also came to visit the pilot at the weekend. For the first time, the four of us sat together at the table: a quiet family dinner with some friendly conversation.

Darkness fell late at this time of year in the Valdai region. In the half-lit twilight, the lieutenant told us about his military career, his flying, and what might come next. In Nikolai's youth, when he was the same age as his son was now, he had often flown on paired patrols over the Scandinavian coast. Sometimes the fighters would accompany Soviet reconnaissance planes during their flights over the Lofoten Islands, where NATO forces were based. However, with each passing year, fighters took off more rarely to patrol the skies, for Russian bases needed to save fuel. Fuel was used only for planes whose pilots were on watch duty, ready to take off if the alarm were sounded.

When it came to long-distance aerial reconnaissance, things were even worse: the number of Russian reconnaissance flights had dwindled to almost none. Only rarely would huge Tu-22 ADM and Tu-95 K-22 long-distance reconnaissance planes, stuffed with equipment, take off with a fighter escort and fly over the north of Scandinavia before turning south over the Norwegian Sea, a route that was nicknamed "going round the corner" among Russian pilots.

Once in a while, the lieutenant got to escort a Russian reconnaissance plane. The fighters would provide cover for these heavy planes when they were carrying out reconnaissance close to foreign bases, airports, and ports. It was inevitably the case that NATO planes would take off to intercept. Usually these planes were F-16 Fighting Falcon fighters equipped with two Sidewinders guided air-to-air missiles. The Norwegians never behaved as rashly as the Americans did; the Norwegians would make the friendly gesture of tipping their wings to greet their Russian colleagues, though they were aware that the Russians' long-distance reconnaissance planes were taking photographs, eavesdropping on transmissions, and probing deep within Norwegian territory.

On the way back, the escorting fighters had little fuel left, so aerial refueling was arranged. A tanker plane waited for them at a set location at an altitude of six thousand meters. A fighter pilot would reduce speed, fall in behind the tanker, and connect his plane to the tanker's fuel hose. The two planes would fly in close tandem until the tanker had finished transferring fuel to the fighter, like circus performers on a wire or mountain climbers on a sheer wall.

Sometimes, in his free time, or more often when he was on duty, the lieutenant would muse, as his father had before him, about whether his sole purpose for existence was really just to oppose the Americans in the skies.

"All I ask is that you don't get shot down," his grandmother Olga said. It sounded like both a wish and an order at the same time. Then in English she addressed God and begged for His mercy, that everyone would return to base and land safely.

"Mom, are you praying?" Nikolai asked, astonished, after she had fallen silent. "That's not like you."

"It's an old prayer that American pilots used to say," his mother explained. "They said it during the war before they took off."

Pavel raised an eyebrow. "American pilots?" he asked, not quite understanding her. "What do the Americans have to do with anything?"

"Really, mom, what Americans?" Nikolai asked in turn. I could see that he was looking at his mother, baffled.

The interpreter glanced uncertainly at me. Then she said, with some hesitation, "I think that we can…" She thought for a moment, then grew more confident. "It's time."

Slowly, often falling silent to regain her composure and listen to the surrounding stillness, she explained the circumstances in which she had served during the war: June 1944, an air base in Ukraine near Poltava… For me, these long-ago events came as no great revelation. I had already known all the details for many years now.

When she finished, her son and grandson were dumbstruck. They found her story completely incredible. Father and son Shilin let her unexpected revelations slowly sink in. The two men sat still as stones, and the strength seemed to drain out of them, though they did at least remain calm and conscious.

"You knew?" Nikolai turned toward me, breaking his long silence and finally moving. "You knew and never told me?"

"I was the one who insisted on that," his mother intervened.

The pilot nodded. "You conspired to keep it secret, then."

"I was afraid they would find out," his mother explained and rapped her knuckles on the table.

Of course, we immediately understood her gesture, and guessed who she meant by "they": informers, bosses of various importance and rank, the USSR's mediocre leaders and their underlings, security agencies, the regime's countless hangers-on. Olga set out a few photographs on the table, the same ones which Steven Creighton had given me in New York. I had left them with the interpreter when we first met in the cafe on the Arbat. Now her son and grandson carefully studied their forebears, captured by the camera in their youth.

Outside the window, night had fallen: a pale darkness, with a trace of light still present over the earth. The water in the lake was still; the motionless water reflected the pale sky, and resembled dull sheet metal or an etching framed by the blackness of the neighboring woods.

Nikolai retired to his own room, from where we shortly heard the sound of his clarinet. I knew that sound. I had heard it on many occasions. The clarinet bemoaned the vicissitudes of life; it creaked and sighed, and with a hoarse and bitter tone it poured out its sadness, wailing, straining, angrily crying and snapping, as if it hoped somehow to alter its fate.

We are all inclined to grumble and complain, but we do not realize that while we are blaming our life for the wrongs it has done us, it is going past. The clarinet jumped from one octave to another, then suddenly fell silent, then started up again. In the pauses, the reverberation of the previous theme would quietly fade away, proving that silence, soundlessness, is the very kernel of the universe.

The sound was of a lone walker on a rain-drenched road, and it floated, cheerless, over the muddy, soaked earth. The soul shrank back at the sound, the heart filled with doubt: where should I go; is that really where I am heading?

Man is subject to despondency, yet despondency is one of the greatest sins. It is akin to a delusion; people lose heart, they lose faith in themselves, and yet even in the parched desert one will encounter wells. Therefore, if one was lucky enough to be born, take comfort and cheer up: you might have never been born at all. What does anyone have to complain about? This is precisely what the clarinet, deep in thought, was expressing on that night.

The pilot put his instrument down. "I didn't know any of this," he said. "But subconsciously I think I guessed. I thought I had no family apart from my son and my mother. Turns out there are loads of us." He laughed. "I just had to spend my whole life fighting the Americans!"

I remembered well how Nikolai Shilin first came to Division X. For years he had been tortured by suspicions that flickered dimly at the margins of his consciousness. The information he had heard from his mother came, as it were, as no news to him at all; it merely convinced him that he had been right all along.

While Nikolai and I were discussing these matters, the young lieutenant raised the clarinet to his lips. Pavel took up the melody where his father had left off, though in a different key. The clarinet's sound seemed to crumble into fragments, rolling like mercury and forming small, shiny balls which merged into a single, swelling whole. The melody poured out in a powerful stream, sparkling and shimmering: a full-flowing torrent of molten silver.

In the clarinet we heard hope, and this hope grew and gathered strength, as clear as a tuned string. It suggested confidence in reaching its goal, that it would come through alive, though it was still at the beginning of its journey.

## 45

After Genoa the ship headed for Barcelona. Along the way we put in at Livorno, where we took on a load of marble chips, after which we made stops all along the Mediterranean coast: Monaco, Nice, Cannes, Marseilles, and finally Sant Feliu de Guíxols, a provincial port a day's journey from Barcelona. Without even docking there, we transferred some of the marble chips to the Spaniards by stopping just outside the port and loading the chips onto a pontoon. I naturally continued my research for Division X. I would leave my cabin to work with the crew and perform experiments with homeostats, devices which determine the ability of personnel to work together as a single team. Cindy locked herself in the cabin and, just as she had promised back in the Bristol Palace hotel in Genoa, she waited for me in the bunk. While Cindy awaited my return, she would read, listen to music on her headphones, write articles, and also work on a book that she had long been planning but never got around to until now.

"What a comfy cabin," she said. "A person has everything they need here to be happy."

Indeed, we had no complaints at all. The week really had turned out well, and we found that a human being does not require very much at all. We were grateful for every day and every night that we spent together, but we did not think of the future, and we did not make any promises to each other. What promises could we make, if we were forbidden to be together by other people, by circumstances, by the regime. We dared not even dream of a life together; we knew we had no future together and that this would never change. "Damn it all," I thought to myself sometimes, "Why did I have to fall in love with an American woman?" That would immediately make me think of the American pilot and the interpreter and their love, cut off so abruptly. They were doomed from the start. Just like us.

The crew naturally figured out that someone was staying in my cabin, though no one had actually seen Cindy, and everyone was very diplomatic and simply pretended that they knew nothing. None of them dreamed of asking questions or showing any interest. I suspect, though, that they gossiped among themselves. What else could you expect with such a juicy topic of conversation: tongues are always ready to wag about other people's love lives.

At Barcelona, we went ashore in the same way that we had come on board in Genoa, that is, carefully and on the sly, so that we would not attract attention. The crew was given leave to go ashore, and did so. The captain's deputy, remaining on watch, pretended this time to be making a careful study of the statue of Columbus standing on its tall column right there in the port. The marina was crowded with yachts, and here La Rambla began, one of the loveliest and most romantic streets in the world. It was an uplifting experience to walk down it, as if it were stirring warm childhood memories.

Over the course of that year, many cities around the world served us as refuges, providing shelter for our homeless relationship. In Barcelona, however, we suddenly felt that we might really be able to live together, that everything had come together wonderfully. Our hopes were stoked by this city, possessing as it did an incredible charm. Surely it was no accident that a poor Catalan, the mad architect Gaudi, had realized his vivid fantasies here in stone. His masterpiece, the Sagrada Familia church on the Carrer de la Marina, is still under construction to this day. It seemed as if even the wildest dreams could come true in Barcelona; one had only to be patient and have faith. No accident, then, that La Rambla brings together unrecognized geniuses, poets, musicians, artists, and performers. Nowhere else had I ever encountered such a large number of eccentrics.

Walking along the boulevard past the Plaça del Rei, past the ample and colorful Boqueria market, and past the Liceu opera house, we arrived at the Plaça de Catalunya, a square which was kept cool by fountains even in heatwaves. Cindy and I jointly decided that if we had the choice we would stay in Barcelona: we thought it the most wonderful place in the world. Honestly though, we would have settled down anywhere, as long as we could be together. As long as we could be together…

Staying in any port would have presented no great hardship. Or in any place where the whims of fate brought me to. Cindy never raised this question. She felt that I should make the decision myself, of my own free will and having thought it through, with no one else's help or interference. Nevertheless, I knew that she would be overjoyed if I decided to stay. That would mean betraying my country, though, however I tried to explain or justify it. The circumstances of my life had no role to play here. No reason I gave would have any meaning or importance; betrayal is betrayal.

Whatever way you looked at it, I could not just turn my back on the oath I had sworn. I did not have it in me to betray my homeland; it was something I simply could not do. Life had me squeezed in a vice between love on one side and my work on the other; it was an iron grip that I could not escape. No matter how hard I tried, I could not break free. The only thing I could do was bitterly regret it. As long as I was working at Division X, the two of us could only meet in brief snatches, once in a while, in different parts of the world, and if we were lucky.

After a week-long stay in Barcelona, my ship was preparing for departure. With the captain's permission, Cindy could have easily sailed on with us across the Mediterranean and then through the Suez Canal. However, in Alexandria we could expect a strict and thorough check of everyone's papers, and so Cindy chose to return home from Barcelona. Three weeks later, the ship arrived in Bangkok, where it would stay for five days, so Cindy immediately flew to Thailand.

From Bangkok the ship headed for Singapore, and there it spent a week lying at anchor just outside the port. I immediately made use of the ship's small boat that was bringing the crew ashore. Cindy had taken the first flight from New York. Our ship then stayed in Singapore for a second week, this time moored within the port. A whole two weeks together was a great blessing for us.

The next port where we could meet was Hong Kong or, as the local Chinese call it, Xianggang. Evening found us sailing through the foggy, winding channels along the shoreline, a rugged series of rocky bays and capes. To port and starboard, countless islands and archipelagos appeared out of the sea and then vanished behind us. Through the wisps of fog, I spotted temples and pagodas among the tropical vegetation: Buddhist, Taoist, and Confucian, with bent tiled roofs, upturned eaves, and sharp corners. On the coastal cliffs and in the mountains, tall buildings towered toward the heavens: brightly lit windows with colorful billboards on their roofs. Skyscrapers rose up one after another, the light from them completely overcoming the darkness of the night and painting the sky with red. I saw, elevated at a great height among the buildings, a network of highways that constantly came together and separated. The cars seemed to be flying of their own accord through the night sky at high speed.

The bays teemed with hundreds of boats, Chinese junks that were like floating homes. Lack of land had led families to live on them for years. Now on their decks children played, braziers burned, and families cooked dinner. Some of the boats were selling fish, bread, and vegetables: floating shops that slowly made their way through the crush in the harbor, the traders deftly tossing their wares from their boat to the customer's. Life was in full swing on the coastal streets under the streetlights, in the bars and shops, and little markets had popped up even on the concrete docks.

It was difficult for our large ship to pass through the narrow and winding straits of Hong Kong. At the East Lamma Channel, myriad junks and boats scurried across the channel and cut our ship off. Odd-looking fishing and cargo boats, reminiscent of medieval caravels with their bulging bows and reared sterns, glided in every direction between Kellet, Waterfall, Telegraph, and Sandy Bay. Innumerable ferries nimbly hurried from shore to shore in the narrow strait between Hong Kong Island and Aberdeen, and they paid little attention to big ocean-going vessels.

As we approached port that evening, the unpredictable South China Sea had a surprise in store for us: its waters burned with a clear greenish flame and there were flashes of fire at the places where the ship's hull was in contact with the water. The sea blazed and shimmered with an otherworldly light, reminiscent of the Northern Lights around the Arctic Circle. I moved from the ship's bridge to the bow and leaned over the side to look down at where the ship cut through the water. A wave, blazing with cold fire, extended from both sides of the ship. The white foam, as if illuminated within, shone in the darkness with an icy metallic luster. An inexplicable glow filled the water down to its depths, and the sea seemed to be so ethereally clear and clean that one could readily see far down and observe in detail the colorful marine life there.

This was the first time I had discovered the hidden underwater world. Countless small fish dashed headlong toward some unknown destination. Schools of fish circled restlessly through the water to escape from predators, merging and dispersing. Larger fish clearly lived down at a considerable depth, and faced no danger there.

As I watched, the movement of each fish, from the smallest fish to the largest, gave off a bright spark in the water. The fish left a trail behind them as they swam, like the vapor trail that fighter jets drag in their wake. A fish would quickly swim off and disappear from sight, but the bright trail would still hang in the water for a long time, gradually fading, until it eventually dissipated. For as far as I could see, the whole sea was streaked with these myriad traces left by the unbelievable number of fish. This is how we human beings are, I thought: we swim through our lives in the dark and we ultimately depart, but we leave a trace that lingers for some time before it fades away.

A more prosaic approach to this strange phenomenon reveals that there is no riddle or mystery to it at all, no mystical cause. On certain days, micro-organisms and minute plankton multiply and phosphoresce in the salt water, which is filled with electricity.

I looked across the water and suddenly, to my great astonishment, I spotted a manta ray. The huge creature, sometimes called a devil ray, is said to be very intelligent and quick-witted thanks to its large brain. The ray was ahead of the ship and a little below the surface, and it was flapping its vast wings like mad. It swiftly bore itself along as if trying to outrace us.

Where was it going in such a hurry, why was it pushing itself so hard, why did it not simply turn around, or disappear into the depths? It was running a big risk, a mortal danger was hanging over it, pursuing it relentlessly, and driving it on. If the ray flagged for even an instant, the steel hull of the ship would run over it. But no, the ray remained always just ahead of the huge metal structure bearing down on it, as if it wanted to prove itself, as if it wanted to convince itself and us of its superiority.

We all think we are capable of much. We overdo it, strain ourselves, throw ourselves into some great effort, we try to catch up with others or outpace them, we go above and beyond and break our backs with the effort, but if you ask why, no one knows. We cannot explain it, and yet many of us act just like that manta ray again and again. Clearly, the ray and we are kindred spirits.

The center of Hong Kong extends like an amphitheater around Belcher Bay, which the locals call Beilou Zaawaan. The steep hills over it are home to the Kennedy neighborhood, a residential area teeming with skyscrapers spreading out over the steep slopes. Finally, our ship put into port in Lai Chi Kok Bay, a suburb of Hong Kong. I had to climb aboard a squat wooden boat in order to reach the city. Shiny copper handrails were fixed onto the dark wood, and there was copper edging on the decks and gangways.

The main thoroughfare, Queen's Road, ran along the coast, and I was immediately amazed by the relentless buzz and activity here. A diverse crowd flowed along without stopping, and cars drove ceaselessly by. Among the general flow of traffic, double-decker buses moved along in no particular hurry, but my eye was frequently drawn to the Datsun taxis: red at the bottom, silver on top, with a massive, shiny metal taximeter under the windshield.

Cindy had told me that we could meet at the closest cafe or bar to the docks. Now, as I walked through the area outside the port, my gaze ran over the delightful signs outside the buildings. These featured large and colorful Chinese characters, while there were fewer English words and these were usually smaller. Not far from the waterfront, I spotted the charming Coral cafe, but I thought it was a bit too far away from the docks and could hardly be our meeting place. On the nearby coastal road, green double-decker trams passed, their sides covered in advertisements. These trams rocked from side to side as they moved, and their general appearance was rather clumsy.

On Queen's Road, skyscrapers stood on both sides of the street like a thick wall consisting of window displays, impressive signage, and mirrored glass and the reflections in it. A host of international companies maintained lavish shops and chic offices here. Law firms and major corporations loved Queen's Road, as did banks. Here was the Chase Manhattan Bank, based in a little hut that reached toward the sky.

Right nearby, somewhat closer to the sea, I saw dark, narrow lanes that were leftovers from colonial times: Li Yuen Street, Chiu Lung Street, Gilman's Bazaar... On these smaller streets, the picture was quite different. Old and squalid buildings, with damp on their walls, hosted haberdasheries, greengrocers, bookmakers, tailors and shoemakers, moneychangers, barbers in hole-in-the-wall establishments, and cheap eateries for the less well-off. Here the local inhabitants, the passersby, and the crowds of visitors were unsightly: their faces were sickly and worn-out, their clothes threadbare, and melancholy and dejection in their eyes. I thought that Cindy would hardly want to come here; I could not even imagine it.

Thus I could only return to Queen's Road and keep searching. At the intersection of Queen's Road and Jubilee Street, I came across a shop that was bursting with ham, sausage, and all manner of meat. A strong smell of smoked foodstuffs wafted through the vicinity and merged with the aroma of the tea and herbs of a long-established Chinese business nearby. The latter's shop window featured a knight in armor, who resolutely affirmed the invariably high quality and unshakable strength of the tea sold within.

Shortly afterward, on the narrow Wing Kut Street that was like a small crack among the dense façades, I found the Super Bar with its furniture built from chrome and brown plastic. I assumed, though, that Cindy would not think to look in here, nor in the McDonald's next door – neither of us cared for fast food.

   

As luck would have it, near the waterfront and close to the ferry terminal, I suddenly caught sight of a large Crocodile shop, a retailer of men's clothing and shoes. I spotted the green sign with the image of a crocodile on it from far away, and right next to it was a charming and cozy little eatery with excellent food just begging me to look inside. I decided that this was a suitable place to wait for Cindy, and moreover its windows offered a view of the waterfront and the wide bridge perched on tall supports, over which flowed a steady stream of disembarking ferry passengers.

The runway for Hong Kong's airport, where Cindy landed, lies on a long promontory jutting out into the bay on the Tsim Sha Tsui peninsula. Planes take off over the water and come in off the sea as they landed. Across the strait, on the opposite shore, the huge Victoria Park sprawls over hilly ground. Cindy arrived at the airport and decided not to take a taxi, which would come the long way round, but to save time by using the ferry, which quickly traversed Victoria Harbor and delivered her to the terminal close to where I was waiting.

From the eatery's window, I saw her as she was disembarking, still some way off. My work at Division X had taught me to maintain control of myself, never to give way to my emotions, and to stay calm under any circumstances. Yet now I felt excitement quicken in my blood, and my heart skipped a beat. My dazzling redhead walked briskly in her high heels among the crowd of Chinese. Her face reddened as she walked, either from excitement or from hurrying, and the wind blew open her cloak. She seemed hardly to be walking at all, but floating through space without touching the ground. I knew of course who she was hurrying to meet, and why there was such impatience in her face, and I involuntarily felt a little pride stir within me.

Obviously, Cindy would soon look into the cafe where I sat, but I did not wait for her. I stepped outside and waved.

How she lit up! A joyful smile, without the smallest hint of pretense, came over her face, and it was so sincere, so natural and lively, that I had not the slightest shadow of a doubt in my mind. Yes, I trusted this woman completely, though in my years at Division X I had grown used to being wary and trusting no one. Cindy waved back and quickened her step, while I rushed toward her, nearly knocking over some passersby.

We met each other halfway among a dense crowd of Chinese and ran into each other's arms. The people around us dodged us and shook their heads judgmentally. It is true that the Chinese are not used to openly displaying their emotions, let alone in public. Usually they behave in a very restrained and modest way, and only we foreigners have no idea how to behave properly. We must have looked shameless and reprehensible. "Shame on them," the Chinese must have thought. "These white people have forgotten what decency is." Russians, however, would retort that shame is not smoke, it does not burn one's eyes.

Honestly, in Hong Kong we did not even bother trying to keep our relationship a secret. Cindy immediately – and, I think, with impatience; of course with impatience – how could it be otherwise? – told me the name of the hotel that was expecting us. Here, halfway around the world where nobody knew us, we abandoned all conventionality and took the risk of embracing on the street, come what may. We dared to do this solely because we were not afraid of attracting any attention from others or of being under surveillance.

It was a pity, of course, that we could not be together, openly and publicly, wherever we wanted. No, we had to roam the earth instead, always being careful and cautious, and what could we do, how could we find any way out of this situation if there was in fact no way out at all? It was not up to us. All we could see in front of us was darkness, a thick fog, and a grim fate, pitch-black anguish, sheer hell.

Today, at least, we did not bother with all that; we gave the future no thought. We shrugged off all our worries and lived for the minute, for the day, or in the best case, for the week. Now the two of us, who were so thrilled and happy to meet again, were hurrying toward our Chinese hotel, when we heard music coming from somewhere. It was a famous melody, something that I had known for many years.

"Shostakovich," Cindy said, and then stopped to listen more closely. I was once again impressed by the breadth of her knowledge, for she was an American, after all, while Shostakovich was a Russian composer. However, Cindy was well versed in the arts; she was a very educated young lady. A little learning hurts no one, so folk wisdom has it; it does no one any harm and costs nothing.

There on the noisy and crowded street, full of traffic and thronged with almost exclusively Chinese people, we could clearly hear a romantic tune by Shostakovich: an organ, and an orchestra principally of strings. The melody soared over the everyday rush, over the countless numbers of people, over the endless flow of traffic, over the noisy street, and over the hectic day.

We stood immobile, as if we had heard a voice from on high. An elderly Chinese man, thin, gray-haired, bald, dressed in old, worn-out clothing and worn felt slippers – presumably a tramp – was listening to this divine music. He stooped to put down his beggar's belongings, a knapsack and a rolled up straw mat. Who was he, where was he coming from, and why had he suddenly halted there on the crowded street?

The music was coming from a small transistor radio. The tramp, apparently in order to keep the radio safe, had taped it to his gray head – an admittedly odd way to listen to music, unexpected and relatively uncommon, to be frank. There was, however, more strangeness and whimsy waiting for us in this place and on this day which Providence had granted us.

While we were standing there listening to Shostakovich's melody, strange people appeared out of the dense crowd, slowly came toward us, suddenly disappeared again amid the maelstrom of human beings, then reappeared as if surging out of the abyss, and finally came right up to us. We stood and gawped at them.

A young Chinese male, his head shaved bald, was resolutely carrying an ancient woman on his back, exactly as older children give younger ones a piggyback. The young man seemed not to notice the weight at all; his burden did not encumber him. The old woman's wrinkled brown face resembled a baked apple, and her withered little body seemed weightless. With humility and meekness, the two of them, dressed in the threadbare clothing of country folk, stepped past us to the accompaniment of Shostakovich. They took no notice of anyone in the crowd, and the crowd took no notice of them.

I do not wish to come across as nosy, but voluntarily or involuntarily, I found myself instinctively wondering who these two were. A second question: and where had they come from? Where were they going? I thought their path might have no end, that they might have to walk for a good long while, perhaps an eternity. They had walked through the centuries and millennia; their road was a long one, with neither beginning nor end.

We watched them go, unable to tear our eyes away. No one else among the crowd noticed them; the Chinese milling around them paid no attention to them. Clearly the Chinese were used to such things, unlike us. It was clear that these people were very different from us.

The strange pair receded into the distance and melted away among the flow of people. Cindy and I exchanged glances. The two of us were seized by the very same thought: reality with its strangeness and quirks is akin to our love. It is just as incomprehensible, unpredictable, and unfathomable. What would eventually happen between us, neither of us knew; we could not foresee or imagine it.

On the way back, my ship put in at Saigon, which by this time the new regime had renamed Ho Chi Minh City. After the war some years before, the situation was still dangerous and unstable. People could be robbed or shot walking down the street at night. Even in the port, which was carefully guarded, the darkness of the night could light up with bursts of gunfire.

I hardly need say it; you have perhaps already guessed that Miss Creighton and I did not see each other in Saigon. We decided against it; in fact, we agreed that it was completely out of the question. My stop there lasted a night and a day. A strategic load was crammed into every hold of the ship, consisting exclusively of straw mats. This was how Vietnam paid for goods provided to it on credit. I concluded, looking at them, that there were enough straw mats for my entire vast homeland, from one end to the other, for every single citizen of Russia. Quite remarkably, our ship was in a position to guarantee every single member of the population, including babies, his or her own personal straw mat.

═══ 46 ═══

For my next journey I boarded a ship named the *Mekhanik Dren*. This was a bulk carrier, and we set off from Odessa to Canada in order to take on grain there. Imagine, Russia had to import grain – pure madness! One could not have imagined such a situation even in one's worst nightmares. Across the country, patients with gastrointestinal diseases were entitled to one white loaf every three days, but only with a doctor's prescription. If we did not deliver our grain, then many people would go hungry, their bellies would be empty. Bread does not come to the belly, the belly has to go looking for bread. If there was not enough grain in Russia to feed the Russians, then the Russians would have to go looking for grain, however far away that might take them. Thus we were obliged to travel overseas. It had come to this. We had lived to see the day. This is how low we had sunk.

I was reminded of an old story. The Russian writer Kuprin was sitting on a train next to an Italian man reading a newspaper. Suddenly the Italian became indignant, and threw up his hands in dismay. Then he read aloud a report that the singer Shalyapin planned to go to Italy to give a performance there. The Italian was outraged, saying that a Russian singer coming to Italy to sing was just like… The Italian thought deeply about the matter for a moment, searching for a comparable absurdity. Finally, he found it: it was just like bringing grain to Russia.

After the North Atlantic with its chill and the waterspouts thrown up by whales, we headed for the Great Lakes via the Saint Lawrence River, passing through the canals and skirting the Niagara Falls. The border between Canada and the United States falls right across a shipping lane, and we often ended up on one side or on the other: in a single hour, we crossed the border seven times.

On the American side, the whole landscape was industrial and urban: bridges, highways, skyscrapers, streams of traffic, gigantic factories, multistory parking lots. On the Canadian side, we were greeted by a rural idyll: green meadows, pastures, small forests, grain silos, apiaries, farms, and small, sleepy communities with little churches and quiet streets set right among the wildflowers.

To my surprise, on these boundless lakes, dead fish bobbed in large numbers. This apparently did not bother anyone; no one thought to point it out or talk about it. I could see that not all was well over there in North America, though it is said that the state of these lakes has improved since then.

The ship made a brief stop in Montreal to take on fuel and supplies. Cindy got in her car and rushed from New York to join me, but my ship had moved on, and she had to drive along the canals and follow the rivers and lakes. Sometimes we caught brief glimpses of each other – she would stand on the shore and smile and we could exchange glances, though without being able to say anything to each other. More often she would drive onto one of the bridges under which the ship was to pass, and look down at me from that vantage point. I would stand on deck, as if I were an actor on a stage, as the ship made its way along, slowly and sluggishly like a boa constrictor, dragging its long metal body. We would then enjoy a brief and silent encounter, a sort of dialogue without a word being said between us.

Eventually, after passing an endless number of islands and making our way through canals and locks, we reached the St. Clair River. The Canadian city of Sarnia, Ontario is located on its banks, with Lake Huron nearby. Stretching across the river, just where it flows out of the lake, is the Blue Water Bridge, and beyond it there is indeed an impressive view of the blue waters of Lake Huron. I watched cars drive this way and that across the bridge, looking as if they were flying along across the sky from Canada to the USA or vice versa. On the American side of the river, I could see the suburbs of Detroit, the famed Motor City. But what did cars have to do with it? We had come, after all, for that damned grain!

When we arrived at the grain terminal with its massive elevator, we saw a number of ships from different countries: Arabs, Indians, Chinese… We meekly took our place in the line among all the other starving nations: those who had come to be fed had to stop and wait their turn. To think that Russia was lining up for bread; the mind boggled! For long decades, the Soviet regime had worked hard, fought boldly, to till the soil and achieve an unprecedented output. And now this.

I should not wallow in self-pity, though, nor look a gift horse in the mouth. In Sarnia, fortune smiled on Cindy and me: we spent a month together, the entire time the ship waited to take on its cargo. We decided not to stay in a hotel, renting instead an apartment in one of the residential complexes on the wide St. Clair waterfront. Our apartment was on the tenth floor and offered a view of the river, the Blue Water Bridge spanning the heavens like a huge stringed instrument, and Lake Huron, looking as vast as the sea.

We settled into a sort of family life. In the morning, after my jog and breakfast, I headed down to the port and boarded the ship, like a clerk going to his office job, and there I would work with the crew, using the homeostats according to Division X's methodology. I ate lunch in the senior wardroom, but at the end of the day I rushed back, burning with impatience, to our apartment. Cindy would make dinner for us, or we would visit a local restaurant.

Sometimes we would drive over the bridge and find a good restaurant on the other bank of the St. Clair River, in the United States. On Down River Street we visited a family-run establishment called The Bridge, which had excellent food, and nearby on Pine Grove Avenue we came across a salad bar that was open twenty-four hours a day. Incidentally, on the other side of the bridge, in a little pull-off next to the road, there was a duty-free liquor store, where we could buy great wine at wonderfully low prices.

Things had come together nicely, and I could not complain. We were never bored – the two of us were never bored together. At the weekends, we took trips further afield and spent the night at motels. We went to Niagara Falls, saw Detroit and Toronto, and drove all over the Canadian province of Ontario and the American state of Michigan. When I first saw the sign in the shape of a blue shield on the Blue Water Bridge with the words "State of Michigan" on it, I remembered one of Hemingway's earliest short stories, "Up in Michigan". A great deal had changed since then, but in some places the original wilderness of the area had been preserved: tiny, sleepy communities, small wooden docks, ancient sawmills that smelled of cut wood and resin.

There is no point hiding it, I was afraid of making any plans or trying to guess what the future might bring. Our romance had been sparked in a completely unexpected fashion, like thunder from a clear sky or snow in the midst of a hot summer. We had not even had time to think about what was going on; our love had flared up in a mere instant, like a forest fire in the dry season. We fell into a swoon, our thoughts grew clouded, the earth gave way under our feet. We did not think about the future. What future could we possibly foresee, in any event, if we were not given the slightest clue? But as long as everything worked out, as long as things went smoothly for us, we were grateful for what we had.

Whatever way one looked at it, ours was a real case of love at first sight. It hit us suddenly and nearly knocked us off our feet. This happens sometimes, albeit rarely, perhaps once in a lifetime. Lightning never strikes twice in the same place, but it can be deadly. Most people survive, but the scars of the burn, the traces of love in one's heart, remain forever.

Here one ought to reflect on something. As long as lovers rarely see each other, as long as they live far apart and their next meeting is no more than a dream, and each encounter is like manna from heaven, their love does not wither or grow dull. Their lives are full of new experiences and they soar above the clouds.

Deep down inside, I must admit, I waited nervously to see how events would play out. If a relationship settles into a well-worn groove, into a comfortable and stable life, then danger lurks in the form of disillusion. It sneaks up on lovers, following ineluctably on their tail, pursuing them hard on their heels. Regardless of what people might say, it is inevitable that one will eventually become fed up with a life that is too comfortable; it grows stale. People's feelings fade, love withers and becomes a perpetual annoyance. Boredom takes the place of the early passion, and gradually it undermines the relationship.

Without freshness and change, people become too used to the rhythm of their existence. Life goes on in the usual way, but beware: habit can destroy even the most blessed of loves.

If you live with the woman you love right there by your side, if you talk together all the time, lie down at night and get up together in the morning, you slowly settle into a routine. The cares of running a household together take over the relationship. Little by little monotony sets in, any sense of joy or novelty melts away, and then one day, suddenly there is no more love; it has sunk without a trace.

The relationship stops being any fun, becoming instead a sad thing, though neither party is to blame. After a long, drawn-out period when a couple's love is ailing, the love dies right out, vanishing as if it had never existed at all. All that is left are memories that nag at you, keeping you awake at night. Admittedly, I was under no illusion; in my mind I was not imagining any kind of idyll. The bitter experiences of former years had led me to expect only disappointment.

But this time, the picture was rather different, and unexpected. Let us start with the fact that I felt like a young man again, someone whose life had just begun, as if from a blank page. The hoary and heavy burden of my past experiences, my failed loves and joyless encounters, seemed to melt away like overnight frost in the morning sun. And I, an educated and level-headed man, a thoughtful and experienced doctor, and an athletic sort, had fallen head over heels in love like a schoolboy, and with an American woman, heedless of whatever danger that might bring.

There was a real danger, and it hung over our heads, ready to fall at any moment. I was serving in the armed forces of a foreign country, and not just in a run-of-the-mill assignment but at the top secret Division X. Frankly, the United States was considered a likely adversary. Who in our respective countries would understand that we were in love? We did not care about high-level politics, but high-level politics did not take into account such a trifling thing as love between two people.

I constantly longed to have Cindy by my side; my attraction to her was irresistible, unflagging, and incurable. In the morning we found it difficult to part for even an instant, let alone for the whole day. It was hard to accept even short times apart, and the mere thought of being separated from her left me sick at heart.

This American woman possessed a natural liveliness. She had not a drop of affectation in her, not the slightest artifice, not a jot of dissimu-lation nor the slightest intent to deceive. Cindy took in the surrounding world with a smile and with a sincere delight in her eyes, as if it brought her joy and wonder. She lived and breathed every moment, happy and free. One did not ever have to expect dishonesty, tricks, dark intentions, or empty words. One immediately noticed in her attractive qualities such as her easygoing nature and her quick wit. Strangely, however, she remained a little enigmatic, as is typical of such deep spirits. She did not reveal all of herself on the surface, but kept some things hidden within her. Moreover, it was as if only one part of her was present, while the other part was somewhere far, far away, in some unknown region which one could not reach no matter how much one wished.

I was amazed at how there coexisted within Cindy a childlike spon-taneity, a penetrating mind, a casual attractiveness, and a seductive charm. Being with her was comfortable, easy, and fun. She radiated light and warmth, an unusual trait in our modern era. And to be frank, peo-ple like me are drawn to the ideal; we want to reach out and touch it.

As soon as Cindy appeared, people could sense her pure spirit, her extraordinary and almost boundless charm. Being around her had such a festive quality, and there was never a dull moment. How could you ever get bored with someone who seems new day after day?

Cindy had made quite a name for herself in journalism. She was considered an important and influential film critic. However, in spite of her solid professional success, in her everyday life she remained completely unpretentious. One observed no arrogance or pride in her at all.

In addition, she was always up for adventure; she loved to hit the road, and her car was always ready for an outing. She could drive tirelessly and non-stop hour after hour, always in her usual good spirits and chipper mood. She was never inclined to moan and complain, or to release her rage on other people around her. I never saw her in a ragged, worn-down state, even after a long journey or a sleepless night. To my amazement, she always maintained a fine appearance and an elegance that was all her own.

Frankly, Cindy's patience and unflagging politeness served as something of a reproach to me. Colonel Creighton had brought his daughter up well. I thought that I was a decently educated man and no slouch myself, but I felt that Cindy possessed remarkable tact and respect for other people's opinions. Such tolerance, incidentally, is something characteristic of the Anglo-Saxon race, unlike, say, Slavs or Jews who can become uneasy or angry when exposed to other views, while ardent Muslims can even erupt into a murderous rage.

I should add that this American woman was the very image of femininity, the sort of person poets of old would have dreamed about. She had a divine figure and sparkling and radiant eyes. Men would do a double-take on meeting this magnificent lady and mysterious stranger who seemed to have stepped right out of their dreams. Men fell for her at first sight, so attractive and alluring was she. I admit that I myself would admire her beauty as we walked down the street, visited the pool or gym, went to local restaurants, or jogged in the park – everywhere we were together in public, and whenever we were alone together. The longer we knew each other, the more I would abandon myself to her perfection, her extraordinary harmony of body and soul.

Without any particular effort, she naturally and easily set my blood pumping; she made me feel crazy for her for days on end, and in any weather she awakened my desire: day or night, morning or evening, night or day.

We made a great couple, it hardly needs to be said. And it was no secret that we could have brought up some fine, intelligent, and healthy children. No matter how you looked at it, nature had endowed us well; we had inherited good traits, and our genes helped, but the most important thing was that there was true love between us. Based on the laws of genetics and common sense, any children we had would be beautiful, there was no doubt about it. In spite of all these musings about our possible futures, though, a sober look at how things really were revealed a picture that was not very encouraging. Disappointment seemed to be in store for us; our story would ultimately be a tragic one with a bitter denouement and pain that would linger long afterward.

The bottom line is that we were doomed from the start. It might seem as if there is nothing wrong with a man and a woman wanting to be together and live happily ever after. In any country in the world, we would have faced no insurmountable obstacles, no minefields, deep moats, or towering walls. But circumstances were against us; we simply could not make it work. Whether we liked it or not, we had been ordained to grow up on opposite sides of the barricade. Our troubles were all down to politics. What hindered us was the quarrel between our nations, their opposed ideologies, their enmity, the Iron Curtain, and the Cold War.

Cindy lived on a different planet, and was unable to come to where I was. For my part, I could not drop anchor the other side of the hill, as we tended to call the West. In spite of my dislike for the regime, I was not the sort of person who could simply forget about his oath. I was not one of those people for whom honor and a conscience are silly, old-fashioned concepts, mere hollow sounds and empty words.

Needless to say, I was not serving the regime itself, misguided as it was, nor politicians. I was serving my country. After all, politicians and regimes change, but the country remains.

Let us try to do without pathos and ardent declarations here. I do not care for lofty speeches and feverish patriotism. But I was simply unable to ignore my convictions or leave my homeland. Even for the sake of love. Our unexpected and dizzying love had suddenly come to seem like a fragile little boat in a storm-tossed ocean, and any minute now a crushing wave would come roaring over our heads. But the truth is, how could anyone survive on such fault lines, who could ensure safety for their love when the whole world had gone crazy? One cannot argue with an earthquake, the poet Goethe once said.

By and large, we did not discuss plans for the future. It was already clear to us that there was no hope, that a danger loomed that was unstoppable and coming ever closer. Soon we would have to part, we would have to say goodbye to each other for good, once and for all.

Outwardly, Cindy did not show her unease. She was able to maintain control over herself. Nevertheless, a hint of sadness would pass over her face, her lips would quiver and her bright eyes would momentarily lose their luster. I could imagine how difficult things were for her, how unpleasant thoughts must be tearing at her, for after all, any woman needs certainty, and her thoughts inevitably turn toward the future, trying to guess at what might be, and worrying about it.

Let me repeat: it would have posed no difficulty for me to settle down in any country I visited. Cindy did not even bring the subject up; it was evident that she wanted me to make the decision on my own, according to my own judgment and feeling, and without any pressure. She would not, it seems to me, have been satisfied with a decision that was not freely made. She waited patiently and remained silent, not saying a word. She humbly accepted her lot and lived in the moment for as long as our relationship was allotted to us, though every day brought us closer to an inevitable separation.

I could suffer and grieve as much as I wanted, I could wail, cry out, even kill myself, but I could never expect mercy or indulgence. It would be pointless to beg for it. As everyone knows, the Soviet authorities did not heed anyone's pain, they were utterly without sympathy, and they had no sense of compassion. The USSR's bosses simply paid no attention to individual human beings.

Meanwhile, relations between our countries remained frosty. The downing of the Korean plane had worsened them to an extreme degree and given a renewed impetus to the Cold War. In other words, we could not even hope for a miracle.

In addition to all this, I had not been lucky with this ship's captain. He would remind me that his authority extended to me as well. He demanded that I explain myself. My disappearances and my absences from the ship drove him crazy. Somehow, he and I never quite established the right rapport.

I could understand how Captain Sinchenko felt. In spite of many years of faithfully doing his duty, he had never been given a ship of his own to command. Within Black Sea Shipping, he was occasionally assigned to command other vessels when their captains went on leave. This meant that he had been roaming from one ship to another, month after month, for umpteen years already. He was a tiresome man, arrogant and constantly puffing himself up. He liked to nitpick and boss people around, and he was malicious and inflexible. Day after day he would get on someone or another's case.

He was also unable to admit to any mistakes of his own. He would invariably insist that he was right. Sinchenko kept very aloof from his crew; for him proper subordination was more important than all else. His crewmen hated and feared him, though they were forced to endure his whims, because a captain has unquestioned authority on board his ship. If he had so wished, he was completely capable of making his crew members' lives pure hell, of subjecting them to the most brutal punishments. Moreover, he could easily kick any man off the ship and deprive him of permission to travel abroad, or of any livelihood at all. Sinchenko was infamous for this; he was constantly poisoning the mood on board his ship and hounding his men. Even the first officer – who was the Communist Party's eyes and ears on the ship, constantly enforcing the Party line and monitoring the crew's level of devotion to the Soviet regime (while remaining suspicious of every one of them) – could not hold a candle to the captain.

Sinchenko was never able to accept the fact that I was not subordinate to him. It drove him crazy that I did not report my doings to him, that I did not ask him for permission, that I came and went as I pleased. I tried to reason with him, saying that I had my own schedule and my own affairs to attend to, but my explanations fell on deaf ears and my efforts were in vain. Ultimately, the only thing I could do was to ignore him and get on with my own business.

I eventually discovered that he had been sending a barrage of radiograms to the USSR to complain, saying that this passenger was breaking the rules, going off somewhere, meeting with unknown people, and acting suspiciously, as if he intended to betray his country or to defect.

For my part, I sent a radiogram to Division X. The radio operator alerted the captain, but the latter was unable to make anything of the message, because I had written it in code. In the message, I reported that the ship's captain was obstructing my work. Apparently Sinchenko was given quite a tongue-lashing, for he got off my case immediately, and held his tongue when dealing with me. Thereafter, he would simply stare at me silently and with a scowl, probably nursing hopes of revenge.

However, security at Division X always looked thoroughly into any report. Every message was examined, even those sent anonymously, and I knew that Sinchenko's complaint would be carefully studied from every angle. As long their investigation was active, it would be up in the air whether I would be sent abroad again. I might not see Cindy again for a long time, and in fact it was unclear if I would ever see her again at all. In any case, if Soviet counterintelligence discovered that I was carrying on a relationship with an American, it would be off with my head.

Cindy and I often encountered the captain ashore. We first spotted him in the town park, where he was standing on the deck of an old steamboat, a monument to all the North American steamboats that had once connected this vast continent. The captain then hurried to the block-long shopping mall at the intersection of Christina Street and George Street, near the Capitol Movie Theater and a tavern whose yellow sign showed a young cowboy in the saddle.

Once, in a small round square at the corner of Wellington Street, we came across a bronze soldier with a flat helmet, a modest monument to all of the town's citizens who had fallen in wartime: sixty-eight men in World War I, one hundred and three in World War II, and sixty in the Korean conflict. I thought of how many wars, campaigns, and losses there had been in the world, such countless numbers of them. Not to mention all the many secret conflicts and battles which few knew about. Cindy and I stood there in silence to pay our respects to the fallen soldiers, and I saluted them according to military custom. The dead do not ask for much, but they do need remembrance and respect.

We had just set off again when we saw Sinchenko on Vidal Street. He was popping in and out of various shops and had a worried look on his face. The Soviet merchant navy, from the captain down to the most junior sailor, made their living from trading in certain goods; the official salary they received was a meager one. For their travels abroad, these Soviet sailors, who lived under socialism and all the shortages that came with it, were given a small amount of foreign currency, with which they would buy ordinary products that were cheap abroad: clothing, cosmetics, fashionable items. Back home, the sailors would sell the items to middlemen, in what was a well-established market. There was in fact a whole industry based on making up for the paucity of products then available in the USSR. These shortages did not affect the Soviet *nomenklatura*, senior Party figures, and people with connections to them, who could do their shopping in special, exclusive shops. The elite walled themselves off from the rest of the population and lived relatively carefree lives.

Such trading demanded a great deal of physical effort and patience on the part of the crewmen. The sailors would visit shops and wholesalers in a foreign port, usually more than once. They would start by getting a price from various places and trying to wrangle a discount. They would end up buying from the place offering the most favorable terms, leaving the other shops empty-handed. That was how competition worked in this market; it all came down to self-interest.

As the captain walked around town, he was accompanied by two crew members, as stipulated in regulations. Sailors on shore leave always went in threes. Even the captain was forbidden from going ashore alone – this was a hard and firm rule. It is therefore easy to imagine how much my independence, my ability to move around freely and decide my own life, annoyed the captain. I feel sure that Sinchenko often wondered why this other person was allowed to do so while he, the captain of the ship, was not. This would naturally give rise to a burning envy, and it would lead him to ask if the Soviet regime trusted him less than this mysterious passenger of his that had come aboard his ship for some strange reason.

One Saturday, Cindy and I were walking hand in hand along the waterfront, past the floating dance-halls, clubs, and restaurants established on old barges that had long since been moored forever along the shore. The largest and most ancient of these barges was adorned with a few wooden billboards depicting antique cars and elegant couples in a retro style: dapper gentlemen and sophisticated ladies dressed to the of the twenties and thirties, the short respite between the wars which Gertrude Stein called the Lost Generation.

We found ourselves recalling the writers whose works celebrated that era. Cindy knew the cinema and literature of those decades well, and our opinions and favorites usually coincided. We rejoiced once more that our thoughts were running along the same lines.

It was a warm, sunny day. The St. Clair riverfront was empty save for a few other people some way off. There was a plastic bottle lying next to a trash can. I gave it a kick, like a rambunctious little boy, and sent it flying across the grass. Cindy immediately joined in and treacherously sought to make the bottle hers. A game started up, a wacky combination of football, hockey, and rugby all in one. I ran toward the bottle, but Cindy caught up and grabbed at me. I dodged her, and we darted about here and there, shoving each other, completely carried away. We had given into the sort of childish silliness typical of lovers.

At that place on the waterfront, Nelson Street, Maxwell Street, and London Road all begin. Suddenly Captain Sinchenko came strolling down one of those streets. He was accompanied by the ship's electrician and a senior officer. All three of them were lugging big plastic bags full of purchases; they had clearly found some good deals. When my fellow Soviets, so weighed down by their burden, caught sight of us, they completely froze and nearly fainted from the shock. It was easy to understand why: it is not every day that you see a women's football–rugby–

hockey team competing with a men's team. Both teams interrupted their match and calmed down: before the eyes of these spectators, we left the field, and as we walked off we exchanged lively glances and found it hard to keep from laughing.

The following Monday, I was studying the crews and investigating how they worked together under extreme circumstances, when I was suddenly summoned to the captain's cabin. Sinchenko had already been doing a good deal of drinking, and on the table before him were assorted bottles of various sizes: whiskey, tequila, rum, and vodka. The captain seemed very cordial, and with a hospitable gesture he invited me to the table.

"Be my guest. What would you like to drink?"

"Thank you, but I have work to do." I turned him down politely, not wanting to ruffle his feathers.

"What work? What you're doing isn't serious, it's just a game. Have a drink. Drink brings people together. Helps them talk."

"Captain, I have people waiting for me."

"So, he doesn't want to drink," the captain said with a wry smile and a bitter expression on his face. "He doesn't want to. He doesn't like the captain. I get it, I get it. He thinks he's too good for us, he's better than everyone else. They send whoever they want to this ship, and the captain has to accept them and make sure everything's alright for them. God-damn aristocrats!"

"If there is nothing else, I'll be on my way."

"You can go when I dismiss you. You're on my ship now, and I'm in command here!" He filled a shot glass and drained its contents, then popped an olive into his mouth and chewed it thoughtfully. He sudden-ly asked, with great interest, "Who was that woman? Is she American?"

"What is it to you?"

"She's a looker! But aren't you afraid someone's going to snitch? They won't look too kindly on you fooling around with an American like that."

I could feel the cold breath of my native country on my back; danger was suddenly blowing in from that quarter. Sinchenko was apparently threatening me. He wanted to show that he had me in his power and that I should not try to oppose him in any way. It was a clear hint – an overt threat. Outright blackmail, even; Sinchenko was evidently trying to extort something from me, and I could only ask him straight out.

"What do you want?"

"You could introduce us…"

"Of course. I'll just chuck everything and do it."

 

The captain poured himself another shot and drank it. Then he stabbed a snack with his fork, but he did this with disgust and an unsatisfied look on his face, as if he did not actually want to eat or drink at all but simply felt forced to.

"Tell me," Sinchenko asked with undisguised resentment, "Why do some guys get everything and others get nothing?"

"What do you mean? In medicine, there is the concept of the dominant, Ukhtomsky's law 'all or nothing'…"

"Don't give me that! You're a doctor, but you're not in a hospital treating sick people. You don't make house calls and do all the hard work."

"I've done that. Treated sick people, worked hard. Then I was called up into the army."

"Yeah, they sent you to faraway places. Chukotka, Sakhalin."

"Wherever they sent me, that's where I served. The top brass knows best."

"It's all been so easy for you. Everything's worked out great. It's like success just comes to you. Hot women cling to you. The rules don't apply to you, you're *special*, and you can go on shore alone."

"I always travel alone, wherever I go in the world."

"There, you see! They trust you. You smart, educated guys are all like that. But I've been a captain, sweating blood, and yet I get nothing."

"If you've been sweating blood, that's not good. You ought to see someone about that."

"Very funny, wise guy! You don't even go shopping with us. Apparently you don't need to. You've got plenty of money."

"Captain, I'm going now. I have work to do and not much time…"

"Are you going to introduce us? Or are you afraid I'll steal her off you?"

"You're not good enough," I retorted vindictively. Then I turned around and walked firmly out of the door, leaving the captain alone with his bottles.

After a month of waiting, the ship moved to the dock with the grain elevator in order to take on our cargo. The hatches were opened and grain poured down into the ship's hold in a thick stream. Wheat came tumbling down like manna from heaven.

The mission we had been sent on was a shameful one. This precious cargo was sustenance for a country that was so rich and yet went hungry. It is hard to imagine anything worse. My God, to thee I pray, a hungry stomach is deaf to reason. Don't leave us without food. Give us this day our daily bread.

In two days we had filled all the ship's holds to the brim. The ship set off from the dock, and with its foghorn it tooted farewell to the town of Sarnia. For Cindy, standing on the riverside, the sound of the ship's horn brought sadness, for it meant separation.

══ 47 ══

Just as I had foreseen, when Captain Sinchenko sent in his complaint, Division X's own security launched an investigation. I was not formally accused of anything, and they said nothing to me of any suspicions they might be harboring, and I continued to work on secret topics, see patients, and travel to other military facilities on official business. I was no longer sent abroad, though.

As long as the investigation was ongoing, I naturally could not see Cindy. Then, abruptly, my country collapsed like a house of cards, and the investigation ended all by itself. No one cared about me any more. Moreover, rumors were already circulating that Division X was to be disbanded.

Once, when I visited Moscow, I entered the central telecommunications building and placed a call to San Francisco. I could permit myself to do this now that the country to which I had sworn my oath had fallen apart, disappeared completely, vanished from the face of the earth. The more so because Division X itself had been rapidly and unceremoniously shut down. Because we were no longer needed, and because there was no money anyway, we were all discharged from the army. I was a free man. As the old Negro spiritual went in America: "Free at last, free at last!" Now that I was no longer in the army, I was released from all restrictions in terms of what I could do or say.

To earn a living, I worked as a district medical officer in the town of Zvenigorod near Moscow, the same district where Anton Chekhov had once worked as a doctor. I also had a part-time position at the local emergency room. I was not starving, at least. Though I was not exactly living in luxury, I could get by. Still, after Division X, life became very dull indeed. My travels abroad were all behind me, I was no longer paid in foreign currency or able to roam across foreign countries, I never stepped across the border, and I now had to be careful about my spending: one had to live more modestly. Gentlemen, modesty is fitting!

I am not used to complaining about the whims of fate and changes of circumstances, but now I had to travel day and night among the villages and treat ill farmers, giving succor to the sick. What I missed most was our scientific work at Division X: the valuable results we had obtained there were going to waste. Plus, other countries would be interested in getting their hands on them, and now anyone with secrets to sell was doing so. If I had remained abroad, I too could have probably made a killing from what I knew. That was not in my nature, however, and although my old country had disappeared, my convictions remained.

It was still night on the West Coast. The phone kept ringing and ringing, while I waited and waited and imagined the vast night-time spaces across which my signal was passing. I had already lost all hope when I suddenly heard a sleepy voice at the other end. Half-awake, Colonel Creighton could not understand who was calling and why.

Once my voice finally reached the sleepy American and he realized who it was, he let out a long moan and then fell silent. I told him that I had seen the interpreter recently, and she had changed her mind. Even from so unimaginably far away, from the other side of the world, I could still sense the turmoil inside the man. I realized that my call had stunned him, nearly knocking him off his feet.

The colonel breathed heavily into the phone, as if he had just come in from a run, but he gradually pulled himself together. He shrugged off the last remnants of sleep. After all, he could hardly go on thinking about sleep when his life had suddenly taken such a sharp turn. The American, making an effort to control his excitement, said with great determination, "Thank you, sir. I am forever in your debt. I want to see you all as soon as possible. You can't imagine what you've done for me. Give me an address, and I'll immediately make arrangements. I'll contact the State Department and get our embassy in Moscow to arrange visas for you quickly."

I headed back to Zvenigorod and returned to my job of driving through the villages in an old, rundown ambulance. The interpreter and the pilot, meanwhile, were invited to the American embassy. There the consul amiably told them that they could have visas for whatever dates they wished. This sudden visit to the embassy seemed unreal. The consul was remarkably friendly, and he looked at these two with sincere interest and unfeigned curiosity: the message that the State Department had sent him must have been impressive indeed if it had surprised even this experienced campaigner.

"Will you be staying in the USA?" the consul asked, a wide smile on his face. "I think that would be no problem. First you'll get a Green Card, then you'll be offered American citizenship."

Shilin was amazed. "Is it that simple?"

"Oh, no, it's not usually that simple at all…" The consul flashed a charming smile at his visitors. "But your story is a remarkable one. It's my pleasure to be able to help you. It's a great honor for me."

"Thank you." The interpreter nodded curtly. "I am very grateful to you, but please don't worry. I shan't be putting anyone to any trouble."

"Excuse me?" the consul looked at her blankly.

"I'm not going," the interpreter told him calmly, as if she had long since thought about the matter and made up her mind.

"What?!" The consul raised an eyebrow, perplexed. "But you wanted to go!"

"I did want to go," the interpreter agreed. "But that was a long time ago."

"And from what I hear, you took such a risk. They arrested you for it."

"Yes," she replied and softly smiled, as if indulging him. "June 1944. But that's all just water under the bridge now."

The consul, taken aback, fell silent and, judging from the bafflement on his face, he was thinking about what a mysterious and enigmatic country Russia is. But he was an American and he summoned all his strength to try and convince her. "You suffered so much. They treated you so terribly. After everything that happened, do you really not want to change your life for the better?"

The consul was genuinely unable to understand what was happening. He assumed that he had simply not explained the situation clearly enough but if he just tried harder he would eventually make these two people understand just how lucky they were, and they would stop being so stubborn. After all, a lot of Russians dreamed of getting a chance like this, as the consul knew very well first-hand. Nevertheless, no matter how hard he tried to persuade the woman sitting in front of him, she simply shook her head.

"If you ask me, you're making a big mistake," the consul, now visibly flustered, told her. "I can guarantee that there'd be a lot of interest in your story. TV, magazines, Hollywood. In America you could become a big star."

The interpreter smiled bashfully, as if she were a little ashamed that she was being compelled to disappoint the consul and indeed all America. "Me, a star?" she muttered.

"But you wanted to go," the American tried to convince her, with a fervor that was untypical of the diplomat that he was.

"I did," she agreed. "I wanted very much to go. More than anything else in the world."

The consul seized on her words. "There, you see," he said. "We'll see to everything. I've received orders to provide you with as much assistance as possible. You will have no problems. You've waited so long, but better late than never."

"It's too late now," she said, and gave a sad smile; and behind the sadness it was not hard to sense real grief and regret, and a belief that everything was in the past now and there was no sense trying to change anything.

Some of my fellow Russians would have chided her for being so silly, reproaching her for her stubbornness. After all, for some Russians, the USA was their dream, a place they longed for but could never reach.

When Shilin described to me their visit to the consul, I pictured the long line stretching outside the American embassy on Novinsky Boulevard. There, Russians stand freezing as they wait their turn, and all the while they silently pray, "Please don't refuse me a visa, please don't refuse me a visa." Yet the interpreter had turned the offer down, and there was no power in this world capable of changing her mind.

"Are you afraid of something?" the consul asked, in the hope of determining the real reason for her refusal. "Is someone threatening you? Putting pressure on you?"

"No," Olga replied curtly.

"I want to assure you," the consul boasted, "you will be under the protection of the US government."

The interpreter nodded to show that she understood. "Thank you," she said. "But that is not the reason. I just don't need any more drama in my life."

A silence hung over the room. The consul could only throw up his hands helplessly. Then he turned his attention to the pilot, expecting trouble from him, too. "What about you?" he asked Nikolai Shilin, unable to hide his disappointment at Olga's refusal. Usually it was the Russians who begged the consulate staff for help, tears in their eyes as they implored the consul, but now he had readily offered his assistance only to be turned down. Indeed, Russia was a mysterious country.

"I'll go," the pilot replied without further ado. "I've been dreaming of it for a long time."

   

The consul sighed in relief, as if a great burden had been lifted from him. He had never before had to convince a Russian to travel to America.

"If you want to, you can stay there," said the consul, who had never, in all his time in Russia, had to utter such words. Russians had so often begged him for exactly that, that he truly believed that living in the USA was the greatest prize any Russian believed he could win. "Your father lives in California. In San Francisco. One of the finest cities in the world," he went on, like a seasoned tour guide.

The pilot smiled. "I'm aware of that."

"And your half-sister lives in New York."

"Yes, fortunately," Shilin agreed. "New York is also one of the finest cities in the world."

The consul did not catch his sarcasm, however. Sarcasm was not provided for in his job description, let alone when he was actually in the office and attending to his official duties.

"Apply for your passport and then call me," the consul said, now beaming with joy. He handed the pilot his card and then looked inquisitively at the interpreter to see if perhaps she had changed her mind.

But she had not changed her mind, and the two visitors left the consulate. She never reconsidered her decision then or at any other time, and I saw no regret on her face, though who knows what she really felt deep inside.

The pilot spent the next few days standing in lines at government offices. It took a little over two months for him to receive his passport. His application was forwarded to the security services, who carefully vetted anyone who had had access to secrets. After much chicanery on the part of the state and long hours standing in line, the pilot finally received his long-awaited passport. He then obtained an American visa and booked a plane ticket to San Francisco.

"You know," he confided to me, "I feel like I'm dreaming. Am I really about to fly to America? It's so crazy! After all, I've spent my whole life fighting America. I can't believe it, it just seems too good to be true."

For all those years the pilot had heard talk only of America, day after day. The Soviets called America their worst friend, their bosom enemy; they repeated the same lines over and over again to brainwash everyone, and nearly the entire country believed them.

To Shilin, America had always been something unreal, though he had often encountered Americans in the skies. Sometimes it seemed as if America did not really exist at all, that it was just something drawn on a map, an illusion that everyone kept talking about. While the pilot had been serving in the Soviet military, he had been certain that he would never get the opportunity to visit the USA. It was something out of his wildest dreams.

Now – just think! – he would get to see the place with his own eyes, and if he wanted to, he could even stay there forever. Needless to say, Shilin had been feeling restless of late, sleeping poorly and burning with impatience. He found it hard to believe that he would soon be overseas and would be seeing his close kin: his father, his brother, his sister, whom he did not know and of whom he had not dared even think until recently.

Even when he was holding his plane ticket in his hand, Shilin could not get used to the thought that he was going to fly to America. He had only to let the thought enter his head to feel instantly stunned: was he really about to fly off?! He would look over his ticket again as if to convince himself once more that, yes, he really was going, that there was no trickery here, America really was waiting for him.

Meanwhile, the date of his departure approached. For some strange reason, the pilot felt increasingly out of touch with reality; he was absorbed in his own thoughts and seemed to be somewhere else, off in space.

At times the pilot would suddenly start to make plans. He was impatient to get to America and discover it for himself. He felt as if he had been separated from the country for his whole life and now he was already seriously considering staying there forever.

"Am I really going to miss anything here?" he asked me once. "My tiny pension? The stupid government? The damned bureaucracy? All the mistreatment I've been subjected to? Over there I'll be treated like a human being. And who the hell knows, maybe I'll even get to fly again."

However, all of us who knew Shilin were in for a shock. Shortly before his departure for America, I felt uneasy and restless, akin to the feeling that had come over me at New York's airport before the departure of Korean Airlines Flight 007 New York – Anchorage – Seoul. My anxiety grew stronger, as if something was about to happen – even, perhaps, a foreboding of some great tragedy.

According to Division X statistics, in one third of cases a person's forebodings end up being justified. Not enough to start a panic, but I am saying that one should not discount noetics, the science of intuition. I did not know exactly what danger loomed, but my concerns were definitely linked to Shilin. Was everything about to repeat itself, did life really go round in circles? Had a path been laid for each person which another had already walked?

On the eve of his departure, the pilot suddenly gave up his plane ticket, got in his car, and hurried from Moscow to the Valdai region. He did not bother to explain why; he simply felt that he had to abandon everything and set off – in order to save himself, as I thought then.

I arrived in Ostashkov in the middle of the night. My train arrived shortly before dawn, and a few streetlights were glimmering in the fog. It took me half an hour to make the journey on foot from the train station to Fishermen's Street at the southern outskirts of the town, a neighborhood that had long borne the name America. The door was opened by a pretty young lady whom I had never met before. As I stepped inside, I was astonished to discover people unknown to me sleeping in all the rooms of the house and even outside. The house was as packed as a provincial inn on market day.

The young lady told me that a neighboring family was holding a wedding, and the pilot had invited the guests to stay in his home. It was cramped inside, and I was unable to find a place for myself among all the snoring, drunken muttering, and moaning guests, so I gave up and headed for the hayloft behind the house. I did not manage to get any sleep, however, for as soon as I drifted off I was awakened by Shilin. It took me a moment to come to.

"Wake up!" he said and shook me by the shoulder. "Come on, get up!"

"What's going on?" I stared drowsily at him, unable to grasp why he should be waking me up at such an early hour.

"Ssh, quiet. People are sleeping."

"I'm sleeping too."

"But I need you right now."

I covered my head with the blanket in the hope of getting rid of him, but it did not work. He pulled me up from where I lay and then led me to the lakeshore. Seliger was wrapped in a whitish fog. The night was nearly past, but the space around us was still filled with a pale, watery murk. As it gradually grew lighter, we could see the dense motionless veil over the lake, muffling all sound. A heavy silence hung over the whole town and its outskirts, its houses and fences. The silence seemed as strong and unassailable as a fortress. The black outlines of a few scattered buildings resembled old and tattered haystacks in the fog on the lakeshore. As we looked around, the trees, fences, and boathouses lost their features and became indistinguishable, as if they had been plunged into lime mortar.

It was cool, and we felt a night-time chill on our faces and at our backs. As dawn came, the fog grew thicker, and it came to cover the entire shore as if it were falling into ranks. The hour for dew arrived, and a cold dampness appeared on the lakeside grass and bushes and on the wooden piers, and moisture gleamed on the chains by which Shilin's boat was moored. We had to wipe the benches of the boat off before we sat down at the oars.

Trying not to make a sound, the two of us pushed the boat into the water and rowed away from shore. We were surrounded on all sides by white gauze; we were floating in a thick milk. The rhythmic lapping of the oars in the sleepy silence seemed exaggeratedly loud.

With some difficulty, our boat cut through the fog, as if through thick glue. We were constantly pushing through a narrow gap which immediately closed behind us at the stern. Once we reached the main channel of the lake, Shilin started the engine, and we began to move slowly away from Ostashkov. The town was invisible in the fog, and the strange idea came to me that we might only have to proceed through the fog and suddenly we would come upon the magical city of San Francisco. In other words, it was right there next to us, so did one really need to travel half a world away to find it?

It was a glorious thought. I immediately understood its import and shared it with the pilot. He nodded appreciatively.

The two of us, one dressed in an old, well-worn padded jacket and the other in a shabby soldier's peacoat, both in high rubber fishing boots, made our way over the water. The engine rattled, sounding as if it was suffering from shortness of breath. A dense fog covered the shores, but we knew that behind the dense, milky curtain, a vast city sprawling over steep green hills was lurking: neatly kept streets, skyscrapers, wild inclines along which little streetcars crawled, wide promenades, countless moorings for boats, yachts, and ocean liners.

"If you wanted to, you could live there," I reminded the pilot. He nodded. I thought about what it would be like for him to arrive there on the other shore after living in this Russian backwater with its snaking cobblestone streets, its waste ground and bad rural roads, the paths through the grass, the picturesque ravines, the humble yards of houses overgrown with burdock and goose-foot, the stacks of firewood, the little churches on the hills, the old homes with stone foundations that had once belonged to merchants, the scattered wooden cottages with traditional bathhouses outside and gardens where scarecrows stretched their arms wide, as if longing to embrace everyone.

Just think, all his life, since he had first taken off into the skies, Nikolai Shilin had been opposing the Americans, trying to defy them, to drive them off, to harry them wherever he could, and he had moved all over the world in order to find them and stop them, as if he had been born solely for that. And now he had turned out actually to be one of them. I even said that aloud, "You are one of them yourself."

The pilot nodded in reply, and an amused smile passed across his lips. "I've been thinking about that constantly," he said.

We are all joined to others. No one has ever existed completely apart, alone unto himself. The lines of fate intertwine, intricately converge and diverge, whether we like it or not. It is hard to imagine how Shilin would have lived with himself if he had shot down that Korean airliner. "God spared me," he would often say. But so what, he reproached himself, people were killed nevertheless. Even if he had not killed them, he had not been able to save them either. The victims constantly came to his mind, refusing to let him go. So many years had passed since then, but he remained just as tormented and unable to forgive himself.

At a gentle speed – it would have been dangerous to go any faster when visibility was so low – we crossed the reach off Ostashkov. To our left were the green islands of Voronye and Klichen. The main channel of the lake gave a wide berth to the densely overgrown Gorodomlya Island. There, among the hills and rocky outcrops and protected by the thick vegetation, a mysterious settlement was hidden, one that resembled a European town, German, say. From sea and air the island was carefully monitored by sentries and sensitive surveillance devices. The settlement there had no address, just a single postbox behind which unspeakably secret laboratories and factories were masked.

For odd reasons peculiar to Russia, in Ostashkov every drunkard, every child, and all the old women sitting outside their homes knew that guidance systems for satellites and missiles were being produced there on Gorodomlya in conditions of the utmost secrecy. Nevertheless, the island continued to hide away its great mystery, and Ostashkov locals and visitors alike felt a burning curiosity about it.

That orderly and well-kept settlement had appeared on Gorodomlya soon after the war. Among its first inhabitants were a large number of Germans, remarkably enough. German engineers were brought here from Peenemünde in the Pomerian region of north-eastern Germany, where Wernher von Braun's research center had developed the V-2 rocket. The crafty Americans had managed to spirit Von Braun himself across the ocean, but his colleagues brought to Lake Seliger did good work to assist their recent foes.

Gradually, the island came to have a stadium, swimming pool, gym, and movie theater, and while the population of the surrounding country faced hunger in the post-war years, Gorodomlya enjoyed abundance. They had plenty of good food, which was understandable, as those who had ordered the building of the facility were willing to pay generously to keep the men well-fed.

Yet it has long been known that this heaven on earth for a chosen few was in fact a golden cage. A strict guard had been set over the workers at the facility, and it was completely isolated from the mainland. The men paid for their abundance and comfort with their freedom; no wonder they say that captivity may allow a person to eat his fill, but it never brings happiness. Life on the island was comfortable, but only a few were ever permitted to leave the secret facility.

Our boat's trace in the water split into two at the stern and cast up gentle waves that rocked the buoys demarcating the channel. Boats were forbidden not only to moor at Gorodomlya but even to approach it: its sentries kept watch day and night, as if an outsider even coming near could change the course of the rockets produced there, and cause them to miss their targets.

We passed a buoy that was barely visible in the fog, and the pilot turned the wheel to the left to point us north where there awaited us, seafaring adventurers that we were, an unknown, undiscovered land, *terra incognita*. We continued to make our way across the lake, concentrating unbrokenly on finding our way in the fog. Our journey across the mist-blanketed water was like life: we had to feel our way along without knowing what would come next. Gradually, however, the fog that had covered Lake Seliger overnight now thinned, melted away, and swirled like white steam over the water. The fog to the right of our course, over the eastern shore of the lake, acquired a copper tinge, the first sign of the still unseen sun.

Maintaining our speed, we proceeded north and slightly west, where the last traces of the night still lingered. As Shilin steered the boat, he stared intently at the horizon, still barely discernible. The rattle of the boat's engine merged with the splashing of water, and on all sides we were surrounded by the flat, silvery surface of the lake, bounded far off by forest which gradually spread out and took on detail in front of us.

Shilin looked abstractedly around without seeming to see anything. Naturally, over the recent weeks he had been overcome by doubts and uncertainties, like a young man who has just started out in life. Well, that can be explained: his life had passed a critical junction and then gathered pace for the downhill run: everyone go home, the party is over!

Just three months ago, Shilin had known nothing of his origins. He had resigned himself to believing that everything destined to happen in his life had already happened. Everything important was already behind him. The future promised nothing. He should not fool himself that something big was going to happen; he should not hope that some change for the better would come. A middling banality awaited him. He would live out the rest of his days scraping out some kind of existence and wasting his life away.

Over these last three months, since the evening when his mother had made her revelation, Shilin's life seemed to have performed something of a trick – turned a somersault, done a handstand. Now, as in his youth, reality seemed to wink slyly at him, and just as in his youth, a glimmer of hope flared up within him and his blood quickened. Why be surprised, then, that in the middle of the night, he had suddenly been seized by an interest that had not visited him for a long time.

This was the reason why Shilin was so restless as we crossed Lake Seliger. The pilot, just like a young man only now starting out in life, felt that he was standing at a crossroads. He had to choose now the road that he would follow. For the first time in many years, something depended on him; he would decide for himself what he would do. Life had become full of novelty again, once more inexhaustible and full of surprises. Now it was time to exclaim, "No! The party is just beginning!"

This feeling of newness and freshness nearly knocked Shilin off his feet. In the army no one had any doubt: America is the enemy. Commanders and Communist Party officials hammered away at this simple truth. It is one thing, though, to take that lesson to heart, and quite another thing to meet the Americans in the skies, fly right alongside them, and look them in the eye. Both sides, bristling with their deadly armaments, moving in a ritual dance: look how strong we are, don't mess with us, get lost or we'll teach you a lesson.

And now imagine what it feels like to discover overnight that you are one of them, one of those whom you have considered your enemy all your life. It was a staggering revelation. The news had sideswiped Shilin, and he was unable to get used to it. He was still not used to it.

The fog over the lake dissipated and scattered in clumps. Visibility had improved and now we could see further. The wide channel between the long, jutting Lebed Peninsula to the west and the village of Peska to the east gradually turned into the Krestets reach with its many bays and islands. People whose roots in the region went a long way back called this reach by its old name of Strogan.

Anglers sat fishing on ramshackle piers set on the banks. Some were standing further out in the water, while others fished from boats on either side of the main channel.

"Now I understand why they used to call me 'the American' back in the camp," Shilin broke the silence. A slight smile passed across his lips. The truth had leaked out from the camp's office, where prisoners' case files were held in a secret archive. Rumors rippled outward like a stone dropped in water, and the nickname stuck.

"By the way," I complained, "I still have no idea where we're going. No one's bothered telling me."

"You could have guessed by now," the boat's helmsman reproached me. "You do know how to read other people's thoughts, right?"

"When I was in the army. I'm just a civilian now, a simple rural doctor. So, no thanks! I'm under no obligation to do it."

"Altruism's dead, huh?"

"As a dodo."

"Call yourself an officer!"

"I was. I'm a reservist now, so far down the list that no one'll ever call on me," I said, explaining my current position in life, the universe, and everything. I repeated it once more just to make it clear: "I'm a spare."

"Being saved up for a rainy day. Your belt won't pull your shoulder. A thrifty guest always carries a spare spoon with him." The pilot expressed himself in an unsophisticated, folksy fashion.

"You've grown bolder, my friend! Have you forgotten about your diagnosis? The Reds will come and you'll have to answer to them. They won't forgive you."

"I'm going to America. I've got close relatives there."

"Why didn't you even mention them on the forms?" I mocked him like an old Soviet bureaucrat. "Were you hiding it?"

"I didn't know myself back then."

"The soldier was hiding it. Relatives in another country! And not just anywhere, but America, the very lair of imperialism! What could be more terrible for a Soviet officer? There's not a single hospital that would admit a patient with that diagnosis. Might as well send him straight to the morgue."

"I'm going to America," the pilot said, uttering these words dreamily. "I'm going to become a rich Yankee. You'll envy me yet."

     

"Maybe I will envy you," I agreed. "Incidentally, I could have stayed there myself."

"And?"

"I didn't stay there, as you can see."

A ship overtook our boat, in the same channel. It tore past us in the water with its huge white hull, driving up a powerful wave that rushed toward the shore and rocked the nearby boats and the fishermen's floats. Early-morning passengers crowded on the deck: the ship made regular tours of the lake's nearer and farther reaches, its islands big and small, and the isolated villages which were connected to the outside world only by boat. Such a big circle around the lake took a whole day. The ship was used by local villagers, by people gathering mushrooms and berries, by fishermen, tourists, and local officials traveling around on business. One also encountered strange wanderers and pilgrims who wished to visit sacred places.

At the ship's stern, over the water churned up by its propeller, gulls cawed. They had grown used to passengers throwing them bread. The gulls flew up and down and, in eager expectation of a treat, hovering for a long time in the air, ready to snatch in mid-flight any piece thrown their way. Any such ship that crossed Lake Seliger was accompanied by gulls for the length of its journey.

When our boat left the channel, the pilot turned left. It was now obvious where we were heading. Stolbny Island rises up over the water, looking like the legendary city of Kitezh emerging from the depths of a lake. Even at a distance, we could see the domes of the awesome Bo-goyavlensky Cathedral towering into the sky. It resembled Saint Isaac's Cathedral in Saint Petersburg, and this was no wonder as they shared the very same design.

As we approached the island, towers, walls, roofs, and domes crowd-ed before and above us. A high granite embankment ran around the southern end of the island, pierced by a shallow inlet. An archway cut into the wall, looking like something out of a fairy tale, led to the mon-astery grounds, which were entirely surrounded by old buildings and churches, of which All Saints was the most impressive.

═══ **48** ═══

The Nilov Monastery is a legendary place in the Orthodox faith, like the Kyiv Pechersk Lavra, or the Solovetsky or Valaam monasteries. Back in time immemorial, a hermit named Nil had settled on this then uninhabited island. He had sworn a shocking vow: for the salvation of his soul, he forbade himself to lie down or sit. He spent his entire life standing, like a pillar – *stolb* in Russian, hence the island's name Stolbny. How can a person live standing up? How could they work, eat, and sleep all the time like that? If anyone wants to find out, let them try it for themselves and see if they can avoid sitting or lying down for even a single day.

After the Revolution, the Bolsheviks naturally closed the monastery down and built a camp for political prisoners on the island, as had happened with the Solovetsky Monastery. Before the war, the camp held Polish officers who had escaped to Russia after their defeat at the hands of the Germans. Once in Russia, the Poles had hoped to fight with the Russians against their common foe, but instead, thousands of wounded, ill, and starving officers, the cream of the Polish army, were imprisoned in this former monastery. Subsequently, at Stalin's order they were all taken to the Smolensk region and shot in the Katyn Forest there.

In the years that followed, the island had simply been left deserted, the holy monastery abandoned to the elements. Local people would come on their boats and plunder the buildings of their metal, brick, and stone. They ripped off the doors, the window frames, and the wooden staircases and floorboards. With no one to take care of it, and now fully exposed to the wind and rain, the monastery quickly fell apart. The gardens, orchards, and paths around the monastery grounds were overgrown with weeds. It soon became hard to believe that this monastery had been renowned across Russia for its home-grown fruit and vegetables. The old buildings collapsed or were covered by moss and mold, and instead of windows only black holes gaped in their façades. Mere ruins were left on the site of a once-flourishing monastery. It was sheer destruction, an abomination of desolation.

After the collapse of Communism, the island and its monastery were given back to the Church. The new abbot and the first monks immediately got down to restoring the place. After the terrible devastation, the monastery recovered and came back to life. The monks began by hauling away the heaps of rubble and rubbish. They replaced the windows, repaired the walls, and made the cells habitable once more. Soon, in one of the churches where an iconostasis had partially survived, they began holding services again. Believers started to arrive in this holy place, as if the intervening years had never happened.

In one of the cellars, the monks fired up the oven and began to bake bread. A carpentry workshop was set up on the grounds, and the monks worked tirelessly. Sometimes workers were hired from outside, but there was not enough money, and so the monks had to make do with their own efforts and whatever blessings came their way. Among the visitors from near or far who came to pray, there were sometimes competent stonemasons, plasterers, and woodworkers, and anyone who wanted to could help dig the earth or carry boards. Some of the visitors stayed on the island to lend a hand in the restoration of this ancient and sacred place. They worked together with the monks and everyone ate from the same pot.

Some of the spiritual seekers settled down on the island, and some were even tonsured as monks. Everyone was given a job to do, as befitted their skills and talents. Often, the monastery received contributions from vacationing tourists, fishermen, and mushroom pickers who had come to visit the Valdai region. When they heard about the monastery's needs, they selflessly offered their help and, as they left, they promised to visit again the next year.

Indeed, they often returned, visited more than once, and toiled at the monastery as if they had to atone for the sins of the Soviet regime and the outrages against the monastery. It sometimes happened that people felt compelled to leave their homes and cities, their comfortable and settled lives, and head for the monastery, where they would rise at dawn every day and work wherever they were directed to, without ever expecting remuneration or recognition.

The devout volunteers were even complemented by atheists, and both groups worked zealously, as if they were atoning together for past sins, whether their own, someone else's, or the sins of the regime they had served for so many years.

Shilin sometimes provided assistance to the monastery himself. The deacon who took care of the monastery's living quarters often tried to convince Shilin to lend a hand, for workers who had technical skills were greatly valued.

It was a strange feeling for the pilot to visit Stolbny Island. He had never been involved with religion before in his life; he had always kept his distance from it. The army tended to avoid the Church, considering it a hostile power that undermined soldiers' readiness and morale. Even a little curiosity about religion could land an officer in deep trouble; fleeting rumors or gossip were enough to destroy his career. Over all the years that the pilot had served, he had thought of religion as something only for ignorant, unlettered, and elderly people. It seemed to him that the Church was barely holding on, that its days were numbered.

Shilin had glimpsed the Church only from afar, though. The military bases where he had lived, as everyone knows, had no churches on them. Instead, the only figures caring for soldiers' souls were Communist Party officials, a mass of faceless creatures who eschewed any meaningful work.

Shilin was amazed when he observed that many people could not imagine life without the Church. At the surface of people's lives, where the foam stirred up by the Communists bubbled, there was of course no place for the Church. However, below the surface presented to the regime lay a different life, one free of all the Communist bombast, the loud slogans and appeals that had taken over the country.

To Shilin's surprise, the hard-pressed people of the USSR, though they were worried about getting by and finding enough food, continued to baptize children, bury the dead, have religious weddings, confess, repent of their sins, pray, and beg God for His protection. He had to leave the army first before he could see this other side of the Soviet reality.

Made no mistake, however: in spite of these musings Shilin did not enter the Church, though; he did not become a believer. He had never acquired the habit of praying, and he did not want to force himself to start doing so now. The pilot winced when Russian politicians who had come out of nowhere and rose to power suddenly turned into devout Christians. In order to keep up with the latest trend, numerous officials of all stripes, though they had recently been Communists, were now suddenly discovering Orthodox feelings inside them which had supposedly lain dormant until now.

Russian television began to broadcast church services. These newly-minted devotees of the Church stood through the service where everyone could see them, there in front of all the cameras, and they frequently made the sign of the cross, albeit often with the wrong hand – they would furtively glance at their neighbors, like bad dancers trying to copy the right moves from others. All their lives they had rejected religion, calling it the opium of the people. They had continually disparaged the Church and persecuted its priests. Now they had supposedly changed their ways overnight and were entering the Church in droves. As they stood in church, people who just yesterday had been Party members and ardent Communists – many of them former KGB – now looked like bad actors who did not know their lines and looked around helplessly in search of a prompter.

A breed of new celebrity priests popped up, of whom the pilot disapproved. They posed for the cameras as they blessed fancy new shops, car dealerships, warships, and missiles. These priests loved to visit big events and lavish receptions and indulge in gluttony. Shilin was unable to trust these shepherds of the flock – indeed, how could he when their hypocrisy was so blatant?

The Church had gone from an unloved stepdaughter to an almighty fad, a way to show off. Shilin did not believe that the Russian population had really gained a sudden insight, undergone a transformation, and attained holiness. To him, the long lines of people stretching before the exhibited relics of whatever saints represented nothing but paganism and medieval obscurantism.

Shilin had never visited churches, though he maintained some interest in them. For him, they were unfamiliar territory that he had heard much about but knew little of first-hand. He was brought to Stolbny Island by the simple curiosity that has always led people to visit foreign lands.

The monk responsible for visitors quickly recognized in Shilin a skilled person whom the monastery could use. During his occasional visits to the monastery, Shilin restored to working order a compressor no longer needed by a local farm, and repaired old pumps that the railway had sent off to the dump.

His mother's recent revelation of how he had come into the world had unsettled him, and he was often given over to reflection. He spent some time thinking it over, and decided that things could not have just happened by themselves, randomly, separately from everything else and unconnected with the general flow of life. He became inclined to take any news as a sign, as a reflection, whether overt or masked, of the essence of things.

Our boat came up to the island, and I started to fathom what had brought us here. It was hard to imagine what might have happened to the pilot if he had been the one to shoot down the Korean airliner. From time to time, he would stop and look intently back at the past, at the events of long ago. He would vividly recall what had happened back then; the image was clear in his mind, and he remembered every detail.

Sometimes, though, once in a while, he imagined events which had not actually happened, but which might well have. In sharp, bright colors, as if in a prophetic dream, the pilot watched himself press the button and send a missile flying toward the target. Fear rose up within him; he was gripped by a chill and dank horror.

Yet alongside this bitter imagining was a comforting thought, a consolation: someone had saved him. Some inexplicable power had held him back and rescued him. He could not leave such mercy unanswered, and he decided that his work at the monastery would be his response. In doing so, Shilin did not realize that he had thereby made a secret vow and surrendered his will, just as the monks had. Who could have told him or advised him?

"I'll accompany you back," Shilin suggested, after we had taken tea in the monastery's dining hall.

We walked across the grounds and through the archway leading to the lakeshore. The space under the arch was dimly lit, and in front of us the sunshine sparkled on the water. We might have thought that we were walking through a tunnel with a blinding light at the end of it. As we stepped out from the archway, the vast surface of the lake opened out before us and stretched, like a veritable sea, for as far as the eye could see.

"Why don't you head off?" Shilin mumbled. "Take the boat." He hid his eyes from me, embarrassed, and his gaze wandered across the lake, the distant islands, and the rooftops of the nearby village of Svetlitsa sprawling among the shrubs and low forest on the other side of a canal spanned by a bridge. "Just go ahead."

"What about you?"

"Maybe I'll stay," he answered evasively.

"In the monastery?"

"I'm doing some work here. The monks asked me to help."

"What about America?"

"America's not going anywhere. We'll see. I want to be somewhere quiet and think. I think better if I'm working."

The pilot collected only his clarinet from the stuff we had brought in the boat. I was amazed, but I kept silent – what would I question him for if his mind was already made up?

## 49

Thus I ended up spending the month of August alone on an uninhabited island on Lake Seliger. I caught fish, gathered mushrooms, cooked my own meals over a campfire, and gradually forgot what it was like to talk to other human beings.

For those who may have forgotten, let me say again that the hilly island was surrounded by deep channels on three sides, but on the fourth side a wide reach opened up. Over the summer, the grass on the island had grown nearly up to my waist. My tent stood on its lonesome on a hilly, forested cape from which I had an endless view around me: the watery expanse of the lake and other shores far away at the limits of my sight. Gulls flew over the island and the water and squawked insistently. Far off, a few buoys bobbed in the water, demarcating the main channel on which ships would glide past me and then disappear beyond the horizon.

I would sit down on a steep bank over a backwater to fish, or sometimes I headed down through a narrow, rocky gully to a sandy neck, or I rowed some distance away on an inflatable boat and fished where the water was deeper. Lake Seliger gave me total silence, and the wild Russian nature helped me get my thoughts in order. By late August, however, my untroubled existence came to an end: a feeling of unease was creeping over my mind, hinting that changes would shortly come.

My premonitions have never led me astray. This phenomenon relates to the noetic sciences which we studied at Division X. Though much time had passed since those days, my ability to think intuitively had remained, and was now making itself felt once more. Again, as usual, anxiety came over me, suggesting that somewhere out there certain things, as yet unknown, were ripening, inexorably coming nearer and altering the course of events.

In late August, the island's quiet backwaters were teeming. Fish were coming toward the shore as if someone had been intentionally feeding them. I tried a variety of bait, but ultimately I established that the large perch and pike were most likely to go for live bait, for fish such as bleak, gudgeon, or small roach.

Over whirlpools it was possible to catch good-sized bream and ide, and in the early morning I often sat fishing with a worm on my hook. On the last day of August I awoke before dawn, as if someone had shaken me. Something was happening out there in the world.

I lay there, motionless, remembering what day it was. Long-ago events flickered in my memory: America, New York, late August, the big airport by night. Now, just as I had then, I felt a premonition, but a premonition of what exactly, I was still not sure.

As the sun came up, my unease grew stronger by the hour. My intuition gradually emerged from its initial, drowsy state. The signals became clearer, and I could distinctly feel a sense of some impending change gnawing at me.

Experienced people know that at moments where you feel uncomfortable, it is best to find something to take your mind off it. If you can just distract yourself somehow, then the discomfort subsides, the waiting does not weigh so heavily on you, and you are less likely to wonder endlessly what it is all about. The best choice is to kill time by cooking a big and complicated dish, and in doing that you can make time fly by without evening noticing it. The pike-perch I had caught gave me an appetite for the traditional Russian soup we call *ukha*, and making that soup is an immersive activity indeed.

Russian *ukha* is a dish for real connoisseurs. It is not like ordinary fish soup from other countries, the French *bouillabaisse*, for example. I must emphasize that one should start making *ukha* immediately after the fish is caught, when it still smells of the lake or river, of pure fresh water. Some gourmands even cook the fish alive, which lends the soup a very distinct taste and aroma.

To make real *ukha*, you need, for example, sterlet, perch, pike-perch, sturgeon, or whitefish. The noble pedigree of an *ukha* is determined entirely by the fish used for it. This means that other types of fish, for example, bream, gudgeon, burbot or roach, cannot provide you with a true *ukha*. Those fish are suitable only for more ordinary fish soups.

When making *ukha*, connoisseurs never put fish from different catches into the pot. Genuine *ukha* is made solely from one species of fish, and the particular varieties of *ukha* are typically referred to based on the fish used to make them.

Generally one does not scale the fish first. The whole fish is plunged into cold, clear water and heated over a low flame. In just a few minutes, my pike-perch had dissolved into an amber-colored liquid and turned the water into a thick, fatty broth. I then added some sorrel that I had collected in the meadow, potatoes, onions, and tomatoes, and seasoned the broth with black pepper, salt, and bay leaf.

By the time the *ukha* was finally ready, the day had already peaked and the sun was no longer so hot. There was still some time left before the sun went down, but the surrounding silence already held a hint of sunset. I heard a motorboat coming from beyond the buoys marking the channel. The vast expanse of the lake was filled with a thumping sound. A small boat came down the channel and then made a turn for my island. The weak sound of the boat engine pierced the sultry late afternoon with its irksome rhythm.

Even while the boat was still approaching, I could see that it was full of people. At this distance, I was unable to make out their faces, but the humming of the boat's engine grew ever closer and the people on board gradually acquired detail.

I stood there waiting, and squinted to see who it was. Pavel, Nikolai's son, was steering the boat. Next to him sat Olga, the pilot's mother. The other passengers seemed unfamiliar, but as the engine bore the boat along closer to me, I suddenly realized that I knew them.

I recognized the American Colonel Creighton, his son Michael, and… the power of speech deserted me; I could not say it aloud… I could not believe it, it was simply unbelievable. To my great surprise, Cindy was there, too, on the boat, Cindy, whom I thought I had lost forever. What can I say, where could I find the words?

It is hard to come to terms with unexpected happiness; one is afraid of scaring it off. Happiness is like a skittish bird: one wrong move on your part and it will fly away forever. Any mistake would be costly, and my disappointment and sorrow would know no bounds.

It is true that happiness is not a horse; you cannot harness it to a shaft, you cannot catch it by the tail, and you cannot put a bridle on it. Happiness is a free bird which lands wherever it wishes. They say that one must be born under a lucky star to be happy. But remember, O fortunate one, remember and never forget: happiness and unhappiness are always close alongside each other.

Nevertheless, she was here. My eyes were not fooling me. Only my brain was holding out, unable to believe, for according to reason or common sense that could not be Cindy right there on a boat on Lake

Seliger. She was expected in Venice now, where the film festival was held year after year at the very beginning of the fall. Yet she really was here, and coming ever closer to me. In the end I chose to believe that indeed, after three years of being sundered from my love, I would finally see her again.

Besides those whom I had recognized, there was a young man in the boat, the same age as Lieutenant Shilin and vaguely resembling him. I realized that Colonel Creighton was accompanied by also his grandson, Michael's son.

There was something else. One detail, after a moment of confusion, attracted my keen attention, awakened my burning curiosity, and left me stunned. I felt suddenly paralyzed, unable to move, as if my body had failed me. My thoughts scattered, they ran wild, and I felt like I was beset with hallucinations. Then I realized that the scene before me was entirely real, and a torrent of thoughts flooded over me. Confusion filled my mind, and all hell broke loose inside my head.

In her hands Cindy was holding a little girl, a blonde-haired angel, a gift from God. She was only two years old, or two and a half, and I racked my brains trying to figure out how long it had been exactly since I last saw Cindy. When had we last met? I could simply not help but do the math. Could any man be expected to do otherwise?

As the boat came up to the sandy neck, Pavel cut the engine. The ensuing silence hung heavy in the air. The boat silently glided up to the shore, and the only thing one could hear was the ever so slight sound of the water splashing and murmuring under the boat.

I stood motionless on the shore, silently awaiting my visitors. They were coming ever closer, but time seemed to have stopped; it dragged endlessly, as if an invisible thread were being unwound. The boat softly ran aground on the sand, and the young American deftly jumped ashore and carefully helped Olga out. Lieutenant Shilin offered a hand to Colonel Creighton, but the latter smiled and refused the help, effortlessly hopping out of the boat like a marine trained for amphibious landings.

I walked out into the water, up to my knees, and took Cindy's daughter from her. I trusted only my own eyes, and now it was time to take a closer look at the little girl. We were related, there was no doubt about it.

"She's yours," Cindy whispered, smiling through her tears. "Let me introduce you to Miss Catherine."

Colonel Creighton came up and, without saying a world, hugged me and thumped me on the back. His daughter wiped her wet face and waited for her turn.

 

The colonel's son Michael lined up behind his sister and offered me his hand. "You were right," he admitted, somewhat embarrassed, and I supposed he was referring to that first night of the fall long ago, when Korean Airlines Flight 007 took off from the New York airport.

In the interim, the air force major had made his way up to colonel, thus matching his father's rank. Now the American side of the family counted two colonels and one lieutenant. The young man whom I was only now meeting for the first time was the son of one colonel and the grandson of another, and he too was an air force pilot. How could it be otherwise, if heaven ordains our destinies?

The whole Creighton family had mysteriously appeared on Lake Seliger. Circumstances had happily erected no barriers against them; on the contrary, things seemed to have come together to make everything easier for them. The international situation was favorable at that time, and that had played into their hands. The Americans, to my astonishment, had made it all the way out to the Russian wilderness, though I can imagine what an effort the journey must have been. Still, experienced travelers, if they so desire, can reach the most inaccessible corners of our planet.

The sun was nearing the horizon; August was coming to an end. Fall was approaching, and we would now spend its first night together, as we had done so long ago. The first thing I needed to do, of course, was to feed my guests: the fresh *ukha* was just what we needed. While my guests were eating, I took my tent down and shoved everything into my backpack, as we had no reason or desire to linger on the island. Soon we were on our way, sailing together into the sunset, across the vast lake toward the distant shore.

## 50

Stolbny Island was usually visible from far off. There on the vast stretch of the lake, one caught sight of its church domes, the roofs of buildings crowded closely together, bell towers, and crosses.

"Goodness, how lovely!" Cindy sighed in admiration at the view. The entire Creighton family were unable to tear their eyes away.

It was easy to understand why: with its crosses soaring upward, the monastery seemed to float in mid-air, and it was reflected below in the clear waters of the lake. Pavel reduced the boat's speed and the engine's sound died away almost to nothing. The boat gently made its way across the wide reach. Hardly breathing, the Americans stared at the island, as if spellbound. The scene was too powerful to take in: the sacred place that traced its history back to the ascetic Nil was wrapped in a boundless peace and surrounded by a wide blue sky. I too was just as impressed as if I were seeing it now for the first time.

Naturally, the whole way to the island, I held little Catherine in my arms. She slept there, warm and tight, and she clearly felt safe and secure. The boat had nearly reached the island when the enormous setting sun touched the water. The water, forest, and shore were tinted by the copper light of sunset, the colors flowed over the water, the shallows, and the embankment along the shore. We turned the engine off and rowed under a bridge, and then soundlessly floated down a channel next to the monastery. Before us was an enchanting array of walls, towers, pointed roofs, ponds, and green hills. Now, at the threshold of twilight, everything felt sad and weary, a perennial trait of Russian nature. We seemed to be floating toward a wild, deserted place, and the infinite calm of the monastery awoke in us a certain anxiety that would be difficult to express in words.

In the silence of the evening and the stillness in the depths of the island, a sound now faintly reached us. It gradually grew stronger and radiated across the area, wound its way through the splayed branches and danced among the willows at the shore. Sometimes the sound soared up over the crowds of mighty trees, then swirled through the void, fell downward, and dissolved into a spray. I recognized a familiar clarinet.

The instrument's voice criss-crossed the vicinity, and all of us in the boat fell silent. We raised and lowered the oars at a soporific, measured pace, the rowlocks quietly creaking, and the boat glided smoothly across the sleepy waters. The Americans listened to the clarinet in a daze, as if oblivious to all else. The clarinet's presence seemed to represent a strange wonder, the caprice of some pagan deity who dwelt here.

Truly, the real world had faded away. The clarinet went from being a mere musical instrument to an expression of someone's fantasy; it turned into a dream-like hallucination. We did not take part in this, we were simply present, random onlookers who had been taken by surprise. The clarinet's sound passed over the shore and spoke of the long and difficult road which fate had ordained for it.

The old colonel now began to root through his baggage. He hunted out his flute case, and opened it to take out the instrument which he always kept by his side. For a time he listened carefully and intently to the monologue of the unseen clarinet player, and then finally he made up his mind. Timidly, the flute took up what was being played on the clarinet, as if trying to fall in step. It muttered in confusion, tongue-tied and not quite able to get in sync with the other instrument.

Soon, however, the flute grew stronger, as if it had become more confident that it was capable of a real duet. Nevertheless, the flute was still beset with doubt, and none of us there in the boat knew how the clarinet would greet this other instrument. Would the clarinet accept the flute, call it to come closer, or would it reject the flute and insist on making its way alone?

Neither. To our surprise, as soon as the flute found its footing and rose to its full volume, the clarinet fell silent, as if this outsider was a nuisance. The whistling of the flute now sounded alone around us, like a moth floating and shimmering in the dusk. Its voice, a little hoarse, swept weightlessly over the water, so still now in the evening, and flew off into the meadows, the fields, and the forested hills, where it sank and melted like fleeting snow.

The clarinet remained silent. We in the boat felt uneasy: would it really not greet us, would it maintain silence, as a hermit shuns other people? The venerable Nil, the founder of this monastery, had remained aloof from any visitors; he had sought to avoid the madding crowd.

Meanwhile, the sun was setting over the lake, and the sky to the west lit up as if a vast fire had been ignited over the heavens. Our rowers, the two lieutenants, let go of their oars, and the boat lay there in the water and the stillness. Everyone was listening carefully to see if the clarinet would recognize the flute, meet it halfway, answer it, or call it closer. Yet the clarinet maintained its stubborn silence, as if it were carefully considering the situation, or running away and hiding. If the flute were out of sight, the clarinet seemed to think, then it would be out of mind, too.

Now that it had not been met by any reply, the flute faltered. Timid, uncertain notes appeared in its playing, and it started to die out like a fire deprived of oxygen. Soon it fell silent entirely, as if a cork had been stuck into it and it was firmly muted forever. Now silence set in again, a silence as vast as the space around us.

We all felt a sense of alarm. The silence surrounded us like an unassailable fortress. It was obvious that we could expect nothing. The clarinet was not going to reveal itself. It was secretly peeping at us through the foliage and did not care to meet us. In spite of our hopes, it seemed to reject us as unwelcome visitors and did not want to be disturbed. It had obviously shied away from us, had sunk like a fish to the bottom, and would not make a sound.

All of us now felt awkward and uncomfortable; we were overcome by doubt, and it left a bitter taste in our mouths. None of us had any idea what to do. We might, of course, step ashore and undertake a search, but on the other hand, one cannot demand a person's love and affection, as everyone knows. Honestly, it might be better to turn straight back.

Our hopes were fading by the second. The Americans looked utterly discouraged, that was obvious to me. The question rose unbidden in their minds as to whether they had made a mistake in coming all this way when they had no idea of how they would be greeted. Perhaps they had acted recklessly.

How long exactly we sat there in this state, I cannot say. It felt like an eternity; longer, even. When everyone was already convinced that there would be no continuation to the story, there suddenly came a twist, in the blink of an eye. Colonel Steven Creighton brought the flute back up to his lips, took a deep breath, and played with extraordinary inspiration and ease that left us astounded.

From the very first notes, I recognized a melody which was very popular in America: "America the Beautiful". In the United States it was often played to stir up patriotic feeling among the country's citizens. Already for two centuries, people have sung it with great abandon. "Oh, beautiful for spacious skies, For amber waves of grain…" This song, which the church organist and choir director Samuel A. Ward wrote in the nineteenth century, is generally considered to be a hymn, but the liveliness of its melody and its catchy beat quickly turned it into a hit song. Americans have even occasionally proposed that it be made the national anthem. It has especially touched the hearts of the immigrants who have come from all over the world to America in search of a better life.

Indeed, "America the Beautiful" has been sung by patriotic Americans and immigrants alike, by huddled masses from all over the world. Needless to say, in Russia such a song might sound rather inappropriate, as if seeking to offend the listener or showing hostility, but now it fitted perfectly, and swiftly did away with the unease that we all felt.

With great inspiration and exhilaration, the flute played this melody in the deep silence after the setting of the sun. Twilight had not yet come, but it was growing ever closer, and the flute's voice sang clearly over the dark water. Its pure and solitary sound hovered in the air over us, and may well have been heard in the neighboring villages and distant stretches of the island, too. We all listened intently, and cast off all the cares of life, and we did not expect anyone to intervene and complain.

Then the clarinet, too, spoke up. It happened so suddenly that everyone initially assumed that they had misheard. The clarinet seized on the flute's melody and ran after it. The song grew louder, the two instruments singing as two powerful voices: "America! America! God shed his grace on thee!" All of us in the boat could now breathe freely again; not a trace remained of our former anxiety. We ourselves knew that America is a beautiful country. The clarinet itself had no doubt about that, and it sang loudly and unabashed before the whole world. Russia, too, is a beautiful country, albeit one that has suffered great misfortune.

Young Colonel Michael Creighton, his lieutenant son, and Cindy all regretted that they, too, had not brought their instruments along. Goodness, just imagine what an orchestra they could have formed! If I had known how to play an instrument myself, I would have readily played along with the Americans. Yet what instrument could I have played with a child in my arms? I will be honest, however – I do not want to mislead anyone – thus far I have never taken up an instrument.

Meanwhile, little Cathy woke up, though she did not seek to crawl away from my arms or put up a fight. But I would not have minded anyway: children in general, and daughters especially, should be nurtured and cherished. I silently recited to myself the words of an old lullaby that I had once heard from an old woman from a Pomor village in northern Russia on the White Sea.

I do not know what awaits us, what tomorrow will look like. It is not for nothing that our ancestors instilled in us the belief that you cannot trust tomorrow, that tomorrow is a sneaky character who will find ways to trick you. Now, however, who would object to a little optimism? My sense of foreboding had gone to sleep, all my professional training was telling me nothing. I did not presume to look into the future and augur what it would bring, and in the meantime, we were all together, and all was well in the world.

*1983–2003*

*Zvenigorod – New York – Venice – San Francisco – Sevan (Armenia) – Hong Kong – Sarnia (Ontario, Canada) – Vladivostok – Olga Bay – Terney – Odessa – Genoa – Saigon – Bangkok – Krasnoyarsk – Singapore – Barcelona – Ostashkov – Moscow*

# The Flying Dutchman

## by Anatoly Kudryavitsky

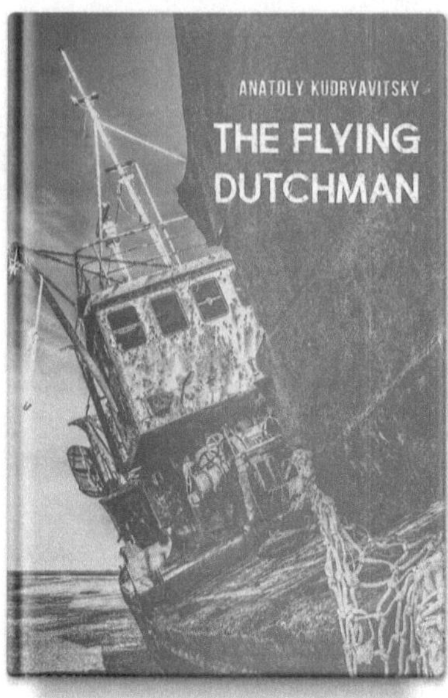

Some time in the 1970s, Konstantin Alpheyev, a well-known Russian musicologist, finds himself in trouble with the KGB, the Russian secret police, after the death of his girlfriend, for which one of their officers may have been responsible. He has to flee from the city and to go into hiding. He rents an old house located on the bank of a big Russian river, and lives there like a recluse observing nature and working on his new book about Wagner. The house, a part of an old barge, undergoes strange metamorphoses rebuilding itself as a medieval schooner, and Alpheyev begins to identify himself with the Flying Dutchman. Meanwhile, the police locate his new whereabouts and put him under surveillance. A chain of strange events in the nearby village makes the police officer contact the KGB, and the latter figure out who the new tenant of the old house actually is.

Buy it > www.glagoslav.com

# Nikolai Gumilev's Africa

Gumilev holds a unique position in the history of Russian poetry as a result of his profound involvement with Africa. He extensively wrote both poetry and prose on the culture of the continent in general and on Ethiopia (Abyssinia, as it was called in Gumilev's time) in particular. During his abbreviated lifetime Gumilev made four trips to Northern and Eastern Africa, the most extensive of which was a 1913 expedition to Abyssinia undertaken on assignment from the St. Petersburg Imperial Museum of Anthropology and Ethnography. During that trip Gumilev collected Ethiopian folklore and ethnographic objects, which, upon his return to St. Petersburg, he deposited at the Museum. He and his assistant Nikolai Sverchkov also made more than 200 photographs that offer a unique picture of the African country in the early part of the century.

This volume collects all of Gumilev's poetry and prose written about Africa for the first time as well as a number of the photographs that he and Nikolai Sverchkov took during their trip that give a fascinating view of that part of the world in the early twentieth century.

Buy it > www.glagoslav.com

# A Brown Man in Russia
## Lessons Learned on the Trans-Siberian
### by Vijay Menon

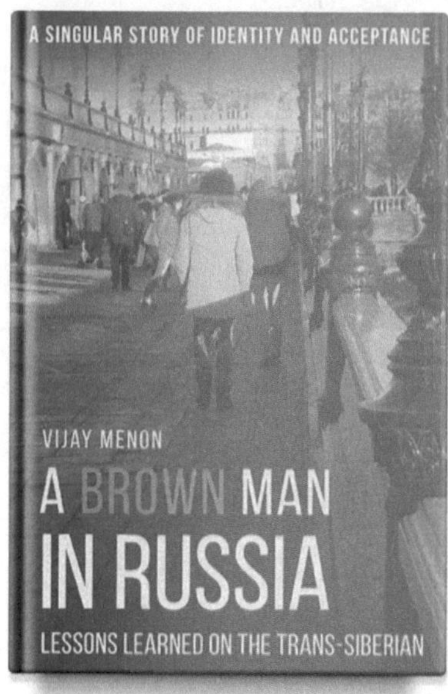



A Brown Man in Russia describes the fantastical travels of a young, colored American traveler as he backpacks across Russia in the middle of winter via the Trans-Siberian. The book is a hybrid between the curmudgeonly travelogues of Paul Theroux and the philosophical works of Robert Pirsig. Styled in the vein of Hofstadter, the author lays out a series of absurd, but true stories followed by a deeper rumination on what they mean and why they matter. Each chapter presents a vivid anecdote from the perspective of the fumbling traveler and concludes with a deeper lesson to be gleaned. For those who recognize the discordant nature of our world in a time ripe for demagoguery and for those who want to make it better, the book is an all too welcome antidote. It explores the current global climate of despair over differences and outputs a very different message – one of hope and shared understanding. At times surreal, at times inappropriate, at times hilarious, and at times deeply human, A Brown Man in Russia is a reminder to those who feel marginalized, hopeless, or endlessly divided that harmony is achievable even in the most unlikely of places.

Buy it > www.glagoslav.com

- *Don't Call me a Victim!* by Dina Yafasova
- *Poetin (Dutch Edition)* by Chris Hutchins and Alexander Korobko
- *A History of Belarus* by Lubov Bazan
- *Children's Fashion of the Russian Empire* by Alexander Vasiliev
- *Empire of Corruption - The Russian National Pastime* by Vladimir Soloviev
- *Heroes of the 90s: People and Money. The Modern History of Russian Capitalism*
- *Fifty Highlights from the Russian Literature (Dutch Edition)* by Maarten Tengbergen
- *Bajesvolk (Dutch Edition)* by Mikhail Khodorkovsky
- *Tsarina Alexandra's Diary (Dutch Edition)*
- *Myths about Russia* by Vladimir Medinskiy
- *Boris Yeltsin: The Decade that Shook the World* by Boris Minaev
- *A Man Of Change: A study of the political life of Boris Yeltsin*
- *Sberbank: The Rebirth of Russia's Financial Giant* by Evgeny Karasyuk
- *To Get Ukraine* by Oleksandr Shyshko
- *Asystole* by Oleg Pavlov
- *Gnedich* by Maria Rybakova
- *Marina Tsvetaeva: The Essential Poetry*
- *Multiple Personalities* by Tatyana Shcherbina
- *The Investigator* by Margarita Khemlin
- *The Exile* by Zinaida Tulub
- *Leo Tolstoy: Flight from paradise* by Pavel Basinsky
- *Moscow in the 1930* by Natalia Gromova
- *Laurus (Dutch edition)* by Evgenij Vodolazkin
- *Prisoner* by Anna Nemzer
- *The Crime of Chernobyl: The Nuclear Goulag* by Wladimir Tchertkoff
- *Alpine Ballad* by Vasil Bykau
- *The Complete Correspondence of Hryhory Skovoroda*
- *The Tale of Aypi* by Ak Welsapar
- *Selected Poems* by Lydia Grigorieva
- *The Fantastic Worlds of Yuri Vynnychuk*

- *The Garden of Divine Songs and Collected Poetry of Hryhory Skovoroda*
- *Adventures in the Slavic Kitchen: A Book of Essays with Recipes*
- *Seven Signs of the Lion* by Michael M. Naydan
- *Forefathers' Eve* by Adam Mickiewicz
- *One-Two* by Igor Eliseev
- *Girls, be Good* by Bojan Babić
- *Time of the Octopus* by Anatoly Kucherena
- *The Grand Harmony* by Bohdan Ihor Antonych
- *The Selected Lyric Poetry Of Maksym Rylsky*
- *The Shining Light* by Galymkair Mutanov
- *The Frontier: 28 Contemporary Ukrainian Poets - An Anthology*
- *Acropolis: The Wawel Plays* by Stanisław Wyspiański
- *Contours of the City* by Attyla Mohylny
- *Conversations Before Silence: The Selected Poetry of Oles Ilchenko*
- *The Secret History of my Sojourn in Russia* by Jaroslav Hašek
- *Mirror Sand: An Anthology of Russian Short Poems in English Translation* (A Bilingual Edition)
- *Maybe We're Leaving* by Jan Balaban
- *Death of the Snake Catcher* by Ak Welsapar
- *A Brown Man in Russia: Perambulations Through A Siberian Winter* by Vijay Menon
- *Hard Times* by Ostap Vyshnia
- *The Flying Dutchman* by Anatoly Kudryavitsky
- *Nikolai Gumilev's Africa* by Nikolai Gumilev
- *Combustions* by Srđan Srdić
- *The Sonnets* by Adam Mickiewicz
- *Dramatic Works* by Zygmunt Krasiński
- *Four Plays* by Juliusz Słowacki
- *Little Zinnobers* by Elena Chizhova
- *Duel* by Borys Antonenko-Davydovych
- *The Hemingway Game* by Evgeni Grishkovets
- *Mikhail Bulgakov: The Life and Times* by Marietta Chudakova

*More coming soon...*

www.ingramcontent.com/pod-product-compliance
Lightning Source LLC
Chambersburg PA
CBHW030835190726
48285CB00004B/1227